D1134744

Shades of Travis McGee

John D. MacDonald

SHADES OF TRAVIS McGEE

THE QUICK RED FOX
•
PALE GRAY FOR GUILT
•
DRESS HER IN INDIGO

NELSON DOUBLEDAY, Inc.
Garden City, New York

Contents

The Quick Red Fox

1

A BIG noisy wind out of the northeast, full of a February chill, herded the tourists off the afternoon beach, driving them to cover, complaining bitterly. It picked up gray slabs of the Atlantic and smacked them down on the public beach across the highway from Bahia Mar. It rattled loose sand across the windshields of the traffic, came into the cramped acres of docks and boat basin, snapped the burgees and went *hoooo* in the spiderwebs of rigging and tuna towers. Fort Lauderdale was a dead loss for the tourists that Saturday afternoon. They would have been more comfortable back in Scranton.

I was cozied up in the big lounge of the *Busted Flush*, my houseboat moored at Slip F-18. My electric heat was turned to high-high. I was stretched out on the big yellow couch and clad in ratty old wool slacks and an old Norm Thompson flannel shirt, faded to a sky blue over the treasured years.

A few days earlier I had junked my old speakers in favor of a pair of AR-3s, and had bracket-mounted them on the far wall. The Scott tuner was locked into WAEZ in Miami, and the Fisher amplifier was driving the new speakers very handsomely. They were broadcasting that Columbia recording of Bernstein conducting the Shostakovich *Fifth*, one hell of a big bold heroic piece of music, and I had the gain high enough to do it justice. You could shut your eyes and float on it.

Skeeter was across the room, hunched over her drawing board. She was wearing gray corduroy coveralls, too big for her. All her clothes always seem too big for her. She is thirty, I think, and looks eighteen. She has cobweb-blond hair, constantly adrift, a Raggedy Ann face, and a narrow graceful immature figure. She is not very well organized, but she makes a pretty fair living doing illustrations for children's books under the pseudonym of Anna-mara. My friend Meyer

found her on the beach a year or so ago. That hairy, ugly, charming
fellow can walk down a beach and collect rare people the way anyone else might pick up a left-handed whelk.

She worked with the tip of her tongue sticking out of the corner
of her mouth. She was doing line drawings of a dissolute field mouse
named Quimby. She was working at my place because they had
repainted her apartment three blocks away, and the smell made her
nauseous, and she had a deadline to meet. Once upon a time, when I
had been feeling shattered by the loss of someone very dear to me,
we had drifted sideways into a brief affair. We had found we weren't
very good for each other on that kind of basis. We seemed to bring
out a talent in each other for chipping away at the weak points. The
infighting got a bit bloody, and though we felt obligated to pretend
otherwise, it was a relief to both of us to call it off and find our way
into a casual and offhandedly affectionate friendship.

At the big parts of the music she would use her drawing pen to
help Bernstein conduct, and then go back to mouse work. She had
uncovered an unexpected talent for making Navy grog, and I had a
mild and pleasant glow from the ones she had fixed me. She had
made her own weaker. Quimby demanded her sober attentions.

Into the resonant blare of the music came the frail little overpowered *bing-bong* of my bell. I have a button board affixed to a dock
post, and a chain across the dock end of my small gangplank.

I got up and went and took a look. It was a tall girl out there, a
tall girl in a severe dark suit, with a purse that managed to give the
same impression as a briefcase. She stood erect, pretending there was
no wind at all. She looked as if she might be going around enrolling
people in a business school. As I peered out at her, she punched the
button again. There was no hesitancy about her.

I went out onto the rear deck and up the broad short slant of
gangplank to face her across the chain. Her survey of me looked
inclusive, and I couldn't tell if she registered approval or disapproval.
I get both kinds. I am extra big. I have been out in the weather. I
look lazy and am. In the words of a Texas chick one time, I look as
if I had been there and back.

She had black hair, short and crisply curly. She had vivid dark
eyes, heavy black brows, a rather long face, high flat checkbones and
a ski-jump nose. The mouth saved the face from austerity. It was full
and broad and nicely modeled. She looked fashionable, competent
and humorless.

"Mr. Travis McGee?" she asked. She had a furry contralto.

"Himself."

"I am Dana Holtzer. I couldn't reach you by phone."

"It's turned off, Miss Holtzer."

"I would like to talk to you about a very personal matter."

Sometimes it does happen that way. She had a money look. No jewelry. Earned money. She looked handsomely employed, and she didn't look as if she was in any kind of jam. An emissary for somebody who was. Had she come along a couple of months sooner, I could not have cared less. But the kitty was dwindling. I was soon going to have a cast about for some profitable little problem. It is nice when they come walking up and save you the trouble of looking.

But caution is always essential. "Are you sure you're talking to the right guy?"

"Walter Lowery in San Francisco mentioned your name."

"What do you know? How is old Walt?"

"All right, I expect." She frowned. "He said to say he misses playing chess with you."

So it was all right. Walt and I never played chess in our lives. Not against each other, at least. But that was the identification tag, if he ever sent anybody along. There are the nosy ones, and the troublemakers, and the cuties, and the official investigators. It is good to have a way to weed the doubtful ones out.

"So come in out of the wind," I said, unhooking the chain, rehooking it after she had eased by me. She was long-waisted, with sturdy shapely calves, moving with the grace many women with that kind of build have. Her back was flat and erect, her carriage good.

I opened the door and ushered her into the blast of music. Skeeter gave her an absentminded glance, a vague smile, and continued her work. I left the music on and took Miss Holtzer on through the lounge and past the galley to the little dining booth. I closed the door from the lounge to the galley corridor.

"Coffee? Drink?"

"Nothing, thank you," she said, sliding into the booth.

I poured a mug of coffee for myself and sat opposite her. "I'm not interested in every little thing that comes along," I said.

"We're aware of that, Mr. McGee."

"You do know how I operate."

"I think so. At least, I know what Mr. Lowery said about it. If something has been taken from someone, and there is no way to get it back legally, you will make an effort to get it back—for half its value. Is that correct?"

"I have to know the circumstances."

"Of course. But I would rather have . . . the other party explain it all to you."

"So would I. Send him around."

"It's a woman. I work for her."

"Send her around."

"That's impossible, Mr. McGee. I have to take you to her."

"Sorry. If she's in enough trouble to need me, she's in enough trouble to come ask me herself, Miss Holtzer."

"But you don't understand. Really. She just *couldn't* come here. She would have talked to you if I could have gotten you on the phone. I work for . . . Lysa Dean."

I knew what she meant. That face was too distinctive, even in the darkest sunglasses in town. She wouldn't want to come on such a private mission with a police escort. And if she came alone, the boobs would recognize her at a hundred paces and come clotting around, pressing in as close as they could, standing and staring at her with that curious fixed, damp, silly smile, America's accolade to the celebrity. Ten big movies, four fairly messy marriages, one television-series fiasco and a few high-paid guest spots had made her a household face. Liz Taylor, Barbra Streisand and Doris Day would take the same stomping among the star-dazed common folk. The public is an untrustworthy animal.

"I can't imagine Lysa Dean in a situation where she thinks she'd need me."

I thought I saw a little glimmer of distaste on the rather somber face of Miss Efficiency. "She'd like to talk to you about it."

"Let me see. Walter did a script for her once upon a time."

"They've been friends ever since."

"Would you say her problem fits into the way I operate?"

She frowned. "I think so. I don't know all the details."

"Aren't you in her confidence?"

"On most things. But as I said, I don't know *all* the details of this. It's been a personal kind of thing. But it is . . . something she wants to get back. And it's valuable to her."

"I can't promise anything. But I'll listen to her. When?"

"Now, if you could manage it, Mr. McGee." The symphony

ended. I got up and went and turned the set off. When I came back Miss Holtzer said, "We'd rather you didn't mention this to anyone. Even her name."

"I was just going to run out and tell a few friends."

"I'm sorry. I've gotten so used to trying to protect her. She's beginning a promo for *Winds of Chance*, starting Monday. The world premiere will be next Saturday night in eight Miami theaters. We came early hoping for a chance to see you. She's staying at the house of a friend now. She'll move over to the hotel penthouse on the beach tomorrow evening. She'll have a full schedule, starting Monday."

"Have you worked for her very long?"

"Two years. A little over two years. Why?"

"I wondered what you call yourself."

"Personal secretary."

"She tote a big staff around?"

"Not really. On the road like this there's just me and her personal maid, her hairdresser and the man from the agency. Really, I would rather you asked her the questions. Could you . . . get ready to go see her?"

"In Miami?"

"Yes. I have a car waiting, Mr. McGee. If . . . I could make a call?"

I took her into the master stateroom. The phone extension is in a compartment in the headboard. She looked up the number in a black leather notebook from her big purse. She dialed the operator and made it a credit-card call. "Mary Catherine?" she said. "Please tell her that our friend is coming back with me. . . . No, that's all. . . . Pretty soon now. Thank you, dear."

She stood up and looked around the room. I could not tell if the huge bed repelled her or amused her. I was tempted to explain it. It startled me that I should want to tell her that it had been part of the furnishings when I had won the craft in a long poker siege in Palm Beach. The man wanted another advance to stay in the game, this last time putting up his Brazilian mistress as collateral, under the plausible assumption that she too went with the boat, but his friends saved me the delicate problem of refusal by leading him gently away from the game.

Miss Holtzer did not look particularly austere. She just looked as if she might put people in handy categories.

She decided she would pour herself some coffee while I changed, if that was permitted. I put on the very infrequent necktie and a fairly heavy suit. When we went back into the lounge, Skeeter said, "Hey, both of you look at this lousy mouse a minute."

She showed us the drawing just completed. "This is when Quimby finds out for sure he's really a mouse. That cat just told him. He's crushed. He thought he was a real small pedigreed dog. But I think maybe he looks more scared than crushed. When you look at it, is it as if he's scared of the cat?"

"It's absolutely charming!" Dana Holtzer said. "What a horrid thing, really, to find out that all along you've been a mouse."

"Quimby can't adjust," Skeeter said.

They smiled nicely at each other. "Dana Holtzer, Mary Keith— known as Skeeter. We have to run. Skeet, make sure you lock up if I don't get back before you go."

"Sure. What's bugging him is all that trouble learning to bark."

"Forage if you get hungry."

But she was back at work, insulated and intent. Miss Holtzer and I headed into the wind, toward the parking areas. She said, "That's a dear strange girl, and very talented. Is she a special friend?"

"They've just painted her apartment so I told her she could work on the boat. She has a deadline."

Within another three steps, Miss Holtzer had tucked the escaping loose ends of personality back into her executive secretary shell. I had a memory of how pleasure in the mouse had brought her alive, younger and surprisingly more vivid. But it was not in her manner or habit to give anything away. She would do her job, reserved, armored, efficient. She was not being paid to react to people, or to show her own reactions, if any.

A glittering black Chrysler limousine was waiting, tended by a middle-aged man in dove-gray uniform with silver buttons. He touched his cap and opened the door for us. He looked like a television U.S. Senator. And he had that uncanny ability of the skilled chauffeur to drift a big car through traffic with such rhythm that the bunglings of other drivers seemed like an untidy and unimportant mirage.

"Miss Dean's car?" I asked.

"Oh, no. It belongs to the people where we're staying."

"When did you get in?"

"Yesterday."

"Incognito?"

"Yes."

"That's a good trick."

"Chartered airplane," she said.

There was glass between us and the barbered neck of the skilled driver. Her face was turned away from me, looking placidly out at the gray day.

"Miss Holtzer."

"Yes?" she said, turning with polite query.

"I'd like to know if I am right or wrong. I get this impression of quiet disapproval."

I thought I saw a flicker of bleak amusement. "Is that sort of thing so important to you, Mr. McGee?"

"I've never thought so."

"Mr. McGee, in the past two years I've been sent on so many curious errands, I would have become quite worn out if I'd tried to make value judgments about them."

"Then you avoid having opinions?"

"Except where it is expected of me. She pays for opinions, Mr. McGee. Legal opinions, tax opinions, artistic opinions. She listens and makes up her own mind. She doesn't particularly care for volunteer opinions."

"And the job pays well?"

"It compensates me for what I do."

"I guess I better give up."

With an almost imperceptible shrug, she turned again to look out her window, presenting me with the nice modeling of the strong line of her throat, the neatness of an ear set into a casualness of cropped black curls, a fringe of black lashes visible beyond the smooth line of her cheek, a faint and unobtrusive and understated fragrance of mild perfume.

2

THE HOUSE was on a private island, over a small causeway from one of the main causeways between Miami and Miami Beach. A gardener swung the ornate gate open for us. We turned into a winding crunch of gravel between lush and carefully tailored jungle, rounded a buttress of pink and white stucco, parked in a small walled area by a garden.

It seemed to be a back stairway. Miss Dana Holtzer led me up half a flight and into a shadowed hallway. I sat on a Babylonian throne under a black gleam of hanging armor. There was no sound in the house. None. She came back, hatless and purseless, and beckoned to me with all the gravity of a head nurse. I followed her down a paneled and carpeted corridor. She rapped on a fortress door, pushed it open for me and stood aside, saying, "She'll be with you in a moment."

She closed the door and left me alone in what seemed to be a guest suite. I was in a long room with a high ceiling. Plum carpet. Paneling. Seven arched windows along one wall, high narrow windows with leaded panes, deep sills. Black Spanish furniture. The center portion of the room was sunken. At one elevated end was a canopied bed. At the other end was an elevated portion with a conversational grouping of furniture around a small slate fireplace. The sunken portion was furnished in rather formal fashion. On the bed level there were two doorways. One, ajar, opened into a dressing room area. I could see pieces of matched luggage in there. The other door was closed, and I could hear an almost inaudible whisper of running water.

Though the draperies of all the windows were pulled aside, the room was not particularly bright. I went to a window. Tropical trees shaded it. Looking down, I could see patches of shaded green lawn. Off to the left, through foliage, I could see one bright corner of a white swimming pool.

The bathroom door opened suddenly and Lysa Dean came out. She was not smaller than I had expected because I was prepared for a woman smaller than she had looked to me on the VistaVision screen, in living color, in close-up, each slanty gray-green eye as large as a Volkswagen sedan. She came across the bedroom elevation and down the three steps toward me. She made the absolute most of those three steps. She wore flat sandals with gold straps. She wore fawn-colored pants in a fine weave. They fitted as tightly as pants, or paint, or a tattoo, could fit. She wore a strange furry blouse, with a big scooped neck and three-quarter sleeves. It looked as if Skeeter's Quimby and a couple of hundred of his relatives had contributed their pale belly fur to this creation. Around her slender throat was knotted a narrow loose kerchief of green silk precisely matching the single jewel she wore, an emerald as big as a sugar cube on the little finger of her left hand.

She came swiftly toward me, hand outstretched, her smile full of the warm delight of a woman welcoming the returning lover. "So good of you to come!" she said in her light, breathy, personal voice. As I took her hand she turned slightly so as to face the bright and shadowed daylight. It is the most cruel light a woman can accept. Her hand was small and dry and warm, a trusting little animal as intimate as her voice.

They have the distinctive occupational tricks. A lot of expressive business with mouth and eyebrows, animation with gestures.

I could remember, quite vividly, a long conversation with a stunt man named Fedder. Arthritis had forced him out of the business.

"Don't let anybody tell you they're not worth the effort," he had said. "A lot of them aren't. You got to look close to see which type. They all have to be damned good-looking and well-built. So suppose you get a chance at one who's a pretty good little actress. Let it go. The thing there, they sublimate. That's a word I learned once. They take all that steam and they shove it into their work and there isn't enough left over for bed. Now suppose you got one *thinks* she's a hell of an actress, but she's a ham. You skip her too. She'll take all that ham to bed with you and be so damn busy watching herself her heart won't be in it. The ones to wait for, and go a long way out of your way to get, they're the ones that plain started off with such damn good glands they don't have to do any acting. The camera picks up how good they'd be. Man, they can't rest from tracking it down and trying it out. The next one is always going to be the biggest and best yet. They've got what you call a real strong interest."

I had the feeling Fedder would approve of this one. I had not expected her to have such a genuine flavor of youthfulness. By every way I could measure it, she had to be about thirty-three. Yet she was a young girl, and not in any forced way. She had the slimness, the clear-eyed look of enormous vitality, the fine-grained and flawless skin, the heavy swing of burnished hair. Her impact, so carefully measured it seemed unaffected, was of a kind of innocence aware. A gamin sparkle, hinting at a delicious capacity for naughtiness.

But I had known enough of them to know that this was but one role. The enticing woman who is not in the industry will have five or six faces to wear. One like this would have dozens, and this was the one she had momentarily selected for me.

She had the showbiz trick of close-range conversation. Normal people keep their faces a yard apart. Eight inches is the focal distance on the Coast. Eight inches keeps you aware of the girl-breath heat against your chin, and the upthrust breast bud an inch and a half from your chest.

"Any friend of Walt's . . ." I said inanely.

"I treasure that man." She backed away a quarter step to give me a cock of the head and an urchin appraisal. "He said you were big, but he didn't say how huge, Travis. Trav? He called you Trav, I think. I'm Lee to my friends. Dear Trav, he told me you were big and rough-looking and sour and sometimes dangerous, but he did not tell me you are so terribly attractive."

"A veritable doll," I said.

"It's so wonderful of you to agree to help me."

"I haven't."

She was quite motionless for a thoughtful second, her smile in place. The capped teeth gleamed, between moistness. Green of iris speckled amber near the pupil. Delicate geometry of the hairs of red-gold brows. Fantasy length of the darker lashes. Faintest of fuzz on her upper lip. It was an unusual and grotesquely familiar face, the features slightly sharp, extremely sensuous, unmistakable. With her head slightly bowed, looking up at me through her lashes, the gold-red weight of hair at the right side of her face had swung slightly forward. Suddenly I knew what she reminded me of. A vixen. A quick red fox. I had seen one in heat long ago on an Adirondack morning in spring, pacing along well in front of the dog fox with a very alert and springy movement, tail curled high, turning to see if he still followed, tongue lolling from between her doggy grin.

She turned abruptly away, walking toward the elevated part of the room where the chairs and fireplace were. "But you will help me," she said in a small voice.

I followed her. She sat on a small couch and pulled her legs up. She took a cigarette from a table box. I held the light for her. She huffed smoke from the delicate oval nostrils of the slightly pointed nose, and as I sat in a big chair half facing the couch she smiled across at me. "You are refreshing, Trav McGee."

"How am I managing that, Lee?"

Her shrug and laugh were self-deprecatory. "You don't say what I always hear. I loved you in this. I adored you in that. I see every picture you make. You look better off the screen than on, actually. You know what I mean."

"I'll go through all that when I ask for the autograph."

"You know, you are sour, aren't you? Or are you afraid of seeming to be impressed? Or don't you give a damn? It's a little unsettling, dear."

"Your Miss Holtzer unsettled me the same way."

"Dana is a gem. When she reacts, she lets you know it."

I shrugged. "I loved you in this. I adored you in that. You look just fine in person."

Again she was motionless. It was an odd feeling to be so close to her. It made me aware of the uncounted millions of men all over the world who had stared at her image, coveted her, lusted after her, mentally stripped her and plundered those silky little loins. I wondered how many secret, solitary orgasms had been engineered with her in mind. The unmeasurable scope and intensity of all that vast and anonymous wanting gave her a curious physical impact. True, she had spent years being starved, pummeled, flexed, rubbed, plucked, burnished, perfumed and trained into the absolute peak of lovely physical condition. Without a chromium ego and a savage will she could not have endured it so long. But one could also believe that, as sex symbol, she also carried sex to an ultimate otherwise unknown—providing ecstasies unimaginable, greater heats, deeper spasms, longer agonies than mortal woman could know. And this, of course, was the nonsense a man must guard himself against. Her physical confidence, approaching arrogance, would lead the unwary to believe it.

"Excuse me, please," she said politely, and hurried the length of the room, toward the dressing room. A girlish graceful haste, forever eighteen. She came back with a large manila envelope and put it on the table beside the cigarette box.

"That big chest down there is a bar. If you want to fix yourself anything, I would like some of the sherry. Just half a glass, please."

As I walked to the bar, she raised her voice and said, "It is so terribly difficult to know where to start, dear. You don't seem to make it any easier for me."

"Just tell me the problem. You told Walt, didn't you?"

"Just some of it. But I would guess you want to . . . know all of it."

"If I'm to help you."

As I carried the drinks toward her, she said, "Celebrity! If all the ones who'd like to be one could only know what it means. You become such a target, actually. Slimy schemes to fasten themselves onto you for the free ride. You cannot make a single careless move."

This was a new pose. She sipped her wine. I sat down. The suffering celebrity. Public responsibility.

She gave me a sad smile. "It isn't worth it, you know. But you have to get into it as far as I am to realize it isn't worth it. And then it's too late. You can't get out. They still follow Garbo. How long since she made a picture? A thousand years, at least. Oh, there have been some satisfactions, of course. But the things I really treasure—contentment, friendships, peace of mind, marriage—none of those things could survive all the rest of it. There is a terrible loneliness, Trav. Like being on top of a mountain, alone."

"They pay you for it."

"And they pay very well indeed. I've had good advice. I have quite a lot of money. Of course, it is invested in a lot of things, but if I should take it all out, it would be quite a large sum. That's why I did try to . . . buy my way out of trouble."

"Blackmail?"

She put her glass aside and got up quickly, pacing about in an agitated way. "Can you see how valuable it is to me . . . how *essential* to have a little time when I can be myself? Like here with you now. We can talk like two people. I don't have to pose with you. I have to forget sometimes that I am Lysa Dean, and just be plain Lee

Schontz from Dayton, Ohio, the fireman's daughter. Sixteen-ten Madison Street." She whirled and stopped with a leg-warmth against my knee. "You can understand that basic human need, can't you?"

"You can't live up to the public image at all times."

"*Thank* you for understanding!"

This was another role. I guessed it was a speech out of an old movie, edited to fit the present need.

"And when I do . . . forget, that's when I'm most vulnerable."

"Sure."

"I *so* want you to try to understand me. I'm not really very complex, Trav. I am the same as everyone. I have times when I feel desperate and self-destructive. I have times when I do foolish things. There are times when I do not give a damn what happens to me."

"Sure."

She reached and drew her fingertips across my cheek and whirled away and sat on the couch again. "I know you're not a prude. I can sense that. This has to be as if I'm talking to my doctor or my lawyer. But I do feel so terribly shy about this."

"What happened?"

She sighed and made a rueful face. "A man happened to me. Of course. He was a very exciting chap. Exciting to me, at least. It happened a year ago last July, over eighteen months ago. We'd just finished shooting *Jack and the Game*. I was literally exhausted, but I went off with Carl. Carl Abelle. He had a ski school. We'd never had a chance to really be alone. He found a place for us. An absolutely fantastic little house. Do you know California? It was just below Point Sur, and clinging to the rock by its fingernails. Friends of his named Chipmann own it. They were in Switzerland. They have another house there. It was just the two of us . . ."

Her voice trailed off into uncertainty.

"Yes?"

"Trav, I am under the most terrible disciplines most of the time. I do work very hard."

"So when you let go, you let go?"

"More than most, I guess. Just a little time of not watching every ounce and every quarter inch, every blemish and drink and calorie and bruise . . . God damn it, to be a woman for a change. Fry eggs, let my hair go, get stoned, have a ball. I'm naturally a very passionate woman. But I keep it all under control. Until a time like that a year and a half ago. With Carl. That's what I try to do. Get away like that, with a certain kind of man. Then everything that's been saved up . . ."

"Birds and bees. I didn't think you went into a convent when you had time off, Miss Dean. I don't follow this routine."

"It's just to explain how things happened. It was such a very *private* place. Carl would drive off to buy food and liquor. There were steps cut into the stone, down to a little beach way way down that you couldn't use at high tide. There was a terrace on the ocean side, twenty feet square, about. It was a little offset so you could get morning sun too. A low broad wall around it. And a great stack of weatherproofed sun mattresses and pillows in all kinds of colors. We'd arranged it so we could have three weeks alone. Maybe that was too long. I guess it was. We were marvelously right for each other, in a purely physical way. We knew that before we went there, of course. Except on a ski slope or in bed, Carl isn't very stimulating. It was very intense for about a week, I guess. Day and night all mixed up. Eat when you're hungry, sleep when you're sleepy. When the edge was gone, we both started drinking more. And we spent more and more time on the terrace in the sun. I knew I was getting too brown, but I was too lazy and relaxed to give a damn. I was drinking a lot of vodka. Hot sun and vodka kept me in a sort of permanent daze. We'd make love there in the sun, all slow and sweaty and, I don't know, remote somehow. The thing is, we felt so *private*. You'd see a boat way out, or an airplane far away, or hear a truck sometimes on the highway. The phone was cut off. I had a little radio. You have to understand that nothing seemed important, absolutely nothing at all. Do you understand that, Trav?"

"I've been there."

"Anyway—it must have been just about at the end of two weeks—we needed things and Carl drove to town to get them. He left in the early afternoon sometime. And he was gone so long I began to get damned annoyed at him. I belted the vodka pretty good, so by the time he did come back, I was getting kind of sloppy and confused. He came skidding back into the driveway with two cars following him, and the whole drunken bunch came marching into the house bellowing some goddam German skiing song. Five fellows and three girls. He'd known one of the girls up at the Valley. He ran into them in town, and had drinks with them, and decided we should have a house party. They damned near fell over when they saw who his girl was. They'd brought tons of food and beer and liquor and cigarettes from town. I was sore at him, but I thought that as soon as they had recognized me the damage was done, if any, and the hell with it: I guess I was getting bored with Carl and I lost my sense of caution. They were swingers, every one. The girls were darling. The fellows were fun. I guess there's no good way to avoid telling you all, dear. It was a very scrambled evening, all things considered, and by late afternoon the next day the last holdout, the girl they called Whippy, she got tight enough to let Sonny peel her out of her swimsuit and get her into the fun and games on the terrace. It just seemed to be a crazy time for everybody, and nobody seemed to care much, and you saw everything and did everything through a kind of sleepy crazy haze so that in my memory it's all jumbled up. It was the first and last time I was ever in a situation like that. It's sort of standard practice on the Riviera, with those car-light signals and horn signals to get recruits and all. It didn't offend me. In some ways it was very exciting. But it was just too dangerous for anybody in my position. And I hadn't *wanted* it to happen. Carl brought them back to the house and it just went on from there, and lasted—oh, four days, I guess. When I got back to Brentwood it took me *weeks* to get back in shape. It all seemed like a dream. Then one day toward the end of August I got a big envelope in the mail. There were twelve photographs in it. Eight-by-ten glossies. There is a great deal of difference between remembering something and seeing it . . . like that. Seeing yourself . . . God! I flipped my lunch."

"It came by mail?"

"Yes. To my home. God only knows how Dana didn't get to it first. There was a note with it. I saved it. I put it in my wall safe. Here it is."

She took it out of the envelope and handed it to me. It was done with a carbon ribbon on an electric machine, with several strikeovers.

"Save the envelope?"

"Not that one. It was mailed at the main post office in Los Angeles. Not special or anything like that. Not even marked Personal on the outside. The address was typed with the same type as that note. No return address. Go on. Read it."

It read as follows:

Lysa, dear: You are practical. You know how the industry makes book. So you have no choice, of course. I have ten complete sets of the enclosed and a good idea of how to distribute them. I recommend the investment. Installment plan, ducks. Ten thousand in used hundreds each time. Wrap in plain white paper. Tie securely. Each Sunday night starting a week from next Sunday, you or your dark secretarial type takes a drive. At midnight, precisely, pull into the Narana Kai Drive-in at Topanga Beach. Order something, then walk alone, with the packet in plain view, over to the public pavilion. Walk to the far edge of the concrete, next to the public phone booths. A phone will begin to ring. Count the rings carefully. Wait and it will ring again the same number of times. Go back to your car. Leave the drive-in at exactly twelve-thirty. Take note of the exact mileage on your speedometer. If it says, for example, eight and six tenths and the phone rang seven times, when the mileage ends in five and six tenths (simple addition, dear), be ready. You will be heading west on 101. Be over in the right lane, your right window open, packet in your little right hand. Look for a light ahead and off to the right. Slow to thirty-five and get just as far right as you can. When you see a little green light blink twice, toss the packet out onto the shoulder immediately. If it blinks red twice, take the money home and come back the following Sunday. Each time you will receive the negative of one picture and all the prints made from that negative. They will come in the mail. If all goes well, and if you have no clever and silly ideas, we should be through with this whole affair in twelve weeks.

"So damned complicated," she said.

"Actually pretty shrewd. Two people could manage it with very little risk. One at the drive-in and pavilion to check you or Miss Holtzer out, then, after you've heard the rings, phone up the road for his buddy to get into place at the designated spot. He gets a chance to see that nobody is hiding in your car. He follows you out of the lot, tails you until it looks safe, then passes you and gets there first and gives a headlight signal to his buddy to use the green lens on the flashlight. Not bad at all. Very difficult to trap them. What went wrong?"

"Nothing. At least not then. I paid. One night there was a red light. I don't know why. It took thirteen weeks. I got the stuff in the mail. The worst ones came toward the last. Dana made the deliveries. Her nerves are better than mine, I guess."

"Maybe you should have sent word you weren't in the market."

She jumped to her feet, flushing. "Don't be dull, McGee. Close to seven million went into *Winds of Chance*. Risk money. The character who wrote that note knows this industry. He knew how I had to jump. It isn't like the old days, where you could count on studio protection. Each picture is a separate packaging operation. There are just about ten men these days who can put the really big packages together. If each one of them got a set of those prints, why should they take any future chances on me? Those pictures are poisonous. What's a hundred and twenty thousand compared to my potential? I liquidated some holdings that weren't doing so good, and took my tax loss, and paid off. Don't tell *me* what I should have done!"

It was a good act and I had to admire it. "How can I help you if all you give me is a smoke screen?"

"What the *hell* do you mean!" she shouted.

"All the industry cares about is money in the bank. Your name on a picture puts money in the bank. The days are long gone when you had to be a dear little buttercup all the way. In our culture there is going to be no huge concerted public censure to drive you out of business. If you get a little rancid, the PR people have you endow a dog shelter, and all America loves you. Drop the act."

The faked indignation was turned off in an instant. She sat again, looked at me with sullen speculation. "Smart-ass," she said.

"What is it, then, that made you pay off?"

"A few little things. A while back I swung my weight around too much. It delayed the wrap-up and bumped the budget, and some people decided maybe they didn't want to work with me. But I smartened up and settled down. I could read what it said on the wall. You know, like Monroe and Brando. But it left them edgy. Also, there've been a couple of little things from time to time. Not as bad as those pictures, but . . . along that line. It just didn't seem to be the right time to make them feel any more insecure."

"And?"

"Boy, you really want everything, don't you?"

"I've learned that it helps."

"I have a very dear friend. He's very devout and very conservative and he owns great big vulgar hunks of California and Hawaii. If he can get the right paper signed by the Vatican and get loose, I'll never have to take any crap from anybody again as long as I live. And one of those sets of prints would have gone to one man who would have felt obligated to give my friend a look at them. And that would have torn it."

"So those are the real stakes?"

She moistened her lips. "Under community property, one half of about eighty million, honey. I am his dear faithful little darlin'. It made the whole thing a lot more . . . chancy. Otherwise I would have borrowed some muscle from an old buddy in Vegas and turned them loose on this clown photographer. They'd be smart enough to handle that, but they're not smart enough to handle what I need now. Actually, if Mr. X had no knowledge of my friend, and how long it takes to bull something through that Vatican crowd, he made a very stupid pitch. But with my friend in the background, there was just too much chance it might backfire. Before you bet, you count what's in the pot. All my potential plus my friend's heavy purse. So I paid off."

"And hoped that was the end of it. And it wasn't. Incidentally, can he clear you with his church?"

"I was never married in his faith, so nothing counts. I get a clean bill. By the way, McGee, Dana doesn't know a thing about my plans for my friend."

I asked her how she thought the pictures had been taken. "It had to be a long lens," she said. "You can see the flattening and foreshortening effect. Off to the left, south of the house, I remember a little rocky ridge higher than the house with some knotty little trees clinging to it. It had to be from there. The angles match. But he had to be part mountain goat, and it had to be a tremendous lens."

"Is there any clue at all in that letter itself, any hint that's made you think of a specific person?"

"No. I read it over and over. He's been around the industry in some connection, and I think he tried to sound as if he knew me, but he calls me Lysa instead of Lee. That could be a cover-up, of course. And it has a phony kind of limey slant to it, calling me ducks."

"What size were the negatives?"

"Little. Like so." She indicated a 35mm frame size.

"You checked them against the prints each time?"

"Sure did. But in a lot of cases the prints were just an enlargement of part of the negative, even less than half sometimes."

"So you were all paid up well over a year ago. And you thought it was over. When was the next contact?"

"Two months ago. Less than that. Early in January. An old friend, trying to make a comeback, was opening at The Sands in Vegas, and a bunch of us were rallying around to give him a good sendoff. It was in the papers that we were all going to be there. Dana was with me. We had a suite at the Desert Inn. Somebody left this envelope for me at the desk at The Sands. I guess they thought I was staying there. They sent it over. Dana got it. I was just waking up from a nap. She came in with the damnedest expression on her face and handed it to me. She had opened it. It was another set of the pictures. There wasn't any return address. The desk had no idea who had left it off. Dana wanted to quit right then and there. She is a strange gal. I had to explain the whole thing the way I explained it to you, Trav. She knew right away that it was the same thing that had cost me all the money. She still wanted to quit. I had to beg her to stay. Our relationship hasn't been the same since she saw the pictures. I don't blame her. I'd still hate to lose her. This is the envelope. You can see how it was addressed. Somebody just cut my name off the front of a fan magazine, something like that. Here is the note that was with it."

It was quite different. Individual words and letters had been cut from newsprint and newspaper stock and pasted to cheap yellow copy paper. It said: "Shameless whore of Babylon you will be cut down by the sord of decency and money will not save your dirty life this time but you better have money ready you whore of evil I will come to you and you will no the truth and I will set you free."

She hugged herself. "That one just scares the hell out of me, Trav. It's kind of sick and crazy and terrible. It just isn't the same person. It can't be."

"So you went and saw Walter?"

"No. I just got more and more jittery the more I thought of it. I'm still shook. I was at a big party at the Springs and I got a little stoned and made a scene and dear Walt was there and he took me for a walk. I hung onto him and cried like a baby and told him my troubles. He said maybe you would help. I guess you can say something was stolen from me. My privacy or something. And somebody wants to steal my career or maybe my life. I don't know. I've been carrying cash around with me. In thousand-dollar bills. Fifty of them. I don't expect you to get back what I paid. But if you could, you could keep half. And if you can get that nut off me, you can have the money I'm carrying around."

"Are the pictures in that envelope?"

"Yes. But do you have to see them?"

"Yes."

"I was afraid of that. I am not going to let you see them until you say you'll try to help me. Every time I think of that note I feel like a scared kid."

"It's a very cold trail, Lee."

"Walter said you are clever and tough and lucky, and he said being lucky is the most important." She gave me an odd look. "I have this feeling that my luck is running out, darling."

"How many people know about this?"

"The four of us, dear. You and Dana and me and Walter. But you know more than the other two. Not another soul. I swear."

"Wouldn't it be logical for you to tell Carl Abelle?"

"Sweetie, when one of those things is over, it is over all the way. Enough is enough forever."

"Could he have set you up for it?"

"Carl? Definitely no. He's a very sunny type. Very simple needs and very simple habits. Totally transparent, really."

"Usually I gamble expenses, then take them off the top before the fifty-fifty split. But this is a little too chancy for that."

"Expenses guaranteed up to five thousand," she said without hesitation, "and when that's gone we'll talk some more."

"Walt must have said I could be trusted."

"What other choice do I have? That's one thing about this. There hasn't been any trouble making decisions. There's been just one way to go. Will you try? Please? Pretty please?"

"Until it looks hopeless."

She scaled the envelope into my lap. "God knows I'm not the shy type, sweetie, but I don't think I could watch anybody look those over. I'll take a walk. Take your time."

She went to the heavy door and let herself out quietly.

3

After a little time I put the twelve photographs back into the envelope. I took a slow turn around the room. I am too big a boy to be churned up by the explicits of other people's kicks.

Nor did I feel any compulsion to make moral judgment. These were modern animals caught in black and white at their silly play. Such sport was not for me, and very probably not for anyone whose friendship I claimed. There seemed to be some kind of severe selection involved. An acceptance of that presupposed an inability to accept or believe in a lot of other things. Personal dignity, for one.

But something still bothered me, something I could not quite define. So I took them out and shuffled through them again. The clue was there. It was the terrible loneliness on their faces. Each one of them, in all that lazy confusion of intimacies, in that lexicon of clinical descriptions, looked utterly, desperately alone.

And they were beautiful people. Lysa Dean was the featured player in every shot, and her body was as superb as its promise.

I felt as if I had glimpsed the edge of some great paradox. The grotesque ultimate of togetherness is the final loneliness of the human spirit. And once you had been that far out on that barren limb, there was no chance of ever coming all the way back.

I shrugged and looked at them again to see if they told me anything about time lapse. I put them away again.

From the varying lengths of shadow in the pictures, from the changing positions on the sunny terrace, I could tell that they had been taken over a matter of hours, perhaps on separate days.

Soon she returned, coming in with a look half challenge, half calculated demureness. "Well?" she said.

"It doesn't look as if it was a hell of a lot of fun."

That response startled her. She stared at me. "Oh, you are so *right!* You know, it seems to me as if it was all a thousand years ago. I guess I've been trying to fade it out of my mind. Oh, Christ, there's kind of a sickly excitement about it, I guess. But what I remember now is being constantly cross and irritable and impatient. And sleepy. Just terribly sleepy and never being allowed to sleep long enough, and having the feeling that all the rest of them were just one . . . one *thing* somehow. Not like the pictures."

"Are these exactly like the other pictures you got?"

"They are the twelve exact same shots, but not exactly like the others. These are fuzzier and grayer, sort of. Not as sharp. But I didn't save any of the others to compare, of course."

"We have to look through these together so you can give me the names to go with the faces, Lee, and tell me what you know about each one."

"I suppose it has to be done."

"Like a trip to the dentist. I think there's at least one fair picture of every other person in the group."

She made a face. "Those pictures are such a big boost to my pride, Travis. It does something for a girl to look like a fifty-peso floozy in a back-room circus in Juarez."

I turned a light on and we sat at the desk in the sunken part of the room. I found a pencil and paper. I pointed to the pictures and asked the questions. She answered in a thin small breathy voice, her face half turned away. I took the following notes.

1. Carl Abelle—about 27—six-footer—husky—blond—has left the Valley—try Mohawk Lodge near Speculator, New York.
2. Nancy Abbott—about 22—tall, dark, slender, heavy drinker, good singing voice, believed to have been divorced, perhaps daughter of an architect. Took ski lessons from Abelle at Sun Valley. Believed to be a houseguest of . . .
3. Vance & Patty M'Gruder, perhaps of Carmel, married couple in middle twenties, apparently well-off, Vance a sailboat buff, ocean racing, etc., have house in Hawaii (?), husband very tanned, short, broad, muscular, going prematurely bald, wife lush & fair, very long blond hair, quarrelsome, strong English accent.
4. Cass—could be first name, last name or nickname. Seemed to have known M'Gruders previously. About thirty. Dark, hairy,

handsome, very powerful—amusing (?). A painter, perhaps. Friend of . . .

5. Sonny, a little younger than Cass—slender, cold-eyed, flavor of violence, untalkative, occupation unknown, who had brought along . . .
6. Whippy. About nineteen then—copper curls, freckles, perhaps waitress or clerk, scared of Sonny.
7. Two college boys from the East on summer trip—apparently joined group at bar where Abelle ran into Nancy Abbott. Boys about 20 or 21—Harvey a big blond cheery one, Richie smaller dark nutty one. Cornell.

On the clearest prints of each I had marked the corresponding number from my notes. I could sense Lee's relief when I put the photographs back into the envelope.

"Who got it all started?" I asked her.

She tightened up again. "Why? What do you mean?"

"I don't think a camera gets that lucky. Somebody had to set you up. Or maybe the real target was somebody else, and you turned out to be a bonus."

"It was a long time ago, and I was tight most of the time."

"Tell me what you can remember of how it got started."

She got up slowly and went over and rested her fists on a window-sill, staring out, the fox-pelt hair softly back-lighted. I leaned a shoulder against the wall by the window. She talked. Her voice was small. I could not see much of her profile because of the way the hair swung forward. Round of forehead, soft snub tip of nose. I did not press her. I let her find her own words in her own time. Her memory was more acute as regards textures than incident. Six men and four gals that first evening and night. Four places to go—two bedrooms, a long couch in the living room, the leathery sun pads on the terrace. It was a prowling thing then, pursuits and tensions, Lysa Dean a primary target for all but Carl, low lights and ultimate arrangements, and some re-pairings when partners slept.

In phrases and fragments, theatrical sighs and beautifully timed hesitations, she painted the flavor of the hot bright terrace on that first full day of house party. Pitchers of Bloody Marys, vodka haze, arrows of white sunlight through squinting eyes, compulsive beat of the music on the portable radio, oil and aromatics of sun lotion, jokes and tipsy laughter. A game of forfeits, with the rules rigged so that to play was to lose, and to lose was to soon be naked.

In half-sleep, mildly and amiably drunk, after the game had ended, she had fended off the increasing insistence of Cass, whining at him irritably when he became too bold. Finally, propping herself up to drink again, she saw several sound asleep, and saw others who were accepting what she had refused. So, squeezing her eyes hard shut to achieve the illusion of privacy, she had surrendered herself to Cass and her own responses.

She straightened and turned toward me and hooked the fingertips of both hands into my belt, leaned her forehead against my chest. She sighed and said, "Then I guess it stops mattering so much. I don't know. You just seem to learn how to turn one whole part of your mind right off. It's all just something that happens. Everybody is in the same boat. So it doesn't seem to make any difference any more. Nothing does."

She sighed again. In the cold soft light I could see the scalp, clean and white as bone under the coppery spring of hair. "I don't know who started it. Patty was bossy. I can remember people getting mad. Whippy cried sometimes. Cass knocked Carl down once, I don't know why. One of those college kids, the big one, kept getting sick. He couldn't drink. It's all so vague, sweetie. If you watched, and you were all turned off, it was just sort of stupid and boring, and if you'd started to hum a little, you could get into that one or set up something else, or go take a shower, or go make a sandwich, or go build another pitcher of drinks. It just . . . wasn't all that important."

She slid her small hands around my waist, laid her cheek against my chest and held tight. I stroked her hair.

She took the deepest breath of all and said, "Listen to me! God, I know it was important. There are some kinds of poisons, I heard you look as if you got over it, but you never really do. I wish somebody could stick a knife in my head and cut out those four days and nights, Trav. A girl thinks about herself a different way, after that. I have this lousy dream ever since. I've fallen into this empty white swimming pool and the sides are too high to get out. The pool lights are on so it's bright as a stage. And there are six ugly snakes in there on the tile, all after me. I can run and dodge fast enough to keep away from them no matter how they try to hem me in. They all look exactly alike. Then I keep calling for help and suddenly I see that the walls are all kind of coming in. It is getting smaller and smaller.

Then I know they are going to get me. As the place gets smaller the snakes get bigger, and I scream and wake up, all sweaty and trembling. Just hold me tight, Trav. Please."

She was trembling and I wondered if it was faked.

After several minutes she quieted down and moved away from me, shoved her hair back with the back of her hand and said, with a funny little shy smile, "You don't want me, do you? I could tell. Just from your hands. Kind of gentle and . . . fatherly and remote. God, I wouldn't blame you for not wanting such a public piece."

"It's not that."

"No? You are certainly not one of those, sweetie."

"No. Well, in all honesty, if that's what you want. I guess the pictures have something to do with it. A man likes the illusion of exclusive option, even on the most temporary basis, I guess. But with or without pictures, let's just say I'm not a trophy hunter."

"What the hell does that mean?"

"Every red-blooded American boy should ride a bike no hands and win some merit badges and go to bed with a household name. Some of them don't get over it, that's all. I had my celebrity innings, but I'm not a locker room historian. I outgrew my bike too, Lee. It's a big scene here. Rich silent house and the closed door and your tight pants and that rostrum-type bed. And mutual attraction. But it isn't worth it. It would be like being taught to dance by your elder sister. She would keep trying to lead, and giving irritable little instructions, and counting out loud and spoiling the music. Then she would give you a patronizing pat and say you did just fine."

For a moment she had the malignant rigidity of a temple demon. Then an urchin grin, seen often in your favorite movie palace, broke it up. "My God, you *are* a strange one, McGee. You wouldn't want me as a gift, eh?"

"Not unless and until it could be more than this for us, Lee."

"You mean like real true love?"

"Affection, understanding, need and respect. You can be sarcastic about that too, if you want. Bed is the simplest thing two people can do. If it goes with a lot of other things, it can be important, and if it goes with nothing else, it isn't worth the time it takes."

She strolled over and curled up in a big chair and pondered me, finger laid against the side of her small nose. "The next time around, Mr. McGee, can you arrange to show up in Dayton about fifteen years ago?"

"I can make a note of it, Miss Dean."

"I've been through too many mills this time."

"Not necessarily."

"But you said respect."

"Once in a while you stop posing for me and remembering lines from old movies, and then I could respect the person that shows through."

"It could be strange to have a friend like you. I have no female friends, really. And just two male friends, fine old guys, both in their early sixties. I love them dearly. Males in your bracket are either studs or competitors, sweetie, or they want to find an angle to get rich off me."

"We might end up friends, Lee. I better go along. I am going to take these pictures along." As I picked them up from the desk she hopped up out of the chair and came running over and grabbed at the envelope. I did not let her pull it out of my hand. I said, "Either you trust me all the way, or I get off right now, Lee. I need them for information and leverage."

After looking at me with a long and searching intensity, she let go. "I never thought I'd let anybody even see those. Trav, will you be terribly careful?"

"Yes."

"I can send Dana over with the expense money tomorrow. Will that be all right?"

"Fine."

"Please be careful with those pictures. If they get out, my career is dead right now. And . . . as you must damn well know, it is the only thing I have left."

Tears balanced on her lower lids, and one broke loose and tracked her cheek. It did not look real. A makeup man had darted onto the set and put them there with an eyedropper. Pure glycerine. Maybe they weren't real. She would have learned to cry almost at will, and cry in a way that would leave her as lovely as before.

"You be careful, Lee. I don't like the sound of that note. Sexually disturbed people try to be the sword of the Lord, going around slaying the sinful. See that you get pretty good protection this week in Miami."

She walked me to the door. She caught at my arm, gave me a quick kiss, as soft and trusting as a child's, then went down the corridor with me, found Dana Holtzer in a small room, typing, and turned me over to her. Dana got up and took me down the stairs and out to the waiting limousine. I saw the quick and wary way she glanced at the envelope I was carrying, and caught a flavor of total disapproval.

The driver's name was Martin. She told him to take me back, or to wherever I wanted to go. It was after five. I had him stop where I could phone. I phoned Gabe Marchman in Lauderdale and told him I had a problem. He said it was convenient to bring it right over.

On one of those hunches that may save your life, though you can never prove it one way or another, I had Martin drop me off downtown. I went into one end of a big drugstore and out the other and into a cab.

Gabe Marchman was a great combat photographer. You have seen his name on those classic Korea things. A land mine smashed his legs all to hell. While convalescing in Hawaii, he met and married a very rich and very beautiful little Chinese-Hawaiian girl named Doris. Gabe looks like a sawed-off Abraham Lincoln. He is still on crutches. They have six kids. With his mobility gone, he has gotten into another aspect of photography. He has one of the most completely equipped private labs in the South, taking up a wing almost as big as the main house. He does experimental work, and problem assignments for large fees. He is a sour little man, adored by all who get to know him.

Doris, blooming large again with child, sent me on through to the lab. Gabe grunted at me. I said I wanted to know as much as possible about some pictures I had with me. We were in his print room. He turned on more intense lights. He levered himself onto a stool and spread the dozen pictures out in a row on top of the work table.

From his lack of reaction, they could have been pictures of puppies or flower gardens. "Whadaya know about 'em?" he said. "Just technically."

"They were taken a year and a half ago in California on thirty-five-millimeter film. The person involved estimates that the only place from which they could be taken was about a hundred yards away, but that is just an estimate. The person involved saw another set of prints over a year ago, and they were just like these as far as subject matter, but these seem to be fuzzier and grayer."

He grunted and got out a large magnifying glass and began to go over them very carefully, one by one.

I said, "I forgot something. My client saw and destroyed the negatives. The negatives included more than in a lot of these pictures."

He continued his careful examination. Finally he swiveled around. "Okay, we accept the hundred-yard distance. I would say it was probably Plus-X using a very fine telephoto lens, one thousand millimeter. Maybe the f/six-point-three Nikkor, a reflector type with two mirrors. It's only about so long and weighs three or four pounds. It was used with a tripod or some other kind of solid rest. With thirty-five millimeter, a lens that size gives you about a twenty-power magnification, so at a hundred yards it would give the same as a normal lens fifteen feet from the subject. These three are the only ones where he printed the full frame. Now, if he printed about half the frame, it would be like being seven or eight feet away from the subject. And this is the average for most of these. Just this extreme close-up was done from maybe a quarter or less of the negative, showing the woman at a viewing distance of about three feet, with less definition. There's good depth of field and all motion is frozen, so a hundred yards away I'll buy. Okay so far?"

"Yes."

"Assuming the same guy who took the pictures made the original prints, he's a good workman. Excellent exposure, good edge-to-edge definition, and when he masked the negatives and did his printing, he had good quality control. You can tell that he did some burning in and dodging, and he couldn't help using a pretty good sense of composition. I would say he took a hell of a lot of shots, maybe several hundred, and came up with the best ones. Very sharp, very clear, and he made high-gloss prints. I'd say definitely a pro, if that's any help to you. Now then, some clown got hold of a set of the prints. See this little flare here on this one and this one. That's where his lighting kicked back off the gloss. He had a set of copy negatives and a new set of prints. This is crappy paper, and he butchered his developing and butchered his printing solutions and times, but there was enough quality in the prints he copied so that all in all it comes through not too bad. The guy who did the originals would be incapable of doing such cruddy work the second time around, even if he was operating in a motel closet. But, having the copy negatives, he can make any number of these poor prints. Your client destroying the original negatives means nothing now. It is unmistakably her in every one of these. I would guess she's the one you're working for."

"Yes. Now I wonder if you can do something with these."

"I was afraid of that."

"From these can you make another set of negatives, and a set of prints that are a little different than these?"

"McGee, if you start out with crud, you end up with crud. I can't get back to the original print quality. I can print for more contrast and clean up these whites a little, but a close focus on fuzz gives you fuzz."

After an original reluctance, he began to get interested. He used a copy camera, a larger negative size, a copy film with a fine grain. By the time he had developed the negatives, Doris began to howl for a little cooperation, so he hung them up to dry and we went in for drinks. The nursemaid had taken over the bedtime routines. The older ones trudged in to say their well-mannered good nights. Doris cooked and served an old Chinese-Hawaiian specialty—broiled steaks, baked potatoes and tossed green salad. The three of us, in front of the big fireplace with a very small fire, revamped the State Department, simplified all tax legislation, tore down half of Florida and rebuilt it in a more sane and pleasing fashion.

Then we went back to work. He would put a negative in the enlarger and focus it on the base, and I would tell him what I wanted. Then he would go to work. He would cut a piece of masking paper to fit Lysa Dean's projected face. He would use sufficient exposure time to give him opportunity to dodge and burn in so that the face of someone else was emphasized. I ended up with fourteen useful prints, on double-weight paper. Some of those that took in more people were duplicated, altered slightly to highlight one and then another.

Somewhere in the processing they ceased to have any fleshy impact. They became problems in light and shade and emphasis. He put them in his high-speed dryer, and after he had flattened them in a bonding press, I studied them under the bright lights. Lysa Dean's features were white censored patches. Gabe was careful to give me the negatives as well as the test prints which hadn't worked out. We argued price, with me trying to increase it, and agreed on a hundred dollars. Doris had gone to bed.

He crutched his way to the door with me, and came out with me into the cold windy night.

"Taking a little trip, I suppose," he said.

"Yes."

"None of my business. I suppose somebody got too greedy."

"That's usually the way."

"You watch yourself, Trav. A little animal like that, if she'd see a way out by pushing you over the edge, she'd take it. That's an interesting little face, but it isn't a good face."

The taxi slowed, putting his spotlight on the numbers. He turned into the drive. When I looked back I saw Gabe still standing there.

4

WHEN I got back to the *Busted Flush* I saw my lights still on. It was a little past eleven. The lounge door was locked. I went in and found Skeeter sound asleep, face down on the yellow couch in her baggy gray coveralls, one frail long-fingered hand trailing on the floor. Drawings of Quimby were propped everywhere. They were wise and funny and good. I admired them. In the middle of the floor was a big stamped brown envelope and a note to me:

"This LOUSY mouse. I am pooped out of my mind. PLEASE would you stuff him in this envelope. He is all weighed in and everything, and PLEASE would you seal him and run him to the P.O. He's an airmail-SPECIAL mouse. Honestly, I had to sleep or DIE!!!!"

I looked down at her. It was typical. God knows how long she'd gone without sleep or when last she had thought of eating. Perfectionists who meet deadlines are usually pretty whipped out.

I went through to the bow of the *Flush* and put my dirty pictures in the hidden safe. It might not take an expert all night to open it, but he'd sure raise hell finding it first. I assembled Quimby and sealed him and turned off one of the lights.

She stirred and raised a sleep-bleared Raggedy Ann face, shoe-button eyes peering, cobweb hair afloat. "Whumya timezit?" she mumbled.

I squatted beside the couch. "You eat anything?"

"Huh? Eat? Uh . . . no."

I knew the problems. I had lived with them. I went into the galley, picked cream of mushroom soup, opened the can, heated it, poured it steaming into a big two-handled mug. She was gone again. I sat her upright and fitted the mug into her hands. When I was sure she was going to keep on sipping at it, I left and took Quimby to the post office and dropped him into an airmail slot.

By the time I got back, the empty mug was on the floor, and she had sagged off to sleep again. I picked her up. The fool girl seemed to have no substance at all. My guest stateroom would have to serve. I carried her in there and then, instead of dropping her into the bed and covering her over, on a strange and lonely impulse I sat on the bed still holding her in my arms. A faintness of marina lights came through the ports. Water slapped and licked at the curve of the barge hull. Mooring lines creaked.

She put her arm around my neck and said, "I thought we gave up on this."

"We did. I thought you were asleep. Go back to sleep."

"I was asleep, damn it. What's this brooding sorrow bit anyway? It's the tenderness keeping me awake."

"I guess I wanted to hold onto you. That's all. Go to sleep."

"Why should you want to hold me? My God, Travis, we ripped each other up pretty good and got over it a long time ago."

"Why do you have to know everything? That's one of your problems."

"I have to know because I can't go back to sleep, that's why."

"Okay. I don't have too many illusions. I just ran into something rotten, that's all. I don't feel shocked. Just sad."

"It was a rotten girl?"

"I don't know. It's a kind of waste, I guess. Go to sleep."

She settled herself more snugly into my lap, arm around me, face in my neck. In a little while she drifted off, and the arm fell away. Her breathing turned deep.

I guess it can be touching. A special kind of trust. Something warm to hold. The way a kitten will drowse in your lap, totally confident.

Holding something alive, warm, sleeping is like handling fresh moist soil under the sun's heat. Restorative.

After a little while I had the idea that it would be an act of good fellowship to peel her out of those coveralls and slip her into the bed. A nice gesture. Sure. This is how McGee kids McGee.

I gave a little shake like a hound coming out of water. During that little time when it had been good, before we had started sawing chunks off each other, I had discovered that narrow little body to be amazingly strong, curiously luxurious. And I had the lonelies.

So I stood her on her feet and held her until she could stand up. "What the hell!" she said.

I stood up and kissed her, gave her a swat on the fanny and told her to sleep tight. I heard the coverall zipper before I got the door entirely closed behind me.

I showered with the strange feeling I was washing off the sweat and sun oil I had acquired on a bright terrace three thousand and more miles away.

I put on a robe and went topside for a nightcap pipe, a load of Irish aromatic in a battered old large apple Comoy. I perched a haunch on the sundeck rail. The wind had died, but the surf still made that endless freight-train sound on the beach. Across the way the Alabama Tiger's perpetual floating house party was muted down to a few girlish squeals and somebody playing bad bongo. Meyer's craft was dark.

Go mention it in the locker room, McGee. There you were with Lysa Dean, and she had on these skin-tight pants, fellas, and there was that big damn bed over there, and her hanging on me, sighing. Go on, McGee. Go *on*, man!

Boys, once when I was riding my bicycle no hands, I hit a stone and removed about one half a square foot of hide from assorted painful places. And once upon a time I won free dancing lessons from Arthur Murray because I knew, right off, what happened in 1776.

When I got up in the morning Skeeter was gone, leaving the bed unmade and no coffee in the pot. But she left a drawing on the sink in the head. A rangy mouse who looked extraordinarily like me sat holding a Skeeterlike girl mouse asleep in his arms. The caption said, "Notorious mouse spares innocent prey. Vitamin deficiency suspected."

After breakfast I phoned her. She said her apartment was smelling much better, thank you.

"McGee," she said. "We might be turning into friends. That's pretty good, don't you think?"

"You're too dangerous on any other basis. What's with this vitamin gag?"

"I guess I was just sort of asleep. You started breathing hard. Then pow! On your feet, girl. And you went off like you used starting blocks."

"Friends play fair, Skeet."

"Well, hell. I don't know. I hadn't decided. You were blue. I practically had a Band-Aid complex. Woman's work or something. I passed the buck by sort of sleeping. Anyway, I was terribly tired."

"Quimby is a fine mouse."

"Trav, dear, I am going to sleep for three days, and then you can take me fishing."

"Deal," I told her. She hung up. It was a sad thing that we had a strange sexual antagonism that made us want to chop each other to bits. We had to cut deep to see how much it would hurt. And it hurt aplenty. You can't live with that. But you can learn to live very nicely without it.

At eleven o'clock Dana Holtzer, as carefully poised as an unfriendly diplomat delivering an ultimatum, arrived with the money. Five thousand in cash. She had a receipt form for my signature, made out in the form of a letter of intent. The money was for "expenses in connection with research for a moving picture as yet untitled, to be purchased in treatment form at a price to be negotiated . . ."

Apparently I was dealing with something called Ly-Dea Productions. She had a file copy of the letter for me. She sat erect on the cushioned top of one of the stowage lockers along the lounge wall under the ports. She wore no hat. She wore a tailored navy blue suit with pleated skirt over a crisp white blouse. I could see no concession to anything in the set of her heavy mouth, the waiting attentiveness of very vivid dark eyes. Had I not seen her reaction to Skeeter's mouse, I would have given up on her.

"Tax reasons," she said.

"Of course," I said, and signed her copy. She refolded it briskly and tucked it away.

I wondered if anything would dent that efficient calm. I expected her to get up and trot off. But she had something else on her mind, yet wanted me to make a move first. I could guess why she had no particular enthusiasm for me. Her confidence would be given to large organizations with computers in the air-conditioned basement to tell the other machines which cards to drop into the slot. Lysa Dean was in trouble. When you are in trouble, you go to a J. Edgar Hoover, not to an obviously shopworn beach bum, a marina gypsy, a big shambling sharpshooter without an IBM card to his name. To Miss

Holtzer I would look like more trouble, not less. My khakis were faded to pale beige, and the toes were out of my topsiders, and the old blue sweatshirt was fringed at the elbows. So I just fell into a chair, hooked a leg over one arm of it and watched her mildly.

She took it well and took it long, and then the pink climbed up her throat. "Miss Dean should be the one to tell you this," she said.

"Tell me what, dear?"

"She could answer any objections better than I could. The agency is sending a competent girl out, to take over for me temporarily with Miss Dean. I'll catch her up to date this evening." She took a deep breath. "Miss Dean has assigned me to work with you on this matter, Mr. McGee."

"That is absolutely ridiculous!"

"Believe me, it wasn't my idea. But in all fairness, it does have some merit. I can get through to her immediately at any time. There may be information about her you might want to have, and information about her friends and associates. Also, I may be able to take some details off your hands: travel arrangements, accommodations, notes, financial records. Miss Dean would feel . . . more at ease about all this if I am with you."

"I work alone, Dana. My God, I don't need any Katie Gibbs-type services, believe me. I wouldn't know how to act with you trudging behind me with a notebook and a ledger. In a thing like this I might have to do a lot of . . . impersonations."

"I am quite flexible and resourceful, Mr. McGee."

I stood up. "But you don't belong in this sort of thing. It looks as if it would be pretty messy, if I have any luck at all."

"I said yes to Miss Dean, but I do have one reservation. I must ask you if . . . if you are employed to kill anyone."

I boggled at her. "What?"

"That's a risk I wouldn't care to accept."

I sat down and I laughed. She let me laugh it out, without a smile, with quiet patience. When I was through she said, "That's answer enough. I had to ask. I have to think of risks."

"Miss Holtzer, I don't know if I could stand the continuous weight of your disapproval."

"What does that mean?"

"I understand you saw those pictures by accident, the ones left at the desk at The Sands, and you wanted to quit then and there. Life is full of a number of things, Miss Holtzer, and many of them get a little grim from time to time."

Her dark eyes flashed. "Do they really?"

"Haven't you noticed?"

With a thoughtful expression she took cigarettes from her purse, snapped her lighter, huffed a dragon plume of smoke toward me. "What I tell you now is, of course, none of your business. But I think we should understand each other a little bit in the beginning. My personal life is out of bounds for any future discussion. I am in the business of selling skills: tact, great energy, adequate intelligence and total loyalty. I sell this package to Lysa Dean for thirty thousand dollars a year. Assigned to you, you get the same package. When I saw what those pictures were, I went through them to see how damaging they might be. I read the note. To me it meant that Lysa Dean was not as good a gamble for me as she used to be. I worried about that before, when I went through that thirteen-week charade."

I saw her hand tremble slightly as she lifted her cigarette to her lips.

"I am married, Mr. McGee. Or was married. My husband was epileptic. He was a talented writer, with a few very substantial television credits. Marriage was a calculated risk. We had a child, a boy. At first he seemed quite normal. Then we learned gradually that he was so seriously retarded an institution would be the only answer. It had no connection with my husband's difficulty. We had to get away after we put the little boy in. He would never know us, or anyone. Bill had made a good sale. It was a good trip, actually, as good as two emotionally exhausted people could expect. We got well enough to head home. We stopped at a place at night for coffee, along the road. It was a bar. We were not drinking. Bill had a sudden seizure. They never lasted long, but they were quite violent. An off-duty police officer thought he was a murderous drunk and shot him in the head. He did not die. He is permanently comatose, Mr. McGee, with tubes for feeding and elimination, and the alcohol rubs to keep bed sores from rotting him away. It is a medical miracle, of course. That was four years ago. I need that thirty thousand. It is barely enough for me and my family. If Lysa Dean is going down the drain in a messy way, it is my responsibility to leave her before it happens and go where an equivalent job has been offered. The job might not be open if I was in any way connected with scandal. Yes, Mr. McGee, the world can get a little grim from time to time."

"What can I say?"

"Nothing, of course. I thought it would be easier to tell you now before you said more things you might regret later, that's all. You haven't hurt me. I'm not certain anything could hurt me, actually. I am sorry it is all so soap opera. I haven't the . . . self-involvement necessary to make moral judgments. Lee was terribly foolish. The pictures offend me because they are vulgar. And they endanger me. If you can't work things out for her, I will have to leave her. I think she senses that."

"Maybe you could be some help."

"Thank you."

"Drink?"

Her smile was small, and perfectly polite, and totally automatic. "Bourbon, if you have it. Weak, with lots of ice and water."

I do not think she wanted it, but knew I wanted a chance to pull myself together, get the taste of my own foot off my front teeth. I had looked at the empty reserve and guessed repression and disapproval. She was merely burned out. Wires had crossed and a lovely machine had fuzed and quit, become a useless lump for her to carry around the rest of her life. I felt like a jackass adolescent who'd tried to tell a dirty joke in front of real people.

When I went in with the drinks, she was standing with her back to me, feet apart, sturdy calves braced, fist on a rich curve of Mediterranean hip, head cocked, looking at a painting.

"Like it?"

She turned with a swift grace. "Very much."

"Syd Solomon. He lives over in Sarasota. It's part of a Bahama series he did a few years back."

"It's very rich. Are you a collector?"

"Sometimes. I've got about five things aboard and maybe a dozen in storage. Every so often I switch them around." She sipped her drink. "Is that all right?"

"Yes. Thank you. What do you drink? What is that?"

"Lately Plymouth gin on the rocks with two drops of bitters." I could almost hear the little click as she filed that away. I had acquired a drinkmaker.

She went back to the upholstered locker and sat and said, "By the way, my expenses won't come out of what I brought you. Is there anything I can start doing today? My desk is fairly clean and the girl won't be in until later."

I left her there and went to the safe and took out the envelope. I put Lysa Dean's pictures back in the safe and brought out the ones Gabe had made. I handed them to her. She looked at three of them, and then looked at me with faint surprise and fainter approval. "You had this done, or did it, since you left her yesterday?"

"I had it done."

"It's quite clever. I see, I think, what you have in mind. These are no danger to her. Are the others safe?"

"Yes." I waited until she had glanced through the set and put them aside. "Would you take down a few things?"

A notebook, gold pen and attentive expression appeared with impressive speed. I gave her Gabe's full name and address. "Make out a check for a hundred and mail it to him for the photo work. The checkbook is in the desk drawer over there. See if you can get a line on a Carl Abelle, possibly a ski instructor at the Mohawk Lodge in Speculator, New York, previously at Sun Valley. Phone him and fake it so that he won't be left with a lot of curiosity. If he is there, find the best way to get there, and reserve us through for Tuesday."

"To stay at that lodge?"

"Let's save that until we get a look, if he's there. Next, see what you can dig up about a Mr. and Mrs. Vance M'Gruder. Their home could be in Carmel. Ocean-racing type. It's a small fraternity, so it shouldn't be rough." I went over and sat beside her and handed her my notes. "These are the names and numbers of all the players, as much as she could remember." I identified them in the pictures for her. "All clear?"

"Yes, sir."

"Yes, *Trav*. Can we do it that way, Dana?"

"Of course, Trav."

"When will you get loose?"

"Actually tonight, about midnight. The new girl is taking my accommodations at the Sultana at Miami Beach. Suppose I check in Monday morning with you right here. Nine?"

"Make it ten. Or you can come right here tonight when you're through. There's an extra stateroom. With a lock on the door."

She nodded. "It would be simpler. Lock or no lock, Trav, that's one problem I don't expect to have, and know how to handle if I do."

I went to the desk drawer, tossed the extra key to her. She caught it with a deft twist of the wrist. I explained it was to the lounge door, in case I was asleep when she got in. I took her on the tour. She said it seemed very comfortable. I was glad that with a morning attack of the neats, I had made up the Skeeter-tousled bed afresh. She went to the galley and rinsed her glass and set it out to dry. She went to my desk, wrote Gabe's check, altered my dwindling balance, and presented me the check for signature, saying, "Perhaps you would like me to deposit some of that cash tomorrow? I made a note of the account number."

"Half of it, I guess. Thanks. Remind me tomorrow."

I was asleep when she arrived. The little *bong* of my warning bell alerted me. When anybody comes aboard it rings. Once. That is always enough. I hate unfriendly surprises. I had left a light for her. Gun in hand, I prowled naked to the interior door to the lounge, opened it an inch and looked through, out of darkness, saw her open the door, reach back and get a big suitcase and come in with it, moving quietly. It was ten of one. I went back to my bed, behind the closed door to the master stateroom.

She was a quiet woman. A thread of light appeared under my door. In time I heard water running in the head. The thread of light went out. Soft click of latch of the other stateroom. Night silence. A faint music from some other boat. Grumble of a truck on the drive. Distant whistling scream of a jet.

A woman aboard, quite unlike any I could remember. This was a staunch one. A lot of people can be gutsy when there is a tiny morsel of hope. Damn few keep plugging when there is none. The human animal is basically selfish. Neither the damaged kid nor the lost husband could ·know what degree of care they were getting. Society could not let them perish if she ceased her support. They could not accuse her. But she had a moral obligation so strong, any other course was inconceivable to her. They were her family. There was no other consideration for her. Life had burned her out, but what was left was considerably more woman than was Lysa Dean.

The night thoughts of Dana Holtzer depressed me. Self-evaluation. It is the skin rash of the emotionally insecure. I felt as if I had spent a lot of years becoming too involved with some monstrously silly people. McGee, the con artist. I would fatten myself off their troubles, and then take the money and coast for a time, taking my retirement in early installments. I was not a very earnest or constructive fellow.

But, I thought, what are the other choices? I am not a nine-to-five animal. I cannot swallow the myths which say that nine to five is a Good Thing because that's the way nearly everybody else gets stuck. I cannot be an orderly consumer, with 2.3 kids and .7 new cars a year, and an after-hours secretarial arrangement. I am not properly acquisitive. I like the *Busted Flush*, the records and paintings, the little accumulations of this and that which stir memories, but I could stand on the shore and watch the whole thing go glug and disappear and feel a mild sardonic regret. No Professional American Wife could stomach that kind of attitude.

I went to sleep feeling critical of the restless animal called Travis McGee and awoke to the sunbrightness of nine in the morning coming through the small shaggy draperies in the stateroom, awoke to a scent of coffee and some furtive clinking sounds from the galley.

After I showered, I went out to find her as full of utterly impersonal morning cheer as a waitress in a good hotel. She said she had slept well, thank you. It's a lovely day. The wind has stopped. It's much warmer.

She said she had taken a chance on the eggs. I said scrambled was just fine. The juice was cold, coffee fragrant, bacon crisp, eggs medium. She served us in the booth. It was a pleasure to watch her move. She gave no impression of haste. Yet each movement was sure, and flowed into the next one without hesitation, and so things got done with a fascinating quickness.

She was wearing gray flannel slacks and a yellow sweater. She looked better in slacks than I would have guessed. She did not look really good. That long-waisted figure was a shade too hearty in the seat and hefty in the thigh to look splendid in slacks. Venus de Milo would have looked like hell in stretch pants. They look just fine on the gangly just-ripening teenagers, or on the calculated slimness of a Lysa Dean. But there is something forlorn and slightly touching about the rump of the mature female who fills them all too well. Dana could not have managed stretch pants, but she did sneak by with the beautifully tailored slacks. They were high-waisted enough to fake a little figure correction, and she was wise enough to wear sandals with about an inch and a half of heel to get her center of gravity a little farther from the deck.

As we sat eating our breakfast, I could see why she was worth a lot of money to a Lysa Dean. She had the deft knack of fitting herself to every situation and operating efficiently with a minimum of fuss.

There was no sycophantic flavor about her. She knew her own dignity.

I told her about the *Busted Flush* and how I had acquired it. It is one of my more polished routines. I don't expect people to roll on the floor, but I generally get a little more amusement than I got from her. Her laugh was polite and came in the right places.

Over coffee and cigarettes, the little notebook came out.

"I had a chance to spend quite a bit of time on the phone, Travis. Carl Abelle is at the Mohawk Lodge. He operates their ski school on some sort of franchise arrangement and runs the ski shop. It would be impossible to stay there. They are booked completely. If you want to go there first, we are reserved out of Miami to Kennedy, arriving at two-fifteen tomorrow. There is a feeder flight which will get us to the Utica-Rome airport at four-ten. It is about a sixty-mile drive from there to Speculator up Route Eight, and the roads are clear."

"What do you mean, *if* I want to go there first?"

"Let me tell you about the others. The M'Gruders are divorced. I couldn't locate her. He has remarried, just a short time ago. They've gone cruising down the Pacific coast to Acapulco, and it is possible they may be on their way back by now. I think I will be able to get a line on his ex-wife. But, having a little extra time, I thought I would see what I could find out about Nancy Abbott. Your notes said her father might be an architect. I checked standard reference sources and found a West Coast architect, Alexander Armitage Abbott in San Francisco. I have a friend in San Francisco, one of Bill's old friends actually, who knows everyone. The architect has a daughter named Nancy, age twenty-four, with matching physical description, so it must be the same one. She has had one annulled marriage. She is a problem drinker. She has been in so many messes, the family has sort of washed their hands of her. He said he would make a couple of calls and phone me back. He did, and said she is in Florida, at some sort of voluntary alcoholic retreat down at Bastion Key. It's called Hope Island. Do you know about it?"

"I took them a customer once. I took her back there three times, but it didn't stick. The same guy may still run it."

"A Mr. Burley? I looked it up."

"That's the one. He gave it a good try with my friend. But she borrowed a car, finally, and drove it into a cypress swamp at about a hundred miles an hour."

"I wondered if . . . as long as she's so nearby . . ."

"Right. We'll go down there tomorrow. Cancel us out on the flight north, and don't set it up again until after we've seen her."

"You have a car?"

"In a manner of speaking. After you left yesterday I was wondering what you think of all this."

"I thought I made that clear."

"I mean what you think of it as a woman."

"Is that pertinent?"

"Perhaps. It might help me in talking to the Abbott girl."

She thought for a moment. It was a long strong face, flat planes in the cheeks, very dark and vivid and lovely eyes, a prominent and forceful nose, broad firm mouth.

"I would say this, I guess. Lee isn't a suggestible child, you know. She's had four marriages. And other relationships, some of them not particularly wholesome. But she's always been pretty cautious. She is very frankly and happily promiscuous, but the situation in those pictures I would say is not her natural style. She was lulled into it somehow, and damned uncomfortable about it later on, and still is. I wouldn't know how those other females reacted to it. But I don't think it is accurate to think of Lee as just another woman getting involved in something messy."

"What do you mean?"

"She is a property, Trav. She has few personal rights and privileges. She's just worth too much money to too many people. They can't afford a blemish on her. I've gotten used to thinking that way about her. So when I look at those pictures, I see them in terms of risk. Like watching a clown juggle priceless glassware. Those men were aware of it, of course. The unattainable goddess suddenly right there within reach, tired and drunk and sweaty and willing. They talk, you know. It spreads like ripples. It has had a lot of time. Little hints and rumors are coming back home to roost. She's scared of that, too. She'll be all right until one picture doesn't pay off. Then there could be some reluctance. Why take a chance?"

"How will this picture do, this *Winds of Chance?*"

"Very well, I think. It's the kind of part she always does well. Coffee?"

"Thanks."

After she poured it she hesitated by the table, empty pot in hand.

"You didn't say anything about how you'd like me to dress, Trav. I thought. . . . I imagine women have stayed here with you. I'd be less conspicuous if I . . . stayed with resort clothes."

"You do fine. Use your own judgment."

5

ON THE way down to Bastion Key, Dana was delighted with my stately and ancient pickup truck. It is painted a hideous electric blue and called Miss Agnes by all who know her. It is one of the largest of the old Rolls breed, and some owner of long ago, perhaps after bashing her up, did a backyard job of converting her into a pickup truck. She is high and solid. It takes a long time to move her up through the gears, but when you have a chance to get her up to eighty, she will settle into it all day long in a rushing ghastly silence. She eats gas but holds a little over forty gallons at a time.

I liked Dana's delight. It reminded me of the way she reacted to Skeeter's mouse. I knew I had to watch it, or I would be trapped into the hopeless project of trying to find ways to delight her, to bring out that little spark so deeply buried.

At Bastion Key you turn right off the highway beyond the town and follow a shell road out to a little short causeway that leads over to Hope Island. It is not a luxurious retreat. Stan Burley is the Schweitzer of the gin bottle. The buildings are surplus barracks he brought over by barge long ago. He and all of his small staff are reformed drunks. If he has room, he takes you, at whatever you can afford to pay. He has some theories. They work for him. If you took a seven-foot chimp and shaved every hair off and painted him pink, you'd have a recognizable version of Stan Burley. His graduates who stay dry send contributions regularly.

Before I could turn the motor off, Burley was striding toward us from his little screened office. It was warm and bright, eleven o'clock on Tuesday morning. The Florida bays were blue.

"Ho, McGee," he said, hand outstretched toward me, looking with a keen expectation at Dana, doubtless thinking her a new guest.

I introduced them and said quickly, "We've come down to talk to one of your people, Stan. If possible. Nancy Abbott."

The welcoming light went out of his face. He gnawed his lip. "Miss Holtzer, you go wait in my office a minute, and Jenny will give you a nice glass of iced tea." She nodded and walked away. Burley led me over to a wooden bench in the shade.

"What's it about, Trav?"

"She was involved in something a year and a half ago. I want to ask her some questions about it. Is she all right?"

He shrugged. "She's dry, if that means very much. Has been since October. I shouldn't tell you a damned thing about that one. But you worked so hard with me that time with Marianne. God help us, we fought hard, but we lost that one, boy. I'll have to tell you, it's on my conscience having her here, this Nancy. It isn't the place for her, but no place is, not any more. Did her father send you?"

"No."

"A retired policewoman brought the child here in October. Sick drunk and down to ninety pounds. The D.T.s and the spasms. Pitiful. I got a thousand then, and I get a thousand a month from a San Francisco bank. I write the bank a condition report once a month. After we began to bring her out of it, she puzzled me. I had a doctor friend look her over. Drunk is only part of it. But the thousand a month takes care of a lot of other ones. I'm an evil old man, Trav."

"What's wrong with her?"

"Physically she's as healthy as an ox. She's only twenty-four. She had nine years of drinking, the last five of them heavy, not long enough to damage her. Mentally, you name it, she's got it."

"She's mad?"

"Boy, she isn't sane. What they did, they got too eager with her long ago. Some people who thought shock treatments were the answer to all. A cure for anxiety and depressive symptoms. As far as I can figure, she had over twenty complete series. That and the alcoholic spasms, there's degenerative damage. She doesn't track too well. She can't handle abstract concepts. She's trapped in a manic-depressive cycle. You hit her at her best. She's on her way up now, but not up too high yet. This is her happy time. She could manage in public pretty well if too much wasn't demanded of her. Pretty soon she'll get real wild. Violence, compulsive nymphomania, such a craving for drink she'd kill to get it. Then I put her under restraint.

Then she falls all the way down to the bottom. She won't speak for days. Then she starts to slowly build again."

"How is her memory?"

"Sometimes good and sometimes gone."

I looked at that tired simian face and remembered the way he had talked of Marianne. Of love and destruction.

"What did it to her, Stan?"

"Her? The father did it. The adored, talented, mighty father. It was an ugly marriage. The poor child was too much like her mother, so the father couldn't help despising her. He rejected her. So because she couldn't understand why—just like Marianne—she grew up with a conviction of her own worthlessness. Ah, that's where the compulsions start, McGee. People can *not* endure inexplicable worthlessness. So they establish the pattern of proving themselves worthless. For this child it was sex and drink. The guilts made her emotionally unstable. She was after destruction. The shock treatments and the spasms have done the job for her. She's a destroyed personality. Where can she go? Nothing much can be done for her now. Here is as good as anywhere. Sometimes she is very sweet."

"I don't want to upset her."

"What do you want to ask her?"

"If she can remember some names. If she can remember some pictures being taken."

"Pictures?"

I opened the envelope, sorted out two of them and handed them to him. His face puckered with concern and sorrow.

"The poor kid. See what she's saying, in effect? Love me, love me. Rejection by the father, rejection by the young husband, a butchered abortion, a year in an institution when she was seventeen, for hit and run."

"What would showing her these do?"

"Trav, nothing can do her much good or much harm."

"Will she talk to me?"

"In this part of the cycle she's very outgoing. She might get agitated. It might strike her as funny. I don't know. It might accelerate this phase of the cycle. I can't see as that would do any harm."

"Should you be there?"

"I think you'd get more out of her alone. When there's two people or more she wants to be entertaining. She reacts too much. She talks better to one. My God, boy, those are some pictures! A year and a half ago? I guess she was bad off then, but it would take a trained man to see it. Now anybody can see it."

"What's the best attitude toward her, Stan?"

"Just natural, friendly. If she says nutty things, just steer her back to what you want to talk about. Don't look shocked and don't laugh. We're used to Nancy around here, and every drunk in the world has heard everything there is to hear. Treat her as if she was . . . a bright, sweet, imaginative child."

"Where is she?"

He took me over to the office and pointed. "Go around the dining hall, and the path to the beach starts on the other side of it. I saw her heading that way about twenty minutes or so ago."

I heard her before I saw her. It was a narrow beach, more shell than sand. It was a lovely contralto voice, very rich and full, singing, with maximum feeling, that cigarette commercial about filter, flavor, flip-top box. She was sitting on a palm log about a hundred feet up the bright beach from where the path exited. As I walked toward her, she heard my steps crunching the shell, stopped singing, turned and stared at me, and then stood up and came toward me with a warm and lovely smile of welcome, teeth very white in her sun-darkened face. "*Hello* there!" she said. "I'm Nancy. Are you one of the new ones?"

She wore pale blue Bermudas, and a man's white shirt with the tails knotted around her waist. Her dark hair was in braids. She was tall and lithe, and her eyes were a dark clear blue. After a mental hesitation, I realized she made me think of Jane in the very oldest Tarzan movies. She was barefoot, unwincing on the shells.

"I'm just visiting. My name is Trav."

"Are you visiting Jackie? She doesn't throw up as much. Maybe she can go home. Just to visit."

"As a matter of fact, I'm here to visit you."

All the warmth and light went out of her face. "He just sends people. Tell him I don't give a damn. Now now. Not ever. Screw him. Tell him that."

"Nobody sent me. I just know some people who know you. I was down this way. So I stopped in. That's all, Nancy."

"What people?"

"Carl Abelle. Vance and Patty M'Gruder."

Scowling, she turned away from me and went back and sat on the

log. I followed and stood near her. She squinted up at me. "I know
that Carl. A strong back and a weak mind, believe me. He had that
stupid idea. The perfect orgasm. Can you imagine? Maybe he
thought it worked me up. Damned coward. Too scared to light a fire
in that line shack. My God, it was always cold in there, way up on
that ridge, with Auntie thinking I was on the slopes all day. He stole
a key from the office. Fifty dollars a day she was paying him for personal instruction. We'd pile everything on that bunk. What was he
trying to get? Tell me that? You either come or you don't. Right.
And I almost always do, no matter how quick they are the first time.
Last week or last year I was trying to remember Carl's name. My God,
he was beautiful on skis. When we'd leave that cabin he'd push me
down in the snow and rub snow on my face to get me all pink and
outdoorsy-looking, and then guide me down the slopes, all the way to
the lodge, half stoned on that brandy, like dreaming and floating.
But he said some real dumb things. What was I then? He probably
told you. Nineteen? I guess so. I'm remembering better. You ask
Stan. He'll tell you. But what good is it? I mean, some of the things
you remember. Sit by me. But please, I don't want to talk about
those puke M'Gruders. I don't have to, do I?"

"No."

"What have you got there?"

"Some pictures."

"May I see them, please?"

She held them in her lap. She looked at them slowly and solemnly,
one by one. I watched her face carefully. She sorted one onto the
top. She stroked a thumb along the line of Sonny's back. "Burned,
burned, burned," she said softly.

"Sunburned?"

"Oh, no. He hit a wall. It was his supercharged Merc with special
cams and like that. I wore the big red hat so he could spot me, and I
sat on the wall by the pits that day. We towed that car all over everywhere, and it burned him up in Georgia. It bounced and
bounced." She stroked her thigh. "Sonny liked me in whore clothes.
He bought them all. Tight short skirts and tight bright sweaters, and
he said I had to swing it when I walked. Proud as a rooster and mean
as a snake, Sonny was."

She ran her thumb across his image on the photograph.

"This one right here. Sonny Catton. He took me along when the
party pooped out. I was with him maybe two weeks, and he kept

beating me up, for taking another drink, or somebody making a pass at me, or sometimes just from remembering things from the party. Like this picture here, me with this one. What was his name? Cass? Cass something. He drew funny pictures of people. He gave me one of me and I lost it. You know, I've lost every single goddam thing I ever owned? I got sick of him hammering on me and I went home and what do you know, my fa-fa-f-f . . . the man who married my mother, *he* had pictures like this. He said tell my friends it was no sale. They could publish them in the *Chronicle*. Boy, what a smack across the face he gave me! His face was like a stone. I guessed it bugged him to see pictures of his wife laying people. Wife! Did you hear that! I'm his d-d-daugh-daughter. Made it!"

My skin had the cold quivers, just below the nape of my neck. "What did you do then, Nancy?"

"Are you another doctor? For a thousand years I've been up to my hips in doctors. I was a woman when I was fourteen, and when I got caught doing it, that was when they sent me to the first one, and I could tell he would have liked it too, if he could get up the nerve. He used to get sweaty and clean his glasses and walk around. They all make a big thing out of stuttering when I try to say . . . ef ay tee aitch ee are. Are you going to give me tests?"

"My name is Trav. I'm not a doctor."

"Trav. Trav, why did he tell you to bring me these pictures? They aren't even the same. There were more of me. Hey, you know who this was? This one with no face? A very famous movie star. Lysa Dean! Honestly, I'm not kidding. She's just a little thing, but so gorgeous."

"Who took the pictures?"

"How should I know? I didn't know *anybody* took any pictures until I walked into his study and he had them. He gave me money and I caught up with Sonny again. I was with him a long time. Months, I guess. All over. Wherever he raced. I remember the day he died and the next thing I remember is in the hospital in Mexico City. *Somebody* had to take me down there, but who? I couldn't have *wandered* down there, could I? Somebody dumped me in the hospital parking lot in the middle of the night, I found out later. I had bronchial pneumonia and two broken fingers. I was hallucinating and I had a dose of clap. When I could tell them who I was, they wired . . . him. As soon as I could be moved, he sent people to bring me back and put me in . . . Shady Rest? Refuge Mountain?

One of those crappy names. How do you expect me to remember. I can't even remember being brought *here!*"

"How did your father get those pictures anyhow?"

"How do I know? He thought I knew all about it. He thought it was friends of mine, and we cooked it up to get money out of him."

"This is a pretty good place to be, Nancy."

"I guess so. I guess I like it. Sometimes I get very very nervous. After that I get sad. I'm sad a long time. I hum sad songs all day without making a single sound."

"Did anybody at that house party say anything about pictures of Lysa Dean?"

She turned toward me with an exasperated look. "You know, you get to be a terrible bore about those pictures. No. Nobody said anything. I didn't see a camera. Let's drop it, shall we?"

I put the pictures away. "Why are you mad at the M'Gruders?"

"I don't want to talk about it."

"Then we won't."

"You know, you are terribly nice, Trav." She smiled at me, all abeam with innocence. She put her hand on mine.

"Thank you. You're a nice girl."

"I'm a slut, darling. I'm a drunk and a slut. May I ask you a very personal question?"

"Of course."

"Why don't we go over in the bushes a minute, sweetheart?" She tugged at my hand quickly and strongly, trying to press it against herself. I yanked my hand away. "It keeps me from getting nervous," she said. "Please, honey. Please, please, please."

I stood up quickly and she jumped up to try to press herself against me. I held her off with my hands on her shoulders. She dipped her head sharply to the side and licked my hand.

I shook her. "Nancy! Nancy! Cut it out!"

She shuddered, smiled sadly, backed away. "It never makes any difference to a man. Why should you care one way or the other?"

"I have to get back. It was nice to visit with you."

"Thank you," she said politely. "Come and see me again." She squared her shoulders like a child about to recite. "When you get back there, tell my f-f . . . tell him I am being a good girl. Tell him that . . . I am getting good marks."

"Of course."

"Good-by."

I walked the hundred feet to the entrance to the path. When I turned and looked back at her, she shook her fist at me and yelled, "You ask that Patty M'Gruder why she kept locking me up! You just ask that goddam bitch!"

Halfway back to the compound I stopped in the path and leaned against a tree. My knees felt strange. I lit a cigarette, took one drag and threw it away. Stan Burley was in the small office talking to Dana. He got up and brought me some iced tea and said, "How did it go?"

"I don't know. Her memory was pretty good. It damn near broke my heart listening to her trying to call him father. What's the matter with that son of a bitch? He threw her away. He threw away a pretty good person, I think."

"Was she any help?"

"I don't know. I have to check it out. Stan, she made a hell of a direct pass at me."

He raised his ridged monkey brows. "Little early for that. I'll start keeping a close watch on her. Thanks."

"What's the prognosis?"

He wiped his hand across his face. "I don't know. The highs don't seem to get any higher, but the periods of apathy seem deeper and seem to last a little longer. And when she comes up out of them I have the feeling . . . there's a little less of her. She's lost some songs she knew a month ago. She's getting a little more awkward and untidy feeding herself and caring for herself. I . . . I guess we'll keep her here as long as we can. She loves the beach so. She hates to be locked in. This place has the illusion of freedom. Maybe a big institution could arrest it, or even improve her a little, but never enough to let her out into the world. She isn't dangerous to anyone. She's a victim. He made her a victim."

"What happened to her mother?"

"She died in a hotel fire when Nancy was seven. She was with a lover at the time. Nancy has a strong body. I am afraid it will keep going long after the brain is gone. Maybe for another forty years or more. There is a brother. Older, and from all reports, extremely righteous. Nice to see you again, Trav. Nice to talk to you, Miss Holtzer. It's a strange world, you know. We can defend ourselves from our enemies, and even from our friends, but never from our family. That tyke was sent to boarding school at age seven. She had lovers at fourteen, alcoholic dementia in a mild form at fifteen, and her first shock treatments at sixteen. I am off to paint chairs. My cure for depression and indignation. Come by any time, either of you."

We stopped at a fish house in town for lunch. We had the privacy of a corner booth. I told her about the dead one. Sonny Catton. I told her about the eight pictures, the slap, the hostility toward the M'Gruders, her final strange comment.

"From the way you look it was rough, Travis."

"I guess so. I don't know why it rocked me so. I guess because she looks so fresh and clean and bright. I guess a man gets the feeling . . . a lovely mixed-up girl, if you could take her along, love her, treat her well, she'd shape up. But you know you can't. Maybe the last one to be in a position to do anything was Catton, but he wasn't the type for it. I guess she got handed around quite a bit, with none of them doing her much good."

I told her about Carl Abelle. The corners of her strong mouth turned downward in an ironic smile. "The Galahad of the slopes. I met him once. I'd been working for her just a matter of weeks. It was quite a while later they went off to stay in that Chipmann house. He was pretty gorgeous. Dark blond curly hair, huge shoulders, bronzed face, custom sports coat, silk ascot, and a little faky German accent. Hair a little much over the ears. You know. A little wave there too. Lots of huge white teeth, and a very Continental handshake. The almost too typical Hollywood stud."

"Smart enough to rig a blackmail thing on Lee?"

"Oh, I doubt it. I doubt it very much. It couldn't have been his idea in any case. Somebody could have bullied him into it. I think he would shatter quite easily under pressure. Only a damn fool would have tried to use him that way. He would crack too easily. And it wasn't a fool who arranged it all."

"Have any ideas?"

"Who there had money or reputation or something to lose? Lee, and the architect's daughter, and the M'Gruders. Cass apparently, and Sonny and Whippy and the college boys and Carl would be very small fry, not worth the effort compared to the others."

"Agreed. Keep going."

She shrugged. "There's nowhere else to go. We know that two out of the three were contacted. Lee paid off. Mr. Abbott apparently

didn't. And we'll know about the M'Gruders later on. We should go
to San Francisco, I imagine. After Abelle or before?"

"After."

"Tomorrow?" I nodded. She slid out of the booth. "I'd better do
some phoning right now then." She walked to the cashier for change.

When we got back to the boat, Dana checked her copy of Lysa
Dean's promo schedule and found that Lysa would be starting a rest
hour in about another fifteen minutes. She waited twenty minutes
and phoned her on a private line that did not go through the hotel
board. They talked together for about fifteen minutes. Then Dana
called to me, holding the phone with her palm over the mouthpiece.

"She wants to talk to you. I've caught her up to date on all of it."

When I spoke to her, Lee said in a lazy drawl, "Sweetie, how do
you like the little giftie I sent you?"

"I beg your pardon?"

"The highly efficient tragic figger, stupid."

"Oh, fine, just fine."

"She'll keep you honest and keep you scrambling, dear. I miss her
already. Little things are starting to get fouled up. So don't keep her
too long."

"I didn't make any request, you know."

"Oh, don't be stuffy! And by the way, McGee, don't waste your
time in any idle hopes. She's quite something in a sort of swarthy
hearty way. The look of banked fires or something. Some of the
greatest experts in the industry have taken their Sunday hack at that,
dear, and wandered glassily away with icicles forming on their
whatsis. It's sort of an in-group joke."

"I'm laughing myself sick."

"You are really a wretched chap, aren't you? Why do I still like
you? I understand the Abbott girl is out of the ball park."

"Did she seem odd to you at the time?"

"Not particularly. She kept belting herself pretty good, so who expected too much sense? And she was pretty rowdy now and again.
Roughhousing into other people's little games. She kept talking
about her dear daddy. And singing that song at very strange moments. 'My heart belongs to' and so forth. When you see Carl, dear,
grasp his hand, smile, give him my love, and kick him solidly in the
jewels. I would pay a small bonus for that."

"Just one thing. Is that little accent of his genuine?"

"God, no! It's for the ski trade."

"Are you getting good protection?"

"So far it looks fine. Take care of yourself. Dana will keep me informed."

"Want to speak to her again?"

"Good-by and love to you both. Happy hunting."

I hung up and said, "You plan to keep her informed?"

She had taken the checkbook from the desk drawer to post the cash deposit she had made. She looked over at me, one dark eyebrow lifting slightly. "In that business, she's so used to intrigue. Everybody watches everybody. And if you work *for* somebody you have to be at a certain established level, a pecking order. She's just trying to fit you into the ranks, Travis, somewhere between a script writer and an associate producer. She doesn't know it won't work, but there's no point in . . . in making a point of it. I'll tell her what she should know, and enough to keep her happy, and no more or less than that. Okay?"

"Divided loyalty?"

"Not really. You are both after the same thing, aren't you?"

"Should that be a question?"

"Mr. Burley told me about a girl named Marianne. I don't have as many questions about you as I used to."

"I'm reasonably honest, Dana, in my own way. That's about as far as I can go with it. Maybe I have a price. Nobody's come up with just the right amount yet. But maybe next time. Let's see how quick you can get us out of here, Efficient Girl."

6

SHE MANAGED to switch it to earlier arrangements on Wednesday. By noon, in a gray February world, we had come down through snow flurries to land at Albany and had taken off again. When the snow ended the sky was a luminous gray. I looked down at the winter calligraphy of upstate New York, white fields marked off by the black woodlots, an etching without color, superbly restful in contrast to the smoky, guttering, grinding stink of the airplane clattering across the sky like an old commuter bus.

Dana seemed pensive. She had tilted her window seat and had her face turned toward the window, and I could not tell whether her eyes were open or closed. I looked at her still hands resting in her lap, against the nubbly fabric of her suit skirt. You look at hands long enough, you can turn them into animal paws. Her hands were a little larger than perhaps they should have been, the fingers very long and firm, the nails oval, quite narrow, convex. The pads of fingers and palm were heavy. The backs of her hands were very smooth and youthful. You look at hands as animal paws, and you think of the animal aspects of the human, and suddenly you are back on that Pacific terrace, seeing that final and most dangerous form of gluttony.

Perhaps, I thought, the most absolute way of categorizing people is by what they are capable of and what they are not capable of. Temptation does not deliver most of us into evil, because temptation is a constant and evil is a sometime thing with most of us.

So far I had seen only two people whose pattern of life had led, almost implacably, toward that terrace. One of them had been on exhibition all her adult life, driven by restless greed, emotional instability, a desire to be noticed. Her artificiality had made this just another act, not particularly real to her while it was happening. The younger one had become food for Jack London's Noseless One long before Carl Abelle and the M'Gruders led her onto that terrace. It, like Mexico, like the tour with Sonny Catton, was just another part of the self-destruction.

I would never talk to Catton. Perhaps it had not mattered a damn to him one way or the other. For the soul to be offended it must first exist. Perhaps to snake-mean Sonny, broads were broads were broads, and if they came in a bundle instead of in separate rooms, he could not care less. He had brought one along and discarded it for one that suited him better. Perhaps for him it was like an exchange counter.

I could not be Sonny. I had the old illusions, including the one that maybe I might be gaining a little bit, just a very damn little bit, in wisdom as my time went by. And wisdom says there are no valuable goods on the bargain counter. Wisdom says the only values are the ones you place on yourself. And I have locked myself into this precarious role of the clown-knight in the tomato-can armor, flailing away at indifferent beasts with my tinfoil sword. A foible of the knight, even the comic ones, is the cherishing of women, and perhaps even my brand of cherishing is quaint in this time and place. Though I have faltered from time to time, I do want the relationship, if it does become intimate, to rest solidly on trust, affection, respect. Not just for taking, or scoring, or using, or proving anything. That knocks out group adventures right there. Not for recreation, not for health rationalizations, not for sociologically constructive contacts. But because she is a woman, and valuable. And you are a man, and equally valuable. There are more than enough girls and boys around. Break down, McGee. Say it. Okay, for love and love alone. They are people, goddam it, not pneumatic, hydraulic, terrace toys. Not necessarily Heloïse and Abelard, Romeo and Miss Capulet, or even Nappi and Jo. But just a crumb of some kind of love there, lad. Love that makes her sweet to hold, warm to murmur to, after no more fireworks are left in the park. And you can't do that with a terrace toy.

Dana rolled her head toward me and smiled and said, "I was almost asleep." She put a fist against her yawn. "You know, when you are thinking of something and then it all turns crazy and then it turns real again, and you know a dream got mixed into it."

"Tell me the crazy part."

"It's just plain dull, Trav, really. I was wondering if the car would be there as I ordered, and then suddenly I was remembering the last time you and I wanted a car—we didn't ever, of course—and we walked out and got into it and it didn't have any wheels. You were furious and you kept saying they always did that to us. And I was thinking that this time I would look for the wheels before signing the slip, and suddenly I realized how nutty that was. I suppose some psychiatrist would have a ball with that."

"I suppose he'd say you were realizing I can't get anyplace with you."

I said it off the top of my mind. She looked at me for another moment and then said, too casually, "I guess you could make it mean almost anything." She turned her face away again, and I saw the redness climb her throat and up her cheek, suffuse her forehead and slowly die away. It had been too logical a guess, and she had for a moment accepted it, and then taken the next step of translating what it meant to dream that this time she'd look for the wheels before signing the slip. I realized I had innocently created the sort of awareness which would keep her doubly on guard against any kind of emotional involvement with me, no matter how minor.

She arranged the car while I claimed the luggage. When she got in beside me, she had a marked map in her hand. She showed it to me and said, "Just the general idea. I'll call the turns." A most valuable gal.

"Food?" I asked.

"Woops," she said, and scrambled out and hustled back into the terminal. She came out with new marks on the map, and we went a few blocks out of our way into North Utica into one of those Italian-Tourist-Close-to-Motels enterprises called the Diplomat. It wasn't going to excite any far-flung gourmet exclamations, but the shots of antifreeze were excellent protection against the 35-degree afternoon, the lowering sky, the chill moistness of the air. Hot Italian sausage with spaghetti *al dente* was a similar precaution.

You know how it is. You wonder. We had drifted into a silence not entirely comfortable. I hadn't seen much lift or life in her. If we were going to spend a lot of time together, it could become a drag. So you wonder, and you think something up. When you say it, you more than half expect a totally blank look and some kind of query like, for example, "Hah! What's that?"

So when she just started to wind a fork of spaghetti, I said to her, "By God, Myra, I bet you forgot to turn the thermostat down."

Her fork clattered on the plate and she said instantly, "I forgot to turn it down? Frank, dear, it was on *your* list. Remember?"

"Of course it was on my list. I reminded you and crossed it off."

"I'd think that once, just once, you could . . . what was it set for?"

"Seventy-five. What else? Sixty-eight is enough for normal people. Y*ou* have to have seventy-five."

"Oh, God, all that lovely oil. Darling, maybe we could phone the Hollisbankers."

"So how do they get in?"

She hesitated a moment. "I have it! With Helen's figure, Fred could slip her under the door."

I broke up. A clear victory for her side. You never know until you try. We laughed like a pair of idiots, and then her very next chuckle turned into a strangled howling sob and she jumped up and fled for the ladies' room, nearby lunch customers staring at her and me. She had finished most of her lunch. I finished mine. I would say she was gone a good ten minutes. When she came out her color was not good. Her fine eyes were red-rimmed. She slipped meekly into her chair. She told the waitress she was finished. Just coffee, please.

"I'm sorry," she said to me. "I didn't expect that. It got a little too close. All of a sudden. I'm sorry, it was just a little too much like . . . another game I used to play. Don't look so concerned. It wasn't your fault."

"I won't try it again."

"That's probably better."

The coffee came. The silence was laborious. As we were getting ready to leave, she suddenly gave me a strained and vivid smile and reached a trembling hand across to touch my wrist and said, "Darling, did you remember to mail the cards to Mom and Sis?"

"I mailed them. Your mother got the one of the bucks with their horns locked."

She pursed her lips for a moment, and I knew she was thinking how to cue me so I could win. "I wonder if Mom will think there's some kind of symbolism there, dear, and get upset or anything."

"Baby, fighting over dough is the thing she does best."

She laughed. Acknowledgment of defeat. Bad jokes win. Her eyes glistened, but she laughed. I was proud of her for coming through, but I could not help feeling guilty too. She had her adjustment, her acceptance. It wasn't fair to stir her up. It wasn't fair to her for me to want to see her lift a bit, to see what she looked like behind the iron control. Two games had set a pattern. We were Myra and Frank. If I tried another round, she would feel obligated. So I would leave it up to her to start the next one. And she would know I was leaving it up to her and why. That was the funny thing about us, back in the beginning. I had the absolute confidence in her knowing what I was thinking.

We went north up Route 8 into the hills. We went through a village named Poland. It looked like a Christmas card. The roads were dry, the snow banked high. It was the sort of town that you do not particularly want to live in, but wish you had come from. It looked like a very good place to be from.

Farther up into the Adirondack Forest Preserve, the air was clearer and colder. The heater in the little sedan was comforting. Winding road, winter lakes, blackness of the evergreens against snow, tree-stubbed hills like the humpbacks of old browsing beasts, eating away at eternity. At least we had changed the quality of our silences. Or that lovely land had changed it.

Speculator, at almost four in the afternoon, was about the size of Poland, but with about one-fifth the charm. Progress had begun to clomp down its main drag, whanging at a tin drum, sending off little clusters of neon. The ski kids were roaming the area, hooting their rut cries at each other, speckling the snowbanks with their bright empty beer cans. I parked in front of a big supermarket-type general store called Chas Johns, where all the fluorescence was on in the gray dullness of the overcast afternoon, and Dana called from an outdoor phone booth. She was back in a few moments and said, "They say he went down to Gloversville to pick up a railway express shipment of skis or something, and they expect him back at six."

"So, accommodations, I guess. I want a chance to measure him a little, get the right time and place to break him open."

"Remember, he'll recognize me."

"I know. And I may need you for the finale, after he's gone soft. We'll see."

"It's strange. You make him sound like a locked box."

"That's what they are, Dana. And usually somebody skimped on the design. Bad welds and a dime-store lock."

There was a small and relatively new motel jammed into almost the center of town at a strange angle. I made a try. The gentleman in command said he had one twin-bed room only because he had a cancellation, and he could let it go for one night only, because he was reserved from Thursday right through the weekend, and so was everybody else. It was good snow and a good forecast, and it looked like one of the big weeks of the season.

I went back out and got in behind the wheel and said, "Dana, I can't help how this sounds, believe me. It's a high-school routine all the way. You can go in and ask him." I told her what I'd learned, and said, "Suppose I take it and you drive back down to Utica and stay there and come on back out in the morning."

She hesitated for four seconds and then said, "If you'd just do something about that horrible snoring, see a doctor, anything, then we wouldn't have to go through this all the time."

"Myra, I freely admit I do breathe a little heavy."

"A little heavy! When you get going, the neighbors run out into the night screaming 'Lion, Lion.'"

"Only when I get over onto my back, dear."

"Then you have a back on both sides. Anyway, dear, I'll sleep so well in this mountain air, I don't think you'll bother me tonight. But do try to hold it down to a dull roar."

"You act as if I enjoyed it."

"Because, my pet, you *sound* as if you were enjoying it."

A car came in and I was afraid we would lose the room if we waited the game out, so I went in and signed us in as T. McGee and wife. The two three-quarter beds seemed to crowd the room. We did a lot of polite walking around each other, getting organized. An electric wall heater kept the room reasonably comfortable. With one quick trip to the ice machine, and with a considerable magic, she materialized a squat broad silver cup, the right amount of gin on ice, the two drops of bitters.

"The celebrity treatment?" I said ungraciously.

"I wouldn't want to get out of practice."

"Well . . . thanks. It's fine."

"You are so welcome, Travis."

We decided it would be best to leave her right there while I took the first little prod at Carl Abelle. The Mohawk Lodge was seven or eight miles out Indian Lake Road, over some impressively hilly highway. The grounds were aglare with floodlights against snow. The establishment was garishly new, pale varnished pine, A-frames, Swiss-kwaint gables. The sign advertised three tows, eight downhill runs, instruction, beginners' slope, Icelandic bathhouse, prime steaks, cocktails. The whole place was noisy, bursting at the seams, with much coming and going and giggling and hooting.

I worked my way into what seemed to be the main lounge. An ox could have been roasted on a spit in the fieldstone fireplace. The ceiling was low, beams huge. There were a lot of overstuffed couches and chairs, and deep rugs underfoot. There seemed to be a great number of young people sprawled on the floor. I saw several legs in casts, arms in slings. Sweating waiters brought drinks from a corner bar, stepping over and around the people, grimly ignoring the shouts for service. A big stereo juke made loud rock music, and some snow bunnies were energetically trying to revive the Twist, wearing their indoor-fireside-snuggle-pants rather than their outdoor togs.

I angled toward a waiter and stuffed a bill in his shirt pocket. It bought me four seconds of attention. "Carl Abelle," I asked.

He pointed with his head and said, "Red jacket."

Abelle was leaning against a paneled wall. He wore a red blazer with an Olympic pocket patch, silver buttons, a white silk ascot. He stood with his head bowed, a dainty little snow bunny in each arm. One of them was talking directly into his ear. She writhed and she worked her face in the curious manner of many women telling a dirty joke. I held off until she had made her point. Silvery glissandos from the girls. A hohoho from Abelle. I moved in and the three of them looked up at me with the polite glaze the in-groupers give the outsider. I wasn't wearing the garments.

The girls looked very young, and the out-of-doors had given them both a lovely healthy flush. But their eyes looked wise and old. Carl looked magnificent. The bronzed blond hero, white of tooth, clear of eye. But somehow it all looked like makeup. And in spite of the tailoring, he seemed to be getting a little thick around the middle.

"Abelle?"

"Yesss?"

"I bring you a message from friends."

"Zo?"

"From Cass. From Vance and Patty. From Lee and Sonny and Whippy and Nancy and the whole gang."

"I know zose people?"

"Yes, you know zose people." I didn't say any more. I let him hang there. He added them up. He wasn't very good at it. His face got sulky and wary.

"Oho," he said. "Would you mean Miss Abbott? And the M'Gruders?"

"And the Cornell boys too."

"Giff them all my best regards, ya?"

"That wasn't exactly the message, Carl."

"Zo?"

"If we could take a two-minute walk."

He hugged the bunnies, whispered to them, sent them off toward the fireplace with an identical little stroke at each upholstered little behind.

"Now we can talk here, Mister . . . ?"

"It's something in the car I want to show you."

"Bring it in."

"I'm sorry. I have to follow Miss Dean's instructions."

He gained a little confidence. "Zo, you work for her. A very lovely little lady, ya?"

"She sends her very special regards."

He puffed up nicely. But then he remembered the names I had given him. He was not intellectualizing anything. He merely had the animal's awareness of something not quite right. "What could that dear woman send me you could not bring in?"

I winked at him most solemnly. "Herself."

He puffed up and he glowed. "Of courze!" He nudged me. "I understand."

"She isn't exactly waiting out in the car, you understand. She's at a private lodge down by the lake. She heard you were here. She said it was a very pleasant surprise. She's staying with old friends. Incognito."

"She sent you to bring me there?"

"On impulse. You understand."

"Oh, of courze!"

"Shall we go?"

He nibbled at his mouth, an Airedale frown between the hero brows. "I must come back later. Social obligations here. But yes, it would be rude not to go at once."

We went out to the rental car. His red blazer was handsome in the floodlights, between the snowbanks. He strutted. There was a Teutonic wrinkle across the back of his neck. Maybe it had grown there in response to the faked accent. I had two inches in height, and he had at least fifteen pounds in weight. I couldn't risk taking any sporting chance with him. He might know how.

I hurried past him and opened the car door for him. He accepted it with regal satisfaction. As he started to bend to duck into the car, I screwed my feet firmly into the packed snow, pivoted very smartly and, with the best right hook I have, made a very good attempt to drive that middle silver button of the jacket right through to his backbone. These little melodramas always make me feel like a jackass. But you must do them briskly. A sudden, merciless, ugly violence is the great leveler. Men revert to childhood. The night is full of spooks and ghosties, and they are reminded of death. A man whipped in a fair fight retains stubborn remnants of pride and honor. A man rendered helpless without warning is much more suggestible. With a great gassy belch, he doubled. With hands clasped together, I chopped down against the back of his neck, off to one side, just below the mastoid bone. As he crumpled, I body-blocked him into the car, kicked his dangling legs inside and slammed the door. I imagine it took about three and a half seconds.

I got behind the wheel. He was wedged partially under the dash. His relaxation was total. I could hear him snore. A few hundred yards down the highway I pulled over, hauled him onto the seat, removed his white silk scarf and tied his wrists together with it. I tied them together in crossed position, under his husky thighs. He toppled over against the door and moaned. Pathos in silver buttons. The world is shiny and the surface is a little too frangible. Something can reach out of the black and grab you at any moment. Everybody wears a different set of compulsions. You can be maimed without warning, in body or in spirit, by a very nice guy. It is the luck of your draw. I did not feel like a nice guy. His red coat was a little too brave and pretty. Now it was a child's toy on the beach after the child drowns. This one was not villainous. He was just a silly stud. A ski-slope, and less reptilian, version of Harry Diadem, a specialist in racing wax and erogenous zones.

I drove on down into Speculator, looking for a place to take him. The snowbanks made it difficult. I turned west on Route 8, and after about a mile I found a darkened structure on the right, some sort of building supply establishment. The drive and parking lot in the rear had been plowed out. Nearby houses were dark. I could see no pedestrians in the glow of the spaced streetlights of the village. No traffic was coming in either direction at the moment. So I turned in quickly, skidding the back end, bumping it off a snowbank, turning off the car lights as I reached the parking lot. I backed it around behind the building, ready to head out. I got out quickly, looking around to see if I had attracted any attention. Snow laid a silence across the land. A dog barked, a comfortable distance away. Night sky speckled with silver. Bare trees in silhouette. Moving flicker of light as cars went by. It was about 20 degrees, I guessed, not too uncomfortable with no wind.

I opened the door on his side. He was coming out of it enough to strain for balance, but he came rolling out, onto the packed soiled snow of the parking area. I bent, braced myself well and picked him up, the two hundred and twenty or so pounds of him, striving to make it seem effortless. The mature male is seldom picked up. It resonates the lost memories of babyhood. It induces a feeling of helplessness. I walked four strides with him and dropped him into the slope of the five-foot bank of bulldozed snow, dropped him butt first, as into an armchair. He chunked down into it, tilted slightly back, feet free, knees up, lashed wrists holding him hunched and about as helpless as a man can be.

He shook his splendid leonine head slowly and said, "Sick. Real sick. Please."

When anything begins to fit their television or movie preconceptions they try to move toward the hero role. So one must give it a flavor they can't comprehend. Cops are good at it. Jocular. You can learn a lot from cop technique.

I stood close and reached to him and rumpled his blond locks with the casual affection you extend toward a small boy. I chuckled. I patted his cheek three times, and on the fourth pat I gave it a little more steam. It was not a blow, yet not a pat. It was a sharp demand for attention. Pay attention to teacher, boy.

My eyes had adjusted. I could see him clearly. Things had moved too quickly for him. He was staring at me with a dumb willingness to ingratiate himself. It was exactly the right attitude. It was a cheap tin box and a joke lock, and it had opened at a touch.

"Carl, baby, Lee is over a thousand miles from here, and she wouldn't say hello if she met you on the street."

"What are you . . . ?"

"She's a big investment. The people I work for get very nervous about her. You can understand that, Carl, baby."

"I don't know what you . . ."

"They are very very annoyed with you, sweetie. You've been very stupid and very naughty. And you've gotten their investment very upset. You shouldn't have played ball with the people who wanted to give Lee a hard time. You should have realized we'd come after you sooner or later, baby."

"This is some kind of a mis . . ."

"Don't play dumb. It's too late for that. You have had it. They don't give me much discretion. At the very least, Carl, I have to break you up a little. Like two or three weeks' worth. And at the very most, I get my little shovel out of the truck and stick you under this snow."

The bulge of his eyes tipped me, so when the mouth opened wide for a roar of terror and protest, I packed it swiftly with a handful of snow. After he had coughed and huffed and spat, I used a handkerchief to wipe the snow water off his face. His teeth clittered. He was melting himself wet, but it was fright and cold both.

"Please!" he said. "I don't know what . . ."

I rumpled his hair again. "The *pictures*, sweetie! The photographs, the pics, the way she got set up for it on that terrace. Like this one."

I had it in an inside pocket, folded once. I held it in front of his eyes, a lighter flame off to one side. A Lysa Dean sandwich. I put it away when he closed his eyes.

"Oh," he said weakly. "Oh, God."

I said softly, "Now can you tell me a *good* reason why you shouldn't die young, sweetie?"

7

I GOT back to the motel room a few minutes before nine. The door was unlocked. As I came in, Dana got up from the room's only armchair and came toward me, silhouetted against the lamplight.

"You were gone so long," she said.

The room was warm. I took my jacket off and stretched out on one of the beds. "A long time and a long way away," I said. "Scratch one ski instructor. We can leave now, if you want."

She looked down at me for a few moments, and then went and fixed another drink in that silver cup. I perched on one elbow and sipped it. "A lot bigger than the last one," I said.

"It seemed like a good idea."

"You've got good instincts." She sat on the foot of the bed. I shifted my feet to make room for her.

"Did . . . you hurt him?"

"I didn't leave a mark on him. I just finished sneaking him to his room up there at the lodge. He didn't want anybody to see him. His legs didn't work very well. I had to help him out of the car. I had to walk him, with my arm around his waist. He was crying like a kid. He had the snuffles. He kept telling me how grateful he was I didn't kill him. He likes me. It's a quick dependency relationship, something like getting emotionally hooked on your psychiatrist. At his door I patted him on the shoulder and told him to get a good night's rest. No, Dana, I didn't leave any visible marks. But I left the other kind. They last longer."

After a silence she said, "Trav, why do you do this sort of thing if it bothers you so much?"

"Maybe I like it. Maybe that's what bothers me."

"Look at me and tell me you like it."

"Okay. So it was just smart-ass talk. I left him with less. Less assurance, less faith, less confidence. Maybe his mask will start to slip a little from now on. The tone of voice won't be exactly right. The snow bunnies will detect it. And one of them will be a little too knowing, and push the right buttons, and big Carl Abelle will come up impotent just once. Once is all it will take, because that's about all he's got left."

She put her hand on my ankle, a light quick touch, like a pat of assurance. "Travis, if you can feel this way, and keep on feeling this way, isn't it all right for you? What if you should become indifferent to . . . this business of opening people up like little dirty boxes?"

"Maybe I care less now than I did a few years back."

"Is Abelle so valuable?"

"Isn't that the key to it, Dana? This act of judging the value of anyone? Is it something I am entitled to do for money? If we're judging value, why am I working for your boss?"

"Why am I?" We watched each other. Suddenly she grinned. "Don't try to fool me or yourself, McGee. If you'd learned anything important from him, you wouldn't be acting like this."

I admitted it. She fixed me a new drink. I told her what I had learned. Not very much. He was certain of one thing. No one had followed Lysa Dean to the Chipmann house. None of the playmates could have tipped anybody off that she was there, because he had not said who he was shacked with, and after they all got there, no one left until it was all over, and the phone was disconnected. Cass was Caswell Edgars, a San Francisco artist. Abelle had not known that Nancy Abbott had gone off with Sonny Catton, nor that Sonny was dead. He had confirmed that Nancy had been houseguesting with the M'Gruders in Carmel, and had said that Vance M'Gruder was a friend of Alex Abbott, Nancy's elder brother.

"Nothing else?" she asked.

"Just guesses. But how good are they? A terrorized man tries to please, like a hypnotic subject. Rule out the Cornell boys. Rule out Cass Edgars and the waitress. And, according to Abelle, we can rule out Lysa Dean too. Security was good. So who was the target? Nancy Abbott? Vance M'Gruder? Patty M'Gruder? There's money there. Blackmail targets. Miss Dean was pure profit. The pictures sent Nancy's father were not the same as the ones sent Lee. Okay, so the fellow took perhaps a dozen rolls. Two dozen. Two hundred and fifty to five hundred shots. He could have another set to sell Vance, another to sell Patty, maybe a set for everybody until he could find out which ones had the money. Maybe he started out, for God's sake, after nesting water birds and hit a jackpot on the terrace a hundred yards away."

"But the idea of it being an accident doesn't appeal?"

"No. Before they bought the groceries, they all knew the name of the absentee owners of the house where they were going. If it was set up, either somebody in the group, during the milling around before they took off in the cars, tipped the cameraman off, or they were being followed. Somehow I like the first choice, Dana. It goes with the way the party developed, as if it was being staged that way."

"Could he tell you who started it?"

"He said it just happened. Everybody tight. One of those real swinging parlor games, revised for a sun terrace. Somebody gets blindfolded, crawls around, and the first person they touch has to hold still, not make a sound, and be identified by touch. Guess right and the one identified loses one item they're wearing, and gets the blindfold. Guess wrong and the guesser loses one item and tries again."

"Sounds gaudy."

"He said nobody really started it. They made up the rules as they went along."

"With much jolly laughter."

"It's a funny thing about Abelle. He had absolutely no idea any pictures were taken. But he did have the feeling that something was wrong. And he is not a sensitive guy. He couldn't put it into words. After the group had broken up and he was alone again with Lee, he had the feeling that something was going to work out badly for somebody."

"Wouldn't anyone have that feeling after all that?"

"If it was new to them, I guess so. But Abelle has had that kind of group action before and since, and the other times didn't hit him that way. *Something* gave him that feeling. *Somebody* made him react that way. But he was drunk. I couldn't dig it out. He had the feeling somebody was going to kill somebody sooner or later, because of that house party."

"Where do we go next, Travis?"

"I want to know how Nancy Abbott's father got her pictures, and if there was any more contact."

I put the silver cup aside. It seemed that moments later Dana was gently shaking me awake. There was a delicious aroma in the room. She had walked to a place almost next door called the Log Cabin Restaurant, eaten there and brought me back a huge bowl of home-made clam chowder and a broiled hamburger as thick as her wrist. It tasted as fine as it smelled.

I awoke again. The room was dark. My shoes were off. There was a blanket over me, but the cold had awakened me. A glow of the sign outside came through the blinds, and I could see the sleeping shape of her in the other bed, hair dark against the pillow. I made a silent trip to the bathroom, came back and undressed to my shorts and slipped into the cool sheets and was asleep in an instant. You can seldom guess what will exhaust you emotionally. That hulk of brave muscle had been a weak and pretentious child. In my dreams I heard him sob. Oh, please don't. Oh, please. Oh, please, mister.

She had flight schedules indicating we could do better out of Syracuse. So we got an early start and went down to the Thruway and west to the Syracuse airport, through a cold gray morning and some tentative snow flurries. She found the best way out, through to Chicago and then nonstop to San Francisco. I noticed something about her, in the ticketing and the baggage arrangements and turning in the rental car, and even with the stewardesses. With absolutely no fuss at all, she got the maximum service merely by an attitude—smiling and polite—which seemed to make anything less than perfect service unthinkable. She could raise one eyebrow and bring a porter hustling from eighty feet away. It is a rare gift. I tried to take over some of the chores, but it seemed to make her feel uncomfortable. It was her job and she was used to it, and she knew how to keep everything straight. I had all the benefit of her efficiency. People stared at me as though trying to remember where they had seen me. This knack of getting exactly what you want exactly when you want it is something shared by great ladies, royalty and the very best executive secretaries. Also I must admit that her strong and handsome face and the sparkling intensity of her dark eyes gave the impression that if things did not go her way, all hell would break loose immediately. But it was odd to have someone else taking such efficient care. I began to feel a little like the honeymoon bride of an important widower. Or a boy being taken to camp by one of those supermothers.

She tried to resist being given a window seat. After we'd latched the seat belts, she checked her little notebook and said, "We'll have an hour and fifty minutes in Chicago. I'll make some phone calls from there. Are you perfectly comfortable, Travis? Is there anything you'd like?"

"You'd better hustle up forward and help them with the checklist for takeoff, honey."

Her mouth tightened and her face got slightly red. "I'm not trying to be officious."

"You are a little overwhelming, Dana."

"You could do it all just as well. But why should you?"

"Okay. Thanks. You're very good."

It was not gracious. Most of my women have not been particularly useful outside the home. I looked at her emotionless profile and sighed and said, "Aw, come *on*, Myra."

Reluctantly her mouth softened. "You get these ugly moods, Frank."

"I keep worrying about how things are going back at the office."

"Honey, I bet they hardly know you're gone."

"Oh, thanks. Thanks a lot. That's a big help." She was laughing with me. Her eyes laughed too. It went deep. That kind of affection is seriously underrated among the hack and grab set. To whom should they give trust? To someone who likes them. When she laughed or smiled broadly I could see that one of the eyeteeth, the one on the left, was set in there aslant, making a little overlap with the tooth in front of it. When an imperfection looks very dear to you, heed the message. Lysa Dean's teeth were mercilessly perfect. No message there. Maybe some of my awareness made a little mark. Dana Holtzer suddenly stopped the real laughter, and went along for a little while on some fake laughter, and then folded herself back into herself, out of sight and out of reach, becoming once again the secretarial presence beside me, smart in wool, laced, girdled, hammocked and erect, her neck severe, eyes distant, seat belt pulled tight for takeoff.

Alexander Armitage Abbott, A.I.A., lay dying in room 310 of University Hospital in San Francisco. There was a waiting room at the end of the corridor. A gray rain which was going to continue forever streaked the waiting room windows, obscuring the view of gray hills. It was Friday afternoon. Dana and I sat like dulled passengers in a heavy train sidetracked at the end of noplace. She put a frayed magazine back in the rack and came over to sit beside me on the couch.

"You're doing fine," I told her.

"I don't like that young man. Or his wife."

"It shows a little. It doesn't hurt anything. They're not anxious to be liked."

The young man came back. Not as young as he looked, or perhaps tried to look. Nancy's brother. Alex. Meaty, dark, bland. The kind who have a smell of pine and a perfect manicure. He gave us a smile of measured sadness and sat facing us. "Sorry about the constant interruptions. You know how it is." He shrugged. "One or the other of us should be with him. It seems to help him a little. Elaine is being so good about it. You have no idea."

"I guess he wouldn't want to see Nancy," Dana said innocently.

"God, no!" Alex said. "I believe, I really believe that he might have lived years longer if it wasn't . . . for all the shame and heartbreak she's given him. She's my only sister. But I can't be the least bit sentimental. Some people are just born rotten." He made a helpless gesture. "Nothing we've tried to do for her has done any good. She's made life difficult . . . for all of us."

"You understand our viewpoint in this, Mr. Abbott," I said.

"Of course. Of course. I appreciate the fact you want to handle this on a completely informal basis. I think I understand her present condition, as well as Mr. Burley's concern. And I am perfectly willing to write to him personally guaranteeing the thousand dollars a month for as long as . . . as she can remain there. Frankly, I was responsible for the selection of the retreat. I wanted her just as far from San Francisco as possible. Dad is leaving her nothing, of course. But I can tell you in confidence that the estate is . . . sizable. And I would consider it a moral obligation. I'm very glad you and Miss Holtzer had to come here on another matter. It's good to talk this over."

I sensed that he was trying to brush us off. Thanks and good-by. He was an elusive fellow. "We haven't settled it yet, Mr. Abbott," I told him. "Mr. Burley has certain moral obligations too, and he is aware of them. He is not set up to give her the mental care she needs. Under the present arrangement, he can't afford to bring someone there at regular intervals to treat her there. We are functioning here merely as . . . friends of Hope Island, Mr. Abbott."

"I understand, but . . ."

"If the monthly fee could be doubled . . ."

"That's out of the question," he said with a regretful air. "I guess it would be better if Mr. Burley did arrange commitment to a mental institution, if that's what he thinks she needs."

"There's just one small problem," I said. "At times she seems perfectly healthy and rational. And she has built up a whole structure of conspiracy. We understand that it isn't true, of course, but it does sound very plausible, and if she went to some other place, they might think it necessary to make a complete investigation."

"I don't believe I understand," he said.

I glanced at Dana and nodded and she took over. "Nancy insists that a year and a half ago you put her in the custody of some people in Carmel named M'Gruder."

"In the custody!" he said indignantly. "It wasn't like that at all. They were just helping me out. They knew Nancy, of course. They knew she could be a problem. It was just a case of getting her away from a very unsavory group she was running with, and . . ."

"I am just telling you Nancy's story. We all know she isn't well, Mr. Abbott. She claims that the M'Gruders, as a favor to you, got her drunk and got her into a situation where certain pictures were taken of her under compromising circumstances. These pictures were then sent to your father so you could be certain you would be the sole heir. She claims you and your father then tried to put her away, but she fled and remained at large for quite a while until you caught up to her and sent her to Hope Island."

Dana did beautifully with it. I watched his face. He had a big choice of reactions. He tried for amused indignation, and almost made it. But not quite. You have to watch for the not quites.

"Do you mean to tell me she could make anyone believe such nonsense?"

"Not necessarily," I said. "They might want to check it out."

"But why?"

I nodded to Dana. She took the picture from her big purse. I slipped it out of the envelope and leaned and handed it to Alex Abbott. He held it in two trembling hands and stared at it. He swallowed convulsively. In a small voice he said, "This one wasn't . . ." He caught himself. "She had this? My sister had this?"

"This is one of several. Mr. Burley has them in his safe."

"But where would she get them? She didn't have them when she was taken down there."

"They came to her in the mail," I said. "Mr. Abbott, what was it you started to say? This one wasn't . . . This one wasn't what?"

He opened his eyes very wide. He smiled sadly. "I guess I should be frank with you people."

"We would be most grateful," Dana said.

"I will admit that I made a mistake when I . . . arranged her visit with the M'Gruders. I knew them as a lively couple. I thought they would keep her amused and out of trouble. I had no idea they went in for this sort of thing." He handed it back to me.

"I would think you would act a little more angry," I said.

"To tell you the truth, there were other pictures of Nancy. They were mailed to my father, with a note demanding money. He had a very nasty scene with Nancy. She left. He showed me the pictures. He was wretched. Heartbroken. He asked me to destroy the pictures and I did so, very gladly. Several days later, after Nancy was gone, someone phoned my father about the money. He told them to go to hell, that they could do any damn thing with the pictures they pleased."

"He didn't contact the police?"

"No."

"Did the man on the phone threaten him with anything?"

"No. Dad said the man was quite polite. He seemed to have some sort of lower-class English accent. He said he might phone back later on, but as far as I know he never did. In one of the pictures it was . . . well, it was Vance M'Gruder and my sister. I can tell you that I was furious with him. I went down to see him. He was alone at the house. Patty had left him. I learned later their marriage was being annulled. He didn't seem guilty or ashamed or anything like that. Just terribly indifferent. I couldn't make a dent on him. He said he was not and had never been in the nursemaid business, no matter what impression I may have had. He did not know or care where Nancy was. I actually thought I might find her there with them. I wanted to know who had taken the pictures at that . . . circus."

"Did he know?"

"He said that nobody at the party had taken them. He said it had to be someone with a long lens."

"Did he seem surprised to know pictures had been taken?"

"No. I wondered if he'd been approached for money also."

"Did you ask him?"

"No. He seemed cross and impatient and anxious for me to go."

"Did you know any of the other people in the pictures you saw?"

"Aside from the M'Gruders, just one fellow, an artist I—." He stopped suddenly, frowning at us. "Why are you so curious about the pictures, Mr. McGee?"

I shrugged. "I guess it's only natural. Mr. Burley was curious too. They do have some bearing on the girl's evaluation of herself. I suppose if she feels it was a conspiracy, a trick, she feels better about it."

"Mr. McGee, if Nancy ever had any hopes of inheriting half the estate, she spoiled her chances long before those pictures were taken, believe me. Naturally I'll support her as long as she lives. But what you ask seems . . ."

"Oh, I don't think she could cause you much trouble, Mr. Abbott."

"I don't see how she could cause any."

I smiled and shrugged. "An institution might call in somebody to give her legal advice. You know how it is. Contingency basis. And you say the estate is sizable. She does sound plausible. All it could do, I guess, would be delay the probate."

He studied his thumbnail. He bit a small piece out of the corner of it and got up and went to the steel window and teetered back and forth, heel to toe.

"You say she seems happy there at the island?"

"She has friends there. And the illusion of freedom."

Without turning, he said, "And this deterioration you mention. It is progressive?"

"From all indications."

"I imagine that if I footed the bill for additional care for . . . say another six months, by the end of that time she . . ."

"Let's say eighteen months."

"I'll take my chances on a year. No more."

"I will so inform Mr. Burley."

He looked at his watch. "Elaine gets nervous if I leave her in there too long. Uh . . . thanks for the report. Good-by." He walked out without looking directly at either of us.

On the way down in the elevator, Dana looked at me and slowly shook her head. "You are very damn good, Trav. You are better than I realized. You are shameless. You are a bastard, Trav. You know very damn well he thinks you are going to split the increase with Mr. Burley. He thinks you are going to bring suit in her name if he doesn't play. And you sat there, so righteous and kindly. Oh boy, oh boy."

"A man like that can't believe anything that doesn't sound crooked."

"A man like that makes me want to go scrub. They better not leave him alone with dear Dad. He's impatient."

Before I started the car I turned to her and said, "Itemize."

"What? Oh. He didn't have the pictures taken. The man who took them or had them taken has a cheap British accent. M'Gruder knew about the pictures. And something else. Let me think. Oh, the M'Gruder marriage was annulled. Did I miss anything?"

"You are very good too."

"I am afflicted with an orderly mind."

And so we drove back to the heart of the city. San Francisco is the most depressing city in America. The come-latelys might not think so. They may be enchanted by the steep streets up Nob and Russian and Telegraph, by the sea mystery of the Bridge over to redwood country on a foggy night, by the urban compartmentalization of Chinese, Spanish, Greek, Japanese, by the smartness of the women and the city's iron clutch on culture. It might look just fine to the new ones.

But there are too many of us who used to love her. She was like a wild classy kook of a gal, one of those rain-walkers, laughing gray eyes, tousle of dark hair—sea misty, a lithe and lively lady, who could laugh at you or with you, and at herself when needs be. A sayer of strange and lovely things. A girl to be in love with, with love like a heady magic.

But she had lost it, boy. She used to give it away, and now she sells it to the tourists. She imitates herself. Her figure has thickened. The things she says now are mechanical and memorized. She overcharges for cynical services.

Maybe if you are from Dayton or Amarillo or Wheeling or Scranton or Camden she can look like magic to you because you have not had a chance to see what a city can be. This one had her chance to go straight and she lost it somehow, and it has been downhill for her ever since. That's why she is so depressing to those of us who knew her when. We all know what she could have been, and we all know the lousy choice she made. She has driven away the ones who loved her best. A few keep trying. Herb Caen. A few others. But the love words have a hollow tone these days.

8

Investigating a cold cold trail can be deadly dull and very discouraging. This one worked pretty well, perhaps because there were two of us, two sets of hunches, two sets of ideas, two methods of approach.

We found Caswell Edgars in Sausalito. He looked twenty pounds heavier than in the pictures. He was living in a pigpen litter in the expensive home of a skinny driftwood blonde on the far side of fifty. She was there too, in extremely tight pants and a high girlish giggle. Any minute now Cassie was going to start working hard getting ready for a one-man show she was going to arrange for him. They had a music system that would have blown the walls out of a less substantial structure. She had soiled ankles, a grubby neck, and a black eye which had faded to saffron. They were hooked on something. From the way they acted, I suspect one of the hypnotics. The house smelled like old laundry. There was a loose and dangerous and desperate flavor about the alliance, and it was easy to imagine that in their blundering they would sooner or later manage to set fire to the place and scream with laughter until they found all exits blocked. She kept talking about poor little ole Henry, who seemed to be a husband, but I could not determine if he was living or dead. If dead, it was conceivable he was buried in the yard, under the weeds. Edgars knew absolutely nothing about any pictures. But he had no difficulty remembering the occasion. He had musician talk which he didn't do too well. "Man, that was a bash. That little movie piece was pure stone fox. The boss fox of all time. Somebody trying to scuffle her with the pics? You never said, man."

"No. I never said."

"Sonny traded the waitress for the tall brunette, and then he burned. It's a harsh way to make bread, man, that chance of burning. I read it someplace."

"Put on my records, Cassie doll baby bug, huh?"

I don't think either of them noticed we'd left, or cared particularly. Though it was warm in the car, Dana shuddered.

"Scratch one more contestant, Dana doll baby bug."

"Please don't," she said in a thin voice.

"Like they say, lives of quiet desperation."

"Trav?"

"Yes?"

"I think that terrace was a damned unlucky place to be. Sonny Catton, Nancy Abbott, Carl Abelle . . . and Caswell Edgars."

"Punishment from on high?"

"I don't know. Maybe. Maybe it can happen, Trav."

She took care of Carmel with some phone calls. The M'Gruder place had been sold almost a year ago. We had less luck with newspaper accounts. I did dig up some background on M'Gruder. There had been an elder brother, killed in a war. M'Gruder's father had invented a little gadget. Every cracking plant in the world had to have one or two of them. Vance M'Gruder had married one Patricia Gedley-Davies some three years ago in California, after apparently importing her from London. She had crewed for him in smaller sailboats. There was no social prominence, nor any attempt apparently to achieve any. But there was money, and so one would think the annulment would be more than a six-line paragraph on page 36. It had happened about two months after the house party.

Dana Holtzer sat in my hotel room with her shoes off and her feet up, frowning thoughtfully after having made a Sunday afternoon call to Lysa Dean.

"This annulment thing," she said. "What you think of, in a state with a community property law, it's the cheap way out."

"Yes, indeed."

"And this was a closed session or closed hearing or whatever you call it, just the judge and them and a lawyer, and everybody agreeing to everything, and a declaration by the judge that the marriage had never existed in fact or something. And this wasn't a humble woman, Trav. Sort of noisy and bossy. Let's say she came from nothing, and she married a rich man. Would she give up without a battle? What made her give up without a battle?"

"And where is she?"

We couldn't answer our questions, but we could look for answers. I decided we would split up on Monday, to save time. I would pursue a small idea of my own. She would use Lloyd's Register as her guidebook and work the boaty people, the ocean-sailing types, with appropriate cover story, and see what she could get in the way of gossip.

It rained all day, matching the mood of the offices I visited. Investigation agencies have very little need for decor. They like to keep the overhead down. Their usual customer does not shop around, looking for better draperies. Most of them are sad, soft, pale, meaty people. They operate with about the same verve as the people who come to spray your home with bug juice.

I had my lines down pat by the time I hit the third one. My name was Jones, said with that emphasis which indicated it was anything but Jones. My employment was "managing my own investment program." That brought a little flicker into tired eyes. My young Italian wife was playing around. I was positive of two men. Perhaps there were three. I wanted somebody who could get some flagrant pictures of her, very quietly and inconspicuously, without her knowing. Then, with the pictures in hand, I could dicker with her and get out of the marriage without too much expense.

No, sir, we don't do that kind of thing.

Who does? Where should I go?

I just wouldn't know, mister.

At four o'clock I hit one who was sufficiently unsavory and hungry. He had the cop look. Not the good cop look, but the apple-stealing look. It was a very good guess that he had been busted for the wrong combination of greed and stupidity, and that he wasn't going to do too well in this line of work either. He had a desk in one of those warehouse offices, the kind where you get the desk, the mail drop, switchboard service and an hourly rate on secretarial help—along with a ragtag collection of phone solicitors, speculators in distressed merchandise, independent jewelry salesmen and so on.

He listened to my story and looked at me with the concealed anguish of a toothless crocodile inspecting a fat brown dog on the riverbank. He wanted to know how to get at me. We hitched chairs close and hunched toward each other. He had that breath which exceptionally bad teeth can create.

"Now, Mr. Jones, maybe I can help and maybe I can't. A thing like this, it would be strictly a cash arrangement. You unnerstand?"

"Of course."

"Now I've got a guy in mind. He's tops. What he goes after, he gets. But he comes high."

"How high?"

"Considering the risks and all I would say this guy couldn't be touched for less than five thousand, but he's a real pro, and he will come up with shots of that little two-timing wop that'll nail her but good. This guy, he's got all the techniques and equipment, but he's funny. He dooesn't feel like working, he doesn't work."

"I never heard of such a thing."

"Like an artist, like, he's got temperamental, you know?"

"I guess I know what you mean."

"What would happen, he would work through me. Now I don't want to be wasting my time trying to talk him into anything. What I need, I need a guarantee of good faith on your part, I mean that you want to go ahead at least far enough to take care of the first part of the trouble I'm going to, namely trying to get him on the phone long distance."

I took my wallet out below the desk edge, took a hundred-dollar bill and put it near his elbow. "Is this okay?"

A big paw fell on it and it was gone. With the back of the other paw he wiped his mouth. "Just fine. Now you go wait out in the hall. There's a bench out there to sit on."

I sat for nearly fifteen minutes. Odd-looking people came and went, tenants and clients and customers. Underside people. The ones that somehow seem to be clinging to the damp underside of reality. The ones that look as if they could truly astonish a psychiatrist or a bacteriologist.

He came out and hunkered in close beside me, to rot my collar with his foul exhalations. "What happened, I can't get him, but the way it looks I got some leads, there's somebody can do a nice job, give me a little time on it."

"Why can't you get the man you were talking about?"

"He's been dead a while. I didn't know that. I didn't hear about it, the ways things are, him out of town."

"What was his name?"

"There are guys around just as good. What I want, you give me how I can get in touch with you, and when I get a good man lined up, one I can guarantee will do this little job, then—"

"I'll give you a ring in a few days."

"On account of I got to do some digging to find the exact right guy for your problem, what about you give me the same figure again as a retainer?"

"We better talk about that if you can find anybody."

After a few more halfhearted attempts, he went shuffling back into his rental bull pen, pants droopy in the seat, hair grizzled gray on the nape of his thick neck.

I made it to the nearest rancid saloon in about eight big bounds, shut myself into a phone booth and called back. I had remembered the name of the switchboard girl on duty. It was posted on her board.

"Miss Ganz, this is Sergeant Zimmerman. Bunco Squad. Within the past twenty minutes you placed a long-distance call for Gannon."

"Who? What?"

"Please give me the name, number and location of the call he placed."

"But I'm not supposed to . . ."

"I can send for you, Miss Ganz, and have you brought down here if you want it that way."

"Did . . . did you say Zimmerman?"

"If you want to play it safe, Miss Ganz, call me back here at headquarters. We have a separate number." I gave her the pay phone number. She had been starting to cool off, and I had to take the chance or get nothing.

In thirty seconds the phone rang. I put my thumb in the side of my mouth, raised my tone level a half octave and said, "Bunco, Halpern."

"Sergeant Zimmerman, please."

"Just a minute." After a ten count, I said, "Zimmerman."

"This is Miss Ganz," she said briskly. "About what you wanted, the call was to a Mr. D. C. Ives, in Santa Rosita. Eight-oh-five, seven-six-five, four-four-three-four. That number had been disconnected. Then he called a Mr. Mendez in Santa Rosita, eight-oh-five, three-eight-four, seven-nine-four-two. They talked for less than three minutes. Is that what you wanted, Sergeant?"

"Thank you very much for your cooperation, Miss Ganz. We'll protect our source in this matter. We may have to ask you for some other favor along the same line in the future."

"You're very welcome," she said.

A nice efficient careful girl. She had to make certain she was really talking to the cops.

Dana got back to the hotel a little after six. She looked pallid and twitchy. Her smile came and went too quickly. She had called me as soon as she got in, and I went down the hallway to her room. A woman in that condition needs to be hugged and held and patted a little. But we weren't on any kind of basis where I could do that.

I lit her trembling cigarette and then she switched around the room and said, "I am now a real drinking buddy of Mrs. T. Madison Devlaney III. I call her Squeakie, as does practically everyone. I poured drinks into her potted plants. Until she passed out. She is twenty-nine. She is two days younger than Vance M'Gruder. She has known him all her life. She has a teeny little voice, ten thousand freckles, ten million dollars, and she's muscled like a circus girl. Swimming every morning, tennis every afternoon, potted every night. No tennis today. Strained ankle."

"What cover story did she buy?"

"Trav, don't be angry, but I couldn't have gotten to her at all without using the best connection I have. Lysa Dean. That opens a lot of doors. And I do have those calling cards."

"I didn't say you shouldn't. I just said don't use her if you don't have to."

"I had to. I told her that Lysa had met Vance. I told her that Lysa was forming a little production company of her own and, as a first picture, was thinking of basing it on one of the ocean races, perhaps the race to Hawaii, and she was asking me to find out just how much cooperation she could get from the people who do own the big boats. It's nonsense, of course, but people know so little about the industry they're ready to believe anything. I made up sort of a plot as I went along."

"So she bought it. That's the important thing. What about M'Gruder?"

"Let me see. Oh, lots of things about M'Gruder. He is a physical fitness nut. He is a fine deep-water sailor. He is fantastically stingy. He gets quarrelsome and violent when he gets drunk. The marriage to Patricia Gedley-Davies was, according to his friends, a grotesque mistake. She said that forty-two times at least. Grotesque mistake. Squeakie and her friends are convinced Patty was a London call girl. I wouldn't say that anyone is particularly fond of Vance, but they are glad to see that marriage ended. They think it was bad form. And so lucky there were no children." She took out her little notebook. "The new wife is supposed to be enchanting. Her name is Ulka Atlund. She turned eighteen a few days before their marriage. Her mother is dead. Her father brought her over here two years ago. He came to lecture for a year at the University of San Francisco and stayed for a second year. He opposed the marriage, then agreed on the basis that, after the honeymoon, she continues her education. They plan to honeymoon for six months. They've been gone two months. Squeakie thinks she heard somewhere that Vance plans to have somebody else bring the boat back from Acapulco. Too much beating into the wind on the way back. She thinks Vance planned to spend that last two months of the honeymoon in his house at Hawaii. Then back to live here while Ulka goes back to college."

"What about the annulment?"

"This is where it gets pretty untidy, Travis."

I got tired of the way she was roving around. I got her wrists and pushed her gently back until the backs of her legs hit the edge of a chair. She sat down and looked up at me, startled.

"Let me tell you something, Miss Holtzer. This whole deal is untidy. The stupendous glamor of Lysa Dean did not suck me into this. You were the item that swayed me."

"What? What?"

"If she'd sent anyone else, the answer would have been no. You looked so staunch and loyal and unyielding and severe. So damned *decent*. You made me feel like an unwashed opportunist. I have emotional reactions to people, Dana, no matter how much I try to deny it. I wanted to prove to you that I am good at what I do."

"But that's absurd!"

I backed away and sat on her bed. "It certainly is. Now, how untidy does this situation get?"

She shrugged. "Squeakie doesn't know for sure. Just second-hand and third-hand gossip. But Nancy Abbott came into it. Apparently, among Squeakie's set, the favorite theory is that Patty M'Gruder had Nancy as a house guest in Carmel, and practically held her a prisoner there, because she . . . Patty . . . had fallen in love with Nancy. The theory is that Vance went along with it because it gave him a chance to get the proof he wanted that Patty had entered into the marriage contract under false pretenses, concealing her real inclinations. Vance used Nancy—Squeakie kept calling her 'that poor poor sick child'—to get the proof, and once he had it, there was no way in the world for Patty to fight his action to annul. It was all handled very quietly."

"That would explain what Nancy yelled at me, about Patty keeping her locked up."

"I suppose so. Patty left. Squeakie's phrase for it was that she slunk away. Somebody saw her several weeks ago, in Las Vegas. Not in one of the big places out on the Strip. Down in town, working at something called the Four Treys. Making change, I think. Some kind of a small job. There certainly wouldn't be many old friends seeing her there. Anyway, Mrs. T. Madison Devlaney didn't know anything about . . . or at least say anything about any pictures. I was lucky to catch her. She and her husband and another couple are flying to Hawaii this week. That whole group seems to be very big for Hawaii. The Devlaneys keep a boat out there."

"You did very well, Dana."

"Thank you. They have a beautiful home. She really got terribly drunk. Did you learn anything at all?"

"I don't know. I traced a man who could have taken the pictures. But he lived three hundred miles away. It looks as if M'Gruder had the pictures taken. I think we can assume that, at least for now. But I can't prove any contact between M'Gruder and the photographer. One thing makes me think I located the right man. He's dead."

"I beg your pardon?"

"Let's say that just for kicks or souvenirs or something he kept one set of prints for himself. He died. Those files got into the hands of somebody who . . ."

"Of course."

"His name was D. C. Ives, possibly. And he lived in Santa Rosita, possibly. We check him out for a vulgar limey accent, and if so it will look a lot more certain."

"Is that what we do next?"

"With one stop on the way, I think."

9

On a bright clear cold Tuesday morning, I climbed the back slope of the ridge. Surf tumbled in, making a continuous roar against the rock. I reached and grasped the small trunk of a wind-dwarfed tree and pulled myself up to where I could look over the top. In my surprise I nearly ducked back out of sight. I had not expected the Chipmann sun deck to be so close. I looked down into it at about a thirty-degree angle. Perhaps that made it seem closer. But it was, I judged, three hundred feet away. It was a special irony that there should be a nude woman on the sun terrace. She was prone on a faded blue sun pad. The wall shielded her from some of the west wind, and she had set up an additional wind screen, one of those made of a shining metal to intensify the heat of the sun. She was of heroic dimensions, a redoubtable female, body brown as coffee beans, hair bleached to hemp, thighs like beer kegs, shoulders like Marshall Dillon. I assumed she had to be Mrs. Chipmann, the dear friend who loaned Carl their house for celebrity assignation. It seemed odd to see the sun terrace in such vivid colors after seeing it so many times in black and white. Her face was turned toward me. She wore sunglasses. There was a half glass of tomato juice on the cement next to the sun pad.

There was absolutely no other place from which the terrace could be watched. She had every reason to think herself unobserved. I eased back, out of sight, and turned and looked down. I could see part of the rear end of our pale gray Avis car parked in the cut where I had left it. I looked around at the immediate area. It was nonsensical to expect to find anything, after a year and a half. But find something I did. It was tucked down into a cleft of stone as if someone had wadded it and wedged it there, a small crumpled cardboard container, once yellow, now bleached pulpy white by sun and rain and weather. I could make out ghost writing on it, white on white. Kodak—Plus-X Pan.

I took it down with me and handed it to Dana as I got behind the wheel. She frowned at it, then saw what it was. She looked at me with a strange expression. "Why should this make it more real? God, could anything be more real than those pictures? But this is . . . like archeology, sort of. It's more . . . first hand."

"Don't get hooked on the feeling, Dana. Investigation can be a disease."

"It's a spooky feeling. I don't like it. It's unfair in a way, Travis. People get so exposed. It dwarfs people, doesn't it? By dwarfing them, it makes you feel bigger. Is that the fascination?"

"I don't know."

"But it *does* fulfill you in some way, doesn't it?"

"Let's drop it, shall we?"

"I'm sorry. I didn't realize it was a sore . . ."

"Shall we?"

"*All right!*"

I drove swiftly southward with the sulks and with a silent woman. Ever since the popularization of the Freud-Fraud, we are all addicted to fingering ourselves to see where it hurts, Mommy. With no one to kiss and make well.

So what if I am hooked on the hunt? All it does is make an orderly life untenable. You trade the kiddies and fireside and regular promotions and appointment to the house committee or the greens committee for a few, a very few, clear clean moments of a savage satisfaction akin to joy. And maybe in the process you keep a little essential privacy. Our dear Uncle owns over 23,000 polygraphs. Lie detectors. God alone knows how many industry owns. Not satisfied any more with giving you the whole series of Multiphasic Personality Inventory tests, they want to make damn well certain you are not merely giving them the answers you think they want. They want to nail you into your permanent box right now, brother. Get in and lie still, and forty years from now we'll bury you.

I get this crazy feeling. Every once in a while I get it. I get the feeling that this is the last time in history when the offbeats like me will have a chance to live free in the nooks and crannies of the huge and rigid structure of an increasingly codified society. Fifty years from now I would be hunted down in the street. They would drill little holes in my skull and make me sensible and reliable and adjusted.

I am, to put it as bitterly as possible, a romantic. I know a windmill when I see one, by God, and I sneer at my white horse. It was appropriate that Lysa Dean should be the damsel in distress. She is such a sweet kid.

"Anyway," I said aloud, "she projects the image of a sweet kid."

Dana was inert for about two seconds, nodding her head, and then she gave a little jump and stared at me. "Don't *do* that!"

"Do what?"

"Get inside my head like that! How did you know what I was thinking?"

"I didn't."

She looked dubious. I glanced at her a few times when I could take my eyes off that languorous and lethargic California traffic. And somehow all of a sudden we were closer. Maybe it is like the learning curve, shaped like a profile of a stairway. We both knew something had happened and didn't know what it was. Her face colored and she turned away. I couldn't really *see* her any more. That was another clue. I could remember meeting a dark-haired, strong-featured, composed woman. A stranger. This was not she. This was Dana. Somebody else. Dana's eyes, Dana's mouth, Dana's hair and ears and body. Individual and unique and not related in any way to anyone previously known. Dana of the dear crooked tooth.

Santa Rosita was a stunted version of the Santa Barbara code of existence. Three industries, electronics, plastics and tourists, and squeeze the bejaysus out of all three. It was sharing the big boom-boom. The incomparably dull tract houses, glitteringly new, were marching out across the hills, cluttered with identical station wagons, identical children, identical barbecues, identical tastes in flowers and television. You see, Virginia, there really is a Santa Rosita, full of plastic people, in plastic houses, in areas noduled by the vast basketry of their shopping centers. But do not blame them for being so tiresome and so utterly satisfied with themselves. Because, you see, there is no one left to tell them what they are and what they really should be doing.

The dullest wire services the world has ever seen fill their little monopoly newspapers with self-congratulatory pap. Their radio is unspeakable. Their television is geared to a minimal approval by thirty million of them. And anything thirty million people like, aside from their more private functions, is bound to be bad. Their schools are group-adjustment centers, fashioned to shame the rebellious. Their churches are weekly votes of confidence in God. Their politicians are enormously likable, never saying a cross word. The goods they buy grow increasingly more shoddy each year, though brighter in color. For those who still read, they make do, for the most part, with the portentous gruntings of Uris, Wouk, Rand and others of that same witless ilk. Their magazine fare is fashioned by nervous committees.

You see, dear, there is no one left to ask them a single troublesome question. Such as: Where have you been and where are you going and is it worth it?

They are the Undisturbed. The Sleep Lovers.

And they fill out an enormous number of forms every year, humbly and sincerely. Each one is given a number to use all his life.

Are they going to be awakened with a kiss? They feel vaguely uneasy about their young. My God, why can't these kids appreciate this best of all possible worlds? What's wrong with these restless punks? These . . . these goddam *dropouts!*

Virginia, dear, through the strange alchemy of the gods, there are a disproportionate number of kids coming along these days with IQs that are soaring toward a level too high to measure. These kids have very cold eyes. They are the ones who, one day, will stop playing with transistors, diodes and microcircuitry and look at Barrentown and start asking the rude questions. Or build a machine that will ask.

In the meanwhile, Virginia, Santa Rosita still exists, and it is as if some cynical genius had designed a huge complex penal colony in the sunshine, eliminating the need for guard towers and barbed wire by merely beaming a gigantic electronic message at the inmates, day and night, saying, You are in heaven! Be happy! If you can't be happy here, you can't be happy anywhere! Vote! Consume! Donate! And don't forget to use your number.

We drove in from the north at four in the afternoon of that first Tuesday in March, and I checked us into two singles in a chain motel—architecture: Lubratorium Moderne. She wanted to call Miss Dean, and I wanted to try the number for Mendez. After a small and cautious hesitation, I decided not to put it through the motel switchboard. Caution can be a way of life. Never leave anything which can be traced, when you do have a choice.

A clear-voiced girl said, "Gallagher, Rosen and Mendez. Good afternoon."

"Uh . . . may I speak with Mr. Mendez, please."

"One moment, sir."

"Good afternoon. This is Mr. Mendez' secretary. May I help you?"

"I would like to speak with Mr. Mendez, please."

"He's on another line. May I call you back, or would you like to hold?"

I held. I riffled the phone book with my free hand. They were attorneys.

"Yes? Hello?" Mendez said in an impatient and harried voice.

"Sorry to bother you. We need an address for the next of kin for D. C. Ives."

"Who is we?"

"Keller Photo, sir. We had a lens for repair. It was under the guarantee, but it took a long time. It had to go back to the factory in Germany, no charge of course, and now we—"

"Miss Trotter? Give this fellow Jocelyn Ives' address."

I heard him hang up. "Hello?" Miss Trotter said. "Just a moment, please." She was back on the line quickly. "Have you a pencil? Miss Jocelyn Ives, Twenty-eight twenty-nine Appleton Way. Phone seven-six-five, three-one-nine-two. Have you got that?"

"Thanks. When did Ives die anyway?"

"Oh, just a few days before Christmas. He held on longer than they thought he could, you know. Days and days, with all that terrible brain damage. It's such a shame. He was *so* talented."

"Well, that's the way it goes."

"I hope they find them some day."

"Don't we all. Thanks, Miss Trotter."

I started out of the phone booth, and then went back in and tried the number she gave me. It rang three times. A woman answered. "Is Georgie around?" I asked.

"You've the wrong number, I expect," she said. I thanked her and hung up. I walked thoughtfully back to the room. I knew that accent. It sounds cockney but isn't. It is Australian.

Dana had just finished talking to Lysa Dean. Miss Dean reported success with the promotion and a good audience response to *Winds of Chance* on premiere night. She was off soon, with group, to New

York for additional promo work, panel shows and so on, four days there and then to Chicago.

I reported what I had learned, and added what I could guess. Dana looked more intrigued than shocked. "Killed, eh?"

"So it would seem."

"He was in a dangerous line of work."

"The quickest way is to give that sister a try."

"Can I come with you?"

"I might strike out. I'll try it alone. Then you can try from another angle."

Appleton Way was dead end. Truck terminals were edging closer to it. Nearby blocks were being leveled for some unimaginable improvement. But the street still had an illusion of peace. It contained multiple housing, old garden courts of pseudo-Moorish styling, faded citrus-tone paint on old stucco. Number 2829 was one of the larger complexes, and her door was off an arched open corridor along the side. A dark door opening into the gloom of a small apartment with too few windows. She looked at me through the six-inch gap the safety chain allowed, and I saw that she was perhaps daughter rather than sister.

"What do you want?"

You have to have a flair for it, an immediate and unthinking appraisal of the vulnerabilities. This one was wary and haughty. I could see that she was a big pale girl, Alice through a strange looking-glass. A twenty-year-old spinster. There are such. A big awkward fatty body in an unlovely jumper. A child face. Reddened nostrils. Pale heavy lips.

"I want to be sure you are Jocelyn Ives. Is there anything you could show me to prove it?" I kept my voice confidential.

"Why should I bother?"

"You do have the same accent."

"Who are you? What do you want?"

"I was associated with him in a certain venture quite a long time ago. I came here to make contact, and I just found out he's dead."

She gnawed her lip and then, to my utter astonishment, gave me a huge conspiratorial wink. She closed the door, unlatched the chain and opened it wide. "Please come in," she said heartily. When she had closed the door behind us, she said, "I do understand why you can't give me your name."

"Uh . . . that's good."

"Back through here. The place is a mess. I'm off work today." I followed her along the murky hallway into a small living room. It was crowded with furniture too large and too expensive for the small apartment. Every surface was covered with large photographic prints, and scores of them were on the floor and leaning against the furniture and the walls. Many of them were matted. With clumsy awkward haste she cleared two chairs. "Do sit down. I've been sorting out. Lens Lab . . . that's a local hobby group . . . they want to put on a show of his best work. At the library. There are so *many*. I get quite confused."

"I can see how you would. It looks like fine work."

"Oh, yes! That's my responsibility now, to see that everyone learns how good Father was. I am going to set up a traveling show also. And there is some interest in Rochester, of course."

"Of course."

She sat facing me and knotted her hands together and said, "I have been so hoping that *somebody* would show up. It's been so terribly difficult for me."

"I suppose it has."

"Poor Mr. Mendez has been doing his best to get everything straightened out for tax purposes. But having quite a large amount of cash turn up has sort of complicated things. And, of course, I couldn't explain the cash. Not to him. If it was supposed to be for necessary expenses, I'm sorry. It's all tied up now with courts and tax people and things. I will get it eventually, I imagine, or whatever part of it they don't take. At least the house can be sold. You know, I have been hoping someone would show up. And you look almost exactly like the kind of man I pictured."

"What can I do for you?"

"I kept my mouth shut, as Father would have wished. And I guess I do not really have to have any posthumous glory for him. He said that was the thing none of you could ever expect. He taught me to be very careful and discreet about . . . the contacts and not to ask him questions. I have been wondering if you could go to Mr. Mendez and explain to him the sort of work Father was doing for you. I think it might make the estate work easier."

"I'm sorry. I have no authority to do that."

"I was afraid so," she said. "Oh, dear. And the ridiculous police will have to go right on thinking it was just someone after his pocket money?"

"I'm afraid so."

She studied me. "Really, how do I know you are what I think you are?"

"We don't carry that sort of identification."

"I suppose not. It wouldn't be very safe, I expect." She looked uneasy. "But why wouldn't you have known he was dead?"

"I've been out of touch."

I now had the shape of it all. There was something unwholesome about her, a greasy sheen to her flesh, a soiled smell in the dark little apartment. But she was his loved daughter. Blackmail needed a cover story. Perhaps it had been her guess at first that Father was in some sort of patriotic undercover work, and when she faced him with it, it was easiest to go along. And, of course, the Enemy had slain him.

I had to find the right way to open her up. I leaned toward her and said, "Jocelyn, I think I can promise you that some day it can all be told."

Tear tracks like the sidewalk marks of snails gleamed on the round pale cheeks, and she made a froggy sobbing sound . . .

10

I LIKED the way Dana listened. She felt no compulsion to fill a silence with questions. She knew there was more to come. I could not see her distinctly. She sat over by the motel windows in darkness. The light was at my elbow, gleaming on the silver cup.

"Ives liked to live well," I said. "He did free-lance photography in Melbourne. Fashion, news breaks, everything. A Hollywood outfit made a movie over there. He got permission to work on the set. His stills were apparently damned good. The stars liked them. The studio brought him over. That was eight years ago. She was twelve. He had about four years of it and did pretty well. And lived well. Then something went wrong. I guess he got himself on that little blacklist they have. I don't imagine it is important to know what cooked him. The girl says it was jealousy. His work was too good. He moved up here to Santa Rosita. His studio was in his home. Weddings, parties, awards, portraits. A nice cover story. She thinks he had some other base in the city. She's so proud of him. Proud of that cynical son of a bitch with his sports cars and fine house and housekeeper."

I got up and collected both silver cups and fixed us another.

"She showed me the clippings. He went on a trip. She doesn't know where. He was gone two days. He came back to the house. He went out again and said he would be back within the hour. That was ten in the evening last December fifth. They found his car, locked, on Verano Street. He was found about a hundred feet away, dragged behind a warehouse, with the top of his skull smashed in, pockets empty, watch gone. They thought he would be dead on arrival, but the heart kept beating for five days. As far as the girl knows, they haven't a clue. Nobody knows what he was doing in that neighborhood. It's mostly industrial small time, empty at night."

After a long silence she said, "Did he leave her anything?"

"Small insurance. The equity in the house. About thirty-eight thousand in cash, already impounded while they check his tax returns. Then a lot of cameras, studio equipment, darkroom equipment, huge stacks of arty photographs."

She asked me if I was certain about Ives. I'd been saving it for her. I told her how I'd wormed it out of the girl.

"So his loving daughter was the one who helped him operate that drop and flashed the green light at you to toss the money out."

Dana shook her head slowly. "And I imagined horrible hoodlums out there . . . and it was that poor simple girl helping Daddy in his spy business. What a total bastard he must have been, to endanger her so!"

And I thought wistfully how easy it would have been for Lysa Dean to have busted it up in the beginning, before it got off the ground. "Ives could trust his daughter," I explained. "And he didn't have to split with her, and she didn't even know what was in the packages. He used her the same way, with variations, on other projects."

"Loyal little helper," Dana said. "Just like me."

"Let's go eat."

She put her sweater on. At the door she stopped me and said, "Trav, you didn't give her any little suspicion that . . . all was not what it seemed?"

"When I left, I told her she could be proud of Daddy. She stood tall and the tears dripped off her fat chin."

She squeezed my arm. In the outside lights, her dark eyes were shiny. "Soft as butter," she said.

"The arm?"

"Idiot, your darn arm is like a slab of redwood. I just meant I'm glad you left her that much."

"I wonder how long she'll keep it."

"What do you mean?"

"Somebody killed him. If they find him, he might have all the right reasons. I think I might talk to a cop."

"Why, dear?" she asked earnestly.

"Dear?"

"Oh, shut up! It was just a . . . reflex."

"You've done it twice today."

"Why will you talk to a cop?"

"Because they very probably know a little more than Miss Ives thinks they know. And we're close to the heart of it now, Dana. Where did D. C. Ives' file copies go?"

My man was Sergeant Starr. Bill Starr. He was a little fellow about forty, very jaunty and bouncy. He was 20 percent nose, and it looked as if that nose had been hit at least once from every possible direction. Under the nose was the abrupt curve of an amiable little smile. He was a clowner, a most happy fellow. He seemed to want you to like him. There was so much nose, there was a danger of misreading the eyes. They were small, cat yellow, and about as soft and mild as cross sections of brass rod.

His tidy little gray office had a rack for cups won in various skills. Several of them were for pistol. He bounced up and perched on the corner of his desk and beamed at me and said, "Why should I play games with anybody, pal? Am I in a buyer's market? Maybe, for residents. If I want to keep a source going. Sure. But I can park your gray tired ass in the tank and keep you there until you get eager to please."

I chuckled as merrily as he and said, "This friend I'm doing the favor for would be terribly upset. No influence here at all, of course. Except the kind of lawyers money will buy. Platoons of them, if need be. I have no record, Sergeant. But careless people have put me in from time to time, here and there. And I have been hit on the head by old-fashioned ones. So it would be an inconvenience for both of us. I'm eager to please right now. And eager to have you please me."

He picked the assorted cards and licenses off his desk and handed them to me. "McGee, there is every identification here except the right one."

"Cards are needed to do a favor for a friend?"

"I'll tell you again. If you have official status then *maybe* you can protect your client. But you have nothing. You *have* to tell me who hired you!"

"But I told you, Sergeant, that we might get around to that, if things go well. Besides, I'm not hired. It's just . . ."

"Oh, God, yes. A favor for a friend." He reached for his hat. "Let's try some coffee."

He drew a car from the pool and we went ten blocks to a drive-in.

The pretty waitress knew him by name and brought us coffee and raised doughnuts.

"I'll start," I said. "D. C. Ives. Sometimes a man has to be killed before people get the idea of some kind of hanky-panky."

"Hanky-panky. Now isn't that sweet! Put it this way. It isn't a legal requirement a man should have a checking account, but nearly everybody with forty-thousand-dollar homes does. An estimate of his take on a legit basis would be fifty or sixty a week. Living expenses better than a thousand a month. So he could be living offa big score from way back, or making little scores as he goes along."

"He was making it as he went along."

"Thanks a lot. I already figured that."

"Did you figure how?"

"It's your turn again, McGee."

"He had a studio and darkroom in his house, and he also had another setup. I'd guess somewhere near Verano Street. A limited setup. A quality enlarger for thirty-five millimeter, a setup for making and drying eight-by-ten prints, no automation for quantity production—almost what you'd expect of an advanced amateur, a one-man operation."

"To do what?"

"Isn't it your turn, Sergeant?"

"Okay. He would do there something he wouldn't want to do home on account of his daughter. When she wasn't in school, she helped him with the home setup. He did a lot of traveling. Short trips. Assignments, he called them. I say it wasn't just a standard smut shop. The requirements in that field are too low. And the pay is low. What do you say it was, McGee?"

"Discreet, careful, expert blackmail. Plus maybe some industrial espionage. And maybe just the long shots of people with the wrong people—the executive talking to the competition, the banker with the tout. Long-lens stuff, up and down this coast. How would he get the work? Some from legitimate agencies, maybe. Some from the great unwashed. With really juicy negatives, he could wring a lot of money out, if the people were important."

"And eventually make a slip and get his head smashed in."

"Probably."

"McGee, if you are trying to do a favor for a friend by getting hold of prints or negatives, forget it."

"They're gone?"

"If he'd been killed immediately, maybe we'd have moved a little faster. We found his hidey-hole. A warehouse corner with its own entrance. It was an area check that turned it up. His prints were on everything. Not much file space for prints, but it was stone empty. No negatives. The file had been locked, and it was pried open. The door had been unlocked and relocked with a key. A good lock. There was a tin money box in the back of the file. It was busted open too."

"What are you holding back, Starr?"

"Me? Me!"

"So all right. My friend is a sick sad girl. She's at Hope Island on Bastion Key in Florida. Her name is Nancy Abbott. She's a drunk. She's been at that retreat for months. Her rich architect daddy is dying, or dead by now, in San Francisco. Ives sneaked some nasty pictures of her a year and a half ago. Now give me the rest."

"I can check that out. The rest? Okay, I found out beyond any doubt that the break-in wasn't accomplished until the day *after* Ives was clobbered. And in Ives' pocket was a key to his little lab. Ives had an employee. Semi-retarded. Samuel Bogen, age forty-six. On and off welfare for years. Trouble twenty years ago. Peeping Tom and indecent exposure, and about four ninety-day falls for that. From what I can find out, Ives used him for scout work, paying him a dollar an hour for washing trays, drying prints, that sort of thing. By the time we got a line on him, Bogen had dropped off the face of the earth. He could be just a harmless spook. Or he could have flipped and bashed his boss. We think we traced him onto a Los Angeles bus. We've had an alert out on him ever since. Medium height, medium weight, glasses, bad teeth, hair brown turning gray, no special identifying marks or characteristics. No family. Left no lead behind in his furnished room three blocks off Verano Street. There is another thing too that makes me less interested in him. At about the right time, a car left the area at high speed. Bogen apparently never owned a car and doesn't drive."

I couldn't risk pursuing the Bogen matter further. I was afraid the little tiger would check it back and come up with Lysa Dean's name.

"So who was involved in the Abbott girl's pictures?" he demanded.

I was ready for that one. "A stock car driver named Sonny Catton. He was killed last year when he hit a wall."

"Where were the pictures taken?"

"Up around Point Sur someplace, at a private home, I think."

"A year and a half ago, you said? So why the heat to get them back now?"

"She was worried about whether he was using them to blackmail her dying father."

"How did you track it back to this Ives?"

"Sergeant, that's a long long story. Let me ask you one. Suppose somebody had some work for Ives. They couldn't get him. So they called Mendez, of Gallagher, Rosen and Mendez, and found out from Mendez he was dead. Does that mean anything?"

"I wondered about that too. Charlie Mendez is clean. Small services for small fees. Like having mail come there."

"Summation, Sergeant?"

"Who, me? Okay, D. C. Ives was very shifty and clever and careful. But one night he forgot to be careful and one of his pigeons got to him. When Bogen heard his boss was dying, he used his own key to get in. He took the dirty pictures and the money and ran."

"So that makes it a dead end for me, Sergeant."

"Are you sure?"

"It was just a favor for a friend."

11

WE LEFT early Thursday morning and drove down to the city, to Lysa Dean's canyon home, secluded behind an impressive pink wall. The staff was cut down to one Korean couple, maid and gardener. When he recognized Dana, he smiled broadly and unlocked the big metal gates for us. It was a hot day. The wall enclosed about one acre. A Mexican architect had done the house for her and her third husband. I guess you could call it Cuernavaca Aztec.

Dana showed me around. The plantings were splendid. The pool was drained. The dogs had been boarded. Walking through the silence of terrazzo, puffy white rugs, dark paneling removed from ancient churches, I counted five full-length oil portraits of the owner. And not one of an ex-husband.

Dana wanted to get different clothes. She showed me how she was set up. A small functional suite opposite the service area, with a rather stark bedroom, a large and luxurious bath, a small tidy office with a row of large gray filing cabinets, a battleship desk. There was a picture in the bedroom, Dana, younger, glowing, intense—holding the new baby in her arms. A young man with a homely, crooked, likable face was staring down at the child too, his arm around his wife.

She saw me glance at it and said, too imperatively, "Please wait for me out there in the office. This won't take a minute."

On an office shelf I saw bound, gold-lettered scripts for the Lysa Dean movies. *Winds of Chance* was among them. I took it down and opened it at random. It seemed highly improbable to me that anyone, living or dead, had ever said lines like that.

I put the script back on the shelf and paced restlessly. There were loose ends. A lot of them. But I could not see how they were pertinent to what I'd been asked to do. I couldn't recover any of the money Lysa Dean had paid Ives.

It seemed reasonably evident that Bogen had gone into business for himself. His note to Lysa sounded as Starr had described him. He would have picked up a few crude lab techniques from Ives. If the police had been looking for him for three months without success, I didn't have much chance of reaching out and picking him up.

We could fly east and catch Lysa in New York. Make a report. Working a complaint through normal police channels, we could get all there was in the files on Bogen. The people responsible for protecting the star could be alerted to watch for anybody who might be Bogen. If she insisted, maybe we could work out a way to trap him, using her as bait. With a little bit of judgment and a lot of luck, I had pushed it about as far as I could.

I could make a few guesses. Bogen had fled with a good piece of money and a whole stack of unpleasant pictures and holed up, perhaps in Los Angeles. He'd fled on December sixth. Those pictures could seriously upset an already disturbed mind. It was highly unlikely that he could have lifted any neat little list of names and addresses. Maybe the pictures covered quite a few of Ives' quiet ventures. If Bogen wanted to get cute with anyone, he would be restricted to those faces he could recognize. Maybe there were a few more celebrity faces in the stack. What was the time sequence? In early January, a month after he fled Santa Rosita, he was out in Las Vegas leaving off the package for Lysa Dean at the desk at The Sands. The columns would have located her for him. No further contact in two months. Was he busy bugging some other famous people who had been captured by Ives' sneaky lens? Was he waiting for Lysa Dean to come back to the Los Angeles area?

At any rate, it would be a comfort to her to know the kind of nut who was running around with pictures that could ruin her, to know his name and his appearance. She would have to decide what that much was worth. I'd dug a pretty good hole in the expense money.

Ives' murder was none of my business. The list of possibilities would have to be as long as my arm.

But I didn't like the way this one was ending. And I couldn't see Lysa Dean being ecstatic about it either.

Dana came out of her bedroom. She wore a pretty green outfit and carried her repacked suitcase. She said, too cheerfully, "Are we ready?"

She seemed very tense. I went and took the suitcase from her. With a quaver in her cheerful voice, she said, "This place gets on my nerves. It never did before. I don't know why. I feel as if I hardly know the Dana Holtzer who lives here. I expect her to come in and ask me who the hell I am."

"Watch out for her. A very icy broad."

She paused in the doorway to look at me, her expression at once vulnerable and wary. "Travis?"

"Yes, honey."

"I can't take too much change. So please don't. Things that get brittle . . . they break, you know."

"I like you. That's all it is."

She nodded. "But we have laughed too much. Do you understand that?"

"I understand that. And you'll be back in harness tonight."

"That picture you saw in there. Did it explain anything?"

"I could have drawn it from memory before I even saw it. You don't have to be explained to me. I don't have to make adjustments with you and to you. Hell with it. Let's go get on our airplane." I tilted her chin up, kissed the corner of her mouth closest to the crooked tooth. A little peck, like cousins. So she smiled, and one tear spilled, and I followed her in flight, *clackety-whack* across terrazzo, green skirt whipping, powerful calves clenching, back very straight and head held high.

We had twenty minutes before they called the flight. Our gear was checked aboard. Early afternoon. I bought a paper. I was scanning it. The name jumped out at me from a small item on page one of the second section. Casino employee slain in Las Vegas. Patricia Davies bludgeoned at doorstep of trailer last night. Once married to sportsman Vance M'Gruder.

Without a word I pointed it out and handed it to Dana. She looked at me, her eyes wide.

"I can't pass that up," I said. "It could be Sammy."

"But . . . our luggage is . . ."

"Dana, you go on to New York. Take care of my stuff at the other end. I'll check this out and be along."

"But I'm supposed to stay with you."

I took hold of her wrists and gave her a little shake. "You have to go to New York. You're a big girl. I don't have to draw diagrams for you. You and I have . . . run out of time."

She held my gaze and her mouth made the shape of that word. Time. Without making a sound. The strength in her face was softened. And younger. "Thank you," she said solemnly. "Thank you, Travis, for knowing when the time ran out."

I released her, turning away, saying, "Your boss expects you. So go ahead." She murmured something about arranging my ticket and went off into the throng. I watched her go, and for an instant had in my mind the grotesque and unworthy image of the time when you feel the tarpon pick up speed for that last, great, heart-busting leap, and see him go high and see him, right at the peak of it, give that final snap of his head that throws your lure back into your lap. The image wasn't even accurate. I'd turned conservationist. I'd let the line go slack and said good-by.

I waited. And waited. Her flight was called. I went to the gate. I did not see her. I went to the airline desk. They checked the manifest for me. Slowly. Sir, the passenger canceled before flight time. I felt fear, worry, irritation. I had played the whole game too loosely, too confidently, and maybe somebody very fast and bright had moved out of the shadows.

I prowled the martian reaches of the terminal, searching for my girl in green. And found her, saw her through the glass front of a men's shop. I went striding in. A clerk was helping her. She gave me a startled and guilty look, then swung all that vivid force of personality upon me, saying, "Darling, I told you I'd forget the shirt sizes. It's *such* a damn nuisance losing luggage. Are these all right? Wash-and-wear, so we could make do with two, don't you think? But what size, dear?"

"Seventeen and a half, thirty-six," I said humbly.

"Two of these in that size, please. And you don't really mind stretch socks too much, do you? Size thirty-three shorts, mmm? No, don't wrap them. I can pop them right in here." She lifted the small suitcase up onto the counter, a cheap one of pale blue anodized aluminum. As she put the articles in, I got a glimpse of some feminine things and some drugstore parcels. She latched it and waited for her change.

"We've got a flight in about twenty-five minutes," she said.

I carried the case out of the store into the waiting room area. I carried it to a quiet space and put it down and turned to her and said, "Have you lost your fool mind?"

She locked strong icy fingers onto my wrist and looked up at me and said, "It's all right. Really. It's all right."

"But . . ."

"I couldn't get the luggage back. It was stowed aboard. It'll be taken care of in New York. Look. I've been a grownup for a long time."

"It's just that . . ."

"Shut up, darling. Shut up, shut up, shut up. Do you want me to draw pictures for you? Stop looking like a spavined moose. Say you're glad. Say something."

I put fingertips on her cheek, ran my thumb along the black gloss of her eyebrow. "Okay. Something."

She closed her eyes and shivered. "Oh, God. No claims, Trav. Nothing like that. Either way."

"Either way."

"Just don't laugh."

"You know better than that."

I read consternation in her expression. "Maybe I'm just not what you . . . maybe you never really . . . you could have been just being polite and now . . ."

"You know better than that too. Shut up, dear."

"I wired New York."

"Kindly excuse delay."

"Dammit, we've never even really kissed. My knees are all wobbly and strange. Please lead me to a drink, darling."

During the flight, in spite of all the persuasive immediate magic of Girl, in spite of scent, closeness, dark eyes to drown in, and the shallow-breathed feeling of expectancy, the workman part of my mind kept moving in old and seamy patterns. We'd made a big swing, and, one by one, we'd been dropping them out of the final count. Carl Abelle, terror of the ski lifts, dangerous as a pratfall on a bunny slope. Sonny Catton, cooked meat in a pretty *whoosh* and bloom of high octane. Nancy Abbott, cooked just as thoroughly but over a lower flame. No point in checking Harvey and Richie, the Cornell kids. Their biggest problem was to find someone, anyone, who would ever believe their story. Caswell Edgars was out of it. And out of just about everything else in the world too. Ives was gone, and violently. So was Patty M'Gruder. If old Abbott, Nancy's father, had any luck left, he was dead by now too. Less violently but

less pleasantly. It was narrowing down. To a yacht bum named
Vance M'Gruder, to a waitress named Whippy, to a retarded little
man named Bogen. It was like going through an empty house, checking the closets. Either it was more complex than I could comprehend, or else it made even less sense. But there was a nastiness somewhere in it that was out of control. I sensed that, and sensed it was
aimed at Lysa Dean, and maybe at me, and I couldn't imagine who
or how. I knew only two things. I was running out of closets. And I
was glad I hadn't been at that house party. So I held the hand of the
girl, and told myself it was a fine world, and filed away my doom
thoughts.

A bored kid built a shiny little model city with his new kit and
when it was finished he gave it one hell of a kick and spewed big
hunks of it out across the desert floor. We tilted down across the afternoon, seeing an unreality of blue pools and green fairways against
that old lizard-skin brown of the everlasting desert. We came in with
a batch of pilgrims—the brand-new ones trying to be cool about their
interest in the air terminal slots, about all the hawking and proclaiming and loud instant promotions. All the old pilgrims wore the
memory of pain and were impatient to get to that certain table at
that certain place, in time for crucifixion. I noticed a pair of ap-
praisers as our group came through the gate, backs against the wall,
staring left and right, somnolently vigilant, bouncing the little black
glances off the pilgrims like aimed bb shot. They have the index
memories of the ten thousand faces in disrepute in Slotsville, plus a
feel for new trouble on the way—the ones who have come to get it
any way they can, including using a gun on the winners. My lady
performed no transit services this time. It was a fine and pleasant dis-
tinction related to the absolute silence of the airplane ride, the hand
tightly held, the dark eyes hooded. She stood foursquare, still and
humble, patient and sensuous, while I, with no bag to retrieve, went
off to dicker for a vehicle and, with ironic impulse, took that most
typical of game-town cars, a big air-conditioned convertible, this one
in metallic blue-green, white leather, ominously silent as Forest
Lawn.

There had been a place I liked, way out on the Strip, an utterly
gameless and consequently expensive motor house called the Apache,
and I knew it would be meaningless and would astonish her should I
consult her. At the desk I said I had been there before, knew I

wanted a double cabana at the pool, gave the porter a dollar to let me have the key and find my own way.

It was a great long room in gold and green, with two huge beds, all of it too bright in the dazzle of poolside sun. I pulled the cords that creaked the heavy yellow draperies across the acre of window wall, turning the room into a shadowy gloom of gold. The whisper of the hushed cooled air made it an oasis, a thousand years from yesterday and ten thousand years from tomorrow. Every fifth breath she took was very deep, with a little catch, like a hiccup at the high end. I put my hands upon her, at waist and nape of neck, stopping her sleepy sway. The man who sits in the steel office and throws the switches and pushes the buttons can rest his hand on his desk and feel, more like a low-cycle sound than any measurable vibration, the power that thrums in the bowels of the light plant. She felt unyielding and I could not guess how it would be for us. Then she gave a little crooked sigh, turned her mouth upward to me, leaned with heat and softness and purpose.

There is one kind of rightness that is an almost rightness, because it is merciless and total and ends in a deathlike lethargy.

Then there is another kind of almost rightness that can never be finished.

Both of these make you strangers to each other. Both of these things make you untidily anxious to give and receive reassurances.

But with Dana it was that rare and selfless rightness which moves with but the gentlest hiatus from one completion to the next, each a growth in knowing and closeness while, unheeded, the deep sweet hours go by. After all the fierceness is gone, it then astonishes by returning in that last time which ends it without question for now, and she is spent and dies there, slumbrous and fond.

I fought sleep. I made myself get up. I covered her over and went and showered and dressed. I turned on a meager light in the room and sat on the bed, pushed black curls aside, kissed the sweet nape of a musky neck. She turned to peer up at me, her face soft and emptied and young. "Yuhraw dress!" she mumbled in accusation.

"I'm going out for a little while. You sleep, honey."

She tried to frown. "Y'be careful, d'ling."

"Love you," I said. It doesn't cost a thing. Not when you do. I kissed a soft and smiling mouth, and I think she was asleep before I stood up. I left the low light on and let myself out.

I walked toward the main buildings feeling all that strange ambivalence of the conquering male. Goaty self-esteem, slight melancholy, a mildly pleasant and unfocused guilt, a tin-soldier strut.

But something more than that with her. A feeling of achieving and establishing identities, hers and mine.

There had been no dishonesties. And so, in all that total giving and taking, I had been aware of her as Dana, so vital and so enduring. The slight physical strangeness of the very beginning of it had lasted but a very short time. Then she was all known and dear. As if we had been apart for a very long time and found each other again, quickly getting over the awkwardness of separation.

After that it was a knowing and re-knowing in a profound way which has no words. It became a symbolic dialogue. I give thee. I take thee. I prize thee.

And there was also the fatuous feeling of enormous luck. It is such a damned blind chance, after all.

I worked my way through two bemused gin and bitters while they seared my steak. Over coffee I stopped marveling at myself and got a local paper and read the more detailed account of the murder of Patty M'Gruder.

Then I drove downtown and parked and wandered through that strange area of cut-rate stores, pastel marriage chapels, open-sided casinos bathed in a garish fluorescence. Spooks trudged amid the tourists, and the cops kept a close sharp watch. Old ladies yanked at the handles, playing their dimes out of paper cups. Music bashed across the dry night air, in conflict with itself, and in the noisier alcoves one could buy anything from a dream book to a plastic bird turd.

The Four Treys was a long bright narrow jungle of machinery. What happened to the old-fashioned slot machine? Now you can pull two handles, hit three space ships and an astronaut and get a moon pot, which is one and a half jackpots. The change girls sat behind wire, popping open the paper cylinders of silver, dumping it into paper cups for the people. At regular intervals came the clash of money into the scoop and a shrillness of joy.

I had just wanted a look. I need no directions. Presently I got back behind the wheel of the luxury device afforded me by a famous movie star and drove off again through the neoned light.

12

THE TRAILER park was called Desert Gate. I had to go down through town and out the far side to get to it. It was a little after ten o'clock when I got there. Some orderly soul had set it up with the requirement that all trailers be parked in herringbone array on either side of a broad strip of asphalt going nowhere. The entrance was an aluminum arch, tall and skinny, with a pink floodlight on it.

The trailers were large, all snugged down off their wheels, with little patios and screened porches added. About half of them were dark. Patricia had lived in—and died in front of—the sixth one on the left. It was lighted. I parked and went to the porch door. As I raised a hand to bang on the aluminum frame, a big woman appeared, silhouetted in the inner doorway.

"Whatya want?"

"I want to talk to Martha Whippler."

"Who are you?"

"The name is McGee. I was a friend of Patty's."

"Look, why don't you go away? The kid has had a hard day. She's pooped. Okay?"

"It's all right, Bobby," a frail voice said. "Let him in."

As I went in, the big woman stood back out of the way. When I saw her in the light I realized she was younger than I had thought. She wore jeans and a blue work shirt, sleeves rolled high over brown heavy forearms. Her hair was brown and cropped short and she wore no makeup. The interior was all pale plywood paneling, vinyl tile, glass curtains, plastic upholstery, stainless steel. A slight girl lay on a daybed, propped up on pillows, long coppery hair tousled around her sad wan face. Her eyes were red. Her lipstick was smeared. She had a drink in her hand. She wore a very frilly nylon robe. Though she was a lot slimmer, I knew her at once.

"Whippy!" I said, and then felt like a damn fool for not having figured it out.

It startled her. She stared at me with disapproval. "I don't know you. I don't remember you from anyplace. People call me Martha now. Pat wouldn't let them call me by my old name." There was something quite solemn and childlike about her. And vulnerable.

"I'm sorry. I'll call you Martha."

"What's your name?"

"Travis McGee."

"I never heard Pat say your name."

"I didn't know her well, Martha. I know a few other people you might know. Vance. Cass. Carl. Nancy Abbott. Harvey. Richie. Sonny."

She sipped her drink, frowning at me over the rim of the glass. "Sonny is dead. I heard that. I heard that he burned up, and it didn't mean a thing to me."

"Nancy saw him burn."

She looked incredulous. "How could that happen?"

"She was traveling with him then."

She shook her head in slow wonder. "Her traveling with him. Oh, boy. Who could imagine that. Me, sure. But her? Gee, it doesn't seem possible, believe you me."

"Martha, I want to talk to you alone."

"I bet you do," the big girl behind me said.

"Mr. McGee, this is my friend Bobby Blessing. Bobby, whyn't you go away awhile, okay?"

Bobby studied me. It is the traditional look they reserve for the authentic male, a challenging contempt, a bully-boy antagonism. There seem to be more of them around these days. Or perhaps they are merely bolder. The word is butch. Having not the penis nor the beard, they damn well try to have everything else. One of the secondary sex characteristics they seem to be able to acquire is the ballsy manner, the taut-shouldered swagger, the roostery go-to-hell attitude. They have a menacing habit of running in packs lately. And the unwary chap who tries to make off with one of their brides can get himself a stomping that stevedores would admire. These are a subculture, long extant but recently emerged from hiding. In their new boldness they do a frightening job of recruiting, having their major successes among the vulnerable platoons of those meek girls who, like Martha Whippler, are abused by men, by the Catton kind of man, used, abused, sickened, shared, frightened and . . . at last, driven into the camp of the butch.

"I'll be where I can hear you call me," Bobby said without taking her stony stare from my face. She went out, rolling her shoulders, hitching at her jeans.

I moved closer to Martha and sat in a skeletal plastic chair half facing her. She looked down into her half of a drink and said, "You named the people that were there that time."

"And left one out?"

"That movie actress," she whispered.

"Have you told people about her being there?"

"Oh, nothing like that ever happened to me before. I couldn't *tell* anybody about it. I mean, I could talk to Pat about it sometimes. You know. I used to have nightmares. She took me back home with her from there. I knew . . . I always knew she would rather it was Nancy."

She looked wistful. She had a cheap, empty, pretty little face, eyebrows plucked to fine lines, mouth made larger with lipstick.

"Did you ever get to see the pictures?" I asked her.

Even the most vapid ones have an urchin shrewdness about them, the wariness of the consistently defensive posture.

"What pictures?"

"The ones Vance had taken."

"For hours and hours today they kept asking me questions, questions. How do I know you just aren't another smart guy?"

"I can't prove I'm not." I hesitated. She was suggestible. I wanted the right approach, without fuss. Grief made an additional vulnerability. Kindly ol' McGee seemed the best bet. I shook my head sadly. "I'm just a fellow who thinks Patricia got a very bad deal from Vance M'Gruder, very bad indeed."

Tears welled. She snuffled into her fist. "Oh, God. Oh, God, yes. That bastard. That total bastard!"

"Some of us have never understood why Pat didn't fight it a little harder."

"Gee, you don't know what she had stacked against her. That rotten Vance had been planning it a long time. He got some kind of morality report on her from the London police from way before they were married, I guess to show that she knew she shouldn't get married. And then he had the tape recorder things of her and Nancy at their house, and her and me at their house, and the pictures he hired that man to get, following them around. It must have cost an awful lot, the whole thing, but as Pat said, it was a hell of a lot cheaper than California divorce. She couldn't get a lawyer to agree to fight it. I mean, after all, there wasn't any question about the way she was."

"Did you get to see those pictures, Martha?"

"Oh, sure. The funny thing, they made it look like nobody else was around at all. I don't know how that man got those pictures so close, Pat with me and with Nancy and with Lysa Dean, just one with Lysa Dean, one where you couldn't tell it was Lysa Dean unless you knew."

"So by the time you saw those pictures, you and Pat were together?"

"Yes. The rotten thing he did, we went up to the city to see some friends of hers, and we came back to Carmel, he was gone and the locks were changed, and our personal stuff was piled in a carport, and there was a man there to keep anybody from breaking in or anything. The way it was, she was still trying to get over being in love with Nancy, and maybe she never did. I guess maybe she never did get over it. But I did try to make her happy, I really did."

"Why would somebody want to kill her, Martha?"

She sobbed again and blew her nose. "I don't *know!* I just don't *know.* That's what they kept asking me. Gee, we lived real quiet here, over a year now, and for a long time we've been working the same shift at the Four Treys, me as a drink waitress and her on a change booth. Just a few friends. She hadn't got interested in any other girl or anything, and nobody was after me like that. There was just one thing."

"What do you mean?"

She frowned and shook her head. "I don't know. It started weeks ago. Before that, whenever she'd think of Vance she'd go into a terrible rage, and sometimes she'd cry. Weeks ago she got a letter from somebody. She didn't let me see it and I can't find it so I guess she destroyed it. She was kind of . . . far away for a few days after she got it and she wouldn't tell me anything. Then one day when I was out, she made long-distance phone calls. She really ran up a terrible bill. Forty dollars and something. And later she made a few more calls. Then she got very pleased about something. She'd be grinning and humming around and I'd ask her why she felt so good and she'd say never mind. Sometimes she would grab me and dance me around and she'd tell me everything was going to be just fine, and we were going to be rich. It didn't matter so much to me. I mean, we were doing all right here. We didn't *have* to be rich. I don't know if it had anything to do with her being murdered last night."

"Where were you when it happened?"

"I *heard* it! My God, I was in bed half asleep. I was sort of worrying about her. I've got a virus and I was off work. She was supposed to be finished at eleven and home by quarter past, but it was a little after midnight when I heard the car motor. I could tell it was ours, it's such a noisy little car. I'd left one light on for her. I wondered what she'd bring me. She'd bring me a little present if I was sick. Some kind of joke, sort of. The car stopped out there and I heard the car door, and then just outside that screen door, she yelled 'What are you . . .' Just those words. There was a kind of a terrible crunching sound. And a falling sound. And steps running. I turned on the lights and put my robe on and ran out and she was just outside the door on the ground, and her head . . ."

I waited several minutes while she slowly and painfully pulled herself back together.

"She was so alive," Martha moaned.

"But several weeks ago she stopped being mad at Vance?"

"Yes. But I don't know what it means."

"After she was locked out of the house, she did have a chance to talk to her husband?"

"Oh, several times. She begged and pleaded."

"But it didn't do any good."

"He wouldn't even let her have her car. He said she was lucky to keep the clothes she'd bought. Finally he gave her five hundred dollars so she could afford to go away. I had about seventy-five dollars. We came here on a bus and got jobs. He was nasty to her."

"Martha, does the name Ives mean anything to you? D. C. Ives?" She looked blank. "No."

"Santa Rosita?"

She tilted her empty little head. "That's strange!"

"What do you mean?"

"Just a couple of days ago she was singing that old song. 'Santa Lucia.' But she was saying Rosita instead of Lucia, and I said she had it wrong and she laughed and said she knew she did. Why did you ask about that? I don't understand."

"Maybe it doesn't mean anything."

"But if it has anything to do with who killed her . . ."

"Did she have any kind of appointment coming up?"

"Appointment? Oh, I'd forgotten. Just the other day she said she might have to take a little trip. Alone. Just for a day or two. It made me jealous. She teased me and let me get real jealous, and then she said it was a kind of a business trip, and she'd tell me all about it later."

"Where was she going to go?"

"Phoenix. Gee, we don't know a soul in Phoenix."

"How soon was she going?"

"I don't know. It sounded as if she meant real soon."

I couldn't shake loose anything else of interest. She was worn out. But she was still alert enough to ask again who I was and what I wanted. I had to answer a question with a question.

"What are you going to do now, Martha?"

"I haven't thought about it."

"It's your chance to get out of . . . this kind of situation."

Her little mouth firmed up. "I don't know what you think you mean by that. Listen, Pat got me out of a lousy situation. I don't want anything like that again ever. What do you know about anything?"

"Don't get sore."

"Why shouldn't I? Jesus Christ! Anything you people don't understand, it has to be lousy. Pat always said that. The world doesn't have to be your way. We never asked anybody to approve or disapprove. It's our own business. Who did we hurt?"

"You?"

"Me! That's some joke. That really is. Honest to God, when I remember the way it used to have to be, when I thought that was the only thing there was, boy, it makes my stomach turn right over. I've got friends who want to take care of me."

"I bet you have."

She stared at me, narrowed her eyes, threw her head back and yelled, "Bobby! Bobby!"

I left without any particular haste, but without delay either. Even so, they were between me and my car. Bobby had a friend, equally sizable. In the angle of the light the friend looked like the young Joe DiMaggio, but with a black dutch bob, and wearing desert rat khakis. Joe carried a putter. The gold head and chrome shaft glittered.

They separated and moved in from either side.

"Don't make any stupid mistakes," I said, coming to a halt.

Joe had managed to train herself down to a good imitation of a baritone. "You bassars got to get a lesson not to come around here bothering the brides."

"What have you got here?" I asked. "A colony?"

"Smart-ass," Bobby said as they moved in.

They generally do very well against the unindoctrinated male. There is a chivalrous reluctance to hit a woman. Martha had come to the trailer doorway to watch the sport. I had learned a painful lesson long ago when reluctance had slowed reaction time, and I had spent the next several days walking around like an eighty-eight-year-old man. It is the type of mistake you are not likely to make twice in one lifetime. And these two were more dangerous than male thugs because their aberrations fired their hatred of the authentic male. They might not know when to stop hitting.

The light was tricky and the putter made me nervous. If I tried sweet reason, she was going to try to sink it into my skull. So I moved with no regard for chivalry. I feinted toward Bobby and lunged at Joe. I got a hand on the putter shaft before she could build up any momentum with it. I wrested it out of her hand, reversed it, sidestepped her and laid the limber end of it across the seat of those khakis. It made a little whirring in the air and a mighty crack on impact. Joe leaped high and, probably much to her own disgust, gave a high girlish scream of anguish. I turned in time to see Bobby hurl a rock at my head. It tickled the hair on the crown of my head, and the fright lent considerable enthusiasm to my pursuit. Bobby turned in flight. I welted her three hearty times across tight denim, and she joined her yelps to those of her buddy. Joe grappled with me, trying to trip me. She was sobbing in frustration, and she smelled like a mule skinner. I spun her away and whacked her another beauty. She screamed and gave up and started running toward the trailer.

Bobby made the mistake of running right along beside her, about five feet away from her. I sped into the gap with forehand and backhand. Martha Whippler had come to the doorway to watch them brutalize me. They nearly trampled her in their haste to get out of range. They sounded as if they were trying to yodel. I laughed, hurled the putter well out of the colony and drove away from there.

Back in the muted silence of the big room at the Apache, Dana slept on. Remembering that the Apache food service would be closed, I had stopped at an implausible delicatessen in town. I turned more lights on. I unsacked my purchases, pried the top off the beef stew with noodles. It was still steaming. I carried it over and sat on the floor beside the bed and wafted it back and forth in front of her face. Her nose twitched, twitched again. Suddenly her eyes opened wide. She focused on me. She gave a great start.

"Hey!" she said. "Hey now!" She gave a great creaking, stretching, shuddering yawn and then reached for the container. She hitched herself up, arranged the pillows, tucked the sheet around her, under her arms, and lifted a huge plastic forkful into the greedy waiting mouth. "Oh!" she said. "Oh, my God, Trav, nothing has ever tasted like this."

I moved a small table close to her elbow, brought over the garlic dills, the hot tea and the strawberry cheesecake. I sat on the foot of the bed, admiring her. When the edge of hunger began to be eased, she began to be uncomfortable.

"Did you eat?" she asked.

"Like a wolf."

She poked at her tangled hair. "I'm a mess, I bet."

Her dark vital eyes were puffy, shadowed with fatigue. Her lips were swollen, pale without lipstick. There was a long scratch on her throat, three oval blue smudges on the front of her left shoulder, where my fingers had bruised her.

"You look just fine, Dana."

Her face got pink. She would not look directly at me. "I bet. Uh . . . what time is it?"

"Twenty of one."

She said she would finish the cheesecake later. She asked me to please turn my back. She lugged our suitcase into the bathroom. I heard her take a quick shower. In a little while after the water stopped, she came shyly out, hair brushed, mouth made up, and she was wearing a little blue hip-length nightgown, diaphanous, with lace at throat and hem. Rather than making any attempt to model it, she scuttled for the bed in a knock-kneed half run, slightly hunched over. She piled in, covered herself and said, blushing furiously, "It isn't exactly what I thought I was buying."

I laughed at her. She frowned part way through the cheesecake and then managed a timid smile, a direct but fleeting glance. "I'm not used to this sort of situation, Trav. I'm sorry."

"Don't be. Nobody else is."

She swallowed and looked pained. "I was so . . . I don't know what you must th . . . . I never . . . oh, *hell*, anyway!"

"Stop fussing. So it's a new relationship. We are something to each other we weren't before. And took a risk. You know that. Somebody, Hemingway maybe, had a definition of a moral act. It's something you feel good after. And coming back here to you after where I've been makes us seem like the innocence of angels."

She showed her concern. "What happened, dear?"

The cheesecake and tea were long gone by the time I finished with the facts and the speculations.

She looked dubious. "It seems like an *awful* lot of guessing."

I went through it once more, in précis form. "What do we know about M'Gruder? He is feisty, rich, ruthless and stingy. And, with no occupation, he is highly mobile. He's brown and fit and damned callous. Okay, as the purchaser of a service, he got into direct contact with Ives. Ives, seeing a golden opportunity, recognizing Lysa, took all the pictures he could get, hundreds of them, knowing he could crop and enlarge to exhibit every relationship that went on during those four days. Assume that when M'Gruder learned where the party was going to be, he got to a phone and alerted his hired photographer. We know one thing about Ives. He was greedy. He did his job for M'Gruder and got his fee. He collected big from Lysa Dean. He took a hack at the Abbott money and struck out, because Nancy was past protecting.

"Now we have to guess. M'Gruder was hot to marry the young Atlund girl. Her professor father disapproved. M'Gruder won him over. I think that with a Swedish girl's traditional respect for parental authority, the professor had to be won over or there would have been no marriage. I think Ives made the mistake of trying to blackmail a previous client, someone who knew who he was and where to find him. The timing fits. Ives threatened to show Professor Atlund the terrace pictures featuring M'Gruder. Anything that rancid would have bitched the marriage forever. The professor would not have his dear girl marrying a libertine like that. Ives did not think M'Gruder dangerous. Maybe he underestimated his stinginess. M'Gruder followed him, saw a good opportunity and smashed the top of his head in. A couple of weeks later he married his Ulka.

"Take it a step further. We have to assume that Patty M'Gruder learned the name of the photographer from Vance. He would delight in telling her how smart he had been, how cleverly he had cut her loose from the M'Gruder money. He would want to rub her nose in it. He would *have* to hate her. He is a very virile type, and it would be an outrage to his pride to realize his English wife had merely pretended pleasure with him and actually preferred girls. Patty got a letter from somebody. Gossip, perhaps. Vance's child bride and the problem with the professor. It started her thinking. She had known of Ives' death. She knew Vance. She knew him damned well, and how his mind operated, and his capacity for violence. Somehow, checking this out by phone, she became convinced Vance had done in Ives. So she sent a letter to Vance. It would be a very veiled hint. Come through with the money you cheated me out of, boy, or the Santa Rosita police are going to take an interest in you. Words to that effect. He couldn't risk that. I'd say he'd write back something about planning to be in Phoenix and be willing to discuss her financial situation at that time. She would realize she had struck gold. Now he could not risk being publicly in Las Vegas. When women die, they check out their ex-husbands. I say he set up a good solid alibi in Phoenix and came over here last night and killed her. He smashed the top of her head in. He would imagine he had no other choice. She hated him as much as he hated her. She would show no mercy. She would bleed him forever."

She thought it over. "I guess it does make sense. But, Trav, is it our problem? Isn't Samuel Bogen our problem, really?"

"At this moment, my darling Dana, some very shrewd cop may be checking out some small slip M'Gruder made. The death of Patricia *has* to require he be checked out. So they grab him for murder first. Do you think he would maintain a chivalrous silence? He would want to lay all the facts on the line, with little distortions here and there, to try to show justification or at least a plausible excuse for murder. Once they round up Cass and Carl and Martha Whippler and start questioning them one at a time, how long do you think Lysa Dean would stay in the clear? Make up a headline, honey. Star Implicated in Orgy Murder. She'd be even worse off. I have to find out how good these guesses are. If she's going to be in the soup, the best I can do is warn her. Maybe she can take some steps. Long-term contracts. Public relations advice. Something."

Dana frowned. "I see what you mean. But he could have just *said* Phoenix."

"I think he's there. It's close. I want to check it out."

"All right, dear."

I patted her on the foot. "I like obedient women."

She yawned. "I just feel terribly passive, I guess."

"Entirely, completely passive?"

She pursed her lips. She tilted her head. She laid a finger alongside her nose. "Well . . . I wouldn't go so far as to say *that*."

13

I HAD the random idea of poking around the Four Treys to see if I could find a small hint of a visit from Vance M'Gruder the night of Patty's death, but my few small memories of the hard-nosed vigilance of the Las Vegas cops outweighed the impulse. They deal, day and night, with every kind of spook and hustler in the world, and they would be focused very intently on this murder, and I did not relish the prospect of being bounced up and down while trying to explain my passing interest.

Besides, if M'Gruder was as bright as I imagined, he would not have put in an appearance in the stage lighting of any of the downtown casinos. He would have her Desert Gate address. Once he got to town it would be no great feat to find out when her shift ended. As I shaved I tried to guess his most plausible mode of transportation. It was just about three hundred miles to Phoenix. I decided that if I were doing it, I'd settle for a good fast car. With enough muscle under the hood, and the right kind of springing for the mountain curves, you could safely call it a five-hour run. Leave Phoenix at six and arrive at eleven. Spend an hour hunting her down and killing her. Back by five-thirty in the morning. Sneak into the bridal bed. A private car was safer than a bus, a scheduled flight or a private plane. Cash for gas. No records, no fellow passengers. Properly done, casually done, he could have people convinced he had never left at all. If he had the cold nerve necessary to make that earlier run to Santa Rosita . . .

We walked to the dining room for breakfast, my lady wearing that green which was all she happened to have. My drowsy lady walked close at my side, without haste, her smile as inward and bemused as that of the Mona Lisa. She hugged my arm and beamed up at me and gave me a sleepy wink. And then she yawned.

Between us we ate a mountain of wheat cakes, a bale of bacon.

I found a Phoenix paper in the lobby rack, checked through it and found a society editor by-line. I coached Dana and put her into a phone booth with a fake name and a reasonably plausible cover story. I stood outside the booth and saw her eyes go fierce and bright. She gave me a savage little nod. When she came out, she said, "What a sweet woman! The M'Gruders are staying with a couple named Glenn and Joanne Barnweather. She spake their names with social awe. Old friends of his, apparently. They flew in from Mexico City about five days ago, she thinks. She had an item on it. They're staying at the Barnweather ranch out beyond Scottsdale. You were sure, weren't you?"

"Not completely. But I'm beginning to be. So let's go take a look at them."

We went back to the room and packed. A tremendous chore. She made a housewifely ceremony of it, trotting around the room in a charade of seeing that no meager possession was overlooked, earnest frown between her eyes, white teeth biting into the fullness of underlip.

I caught her as she went by, planted a kiss upon the frown lines and told her that she was a fine girl. She said she was glad I thought she was a fine girl, but it might be a pretty good idea to just leggo of the fine girl or maybe we wouldn't be out of there by noon, which she had happened to notice was checkout time.

We were on our way with the top down heading toward Boulder City by noon, after one quick stop at a department store for a stretch denim skirt and halter top and bright yellow scarf for her, white sport shirt for the driver.

The car was heavy and agile. The day had a honeymoon flavor. The sun and the dry wind baked us. We laughed. We made bad jokes. She slanted dark eyes at me, lively with her mischief. This was the way I had wanted her to be. Totally alive and free, not tucked back into her own darkness.

But, totally alive, she was an impressive handful. This was not some pretty little girl, coyly flirtatious, delicately stimulated. This was the mature female of the species, vivid, handsome and strong, demanding that all the life and need within her be matched. Her instinct would immediately detect any hedging, any dishonesty, any less than complete response to her—and then she would be gone for good. Wholeness was all she could comprehend or accept. For now there were no shadows in her eyes, no hesitations as a bad edge of memory stung her. Even in this pursuit of murder, it was a fine fine world.

When we stopped for lunch in an outdoor patio in heavy shade, I looked at her and said, "Why?"

She knew what I meant. She scowled into her iced coffee. "I guess way back after you came back to the room after seeing Carl Abelle. I don't know. You could have stomped around, the hard-guy grin and all that. But you felt bad about hurting and humiliating him. And he isn't much, certainly. So I figured out you don't go around proving you are a man because you are already sure you are. It isn't all faked up. And in the same way you didn't have to try to use me to prove what a hell of a fellow you are. Even though we were both . . . being attracted in a physical way. I know this sounds as if I'm some kind of an egomaniac, but I just thought well . . . heck, if being a man is a good and valid thing, then there should be like an award of merit or something, an offering. In Abnertalk, namely me. As if I'm so great."

"Don't do that to yourself, Dana. You are implausibly . . . astoundingly, unforgettably great. And I don't mean just in a . . ."

"I know. It isn't me, and it isn't you. Let's not talk about it. It's the total of us, the crazy total. I'm not going to talk about it, or think of what comes after. Okay? Okay, darling?"

"No talk. No analysis."

"We are kind of beautiful," she said. "It's enough to know that, I guess. Alone I'm just . . . sort of efficient and severe and a little heavy-handed. Defensive. Alone you're just sort of a rough, wry opportunist, a little bit cold and shrewd and watchful. Cruel, maybe. You and your sybarite boat and your damned beach girls. But we add up to beautiful in some crazy way. For now."

"For now, Dana?"

"I'm no kid, Travis. I know hurt is inevitable always."

"Shut up."

"I talk too much?"

"Only sometimes."

So off we went, to Kingman, to Wikieup, to Congress—up into cold places, down into heats—to Wickenburg, to Wittman, and down into the richness of the old Salt River Valley where Phoenix presides over the boom that threatens never to quit. It has become a big fast rough grasping town, where both the irrigation heiresses and the B girls wear the same brand of ranch pants.

The sun was low behind us as we came in, breasting the outgoing traffic of the close of Friday business. I cruised and settled for a glassy sprawl called the Hallmark, a big U of stone, teak and thermowindows enclosing a great green of lawn and gardens, a blue of water in a marbled pool in the shape of a painter's palette. In a nearby specialty shop, still open, we let Lysa Dean refurbish our dwindled wardrobes to the extent of swim trunks for me and a swimsuit for the lady. We fixed ourselves tall ones of gin and bitter lemon. Dana swam with utmost earnestness, chin held very high, using a stroke I told her was early sheep dog. In the bathroom, in fading light of day, her body bore the halter marks of the long sunny ride, her broad flat breasts pale, responsive to soapy ablutions cooperatively offered. In a predictable haste, I toted the untoweled seal shape of her, dripping, to bed, a firm, lithe, gleaming, chuckling burden which seemed to have no weight at all. Ceremonial celebration of our twenty-fourth hour.

Eased and complete, in mild and affectionate embrace, we took up the duty of talking about M'Gruder, weighing the merits of the possible methods of contact.

I could not tell her precisely what I hoped to accomplish. If M'Gruder was the man, I wanted to stir him up. I didn't want him to believe he had any chance at all. A man running is a dead man. A trial would finish Lysa Dean as well. And when you take someone's money for expenses, there is a morality involved. He would have some confidence he had gotten away with it. I had to blast that out of him and set him running. And arrange a chase.

The Barnweather number was listed. We went over it carefully. I coached her. She added a few ideas. There was a phone extension in the bath. I went in there and listened.

A servant said the M'Gruders were in the guest house. He gave Dana another number to call.

A man answered. A cultivated baritone, loosened slightly by drink, admitting that he, indeed, was Mister M'Gruder himself.

"You don't know me, Mr. M'Gruder."

"From your charming voice, that is my loss, my dear. What is your name?"

"I've just picked a new name for myself. I wondered if you'd like it. Patty Ives. Do you like that name?"

It was a slow five-count before he spoke. His voice was under careful control. "You sound as if you thought you were telling me something. But I am afraid I don't follow."

"I guess I do have you at a disadvantage. I know so *much* more about you than you know about me."

"I don't wish to be rude, but I don't like guessing games, whoever you are. So if you don't mind . . ."

"I thought we might make a date for a quiet talk, if you would like to sneak away from your little bride, Vance. We have mutual friends. Carl Abelle. Lysa Dean. Cass Edgars. Nancy Abbott. Martha Whippler. Of course Sonny Catton is dead. Poor Sonny."

Again I could have counted to five. "I think you might be a very foolish girl."

"Foolish, but not very greedy. And very, very careful, Vance."

"Let me put it this way. You might have something you think is valuable. But suppose it is only an annoyance?"

"Oh wouldn't it have to be a *lot* more than that!"

"You are talking in circles, my dear. I am quite certain I can be forgiven for old indiscretions. Life with my ex often became very unwholesome. Mrs. M'Gruder is aware of that. I've reformed. The police were here yesterday afternoon, cooperating with the Las Vegas police, I imagine. To make certain I hadn't killed Patty. I'm not sorry she's dead. I'm not that much of a hypocrite. She was a horrid woman. I had to get free of her in any way I could. All this is none of your business, of course. But I didn't want you to think you've alarmed me. You just make me feel . . . irritable. Please don't phone me again." Click.

I reached and put the phone on the hook and then sat back on the wide yellow rim of the little triangular tub. In a few moments Dana appeared in the bathroom doorway. She had put on my sport shirt. She leaned against the doorframe and said, "Well?"

"I don't know. I just don't know. Either we're dead wrong, or he's got the nerve of a headwaiter. So much points his way. Damn it, it *has* to be him. We're going out there."

"Just like that?"

"We're going to be invited out, I hope."

There is one theory that there are but a hundred thousand people in the United States, and the rest of the 189,900,000 is a faceless mob. The theory further states that any person in the hundred thousand can be linked to any other by no more than a three-step process. Example: Ron knew Carol's brother at Princeton; Carol's husband worked with Vern at the Ford Foundation; Vern's cousin met Lucy at the film festival. Thus when Ron and Lucy met as strangers, and sense that they are each members of the hundred thousand, they can play a warm and heartening and satisfying game of who-do-you-know and, with little cries of delight, trace the relationship.

By dint of past endeavors I had acquired provisional membership in the group, and it seemed likely to me that Glenn and Joanne Barnweather would be solid members. So I had to tap other members most likely to know them. I tried Tulio in Oklahoma City and drew a dead blank. I remembered Mary West in Tucson. She knew them, but not well. But she did know Paul and Betty Diver in Flagstaff who knew them intimately, and she was certain she could get Betty to play along. If there was any hitch, she would phone back. If not, I would hear from Joanne Barnweather directly. She briefed me on what I'd have to know about the Divers.

We had a twenty-minute wait before the phone rang. "Trav McGee?" a woman asked. "This is Joanne Barnweather. I just got a call from our very dear mutual friend, Paul Diver, saying you're in town. Could you come out to the place? Are you free?"

"If I can bring along a gal."

"Of *course* you can, dear. Glenn and I will be delighted. We've got some people in to meet our houseguests and we're just churning around here, very informal, drinking up a small storm and waiting for time to throw a steak on. Do come as you are. We'll be delighted to see you." She gave me directions.

Dana had been nestled close to me, listening. When I hung up she gave me a look of mock admiration. "You are a scoundrel, McGee."

"Darling, go put on your green."

"She said to come as we are."

"Then at least button my shirt."

14

On the way out, under a chilly spangle of stars, I had briefed Dana on how we'd handle it. She was to stay away from M'Gruder, target on his young Swede bride if possible. I would do what I could with M'Gruder.

The Barnweather place was a simple little quarter-million-dollar ranch house a few hundred yards into a lot of rocky acreage, with fifteen cars glinting in the starlight, music and festive sounds coming from the flood-lighted pool area.

I sensed that Dana took a deep breath and braced herself as we walked toward the party jabber. There were infrared heaters focused on the broad terrace area at the house end of the pool. A gleaming, beaming little fellow in a red coat tended bar. These were a pack of the young marrieds, the success-prone ones. The tense and girlish mothers of three and five and seven young, their beefier husbands, expansive with bourbon and land deals. About thirty-five people in all, forming and reforming their little conversational groups. Dress was varied, all the way from shorts and slacks to some of those fanciful ranch coats on the men, the pale whipcord jobs with the pearl buttons and pocket flaps. The audible talk had that Southwest flavor so quickly acquired by the people who move there from Indiana and Pennsylvania.

When we hesitated, a slender pretty woman came smiling toward us, holding one hand out to each of us. "Trav? I'm Joanne."

"And this is Diana Hollis." We had decided it was possible Lysa Dean had spoken of her girl Friday to M'Gruder, and the name was just unusual enough to stick in his mind.

"So glad you could come, dears. Come meet the group."

She steered us over for a drink first and then swung us through the throng, rattling off the names and identifications. Glenn was one of the burly ones in whipcord. Joanne made a little more special thing of the introduction to their houseguests. Vance M'Gruder was a little balder, a little browner, a little taller than he had seemed in the pictures. He was a type. The totally muscled sportsman—muscles upon muscles so that even his face looked like a leather bag of walnuts. Polo muscles, tennis muscles, sail-handling muscles, fencing muscles—the type who does handstands every morning of his life, works out with professionals whenever possible, and has a savage and singleminded desire to whip you at anything you're willing to play with him, from squash racquets to tetherball. He had the personality to go with the body—a flavor of remote, knowing, arrogant amusement.

His young bride was one of the most striking females I have ever seen in my life. You had a tendency to speak to her in a hushed voice, an awed voice. The Swedes grow some of the finest specimens of our times. This Ulka Atlund M'Gruder was big enough for M'Gruder to keep her in flat heels at all times. She wore a woolly tangerine-colored shift. Her arms were bare. The others were bundled in jackets, sweaters, tunics, shawls, stoles. She looked as if she had enough animal heat to keep her entirely comfortable at 30 below. Her body, under the touch of the fabric, was ripe, leggy and entirely perfect. Without makeup, her features were almost those of some heroic, dedicated young boy, a page from the time of King Arthur. Or an idealized Joan of Arc. Her tilted gray-green-blue Icelandic eyes were the cold of northern seas. Her hair was a rich, ripe, heavy spill of pale pale gold, curved across the high and placid brow. She had little to say, and a sleepy and disinterested way of saying it. Her eyes kept seeking out her husband. Over all that stalwart Viking loveliness there was such a haze of sensuality it was perceptible, like a strange matte finish. It was stamped into the slow and heavy curve of her smile, marked by the delicate violet shadows under her eyes, expressed by the cant of her high round hips in the way she stood. Though by far the youngest person there, she at the same time seemed far older. She had been bolted to the bowsprit of an ancient ship for a thousand years. And every woman there hated her and feared her. The look of her confirmed my guesses about Vance M'Gruder. Wearing this one like a banner or a medal was the ultimate cachet of competitive masculinity. She had a strange primitive flavor of sexual docility. She was indentured to M'Gruder, totally focused upon him, yet were she taken from him by someone with more strength and force and purpose, she would shift loyalty without question or hesitation. A man like M'Gruder would go to any length to acquire her. And he had. I was certain of that. I thought of M'Gruder's past habits and inclinations, and I wondered if, when his physical resources began to flag, he would stimulate himself by corrupting her. A woman to him would be something owned, to use as he wished.

Later, standing in a group with M'Gruder, I looked over and saw Dana alone with Ulka, talking quietly to her. Ulka nodded. She was watching Vance. I could not get anywhere with Vance. I tried to play do-you-know with him, bringing up the names of some of the Florida sailboat bums I know. Yes, he knew them. Sure. So what. I guessed he could not become interested in trivia. He had taken two horrible risks to acquire and keep the Viking princess. Maybe somebody was getting set to drop the noose on him and end it. Apprehension could make small talk almost impossible. I could not comprehend M'Gruder's promise to put this creature back into college. I found it hard to believe that a professorial type had spawned her. In days of old whenever one of these rarities appeared, one of the king's agents would run to the castle with the news, and the girl child would disappear forever into one of the royal suites, and her family would get a little sack of gold coins in exchange. In these more random times they are grabbed off by oil men, celebrity athletes, television moguls and M'Gruders. But the man who has one stays nervous because, unless you are a king, you don't really get to own it. It is on temporary loan from providence.

Later I sat near Ulka in a big game room in the house while she carved and chewed her way through a huge rare steak, knife and teeth flashing, jaw muscles and throat working, her eyes made blank by a total concentration on this physical gratification. The effort made a sweaty highlight on her pale brow, and at last she picked up the sirloin bone and gnawed it bare, putting a slick of grease on lips and fingertips. There was no vulgarity in this hunger, any more than when a tiger cracks the hip socket to suck the marrow.

The party fragmented, and there was room enough for them to roam all the house and grounds, various degrees of alcohol dividing them more positively than social class or business interest. I had lost track of Dana, and I went night-walking in unhurried search. Skirting a tall cactus garden, floodlighted in eerie blue, I heard, off to my right, a conspiratorial rasp of female venom. "Bastard! Bastard! Bastard!" It was more contemptuous than indignant. I sought to move quietly out of range. I did not care how husbands were gutted in this desert paradise. I imagined it was done the same as elsewhere.

But the male voice stopped me. "All I want to know is where you . . ." The rest of the sentence was lost. He had raised his voice to cut her off and lowered it as she fell silent. But it was Vance M'Gruder.

"You are so smart! You are *soooooo* smart! Oh, *God*, what a brilliant mind I married!"

"Sssh, Ullie. Don't shout!"

"Maybe it was one of my Mexican boyfriends. How about that? Hah? How about that? And just what would you do about it?" Sweet voice of Ulka Atlund M'Gruder, bride of two months. And where was the sleepy remote smile? The placid acceptance? This was the malignancy of a taunting woman, an emasculating woman. He shushed her again and they moved off, out of range. I circled and discovered I had been near the path that probably led over to the guest house.

I admit feeling a certain dirty little satisfaction. It was as if the fox had made one leap just high enough and found out the grapes actually *were* sour. Here was this brown hard bundle of sport muscles trying to kid the calendar by wedding the glorious child bride, and now all his game skills and all his money and his social standing were no defense at all against that killer instinct which could launch her right at his most vulnerable point, his aging masculinity. Seeking paradise, he had embraced a sweet disaster.

The party dwindled. Laughter was drunken. A group sang "The Yellow Rose of Texas."

I stood with Dana, saying good night, and Joanne Barnweather swayed against us, and said, "You all come riding tomorrow morning, you hear? Got lovely horses. Jus' lovely. Diana, sweetie, like I said, I got stuff'll fit you. Don' worry 'bout it. Jus' you all and us and the M'Gruders. You know what, Diana? Ulka liked you. She wants you 'long. How about that anyhow? To find out she likes anybody. Crissake, we've known Vance forever and we love the sweet ol' son of a bitch, and it was great he got loose from that limey dyke, believe me, but hones' I can't figure this Ulka. Sheese! A zombie, thass what she is. I shouldn't talk like this, but I'm a wee little bit stoned, sweeties. What you do, you get here like nine in the morning, okay?"

On the way home Dana said, "Horses scare me."

"How did you make out?"

"Didn't you hear? She likes me. But I never would have been able to tell. Trav, that child has very limited reactions, really. I had a friend who got like that once. They said finally it was a hypothyroid condition. She sort of drifted, slept fourteen hours a night and couldn't keep track of conversations. Believe me, dear, I tried. I really tried. I had about forty minutes alone with her. I tried to drop key words into it to get some kind of a reaction. After a long struggle I did find out that her husband played poker last Wednesday night. He loves a good poker session, she said. She said he didn't come back until Thursday just before noon. I practically had to shake her to get that much out of her."

I did not tell Dana I felt uneasy. I had the feeling the play was being taken away from us. I had made a move. Now either this was all in innocence, or M'Gruder was making one. I resolved to handle myself as though he were making a move. Violence is the stepchild of desperation.

We both had to borrow gear. Glenn Barnweather's pants were too short in the leg and big in the waist for me. Dana had a slightly different problem with Joanne's twill britches. The waist was fine and the length was good, but in thigh and bottom Dana filled them to bursting. The stable hands saddled the mounts while a rather shaky Joanne doled out therapeutic rum sours. Joanne assigned the mounts. Dana, as a novice, got a rather plump and amiable mare. I was given a hammerhead buckskin with a rolling eye. He sensed a certain incompetence and tried simultaneously to nibble my leg and bash me into a post. I sawed him and kicked him into a dubious docility. By all odds, as we went clattering and snorting up a long baked slope, Joanne and Vance were the best of the group. Elbows in, heels correct, moving like a part of the animal. Glenn on a big red stallion was a close second. Ulka and I were about on a level. She looked glorious in pale blue denim with a white cowgirl hat on the back of her fair head, laced under her chin. Ulka seemed much merrier than on the night before. But Vance looked wretched. He had a greenish look under his tan. His eyes were bloodshot. With the air of a man under great tension he had knocked down three sours in rapid order before mounting.

Joanne chattered about the ranch and what they were eventually going to do with it. She pointed out where things would be. My damned horse kept trying to stumble to see if he could loosen me a little bit, then hurl me the rest of the way. For a time I rode beside Ulka. She dipped into a pale leather pouchpurse she wore looped around one wrist and got out cigarettes, leaned and gave me one, then leaned and after several near misses, managed to give me a light. We smiled in wordless idiocy at each other. Her big breasts bounced very firmly under the denim. Her classic nose was shiny. I lost her when my horse moved up from a canter into a full run. He didn't seem to like a canter. He tended to drop back into a spine-shattering trot or suddenly go like hell. He kept me busy. Suddenly everybody, at Glenn's suggestion, went careening across rocky flats toward a distant stand of trees. My horse was beginning to take me a little more seriously. We were spread out. Dana was up with Glenn, hunched toward the horse's neck, perhaps grasping at the saddle horn, pale pants bouncing. Joanne was at my left and a half a length ahead of me.

That was when Ulka Atlund M'Gruder gave her terrible, piercing scream. The horses had violent reactions. I went up with mine and came down with mine, then spurred him forward and caught at Dana just as she began to slip off the side of her mare's neck, hauled her back toward the saddle. Glenn had taken off to the left. I looked and saw M'Gruder's horse running wildly in that direction, with a terrible ragdoll figure bounding along the rocks beside the rear hooves. It slipped free and lay still, wet-shining with some patches of red. Ulka dismounted and, screaming again, ran stumbling across the rocks to drop beside the figure. I dropped off and knotted my barbarous steed to a dwarfed bush. Dana's mare suddenly took off, heading for home. Joanne reined around and set out after Dana. I ran over to the body. It took one look to identify it forever as such. I pulled Ulka to her feet and walked her away from it. She was shuddering, over and over.

"He just leaned forward and slipped off," she said in her thin little voice with just a trace of accent. "He slipped off but his foot was caught. He just leaned forward and slipped off. Oh, my God." She dropped onto her knees and haunches, face in her hands.

They brought the body back in a jeep and transferred it into an ambulance near the Barnweather house. The necessary red tape was handled with dispatch. We all agreed that M'Gruder had not seemed well. Ulka said that he'd had a stomach upset and had not slept. She rested in Joanne's bedroom. Joanne and Dana were with her. Her father was notified. He would arrive in Phoenix Sunday morning to take her back to San Francisco. The funeral would be there. M'Gruder's lawyer was notified. Reporters hovered around, sitting in cars, looking irritable.

I sat in the terrace shade with Glenn Barnweather. He kept shaking his head and saying, "Hell of a thing, hell of a thing," and then fixing himself another stiff bourbon.

"He certainly had everything to live for," I said.

"Christ, you ought to see his place in Hawaii. Her place now, I guess. You know why it hits her so damned hard having it happen right now? I got woozy last night. If I'd gone to bed, I'd have been sick. I took a little walk. Sounds carry in the night. They were having one hell of a battle last night. Screaming at each other. I couldn't hear the words. It went on a long time. You wouldn't think she could get that worked up, would you? Maybe it was their first fight. I had the idea he was in charge. Maybe he thought so too. A man married two months and he can stay out all night for poker when there's that item home in bed, you *know* he has to be boss."

"Poker?"

"Down in town at the club last Wednesday. It's a regular thing. All-night session once a month. He dropped about two thousand. I got some of it. I would have had more, but he came back pretty good toward the end."

When you sell yourself something, and all the parts fit, you resent the hell out of having somebody kick the foundation out from under it. You want to grab the structure to keep it from falling down.

"He played all night long?" I said, looking at that big red earnest face, looking in vain for any hint of lie or evasion.

His fleeting grin was mildly lewd. "Well into the bright cruel light of day, McGee. I can understand anybody being startled, after a good look at that Swede bride. Maybe poor Vance had to take a breather. She looks like one hell of a project."

My pretty tower fell down. Fallacious suppositions make a hell of a jangle when they hit the dirt, particularly when you dislike the person you've nominated. I'd heard one little piece of that quarrel too, a piece that could be related to the previous Wednesday night. Maybe I'd heard him asking her where she'd gone that night. And she taunted him about Mexican boyfriends . . .

"Did Ulka have a night on the town too?" I asked him.

"She was going to, but not what you'd call a real swinging situation. One of Joanne's concert things. I miss every one I can. Cocktails and a dinner party and a concert party. It was all set up, and Ulka decided not to go, and Joanne went alone."

"Maybe Ulka went out later. Did they have a rental car?"

"I loaned them the Corvette I bought Jo. It's the three-sixty, and it's just too much car for her. It scares her. Vance was wondering about buying it and they could drive it to San Francisco and have the rest of their stuff shipped. Okay with me, but we didn't get around to making the deal. It's new. About fifteen hundred miles on it. It scares Jo. She gets absentminded and gooses it and it scares her."

"Was that Wednesday night the only time they've been apart?"

"He stuck pretty close to her."

"They drive around in that car much?"

"We were keeping them too busy. What's this all about?"

I shrugged. "Nothing. Idle chatter." After some small talk, he fixed himself another drink and ambled off into the house. I went down the path to the guest house. The Sting Ray was in the carport, top down. I looked at the speedometer and then walked slowly and thoughtfully back to the main house. I couldn't tell Glenn what was on my mind. The toppled pieces of my theory suddenly looked good again. I was putting it back together, with a new name on it. The problem was motive. A weird guess stopped me in my tracks. I took long strides the rest of the way to the main house.

I whispered to Dana in the hallway. "Honey, just keep anybody from going into that bedroom. Make any excuse you can think of."

"You look so strange, darling."

"I feel strange."

"Can you tell me?"

"When I'm sure. Then I can tell you."

I went into Joanne's bedroom and closed the door behind me. It was a long room. The draperies were drawn. It was early afternoon. Ulka reclined on a quilted yellow chaise with a fuzzy yellow blanket over her lap. Her slanted eyes were reddened. She was still in her stretch denim, and drifting on the air-conditioned chill was the faint effluvium of saddle horse. She watched me with apparent unconcern as, without greeting, I pulled a hassock over close to the chaise and sat facing her. She had so much presence I had to remind myself she was, after all, just an eighteen-year-old girl, with the very last diminishing hint of a childish roundness in her cheeks.

Silence is a useful gambit, but I could not tell if it was having any effect at all upon her.

"Well, Ullie," I said.

"I will never let anyone else ever call me that, all my life."

"That's very sentimental, Ullie. Very tenderhearted. I guess you are a very tenderhearted girl. You didn't want your father upset, did you? Those pictures Ives took of your husband-to-be would have upset the professor. He would have forbidden the marriage. And you are a dutiful daughter. Ives was a very greedy fellow. He knew how badly Vance wanted you. He must have asked for a great deal of money. You know, it wasn't smart of Ives to blackmail his previous client with the pictures he took, because Vance knew him. Ives must have decided Vance was incapable of violence."

She frowned and shook her pretty head. "Ives? Pictures? Blackmail? Why do you come in here with this crazy talk?"

"Ives had to get it in one big chunk because as soon as you were married to Vance, there was no more leverage Ives could use. I guess Vance must have confessed the problem to you and showed you the pictures, perhaps to see if you would marry without Daddy's permission, so he could save a bundle. It's pretty sad and funny, Ullie. Your great respect for your father, and no respect for life."

"You should not call me Ullie. I will not permit it."

"Vance must have thought it was just a marvelous accident when Ives got killed. All he cared was that it got him off the hook, and when no confederate appeared to pick up where Ives had left off, he knew he was home free. He was going to have the girl, the gold ring and everything. His tragedy was in slowly finding out what a psychotic bitch you really are."

"Who are you? You must be mad, entirely."

"Let's check it out together, Ullie. No one suspected Vance. Patty, his ex-wife, was the only one in the world in a position to brood about it and begin to add two and two. And finally she got an answer and checked it out as closely as she could, and knew she had Vance right where she wanted him. She had every reason to want to get back at him. Believing Vance had killed Ives, and knowing that he could be a good big source of income to her for the rest of her life, she got in touch with him. I think we can figure out how that went wrong, Ullie. Vance could prove where he was on the night of

December fifth. But where was his darling girl? Quite a husky girl. And someone who could get close to Ives and close to Patty at night, in lonely places, whereas Vance couldn't have managed it. After you'd bashed Ives, Patty was a necessity. Clumsy murder is like housework, dear. Once you begin, you're never really finished."

"All this is so absurd, and so boring."

"Patty would have persisted, and sooner or later Vance would have had to face the idea that you killed Ives. Maybe he couldn't stomach that. Maybe he would have turned you in. He was finding out that his marriage wasn't what he had counted on."

"We couldn't have been happier!"

"Ullie! Ullie! What about the Mexican boyfriends? Just little flirtations, I imagine. Just enough to keep him off balance, make him sweat."

"How could you—" She stopped. I could guess she remembered how he had tried to shush her. Her breathing had gone slightly shallow and there were spots of color in flawless cheeks. I saw her recover herself with an effort, slowing and deepening her breathing.

"I don't imagine Vance really wanted to play poker. You left unobserved, you got back unobserved. Home free. But all it would take would be legwork, Ullie. One of those plodding methodical checks of every gas station along the way. You didn't have the range. Some little joker is probably still dreaming about you—the most beautiful girl he ever saw, coming in out of the night in that Sting Ray."

"So? I got very restless. I took a drive. I drive very fast. Can I help it if Vance got very suspicious of me, if he got very foolish ideas? You don't know how it is . . . how it was. He wanted to be . . . so very young and lively and fun, to be like boys I know. But really he wanted things quieter. I could see strangers laughing at him. He should have had *dignity!* Certainly I wanted all that money and travel and clothes and fun. A professor has a shabby little life. All my life I knew the husband I would have, older and very rich and strong, to buy me everything and adore me, to sit and smile at me and admire me when I danced with all the young men, and trust me. When I'd found him I could not lose him. But every day was a contest to see . . . which one of us was younger. He did not understand how love should be a perfection. All he cared was how many times he could take me. He thought that was another way to be young. Why did he have to prove so much? I can tell about you. You would understand. You are older too, but not as old as he was. You are stronger, Travis McGee. There is the money now. I listened when you told Joanne about your funny little boat with the funny name." She closed her eyes for a moment, opened them wide and looked at me. "You see, I have always . . . felt like a special person. As if my life would be . . . beautiful and important. Things happen in strange ways. Vance was not the one. But suddenly you are here. It is strange. It is so strange the way we both have that little feeling it would be . . . what was planned for us all along."

It was such a fabulous con job, I could feel the dirty dreams seeping into my mind. Help her cover up the mistakes she'd made. That was the unspoken offer. And you get the girl on a platter. Mmmm . . . trade the *Busted Flush* for a really good motor sailer, crew of three—captain, steward, deckhand—and see how many sheltered coves in the world's oceans had really top-grade moonlight. And, of course, remember never to turn your back to her . . .

"Ullie, dear, we can't get onto a new subject until we finish the first one. I repeat your interesting statement. 'When I'd found him I could not lose him.' But he finally worked himself into a position where you had to lose him. I knew he was prying at you to find out where you'd gone, and I wondered why he thought you'd gone anywhere. Then Glenn told me about Vance thinking he might buy the car. Men who think of buying cars kick the tires and slam the doors and check the mileage. So he checked the mileage, and then he checked it again and found a great big inexplicable addition, taking it up to past two thousand. He hadn't put it on, so you had, and Patty was dead in the same way Ives was dead, and he found himself in a pretty eerie marriage. I'll make a little guess, Ullie. From the way he acted this morning, I don't think he got much sleep. I think he kept digging at you until you opened up and told him the whole thing. Then after you told him, you realized he couldn't exactly forgive and forget. He couldn't handle it. It was too much. Maybe he felt so wretched he didn't want to take any morning ride, but you knew that sooner or later you could maneuver it so that all the rest of us would be ahead of you two."

"Could I be such a monster, darling? Could you believe that of me, really?"

That narrow leather pouchpurse was on the chaise beside her hip. She made a futile grab for it as I took it quickly. It was new. I examined it and found a little area still moist near the bottom seam.

The leather thongs were long and sturdy. Holding it by the thongs, I felt the deadly heft and balance of it. It was like a sock with a rock in the toe. It was a skull smasher, wicked as a medieval flail. I opened the pouch top, reached in and fumbled past lipstick, little comb, cigarettes and matches, and pulled out a rabbit. It was carved of some dense gray stone, sitting hunched, ears laid back, crude, a lump about two-thirds the size of a baseball.

"There is the legwork with the gas stations, and there are the miracles of modern chemistry, Ullie. The tiny little blotch of blood on this, with maybe a sweet little tuft of hubby's hair stuck thereon, scrubbed off nicely right there in Joanne's bathroom. But a police lab can prove it was human blood hereon, though they can't type it. And they can dismantle the plumbing and find traces in the drain in there. I imagine that after Ives and Patty you disposed of the bags. They'd have been a lot messier."

"That's a very old bunny," she said. "It's primitive folk art from Iceland."

"Ullie, a good enough lawyer might be able to plead you sick and buy the experts to back him up. Age would be a consideration, of course. And beauty. Maybe you are sick. I don't know. Perhaps it is just an egoism so intense other people don't seem quite real to you. Murder wouldn't seem real then either, I suppose."

She tilted her head. "Vance cried and cried. He hugged me and said he would get me the best—" She stopped, gnawed her thumb knuckle, looked at me in a speculative way. The admission had been made, and I could not tell if it was inadvertent or meant to look inadvertent. "You can understand, Travis. There's such a thing as thinking of the best for everybody concerned. I'd very much like to have you take me home to father. I know you would like each other, very much. He is very old-fashioned, you know. He would want me to wait a year. Waiting isn't too hard, is it, when you're sure?"

I bounced the bunny in the palm of my hand, dropped it back into the lethal sack, yanked the drawstring tight. I could not even tell if she knew what a desperate game she was playing. She sat up, reached and closed her warm strong hand around my wrist. I was planning the words to tell her I was blowing the whistle when I heard the door behind me open slowly. I realized, as I turned, I had spent a long time with the bereaved widow, and Dana might be having problems keeping people out.

Dana stared in at us from the doorway. "Joanne has to . . ."

"I'm through here, honey," I said. "Tell Glenn to phone the law. This eerie child killed all three of them, and she made so many mistakes it won't be hard to . . ."

I had made the elementary mistake of taking my eyes off Ulka. When the pouch bag was ripped out of my hand, I did not bother to turn around and see what she was going to do with it. I dived to my left, away from the chaise, but bunny rabbit still glanced off my skull and came down onto my shoulder, smashing the collarbone. I sprawled on the floor, with my ears roaring and with lights spangling my vision, absolutely unable to avoid a second and mortal crunching if she had taken time. But a vagueness moved past me with tiger pace, and I made a stifled whimper which was supposed to be a roar of warning to Dana. As vision cleared, as I got onto my knees, I saw Dana go down flat and heavy and hopelessly limp, onto her face. I heard a distant shout of query and alarm. I began the slow crawl toward my woman.

15

I HAD a pretty fair concussion, just enough so that I had blackouts, and they kept shining lights into my eyes, testing my reflexes and giving me mental arithmetic to solve. My right arm, taped across my chest, felt leaden, and the smashed bone caused enough pain to keep them sticking needles into me. It made me groggy, and I kept asking about Dana. Miss Holtzer is in surgery. Miss Holtzer is still in surgery. Miss Holtzer is in the recovery room.

Then it was Sunday morning and I was told that Miss Holtzer was doing as well as could be expected. It is a dim phrase. Who sets up the expectations?

Glenn Barnweather arrived with a big solemn face, a hundred sighs, a sad shaking of the head, a rich smell of bourbon to tell me Ulka was dead. I already knew that, but I didn't know how.

"She took off in the Corvette, northeast out Sixty-five like a goddam road race, and they still can't figure how she got past as many curves as she did. They put a roadblock up there in the straight, way beyond Sunflower, one car blocking the road, and she came down on it at, they estimate, a hundred and thirty or better. Tried to cut around it. Hit the gravel, skidded, hit a rock, went two hundred and fifty feet through the air, hit and bounced and went over a rim and down a thousand-foot slope, bouncing all the way, and the final couple hundred feet on fire. Like you told the cops, McGee, she must have been crazed with grief. That's right, isn't it? Crazed with grief."

"Out of her head completely. Maniacal strength. You've heard of that."

"I've heard of that. And Diana Hollis turns into Dana Holtzer. What goes on, old buddy?"

"We have to try to protect a lady's reputation, don't we?"

"Oh, sure. Hell, what you do is your own business, I guess, but Jo is going to come in here and really blow her stack."

"I guess she checked with the Divers."

"And Mary West, who wouldn't tell her a damned thing. So she's steaming."

"Glenn, how about you finding out just how Dana is. I would appreciate it very much."

"Glad to do anything for an old buddy who tells me every little thing," he said.

He came back in a half hour. "She's one sick gal, Trav. They spent six hours picking little bits of bone out of the front of her brain, right here. And I find out she works for Lysa Dean. That's going to intrigue hell out of Jo. They say Dana's going to be okay." He stood up. "You'll be able to see her by tomorrow."

More officials visited me. I told my tale of hysterical violence again, the young bride crazed by her terrible loss.

Joanne came in. She was furious. After fifteen minutes she was merely resentful, reluctantly accepting the fact there must be some good reason why she'd never find out all she wanted to know. She was decent enough to do some errands for me, like telling the Hallmark to save the room for me, like getting a phone put in, like getting a resident neurosurgeon to come in and give me some straight answers on Dana. He said she should take two months' rest and recuperation before going back to work. I had passed my tests and would be released Monday, unless I acquired some new symptoms. He said not to worry about how she'd act on Monday when I could see her for a few minutes. She would be dazed and semiconscious still and might not know me.

After he left I was planning to try to locate Lysa Dean, but she phoned me, putting one very nervous quaver in the switchboard operator's voice. Lysa was terribly dramatic and terribly concerned about everything, full of elaborate assurances about hospital bills—but shrewd enough to play the whole thing as though I was Dana's dear friend who had accompanied her on her little vacation. She said she and her whole entourage would stop off on the way back to the Coast, but she couldn't be sure exactly when they could manage it.

On Monday I got dressed and paid my bill and had five minutes with Dana. She was in an adhesive turban, face bloated, shiny, streaked with bruise marks, slits revealing dazed eyes, mouth cracked and puffy. She seemed to know me. She squeezed my hand. I could not understand her mumblings. The nurse stood by and called time on me and sent me away. I moved back into the Hallmark. On Tuesday I saw her three times, morning, afternoon, evening, ten minutes each time. She knew me, and her diction was better, but she was unaware of what had happened to her and seemed in no hurry to find out. She had a tendency to drop off and start snoring in the middle of a vague remark, but she did like her hand held.

At midnight on Tuesday I was awakened by a phone call from an abjectly apologetic fellow telling me that Lysa Dean was in residence at the best hotel in town and wanted to see me right away. I told him to tell Lysa Dean to go emote up a rope and hung up. I picked up my phone and told the Hallmark switchboard to leave me in peace until nine the next morning. The pinned bone made dressing too much of a problem. If she wanted me, she knew where I was.

Just as I got back to sleep, forty minutes later, there was a brisk knock at my door. Muttering various Anglo-Saxon expressions, I got up and adjusted my sling and went in my shorts to the door. A portly chap in a black suit entered, followed by a Hallmark porter carrying the luggage which Dana and I had checked on to New York and couldn't retrieve in time.

"I'm Herm Louker," he said with an air of imparting information any fool would know. When I looked blank he said, "From the agency." It was supposed to explain everything.

He dipped two fingers into a breast pocket, pulled out two crisp dollars, crackled them very loudly as he handed them to the porter.

Herm looked somewhat like a penguin. He had the same walk. He wore a hairpiece, with a deep wave. His eyes were cigar holes in a hotel towel. He had gold jewelry. He settled himself into a chair, sliced the end off a cigar with a gold knife, lit it with a gold lighter.

"Let me make myself entirely clear, Mr. McGee. The client's interest is my interest. Aside from loving that little woman personally, because she is all doll, through and through, what I got in my mind is a maximum protection of her interests and mine and the industry's." He held up a fat warning hand. "In addition to that, before we go further, I've got also a nervous stomach, and I want to know no more than I already know. I have been with her in Miami, New York and Chicago, and she was a great little trouper, performing in every way. They love that girl all over America. She is all star."

"So I'd better know how much you know."

"Merely that there has been, we shall say, an indiscretion. Show business people, Mr. McGee, are high-spirited and hot-blooded, and some people can take advantage. What we have going is an unfortunate situation where some character wants to give her a rough time. What the little lady feels is that after you started to perform, then you went off on a tangent. Time has been wasted. We got certain information from you in New York. One Samuel Bogen wanted already by the cops. There is no picture. Fingerprints only. A complete description which could be ninety-five thousand guys including me, almost. So we laid on special guards with that description in mind. Nothing in New York. Nothing in Chicago. No contact. As I get it, certain financial inducements were offered. Our star gets nervous, Mr. McGee. What we need now is some way to bring this to a head. If you can solve that, the little lady says she will live up to her end of your deal. I do not want to know your deal, believe me."

"I had one idea worked out."

"So?"

"I wanted to be part of it. I'm not in top shape at the moment."

"So I see."

"It depends on several things. Could you set up a time for her arrival at Los Angeles by air and give it a lot of publicity around Los Angeles?"

"But naturally. It's done every day."

"The man who is after her is disturbed. I think that except for one trip to Vegas, he's stayed in the Los Angeles area. He might come to the airport. He might be waiting at her house. He may want money. He may want to kill her. He might not even know which he wants."

"Please. It give me cramps."

"You have to know a few things, Mr. Louker. We don't want to endanger your star. You could arrange a reasonably good facsimile?"

"The right size, right dye job, right clothes, dark glasses, makeup, a quick study in the way she waves and walks. Sure. Ten minutes on the phone I've got one, believe me."

"But she gets maximum protection too."

"I would insist."

"Now here is the delicate point, Mr. Louker. If this Bogen is picked up, the cops are going to know the name he is using and the address he is using in about three minutes. Somebody has to be ready to move very quickly. At that address are going to be some things which should be destroyed, or maybe your star's career goes down the drain. Somebody has to be smart and quick."

"Are you going to give me more cramps?"

"Photographs, Herm. Of your star in a circus. A mob scene. If they got out it might not dent her too badly as long as she stays big at the box office. But two dog pictures in a row could cook her."

He got up and tiptoed about, patting his stomach, moaning softly. There was a lot of stomach. It started under his chin and descended in a long penguin curve to his knees.

"How can we get the pictures?" he demanded, more of himself than of me.

"Get a very nimble lawyer, and charge Bogen with stealing them from her. Get them impounded for her identification, then returned to her for destruction, and give him some impressive pieces of cash to hand out if he has to. Hell, you people have given out little gifts other times."

He studied me. "I know you from someplace, maybe? Like in Rome with Manny?"

"No."

"It will come to me. We'll work it out somehow." He took a wad of currency out and counted out a thousand dollars. "She said expenses. You can sign the receipt okay?"

I managed. He wished me well and left, looking gastric.

Dana wasn't very responsive the next morning. After I left her room the head nurse on the floor intercepted me. She was wearing a curious expression, as if she had just discovered that if she flapped her arms hard enough she could fly.

"Lysa Dean came to see her."

"Was she conscious then?"

"Oh, no. Miss Dean was very shocked. She was very upset. I think she must have a very warm heart."

"She must have."

"She left this for you, sir."

I opened it with one hand on my way down the hall. Heavy blue paper, scented. Sprawling backhand in blue ink. "I must see you. Please. L."

The cab took me there. The desk said sorry, she isn't registered here, sir. I gave them my name. Oh. Go right up, sir. She has the west wing on the fourth floor. A cop type guarded the wing. He glanced at the sling and spoke my last name with a question mark after it. Last door on the right, he said.

She sat on a dressing table bench in a white robe. A man was saying rude words over a phone. A thin man was fixing her hair. A girl in glasses was reading her a script aloud in a nasal monotonous voice. She shooed them all out.

"Dear McGee," she said. "Your poor arm, dear. Oh, my God, the way Dana looked. It broke my heart. It really did. I actually wept."

"That's nice."

"Please don't be sullen. We're going to do what you suggested to Herm. They're going to fly a girl in. I'm going to hide out here like a thief, dear. God, things are going to get into the damnedest mess without Dana. They're going to pot already. How could she?"

"I guess it was just thoughtlessness."

She studied me, head cocked on the side. Then she laughed aloud. "Oh, *no!* Really? But when I kidded you in Miami, I never *really* thought you could actually *get* her. You must be very damned . . ."

"You would be doing me one of the world's greatest favors to please shut your mouth, Lee. There's been a lot of dying done. My shoulder aches. Dana is worth ten of you."

She went back and sat on the bench. "At least I know why you two were futzing around out here on my expense money. Making the fun last, eh?"

"That's right."

"Damn you, tell me the real reason."

"The man who took you for a hundred and twenty thousand was murdered. It looked as if M'Gruder might have done it and could be arrested for it sooner or later. Then that house party would have figured in the trial. I wanted to check it out."

The quick red fox stared at me with foxy eyes, instantly aware of the implications. She fingered her throat. "Off the hook on that, eh?"

"Yes. And I have a hunch you'll be in the clear on the other too. I wonder about you, Lee. Take a look at that house party list. Nancy Abbott is beyond hope. Vance and Patty and Sonny Catton are dead. The photographer is dead. Poor little Whippy is trade for the butch."

"Really? What is all this? The hand of God? Punishment? Don't be an ass, McGee. Sometimes the swingers go quicker. Maybe because they don't have their feet braced. If that kind of little fun party could kill, honey, lower California would be shrinking. You know, you do drag a little. Have you noticed it? Oh, hell, I don't want to fight you. It's going to be weeks and weeks before Dana can get back on the ball. That's what they told me. I'll keep her on salary, of course. And there's a sick benefit thing she's entitled to. Scotty will check that all out for her and take care of it. I think . . ."

Herm came to the door and beckoned to her. She excused herself and went to him. They talked a few moments in low tones. He left and she came slowly back to me. "There's a meeting I don't dare miss. Damn it. I did want to see Dana, at least once more. Herm is going to have to smuggle me into town and bring the stand-in along later. McGee, my darling, I've got a thousand things to do . . ."

"You sent for me. Remember?"

She snapped her fingers. "Of course. Darling, you got the thousand expenses? You understand that our deal was to get me completely free and clear. Right? It's all or nothing, you understand. If your plan works, you come to see me and we'll settle up. All right? Darling, I do love Dana like a sister, but sick people depress me so. Could you find some nice little dude ranch or something for her, and a woman to take care. I'll have Victor Scott work out the money end with you. Would you mind terribly? After all, you *must* find each other attractive. I'm entirely clear publicity-wise on this end because, thank God, there isn't a shred to link me to Vance in any way." She patted my face. "Be a dear and take care of our girl. Give her my love, and bring her back to me when she's truly healthy again."

On Thursday afternoon the improvement in Dana was astonishing. The puffiness was gone, but there were saffron marks of the bruises. She wore lipstick. She was propped up. Her smile of greeting was shy.

They let me have an hour with her. She was anxious to know what had happened. I knew it might tire her, but I had to brief her before some official visited her and asked questions. I caught her up to date, including the plan to trap Bogen.

When I got back to the Hallmark at four that afternoon, there was a message to call a Los Angeles operator. When it went through, Lysa came on the phone, yapping with glee and relief. "McGee, darling? It worked, you shrewd, shrewd man! Our own people got him, and took away the nasty little gun he was going to shoot me with.

Shoot the stand-in, I mean. And they went to his nasty little rooms and got all the photographs, and then they turned him and his nasty little gun over to the law. My God, I didn't even know the terrible tension I was under. It's *such* a relief."

"Wouldn't it be nice if you asked about Dana?"

"Give me *time*, for God's sake! All right. How is she?"

"Much, much better."

"That's fine. That's good to hear."

"You and I have a little accounting to do."

"I *know* that. Damn it, what makes you so sour? Give me a chance. What's today? Thursday. Let me look at my book." I waited five minutes and she came back on the line. "Darling, I'll be home Monday afternoon. You fly in and come talk to me about it."

"Talk to you about it?"

"Darling, you don't exactly have a contract, you know. And a frightened person can make some *very* rash promises. Technically, you really weren't in at the kill, were you?"

"Monday afternoon," I said and hung up. I did not know why I had been sour with her. Something was wrong, and I did not know what it was.

On Sunday afternoon I found out what my instincts had been trying to tell me. The nurse and I helped Dana into the wheelchair and I rolled her to the big sun-room, to a private corner.

"Here's the way I have it lined up," I told her. I sat holding her hand. "Ten days before they spring you, then say a week or so more before you can travel, honey. So I tote you east, get you settled aboard, and after a few days we can go cruising. How does that sound?"

She gently, firmly pulled her hand away from mine. She looked away from me. "Travis, you have been very good to me."

"What's the matter?"

"It was all . . . mixed up and crazy. It wasn't me, really. I don't know how to tell you. I'm not like that. I'm married. I don't even know how I could have been so . . . so silly. I think it was because of working for her, maybe. I'm not going back to her."

I put my fingertips under her chin and turned her head and made her look at me. I looked at her until she flushed and twisted her head away. She meant it. A new conception. You could get a hit on the head that could knock love out of you for good and all. When their eyes go that dead for you, there's no way to ever get back. I knew what my instincts had been trying to tell me.

"You don't have to stay around," she said. "I mean, I'm used to looking after myself. I'll be fine, really. I do want to thank you for everything. I feel so sorry about . . . giving you the wrong idea and a lot of false hopes and . . ."

"You can still be honest, can't you?"

"Of course."

"How do you feel about my coming to see you here, Dana?"

She hesitated, then lifted her chin a half inch. "I d-dread it, Travis. I'm terribly sorry. It just keeps reminding me of something I'd rather forget."

Then all that was left us was the good-by ritual, which was, after the details of what to do with her belongings, and my promise to send a nurse to wheel her back to her room, a handshake. McGee, the great lover. This was one I wanted to keep. No, not this one. I didn't even know this one. The one I wanted to keep was the one Ullie had bashed on her way to go kill herself. This Dana wanted to forget that Dana. And damn well soon would. So shake hands with your darling and say good-by and try not to see the evident relief she tries to hide.

The cab deposited me in front of Lysa Dean's iron gates on Monday afternoon. The Korean let me through the gates. The maid let me into the house and then disappeared. The house was as silent as when I had been there with Dana. The big oil portraits of Lysa Dean stared emotionally at me through the half gloom of draperied sunlight.

I roamed and plinked two notes out of the gold and white piano. Lysa Dean came swiftly into the room, in black knit pants and a white silk overblouse, an effective combination to go with gold-red hair in a room of whites and blacks and golds. She wore woolly white slippers and carried a white envelope in her hand. She hurried to me, stretched up to kiss me with the faked sweet shyness of a welcoming child, and took me by my good hand to a vast couch in a shadowed alcove.

"How is dear Dana?" she asked.

"Marvelously improved."

"When can she come back to work, dear? I really need her, desperately."

"She'll have to take it easy for a while."

"McGee, darling, *do* use your influence on her. Tell her Lysa needs her *sooooo* much."

"I'll tell her that the very first chance I get."

"You *are* a huge old sweetie. Now what about the photos I gave you in Miami?"

"I've destroyed the ones I had made, with your face blanked out. When I get back, I'll destroy the other ones . . . unless you want them."

"God, I don't ever want to see them again. Darling, they say that little Bogen is way way off. If he'd tried to fire his rusty little gun, it would have blown his hand off. They are going to put him away."

"So now your life is all neatened up, Miss Dean. And you'll get to marry your dear friend. Congratulations. Is that my money you keep hanging onto?"

She handed me the envelope. I fumbled it open, and saw that it was light, and found that it counted up to ten thousand. It wouldn't count one inch past that. Before I could get the first word out, she was hanging onto me, laughing and teasing, saying, "Now darling, *do* be realistic, after all! I gave you all that nice travel money, and sent you off with quite a handsome and exciting gal, and you had some exciting and delicious adventures, all on the house. I'm really not *made* of money, darling. Taxes are fantastic. Really, when you think of it, I think you are doing terribly well out of this, and some of my advisers would think I was out of my head to give you all this." As she was talking she got the money out of my hand and slipped it into the inside pocket of my jacket, and was going quite directly and efficiently to work on me, with the quickness of a lot of little kissings, and an arching and presentation of all the celebrity curves and fragrances, a lot of cleverness of little hands, and a convincing steaminess of breath and growing excitement, worming her way astride my lap. This was the artist at work, at the work she knew best, operating from a lifelong knowledge of the male animal and quite convinced, apparently, that a good quick solid bang would send the man away too happy to care about being shorted, too dazed to object. Already she was beginning to work her way out of those soft knit pants and simultaneously beginning the little pressures which were supposed to topple me over onto my back on the big couch under a picture of the lady herself.

I got my good left arm in between us and my palm flat against her wishbone, then abruptly straightened my arm, sending her catapulting back, scrambling, slipping on the smooth hard terrazzo, sitting hard on a white furry rug and riding it back like a sled to end up under another picture so soulful the artist had indicated a halo effect.

She bounded up, hair masking one eye, yanking the knit pants up over the white behind. "What the hell!" she squalled. "Jesus Christ, McGee, you could have bust my tailbone!"

I was standing up, fixing my sling, starting toward the door.

"It's okay, Lee baby," I said. "I'll take the short count. You don't have to try to sweeten it. It wouldn't mean one damn thing to you, and it would mean just a little less than that to me."

I left amid a shrieking of ten-letter words, and I was hastened on my way by a hail of elephants. She had a collection. She threw fast, but not well.

I crunched down the finest grade of brown gravel, past sprinkler water pattering on fat green leaves. The Korean let me out. I could feel the meager money weight in my jacket pocket. I stopped and took my arm out of the sling and stuffed the sling in a pocket. The arm did not feel good swinging, so I tucked a thumb in my belt.

I walked and thought of what a weird way to lose a good woman. I saw old men carefully driving lookalike cars with names like Fury and Tempest and Dart. Through a fence I saw a quintet of little girls dashing in and out of the silvery spray of a sprinkler, shrilling. A dog smiled at me.

What a ridiculous way to lose a woman. They do not like pedestrians in that neighborhood. Polite cops stopped, asked polite questions and politely drove me to the nearest taxi stand. I got into the cab and the only place to go was my hotel room, and I didn't want to go there, but I couldn't think of anything else.

When we stopped for a light I saw a magic store, and I asked the driver if he thought they might sell love potions in there. He said that if I was looking for action, just say the word. I went back to the hotel, and seventy minutes later I was on the Miami jet.

Pale Gray for Guilt

"Perhaps no one can be really a good appreciating pagan who has not once been a bad puritan."

—BOURNE

1

THE NEXT to the last time I saw Tush Bannon alive was the very same day I had that new little boat running the way I wanted it to run, after about six weeks of futzing around with it.

So on the test run I demonstrated one of our contemporary maladies: You can't just go out and ride around in car, boat, or airplane— you have to have a destination.

Then you feel purposeful.

So in the early morn on a flat, calm, overcast day I stocked the ice chest on the little *Muñequita* from my ship's stores on *The Busted Flush*, locked up the *Flush*, dropped down into my new playtoy, and, as what faint breeze there was seemed to be coming out of the southwest, I stuck my nose out of the pass to see if I could run north outside. The long, slow gray-green lift and fall of the ground swell was all of a towering five inches high, so I took it a mile off the beaches and fooled with the rpm and the fuel flowmeter, until she was riding right and sounded right and just a hair under 3,000 on each of the OMC 120-horse stern-drive units. I then turned the steering over to the little Calmec auto-pilot, took a bearing on the Lauderdale Municipal Casino and noted the time.

That, of course, is one of the fussy little enchantments of a new boat—new being either brand-new or second-hand new. What you are hunting for is the optimum relationship between fuel consumption and distance. You tell yourself that maybe someday you are going to get caught very short, and you are going to have to squeak back into port with no more than half a cup of fuel left, with luck, and it would be very nice to know what rpm leaves you the least chance of running dry.

But like the exercise of caution in almost every human activity, the fusspots who make it their business to know are the ones least likely to ever have that ticklish problem. It's the ones who never check it out who keep the Coast Guard choppers busy.

The little boat was aimed back up the Florida east coast toward Broward Beach, where I had picked her up on an estate sale from a law firm. She'd belonged to a Texan named Kayd whose luck had run out somewhere in the Bahamas.

It's a funny thing about boat names. She had that *Muñequita* across the stern in four-inch white letters against that nice shade of Gulf Stream blue when I brought her on back to Bahia Mar. Spanish for "little doll." One night Meyer and Irv Deibert and Johnny Dow and I sat around trying to dream up a name that would match *The Busted Flush*. Little Flush? Inside Straight? Hole Card? The Ante? And I forget which one we decided was best because when I got around to changing it, I looked at the name it had and I decided that trying to match it to the name on the mother ship was a case of the quaints and the cutes, and I liked the name just fine. It was a little doll and had begun to acquire in my mind a personality that could very well resent being called anything else, and would sulk and wallow.

I switched the FM-UHF marine radio to the commercial frequencies and tried to find something that didn't sound like somebody trying to break up a dogfight in a sorority house by banging drums and cymbals. Not that I want to say it isn't music. Of course it is music, styled to accompany teen-age fertility rites, and thus is as far out of my range as "Rockabye Baby." FM radio was a great product when it was servicing a fringe area of the great American market. But it has turned into a commercial success, so they have denigrated the sound, and they have mickey-moused the stereo, and you have to really search that dial to find something that isn't either folk hoke, rickyticky rock, or the saccharine they pump into elevators, bus stations and Howard Johnsons.

As I was about to give up I found some pleasant eccentric, or somebody who'd grabbed the wrong record, playing Brubeck doing Cole Porter, and I caught it just as he opened up "Love for Sale" in a fine and gentle manner, and then handed it delicately over to Desmond, who set up a witty dialogue with Joe Morello.

After telling myself that ten of eight in the morning is beer time only for the lowest types, I cracked a bottle of Carta Blanca and stood in the forward well, leaning through the center opening where

I'd laid the hinged windshield over to port, out of the way, forearms on the smoke-blue foredeck shell.

Well, I was on my way to see old Tush after too long, and I had wind in my face like a happy dog leaning out a car window. The wake was straight. The engines ran sweetly in sync. I could feel the slow rise and fall in the imperceptible ground swell. The overcast was starting to burn off, the sea starting to glint. I could see pigmy figures over on the beach by Sea Ranch. Even with the investment in the playtoy, I still had a comforting wad of currency back in the cache aboard *The Busted Flush* at Slip F-18, Bahia Mar.

It had been a fine long hot lazy summer, a drifting time of good fish, old friends, new girls, of talk and laughter.

Cold beer, good music and a place to go.

That's the way They do you. That's the way They set you up for it. There ought to be a warning bell on the happymeter, so that every time it creeps high enough, you get that dang-dang alert. Duck, boy. That glow makes you too visible. One of Them is out there in the boonies, adjusting the windage, getting you lined up in the cross hairs of the scope. When it happens so often, wouldn't you think I'd be more ready for it?

I took my right-angle sight on a water tower just beyond Ocean Ridge, one that measures almost exactly thirty miles north of the Municipal Casino, and my elapsed time was sixty-two minutes. I wrote that down, along with fuel consumption, so I could do the math later, breaking it down in the way that to me is easiest to remember, statute miles per gallon at x rpm.

The wind was freshening and quartering into the south, and though I was still comfortable, I decided it wasn't going to last very long, so I went through Boynton Inlet into Lake Worth. The OMC's were still green enough so that too much constant speed wasn't the best thing in the world, so as soon as I had a nice open straightaway up the Waterway without traffic, I pushed it up to 4,200 rpm, estimating it at about 45 miles an hour. I estimated I had fifty if I ever needed it, and hoped I'd never get in a bind where I needed it. I held her there for five or six minutes, then dropped it way back, getting it to that minimum rpm that, depending on gross weight at the time, would just hold it on the plane. It wasn't a rig I was about to take out and see if I could get to Nassau ahead of Wynne and Bertram and those people, taking those thirty-foot leaps and turning your spine into a concertina every time you smash back into the sea, pulping your kidneys and chomping your jaw into the foam rubber tooth guard. The little *Muñequita* would have had to be turned into a racing machine, with a hundred more horses in each mill, special wheels, a lot more bracing and reinforcement to keep the engines in her, and then she would not be much good for anything else.

Besides, I had been talked into trying it once. I think you could maybe argue the point that it is a little more fun than a hungover, carbuncled cowboy might have while trying to stay aboard a longhorn in a dusty rodeo, but it would be a close decision.

When I reached the bay north of Broward Beach, I had to look at the chart to see at which marker I should leave the Waterway to hit the mouth of the Shawana River. So it was ten thirty of that Tuesday morning, or a little later, when I eased up to one of the finger piers at Bannon's Boatel, put a line on a piling and cut the engines off.

I stepped high onto the pier decking and looked around. He had a dozen outboards tied up, and maybe half as many inboard-outboard rigs, two smallish cruisers, and, neatly aligned in their slips, a dozen rental houseboats, outboard rigged, fiber glass, white with orange trim. I saw that he'd put up the in-and-out storage he had told me about the last time I'd seen him, over a year and a half ago. Fifteen racks wide and three high. The forklift could tuck forty-five boats in there on monthly storage, but only the bottom row was full, and the middle layer half full.

Up the river from his place and on the other side, where it had all been marshland the last time I was there, I could see, maybe a mile away and more, some squat, pale, technical-looking buildings and a glinting of cars in the industrial parking lot next to them.

There didn't seem to be anyone around the little marina building, or around the white cement-block motel with the red tile roof that sat parallel to the river and parallel to State Road 80D, and about a hundred feet from each of them. I remember Tush talking about how he was going to expand the motel from ten units to twenty.

"Now that there's the three kids, me and Janine are taking up two units, and having just eight rentals, I couldn't tell you the times we've had to turn folks away, Trav."

The slab had been poured for the extra ten units, and the block had been laid up to shoulder-high on about three of them, but some kind of a coarse green vine had taken hold and had crawled along fifteen feet of the wall, spilling tendrils down.

Some of the dock pilings sagged. The pennons on the marina building were bleached gray, wind-ripped and tattered.

"Hey!" yelled Tush. "Hey, now! Hey, McGee!" He had come around the corner of the motel and came toward me in a kind of Percheron canter. A big man. Almost as high as I am, and half again as big around.

Long ago and far away we'd been on the same ball team. Brantley Breckenridge Bannon, second string offensive fullback. First string if he could have gotten into his stride quicker, because he was hard to stop when he was in gear. The nickname had started as BeeBee and had been shortened to Beeb, and it was that season it suddenly turned into Tush. He was a man totally incapable of profanity. The most we ever heard from him, even in the most hideous, unlucky and painful circumstances, was a mumbled "Durn!"

Then in one game we tried running a play that was designed to make up for his slow start. They set him out to the right, and on the snap he had to run to his left, go behind the quarterback who had taken some quick steps back and who had faked a handoff to a wing-back slanting right, and who would then spin and stuff the ball into Bannon's belly on a half cut and an off-tackle slant left.

The first time we ran it, and I was offensive left end at the time, a linebacker thought he smelled a pass, blitzed through, saw what was happening, and rolled his shoulders right into Bannon's ankles. The second time we ran it, he had a good head of steam, but there was absolutely no hole at all, and as he tried to spin along the line and find one they tore him down. The third time we tried it, we were fourth and two at their eleven, so late in the game that we had to go for six points, being four points behind. He got a fine start. We got a good jump and cleared him a big hole. But as he went through the hole he was juggling that ball, hand to chin to chest to forearm to hand, too busy to keep from getting hit, and was hit from the side and the ball floated into the hands of their squatty defensive center, who after a considerable pause to realize he actually had a football right there in his hands, took off in a lumpy little grinning gallop out to their forty before he got pulled down from behind. Bannon, on his knees, ripped off his helmet, whammed it against the sod, stared skyward and yelled, "Oh . . . TUSH!"

When things went badly for him on one play in the next game, about four of us yelled, "Tush!" and Tush it became, then and forever.

After he was converted to a tackle, he stayed with an AFL team four years, during two of which, being married to Janine, he saved his money. A pinched nerve in his neck turned him into an insurance salesman and he did well but got sick of it, and then he sold houseboats, and then he bought the ten acres on the Shawana River on which to act out and work out the American Dream.

So after the obligatory thumping upon each other, our words of greeting were drowned out by an oncoming roar, deep and grinding, and three big orange Euclids went by on their six-foot tires of solid rubber, loaded high with yards of wet marl, kicking up a powdery dust that drifted north, across the palmetto and scrub pine flats on the other side of the state road. I saw then that the blacktop was gone, and the right of way widened.

"We're being improved around here," he said in sour explanation. "Everything is going to be first-class. By and by." He stared west, after the fading roar of the big earth movers. "Worries me the way they bucket through here. Janine should be on her way back from town by now, and there's some bad places where she could meet up with them. She does more than her share of driving now that the school bus can't come down here."

"Why can't it?"

"They can't use roads that are officially closed, that's why." He looked toward his waterfront. "What'd you come in. You can't get the *Flush* upriver in this tide."

"Wasn't there a good deep channel?"

"Until they did a lot of dredge and fill upriver. Now the first half mile from the bay up toward me is pretty bad. They say they're going to scour it out, but they won't say when."

We walked out and I showed him the *Muñequita*. He knew that good honest T-Craft hull, the semi-V that Rodney Thompson makes in Titusville. When people from the Kansas flats get the marine fever, it is a dreadful addiction, and Tush had a bad case. He looked over the custom installation of the two dual-carb OMC's and listened to my explanation of why I'd pulled the Chrysler-Volvos the original owner installed. He was intrigued by the special engineering of the Teleflex panel and control system.

I heard myself talking too much. Things were going well for me. And the world was a little sour for my friend Tush Bannon. In repose his broad, heavy, freckly face sagged. So when it happens like that, you talk too much. The small breeze stopped, and the October forenoon heat leaned hard, in that 95°-95 humidity that makes the sweat pop out.

So we went up to the motel and sat in the kitchen alcove under the rackety-clatter of an overworked little window air conditioner, drank beer while he said Janine was fine, the boys were fine, and we talked about who we'd heard from and who we hadn't, and who was doing what. I stood by the window with the cold can in my hand and said, "What's all the big industry over there, up river?"

"TTA," he said with a tangible bitterness. "Tech-Tex Applications. A nice clean industry, except every now and then any fool fish that comes up the Shawana turns belly-up and floats back down. And sometimes there's a funny little smell, sort of like ammonia, and the tears run down your face. But they employ four hundred people, Trav. Big tax base. They gave 'em the keys to the county to move in here."

"But I thought this county had pretty fair zoning and pollution control and all that. I mean Broward Beach is a——"

"Don't you know where you are, boy?" he asked. "You're a good mile west of that county line. You are in Shawana County, Mister McGee. A garden spot. Go right over to Sunnydale, to the County Courthouse, and ever' one of those happy, smiling five commissioners will tell you a man couldn't pick a better spot to live and raise his kids and grow with the county." He astonished me. I had never thought of Tush as being capable of irony. He was a big, amiable, beefy man, with mild blue eyes and stubbly pale lashes and brows, and a pink, peeling, permanent case of sunburn.

I heard a car drive in. He went to the window on the road side and looked out and said, "Oh . . . *no!*"

I followed him out. Janine had gotten out of the car, a very dusty pale blue sedan about two years old. At twenty paces she still had the gawky, leggy look and stance of a teen-ager. She stood in an attitude at once defiant and disconsolate, staring at the left rear corner of the car, which squatted expensively low. Their youngest, about two and a half, stood nearby, scowling, giving the intermittent snuffle of tears not long ended. Janine wore bleached khaki walking shorts and a yellow halter in a coarse fabric. The shorts were darkened with perspiration around her narrow waist. She had cropped her black hair very short. With her deep tan, and the length and strength and slender delicacy of her face, her dark eyes, she looked like a young man, Mediterranean, ready to guide you to the Roman ruins, pick your pocket, sell you fake heirlooms, send you out in a leaky gondola with his thieving cousin.

But the shape of the ears was girl, and the corners of the mouth, and the elegance of the throat, and from there on down no doubt at all, even were she clad in a loose-fitting mattress cover, no doubt whatsoever. And I knew her maiden name was Sorrensen, and she was Wisconsin Swede, and she birthed towheaded Swede kids, and so she was one of the improbabilities of genetic mathematics, of maybe one of the Scandinavian raiders who brought home from a far country a swarthy boy to be a kitchen slave.

Tush got down behind the car and rolled onto his back and wormed his way under it. She said, "It was just a half mile this side of the hard top. I guess the rains dug it out and then the dust drifted into it, and I swear, honey, nobody could have seen it."

He slid out. "Spring shackle."

"She *hit* me!" the little kid said. "She hit me awful hard, Pop."

"Were you going fast, Jan?" he asked her.

She stared at him. She raised a helpless arm and let it flap down. "Oh, good Christ, I was making better time than Phil Hill, laughing and singing because the world is so sweet, and I was probably all boozed up, and I was trying to break the goddamn whatever it is!"

She spun and went by me, giving me a sudden and startled glance of recognition, but too trapped then in the compulsions of the quarrel to deviate from the planned exit.

He shouted after her. "You can say hello to my friend! The least you can do is say hello to my friend!"

She walked ten more strides, shoulders rigid, and then turned at the motel doorstep and, with no expression on her face or in her voice, said, "Hello. Hello. Hello. Come on, Jimmy. Come with mother."

The kid went plodding after her. The door closed. Tush looked at me and shook his head and tried to smile. "Sorry, boy."

"For what? There are good days, medium days and bad days."

"We seem to be getting a long run of one kind."

"So, for starters let's fix it."

He ran it down to the marina shed, where the tools were. We used the forklift to raise the back end. It took two gallons of sweat apiece to punch the busted pieces out, hacksaw some bar stock, clumsy it into place and peen the ends over. We set it down and it sat level, no longer looking like a spavined duck. I stepped on the rear bumper and it didn't come back up as it should. It oscillated, good proof the shocks were nearly gone, and from the way he sighed I was sorry I'd done it.

I got fresh clothes off the boat, and Tush gave me a motel unit to shower and change in. I was just buttoning the clean shirt when Janine knocked at the door. I let her in. She carried a clinking pitcher of iced tea, and her apologetic pride. She wore a little pink cotton shift and a pale pink lipstick.

She put the pitcher down, put her hand out. "Hello the right way, Travis. Like welcome. Excuse the bad scene." Her hand was long and brown and slender, and her grip surprisingly strong. She poured the two tall glasses of tea and gave me one and took hers over and sat on the bed. I counted back and realized that this would be the fifth time I had seen her. And, as before, the chemistry was slightly off, as it so often is with the friend who knew the husband before the husband met the wife. It can be a kind of jealousy, I guess, because it is a reminder of years she didn't share, and of an acceptance of the husband's friendship, which was in no way her decision. She seemed to relate to me with a flavor of challenge. Prove yourself to me, McGee. But you can't, McGee, because you aren't housebroken. Your life isn't real. You drift around and you have your fun and games. You make my husband feel wistful about the debts he has and the girls he hasn't. When you come near my nest, just by being here, you remind my man of the gaudy grasshopper years, and somehow you turn me into some kind of guard, or attendant, or burden.

With some of the wives of old friends I have been able to quench that initial antagonism. They soon find out that I am aware of what every single unwed person knows—that the world is always a little out of focus when there is no one who gives the final total damn about whether you live or die. It is the price you pay for being a rambler, and if you don't read the price tag, you are a dull one indeed.

Jan had obvious warmth. She seemed to have the empathy to realize that I meant her well. But the antagonism wouldn't melt. She could hide it pretty well. But it was there.

I toasted her with tea, saying, "That was a mere snit, Janine. One of the tizzies you get during the hot months."

"Thanks," she said, and smiled. "Tush gobbled and ran. He took over the child taxi service. Come on over in about ten minutes and I'll have a sort of a lunch."

She finished the glass of tea, then poured herself another to take with her. As she moved toward the door she shook her head slowly and sadly. "You know, I think it was guilt mostly. Poor darn little Jimmy kid. What's wrong, Mom? What busted, Mom? Will it run, Mom? So I swatted him a dandy. Much too hard, without thinking. Taking it out on him." Beyond the wry smile her eyes looked wet. "I don't know what's happening to me lately. Oh, how I hate that goddamn car. That goddamn stinking car. How I hate it!"

2

As I waited, sitting in the full huff of the air conditioner, gulping down the tea, I thought of the little dreamworld called Detroit, fifteen years behind the rest of America, as usual.

Janine had nailed it. People hate their cars. Daddy doesn't come proudly home with the new one any more, and the family doesn't come racing out, yelling WOW, and the neighbors don't come over to admire it. They all look alike, for one thing. So you have to wedge a piece of bright trash atop the aerial to find your own. They may be named after predators, or primitive emotions, or astronomical objects, but in essence they are a big shiny sink down which the money swirls—in insurance, car payments, tags, tolls, tires, repairs. They give you a chance to sit in helpless rage, beating on the steering wheel in a blare of horns while, a mile away, your flight leaves the airport. They give you a good chance of dying quick, and a better chance of months of agony of torn flesh, smashed guts and splintered bones. Take it to your kindly dealer, and the service people look right through you until you grab one by the arm, and then he says: Come back a week from Tuesday. Make an appointment. Their billions of tons of excreted pollutants wither the leaves on the trees and sicken the livestock. We hate our cars, Detroit. Those of us who can possibly get along without them do so very happily. For those who can't, if there were an alternate choice, they'd grab it in a minute. We buy them reluctantly and try to make them last, and they are not friendly machines anymore. They are expensive, murderous junk, and they manage to look glassily contemptuous of the people who own them. A car is something that makes you whomp your youngest kid too hard and then feel ashamed of yourself.

I had just been through the bit. My elderly Rolls pickup, *Miss*

Agnes, was as agile as ever which meant about 40 seconds from a dead stop to sixty miles an hour. And she had the same reluctance to come to a stop once she was humming along. So she and I were slowly becoming a highway hazard, the narrow shaves getting narrower. So I had gone shopping, test driving, and found they all had fantastic acceleration, and they'd all stop on dimes, and they all bored me to hell.

So I went looking for a boat I could use as a car. I would keep *Miss Agnes* for back roads and the *Flush* for open waters, and use the *Muñequita* for errands, and if I had to have a car, there was Mr. Hertz trying hard, and Mr. Avis trying harder, and Mr. National hoping they'd run each other into the ground. Anything in Lauderdale that I wanted to buy, and I could lift, if I couldn't buy it right at Bahia Mar, I could go off in the *Muñequita* and buy it. And it was nice to poot along an urban waterway and hear the distant clashing of fenders, gnashing of bumpers, and the song of the ambulances.

Janine and I ate ham and cheese sandwiches at the breakfast bar, and every time Jimmy came stomping by, he got a couple of loving pats from his mother. I had forgotten the names of the older two boys and had to pick them up out of her conversation. Johnny and Joey. Joey was the big kid. Six. Johnny was four and a half.

I realized I hadn't seen Tyler around, the Negro who had been working for them the other times I'd been there, a tall, stringy, cheerful, ageless man, dark saffron in color, with a scholarly face, plus an uncanny knack of diagnosing the ailments of marine engines. I asked her if it was his day off.

"Oh, Tyler quit us . . . it must be eight months ago. Tush was very upset about it. You know how good he was around here. But now . . . it's just as well, I guess, because we couldn't afford to pay him anyway, the way things are."

"On account of the road?"

"And a lot of other things."

"Such as?"

"I think if Tush wants you to hear the tale of woe, he better be the one to tell you. But I'll tell you one thing, Travis McGee!" Her eyes narrowed, and she thumped her fist on the Formica counter top. "We are *not* going to be run off this place!"

"Is somebody trying?"

"You'd best talk to Tush about it."

"Can you get a sitter for tonight?"

"Huh?"

"Wear your pretties and the three of us will go runabouting into Broward Beach and track down some booze and some meat and come home late, singing all the way."

Her narrow face lighted up. "I would *love* it!"

And when Tush got back with the other two towheads, he approved. The sitter was handy. Jan explained they had made a special rate on a houseboat rental to a couple. Young kids. About twenty-one years old. They were in the houseboat where the old yellow station wagon was parked. There was a retired couple in the one on the far end. Those were the only two rented at the moment.

"Arlie and Roger Denn, their names are," Janine explained. "They're a little on the weird side. Sort of untidy looking. He makes little funny figurine things and he makes shell jewelry. She does hand-weaving and she paints these insipid little seascapes, and when they have enough, they fill up the station wagon and go around and sell them to gift shops. Sometimes it takes two days, and sometimes it takes a week."

Arlie Denn arrived for sitter duty right on time, and I could agree about the untidy part. She was a soft, doughy, pallid girl with a long tangle of dark blonde hair, wide, empty, indifferent blue eyes, a little sing-song voice and a mouth that hung open. She wore a man's white shirt, dirty. Pale blue denim walking shorts, ditto. Bare feet, also dirty. I could see why Janine had fed the kids before we left.

Once I had the little boat away from the dock, I turned it over to Tush. And with the sun lowering behind us, we skimmed down the long, broad curves of the Shawana River, past the mangrove and the white herons, and out into the big bay where, corny as any postcard, a ketch was moving northward up the Waterway, sun turning the sails orange, while a ragged flight of pelicans passed diagonally in front of her, heading for the rookery, pumping then soaring, taking cue from the flight leader.

With his big paw on the twin throttles Tush raised a questioning eyebrow, and I made a shoving motion with the heel of my hand. Janine sat on a life cushion on the transom engine hatch, in her pretty yellow dress, her short black hair snapping in the wind, her face alight with the pleasure of speed and change and the rush of the soft evening air after the heat of the day.

At the city marina Tush slowed and we went up the channel and under the bridge, and along the bay side of the beaches. I took it into a place called Beach Marine, where the man said nobody would mess with it. We walked three blocks to a good place I knew. Thirty feet from the restaurant entrance Jan balanced herself with one hand on Tush's shoulder while she changed from the zoris to the high-heeled shoes she was carrying in her straw purse.

The drinks were good, the steaks were good, the evening was al-most good. Every marriage at one time or another is going to run through some heavy weather. Heavy weather comes in all kinds of flavors. Slowly going broke, slowly losing the whole stake instead of making it like you thought you would—that can erode the happiest of hearts. With the two of them it wasn't a continuous thing. It just kept cropping up now and again, and clouding the fun and games.

There was just enough said for me to see the shape of the running quarrel, or argument, or regret. Over a year ago, when they had a chance to pull out, when they had a buyer for the place, Jan wanted to take the loss and get out. Only about a ten-percent loss on what they'd put into it, but that didn't count all the hours of their brute labor. But he insisted it was just a run of bad luck. Nobody was re-ally trying to stack the cards against them. Things would get better. Things always got better.

Except when they get worse.

Tush didn't want to talk about it at all. To him it was like whin-ing. He would let it go just so far, and then he would reach out, grab the conversational ball, and throw it the hell into center field.

But they seemed to have a good time, on average. Maybe a better time than in many months. It was overcast, and there was pink light-ning on three sides of us when we went back across the bay. Tush picked up the markers for me with the hand-held spotlight, with its 45,000 candles and its narrow one-mile beam. We got the boat tied up and the first fat drops were speckling the dust as we made it to the motel. The rain roar was coming. The fat sitter went cantering and bobbling off to her rented houseboat.

Maybe three inches came down in the hour we sat at the Bannons' breakfast bar and drank kitchen whisky and told lies.

Back in my borrowed motel unit, after starting to get ready for bed, I decided I'd better check the *Muñequita* and see if the auto-matic bilge pump had handled the heavy rain and turned off, as promised. The air was washed clean, and the hungry mosquitoes hadn't begun to roam. The wind was rain-fresh, and from the west.

The boat was fine and, as I turned, the bulk of Tush Bannon standing in the night startled me.

"I miss the sound of that old hump-back bridge when the wind's from upriver," he said. "Not much traffic over it, but the timbers would rumble. You get so you don't even hear a sound like that, and then you miss it after it's gone."

"They put a new one there?"

He sighed. "Not there. Three miles further upriver. That hurts. It lost me most of the business I was getting from the people that live on the other side. TTA wanted it taken out. They wanted the road to it officially abandoned. We went to the Public Hearing and made a lot of noise, but what TTA wants from this county, TTA gets."

"Tush, if you need any help hanging on here until things pick up . . ."

"Forget it. Thanks, but forget it. It would just take that much longer to run down the drain."

"Is it all going to go?"

"Probably."

"Can you sell?"

"Sell what? Our equity? Go ask the bank what they think our equity is." He yawned. "Hell, I can always get a pretty good job selling. I can sell pretty good. Trouble is, I hate the work. 'Night, McGee. And thanks again. It was a good evening. It helped. We needed it bad."

I left the next morning. And that was in October, and I kept thinking about them and wondering about them, but I didn't do anything about it. I didn't run up there again. I wish I had. There are a lot of things in this life I wish I'd done, and a pretty gamey collection of things I wish I hadn't done—but the things you don't do leave the remorses around a little longer somehow.

The last time I saw Tush Bannon alive was the weekend before Christmas, late on a Saturday afternoon. It was by the kind of accident so unlikely, one has the temptation to call it fate. My friend Mick Coseen was awaiting a very important phone call from Madrid, and he had given my phone number aboard *The Busted Flush*. So when it was delayed, he asked me if I'd take his car and run down to the Miami International and pick up his date, Barni Baker, a Pan-Am stewardess due in from Rio for a Miami layover. As I was the only other one in the group who knew her by sight, it was more efficient for me to go down.

For company I toted Puss Killian along in Mick's rental convertible. It was a cool, bright day, and the time of year when the gold
coast is as empty as it ever gets. Nervous little men who own points
in the big beach hotels brood about their fifth mortgages, and the re-
tailers give frequent thanks that the Christmas pressure on the locals
makes up for the lack of snowbird money. Puss is a big, stately, random redhead, a master of the put-on and the copout, who believes
the world is mad, so she is the best of companions if you can keep
up with the slants and shifts of her conversation, and merely irritating and confusing if you can't. A little herd was assembling, and it
was shaping up party time.

We put the car in the lot and went in and checked the board, and
the man said that 955 was just touching down. After the passengers
had been herded off and aimed in the right direction, Barni, with her
peer group, came brisk-clicking along, button-big, button-bright, a little candy-package blonde with eyes of widest innocent blue, eyes
casting right and left, searching for Mick, finding me as I moved to
intercept her. Big smile, gracious and wary acknowledgement of the
introduction to Puss. I told her about Mick and his call, about an independent wanting somebody to take over the camera crew because
their chief cameraman had racked himself up on a bicycle in Madrid
traffic, and I said we would be up at the bar on top of the International, and she said just fine and went tap-tapping away, moving firm
and well in her uniform.

In the big blue windowed room high in the air, the cocktail business was still thin, because of the hour, and a familiar face was working the quiet and elegant bar, and he remembered The Drink, and
seemed so pleased with himself in remembering, that we each had
one, sitting and watching the deftness with silent and respectful attention. Two ample old-fashioned glasses, side by side, filled to the two-
thirds line with cracked ice. A big, unmeasured slosh of dry sherry
into each glass. Then swiftly, the strainer placed across the top of
one and then the other, as with a delicate snap of the wrist he
dumped the sherry down the drain. Then fill to the ice level with
Plymouth gin, rub the lemon peel around the inside of the rim,
pinch some little floating beads of citrus oil on the surface of the
drink, throw away the peel, present with small tidy bow and flourish
to the folk. "Two McGees," said he.

"Thank you, Harold," I said.

He had two new customers and when he moved away, Puss

hoisted her glass, tinked it against mine. "The instant drink," she said. "Instant stupidity, or instant rape, or instant permission. Me, what I get is this instant numbness around the chops. Here's to flying quail."

"To what?"

"To stewardesses! You're slow today, lover. You're not relating now and again."

"It's just that I was looking at you. Then I don't hear so well." And looking by chance beyond her, I saw Tush Bannon sitting at a deuce against the wall, the shoulder bulk hunched toward a still-faced girl who sat across from him. She had long, straight auburn-brown hair, a pouty, impassive little face. She seemed to be listening to him with a thoughtful intentness, and she bit at the heavy bulge of her underlip and closed her eyes and slowly shook her head in a prolonged No.

That is not the point where one goes ambling over to the old buddy and whacks him on the shoulder and asks how Janine is. It was a private conversation, so private and intense they seemed to be inside an overturned bowl of thinnest glass, almost visible.

"Know them?" Puss asked.

"Just him."

"I'd say he's going to get called out on strikes. He's lost his cool. The hard sell makes a gal nervous these days."

"Hey!" said Barni Baker, and put her overnight case down and climbed up onto the stool on my right. She wore a little pale green skirt, and she had little gold ladybugs in her pierced ears, and she wanted a bourbon sour.

Puss leaned forward and spoke across me, saying, "Gad, it must be the most marvelous, exciting, romantic thing in the world, jetting around to marvelously romantic places! It's really living, I bet. Those fascinating pilot types, and mysterious international travelers and all. I guess you realize how jealous of you all we earthbound females are, Barni."

There was just the slightest narrowing of Barni's eyes, gone in an instant. She leaned in from her side and said breathlessly, "Oh, yes! It's all my dreams come true, Miss Killian. To fly to all the lovely places in the world." She sighed and shook her pretty head. "But it seems so . . . so *artificial* somehow to have to use an airplane, don't you think? But with my little broom, I can just barely get above the treetops. Have you had better luck?"

"I think having to carry that damned cat makes the difference," said Puss without hesitation. "And wear that stupid hat and the long skirts."

"And it's hard to enjoy the moonlight when you have to keep up that dreary cackling, don't you think?" Barni asked.

Tush came up behind me and said, "Talk to you a minute, Trav?" He turned and walked away before I could introduce him. The gals did not notice. I excused myself and followed Tush. Barni Baker moved over onto my stool. As I went out into the corridor, before the glass swung shut I heard the contralto bark of one of Puss's better laughs, in counterpoint with a silvery yet somehow earthly yelp from Barni. Knife-fighting among the females can spoil party time, and it was nice to know that this pair would get along.

I went with Tush past the elevators to the empty men's room.

"I would have said hello, but you had a friend."

"Friend! With friends like that, who needs, and so forth. She left. Look, I haven't much time. I've left Jan alone with the kids for three days and I want to get back. She said a year ago there was a pattern in this whole thing and we should get out, but I wouldn't believe her. Okay. I believe her now. It's a business deal. A land development deal. And we got in the way."

He was as big as ever, but his face looked oddly shrunken. His hands were shaky. His eyes had a starey look, somewhat like the eyes of people who wear glasses when they have their glasses off.

He tried to laugh. "I thought somebody wanted my marina. So I used money I couldn't spare to get a local lawyer to see what he could find out. Young guy. Steve Besseker. I thought maybe he was the only lawyer in Sunnydale who wouldn't scare. I told him everything that had happened to me, and he agreed it couldn't be coincidence. So he nosed around. Nobody wants the marina, Trav. They want to put together a parcel of four hundred and eighty acres. And my little ten acres is right in the middle of all that riverfront land they want."

"They?"

"All that area is zoned as an industrial park ever since Tech-Tex came in, across the river. Big high lines come in with all the power anybody would need. They're going to dredge the river and the channel so barges can come in from the Waterway. Some big corporation wants to come in, apparently, and they'd pay a nice price for the land."

"So who's putting it together?"

"A local real estate man named Preston LaFrance owns the fifty acres right behind me. Besseker found out LaFrance has an option on the two hundred acres just east of me, at a price of two hundred dollars an acre. It's owned by an old boy named D. J. Carbee, an early settler. On the other side of me, to the west, there's two hundred and twenty acres owned by something called Southway Lands, Incorporated. Besseker found out that Southway is one of Gary Santo's operations. Do you know him?"

"I know *of* him. Like everybody else in south Florida." A few years ago Santo had been the dramatic young swinger, with the touch of gold. Now he is the not-so-young swinger, moving in mysterious ways behind many scenes, behind barriers of privacy and money. The name in Miami has the flavor of penthouses, pipelines, South American playmates, mergers and acquisitions, private jets, and well-publicized donations to local drives in the art and culture areas.

"I don't know the exact relationship between Santo and Preston LaFrance, Trav. Maybe LaFrance is just acting as Santo's agent. Maybe it's a joint venture. Besseker heard a rumor that the plant location experts nosed around the area a year and a half ago and recommended that the big company that wants it could go as high as eight hundred thousand! Seventeen hundred dollars an acre. About the time I learned all this, an old friend came out and told me he couldn't help it, and didn't want to do it, but he had to pick up the houseboats. I still owed on them. He told me that one of the Shawana County Commissioners, Mr. P. K. Hazzard—they call him Monk Hazzard—had hinted that if my friend repossessed his houseboats, he'd get a favorable ruling on a zoning application. So when I told that to Besseker, he said that Monk Hazzard was Preston LaFrance's brother-in-law, and there wasn't any way to prove a thing. He acted funny. He said he had a lot of things coming up and he couldn't promise to give me any more time. They'd gotten to him too, I guess. He has to make a living there."

"All just folks," I said.

He stared at the paper towel rack. He shook his head. "You know my style, Trav. I don't like all this round-and-about stuff. Direct confrontation. I'd seen Hazzard at a couple of those public hearings where they'd messed me up, like about taking that bridge out, but I hadn't talked to him. So I tried to make an appointment and he kept stalling, and finally I took Jan with me and we sat there outside his office until he finally saw us. Smallish man, with a long neck and a little bit of a round head, and big goggly eyes behind his thick glasses. Face sort of like a monkey, and a squeaky voice. I said we were citizens and taxpayers and landowners, and he was a public official, and it was his ethical and moral duty to see that the machinery of government wasn't used to shove me into bankruptcy so his brother-in-law could make a few bucks. You know about humiliation, Trav?"

"I keep getting a little every once in a while."

"He strutted around and he squeaked and lectured. Folks come down from the north and think it's easy to make a living in Florida. Toughest place in the world. He wouldn't look at me. He looked out the window part of the time, and at Jan's legs the rest of the time. He said it wasn't the job of local government to save a man from his own mistakes and bad judgment. He said that the greatest good for the greatest number meant the best possible land use, and maybe a marina wasn't the best use when you think of the tax base and employment and so on. He said he'd overlook the slur on his honesty because a man in trouble says things he doesn't mean. He said people just don't know how much talent it takes to run a small business, and I'd probably be happier in some other line of work. He said that he didn't know whether Press LaFrance was interested in my ten acres or not, but maybe if I could talk to him he might make me an offer, but I shouldn't expect too much because the business was in bad shape. He said that people in trouble get to thinking the whole world is against them, and just because certain necessary county improvements were hurting my business, it didn't mean it was done on purpose. He said thousands of little businesses go broke every year in Florida, and I shouldn't think I was an exception. So we left and Jan was crying before we got to the car. Humiliation and frustration."

"You're bucking the power structure, Tush. You can't hardly win."

"I thought I could. When I saw LaFrance, I went alone. He gave me the same line, as if they'd rehearsed it. I told him to make an offer. He said he wasn't interested. He said maybe if it came on the market later on, he might make an offer on a foreclosure price, but he didn't think it was worth the mortgage balance. A little over sixty thousand, that is. And we put fifty-one thousand in it. So I had to open my big mouth. I leaned across his desk and told him he was never going to get his hands on my property. I'd leave Jan there to run it and go back to sales work, and put every dime I could spare against that mortgage. So they squeezed a little harder."

"How?"

"First they extended that road contract another hundred days. Then they sent out inspectors from the County Bureau of Services, and they condemned my wiring, and the septic tank drain fields, and my well, and lifted my license to do business. With the license gone, the bank said I come up with the whole amount of the mortgage in thirty days or they foreclose. It's way past due. We did well for a while there, Trav. I didn't overextend. If they'd left me alone, I had enough business to pay for the boat-storage rack and the motel enlargement. We were going to have one of the best little operations in that whole area. I tried to see Commissioner Hazzard again. I waited and a couple of sheriff's deputies showed up and said I could either leave or get picked up for loitering. So Jan and I talked it over and decided the best thing to do would be to lay it all out for Mr. Gary Santo. We decided he was probably big enough so that he didn't even know what was going on up there, and would tell them to put a stop to it if he did know. We decided that probably LaFrance just got too eager to do a big job for Santo and do it as cheap as possible. I put it all down on paper. I guess that between us we must have rewritten that letter about nine times, and Janine typed it on the old machine in the motel office, and we sent it down here Special Delivery, marked personal."

"Any answer?"

"Verbal. From that girl I was sitting with. Her name is Mary Smith. I came down and tried to get to Santo. She was as far as I got. She said she'd meet me out here, because she had to catch a flight. Cold as a meat locker, boy. Yes, Mr. Santo had read my letter personally. Yes, he had an informal agreement with Mr. LaFrance. But Mr. LaFrance is not employed by Mr. Santo. Yes, Mr. LaFrance is under considerable pressure by Mr. Santo to produce the results promised insofar as land acquisition is concerned. Mr. Santo feels no personal responsibility for your plight. He is not running a charitable organization. I wanted to know if I could see him in person. No. Sorry. But no."

"Now what?"

"We lose it. That's all. The grace period is about gone. Janine is taking it hard. It's a lot of money and work and time down the drain, and nothing to show for it. I . . . I wish I'd come to you sooner, Trav, before it got to be too late. Maybe you could have figured out some kind of a salvage operation. Your kind of salvage. Squeeze them like they've squoze me." He gave me a strange, puzzled, thoughtful look. "You know, I keep thinking about how I might kill somebody. Hazzard, Santo, LaFrance. Somebody. Anybody. I never thought that way in my life before. I'm not like that."

He grimaced, whirled, kicked the big metal trash basket full of used paper towels. "Aaaah . . . Tush!" he yelled, and went blundering out.

I collected Puss and Barni. It was after six thirty when we got back to *The Busted Flush*. Mick had gotten his phone call, made his deal, and set up a Monday morning flight to Spain via New York. And so, though my mood was somewhat soured, there was song and sport, sunburn and music, beach time and nap time, old and new jokes, girls in the galley, new tapes on the music machine, lipstick and sand and the sometime kiss, and the long heavy look through curl of lashes.

Meyer trooped in and out from time to time with little groups of Meyer's Irregulars and Partisans. We had a slight overflow from the permanent floating houseparty aboard the Alabama Tiger's big cruiser.

Though it looked as it always looks—so informal you don't know who is tied up with whom—there is protocol. There is a very real ingroup unwritten list of things you do and things you don't do, things you say and things you don't say. And if you are the kind of person who can't case the scene and know by instinct what the rules have to be, then the blinds are closed, shades drawn, and the freeze is on. But sometimes, as in the case of one midday visitor on Sunday, someone is so obtuse the action has to be a little more direct.

This one was named Buster or Buddy or Sonny, one of those names, a big loud thirtyish jollyboy type, office-soft, overconfident, far from home on a business trip and out beagling for a broad, confident that he was twice the man any of these beach-bum types could be, ready for a nice little roll and scuffle that he could describe to the other JC's back in God's Country, and hide from li'l ol' Peggy staying back home there with the kids.

So he came up onto the sun deck and sprawled out next to Barni and told her she was cute as any bug in the wide world, and if she would just let him spread a little more of this here suntan juice on that cute little ol' back and this here cute little ol' tummy, why she'd be making him the happiest paper salesman in the southeast territory.

She sat up and frowned into his dumb, happy, smirking face, and as Mick started to get up to heave Buster-Buddy-Sonny over the rail she waved him back. "Music down and out," she said. Puss went to the speakers and turned the volume off.

In the silence Barni said, with a brutal clarity, "Puss? Marilee? Come here, dears. Take a look at this one."

They came and sat close to her on her sun pad, all of them staring at Buster-Buddy-Sonny. "The type I was telling you about," Barni said. "One of the charmers that make life hell for a stewardess."

"Now, don't you badmouth me, you purty thing," he said grinning.

Puss said, scowling, "I see. Of course. All that fatty look around the middle. And that big voice and those dim, nasty little eyes."

"You funning me, you gals?" he asked, his smile fading a little.

Marilee tilted her head. "Mmmm. The kind you don't dare turn your back on when you're on duty. A real snatch-ass Charlie."

"They have this crazy dream, I guess," Barni said, "about how you're going to fall for that meaty charm and go back to their hotel or motel and climb right into the sack. Can you imagine?"

Puss shuddered delicately. "My God, darlings, suppose we were call girls or something and we *had* to sleep with one of those."

"Ekk!" said Marilee.

Buster-Buddy-Sonny stood up and the three lovelies looked blandly up at him.

"Coffee, tea or milk?" asked Barni.

"You lousy little bitch!" said he.

Puss laughed. "See? Just like you said, dear. Typical reaction. Look at how red his face is! Let me guess. He'll be bald in five years."

"Four," said Marilee firmly.

"He needs glasses already and won't wear them," said Barni.

"He's going to grow an enormous belly," Puss said.

"And fall over dead of a massive coronary occlusion when he's forty-five."

"And when he falls over, it will bust his cigar and spill his bourbon."

"And some sorry wretched woman is married to him."

Barni shook her head. "No girl who ever spent any time as a stewardess would ever marry one of those. Look at that mouth on it!

Imagine having to actually kiss something like that and pretend you were enjoying it!"

"And look at the dirty fingernails, will you!"

When Buster-Buddy-Sonny reappeared in view, he was eighty feet up the dock, walking briskly and not swinging his arms at all.

"You girls need your mouths washed out with gin," Mick said. "That was naughty."

"A little friendly castration never hurt anybody," said Marilee.

"Besides," said Puss, "we didn't touch on his *really* filthy habit. Given half a chance, do you know what that dreary bastard might do?"

Marilee, with a dirty chuckle, leaned close to Puss and whispered to her. Puss shook her head and said, "Congratulations, much worse than that."

"Like what?" Barni asked, puzzled.

"If you were stupid enough to let him get just a little past first base, that utter spook would stare right into your eyes and he would kind of gulp and look like a kicked dog and his voice would quiver and he'd say, 'Darlin', I love you.' "

"He would! He would indeed!" cried Marilee. "The lowest of the low. He's the *perfect* type for it. A real rat-fink coward."

Meyer came out of a long and somber contemplation hunched like a hirsute Buddha, reached a slow ape arm and picked up his queen's bishop and plonked it down in what at first glance seemed like an idiotic place, right next to my center pawn. A round little lady who was one of his retinue that week, beamed, clapped her hands and rattled off a long comment in German.

"She says you give up now," said Meyer.

"Never!" said I. I studied and studied and studied. Finally I put a knuckle against my king and tipped the poor fellow over and said, "Beach-walking, anyone?"

But before Puss and I went over, I tried once again to reach Tush Bannon at his Boatel by phone. Once again there was no answer. I felt irritation and depression. And, perhaps, the first little needles of alarm.

3

I AWAKENED at six thirty Monday morning thinking about Tush and his problem. If I hadn't awakened with that idea in mind, I could have gone back to sleep. But it snapped my eyelids up and held them there. And big as the bed was, the custom job that had been aboard the *Flush* when I won her in Palm Beach, Puss Killian had left me in precarious balance on the edge. She was curled, her back to me, and there was a solid and immovable feel to the warm and shapely rear that pressed against the side of my hip. She was deeply recharging all her redheaded batteries, in the deep, slow intake and humming exhalation of sleep of the heaviest and best kind.

So I gave up and got up and showered and came back, and tried to quietly get into a white sports shirt and khaki slacks. But in the muted light as I shoved my arm through the short sleeve I knocked a nightcap glass off the shelf and it smashed on the deck.

She rolled, rose up slowly, glowered indignantly at me and settled back down into her sleep, nestling onto her other side, a long, tangled tassle of red hair falling across her cheek and mouth, stirring with each breath.

I heard furtive galley sounds and found Barni Baker in a hiplength yellow robe, her hair in a kerchief, doing something to eggs. Her eyebrows went up when she saw me, and she whispered, "You too! What's *your* excuse? Don't answer. It's rhetorical. It's criminal to have to talk in the morning. I found this here good-looking roe and these here good-looking eggs, and what smells like good Herkimer County cheese, and if you want me to double the portion, just nod."

I nodded. I poured us some juice. She had the water on. I dumped the Colombian fine grind into the Benz filter paper and slid into the booth. She stared at me as I tried the egg invention. The question was in the lift of a little blonde eyebrow. The response was the circle of thumb and forefinger. When she started to tidy up, I told her to leave it until later, and I carried our coffee seconds in the white porcelain pot topside, and she brought along the mugs.

The morning was almost cold. I dug a blanket out of the forward locker for her to use as a lap robe over her bare legs, and I put on an old gray cardigan I've had for seven hundred years. It could now be classified as a missionary barrel reject.

"I think we could have practiced on the snare drum and tuba down there without bothering those two," I said.

"Mick needs all the sleep he can get. We'll have to leave by ten o'clock to make that flight. They're going to work him to death when he gets to Spain. The picture is behind schedule."

"When do you have to go back to work?"

"Tuesday noon."

"So come back."

"Thanks, but I don't think so. I think I'll turn the car in and hole up and try to do some thinking. You make damned good coffee, Trav. How good is your advice? Like to the lovelorn?"

"The best. But nobody ever takes it."

"So here is a hypothetical case about two loners, about this little ball of fluff who is an airline stewardess who is twenty-seven all too soon, and likes to be where the action is, but lately she wonders if the action isn't getting to be all alike. And there is this very special and talented guy who is a cinematographer, and who is a tough and skeptical thirty-two, who is gun-shy from a sour marriage, and who gets so hooked on his work he can't remember the stewardess's name, practically. And they are together maybe five times a year, maybe five days a time, and it is always the rightest of the right. The workingest of ever, even though they keep telling themselves and each other that it is going to wear off any minute now. So last time the camera guy wanted to marry the airline girl and she said hell no, so she thought about it a lot, and this time she brought it up and said okay and he said hell no, because he was hurt because she said no the last time. Can these two darling kids find happiness, McGee?"

"You get married when there is no other conceivable course of action, Barni-baby. You get married because you are both compelled to marry each other."

"Indeed?"

"Don't get frosty. I'm not putting down your romance. It will either get inevitable or it won't. It won't hang where it is. It will get bigger, or it will start to dry up, and either way it goes will be the right answer at that time. Don't get pushy."

After a long silence she said, "Anyway, the coffee *is* good." She shrugged. "Change of subject. This Puss Killian of yours. I *like* her, Trav. I like her a lot. But there's a funny thing about her. You think she's telling you all about herself, and afterward you know she hasn't really told you a thing. What about her, anyway?"

"I wouldn't know. Don't look at me like that. I've known her for four months. She goes away for a couple of days every few weeks. I could do some digging. But it's up to her. When and if she wants to talk, she can talk. I know that she's from Seattle, that she isn't hurting for money, that she's twenty-four or -five, that she shed a husband not long before she showed up here, that I met her on the beach only because she stepped on a sea urchin and was cursing billy blue blazes and ordered me to come over and do something about it right now. I know she has enough energy for three stevedores, that she can eat three pounds of steak at a sitting, that she can hold her booze, and she would walk up and spit in a tiger's eye if she thought it would liven up the idle hour. And I know that once in a while she goes absolutely dead silent, and all she wants is for you to pretend she isn't there."

"She has a very soft look for you, Travis. When you're not looking at her."

"Troublemaker!"

I tried again and couldn't get an answer out of Tush. I had the long-distance operator run a check on the phone up there, but it was reported in order. At a little after nine I thought I'd better see if Puss wanted to say her good-bye in person or let me relay it. I went in and sat gently on the bed. She was breathing faster. Her hand and arm were twitching as she dreamed, and she made a little whimpering sound. I gently thumbed the hair back away from her face and saw a wetness of tears leaking out of the closed lids.

I put my hand on her bare shoulder and gave her a little shake. "Hey," I said. "It's not all *that* bad, is it?"

She opened wide blind eyes and snuffled and said in a little-girl voice, "But they keep saying . . ." She shook herself like a wet red setter. She focused on me, snuffled again, smiled and said, "Thanks, pal. They were about to cut me off at the pass. Wassa time?"

"Nine fifteen."

"Hmmm. If I'm reading you, McGee, I admire your thinking. It's very good. Stay right where you are while I go brush my teeth first."

"Mick and Barni are taking off in a half hour. I wondered if you wanted to wave bye-bye."

She gave a leonine stretching yawn. "Yes I do indeed. And if you had any sense at all, you big brown knuckly idiot, you'd have come smirking in here at quarter of, not quarter after. Haste makes waste, and what I have is not to be wasted, lad. So set your little clock for siesta time."

"At siesta time we're going to be up in Shawana County visiting some old friends of mine with a problem."

"Really?" She sat up, holding the sheet to her breasts. "Hmm. Then hustle the lady some coffee while she showers. And set your clock ahead."

". . . on location like that," Mick was saying, "it's the time lag that drives you nuts, not getting to see rushes, and see how the color values stand up until you're three days or four past that particular point."

And from the giant shower stall, above the sound of sloshing like unto that which a small walrus herd might make, the three of us could hear Puss in good voice: "With 'er 'ead tooked oonderneath 'er arm, she 'awnts the bloody tow'r. With 'er 'ead tooked oonderneath 'er arm at the midnight hour."

"So I turned around," said Barni Baker, "and there was that sweet little old man yanking away at the lever on the cabin door thinking it was how you get into the men's room, and we're at twenty-eight thousand feet over the Amazon basin. So I got to him at a dead run and steered him gently where he wanted to go. Then he came out and stared at the cabin door and the big lever and rolled his eyes up and fainted dead away. A passenger helped me get him back to his seat and I gave him smelling salts and then I explained to him how the doors are designed so the pressurization clamps them shut so tightly ten men couldn't open them. But he just kept shaking his head and saying O Dear God."

Puss appeared just in time, wearing her big white woolly robe and carrying the half cup of coffee left from what I had taken her as she was stepping into the shower. The ends of her red hair were damp. She gathered little Barni into the big white woolly arms, hugged her, smacked her on the cheek, and told her she was all doll. We went out the aft door of the lounge and waved them off, and watched them get into the car and drive away.

"Nice ones," said Puss. "For such a raunchy old beach bum, you know a lot of nice ones. Like me, for example. I was nice enough to leave our coffee and my cigarettes right beside the bed." She went over to the phone and switched it off. She went frowning to the record bin, made a thoughtful selection of two and held up the sleeves so I could see what she had picked. George Van Eps guitar, and the Modern Jazz Quartet on Blues at Carnegie Hall. I took them from her, put them on the changer, fixed the volume where she said she liked it.

"Coming, dear?" she said with an excessive primness, and just inside the door of the master stateroom I had to step over the woolly whiteness of the robe on the deck just beyond the sill.

The day had warmed up. The *Muñequita* had run handsomely, with a deep drone speaking of a lot more power in reserve. When we had anchored for lunch in Fort Worth, well away from the channel, while we ate the thick roast beef and raw onion sandwiches and shared an icy bottle of dry red supermarket wine, I briefed her on Tush, on how long I had known him, and on Janine and what Tush had told me of his problems.

"No answer at all on the phone?"

"Not a thing."

"Seems odd."

"Seems very damned odd, Puss. The thing is, he isn't a devious guy. And he's caught in the middle in a very devious situation, with large money hanging on it, and old Tush may try to bull his way through, and he could get hurt twice as bad."

When we went up the Shawana River, there was a faint, drifting acrid stink. Our eyes watered. When I came around the last bend, I was shocked at the deserted look of the place. The cheerful white houseboats were all gone. All but one storage rack on the in-and-out boat shelter were empty, and the remaining boat was, at a hundred feet, worth perhaps fifty dollars, outboard motor and all. The moored boats were gone, except for a skiff so full of water there were only inches of freeboard left, and an old cruiser hulk that had sunk in the shallows. The forklift truck was gone.

I tied up and we went ashore. Near the cities, all the old highways of America pass businesses that have gone broke. End of the dream. The spoor of a broken marriage can be kept in a couple of cartons on a shelf in the garage. Broken lives can be tucked neatly away in graves and jails and sanitariums. But the dead business in a submarginal commercial strip stays right there, ugly and moldering away, the frantic advertising signs of the final convulsive effort fading and tattering over the weeds. For every one of them was the big dream, the gala opening, the last dusting and arranging before the doors opened. "We're going to make it big, honey. Real big." Then there is the slow slide into doubt, into confusion, and into the terminal despair. "So we were going to make it real big, were we? Ha!"

It was a silent place. The acrid river slid by. Dry fronds rattled in the breeze. A sign creaked.

Even the two marine gas pumps were gone. I went to the marina shed. The tools were gone. We asked each other questions in low, graveyard voices. There was a shiny new hasp and padlock on the marina building, along with a printed notification from the County Sheriff's Department. There was another on the motel office. I could find no note fastened to anything that told how to get in touch with the Bannons.

"Now what?" Puss asked.

"There's no neighbors, nobody here to ask. I suppose we could run upriver until we come to something."

She stared around. "Gives me the spooks," she said. We'd just reached the dock when I heard a car coming. We went back around in front and saw the phone company service truck lurching over the torn-up road. As I moved to wave him down, he turned in and stopped and got out and stared at us as we approached. He looked to be about fifty, a squatty, leathery man wearing silver-rimmed glasses.

"I'd like to find Mr. Bannon," I said.

"Why?" It was a very flat and very abrupt question, and there was something about the flavor of it that made me wary. So I reached into the old bag of tired tricks and pulled out the one labeled Real Cordial.

"Well, it's like this. Quite a while back, I can't remember how many weeks, I had a bilge pump acting up, and I stopped in here and Bannon pulled it and stuck in a loaner, the idea being he'd fix it if he could or sell me the loaner if he couldn't, but I didn't get back as soon as I thought. Now it looks like he's gone out of business or moved someplace else."

"You could say that. Yes. It surely does. Let me make the disconnect and check in first, then maybe I can tell you what happened."

He donned harness and spurs with practiced ease and walked up the pole. He made his service disconnect at the lead-in terminals, clipped his handset onto the wires and called in. We could hear his voice but not what he was saying. He came down fast, showing off a little. He took off his gear and tossed it into the truck.

"Well, sir," he said, "you got here yesterday morning, you'd had some excitement for sure. You'da found Bannon right here. Promised myself I'd take a look and see where it was they found him. Maybe you'd like to come take a look, mister. Maybe the young lady should kind of wait on us."

But Puss tagged along. He went around in back and looked around, grunted and went over to a sturdy and rusty tripod made of heavy pipe, standing about fifteen feet tall. There was a manual winch with a crank, as rusty as the pipe, and a wire cable that went from the winch drum up through a pulley at the top of the tripod. A big, heavy old marine diesel, cannibalized down to little more than the ponderous block, hung from the taut cable about five feet off the ground.

The phone man sat on his heels and shook his head and said, "Sure a terrible way for a man to do himself. Look there! There's still hair and mess on the bottom side a that engine."

I had thought the stain on the packed oily dirt was merely more oil. Puss went trotting busily away about fifty feet. She stopped and bent forward and coughed shallowly a few times, then straightened up and went over and sat on a sawhorse with her back to us.

"What Freddy said this Bannon done—Freddy is one of Sheriff Bunny Burgoon's deputies and Freddy is the one that found him Sunday morning—this Bannon must have cranked that block up as high as he could get it, and then he fastened a piece of stove wire to that ratchet there on the side of the drum and lay out on his back right under that thing and give the wire a yank. The wire was still wound around his hand. Mashed him something terrible they say." He stood up, spat. "Well, you got to say one thing. It was quick and it was for certain. And I guess the poor fella didn't have much to live for."

"Because he went broke?"

"Maybe I don't have the straight of it. You know how people get to talking and every time they tell something, it comes out different. What I hear, he went off to try to raise some money fast to save the business. So when they come out here Friday with all the eviction papers and bankrupt papers and so on, just his missus is here with the youngest. She wanted them to hold off until Bannon got back, but all the legal steps had been took care of in proper order, and there was just no choice about it. They waited about an hour for her to pack up personal stuff and they helped her load the car. They say she was crying, but she wasn't carrying on. She was crying without making any noise about it. She picked up the other two kids from school, and she left off Bannon's suitcase and a note from her to him with the Sherf, and she just took off. She must have had some travel money saved out, because they say that yesterday after they toted Bannon's body back to Ingledine's Funeral Home, Sherf Burgoon opened that note to see where he could get in touch with her to tell her about her husband, but all it said was she was going to go stay with some girl's first name for a while, and Bannon would have known the whole name, but nobody else does."

He spat again and started to move toward his truck. I walked slowly with him and said, "He seemed like a bright, pleasant guy. He didn't seem like the kind who'd go broke. But you never can tell. Sometimes it's booze, or the dog track, or other women."

He got into the truck and stared out at me. "Not this time. They run this boy off. He was in the way, and they run him off. But you didn't hear me say that, mister."

"I didn't hear you, friend."

He headed back over the lumpy road. I walked around to where Puss still sat on the sawhorse. She looked up at me. With a small frown she said, "My heart bled for you the way you went reeling around in shock, McGee. You really took it hard. Your dear old buddy has gone to the big marina in the sky. The hard way. Came to get your bilge pump! God's sake, Travis!"

I sat on my heels and squinted up at her. Dark red hair and disapproval, outlined against a blue December sky. "Win a few, lose a few, honey," I said.

"What *are* you?" she asked.

I stood up and put my hands on her upper arms, near the shoulders and plucked her up off the sawhorse and held her. Maybe I was smiling at her. I wouldn't know. What I was saying seemed to come from a strange direction, as if I were standing several feet behind myself. I said some nonsense about smelling these things out, about sensing the quickest way to open people up, and so you do it, because if you don't, then maybe you miss one little piece of something you should know, and then you go join the long long line of the dead ones, because you were careless.

"And," I heard myself say, "Tush killed himself but not with that damned engine block. He killed himself with something he said, or something he did, and he didn't know he was killing himself. Maybe he didn't listen very good, or catch on soon enough. I listen very good. I catch on. And when I add up this tab and name the price, I'm going to look at some nice gray skin, honey. Gray and pale, oily and guilty as hell, and some eyes shifting around looking for some way out of it. But every damned door will be nailed shut."

I came out of it and realized she was making little hiccupy sobs and looking down and to the side, and her cheeks were wet, and she was saying, "Please, please."

I released her and turned on my heel and walked away from her. I went a little way up the road. I leaned against the trunk of an Australian pine and emptied my lungs a few times. A jay yammered at me. There were tree toads in a swamp somewhere nearby. Puss came walking very slowly up the road. She came over to me and with a quick, shy smile leaned her face into my neck and chest.

"Sorry," she whispered.

"For nothing?"

She exhaled. "I don't know. I asked you what you were. Maybe I found out, sort of."

"Whatever it is, I don't let it show, Puss. Ten more minutes and I would have been kindly Trav forevermore."

She pushed herself a few inches away and looked up at me. "Just smile with your eyes like kindly ol' McGee, dear, to kind of erase that other . . . that other look."

"Was it that bad?"

"They could bottle it and use it to poison pit vipers."

"Okay now?"

She nodded. "Sure." Her eyes were a sherry brown, almost a tan, and in that good light under the tree I could see the area right around the pupil, a corona of green. "He was a special guy?"

"He was that."

"But can't even a special guy . . . give up?"

"Maybe, but if that one ever had, it wouldn't have been like that."

We walked back toward the dead marina, my arm around her strong waist. "Call it enemy country," I explained. "He's dead, and it solves some problems for some people. And they'll want to forget all about it as fast as they can, and they won't know anything about anything."

I got the camera off the boat, a battered old Retina C-III, and put in a roll of Plus X. I hand-cranked the block as high as it would go before it wedged against the tripod poles. I got wire and pliers out of the toolbox aboard, fastened wire to the ratchet stop. I took pictures as I went along. When I yanked the wire, the great weight came down to thud against the hard dirt with a shock I could feel in the soles of my feet, while the drum clattered and the cable rasped through the rusty pulley. I cranked it up and left it the way it had been.

She watched, and had the grace not to ask why.

I didn't rinse my hands in the river. I waited until we were well out into the bay.

Then I put it at dead slow, right at 700 rpm, and told her to head down the channel. I climbed out onto the forward bow shell and leaned back against the port windshield.

One approach: Go storming into Sunnydale, promising stink and investigations and general turmoil.

Or: Find some kind of cover story that might open up some mouths. See who can be conned. See who can be turned against whom.

Or: Go in fast and quietly and come out with one Preston La-France and take him to a nice, quiet place and open him up.

Or: What if some mysterious buyer picked up the Bannon property? Then the boys couldn't put the whole two sections together. And that might bring them out of the woodwork.

The last had the right flavor, if it could be worked.

But first there had to be a first thing, and it had to be poor Janine. And if I couldn't get to her before the Sherf told her the bad news, I could at least arrive shortly thereafter.

So I hopped down and took the wheel and ran at high cruise to Broward Beach and tied up at the city marina. I left Puss at the drugstore counter and shut myself into a booth and made a person-to-person credit card call to Sheriff Bunny Burgoon in Sunnydale. I yapped at him in the excited tones of a whiter-wash commercial and told him that CBS news had researched him and discovered he was a truly fine law officer, and had they located Mrs. Bannon yet, and her three kids, and it was a great human interest story and we might do a little feature.

"Sure," he said. "Just before Christmas and all that. Yeh. Locate her? Well, not exactly yet, but we're doing everything that any human person could expect or ask for, and that's the truth. We got aholt of her folks in Milwaukee, and they're all upset as any human person could imagine, but they haven't heard a word from her, and they don't know any friend of hers of the name of Connie. Now if it was to go on national television, she'd turn up right off, I imagine. The name is Sheriff Hadley—that's an e-y, Burgoon, B-u-r-g-o-o-n. And I've been elected here three times as Sherf of Shawana County and——"

"Could you read me the note she left her husband?"

"Did you get the name wrote down with the right spelling?"

"I did, Sheriff."

"It's personal-like, but I see no harm in reading it to you, as any human person could tell it's a public service to find that poor lady. Just a minute. Let me see now. Here it is. It goes like this. 'Dear Tush, I'm sorry. This last thing was just the bitter end. Somehow it made me so ashamed. The boys are so upset and confused. I had to handle it alone because you weren't there, and it took the very last bit of strength and courage I had. Don't be angry with me. I'm worn out. I'm going to go stay with Connie for a while. I'm leaving this note and a suitcase with the things you'll probably need with the Sheriff. When you get the details and all straightened out, please phone me. Don't come charging up here, because I might not be ready to see you yet. I have some thinking to do, and then we have a lot of talking to do, about what's going to happen to you and me. Don't worry about me or the boys. We'll be fine. It was all so ugly, the way it happened. I suppose those men tried to be nice, and it wasn't their fault, but it was a terrible thing. Jan.'"

"I certainly appreciate your cooperation, Sheriff. We'll be in touch. Yessir, we'll stay in close touch with developments."

I went back to the counter. Puss was sitting on the stool sipping her cola drink, eyes a bit narrow, and on her lips a dangerous little smile. A plump man with a vulgar shirt and a hairline mustache sat two stools away, blushing furiously. He tried to sip his coffee with trembling hand and spilled a dollop of it into his saucer.

"Darling!" she cried, turning toward me, her voice of such a penetrating clarity it reached all the way back to the remedies for iron-poor blood. "This dear little fat fellow wanted to show me all the sights. What's your name, dear little fat fellow?"

He clapped two bits onto the counter top. "GeeeZUSS!" he muttered. He fled out of the cool into the midafternoon sunlight.

She gazed somberly toward the door. "Seems to have turned chicken. Have you noticed the progressive emasculation of the American male, Travis? Present company excluded, of course."

She finished the soft drink with a rattling slupp amid the cracked ice, cheeks sucked hollow, and stood up in her sky-blue linen boat shorts, and her basque shirt, shook her hair back and smiled benignly up at me. "I counted myself in," she said in a low voice.

"How's that?"

"Since we left the river, I've felt like a bulky package you were tired of carrying around, and you were looking for a coin locker. I never knew Tush. I never met Janine. But I have a very hard nose, dear, and I don't scare, and I want to share."

"I'll give it some thought."

"You *do* that."

4

I HAD to give a lot of thought right then and there to getting a good quick line on Connie. Janine's parents didn't know her. But somebody who had been close to the Bannons would know who she might be. I had to dig through the fragments of old memories and piece something together. I tried walking and thinking, Puss quietly, patiently trudging along beside me.

I found a dark little cocktail lounge, and a dark table in a corner. They had one cocktail waitress, and the small percentage of her that was not bare was cruelly bound and laced into the compulsory bunnyfication of tiny waist, improbable uplift and separation of breast, revelation of cleavages front and rear. She had a tired, pretty, sour little face, a listless manner. When she left with the order, Puss clamped her hand on my arm and stared after her, saying, "Santa Claus is coming to town."

They had their Christmas decoration up. It was a lush plastic spray of mistletoe, affixed exactly where the nubile legions of the Hefner Empire affix their fluffy white bunny tails. It expressed such a perfect comment on commercialized Christmas, it gave Puss a case of gasping chuckles that turned into hiccups, which were soon quelled by her big swallows from the steinkrug of dark beer on draft.

I shoved my memory back to the drinks at Tush and Janine's breakfast bar two months earlier, when we had played what happened to who. And I finally came up with Kip Schroeder, the quarterback who, after seven years of high school ball, New Jersey All-State, and five years of college ball, a couple of All-American mentions, had been held together with wire, tape and rivets. He had been obsoleted by giant strides in nutrition. He was structured like a fireplug, and every year the line he had to see over was higher and wider. But where the hell was he? He and his wife, whose name I couldn't remember, had been best man and matron of honor at the wedding of Tush and Jan. I had to have a football buff, one of those nuts who knew every statistic and what happened to everybody.

I tried the bald bartender, breaking up his murmured conversation with the mistletoe lass. His frown wrinkled the naked skull almost all the way up to the crown of his head.

"I think maybe Bernie Cohn. He does the sports on WBRO-TV. It ought to be a good time to catch him there at the station. Janie, look up the number for the gennaman, and plug the phone in over there, huh?"

It was a little pink phone with a lighted dial. She had to use a lighter to find the baseboard phone connection. She started to tell me the number, then shrugged and dialed it herself and handed me the phone.

I got the switchboard and then I got Bernie, who said, "Yes, yes, yes?" with irritable impatience until I told him my question. Then he sounded pleased. "Let me see now. Schroeder. Schroeder. I'm not drawing a blank, buddy. You can put odds on that. I'm running through the career, up to the last thing I heard. Okay. Here it is. Two years ago Kip was athletic director, Oak Valley School, and that's in . . . just a minute . . . Nutley, New Jersey. Right?"

"Sure appreciate it."

"Did I win you a bet, fella? Express your appreciation by telling all your friends to watch the Bernie Cohn show at six fifteen every weekday on your Big Voice of the Big Bay, WBRO-TV. Right?"

Listless Janie came over when I signaled her, and I ordered two more draft and asked her if I could make a credit-card call on the phone. When she came back with the beers, she said, "He says okay if I stand here while you make the call. You know. On account of any long distance comes in on the bill, it's a deduct on him."

Puss reached out with a foot, hooked a chair over from the nearby table and said, "Rest your mistletoe, honey."

With her first smile, the waitress sat down, saying, "My feet are like sore teeth, honest to God. I worked waitress three years and no trouble, but in this costume the owner says high heels, and now after three months I hurt all over, honest to God."

I got through to area information on my station-to-station call for anyone at the phone listed in Nutley for Kip Schroeder. They didn't have one. They had a K. D. Schroeder. I tried that and got a Mrs.

Schroeder, and she said yes, she was Kip's wife, Alice. Kip was out.

I said I had met her once, and she pretended politely that she remembered me perfectly. I was glad she sounded so bright. I said I was trying to locate a very good friend of Jan Bannon, named Connie.

"Connie. Connie. Can you hold on a minute while I get my Christmas card list? It's laid out even, but we haven't gotten started on it yet."

She came back and said, "I think this is who you want. Connie Alvarez. It used to be Tom and Connie, and he died. I think she was one of Jan's teachers in school. Here's the address I've got for her. To-Co Groves. That's capital To, capital Co, with a hyphen. Route Two, Frostproof, Florida. Frostproof! And you should see the sleet coming down here today. It's worth your life to drive."

I thanked her and told her to give Kip my best, asked her how he was doing. She said he'd had two good seasons in a row and he was happy as a clam. So she asked how Tush and Jan were. What can you say? I said that the last time I'd seen the two of them, they were fine. It wasn't a lie. She said that if I saw them soon again, to tell Janine she owed her a letter and she'd write right after the holidays for sure.

I didn't want to make the next call from there, not with tired Janie listening. So I paid her, and added on top of the tip a little balm for sore feet.

Back toward the city marina, toward the drugstore, and I briefed Puss en route. "She didn't need much travel money to get there. Less than two hundred miles, I'd guess."

In the drugstore booth, on the off chance that Jan might answer, I made the call person to person to Mrs. Alvarez. I heard a maid answer the operator and say she would get Mrs. Alvarez. It was at least two minutes before Connie Alvarez answered, sounding out of breath.

"Yes?"

"Is Jan staying there with you?"

". . . I . . . I'm afraid I wouldn't be interested, thank you."

"Look, Mrs. Alvarez. This isn't Tush."

"Then, perhaps you could explain more about it, Mr. Williams."

"I get the message. She can hear your end of it. Now, listen very carefully. Please. Don't let her answer any phone calls, and keep her away from the newspapers and the radio and the television."

"I suppose there would be some reason for that."

"My name is Travis McGee. I'm going to try to get there this evening. And it might be a good idea if you could have a damned good tranquilizer handy. I'm an old friend of Tush's. I wasn't going to tell you this if you sounded bird-brained, Connie. But you sound solid. Tush is dead. And it was messy."

"In that case, Mr. Williams, I might be willing to listen. Perhaps if you could come out this evening? There's loads of room here. We can put you up, and it will give us a good chance to talk business. I know a little bit about the sort of proposition you mention. I mean, the background data. I'll look forward to seeing you. By the way, we're eight miles northeast of Frostproof. Go north out of town on US Twenty-seven and turn right on State Road Six thirty, and we're about five miles from the corner on your left. I'll turn the gate lights on at dark."

And then came the fat argument with Puss Killian as we walked back to the city marina. At last she said, "Old buddy, you are leaving out one ingredient. You say she was a steady one. Great. She can cope. So maybe she is one of those who can cope with all the mechanics of a situation. A real administrator. But maybe she can't hold people. Maybe it makes her feel itchy to try to hold somebody and hug somebody and rock somebody. I have this rusty nail for a tongue, and I kick where it is going to hurt the most, but I am a warm broad, like in the puppy sense of touching and being touched. Contact with flesh. That's where the messages of the heart are, McGee. Not in words, because words are just a kind of conventional code, and they get blurred, because any word doesn't mean just the same to any two people. And I am very familiar with that old spook with the scythe and the graveyard breath. And I do *not* care to be sent back to Lauderdamndale to sit around in that sexpot houseboat and crack my knuckles. Think of me as a kind of tall poultice. Or a miracle drug. Part of your kit. And if the lady administrator can supply the same item, I will not enter a competition. I will stay the hell out of the way. But this is women's work, and two are better than one, and it is going to be ten times worse for her because she ran for cover, and there will be guilt up to here."

So I scribbled her a list of my overnight needs and sent her off to a shopping plaza winking and glittering in the distance. I checked the marina office and got the name and location of a place that could lift the *Muñequita* out and tractor it over and put it on a shelf. He phoned for me and said they had space. I ran her over and took out all the stuff I did not want to leave aboard. A boat you can check as if it were a 4,300-pound suitcase is a vast convenience for people who never know what they'll be doing tomorrow.

I watched them hose down the hull and put Little Doll tenderly on her shelf, and soon a rental sedan arrived for me, tow-barring the little three-wheeled bug that would get the delivery man back to the rental headquarters. I accomplished the red tape on car and boat, locked the gear in the trunk of the maroon two-door, and got back to the cavelike cocktail bar ten minutes before Puss came striding in with a new genuine imitation red alligator hatbox, a blue canvas zipper bag advertising an obscure airline, two suitboxes and a big shopping bag full of smaller parcels.

By five thirty we were making good time up State 710, aimed like a chalk line at the town of Okeechobee, and Puss was in the back seat, happily unwrapping packages, admiring her own good taste, and packing the items in the oversized hatbox. At last she came clambering over the back of her bucket seat, plumped herself down, latched her belt, lit her cigarette and said, "Now about a few little things aboard *The Busted Flush*, friend. Like the little ding-dong when anybody steps aboard. Like the way it is wired for sound, not the pretty music, but for tape pickup. And how about that cozy little headboard compartment with loaded weapons therein? Also, you have some very interesting areas that look as if you'd have a nice collection of purple hearts, if you got them in a war. And how about the way you go shambling mildly about, kind of sleepily relaxed, beaming at your friends and buddies, kind of slow, rawboned, awkward-like, and you were ten feet from Marilee Saturday night when she stepped on that ice cube on the sun deck and was going to pitch headfirst right off the top of that ladderway, and in some fantastic way you got there and hooked an arm around her waist and yanked her right out of the air? More? How about the lightning change of personality for the benefit of the phone man with the old-timey glasses, the way you turned into a touristy goof so completely I didn't even feel as if I knew you? How about this con you almost worked on me about being retired. How about the way I tried to pump Meyer about you, and he showed speed and footwork like you couldn't believe? How about that kind of grim professional bit with the camera and the hoist and the wire and all, so totally concentrated I could have been walking around on my hands with a rose in my teeth without getting a glance from you? How about my gnawing little suspicion that you aren't going up to Frostproof to comfort this Janine, but to go pry information out of her? Enemy country, you said. Maybe for you the whole world is enemy country, McGee. But somehow it would sort of fit one lousy guess, which would be a batch of official cars screaming up and the boys in blue jumping out, and a big loudspeaker yammering for you to come out quietly or they lob in the tear gas."

"You are a warm broad. You are a warm *nosey* broad."

"So I have this eccentricity, maybe. You know, a social flaw. Some kind of insecurity reaction or something. I start sleeping with somebody and I get this terrible curiosity about them."

"So? I could have the same trouble too. But I haven't asked questions. Or tried to find out things I could find out, without much trouble, probably."

She was quiet for a long time. I glanced at her. Her hands were folded in her lap and she was biting at sucked-in lips.

"Fair is fair," she said. "When it's time to tell you, I will tell you. Not in words, but in writing, so that I get it down exactly right. Not that it is so earth-shattering or anything. But for now, for reasons I think are pretty good reasons, I want to keep it to myself. Fair being fair, if you have good reasons, okay, I ask no more."

So I told her the retirement was accurate, except I am taking it in little hunks whenever I can afford it. "It's a tricky, complex, indifferent society, Puss. It's a loophole world. And there are a lot of clever animals who know how to reach through the loopholes and pick the pockets of the unsuspecting. Carefully done, the guy who has been plucked clean has no way of getting it back. There are a thousand perfectly legal acts that can be immoral, or amoral, acts. Then the law officers have no basis of action. Attorneys can't help. The pigeon might just as well have dropped his wallet into a river full of crocodiles. He knows right where it is. And all he can do is stand on the muddy shore and wring his hands. So I'm the salvage expert. And I've known a lot of crocodiles. So I make a deal with him. I dive down, bring it up, and split it with him, fifty-fifty. When a man knows his expectation of recovery is zero, recovering half is very attractive. If I don't make it, I'm out expenses."

"Or you are a dainty dish for the crocs, man."

"So far I've been indigestible. Now Janine Bannon is a client. She doesn't know it yet. Tush would have been. A client in the classic sense of the legal squeeze. I don't understand the killing. They didn't need that. I know one thing. I have to watch myself on this one. Strangers make the best clients. Then I can play the odds and stay cold. Here I'm too emotionally hung up. I'm too angry, too sick at heart. A dirty, senseless act. So I have to watch it."

She pondered it for a time. "Just one thing that bothers me, darling. How do you find . . . enough new clients?"

I told her how I had found the last one, by combing very carefully through all the local items in the fat Sunday edition of a Miami paper. Of the items I marked that looked interesting, one was an apologetic announcement from a stamp collector's club that Mr. So-and-So, a very long and complicated Greek name, the well-known restaurateur had, at the last minute, decided to withdraw from the exhibition and not show his complete and extremely valuable collection of Greek postage stamps, which had included the famous 1857 Dusty Rose, which had brought $21,000 at a New York auction house in 1954.

I'd called an officer of the Philatelic Society who said the old gentleman was not mad at anybody, that he took a lot of pleasure in exhibiting his collection and having it admired, and that though he had sounded upset, he had not given any reason for withdrawing.

It had taken a little more research to find out what company insured the collection. An agent who said he had never met the old gentleman gave me his card. So I took his card and his name and presented myself to the old gentleman and said we wished to make a new appraisal of the collection. He stalled. The collection was in the vault at the bank. He was very busy. Some other time. So I said we had reason to believe he had disposed of some of the collection.

He broke down. He had been remounting the collection under glass for the exhibition. He had to leave his home for a doctor's appointment. He returned. Twenty-two of the most valuable stamps, including the Dusty Rose, were missing.

"So he was the patriarch of a big family, all very close, all sensitive to scandal, and his wife had died, and he had been remarried for two years to something of the same coloring, general impact and impressive dimensions of the late Jayne Mansfield, a lassy big enough to make two of the old boy, and he was so certain she had clouted his valuable toys he'd been afraid to make a report to the cops or claim insurance. So I followed the lady to an afternoon assignation with the hotel beachboy who'd blackmailed her into heisting the stamps, and after I got through shaking him up and convincing him that the old gentleman had arranged to have her last two male chums dropped into the Florida Straits wired to old truck parts, he produced eleven stamps, including the gem of the collection, and was so eager to explain where and how he had fenced the other eleven he was letting off a fine spray of spit. I helped him pack, and put him on a bus and waved good-bye and had a nice little talk with the big blonde about how I had just barely managed to talk two tough old Greek pals of her husband's from hiring local talent to write a little warning with a hot wire across her two most obvious endowments. A cop friend shook the missing items out of the fence, and I told the old man it hadn't been his wife at all, and he had every reason to trust her. So he hopped around and sang and chuckled and we went to the bank and he gave me thirty thousand cash, a generous estimate of half the value, and he gave me a note that gives me free meals for life in the best Greek restaurants in four states, and the whole thing took five days, and I went right back to my retirement and maybe three weeks later one Puss Killian came along and enriched it considerable."

"Pull over," she ordered. I found a place where there was room to park on the grass between the two-lane road and the canal. She unsnapped the seat belt, lunged expansively over, a big hug, a big kiss from a big girl whose eyes danced and sparkled in the fading daylight.

"Drive on," she said, snapping the belt.

I did. "Whatever it was for, it was nice."

"Well, this is a very long day, and it was partly for way way back, having that coffee-with. And it was for getting so damned scarey furious—because maybe there isn't much real anger around any more. It's for appreciating mistletoe. It's mostly for being what you are, doing the nutty things you do, and letting me for once be . . . Sancho Panza."

"Please! Sancha."

"Of course."

5

THE ENTRANCE gate was very wide, very high, with a floodlight shining on the clean white paint and on the sign that hung from chains from the top of the arch. To-Co Groves, Inc.

It was nine fifteen. We had stopped in Okeechobee for a hasty meal of some fresh bass, fried in corn meal and bacon fat. I turned into the graveled drive and a figure stepped out of the shadows into the headlights, raising a casual hand to stop me. Ranch hat, faded blue denim work jacket and jeans. She came to my side of the car and said, "McGee? I'm Connie Alvarez."

I got out, leaving the door open, shook hands, introduced Puss. Connie leaned in and shook her hand, then straightened again. In the glow of the courtesy light I had my first good look at her. A strong-looking woman, chunky, with good shoulders, a weathered face, no makeup, very lovely dark, long-lashed eyes.

"You would have helped them if they'd hollered, McGee?"

"All I could."

"Me too. Pride. Their lousy, stiff-necked pride. How many good people has pride killed? She's up there at the house thinking the roof has fallen in on her. She doesn't know it's the roof and the chimney and the whole damn sky, and it is a lousy time to have to tell her. What happened?"

"He was on his back on the ground and about five hundred pounds of scrap iron dropped on him from ten feet in the air. Head and chest, I'd imagine. I haven't seen him, and probably wouldn't know who I was seeing if I did."

"Jesus Christ, man, you don't tiptoe around things, do you?"

"Do you want me to?"

"I think already you know me better than that. Are they trying to call it an accident?"

"Suicide. He's supposed to have run a wire to the ratchet stop, lay down and yanked it loose. They found it still fastened and wound around his hand. Yesterday morning."

Suddenly her brown strong fingers locked onto my wrist. "Oh my dear God! Had he gotten the note she left him?"

"No."

I heard the depth of her sigh. "That could have done it. That could have been the one thing that could have made him do it. I think I got to know him that well. I think I know how much Jan meant to that poor big sweet guy."

"Not even that, Connie. At least not that way. He was murdered. But we've got to swallow the suicide story. All of us. We've got to act as if we believed it."

"Why?"

"Why do you think?"

"I think why use amateur talent when you can hire professionals."

"Rest your mind, Mrs. A."

"We'll talk after we get this sad thing done." She leaned abruptly into the car again. "You, girl. Do you dither? Do you bleat and snuffle and carry on?"

"Go grow yourself an orange, lady."

She threw her head back and gave a single bark of humorless laughter. "Maybe you'll both do." She pulled my seat back forward and scrambled into the back seat, rustling the discarded wrapping paper. "Let's go, McGee. The gate light turns off up at the house."

I wasn't prepared for a full half mile of drive, nor for the house at the end of it, big and long and low, with upswept drama of roof lines, something by Frank Lloyd Wright out of Holiday Inns. She had me park around at the side. "I'll have my people take care of the car and bring your gear in. You people use one bedroom or two?"

"Two, please," said Puss.

"Well, at least the thundering herd is sacked out by now. Her three and my two." She looked up at the stars. And we squared our shoulders and went in to drop the sky down upon Janine, to change the shape of her world and the shape of her heart forever.

It was one thirty in the morning when Puss came walking slowly into the big living room, yawning. Connie and I had been sitting for

a long time in the dark leather chairs near a small crackling of fat
pine in the big fireplace of coquina rock. We'd done a lot of talking.

"I think she's good until midmorning anyway," Puss said.

"But Maria better sit there by her just in case."

"She's there, Connie. If Jan wakes up, she'll wake us up. But it
isn't likely."

Puss went over to the little bar in the corner, put two cubes in a
squat glass, poured some brandy over them and then came over and
shoved the footstool closer to me, sat on it and leaned her head
against the side of my knee and yawned again. "She was trying to be
so damn brave," Puss said. "She wouldn't let go, and she wouldn't
let go, and then she did. And that's the best thing. Did you get the
calls through, Connie?"

"I got that Sheriff and told him she knew and she was resting, and
I'd call him back tomorrow and let him know what she's going to do
next. I got her people and got them calmed down. She'll have to
phone them tomorrow. And the boys have to be told."

"Jan said not to tell them," Puss said. "She said it's her job.
She keeps asking how we can be sure he never got her note."

Connie swirled the ice in her drink and then slugged it down.
"Know what I can't forget? Can't and never will? Five years and it's
still so clear in my mind. Every word that was said. Oh, it was a typical brooha. Tommy and I had hundreds of them. Yell and curse, but
it never really meant anything. We both had strong opinions. What
we quarreled about that morning doesn't matter. After he went
crashing out, I ran and yanked the door open and called after him.
'And don't be in a great big hurry to come back!' Maybe he didn't
hear me. He had his jeep roaring by then. He never did come back.
He didn't see the sinkhole and drove into it, and he stayed alive in
the hospital two days and two nights without regaining consciousness, and he died there." She stood up, wearing a crooked
smile, and said, "The guilts. That's what they leave you. Tomorrow
is going to be a long rough day too, people. 'Night."

I was on the downslope into sleep when the bed tipped under
Puss's stealthy weight and she slipped under the sheet and blanket to
pull herself long and warm against me, fragrant and gentle, with
some kind of whisper-thin fabric between my hands and her flesh.

"Just hold me," she whispered. "It just seemed like such a dark,
dark night to be alone." Her words were blurred, and in a very little

while her breathing changed and deepened and her holding arms went slack and fell away.

The four of us arrived in Sunnydale three days later, at a little before noon on Thursday. Connie Alvarez drove the lead car, a mud-caked black Pontiac convertible of recent vintage and much engine. Janine was beside her. When the road was straight, I had all I could do to keep them in sight. Puss mumbled now and again about Daytona and Sebring.

"The whole thing sounds so nutty," she said. "Do you really think that funny-looking little old judge knows what he's doing?"

"That funny little old Judge Rufus Wellington knows what everybody is doing. And he'll have had the whole morning to pry around." I braked at the last moment, pulled the rental around a bend and peered ahead for the distant dot that would be the Pontiac. "Have you got any questions at all about your little game?"

"Hah! Can the gaudy redhead from the big city dazzle the young, earnest attorney with her promissory charms? Will Steve Besseker, the shy counselor from the piney woodlands reveal the details of local chicanery to your glamorous wench? I might have a question at that."

"Which is . . ."

"You were a little vague about the details, McGee. Do I give all for the cause? Do I bed this bumpkin if it seems necessary, or don't you care one way or the other?"

I risked a high-speed glance at her and met the narrowed quizzical eyes of sexual challenge. I said, carefully, "I've always had the impression that if the string on the carrot was too long, and if the donkey snapped at it and got it, he'd lose his incentive and stop pulling the load."

"I resent the analogy and approve the sentiment, sir."

But challenges have to go both ways or there is no equality between the sexes. "On the other hand, I imagine that you're the best judge of your own motivations, and you would be the best judge of the appropriate stimulus and response. Such situations vary, I imagine."

"Are you trying to be a bastard?"

"Aren't we both trying?"

After a thoughtful silence she said, "Just for the hell of it, McGee, what would be your reaction if I said I'd keep the carrot on a mighty short string?"

"Killian, I would have to admit that I am just stodgy and old-fashioned enough to enjoy being the dog in your manger. I like a kind of sentimental exclusivity."

"Romantic exclusivity?"

"If you prefer."

"I prefer, thank you. So be it. I am now motivated to defend my honor. So suppose you watch yours."

The appointment had been set for twelve noon with Mr. Whitt Sanders, the President of the Shawana National Bank and Trust Company. I saw the empty Pontiac in the bank lot and parked near it and sent Puss on her way, wishing her luck. When I went into the bank, I could see Connie and Janine sitting in a glass-walled office in the rear, facing a big man across a big desk. The receptionist took me back, tapped on the door, and held it open for me.

Sanders stood up and reached across the desk and gave me a bully-boy handshake. He had tan hair and a big, sun-reddened, flakey face, a barrel of belly, a network of smile wrinkles and weather wrinkles, big red hands like ball gloves, and eyes that seemed to have the same size and expression as a pair of blueberries. "Mr. McGee!" he bellowed. "Pleasure! Sit right down and rest yourself."

I did and he said, "I was just telling the ladies that my sympathy goes out to Mrs. Bannon in this tragic time. You can rest assured, Mrs. Bannon, that the bank is doing everything in its power to liquidate the properties in question at the maximum figure obtainable. Of course certain unfortunate situations in that area have made it a difficult piece to move at this time, but we have negotiated something which I think anyone would agree is more than fair. As a matter of fact . . ."

And in came little old Judge Wellington with his cream-colored ranch hat shoved back, locks of white hair escaping in random directions, in his dusty dark suit and gold watch chain, carrying a briefcase that had perhaps first seen duty during the Lincoln-Douglas debates, his face remarkably like one of Disney's seven dwarfs, but I couldn't remember which one. "Hidey, Whitt," he said, "New paneling, eh? Purty."

"Rufus! I heard somebody say they thought they saw you over at the courthouse! *Glad* to see you."

"No. I'm not going to let you get aholt of my hand, Whitt. Not with my arthritis laying quiet for a change. So set."

Whitt Sanders looked confused. "Rufus, if you wouldn't mind waiting outside until I finish with——"

"Finish with my client? Now, even a jackass like you knows you can't keep a lawyer away from his client."

"*You* are representing Mrs. *Bannon!*"

"Why not? Mrs. Bannon is a dear friend of Mrs. Connie Alvarez here, and Miz Connie owns and operates To-Co Groves up to Frostproof, right in my back yard, which you may have heard of even down here in the wilderness, it being near three hundred thousand trees, prime Valencia on sour orange root stock, and she has enough legal battles going at all times with the Citrus Commission and the growers association and the concentrate plant she's got a stock interest in to keep me right busy in my declining years."

Watching the bank president, I realized it is possible for a big man to slowly come to attention while seated, and even give the impression of saluting. Connie had taken me on a tour of the groves, and I could see why Whitt Sanders reacted. For the first year after her husband had died, a management outfit had operated the groves on contract. Connie had spent every daylight hour with the crews and every evening studying, and at the end of the year she said she had been willing to take the risk of being able to do the job herself.

When we had come upon a trio of big spray trucks lumbering down the geometric lines, the nozzlemen garbed like astronauts, and I'd asked if bugs were a big problem, Connie had planted her feet, rolled her eyes skyward and chanted, "Kill off the burrowing nematode, the aphid, the rust mite, white fly, white-fly fungus, Mediterranean fly, red mite, six-spot mite, iron mite, Texas mite, mealy bugs, cushion scales, black scales, soft scales, yellow scales, wax scales, snow scales, purple scales, dictyospermum, melanose, citrus scag, mealy bugs and orange-dog caterpillars, and keep killing them off, and if you don't get a hard freeze, you've got half a chance, man, of hitting today's market with a hell of a nice crop, which at today's prices cost me one dollar and sixty cents more per box to raise than I get for them." She had shrugged, scuffed at the sand. "I counted on the over-production and set up a reserve. These prices are going to sink the half-ass operators and that'll cut production back to balance and bring back a fair price."

In the president's office the president said, "I didn't realize you were *the* Mrs. Alvarez."

"So I asked the judge if he could do anything to help my friend here, Jan Bannon."

Janine sat silent and motionless, dressed in darkness and the blueberry eyes of Whitt Sanders seemed to slide uneasily past her.

Sanders said, at last, "I guess I don't know what you're driving at, actually. The business holdings don't fall into the estate because there was an actual foreclosure before the time of death, with all proper advertising and notifications. So title passed. It's a standard first mortgage agreement, Rufus. Title passed to the bank."

"That so?" said the judge. "Funny. I got the impression that when I turn over to you the certified check I got here for ten thousand dollars in the name of Mrs. Bannon, that is going to cover back payments on principal, plus interest, plus fees and expenses, and leave a little over which you can apply on the next payment, and I got the impression that title is going to ease right on back to her."

"But the grace period is up! It isn't possible now!"

Judge Wellington sighed. "Bullshit," said he. Then he swept his hundred-dollar ranch hat off in courtly fashion, nodded toward Connie and Janine and said, "Begging your pardon, ladies." He dropped the hat on the floor beside his chair and said, "Whitt, I can't remember you ever being admitted to the Florida bar, so there's no point in me citing the pertinent and appropriate cases where the courts have ruled that in the cases of widows and orphans, especially where the widow was one of the parties on the mortgage, foreclosure action can be set aside provided the bank has not yet passed title on to a third party in a liquidation of the recovered assets."

"But we've accepted earnest money from——"

"One Preston LaFrance in the amount of three thousand two hundred and fifty dollars, representing ten percent of the agreed price on the foreclosed business property on the Shawana River, and the acceptance of that money did not constitute a change of ownership on the property, and here is the certified check for ten thousand, Whitt, and I request a signed receipt, with the date and the hour thereon."

"I can't accept it until I find out——"

"You take it and you make out the receipt saying you are taking it and holding it in escrow pending the decision of your legal people, or you and me are going to go around and around right here, boy. Besides, here is a situation where, by accepting the mortgage obligation and paying it up to date, Mrs. Bannon is putting that mortgage back on the books, sound and whole, in the amount originally owed and paid down to where this check puts it, and it would seem like a bank officer thinking of his stockholders—and thinking of the State Banking Commission—would snap at the chance to keep from showing a loss. Why do you seem to be holding back, Whitt?"

Sanders patted his red forehead with a handkerchief. "As you pointed out, Rufus, I'm not a lawyer. I don't know what our obligation to Mr. LaFrance might be."

"Absolutely no obligation, I can tell you, but you'll feel cozy hearing it from your own people, so we'll give you a chance to do just that. Suppose we come back at two thirty?"

"That . . . that ought to be time enough. Uh . . . Mrs. Bannon, do you intend to operate the business there yourself?"

"She's going to think about it," Judge Wellington said. "When her husband couldn't keep up on his insurance, he had the good sense to tell the company to apply the cash value to the premiums instead of drawing it out, so she has a little money to give her time to do some planning. We'll let you get on back to work, Whitt."

We left the bank and walked two blocks to the old Shawana River Hotel, and got a corner table in the dark-paneled, high-ceilinged old dining room. Janine was at my right, and the judge across from me. Connie and the judge and I ordered drinks. Jan didn't want any. There was a yellowish look to the tan of her lean, Mediterranean-boy face, and the skin of her face and hands had a papery look.

I touched her hand and said, "Okay?"

She gave me an abrupt nod, a smile that appeared for but a moment. The judge seemed lost in private thought. Finally he gave a dry little cough and said, "McGee, you seem to know what you're trying to do for this little lady, and I know Connie well enough to know she'll go along with some pretty wild ideas. But I've heard a few hints around the courthouse, and a few rumors, and I can put things together, and I wouldn't be doing right by my client not to give advice, whether it's wanted or not."

"I want your advice, Judge," Janine said.

He sipped his bourbon and licked his lips. "These little counties all got what you could call a shadow government. These folks have known each other for generations. They got to putting this land deal together, and there is a little business right in the way and doing pretty good. Expanding. So they use the county government to stunt that business and knock it down to where the price is right. It doesn't take all five county commissioners. Just a couple, plus the other three needing favors themselves sometime, with no need of anybody asking too many questions. You depended on highway trade and river trade, and giving service to local residents. Now they could have kept that road open to traffic and in pretty good shape too while fixing it, and set up a short-term contract on it. There's pollution-control ordinances on the books to keep that river in better shape. They could have denied that Tech something outfit when they petitioned to have the bridge taken out. When you didn't drop off the vine as fast as they wanted, then they put those regulatory services people onto you and really closed you down. Okay, Miz Bannon, you got squoze bad. So what I say is this. I say don't mess too fancy with these folk because in the long run you can't win. You can lay the squeeze right back onto them. I know how these folks think. You just say a hundred and twenty-five thousand, plus the buyer takes over the mortgage. No dickering. No conversations. Let them make the offers. When time starts to run out on them, somebody is going to get nervous and offer a hundred thousand, and then you by God grab it and walk away, and you'll know you've skimmed some good cream off their deal."

"That isn't enough," she said in a barely audible voice.

"But, girl, you'd be hurting them in the place that hurts the most. What are you trying to get out of this? Lord God, you can't make anybody *ashamed* of how they did you, even if they'd ever admit it wasn't just kind of a series of accidents. They just say it's dog eat dog and lots of businesses fail all the time."

"But they had Tush killed."

That little embellishment had been kept from the judge. He leaned forward, his old eyes wide. "You say killed? Now, young lady, I can understand how you could come to believe it was like that, but these folks just don't operate that way. That man of yours worked hard and long and it was all going down the drain, and sometimes a man gets to the point where he——"

"You didn't know Tush Bannon," Connie said. "I did. And Travis McGee knew him longer than either Jan or me. We're not taking any votes, Rufus. We're not talking about probably this or probably that. We're telling you he was killed."

Judge Wellington leaned back, so upset he tried to drink out of the glass he had already emptied. "Well now! Then, it must have been some fool mistake. It must have been something else that went wrong. Then, by God, the thing to do right now is put it in the hands of the State's Attorney for this Judicial District and . . ." He stopped suddenly and frowned at Connie. "By God, I must be getting old. He'd turn it over to the Assistant State Attorney for Shawana County, and the Shawana County Sheriff's Department would make the investigation, and the Shawana County Medical Examiner would do the autopsy, and all these folks are elected to office, and there'd be all the pressure to cover it over and forget it, and even if it went to a Grand Jury if it got that far, who'd get indicted? I'm getting so old I'm forgetting the facts of life. Second childhood. I'm thinking the world is like I thought it was when I was back in Stetson Law School." He scowled into his empty glass. "Maybe bring in somebody from the Attorney General's office to poke around?"

"Maybe," I said. "But first maybe we should blow some smoke down into the burrow and see what comes running out."

He thought and nodded. "Now I see why you want to do what you're doing. I won't say it has much chance of working. But it'll sure stir things up." He gazed at Jan. "Miz Bannon, I know it's a great and sad and tragic loss. And doing something about it can make a person feel better somehow. But don't aim all of yourself at that one thing, of paying somebody back. Revenge. Because it can turn a person sour through and through."

"I don't care what I turn into, Judge," she said.

He met her dark gaze, then opened his menu and said, "We better get our order in."

I went alone to Ingledine's Funeral Home and arrived at quarter of two. It was on a lateral street, and was a small version of Mount Vernon, sat between a Savings and Loan branch and a used car lot. I asked for Mr. Ingledine and the stealthy, earnest, unctuous young man told me that Mr. Ingledine had retired, and that he was Mr. Farris, Junior, and that he and his father owned and operated the establishment, and how could he help me, sir.

We tiptoed past an arched doorway where, under a rose-colored spotlight, a waxy pink and white old man rested, propped up in his bronze box, with floral offerings concealing whatever the box rested upon. Two old women sat on a couch on the other side of the room, holding hands and murmuring to each other.

Mr. Farris, Junior, opened a desk drawer in a small office and took a folder out, and extracted the death certificate signed by the County Medical Examiner.

"We obtained the vital statistics from available local records, sir. You might check them over for accuracy." Brantley B. Bannon, and the age looked right, and he had the next of kin right. The doctor had listed it as accidental death. I asked about it and he said that in the absence of any suicide note or any witnesses, and in view of the fact that he could have been working on the diesel engine, it would have been unfair to assume suicide.

"Would you care to . . . uh . . . view the remains, sir? I would not advise it. It's quite a . . . an extensive and nasty mutilation. There is absolutely no possibility of any reconstruction of the features. And I think it would be wise for you to discourage the widow from viewing the deceased. A memory like that would be . . . difficult to forget."

"What work have you done?"

"Well, a great deal of the blood was gone, of course. We trocared the rest of it as best we could, and the body fluids and so on, and by clamping some of the major vessels in the chest and throat area, we did manage to embalm to a certain extent. Let me see. Oh, yes, we were able to make positive identification so that we do not have to trouble anyone about that. They had at one time sold sandwiches and coffee at their marina, and the County Health Department requires a health card with a photo and thumbprint, and the Sheriff's Department verified the identity by taking a print from the body."

"You've been very efficient."

His smile was shy and pleased. "I am sorry, but I do not quite understand . . . what your function is in this, Mr. McGee?"

"Friend of the family, you could say. Here is a limited power of attorney, notarized, empowering me to make the arrangements in the name of the widow."

He looked at it with a faintly pained expression. "There'll be no services here, I would assume?"

"No. You can expect shipment instructions within the next few days." He led me back into the display room. The lids were propped open, the linings glossy, the handles burnished. They ranged from two twenty-five on up. I picked a three-hundred-dollar box. We went back into the office.

He said, "I'd recommend that we take the remains out of the storage vault and place the body in the casket and seal it, sir."

"I suggest you leave it right where it is, Mr. Farris, under refrigeration, until you get shipment instructions. And then please don't make a permanent seal. There could be an insurance question, on an accident indemnity clause."

"Oh. I see. But you should know that storage is costing eleven thirty-three a day. That's with tax, of course."

"Of course. Now may I see your statement on this?"

He took the statement from the folder and took it into the next room. I heard the slow tapping of unskilled typing. He brought it back and handed it to me. He had added the box and two more days of vault rental. The total was seven hundred and fifty-eight dollars and thirty-eight cents.

"Mr. McGee, I am sure you will understand our position when I point out that it is our information that the deceased *was* a bankrupt, and we will have to have some assurance that . . ."

The certified check for a thousand dollars that I placed in front of him stopped him abruptly. I said, "Is this top copy mine? Just acknowledge the receipt of a thousand dollars on it, Mr. Farris, and when the body leaves here, deduct any further charges from the credit balance and mail your check to Mrs. Bannon, To-Co Groves, Route Two, Frostproof. And I see you have a photocopy of the death certificate, so you can let me have the original? Thank you."

He went with me to the front door, through the ripe smell of flowers in full bloom, through the muted organ music.

He put his pale hand out, smiled his pale smile, and said, "Please express our sympathy to the bereaved."

I stared at his hand until he pulled it back and wiped it nervously on the side of his jacket. I said, "Junior, you could make a tangible expression of your sincere sympathy."

"I don't believe I follow you."

"Before you send her the check for her credit balance, just refigure your bill. She's a young widow with three boys to raise. You padded it by at least two hundred and fifty dollars. I think it would be a nice gesture."

His face went pink. "Our rates are——"

"Ample, boy. Real ample."

Outside I took a deep breath of Shawana County air, but there was something vaguely industrial in it, some faint acid that rasped the back of my throat.

We were moving in, stirring them up with a blunt stick. The old judge, with good law and good timing, was snatching the ten acres right back out of the hands of LaFrance, just when he thought he had his whole deal lined up. And soon he would know a stranger was moving into the game, buying some chips, asking for somebody to deal. When in doubt, shove a new unknown into their nice neat equations and see how they react.

Hungry men think everybody else is just as hungry. Conspiratorial men see conspiracy everywhere. I strolled through industrial stink toward the bank.

6

WE GATHERED again in the bank president's office at two thirty. Sanders had the Bannon file on his desk, and a Mr. Lee, an attorney for the bank, sitting near his left elbow. Lee had a round, placid face and a brushcut. He could have been thirty or fifty or anything in between.

With obviously forced cordiality, Sanders said, "Well, Mrs. Bannon, the bank has decided to accept your payment and mark the mortgage account current and in good order."

Judge Wellington yawned. "You say that as if you had choice in the matter, Whitt. All right. My client is grateful. She thanks you." He opened his old briefcase and pawed in it and took out the papers that had been prepared Wednesday afternoon in the judge's law offices. He flipped them onto the desk in front of Whitt Sanders, saying, "Might as well get this taken care of too, as long as we're all foregathered here. Everything is all ready to record, but what we need is the bank's approval of the transfer of the mortgage from Mrs. Bannon to Mr. McGee here."

Mr. Lee hitched closer to the president as Sanders leafed quickly through the legal documents. He stared at Judge Wellington with a look of astonishment. "But . . . according to this, she's selling her equity in the property for fifteen thousand dollars, Rufus!"

"Wouldn't you call that a pretty good deal? Sixty thousand mortgage balance, and you were going to sell the whole kaboodle for thirty-two five and have a judgment against the estate, if any, for twenty-seven thousand five. So she pays the mortgage down to fifty thousand, then sells for fifteen thousand, which puts her five ahead instead of twenty-seven five behind. Why, this little lady is thirty-two thousand five hundred better off right this minute than she was when she walked in here. Or maybe you just look surprised she did so good. Remember, she's got a good lawyer."

"But we can't just . . . approve this transfer. We don't have enough information. Mr. McGee, we'll have to have a credit report on you, and we'll have to have a balance sheet and income statement. This would be *highly* irregular. I have a responsibility to——"

"The stockholders," the old judge said. "Whitt, you went through those papers too dang fast. Try it a little slower."

He did. He came to an abrupt stop. He stared at Connie. "You'll be the guarantor on the mortgage note, Mrs. Alvarez?!"

"That's what it says there, doesn't it?"

"If you're still nervous, Whitt," said the judge, "go look up To-Co Groves in your D. and B."

"Oh, no. I didn't mean anything like that. It was just . . ."

The judge sighed. "Could we just stop fumbling and get the red tape done so we can get this stuff recorded and set out for home?"

"Excuse me just a moment," Sanders said. He took Mr. Lee out of the office with him and over to a quiet corner of the carpeted bullpen. They held about a forty-second consultation. I hoped I knew exactly what it was about. I looked to the judge for reassurance, and got it in the form of a slow wink, an almost imperceptible nod.

Mr. Lee came back in with Sanders. He was apparently nominated by Sanders to put the matter into careful legal jargon.

"Mrs. Bannon," he said, "whether or not your sale of your interest to Mr. McGee is final at this moment, the bank feels that it is ethically obligated to inform you that shortly after two o'clock this afternoon a local attorney contacted Mr. Sanders here and asked him if the sale of the foreclosed properties had been consummated. When Mr. Sanders said that it had not, this attorney then said he was representing a party whose name he could not divulge, but who had directed him to inquire of the bank if, in the event the properties had not been sold, a firm offer of eighty thousand dollars would be sufficient to acquire it."

Sanders then interrupted, making Lee look exasperated for an instant. "It isn't a firm offer," he said to Janine. "But I don't think young . . . the local attorney would make a trivial inquiry. You see, if your arrangement with Mr. McGee isn't firm, or if he would like to withdraw, this might be a lot more advantageous for you. You would get back your ten thousand, plus the overage above the sixty-thousand mortgage, or another twenty thousand."

Jan had been coached in how to react, by the judge, if Puss had been successful in conning the young attorney, Steve Besseker.

"But couldn't this mysterious party be the same Mr. Preston La-France you were going to sell it to?" Janine asked.

"I don't think it would be very likely that Press would——"

"But haven't you told Mr. LaFrance he wasn't going to get my property?"

"Well . . . yes," said Sanders uncomfortably.

"Then, couldn't he turn right around and make a bigger offer through a lawyer, if he wants it bad enough?" she asked.

"It might be possible. Remotely possible."

"But don't you see," she said, frowning, earnest, leaning forward, "Mr. LaFrance owns the acreage directly behind us. He's been after our property all along. He's schemed and plotted to drive us out of business, Mr. Sanders, so he could buy it, and so he's responsible for what . . . my husband . . . responsible for . . ."

She snuffled into her handkerchief and Sanders, edgy and uncomfortable, said, "Now, there. Now, now, Mrs. Bannon. We all like to have some specific thing or person to blame when . . . when things don't go right. I'm sure Press LaFrance wouldn't——"

"My husband was convinced of it, and that's enough for me," she said spiritedly. "Why, I wouldn't accept any blind offer like that if it was . . . twice as much. Three times as much! I would rather sell it to Mr. McGee for eleven cents than see that man get it!"

Whitt Sanders fussed with the documents in front of him. He looked over at Rufus Wellington. "Rufus, I'd be way out of line, as you well know, if I made any comment about . . . about the re-sources of anybody doing business with us. All I can say is that . . . it is remotely possible the attorney is representing Press LaFrance. But it isn't very damn probable."

"You telling me, Whitt, it's pretty much a known fact around town this LaFrance couldn't scratch up eighty thousand?"

"I didn't say that."

"Around the courthouse this morning, Whitt, talking to the County Clerk, and passing the time of day with your Assessor, I got the feeling things are a little slow lately in the land business in Sha-wana County. Now if this LaFrance is up to his hocks in land deals, he might be like the fella with the itch who was juggling the family china and walking a tightrope, and a bee stung him right square on . . . Sorry, ladies, we'll leave that one right there. Probably got a good-looking balance sheet, all considered, and you got some of his notes, but you won't go one more dime, and you're a little nervous about him." The judge laughed suddenly and slapped his thigh. "By God, Whitt, that explains how come you acted sorry as a skunked hound you couldn't sell off the foreclosure to this LaFrance. He must have some deal in the making that would get him free and clear. He into you a little deep, boy?"

"Now, Rufus," Sanders pleaded. "I haven't told you a thing, and I'm not about to."

"Not in words," the judge said. "But we've set in poker games together, Whitt, and I never had much trouble reading you."

So then the red tape was taken care of, and the necessary documents were recorded at the courthouse. I walked with the judge to his black air-conditioned Imperial and he stopped out of earshot of his driver, who had gotten out and opened the door for him.

"Son, we sure God rammed a crooked stick into the hornet nest and stirred it up. There'll be folk sitting up half the night trying to make sense out of it all, not knowing it doesn't make sense—not the way they're thinking. Make sure you keep back far enough from the hornets."

"I'll be careful, Judge."

"You tell that big sassy redhead she did good. That's as much woman as a man is likely to see in a long day's journey. Where are you meeting up with her?"

"Not anywhere near here," I said. "Back at Broward Beach. She said she could probably get Besseker to drive her over there, and if she couldn't, she could get there somehow."

He squinted into the late afternoon sunlight and said, "There's a gal like that so clear in my mind it's like yesterday, son. And that was nineteen twenty and six." He turned to me with a look of dismay. "And if she's alive anyplace in the world, she's somewhere in her sixties. Hard to believe. Know something? I wrote poems to that gal. First, last and onliest time in my life. You let me know how you make out with that old swamp rat, that old D. J. Carbee, will you? McGee, tell me one thing. Are you going to let the angries get in the way of pumping some cash money out of this for that widow girl and her kids?"

"The money first, Judge."

He looked at his watch and grinned. "The way Connie drives, they're probably halfway back to Frostproof by now."

It took me a long time to find anybody who could give me any kind of clear directions on how to find the Carbee place. He had no phone. He had a post office box in Sunnydale, and it was his habit to come in no oftener than once a week to pick up his mail.

In the end I had to go over the unending construction project that ran by my new property. Florida is full of long-range, unending road jobs that break the backs, pocketbooks and hearts of the roadside business. The primitive, inefficient, childlike Mexicans somehow manage to survey, engineer and complete eighty miles of high-speed divided highway through raw mountains and across raging torrents in six months. But the big highway contractors in Florida take a year and a half turning fifteen miles of two-lane road across absolutely flat country into four-lane divided highway.

The difference is in American know-how. It's know-how in the tax problems, and how to solve them. The State Road Department has to take the low bid, by law. So Doakes Construction says a half-year contract will cost the State ten million, and a one-year contract will cost nine, and a year-and-a-half deadline will go for eight. Then Doakes can take on three or four big jobs simultaneously, and lease the equipment from a captive corporation, and listlessly move the equipment from job to job, and spread it out to gain the biggest profit. The only signs of frantic activity can be two or three men with cement brooms who look at first like scarecrows but, when watched carefully, can be perceived to move, much like the minute hand on a clock.

Of course if some brisk, hustling firm moved into the state and started bidding what the jobs are worth and doing them fast, it would upset the tax tea cart. Some have been foolish enough to try it, and the well-established Contractor's Club has just taken round-robin turns low-bidding the interloper to death. When he has quit for lack of work, things settle down to the cozy old system whereby, through some miraculous set of coincidences, all the big boys have exactly the amount of work they need at all times.

A couple of governors ago, when too many road jobs were not up to specification, somebody ratted and there was a big hassle about the State Road Department engineers and inspectors getting envelopes with cash money therein from some of the club members. Those contractors were restrained from bidding for a little while, and the engineers and inspectors were suspended. But it died down, as it always does, and the companies were reinstated with authorization to bid on upcoming work, and the state employees were put back on the job also, with the governor explaining that men should not be judged too harshly for a "moment of weakness," even though it had been made quite clear they'd had their little moments of weakness every Friday afternoon for a long, long time.

The Shawana County project of repaving 8oD was the same thing on a smaller scale. Though the workday was not over, the only sign of roadwork I saw was one bulldozer and one scraper parked and unattended off the side of the rutted road. I stopped at my dead business property, tore off the official notices of foreclosure, and decided against busting the shiny padlocks with a tire iron. Near the far end of 8oD I found the sand road I was told to look for. It wound through scrub toward the bay shore, and when I drove into the clearing at the end I saw the traditional old Florida shack of cypress and hard pine set high on pilings, so that looking under it I could see the bay water and a crooked little dock with a skiff tied up.

There was a twanging of dogs toenailing the wire of their run, and a heavy throated *Arooo, Arooo* of the indigenous hound. I was standing by the car looking at the hounds when the voice directly behind me said, "Evenin'." It gave me a violent start and when I whirled, I could see from the glint in his faded old eyes that he enjoyed the effect.

In the days before age hunched him and withered him, he could have been nearly my size. His sallow jaws were covered with long gray stubble, and his head was bald except for a sparse white tonsure. He wore torn, stained khaki pants with a narrow length of hemp line for a belt, and an old gray twill work shirt. His feet were broad and bare, and standing near him was like standing near a bear cage, but with a slight spice of kerosene amid the thickness of the odor.

I gestured toward the dog run. "Red Walkers?"

"Got some Walker in 'em. I don't sell no dogs this time of year. Got just one bitch carryin' but she got loose on me just the wrong time, so God knows what she'll drop."

"Mister Carbee, I didn't come by to look at dogs. I came on a business matter."

"Waste of time. I don't buy a thing except supplies in town and send for the rest out of the Sears."

"I'm not selling anything."

"They say that and I ask them to set, and it turns out they are after all."

"It isn't like that this time."

"Then, you come set on the stoop."

"Thank you. My name is McGee." When we had climbed the steep steps and were seated, Carbee in a rocker and me in an old kitchen chair that had several generations of different shades of paint showing, I said, "I just bought the Bannon place on the river from the widow."

"Did you, now? I seen her once and him twice. Heard he kilt himself last Sunday morning when he found he'd lost the place. Great big old boy he was. Him and that Tyler Nigra come on me one morning drifting on the bay. Year ago maybe. Heavy fog, and me out too deep to pole and the ingin deader'n King Tut. That Tyler knows ingins like he invented them. Spring thing busted on the little arm for the gas feed, and that Tyler fixed it temporary with a little piece of rubber, got it running good. That Bannon wouldn't take a thing for it. Neighborly. Couldn't been too much longer after that Tyler quit him. Heard Tyler is working at the motorsyckle place in town. Anywhere there's ingins he's got a job of work. Maybe Bannon knowed and maybe he didn't that when Tyler quit him, it was because no Nigra with sense like Tyler's got is going to stay in the middle of any white man's fussing. If you're going to run that place, Mr. McGee, the first thing you better do is get Tyler back, that is if you're peaceful with everybody."

"I'm not going to run it, Mr. Carbee. I bought it as an investment."

"Lease it off to somebody to run?"

"No. Just let it sit."

I let him ponder that one, and at last he said, "Excuse me, but it don't make good sense, unless you got it for the land value alone. The buildings are worth more than the land."

"It depends on who wants the land."

He nodded. "And how bad."

"Mr. Carbee, I've been checking land ownership at the courthouse. You own the two-hundred-acre piece that starts at my east boundary."

"Could be."

"Ever thought of selling it?"

"I've sold a little land now and again. I've got maybe seventeen, eighteen hundred acres left, scattered around the east county, and except for this hundred right here, my home place, I imagine it would all be for sale if the price was right. You thinking of making an offer? If so, you better come up with the best you can do right off, because I don't dicker. Man names a price, I say Yes or I say No, and that's it."

"Best offer, eh? I better tell you, Mr. Carbee, that I would be gambling on being able to pick up other parcels too, and gambling on being able to do it while my chance of resale is still good, resale of the whole two sections. And I'll tell you right now that if everything *does* work out, I'll make a nice profit, but if it doesn't, I'll have some working capital tied up until I can find some way of getting it back out. The best I can offer on an immediate sale—provided the title is clear of course—would be five hundred an acre."

He rocked forward and slapped his big bare feet on the boards and peered at me. "One hunnerd thousand!" he whispered.

"Less your share of the closing costs."

He got up and stamped over to the railing and spat. I knew the turmoil in his mind. He had wanted to check and see if he had optioned the two hundred acres to Preston LaFrance at a good figure. Two hundred dollars an acre had seemed like a good deal until I named my price. I could assume Tush's investigation was correct, and LaFrance's option was good until April. He wouldn't dare tell me about the option, for fear I would make my deal with LaFrance. And he was afraid that if he told me the land was not for sale, opportunity might move on to some other location and then he might not even get his two hundred an acre.

It was a pretty problem, and I wondered how he would handle it. He came back and sat down. The chair creaked. "Tell you what," he said placidly. "I have to think on that. And I should talk to the man that turns in the government figures for me when I sell things and see where that would put me on taxes and so on. Let me see now. This being Thursday the twenty-third day, that would mean two weeks from today would be . . . January fourth. Then I'll know more what I should ought to do. A man can't jump at a piece of money like that right off. He has to set and taste it a time."

"I understand. But you will have to tell me Yes or No when I see you again."

"One other thing. You said you were taking a gamble. What you might do is figure on maybe me taking some of the risk too, Mr. McGee."

"How so?"

"From what you said, if your deal doesn't work, then you got a hundred thousand tied up and it will take a long time to move that land at that price. But if it goes like you're hoping, you turn a good profit on it. Maybe double?"

"Maybe not."

"Let's think on it being double. One thousand dollars an acre, two hundred thousand all told. So maybe we could get a paper drawed up between us, a contract saying that you give me five thousand cash money in hand that says come next . . . oh let's say April the fifteenth . . . you got the right to buy the land from me for four hundred an acre if you're willing to buy and I'm willing to sell. And if it works out that way, then if you resell it any time inside two years or three, you agree to pay me half the difference between what you bought it for and what you get for it. So if it was for one thousand, you'd for sure clear three hundred an acre profit, and no chance getting stuck with it. Of course if I want to sell on April the fifteenth and you don't want to buy, I keep your five thousand. But if you want to buy and I've decided not to sell, you get it all back."

He looked at me, benign and gentle and O so eager to be agreeable and fair to all. Way up the coast from us were the little nests of the hideaway mansions of the international bankers, and to the south of us was all the trickery and duplicity of hotel and resort syndicate financing. He had the precise look of a man betting into a pair of kings showing, and him with a three in the hole and a pair of threes up, and a perfect recollection of having seen the other two kings dealt to hands that had folded, one of them a hole card inadvertently exposed when the hand was tossed in.

"Mr. Carbee," I said. "I think we'll get along fine. You might even sell me an undivided half interest for two hundred an acre, and we could make it a joint venture."

"It'll be a pleasure to do business with you, Mister."

It seemed to me that old Mr. D. J. Carbee could have floated very nicely in the tricky currents of Hobe Sound or Collins Avenue, and I had a sudden respect for the guile of Preston LaFrance. But I did not envy him the little talk he was going to have to have with the old man just as soon as the old man could catch up to him. There was a shaggy old high-sided International Harvester station wagon parked over near the dog run, and it seemed probable that D.J. would be going into Sunnydale either this evening or early in the morning.

It was full dark when I drove into the city of Broward Beach. The stores were open, because tomorrow was Christmas Eve. Hefty Salvation Army lassies in their wagon-train bonnets dingle-dangled spare change into their kettles, and fat foam Santas were affixed to the palm boles and light standards, high enough to keep the kids from yanking their foam feet off. "Adeste Fidelis" was coming from some- where, possibly a downtown church, electronic chimes that could rat- tle fillings in teeth, and overpowered the retail sound tracks of sprightlier seasonal music. I went through town and out to the beach and parked in the lot of the place I had told her to be, an expansive, glossy, improbable motel called Dune-Away, with a place pasted to it called The Annex, where food and drink was worth the prices they charge, even in the off season, and where if an attractive lassie wishes to be picked up, the hard-nose management will smooth the way, and if she doesn't, those same professionals can chill the random Lothario quickly, quietly and completely.

I looked at the lounge from the doorway and saw her alone at a banquette against the far wall. As I headed across toward her I was aware of a wary waiter also moving on an interception course. But he and I saw her quick recognition and saw her face light up in greet- ing. So he held the table out for me to sit beside her, and went off with our order.

"You missed our boy by ten minutes," she said. "He was very dear. Not my type. One of those narrow-boned dark ones, a bit stuffy. He wants to be with it, but he laughs a little too soon or a little too late, and he seems to sit and steer his car instead of drive it. Let me see. He's thirty-one and he's been married to Linda for five years, and they have two kids and she is a fantastic golfer, and her father owns the Buick Agency in Sunnydale, and he is worried about her drink- ing. He kept giving me a certain business with the eyebrows that maybe he learned in front of his mirror, and I made his hands clammy when we sat close. He didn't have the guts to take a hack at me right out of the clear blue. He'd have to be encouraged so that then he could tell himself he hadn't started it, and he's only human, isn't he? He's very nervous about the impression he makes, and he's steeped in all that radical right wing hoke about conspiracies and a bankrupt America and Chinese bombs, and it was a drag to listen big-eyed to that tired gunk and say Oh and Ahh and Imagine that! He does a lot of civic stuff and joins everything, and thinks of him- self as being the fearless attorney, standing up for right and purity.

As the dear judge would say—Bullshit. He tried to help Tush Bannon, and then when it got a little sticky, he dropped him. Know how he explained it to me? This is precious!"

She paused for the waiter to serve the drinks, then went into an imitation of Steve Besseker: "So long as we are operating under the Capitalistic System, Puss, and remember it is the best the world has yet devised, men will take business risks and some will win and some will lose. I won't deny there were certain pressures on Bannon, but he got so he thought everything was some kind of a plot. He started whining and stopped fighting. That's when I lost my respect for him and washed my hands of him."

"Yes," I said. "That is precious. That is very dear."

"I never met your friend Tush, Travis. But I don't think he ever whined."

"He wouldn't know how. Congratulations. You snowed him very nicely. Have any trouble with it?"

"None! I hitched my chair closer and closer to his and I kept my voice very low and full of secrets, and I kept my eyes wide and I put my fingertips on his arm. I told him that I was employed by Gary Santo and we had investigated him and it was Mr. Santo's decision that he could be trusted with certain delicate and private negotiations involving one of Mr. Santo's operations in this area, and could be trusted not to reveal the name of his client. I explained that it was so hush-hush that if he was foolish enough to even try to reach Mr. Santo by phone or in person, he would ruin everything for himself. But if things went well, then he could think in terms of a retainer of five figures annually. You know, when he began to swallow it, his eyes looked glazed and his mouth hung open. I almost started laughing. So he phoned the query about the eighty thousand to the bank like a good little fellow, and he was *so* upset when he met me later and told me that Mrs. Bannon had regained title and then sold it to some mysterious stranger named McGee from Fort Lauderdale. I thought he would cry. I told him I was sure that Mr. Santo would be convinced that he had done all he could. I told him he would get his instructions from me by phone or in person. I asked him if he would be willing to meet me sometimes, if it was necessary. In Miami, or even Havana or New York. All expenses paid, of course."

"Who told you to say that?"

"I made it up. It seemed like a good idea. I mean it makes him think more about me and not so much about it being a pretty funny way for a man like Santo to do business. Was I wrong?"

"No. I like it. And the final little hook? Did you remember to get that in?"

"Yes, but very casual, and not until he came in here to have a drink with me. I just said that I know the way Mr. Santo's mind works, and he would certainly wonder if there was any connection between a Mr. Preston LaFrance and Mr. McGee, any business connection, and if he could find out in advance of my phoning him about it, it might make a good impression on Mr. Gary Santo."

"Reaction?"

"Nothing in particular. He said he'd try to find out." She shrugged. "He's just a trivial little man, honey, really. And this is the first little whiff he's had of something big and important and kind of glamorous, and he can't hardly stand it. Feed me, please. I'm sitting here aching and gnawing, and I keep looking at that door where the waiters go by with those steaks."

She ate with a savage and elegant precision, and an occasional little sound of contentment. I told her that as a reward for special sly services and for being a persuasive liar, I would stake us to the most elaborate accommodations the Dune-Away could provide.

"And go back in the boat in the morning?" she asked. "Would it be vulgar, dear, if I asked a special favor? So much has happened and I am so pooped, really, that all I can think about is that gigantic, fantastic, marvelous bed aboard the *Flush*, and it would be a nice place to wake up on the morning before Christmas, and I want to get to that bed faster than your pretty little boat can get me there. Possible?"

"Race you to the car, Red."

She was asleep by the time I hit the first stoplight, and slept all the way back, and groused about being shaken awake to walk from the car to the houseboat. I made her stand on the dock while I went aboard and, before unlocking the door, checked the little bulbs behind the sliding panel in the outside port bulkhead of the lounge. The bulbs were out, so I turned the knife switch below the bulb, turning off the little Radar Sentry that monitored the below-decks areas of the *Flush* while I was away from her. Had anyone broken in, their mass and movement would have closed the circuit that lighted the two hidden bulbs, or lighted one of them if by any chance the other had burned out. The gadget can be rigged if anyone wants, to turn on floodlights or sound a siren or even phone the cops. But I didn't want an alarm system that would spook the intruder. I just wanted to know if I'd had visitors, and then I could take the necessary steps to make them welcome if they happened to be still there.

I beckoned her aboard, and she came inside, stumbling and yawning. We shared a shower, and then we shared a lazy, easeful, gentled quarter hour of love, wherein she murmured she didn't think she could but don't go to any special trouble, darling, it doesn't matter that much, and then she murmured that if it wasn't too late for a lady to change her mind, sir, and it was just barely not too late to be able to wait just long enough, and so she rose, and caught, sighed long, and fell away purring. She called me back from my edge of sleep by gently thumbing my left eye open and saying, "Are you there? Listen, for making all these days and nights so full, the lady thanks you. Thanks for letting me come along for more than just the ride, McGee. Thanks for helping me cram three bushels of living into a one peck basket. Are you there?"

"You are O so welcome, lady."

7

MEYER CAME over on Christmas morning with a cumbersome vat of eggnog and three battered pewter mugs. We had a nice driving rain out of the northwest and a wind that made the *Flush* shift and groan and thump. I put on Christmas tapes because it was no day to trust FM programming. Sooner or later daddy would see mommy kissing Rudolph. Meyer and I played chess. Puss Killian, in yellow terry coveralls, sat and wrote letters. She never said who they were to, and I had never asked.

He won with one of those pawn-pressure games, the massive and ponderous advance that irritates me into doing the usual stupid thing, like a sacrifice that favors him, just to get elbow room on the board.

As we finished, Puss came over, shoving her letter into her pocket, and said, "Should we call Jan and say merry, merry? Which is worse, I guess, to call her or not call her?"

"There's one of Meyer's laws that covers it. Tell her, Meyer."

He beamed up at her. "Of course. In all emotional conflicts, dear girl, the thing you find the hardest to do is the thing you should do. So I guess you call."

"Thanks a lot. Trav? Will you do it? Please? Then you can turn it over to me. Okay?"

So I placed the call. Connie sounded too hearty. I guess it wasn't such a great day at the groves. Janine imitated the requirements of friendship and holiday. But there was deadness under her tone of voice. I knew she would not break up, not with that weight of the deadness holding her down. After all the things to say I could think of, most of them so trite I felt like both Bob *and* Ray, I gave the phone over to Puss. She sat at the desk and talked for a long time with Janine, in low tones. Then she said Connie wanted to talk to me again. She said Janine had gone to her room, so she could talk freely. She asked me when the body would be picked up. I said I'd made arrangements and they would come and get it tomorrow. The holidays had caused a delay.

"Any communication from sunny Sunnydale, Connie?"

"Nothing at all. Nothing yet."

As I hung up I turned and saw Puss leaving the lounge, almost at a gallop, and heard her give a big harsh sob.

I looked at Meyer and he shrugged and said, "The tears started to drip, and then she started to snuffle and then she took off."

I filled our mugs and brought him up to date on my financial affairs in Shawana County.

He pondered the situation and said, "It's pretty flexible. There's a lot of ways it could go."

"That's the general idea. To keep my skirts clean I have to have a legitimate sale of my legitimate ownership in that marina and motel. I think that's where I pick LaFrance clean. If he could offer thirty-two five, I'll settle for forty thousand, *and* he assumes the mortgage. He'll have to go for it because that's the only way he'll have a package he can provide Santo—his own fifty acres, my ten, and the option on old Carbee's two hundred. Now this LaFrance is a greedy and larcenous bastard. He was trying to make the deal as sweet as possible for himself by driving Tush into the ground and getting those ten acres cheap. I think he will continue to be a greedy and larcenous bastard, and I think that if I can offer him a little extra edge, for cash under the table, he'll get the cash somehow, and I hope it will be from that brother-in-law of his on the County Commission." I went and checked the name in my notebook. "P. K. Hazzard. Known as Monk. He—meaning Preston LaFrance—is going to be very jumpy, so you and I are going to work a little variation on the old pigeon drop."

His big bushy brows climbed his Neanderthal forehead. "We are?"

"Meyer, I think you'd make a nice plant-location expert, somebody with the authority to make firm recommendations to a nice big fat rich company."

"It is an exact science, my good fellow," he said. "We take all the factors—labor supply, area schools and recreation facilities, transportation costs, construction costs, distance from primary markets, and by adjusting these by formula before programming the computer, we can arrive at a valid conclusion as . . . Travis, what is a pigeon drop?"

"Unlike what might first come to mind, Meyer, this is something one drops *onto* a pigeon."

"You couldn't have made it more clear. One thing. Aren't you on a little dangerous ground on this body-snatching thing?"

"Body-snatching! Me? Meyer! A perfectly legitimate funeral home in Miami is going to pick up that body in a licensed hearse and bring it back to Miami and air-ship it from there to Milwaukee."

"And the place is run by a man who owes you a big favor, and that hearse is going to make a stop at a very well equipped and staffed pathology lab during the off hours, where two more of your strange friends are going to determine if there was some cause of death besides dropping an engine block on him."

"Meyer, please! It's just normal curiosity. Jan gave her permission. Is there an ordinance against it?"

"What about concealing evidence of a crime?"

"If you're nervous about evidence we don't even have yet, you don't have to help me play games with LaFrance."

"So who's nervous?"

"I am. A little."

We sat in silence. The tape had run out and turned off. I wondered if I should go in and give Puss a little comforting pat to cure the Noël blues. Too many pasts crowd in on you at mistletoe time. It's the good ones that hurt.

"Meyer?"

"At your service."

"On the sale of the marina thing to LaFrance, Jan will end up with thirty thousand, net. If we can work that pigeon drop, she'll get maybe fifty, maybe a hundred on top of that. Money won't buy what she's lost, but it would be nice to get her a really good big chunk. If I could find out that Gary Santo knew about what was being done to the Bannons, knew about it and didn't give a damn because he was pressuring LaFrance into assembling the adjoining parcels so he could buy them for resale, then it would be nice to take a slice of his bread too."

"Now *wait* a minute! This is not somebody that goes for your pigeon drop. This man operates very big, my friend. He has lawyers and accountants double-checking every move."

"I was thinking of something legitimate. Something in your line.

Like some kind of an investment where you would know it was going to go sour and he wouldn't. Then couldn't there be some way of . . . funneling money out of the same proposition into Janine's pocket? Hell, Santo is a plunger. With all the protection, he's still a plunger. Some kind of a listed stock, maybe, like those they are rigging on the American Exchange you were telling me about one time."

"So why should Gary Santo listen to Meyer?"

"Because first we build you a track record. You dig into those charts of yours and make some of those field trips and surveys and come up with some very very hot growth items. And I think I've got just the pipeline, once I develop it a little, to feed them to him. The pipeline is named Mary Smith. She has brown straight glossy hair. She is small, and stacked, and she looks sullen and hungry."

"So if the great Gary Santo knew nothing about your friend Bannon?"

"I know Tush tried to get to him and couldn't get past the girl-curtain. He didn't think Santo was the kind of man who'd want the little guy crushed under his wheels. Somehow Santo squeezed La-France and LaFrance squeezed various folk, which happened to include Tush. If Santo knew—and let the roof fall on Tush—for a lousy little crumb of the acreage he needs up there, then I would like to have him get it where it stings. And, if so, can you work up something?"

Meyer got up and plodded back and forth, all hair and simian concentration, and scowling little bright blue eyes. He stopped and sighed. "McGee, I don't know. I just don't know. The problem divides itself into two interdependent parts. First I would have to get a line on a dirty situation like Westec before it leaks out. Those people falsified their earnings statements to keep the stock at a high level so they could pick up smaller companies on favorable merger terms. Then one executive put in for eight million worth of stock, traded on the American Exchange, and he couldn't come up with the money to pay for the stock and that's when trading was suspended. Now *if* I could smell out something like that, heading for disaster, and then if I can pick a few legitimate winners to make him feel as if I——"

"Or as if you *had* picked some winners, Meyer."

He looked startled for just a moment, and then came that broad Meyer smile that turns one of the ugliest faces of the Western World into what one of the articulate lassies among the Meyer Irregulars one season called "a beautiful proof that someday, somehow, the human race is going to make it."

"Dated, official, machine-printed confirmations of stock purchases on official forms from a reputable brokerage house! Hindsight! Perfect! One day, maybe two, in New York, and I can come back with proof I'm such a genius I bought——"

"You had *me* buy . . ."

"Yes. I see. I had you buy highfliers right at the point where they were taking off, and I don't have to go back far, less than a year in every case. Gulton, Xtra, Leasco Data, Texas Gulf Sulphur, Goldfield Mohawk Data. Fantastic performers! Listen, I won't make it too good. If every buy was at the bottom, there'd be suspicion. Like instead of Gulton at fifty dollars a share, you get on at sixty-five."

"Where is it now?"

"It went up to nearly a hundred and ten, split two for one, and the last time I looked it's maybe sixty dollars." He sat down and emptied the nog mug again. "Travis, how rich do you want to be? I can use an old and dear friend who will be delighted to help, so I can get you monthly margin-account statements showing the security position, the debit and so on."

"Say I started a year ago with a hundred thousand."

"Congratulations! You are now worth a quarter of a million."

"Success hasn't spoiled me, Meyer. Have you noticed?"

"All I notice are your criminal instincts, my dear Travis, and how rash you are with your queen, which lets me whip you at chess, and how right now you are too tightened up over this Tush business. You are too close to this one. Be careful. I don't want to lose you. Some terrible people might take over Slip F-18. Nondrinkers, going around saying shush."

Puss Killian came drifting back into the lounge, looking wan. Her face was puffed, her eyes red. She snuffled and then honked into a Kleenex, and said, "Give me that Meyer's Law again, please? The exact words."

"In all emotional conflicts the thing you find hardest to do is the thing you should do."

"I was afraid that was what you said, Meyer. What we all do is make excuses why we shouldn't do the hard things. Like apologize. Like visit the dying. Like spend a little time with bores."

"Stop short of masochism, dear girl," Meyer said.

"I always have. Too far short, maybe. Gad! I feel as if I'd been pressed flat and dried out, like an old flower in a bad book. Do something, gentlemen!"

And so we did. Meyer and I went off in opposite directions, head-hunting. He had a quota of five—three female and two male. I went after two couples. It is an old contest. They can be friends, or acquaintances, or absolute strangers. After the festivities, we rate them on a scale of ten, the measurement being whether or not you'd be willing to spend a month on a small boat with them. We made a good Christmas bag, because there was a compulsion to have a good time. We unfastened all the umbilical devices affixing the *Flush* to her mooring space, and, with eighteen yuletide souls aboard, chugged down into the breadths of Biscayne Bay under clearing skies, edged the old girl as close as I could get her to good beach with good protection near Southwest Point, stayed the night in drink, argumentation, minimal sleep, beach walks, a touch of skinnydipping for those brave hearts who can stand the December waters, and came trundling back up to home base the next day.

Sometimes it doesn't work at all, but this time it had jelled. There had been some good minds, outrageous opinions, furious squabbles, laugh-till-you-cry incidents, games and contests, confessions and accusations, tears and broad smiles. But no sloppy drunks, no broken crockery, or teeth. We aimed homeward tired and content and, for the most part, friends. Waterborne group therapy, Meyer calls it. It restored Puss Killian. Late on Tuesday afternoon as we were scoring our recent boatmates, with Puss as arbiter when we disagreed, she said, "Does anyone else have the feeling that little jaunt lasted at least a week?"

"When they don't seem to," said Meyer, "they haven't worked." Which could be another one of Meyer's Laws, but he says it is too close to aphorism to be significant.

8

WEDNESDAY, December 27th, before Puss and Janine and I had to catch the flight out of Miami to Milwaukee for Tush's funeral the next day, I had a chance to talk with Dr. Mike Guardina at the lab. I left the gals with the car and told them I wouldn't be long, so not to wander too far.

Mike took me into a small office and closed the door, and took a folder out of the locked file. He is thin, intent, strung on taut wires, totally intent on finding out why people die. He is qualified in about all the kinds of pathology they have.

"Trav, the first impression was of too much damage. Way too much to go with the way it was supposed to happen, from what we found on your roll of film once we made prints. So much damage that actually trying to locate any specific tissue damage or bone damage not likely to have been caused by the impact of that weight dropping on him would have been pretty iffy. About all we can say for certain is that there is a good chance he wasn't shot in the head first, nor much of a chance that there was any blow that struck him from behind. Now you *did* want a cause of death to a reasonable medical certainty, but I gathered from your conversation over the phone with me that you want suicide ruled out if possible."

"But if you can't——"

"This is another approach. Take a look at these." He put three 8 x 10 glossies on the desk top. He pointed with the eraser end of a yellow pencil. "This is a blowup of the central portion of one of your pictures, Trav, where you had that block cranked high and you aimed up at it. See these rusty hexagonal nuts along here, toward what we will call the rear end of the block? Look at this one in particular. Somebody apparently tried to knock it off with a cold chisel, and knocked off a third of it before they gave up. Now this next print is full frame, of the chest area of the subject. Note these three marks circled with a grease pencil, and marked A, B and C. This third print is actually a triptych, an enlargement of A, B and C. The area marked A shows a clear imprint or incised impression of that damaged nut. The encircled B area shows the same imprint exactly, and it is about four inches from the point marked A, in a lateral direction across the crushed chest, from right to left. Imprint C is, as you can see from the print of the whole chest area, another inch and a quarter or inch and a half further, going from right to left, from imprint B. But here, as it struck, or would seem to have struck a previously damaged area, we do not have as obvious an identical match. However, if you want me to project the thirty-five millimeter color slides we took of points A, B and C, I think you will see that it is reasonable to suppose that impact area C represents the same deformed nut."

"In simple lousy English," I said, "you are certain that the engine block was dropped onto him twice, and you can make a case that it could have been dropped, cranked up, dropped again, cranked up, and dropped the third time."

"Yes," said Mike. "It wouldn't be consistent with suicide."

Long ago and far away I could see Tush Bannon under the needle spray in the long shower room that smelled of old socks, soap and disinfectant, rubbing up a suds on that barrel chest and bawling, off-key, ". . . and this is my storrrreeee, as you can plainly see. Never let a sailor put his hand above your kneeeeeeee."

"Spare me the slides, Mike. Can I have dupes of these?"

"Got them right here for you. Smaller. Five by sevens. Okay?"

"Fine. And what about a grand jury? Will it make you nervous if we don't do a thing?"

"What could you do with it? Somebody got clumsy. They found him crushed under that thing and so they cranked it up and it slipped and fell on him again and they cranked it up again and locked it. He was obviously dead, so why make a big statement about the crank slipping? We can't prove the third drop, even though I feel certain it happened. You understand what I'm saying, Trav. In a court of law any neophyte defense attorney could set up an area of reasonable doubt you could take a truck convoy through."

"But if there ever comes a time for affidavits?"

"Me and Harry Bayder, and the tape going as we worked, and a resident in pathology taking notes. Time and place, and an accurate identification of the body, and signed statements in the file from all three of us. Just in case. If and when you ever get something else to go with it."

"You are a good man, Guardina."

"Beyond compare, surely. Keep in touch, hombre."

All I could tell Janine, or wanted to tell Janine, was that any last faint possibility of suicide was long long gone. I told her on the way out to the airport. She didn't say a thing. I had my hands on the wheel at ten of and ten after. She reached up and put her long fingers on the ten after wrist. At the chapel in Milwaukee, when we bowed our heads in prayer, I looked down at the underside of my right wrist and saw the four dark-blue half moon marks where her nails had bitten deep. Her parents thought she should have brought her three young sons to the services. They thought Tush should have been shipped sooner and buried earlier. They thought she should come home with the boys and stay. They thought her tailored navy-blue suit was not proper attire for a widow. They thought it odd she had brought along this McGee person and this Killian woman when there were so many old friends who were—or should have been—so much closer in a time of need. They resented not knowing Connie Alvarez. They had remembered that she had been at Janine's wedding, but they let it be known she had struck them as a rather coarse and peculiar person, not at all the ladylike type their daughter should cultivate. They made it clear that it was an affront to them that poor Janine should go back immediately to Florida with these . . . these *strangers*.

On the flight back we had three side by side. Janine was in the middle. She said, turning her face from Puss to me and back, "I'm sorry. They just . . . they aren't . . ."

Puss hugged her and said, "Honey, if you put the knock on them you'll feel like a traitor. Everybody has people, and their people don't want to let them go or admit they're gone when they're gone. They love you. That's good enough. Right?"

"Should I have brought the boys? That's what I keep wondering."

"Ask each one of them when he gets to be twenty-one, dear. Ask them if they felt as if they had been left out of anything," Puss said.

So they sat, holding hands, and Jan fell asleep. Puss gave me a sleepy wink and then she was gone too. I looked out of the jet at December gray, at cloud towers reaching up toward us. Tush was gone, and too many others were gone, and I sought chill comfort in an analogy of death that has been with me for years. It doesn't explain or justify. It just seems to remind me how things are.

Picture a very swift torrent, a river rushing down between rocky walls. There is a long, shallow bar of sand and gravel that runs right down the middle of the river. It is under water. You are born and you have to stand on that narrow, submerged bar, where everyone stands. The ones born before you, the ones older than you, are upriver from you. The younger ones stand braced on the bar downriver. And the whole long bar is slowly moving down that river of time, washing away at the upstream end and building up downstream.

Your time, the time of all your contemporaries, schoolmates, your loves and your adversaries, is that part of the shifting bar on which you stand. And it is crowded at first. You can see the way it thins out, upstream from you. The old ones are washed away and their bodies go swiftly by, like logs in the current. Downstream where the younger ones stand thick, you can see them flounder, lose footing, wash away. Always there is more room where you stand, but always the swift water grows deeper, and you feel the shift of the sand and the gravel under your feet as the river wears it away. Someone looking for a safer place can nudge you off balance, and you are gone. Someone who has stood beside you for a long time gives a forlorn cry and you reach to catch their hand, but the fingertips slide away and they are gone. There are the sounds in the rocky gorge, the roar of the water, the shifting, gritty sound of sand and gravel underfoot, the forlorn cries of despair as the nearby ones, and the ones upstream, are taken by the current. Some old ones who stand on a good place, well braced, understanding currents and balance, last a long time. A Churchill, fat cigar atilt, sourly amused at his own endurance and, in the end, indifferent to rivers and the rage of waters. Far downstream from you are the thin, startled cries of the ones who never got planted, never got set, never quite understood the message of the torrent.

Tush was gone, and our part of the bar was emptier, and the jet raced from the sunset behind us to the night ahead, and beside me slept the two women, hand in hand, their lashes laying against the high flesh of their cheeks with a heartbreaking precision, a childish surrender, an inexpressible vulnerability.

By Saturday, the next to the last day of the year, I was beginning to feel surly and uneasy. I held a slack line. I felt that I had deftly pulled the barbed hook through the underlip of one Preston La-France, and that boating him was inevitable. He had to come aboard the *Flush*, flapping, gills working. The name McGee had suddenly cropped up at too many points in his life. McGee at the bank with the widow. McGee at Ingledine's, making the arrangements about the body. McGee out at the old shack, souring his deal with old D. J. Carbee. McGee, the new owner of the property he wanted.

But the line lay slack on the water, without the slightest twitch or tension. Puss and I drove up to Broward Beach early Saturday morning, turned the car in, and came back down the Waterway in the *Muñequita*. I made a fast run, thinking I might find LaFrance when I got back to *The Busted Flush*. Nothing. Puss was withdrawn, remote, and did not help my mood by telling me she was going away Monday morning for a little while. A few days. No clue as to where or why. And be damned if I'd ask. As she packed a bag it seemed a gratuitous affront that she should hum to herself. What was she so cheery about?

And why didn't Meyer phone from New York? Too busy having a fine time with old stockbroker buddies, probably.

At ten minutes after four the slack line twitched. I tested the tension cautiously. It was still through the underlip. I shooed Puss into the master stateroom and invited Preston LaFrance into the lounge. He came in, grinning, hesitant. A gaunt and ugly and sandy one. Maybe the young Sinclair Lewis, if the old photographs are accurate. Fifty percent hick. Fifty percent con artist. Cowlick. Long lumpy face. Lantern jaw. Nervous cough. Ploughboy hands. Brash sports jacket with the wrong button buttoned. A gangly diffidence overlaying a flavor of confidence. When he looked around the lounge, his expression vague, I had the feeling he saw everything that had any bearing on his own aims and motives, and could price the whole layout within plus or minus three percent.

His big hand was warm, dry and utterly slack. "Mr. McGee, we seem to be aiming in kind of the same direction on a little matter, and what I thought, I thought it might be time to see if we can eat out of the same dish or spill the dinner."

"I guess that depends on how hungry we are, LaFrance. Sit down. Get you a drink?"

"Mostly I'm called Press. Short for Preston. Thank you kindly, and if you would have such a thing as a glass of milk, that would be fine. I had an ulcer and got over it, and they tell me sipping milk instead of kitchen whisky will keep me from having the next one. And I guess you've upped my milk bill by maybe half, Mr. McGee."

"Mostly I'm called Trav. Short for Travis. And we stock milk, because there is very little damn else you can put on cornflakes."

"You are so *right!*"

I brought him his glass of milk, and a beer for me. He sat on the long yellow couch. I pulled a chair a little too close, turned the back toward him and straddled it, forearm along the back of the chair, chin on the forearm, expression politely expectant and benign. It put my face two feet from his, and six inches higher, with the brightest window right behind me. Closeness is a tactical weapon. We do not like our little envelope of anticipated separation and privacy penetrated. It is a variable distance, depending on the needs and necessities of the moment. We endure the inadvertent pressure of the flank of the office worker in the crowded down-elevator at five o'clock. If we are alone with the office worker, if it is male—without overtones of fag—then it is insolent challenge, demanding action. Being jostled in a crowded airport is acceptable; on a wide and empty sidewalk it is not. A fixed stare is a form of penetration of the envelope, carrying different messages according to the sort-out of sex, station, race, ages and environment.

Always we want some separation, some tiny measure of distance regardless of how clumsily our culture mechanizes an inadvertent togetherness. The only exception time is when sex is good in all dimensions, so that even in the deepest joining there is the awareness of that final barrier, an apartness measured by only the dimension of a membrane, and part of the surge of it is a struggle to overcome even that much apartness.

The lounge aboard the *Flush* is a sizeable enclosure, and I positioned myself well inside the area of logical separation. Once you learn the expectations of distances, small and great, you can use them in tactical ways, watching for reaction, for a pulling back, a pained stiffness of expression, an awkwardness. Or position yourself beyond the plausible distance and watch for the forward lean, the advance, the slight what-is-wrong-with-me agitation. It is a kind of language without words, a communication, and incites a reversion to the primitive compulsion of the pecking order, the barnyard messages—You get too close so I peck you back to where you belong.

Press LaFrance sipped his milk, looking down into the glass. He looked to the side and reached and put the half glass on the end table. He then hiked one limber Ichabod leg up, heel on the edge of the couch cushion, long fingers of both hands laced around his ankle, slouching just enough to interpose the knee between us so that he looked at me over the top of it. With that interposition he increased the subjective distance between us.

"Fifty mortgage plus fifteen cash equals sixty-five thousand," said he. "And that is better than twice what any licensed appraiser would put on it."

"For the same use Bannon put it to. A man with his house on fire and a man dying of thirst would put a different value on a glass of water."

"Hard to put a value on 'if,' Trav. Link three or four ifs together and it comes out long odds, so you can't go very high."

"There are some men, Press, who get a little confused between greed and shrewdness. Maybe they are a little bit shrewd, and then they want to buy at the lowest dollar and sell at the highest, and finally it comes out as if they weren't shrewd at all. They end up doing the very same thing as if they were stupid to begin with."

The knobbly face colored a little and the mouth stiffened then relaxed as the color faded. "A fella could have made an offer way back, through a third party, and a fair offer, all considered, but somebody could have been too bullheaded to listen."

"Fair offer?"

"We aren't talking marina, McGee. We aren't talking motel. You know that and I know it. We are talking ten acres."

"Ten acres in the middle of the deal, smack in the middle of it, like a June bug in the birthday cake."

"So I was coming up with thirty-two hundred and fifty an acre for those ten acres."

"Which gives you sixty acres, if you'd gotten it. What did the fifty behind Bannon's place cost you?"

"A fair price."

"One thousand dollars in nineteen fifty-one, according to the tax stamps on the deed as recorded in the Shawana County Courthouse, which comes out to twenty dollars an acre. That was probably a fair price in nineteen fifty-one. We can do a little arithmetic, Press. When you pay me forty thousand for clear title to the Bannon place, and assume the mortgage, then you have a ninety-one-thousand cost figure on the sixty acres, or just about fifteen hundred an acre. That will turn you a profit of five hundred an acre on resale, or thirty thousand, and because you are a reasonable man and because you are in a bind, you are going to be sensible and take it."

He was absolutely immobile for long seconds. I think he even stopped breathing. He dropped the knee, swiveled and got up and peered down at me. "Man, you lost your cotton-pickin' mind for sure! That would be two thousand an acre on resale! The deal with my buyer is for nine hundred. I couldn't pay you any forty thousand and take over a fifty-thousand mortgage! I'd come up with a loss of six hundred an acre. Where do you get this crazy two-thousand figure?"

"Why, Press! You'd make out just fine on nine hundred an acre! You've got old D. J. Carbee screwed. You pay him two hundred an acre, or forty thousand, and you resell it to Gary Santo for nine hundred, which comes to a hundred and eighty thousand. So deduct that thirty-six thousand you'll lose on that sixty acres, and there you are, fat and sassy, and a hundred and forty-four thousand ahead."

He picked up the glass and drained the milk, wiped a chin-drip on the back of his wrist. "D.J. told me he didn't tell you a thing about that option. So by God, you knew about it when you went and offered him five hundred an acre. You upset that old man something pitiful."

"Maybe I was trying to upset you, Press."

He sat down on the far end of the yellow couch. He shook his head like a sad hound. "What in the world are you after, McGee?"

"Money. Just like you, Press."

"You knew I had to show up here. You left a trail and you left loose ends. But you didn't do all this just to charge me forty thousand for something that cost you fifteen."

"That isn't much profit, come to think of it. What do you think I ought to charge you? Sixty? A hundred?"

"Oh, come *on!*" he wailed.

"You can't come up with much. You've got the shorts, haven't you? Overextended?"

"Don't you worry about *me!*"

"But I *do!* I'll tell you what I'll do for you, LaFrance. I'll pay you fifty thousand dollars in cash for your fifty acres *and* the option you've got on the Carbee acreage. Then you're out of the whole thing with a nice profit."

He stiffened. "Hell *no!* Then you got the whole two hundred and sixty acres Santo wants to buy."

"But I wouldn't sell it to him. The price isn't right."

"But you can't move it, McGee, unless you move Santo's parcel at the same time! Calitron has to have the whole four hundred and eighty acres. You know the rest of it, so you have to know that much."

"I know the Calitron Corporation will go as high as seventeen hundred an acre to Gary Santo." It was nice to have the name of the corporate buyer.

Preston LaFrance brooded about it. "He never did let on what he expects to get. But there's not a damn thing anybody can do about that. Hell, Santo can just let his land sit there for ten years. He doesn't have to sweat these things out."

"In a smaller sense, Press, that's my policy too."

He looked startled, and then alarmed. "Now, you wouldn't squirrel up the whole deal by setting on that little ten acres forever, would you. Jesus, man, Calitron will go somewhere else if they get held up! Then where are we?"

"Maybe I've got a buyer who doesn't need that much room. I'm thinking of your health, Press. Fifty thousand and no more worries, and your ulcer will feel fine. You can pay off some of the notes at the bank and make Whitt Sanders happy."

His jaw firmed up. "I'll play it like a Mexican standoff, mister. I'll squat on my fifty and you squat on your ten."

"It's like what you said when you came in. Do we learn to eat out of the same dish or do we spill the dinner? Know what the difference is, Press? I'm not hungry and you are."

He cracked the knuckles of both hands, methodically, one at a time. "Now you said something about being shrewd and being greedy both and how it turns out stupid, Trav. I've been working on this thing one way or another for a year and a half, about. The way things are, I have to make it big, and that's the truth. Not big the way Santo thinks about money, but big for me. I'm leveling with you. I've got to come out of this six figures ahead any way, or with the present timing I'm going to end up way the hell back where I started in forty-six when I got out of the service, and I don't want for that to happen. I had it within an inch of being home free, and you slipped in out of nowhere and bollixed it all up for me. Okay, it was smart business and you're pretty cute. So right now I think it's up to you to find some way to fix it so we get to eat out of the same dish, each to his need. I've got my good option out of old Carbee, even if he is thinking about shooting me since you went to see him. And I got the fifty acres behind your place."

"As long as you're leveling, you can settle one thing that bothers me a little. Back when you found out Bannon wouldn't sell and wouldn't budge, and if you had the shorts so you couldn't offer him enough, why didn't you turn the problem over to Gary Santo. With what he'd stand to make, he could have paid Bannon twenty cents for every dime he had in that business, and bought him a new location."

"I told Santo about that! I had that same idea. It took me a whole month to get to talk to him face to face, and then I had to chase him up to Atlanta, where they were opening up a hotel he's got money in, where he's got a penthouse thing he keeps for himself. I was up there drinking and waiting around maybe an hour and then he was ready to talk and we went back into one of the bedrooms and I told him these Bannons were a nice little family, working hard and doing pretty good, and if he could make them a good offer, which I wasn't in any shape to do, then we were all ready to move. So he said don't bother me with the details, LaFrance. He said that if he had to take care of all my problems, why should I have a slice of the cake. He said that come next May first he'd pay the full two hundred and thirty-four thousand for a clean, clear title to the two hundred and sixty acres to the east of his holdings, or I could forget the whole thing. And that was what I couldn't do, McGee—forget the whole thing."

"So you broke them. You busted them down to a price you could afford. You didn't have any other choice."

"No other choice in the world, excepting to go broke myself. I swear, if it had been my own brother running that place, it would have had to be just the same. But let me tell you, I never did count on Bannon killing himself. That never entered my head one minute. We were having a late Sunday breakfast in the kitchen when I got a phone call telling me what he'd done, and after I hung up and thought about it, I went right in the bathroom and threw up. I swear, it made me sick. I was in bed most of the day. Suzy wanted to call the Doc, but I told her it was just probably something I ate at the hotel Saturday night, at the testimonial dinner for old Ben Linder, retiring from the law, looking like a little old gray ghost the way the cancer is eating him up." He sighed. "You know, having you come out of noplace and snatch those ten acres away from me is like punishment for what Bannon did to himself. It's like getting the word that nothing ever is going to work out right anymore for me, and things used to go so good there for a while."

"Maybe Bannon didn't kill himself."

His sagging head snapped up. "What are you trying to do now? What kind of new game are you playing?"

"Just a thought. I suppose it was pretty well known who was putting the pressure on Bannon and why. Maybe somebody wanted you and Monk Hazzard to be appreciative. Maybe they roughed Bannon up just to prove a lot of real diligence and cooperation and went a little too far. And if Bannon just happened to die on them, it would be a pretty good way of fixing it so that nobody would ever be able to find out that Bannon took a bad beating."

He chewed a crumb of skin off the corner of his thumb. "Suzy said if it was sure going to crush a man's head anyway, he might as well be face down so he couldn't see it falling . . ." He straightened and shook his head. "No. There's nobody around who'd do a man that way. Nobody I know. Nobody Monk knows."

I looked at my watch. "I'll tell you exactly what you do, Press. I'll be up there on Thursday the fourth. I'll have somebody with me who can tell you something you might find interesting. But the only way you can get to talk to him is to have that forty thousand in cash or certified check all ready and waiting, and I'll have a deed and closing statement and so on. Show me the money and then you can talk to the man I'll bring along. Then you can decide whether you want to buy the Bannon place. Because that's the only way you're going to have any dish to eat out of."

He stood up. "Otherwise?"

"Otherwise I just wait you out, and I wait until the Calitron deal is dead, and then I make my own deal with Carbee, because he certainly isn't going to renew that option with you, and then I see if my buyer can get along without your land and without the Santo land, and I think it's quite possible that two hundred and ten acres might be enough."

"You wouldn't be running a bluff?"

"Prove you have forty thousand to get into the table stakes game, and we'll give you a little peek at the hole card. Believe me, it's the last and only chance you've got."

From the dock he looked back toward me, standing on the after-deck. He shook his head and said, "You know, damn it, McGee, it's almost easier dealing with that son of a bitch Santo. At least you know more about what the hell is going on."

I went back in and hollered to Puss that she could come out. I took a yellow cushion off the couch and lifted the little Sony 800 out of its nest and took it over to the desk. We'd used up two-thirds of the five-inch reel of half-mil tape at three and three quarters ips. I unplugged the mike and plugged in the line cord to save the battery drain and rewound it to the beginning. I stretched out on the couch and Puss sat cross-legged on the floor and we listened to it all the way through. I got up just once and held the rewind key down a few moments, and replayed the account of the talk with Santo in Atlanta, and let it continue on from there.

At the end, Puss got up and punched it off and came over and hip-thumped herself a little room on the edge of the couch. "Is that what we've got for a villain, dear? That weak, scared, sly, sorry man? Just scrambling and hustling and trying to keep his stupid head above water? So his stomach hurts all the time, and he threw up."

"Settle for Santo?"

"Maybe indifference *is* the greatest sin, darling. I'll settle for Santo, until a new one comes along. McGee, tomorrow is New Year's Eve."

"So it is. So it is indeed."

"How would you feel about no throngs, dear?"

"I was thinking about trying to prove two is a throng."

"I think two people could purely lang the hell out of auld zyne if they put their minds to it. Is it zyne, or syne or what?"

"It is old acquaintance ne'er forgot."

"New acquaintance ne'er forgot. What happens to people who start on Black Velvets and taper off on champagne?"

"They seldom remember their own names."

"Let's try for that."

A slow gray rain came down all day long on the last day of the year. We kept the *Flush* buttoned up, the phone off, ignored the bing-bong of the regulars who were drifting from boat to boat. It was a private world, and she provided a throng of girls therein. Never had she released all that mad and wonderful vitality for so long. She had come all the way out of the shell she had been keeping herself in for the last few days. We peaked at that point where the wine held us in an unreal place, neither drunk nor sober, neither sane nor crazy, where the funny things were thrice funny, where all the games were inexhaustible, where tears were part of laughter or sadness, and every taste was sharpened, every odor pungent, every nerve branch incomparably sensitized. The ones who are half alive can reach that place, perhaps, with their trips and their acids and their freaking, but reality truly felt, awareness made totally aware, is a magic they can't carry around in powdered form. She was a throng of girls and she filled the houseboat and filled the day and filled the long evening. Some of the girls were ten, and some were fifteen, and some were ten thousand years old. And, like Alice, I had to run as fast as I could to stay in the same place. HAPP-eee New Year, my love . . .

I awakened on Monday with the impression that I might have to get up and bang my head against the wall to get my heart started. The bedside clock was at seven after eleven. No hangover. Just that leaden heavy contentment of an expenditure so total the account was seriously overdrawn. I plodded my way into the vast shower stall, soaped and then stood swaying, eyes closed under the steaming roar, like a horse sleeping in the rain. Finally out of a sense of duty and character I fixed the heads to needle spray and switched it to cold. As I hopped and gasped, I thought dourly of how inaccurate are all the bridegroom jokes about window shades. A long and private holiday with a sizable, sturdy, vital, demanding and inventive lass leaves you with the impression that you had merely rowed a couple of tons of block across a lake, then ran them up to the top of a mountain with a dozen or so trips with a wheelbarrow, then rolled back down the mountain into the lake and drowned.

As with sad and reminiscent smile I was reaching for my toothbrush, I noticed that hers was gone. Okay. So she had packed early. But while brushing, I reached my free hand up and opened the other cupboard. It was bare. She had taken everything of hers, for the first time in all these months.

I rinsed and spat and wrapped the big damp towel around my waist and went in search of her. Of course there was nothing of hers left aboard. She was gone. She had scotch-taped a note to the side of the coffeepot. It was in her freehand printing, using a red ballpoint.

And so, my scruffy darling, cometh an end to all good things. End-

eth with a flourish, what? You are the best that could have happened to me. It isn't Killian and it wasn't Seattle, so don't waste time and money. And nothing you said or did. Your saying and your doing are a memorable perfection. I am just not a very constant type, love. For once I wanted to quit when I was ahead. Think kindly of the girl. Because she did love you, does love you, will love you from here on in. Cross my heart. (Say my good-byes to all the good ones.)

Instead of a signature she had drawn a circle with two little almond shapes for eyes, and a great big curved line for a smile. Three tears were dripping down out of each eye.

But, damn it, I wasn't *ready* yet.

Those were the words in my mind. I read them back and suddenly understood them, and I sat down in the booth suddenly full of self-understanding and self-loathing.

Sure, Puss-baby. We just hadn't reached the cutoff point where McGee would make the break on *his* terms. Which would have kept you from quitting while you were ahead. The key word is 'Yet.' So all that's hurt is pride, you sorry son of a bitch.

I could have done without that kind of self-revelation. I felt like a very trivial and tiresome animal, a sluggish animal sitting slumped in its tired slack hide—hide that bore the small and involuntary marks of fang and claw of the otherwise gentle she-thing now gone for good. Who is the user, Trav baby, and who is the used? And have you ever given anybody anything worth the having.

I clamped my jaw until my teeth squeaked and my ears buzzed. Why such a big hang-up over another promiscuous broad? Town was full of them. Go whistle up another one. Be the jolly old lover-boy, and be glad the redhead left before she turned into a drag, before she started bugging you about making it something legal and forever, and a-crawl with kids.

I like last year's McGee better.

9

MEYER WAS back on the second day of the new year, back on Tuesday at ten in the morning, and came over in his New York garments after leaving his suitcase off on his boat, so eager was he to display the fruits of his efforts.

There were two thin sheafs of brokerage house forms, paper-clipped together. He sat across from me in the galley booth and said, "That batch is the monthly margin account statements."

The forms were printed in pale blue ink on a thin off-white paper. The name of the firm was but vaguely familiar. Shutts, Gaylor, Stith and Company. 44 Wall Street. New York 10004. Established 1902.

"And these are the confirmations of purchases and sales. The prices are correct for the date of sale. The monthly statement of account checks against the confirmations, of course. The monthly statements cover eleven months, including last month. I put in several where you bought at such and such a figure and then sold after they'd gone up just a few points. They went up further and then dropped like stones. I gave you two small losses, short term, on the same basis. In effect in eleven months you built a hundred thousand into almost two hundred and ninety thousand, so that according to the summary, right now you could sell two hundred thousand worth, pay a twenty-five percent long-term gain, and pocket a hundred and fifty thousand, leaving almost your original investment in the securities you'd still be holding."

"What about anybody checking it out?"

"Your account number . . . that number there . . . oh-three-nine-seven-one-one-oh, that's in legitimate sequence. Somebody started an account eleven months ago, then canceled out. It's a small, conservative, reputable house. I can tell you that there is not one other person in the world they would do this for. I had to make so many solemn oaths I've forgotten half of them. If anybody checks back to the margin clerk, he will say it is all legitimate. If anybody tries to go further, they will come upon either Emmet Stith or Whitsett Gaylor, who'll confirm."

"So how did I make payment to them?"

"Always by check on the Bank of Nova Scotia in Nassau."

It was beautiful. There is no way that even a Gary Santo could pry information out of the Bank of Nova Scotia. It is a system some call Zurich West.

I leafed through the sheets. I had bought at the right time. I'd done very well.

"So what is wrong with you?" Meyer asked.

"I'm just great. Nifty peachy."

"You are stimulating. Like a dirge. Where's Puss?"

"Gone for good."

"So!"

"So?"

"So I don't think you drove that one off. So it was her choice. So she isn't the kind who says it is for good and then comes back all of a sudden. With her, gone is gone. So if I were you, I would be just as bad off as you look. Or worse. So if I were you and one like that was gone for good, I'd miss hell out of her and wonder if maybe I'd handled things a little differently somehow, I could have kept her around permanently."

"That's enough about 'so.' "

He got out of the booth. "When you want to be civilized, I live over there on a boat. *The John Maynard Keynes.* Fourteen hundred and forty a year, special annual rate, less a discount for paying the year in advance. Ask for Meyer."

"Okay, okay. These sheets are perfect. You did a hell of a job up there. You are intelligent, crafty, loyal, persuasive and diligent. Puss or no Puss, the job goes on. LaFrance showed. I'll play you the tape. It's interesting. He spilled the name of the company. Calitron. Mean anything?"

"A name only. Listed on the big board. A growth issue, going at thirty times earnings. Volatile. I'll check it out. Play the tape and I'll go away and let you sit and chew your hands and moan a little."

"I'm glad I depend on you for sympathy, Meyer."

"What sympathy should you get? A little arrangement, wasn't it?

A sea urchin arranged the meeting. The urchin didn't wash up, she didn't step on it, what have you lost? Don't answer! Your disposition you've lost. Play the tape before I start to cry."

I put it on. I stretched out on the yellow couch. I closed my eyes. If I opened them quick enough, turned my head quick enough, I would see Puss sitting cross-legged on the floor, scowling as she listened to Preston LaFrance.

When it was through, I turned it off. Meyer sighed. He said, "I think he will have the forty thousand. Even knowing I was hearing nonsense, I could believe you a little. Forty thousand is better than getting poked in the eye with a stick."

"You left something out. Did you find the kind of a company Gary Santo should invest in?"

After the first five sentences I was totally lost. I stopped him and told him to start over again, and give it to me in baby talk.

He sighed; pondered. "Try this. A company has only so many shares of stock issued. The number of shares is called the 'float.' When there aren't many shares, it is called a 'thin float.' Somebody buys ten thousand shares of General Motors, he might move it up an eighth of a point—twelve and a half cents a share—just by the effect of his demand on the floating supply. But if he put in an order for ten thousand shares of Peewee Incorporated, the demand might shove it right through the roof. It might boost it four or five dollars a share. Are you with me?"

"So far."

"Every day in every newspaper it shows you, with the two zeros left off the end, how many shares of every listed stock were bought and sold. People watch like hawks. Two kinds of people. One guy wants capital gains. He wants to buy something for twenty dollars a share, hold it for six months and a day, sell it for forty a share, pay Uncle twenty-five percent of the profit in capital-gains tax, or five dollars, and put fifteen in his pocket. Other characters are traders. They sit in brokerage offices and watch the tape. They want to buy a stock for twenty a share, sell it next week at twenty-five, when it drops down from twenty-six, buy it back at twenty-seven, sell at thirty, buy back at twenty-eight, sell at thirty-five and so on. They pay straight income tax on their net gain. Gary Santo is the first type, the capital-gain guy, because all his income is being taxed at the maximum rate already."

"Still with you, Professor."

"Splendid! Now when something good is going to happen to a little company, the number of shares sold and bought every day goes up. It becomes more active. The price of the stock goes up. So it gets noticed. So more people want to get in the act and make a buck. That creates more demand. The demand pushes the price higher. In every trade, Travis, nobody can buy unless somebody is willing to sell. The more people who want to hang on, the fewer shares floating around, and the higher it goes, because the price has to go up to the point where somebody will say: Okay, I've made enough off this stock, so I'll sell it. I'll put in my order to sell it at two dollars a share higher than it is right now. It is a big snowball rolling *up* the hill. Okay?"

"One thing. What keeps Santo from making a lot of money too?"

"Nothing, if he gets out in time. But look at the credentials I fixed you up with. All splendid values back at the time you bought them, at the time you apparently bought them. Stock prices go up because the company is *making* money, and has the look of making *more* money than before when they make their next earnings report. So the stock I found, Santo will think it has the same beautiful future like these you made the capital gains out of. They are still all hanging up there pretty good. So why should he be nervous? I tell you, he would be nervous if he knows what a terrible lousy stock I found."

"What is it?"

"A dog called Fletcher Industries. I read maybe two hundred balance sheets and operating statements. I started with two hundred and weeded down and down and down, hunting for something that looks okay fine on the surface but is rotten underneath. It could win a prize for the worst stock. It has a thin float. It shows sales and profits going up every year. It has a nice profit margin, nice book value, big words in the annual financial report about a glowing future and so on."

"So what's wrong with it?"

"This I shouldn't even try to explain. Listen, there are maybe eight perfectly ethical and legitimate choices a C.P.A. has when he is figuring profit per share. Each choice makes the profit higher or lower, accordingly. You could find some old conservative companies that make the eight choices so they show the lowest per share profit. Most companies make one choice one way, another, another way, so in general it cancels out. But this little Fletcher outfit, they use every chance they have to make profits look bigger. I reworked their statements. The stock sells right now for fifteen a share. Over the last twelve months the earnings reports say they made ninety-six cents a share. This was up from seventy-seven cents the previous year. Use the most conservative methods and you know what it is? It is a lousy eleven cents the previous year, and it is a four-cent loss this year. Such a statement they publish! The book value is all puffed up. The profit margin is nonsense. Even the cash flow is jiggered up."

"Book value? Cash flow?"

"Forget it. You don't have to know. All you have to know is that no matter how careful Santo is, the published trading volume will go up, the stock will go up, a lot of careless people will jump on the wagon and push it higher. They'll think a big increase in earnings is going on. Or a merger, or a new product. Like with the ones you are supposed to have bought. But this one has no substance. It will go up like penny rockets and when it starts down, it should maybe end up a two-dollar stock where it belongs."

"So we con him into buying it, Meyer. So it goes up and up and he makes a lot of paper profit, and then when it goes down, he sells out and keeps the profit."

"With everybody selling, with everybody trying to save out some profit, who will buy it? No buyers and they'll suspend trading, investigate the heavy speculation, and when it opens again, it will open in the cellar. Santo should lose most or all of his bundle."

"So how does Janine make the money you were talking about?"

"With the forty thousand from LaFrance we start her off, pick up three thousand shares. As it moves, I use the increased market value to pick up more for her. I watch it like an eagle, and then I start pulling her out of it very, very gently, and putting her into a nice solid little sleeper I happened to find when I was looking for this Fletcher dog. It should give her a hundred-percent gain in a year, along with a nice dividend yield."

"How much can you make for her if things work out right?"

"If? Did I hear you say if? You get Santo to bite at it, and I'll do the rest. End of the year? Oh, say the original stake plus a quarter million."

"Come *on*, Meyer!"

"Oh, that's before short-term gains tax on Fletcher. You see, that's what'll lock Santo into it. He'll be hoping to ride the profit for six months. Say a fifty to sixty thousand tax she'll pay."

"You kill me, Meyer."

"Make sure nobody else kills you. It would be boring around here."

For the first time since I knew Puss would never come back, I felt a faint and reluctant little tremor of excitement and anticipation.

Meyer, frowning, said, "You are going to see LaFrance the day after tomorrow? Does that give us time to do everything we have to do?"

"I was just making him sweaty, Meyer. I'll phone him Thursday night and say we'll have to change the arrangement. Don't call us. We'll call you. And I can get a pretty good indication of whether he has the forty all ready."

"You know, you look more like yourself, Travis."

"It's the sympathy that does it, every time."

"An obligation of friendship. What do you do first?"

"Find that little pipeline."

After a long conference Wednesday morning with Meyer about strategy and tactics, and the documentation he ought to have, I went down to Miami. The offices of Santo Enterprises were in an unimpressive six-story office building on North East 26th Terrace, a half block east of Biscayne. Reception was on the sixth floor. A wide corridor, glass doors at the end, and beyond them a paneled room, thick blue rug, an elegant blonde desktable on a raised dais and, behind it with a look of polite and chilly query, a slender princess with white Dynel hair, glowing in the drama-light of a little ceiling spot, who asked me in the beautiful clarity of the English upper class if she might be of service.

When I said I would like to see Mr. Santo, she looked remotely amused. "Soddy, sir, but he is out of the citeh. Possibleh someone else could help you?"

"I'm inclined to doubt it."

"Praps if you might tell me the nature of your business, sir?"

"I'd rather not."

"Ektually, then, there isn't much that can be done, sir. Mr. Santo only sees one by appointment, and he would certainly not relish having his secretry make an appointment . . . blind, as it were. You see the problem, do you not?"

"Why don't I talk to his secretary, then?"

"But you see, sir, I would have to know the nature of your business to know *which* secretry you should speak with."

"Does he have a super-special personal private one?"

"Oh yes, of course. But, sir, one must have an appointment to speak with her. And to make the appointment I should have to——"

"Know the nature of my business."

"Quite."

"Miss, we're both in trouble."

"I wouldn't really say *both* of us, sir."

"If you don't help me a little bit, and when I do get to Gary Santo, which I most certainly will, he is going to wonder what took me so long, and I am going to tell him that I just couldn't get past that limey wench with the white hair under the spotlight."

"But, sir! Really, I have——"

"Your orders."

"Quite!"

"Do I look like a con artist? Do I look like a salesman? Do I look like a pest? Dear girl, aren't you supposed to exercise *some* instinct and judgment about people?"

"Sir, one might possibly say . . . pest, should this go on too much longer. Oh! My word! Are you a pilot? Is it about that . . . currency matter?"

"I am not a pilot. But some currency might enter into it. I just remembered something. Somebody said at one point that to get to Santo with a certain suggestion, they had to clear through Mary Smith. Is that a person or some kind of a code name for something?"

"Mary Smith would be a person, sir."

"A special personal private secretary, maybe?"

"Praps just private secretry, sir, might be suitable."

"Now, please don't tell me I need an appointment with her."

She studied me for a moment, tilted her head, looked slightly quizzical and inwardly—and possibly bitterly—amused. The appraisal was like unto that given a side of beef when the US Grade stamp is not easy to read.

"You could give me your name, sir?"

"McGee. T. McGee."

"This is teddibly irregular. Just a chawnce, y'know."

"Tell her I do card tricks, have never been completely domesticated, and show signs of having been struck sharply in the face in years gone by."

"At least you are amusing," she said.

"Quite!" said I.

"Please have a seat. I'll find out what she says, Mr. McGee."

I sat cautiously in a chair that looked like the slope end of a blue bathtub resting on a white pedestal, and found it more comfortable than it looked. Windowless rooms always give me the feeling of having been tricked. Now they've got you, boy, and they're going to come through all the doors at once. I opened a mint copy of *Fortune* and a grizzled fellow looked out at me with alert and friendly squint of eye, advertising my chummy neighborhood power company. I think I could remember having seen him on somebody's television set shilling an adenoidal housewife into squealing in ecstasy about suds.

The limey maiden murmured into the oversized mouthpiece of one of those privacy telephones. In a little while she hung up and said with a certain air of accomplishment and mild surprise, "She will be out in few moments, sir."

A flush door, bone-white, off to the left of the receptionist opened, and little Miss Mary Smith came through and toward me without a glance at the receptionist. I put *Fortune* aside and stood up. She marched to within four feet of me and stopped and looked up into my face. At least it was not a name they handed around the office. She was the one I had seen with Tush Bannon in the bar lounge atop the International Hotel. The dark and rich brown-auburn hair fell in a straight gloss. I had misread, across the room the last time, the expression on her face. It was not petulance, not discontent. It was a total and almost lifeless indifference, a completely negative response. In a special way it was a challenge. It said, "Prove I should relate to you, buddy." Her eyes were the improbable emerald of expensive contact lenses, made more improbable by just enough eye makeup to make them look bigger than they were. And they were generous to start with. Her skin texture was a new grainless DuPont plastic. The small mouth did not really pout. It was just that both upper and under lip were so heavy it was the only choice it had. They were artfully covered with pink frost. White blouse, navy skirt —that nunnery flavor of offices and hospital wards.

She looked up at me, motionless as department store wax, with two millimeters of query in one eyebrow.

"The eyebrow," I said, "is the exact same shade of those wooly bear caterpillars I remember from my childhood. You'd look for them in the fall to see if they were heading north or south. It was supposed to predict what kind of a winter we'd have."

"So you've verified Elizabeth's claim you're mildly amusing. This is a busy office."

"And I just happened to come bumbling in off the street to bother all you busy, dedicated people."

She took a step back, a quarter turn. "Then, if that's all."

"I want to see Santo. What do I have to say to you? A magic word?"

"Try good-bye."

"My God, you *are* a silly, pretentious little bitch!"

"That doesn't work either, Mr. McGee. The only thing that *does* work is to state your business. If Mr. Santo did not employ people of some judgment to screen out the clowns, his time would be taken up with clowns . . . and eccentrics, and clumsy con men. Do you want him to finance a flying saucer?" She rested a finger against her small chin and tilted her head. "No, you have that deep-water look. A bit salty? This is probably more of that treasure-map nonsense. Spanish galleons, Mr. McGee? And you have some genuine gold coins minted in the New World? I would say we average eight or ten of you people a month. So either you tell me or you don't tell anyone here at any time. Is that quite clear?"

"All right. I will tell you. I will tell you enough so that you will open the door for me to see Santo."

"May we call him Mr. Santo?"

"But I am not going to talk standing here like the last guests at a cocktail party. I want to sit at a desk or a table and you can sit on the other side of it and listen to as much as I care to tell you."

"Or as much as I care to listen to." She turned to the receptionist and said, "I shall be in Conference D, Elizabeth."

"Thank you, Miss Smith," said the humble limey.

I pushed the glass door open for little Miss Mary Smith and followed her down the corridor. Her walk was engaging, as it seemed to involve a conscious effort to inhibit any swing and flourish of her solid little rear end, and was successful to but a limited degree.

Conference D was a ten by twelve cubicle. But the end wall opposite the door was all window, looking out across Biscayne Bay to the improbable architectural confectionery of Miami Beach, with a sunlit glitter and shimmer of traffic across the Julia Tuttle Causeway a little to the north, and the residential islands off the Venetian Causeway about the same distance south. It was a gray room with gray armchairs, six of them, around a Chinese red conference table. On one wall was a shallow gray case, glass-fronted, wherein a very diversified collection of white nylon gears and cogs and rods and bushings of various sizes had been arranged against a Chinese red background in simulation of some of the art forms of Louise Nevelson.

I could be reasonably certain that as we had walked down the corridor, Elizabeth had, as common practice, turned on whatever bug system was used in Conference D. After all, Elizabeth could look through the glass doors and see which door we had entered.

I had learned the right terms from Meyer. She sat across from me, radiating skepticism.

"I am a speculator, Mary Smith. I'm not a trader. My specialty is in the maximized capital-gains area. There is enough income from certain other sources so that the Fed hasn't, and won't, class me as a professional and cut it all back to straight income. Is this over your head."

"Hardly! In fact, you've almost run out of time, Mr. McGee."

"I do *not* want to sell Santo a hot item. I do *not* want him in any syndicate operation. I do *not* want any piece of his action, or even any knowledge of the details just so long as he *does* move in on it. This is not nickel and dime. It's a listed security. Now, usually I operate in a sort of informal syndicate deal. Every man for himself, but we make the same move at the same time. But we've done so well we've got some security leaks. I dug this one out and it's too damned good to get the edge taken off of it by too many leaks. I could probably establish a position in it and then arrange a show of interest on the part of one of the aggressive funds. But they work out in the open, and the blocks they buy are too big."

I looked at her questioningly. "You haven't lost me. And your time hasn't run out," she said.

"So I have the word here and there that Santo will swing when something looks good. And I think he is smart enough to ease his way into it, because if he comes in too hard and fast, it is going to go up the ladder so fast I'm not going to have a chance to use the buying power on the margin account to keep doubling on the way up. He'll have to set it up to work through several accounts, and be willing to sell off blocks of it to kill the momentum if it starts to go too fast."

"You said something about it not being nickel and dime."

"So it would depend entirely on how far he wants to go with it. If he goes in, it will take a million to create the pressure it needs. I would say he could come in anywhere from one million on up to a tops of four. Over four and it would put it too far out of balance and attract too much attention in the long run. Frankly, I'd be hitchhiking, using his buying pressure to get on for the ride up, and taking the chance he can keep the climb controlled. I could assemble syndicate money because the track record is good, but the leaks would hurt. If I had the million, I wouldn't be here. Let's say he can count on three hundred percent long-term gains, if he doesn't plumber it. This is the kind of thing that comes along every three to five years, where all the factors fit like a beautiful watch."

"Mr. Santo has very little tendency to plumber anything."

"That was my evaluation. And when the ride is over, I should be where I won't have to fool with syndicates and Santo. I'll be where I can make my own markets."

"A listed security?"

"And a company in a potentially dynamic growth area."

For the first time I saw the suggestion of a smile on that heavy little-girl mouth. "And absolutely no point at all in asking you the name of it, of course. But I can ask you for . . . bank references?"

"That's a silly question. If he wants to dig around and check me out, lots of luck. He could find worms in the apple. All he'll be interested in is the track record." I took the envelope out of my inside jacket pocket and took out the brokerage account forms and flipped them over to her. "Take a look, if you can read them and interpret them, and then you can give Santo a nice verbal reference."

She went through the margin-account monthly summary forms first, sheet by sheet. Midway through she gave me a sudden green glance of reappraisal. On the last one, the December one, I had penciled beside each stock listed in the security position the January second market value. She checked those values against the purchase confirmations—not all of them, just a random few.

"May I hold these for a few days?" she asked.

"No."

"Can I have them Xeroxed? It would take just a few minutes."

I hesitated. "On one basis, and I can't enforce it. You see them and Santo sees them, and that's it."

"That would be up to him."

"So relay my humble request to the great man, sweetie."

"Do you have to be so sarcastic?"

"Am I supposed to be impressed by Gary Santo? He happens to

be my number one on a list of three possibles. Whoever it turns out to be will make a bundle on their terms while they help me make a bundle on my terms. I didn't come to beg, sweetie."

"You *do* make that clear. I'll be right back."

"If you ever stoop to manual labor around this shop, I think it would be nice if you did the Xeroxing yourself."

"I shall, sweetie. And you just made a nice brownie point. Cautious is as cautious does. We treasure that around here."

She was back in under ten minutes. She did not sit again. I stowed the account forms in the envelope and in my pocket.

I said, "You see, Miss, there's all those chests of gold coin busted open and spilled out right across the white sand bottom next to Hustler Reef."

"That was clumsy, wasn't it? I must stop typecasting. Of course you realize I have no idea whether or not this will appeal to Mr. Santo. The idea, I mean. If it does, he will have to know the security you're talking about, and he will want to have it checked."

"Quietly, I hope."

"Of course."

"When do I get to see him?"

"How can I reach you?"

"I'm going to be on the move. Suppose I phone you tomorrow afternoon."

She shook her head. "Friday. Say at four in the afternoon. Ask for me by name and give my extension number or you won't be put through. Sixty-six."

"Just what *is* your job around here, Mary Smith?"

"You might call me a buffer zone."

"Have I gotten past you?"

"On Friday we'll both know, won't we?"

10

On Thursday evening I reached Preston LaFrance by phone at his home in Sunnydale. I taped it so that Meyer and I could study the playback.

"McGee? Trav? I've been wondering all day——"

"Too much has been happening, Press. I might say that things are shaping up a little better than I'd hoped. I might have some good news for you when I'm able to get up there."

"I need some good news, and you can believe it. When are you coming up?"

"I'll have to let you know. That money we talked about. Have you got it set aside?"

"Let me get one thing straight. I get to know about what's going on before I have to go ahead and buy that damned thing for three or four times what it's worth, don't I? I mean I get a chance to make a decision based on what you tell me?"

"Naturally. But as you must realize, I'm not in this thing for *that* kind of a profit."

"I can figure that out for myself all right. Okay, I've got that money set aside, in case I want to go along."

"You will. I'll have the papers all drawn and bring them along. But one thing has come up which worries me a little, Press."

His voice tightened up. "What? What?"

"Have you had any recent contact with Santo?"

"No. No reason to. Why?"

"I think it would be a very good thing if you make certain he never hears about any kind of deal between you and me."

"I don't understand what you——"

"Did you hear anything about somebody topping your offer that same day title reverted to Mrs. Bannon, and I bought it from her?"

"I sure did, and it puzzled the hell out of me. It come through Steve Besseker here, and he won't say who made it."

"I have it on pretty good authority that Besseker was representing Gary Santo."

"What! The hell you say! Steve?"

"Santo sent some woman up to give him his orders, apparently. A tall redhead."

"By God, somebody was kidding Steve about seeing him over in Broward Beach with a big good-looking redhead sometime just before Christmas."

"It was probably the same day I bought the Bannon property. And it strikes me that the way things are going, Santo would want to know if there is any present or pending agreement between you and me, and he might have asked Besseker to find out."

I could hear him breathing, and then he said softly, "Well, I'll be a son of a bitch! The very next day he asked me if I knew you, and if maybe you were acting for me because, like Whitt Sanders said, that Bannon woman certainly wouldn't have sold to me no matter what I offered her. What's going *on*, McGee?"

"I'm afraid he's gotten wind of the deal I'm trying to pull off, and it would sting him a little. I suppose Besseker will keep him posted on every move you make. Well, we may have to move a little faster than I planned. Santo will hear about you buying the Bannon place from me as soon as the sale is recorded. Until then, keep your mouth shut because I wouldn't want to have it turn out that you end up with no share in either his deal or mine."

"Listen, I can't risk anything like that happen——"

"Sit tight, Press. Hang on. Keep the faith."

As he started to speak again I hung up on him.

About an hour later I played it for Meyer. He listened and then shook his head. "What's the point, Travis? Why are you confounding that dull boy with all this business of wheels within wheels?"

"For the variation of the pigeon drop, my friend. If suddenly the whole world seems more conspiratorial than he ever believed it was, then he'll be in a better mood to stand still for the sleight of hand. Confused people are less skeptical. I was going to use Besseker another way, but it had to be through Puss, and she doesn't seem to be around any more, so I salvaged a piece of the situation anyway."

"But one thing puzzles me," Meyer said. "Here you are worming your way into one kind of thing, directly with Santo. And up there you have your thumb in another kind of pie, but that is Santo's too, but not so direct. Up there you are Travis McGee, this address. And down there in Santo Enterprises, you are Travis McGee, this address. There is the chance that by some accident Santo or one of his people finds out you are into both things. That would immediately alert a man like Santo. He could find the relationship between you and Bannon, and he would smell mice."

"So?"

"Maybe I should have been the one to set up the investment thing."

"It would take the joy out of it. He might never make the connection. I need the chance to look him in the eye, laugh at his jokes, share some booze with him, and then sting him where it hurts. Then he can find out why it happened to him. I'll tell him, given the chance. For the rest of his life, the name Bannon is going to make him feel sick."

"Maybe he has some people who will make you feel sick in other ways."

"And sometimes they almost make it."

"This time they could."

"You always worry. It's nice. If you stopped, I'd worry."

He sighed. "Okay. So look at my expert, specialist, impressive kit. Meyer, the big industrialist."

He had the aerials of the Shawana River area, and the series of overlays marked as planned. He had soil surveys, water-table data, labor-supply data. He had business cards on expensive buff stock, engraved, turning him into G. Ludweg Meyer, Ph.D., Executive Vice President of Barker, Epstein and Wilks, Inc. Management Engineering Services.

"Let us sincerely pray," he said, "that one of these cards never finds its way back to that very sound and good firm."

"It might be therapeutic. It might stir them up. Let me see the correspondence file."

The letterhead startled me. It looked totally authentic. One of the giant corporations that have become household words in these days of electronic fantasy. I stared at him and he beamed at me and said, "It was a bit of luck. So wonder about it. Note that it is from the office of the President of the corporation. That is his name, truly. Note that it is marked confidential. Note the very impressive carbon-ribbon typeface. See the secretarial initials at the bottom. Those are the initials of his actual private secretary. The signature is not great. I copied it from a copy of their annual report. The top letters are background. The key letter is about the fourth one down. There. That's the one. Is it what you had in mind?"

The president called him *My dear Ludweg:* The first paragraph acknowledged the receipt of reports and recommendations, and then the letter went on to say, *I tend to agree with your appraisal of the competitive implications and possible danger to our industry position in that particular manufacturing division should Calitron establish a branch facility in such close proximity to Tech-Tex Applications, Inc. Though the branch facility we now have in the final planning stage is smaller, one could logically assume that proximity to TTA would benefit profit margin to the same extent percentagewise.*

In view of the necessity of moving quickly, and the favorable report our people brought back, you are authorized to make a firm commitment in the name of the Corporation for from 200 acres minimum or 260 maximum either in general area A, or general area B. A separate letter of authorization is appended hereto. In view of the other interest in these industrial lands, you are authorized to bid up to $2 thousand per acre, or a maximum of between $400 thousand and $520 thousand, at your discretion.

"Very nice," I said.

"What should my approach be up there? How should I act?"

"Self-important, influential, crooked and careful of being caught at it. Great letter, Meyer. You are showing more and more talent every time you get into one of these things."

"And getting more and more scared. Isn't this a conspiracy to defraud?"

"Let's say to highjack. Now let me tell you how it is supposed to work."

He buried his face in his hands and said, "I can hardly wait to hear." After I explained it, it took him a long time to smile.

When I phoned Mary Smith at four on Friday, she said, "Mr. McGee, would it be possible for you to have a drink with Mr. Santo this evening at seven at the Sultana Hotel on Miami Beach?"

"I can arrange it."

"The Out-Island Room, then, at seven. Just ask for Mr. Santo's table."

I arrived at the arched doorway a few minutes after seven. A lackey with a face like a Rumanian werewolf slunk out of the gloom and looked at me with total disdain, as if Central Casting had sent the wrong type with the wrong clothes. It was a cold day, and I had put on the Irish jacket. After five or six years, twigs still occasionally fall out of the dark, coarse weave.

"Mr. Santo's table, please."

"And your name?"

"McGee!"

He lit up with joy at beholding me. He popped his fingers and a waiter trotted over, bowed several times, and led me back through the labyrinths of partitions and alcoves to a deep corner, to a semi-circular banquette big enough for six, and a semi-circular table to fit. He pulled the table out, bowed me in, put it back and bowed and asked for my drink order.

At ten after he came on the run and pulled the table out again as the Santo party arrived. Gary Santo, Mary Smith, Colonel Burns, Mrs. Von Kroeder. I measured Santo as we shook hands. He was not as tall as he looked in his pictures, but with all the shoulders and chest so frequently mentioned in his publicity. He was shading fifty, but fighting it and winning the same way those more directly in show business win it, with the facials, the luxuriant hairpiece touched just enough with gray, the laborious hours in the home gym, and the sessions on the rubbing table, and the hefty shots of vitamins and hormones, and a hell of a good dentist. He came on all virility, white teeth, wrestler's handshake, and the knack of looking you squarely in the eye and crinkling his eyes as if you and he shared a joke on the rest of the world.

In resonant boyish baritone he told me I knew Mary Smith, of course, and presented me to Halda Von Kroeder, who had as much thin, pale, graceful neck as I have ever seen, a small, pert head, a tall, slat-thin body, a cascade of emeralds, and a set of breasts so awe-inspiring she gave the impression of leaning slightly backward to keep herself in balance. "So bleezed," she said in a Germanic rasp, then hiccuped.

Colonel Dud Burns had the look of eagles . . . defeathered, earth-bound, and worried about cirrhosis. Gary Santo arranged the group with himself in the middle and, at his left, first Mary Smith and then me at the end, and with Halda and Burns in that order at his right.

Mary Smith was at that daring outer limit where style becomes comedy. There was more eye makeup, and the mouth more frosted. She wore a gray sweater with a great deal of complex stitchery and welts and seams. It came down to within six inches of her knees. Showing under the sweater was two inches of blue tweed skirt. Below the skirt were sheer blue stockings that were a perfect match for shoes with stubby heels and high, stiff tongues. On her head was a wide-brimmed hat shaped much like the hats the novilleros wear in the bullring. It was of a stiff eggshell fabric in a coarse weave. She had it perched aslant on the gloss of the brown-auburn spill of hair, with a white thong under her chin, a blue wooden thong bead at the corner of her little jaw. The sweater sleeves came midway down her forearms. Her gloves and purse matched the eggshell hat. When she pulled her gloves off, she uncovered nails painted a thick, pearly, opalescent white.

She sat bolt upright like a bright and obedient child and smiled at me with wide eyes and careful mouth, and told Santo she would have the regular, which turned out to be a straight shot of Wild Turkey with water, no ice, on the side. When she got it, she went at it with frequent little sippings, each of which must have been three or four drops by volume.

Santo turned finally, after some in-group jokes and conversation I couldn't follow, and faced me across Mary Smith, his back squarely toward the kraut lady.

"Our little Poo Bear here gives you a good mark, McGee."

"Poo Bear Smith?" I asked.

"It's an office thing," she said. "I have this instinct or something. He says what about this one and I say Poo. And that one, and I say Poo. Then the next one I say okay for brownie points."

"She's got a nose for it. Questions, McGee. If I go for it, if I like the flavor of it, how much do you have to know?"

"The day you start and how much you are going to spring for all together."

"Have you taken a position in it?"

"About the same way porcupines make love, but I'm nowhere near as far in as I want to be. It's been moving in a narrow range and I've been buying on the downs."

"Will you need to know my orders?"

"No. I'll have a man tape-watching it."

"There's one place where we have to be coordinated on it, and that's getting off it."

"As carefully as we get on, I hope."

"And the last thing, of course, is the name of it."

"Right here?"

"The other two can't hear, and Mary is the best you've ever seen at keeping her mouth shut. About anything."

"Fletcher Industries. American Exchange."

"Want to brief me a little?"

"Why should I? It's a duplication of effort. If your people can't see why it's as good as it is, you need new people."

"You have your full complete share of mouth, McGee."

"Have you gotten too accustomed to total humility on all sides, Santo?"

"Hush, now!" said Mary Smith. "You both hush. You're both right. Don't you two go all ballsy and wicked when you're going to be helping each other."

Santo threw his head back and laughed his boyish laugh. "Her biggest trouble is making sense. By Wednesday . . . that will be . . ."

"The tenth," said Mary Smith.

". . . phone her and she'll have the Yes or No on it, and give you a probable figure."

"Will do," I said.

He smiled down into her face. He said to her, "I think I like your new friend, Mary. I think he's maybe brought us another winner." He took out his bill clip, slipped some bills out of it, and put them quickly into her purse. "I'm so sure, here's an advance on your bonus. Use it to take him to where the steaks are."

She looked at her watch. "Yes, you'd better start moving it, Gary. Ben will be out there with your luggage. Kiss Bonnie Bea for me."

He made the smallest of gestures and people came on the run to pull the table away, hand him the check for signature, bow the three of them out and away.

We went up the beach in her little red car to what she called one of "her" places, a little bar dark as pockets. Once we were sitting across a very low and narrow little table from each other, so that we had to hunch over it in intimate arrangement, she figuratively rolled up her sleeves and went to work. She had awaited the pass, and for once there hadn't been one.

She had put the strange hat aside. She shook out her gleaming hair. A stray pattern of light rested on a long diagonal across her face, from eyes to lips.

She dipped into her shot like a moth, put it down, picked up the stray lip-drop with tongue tip. "Want to know, Travis? Want the crazy message?" It was half whisper, her voice dragging.

"Message by special delivery. Sure, Mary Smith."

She made her eyes very wide and solemn. Her lips parted. She reached and took my hand in both of hers and pulled it slowly to her side of the table. She turned my slack fist over, then put the nails of her right hand high on the inside of my wrist, and slowly drew her nails along my wrist and over my palm, uncurling my slack fingers as she did so. Holding my fingers down, she dipped her head suddenly, pressed the mouth moist against my palm, lifted her head very quickly and stared at me, her face both sly and fake-frightened.

"Is there more?" I asked.

She turned my hand over and formed it into a fist and, holding it in both her hands, lifted it, held it, her elbows braced on the table. She bumped her chin into the knuckles, closed her eyes.

"Pow," she whispered. "Like right off, the first minute. Pow. I'm *never* like that."

"Comes a time," I said.

"There does indeed, Mr. Travis McGee." She tilted my fist slightly for a better angle, and went across the knuckle ridge with her warm little mouth, taking a gentle little bite at each knuckle and kissing the space between each knuckle. With each kiss, her tongue tip flicked at the closed space between fingers.

"When it's going to be what it's going to be, there's that message, don't you think? An old-timey thing, way deep, that's been waiting for it special. So very rough crazy everlasting special. And you know it too. Don't you? Don't you?"

She sat back there someplace behind those swarming eyes, listening to herself pant, in such a soft little wondrous way. She watched herself work herself up, no doubt measuring the bra-tickle of the nipples becoming erectile, sensing the new softness of thigh and belly. This was one of the new breed who assist the manipulators. Gary Santo, being a manipulator in a large way could be expected to have one who would know her business backward and forward and upside down. He might have two, three or a dozen in the retinue. He would keep them loyal not only with money, but with the feeling of being part of an operating team and performing a function for the team.

Sex with a particularly skilled and desirable woman who could convince you that you were the greatest thing since fried rice was a marvelous gadget for one of the manipulators. The bedazzled male is incautious, mazed, thunderstruck. In that condition he can provide the maximum benefit to the manipulator and the least problem. He will come trundling along in the entourage just to be near his brand-new love-light. He will tell her all he knows and all he hopes, and in a frenzy of team spirit and accomplishment, she will bang him out of his mind and drop him right back where she found him when the manipulator has the last crumb of information he can use. But while he's getting the treatment, he tags along with the team, with the group but not really a part of the group, aware that the team knows the basis for the attraction, aware of a team attitude of kindly contempt for him but so enthralled in his doggy, lolling, bitch-trailing way he will endure the little humiliations to keep getting what becomes more instead of less necessity to him the more he gets of it.

The role requires a woman exceptionally confident and decorative, a woman of a hearty and insistent sexuality, a woman who understands that serving the manipulator in this way is part of the price of the ticket on all the best flights to the best places, and if you want to be coy, or choosy or chicken, you can drop right back to the posture chair and the old electric and the girl's room scuttlebutt about who might get promoted to what. It takes special gals to travel with the team, so dig in and enjoy the special assignments, because between the romps the guy will talk and you tote the crumbs back to Gary and he fits them together.

The manipulators are the brash gamblers putting little corporations together to make big ones, and they are the talent packagers who stick a half dozen special abilities together and end up with the percentage off the top of the network serial show, and they are the showboaters who take on the tax cases of the mighty and fight the Fed to a draw—or a cheap compromise—and they are the inventive money men who direct the conversion of hoodlum funds into legitimate enterprise, and they are the whiz kids who tear down the honest old buildings and stick up the glittery new boxes on the lease-back, write-off, tax-shelter kick, and they are the ones that boost the market price of a stock up and unload and then kick it back down and buy back.

They buzz around the country and the world in little groups,

where everybody is always laughing, and at the resorts and airports
and executive dining rooms, at the padded bars and the swinging casinos, in the groups there are always the Mary Smiths, pert, tidy,
high-style, voracious and completely with it, eyes a-dance, freed by
The Pill to happily pull down the game the manipulator fingers for
her, the new Gal Friday who has become the Gal Friday Night.

It is a new breed that did not exist a few years back, but cultures
seem to have an uncanny way of spawning creatures to fill any need.
So situation ethics, plus profitable manipulation, brought this merry
regiment out of the wings, as if they had been waiting there all
along. It would be pointless to conjecture about immorality or
amorality, or make analogies about whoredom, that word with the
ring of biblical accusation. A Mary Smith would not even be upset,
merely puzzled.

In the diagonal of light she rested her chin against my fist, her two
warm and shapely little hands holding it there, elbow-braced, and
made her eyes huge, then dipped and turned her head first one way
and then the other, to slowly drag first one sheaf of the dense and
fragrant hair across the back of my hand and then the other.

I remembered the shaggy and ancient joke of the young man in
the strange city who had arrived with the phone number of a
hundred-dollar girl. He called her up and was invited up to her luxurious apartment, where she cooked him a gourmet meal, recited
French poetry, played the piano for him and sang with professional
skill. She mentioned that she spoke six languages, had a master's degree in psychology, and had designed and made the gown she wore
on her lovely body. At last as she led him in toward the canopied
bed he had to ask. And so he said, "Please would you tell me how a
girl like you got into . . . a business like this?"

She twinkled up at him and sighed and said, "Just lucky, I guess."

Mary Smith took a deep and shivering breath and said, "There is a
steak, darling, and it is not frozen and never has been, and it is in
the meat-keeper thing in my apartment, which is, God help us, a
con-do-min-i-um, which will never cease to sound like a dirty word,
and the apartment is twelve and a half minutes away, give or take
ten seconds, and the steak will keep for us, darling, until three A.M.,
or until twelve noon tomorrow for a Texan's breakfast for us because I don't have to tend the store until Monday morning, and that

twelve and a half minutes might just be the longest twelve and a half minutes in my life up till now."

The temptation was to accept the whole con. But there is an immense perversity in the male animal at the most unexpected times. And why *didn't* you climb Mount Everest, Sir Hillary? Because it was there, fellow. And I could see her in memory in another bar, by daylight, teeth set in that meaty little underlip, eyes half closed, listening to Tush, and turning her head slowly from side to side in a denial as definite as the slam of a door and clack of the lock. She would be exquisite in all detail, from earlobes to cute little toes to the dimples at the base of the spine. She would be fragrant, immaculate, prehensile and totally skilled, and she would ring all the changes, and pace herself beautifully, and draw me to her pace, and inflate my ego with her breathless astonishment at how it had been the most fantastic and lasting that had ever happened to her and how she had thought it could never even be equaled again, but lo and behold, when it had happened again, it was even more so, and if it ever got to be any more than that, she just couldn't stand it at all; it would blow her out of her mind, and how did we get to be so great, darling, so that really and truly it is as if it was the very first time ever with anybody.

The temptation was to take the man's Ferrari around the track a few times, just to prove to yourself you couldn't get hooked on a great piece of machinery or on the whole speed competition bit.

But it was right there and it was buzzing with it, and how do you sidestep without creating some unhappy suspicions about the whole approach? It would have to be some fancy footwork, and it would have to be on her terms, something she could comprehend immediately.

I slipped into my elk-hide ring-shoes just in time, just as her eyes narrowed and she said, "You're not exactly overwhelming the girl with enthusiasm, old buddy."

"Decisions, decisions, decisions," I said. "I seem to have this hex lately."

She let my hand go. "What's to decide?"

"There is this very pigheaded man sitting in a hotel suite and looking at the phone and getting madder and madder by the minute. I have been trying to unload this and that for cash money so I can get the maximum out of our little gem of opportunity. And he flew down from Chicago because this particular item happens to be worth about twenty thousand more to him than to anybody else in the world, for reasons I will not go into at the moment. So I told him I had to delay our meet because of something that came up, and I would try to get there by eight. And right now it is quarter to nine, and he is the type who feels unsure of who he is right down in the gut where it matters most, the type who to prove he is who he thinks he is might wait about one minute more and cut off his nose to spite his face, or he may have cut it off already and be on his way to the airport. I have been looking at you and trying to get a little controlled piece of amnesia about him, but it doesn't seem to work so good."

She sat taller and gave a little shake like a toy poodle who has just been lifted out of her doggy-bath, and gave her hair a few pats, and gave a hitch at her complicated sweater and said, "Darling, you are an absolute idiot! Why didn't you *say* something? Didn't you think I'd understand? I'm all grown up and everything."

"Let's say I was enjoying myself. I was listening to the message of the Poo Bear Smith."

She reached and patted my arm and with a crooked little smile and a bawdy wink said, "Let's put it this way. The twenty grand won't keep. You hustle and phone him. There's a phone at the end of that hallway over there that goes to the biff."

I went to the phone and lit a match and looked up a random number and dialed it and asked a nasal woman if I could speak to Mr. Bannon. She told me I had a wrong number and hung up, and so I talked for a while over the empty wire to Tush and told him the news of the moment, with a few comments on the weather. He didn't have a thing to say.

I went back to the table and told the chicklet that my man was very frosty, very frosty indeed, but still available for negotiation. She said, "Darling, if you'd lost him on account of me, I was sitting here deciding I was going to make one hell of a try at being worth the whole twenty big ones, but no broad in the world carries a tag like that. I might have choked up and blown the whole match."

"I like a practical woman."

"Can I drop you at his hotel?"

"Thanks, but I gave myself time to go pick up my car at the Sultana, if you want to drop me there."

"And wait for you, I hope, I hope?"

"I guess you better wait at your place, because I am not exactly together on price with this clown yet."

She lifted her purse onto her lap, opened it and dug around inside and took out a little flashlight. She gave it to me and I held it for her while she took out a little golden notebook with a snap fastener. She opened it and slipped the little gold pencil out of the little gold loop and said, "I just realized I'm absolutely starving, dear, so let's say it'll be ten before I get home. This is the unlisted number. And this is the address, on Indian Creek Drive, on the west side going north. Look for a raspberry-colored thing with a white canopy and white awnings and white balconies. Call me first, love, because I want the delicious feeling you're on your way to me."

Again she drove the little red car. She whirred into the Sultana parking area, cutting off her lights as she did so to keep the front boys from noticing us and whistling her up to the entrance. She unstrung her bead, put her hat on the shelf in back, said, "Um" and splayed her little fingers on the nape of my neck and impacted a kiss with sufficient know-how to leave my knees feeling loose and fragile as I strode to my rental car after she had driven away.

At twenty to midnight, aboard *The Busted Flush*, after I had washed up after my plate of scrambled eggs and onion, I got the little sheet she had torn out of her notebook. It was oyster-colored parchment, thin and stiff, with tear-out perforations down the left side. And in the bottom right-hand corner was imprinted, in the plainest imaginable type face, in gold: Love, Mary Smith.

I direct-dialed her number.

It rang five times, and then her muffled, silky voice said, "Mmmmm?"

"T. McGee, ma'am."

I heard a small yowly yawn. "W'time zit, sweetie?"

"Quarter to Cinderella, almost."

"Mmm. I was having the most interesting dream about you. And I have on this interesting little yellow night garment I bought in Tokyo. And I dumped this and that in the big hot tub, and so I smell interesting, sort of like between sandalwood and old rose petals, and something else mixed in. Some kind of spicy smell that makes me think of Mexico. Do you like Mexico as much as I do? How soon will you be here, my darling?"

"That's a very good question."

"I don't like the sound of that, somehow."

"That makes two of us."

"You sound so depressed. Troubles?"

"Out of the blue. Now we've ordered up some food and we're waiting for a third party, and by dawn's early light my guess is that we'll be a hundred miles from here looking at the property in question, on the Tamiami Trail, just this side of Naples."

"Oh poo!"

"I think I'd use a word with a little more bite to it."

She gave a long sigh. "Well," she said, "down, girl. Bear me in mind, will you?"

"Get all the rest you need. And I will phone you precisely at twelve noon tomorrow and we'll get out the old starting blocks again."

"The old track shoes. Bang. They're off. Anyway, as long as you might have some faint idea what you're missing, dear, drive a very hard bargain. You should be motivated, God knows."

After I hung up, I packed a pipe and took it topside and stretched out on a dew-damp sunpad, down out of the bite of the breeze, and looked at the cold stars.

Where is the committee, I thought. They certainly should have made their choice by now. They are going to come aboard and make their speeches, and I'm going to blush and scuff and say, "Shucks, fellas." The National Annual Award for Purity, Character, and Incomprehensible Sexual Continence in the face of an Ultimate Temptation. Heavens to Betsy, any American Boy living in the Age of Hefner would plunge at the chance to bounce that little pumpkin because she fitted the ultimate playmate formula, which is maximized pleasure with minimized responsibility. With a nice build, Charlie. With a lot of class, Charlie, you know what I mean. A broad that really goes for it, and she had a real hang-up on me, Charlie. You never seen any chick so ready, Charlie buddy, to scramble out of her classy clothes and hop into the sack. Tell you what I did, pal, I walked away. How about that?

There had to be a nice medal to go with the National Annual Award. With the insignia of the society. A shield with a discarded bunny tail, and an empty bed, and a buttock rampant on a field of cobwebs, with the Latin inscription, "*Non Futchus.*"

A nice pink and white old gentleman would pin the medal to the bare hide of the chest, as recommended by Joe Heller, while a violin would play, "Just Friendship, Friendship."

The ceremonial kiss on the stalwart, manly, unsullied cheek and . . .

A huff of wind came and flipped the point of my collar against my throat. It ruffled the canvas laced to the sundeck rail. The collar was the tickle of the brisk red hair of Puss, and the canvas sound was her chuckle, and without warning I had such an aching longing for her it was like long knives in my bowels, and my eyes stung.

You never do anything for no reason at all, and you never refrain from doing something for no reason at all. Sometimes it just takes a little longer for the reason to get unstuck from the bottom of the brew and float to the top where you can see it.

I rapped the pipe out and went below. So it wasn't righteous denial at all. Or a lofty, supercilious disapproval. It was the monogamous compulsion based on the ancient wisdom of the heart. Puss had made of all of herself an abundant gift, not just the giving of the body or the sating of a physical want. And no matter how skilled the erotic talents of a Mary Smith, sensation would not balance out that privacy of self that she could not give, nor would want to, nor perhaps could ever give even if she wanted to.

And I knew just how it would have been with Mary Smith, because Puss was all too recent and all too sadly missed. All the secret elegancies of Mary Smith would merely have told me of wrong shapes, wrong sizes, wrong textures, wrong sounds from her throat, wrong ways of holding, wrong tempos and tryings and wrong oils of a wrong pungency. So it would have become with her a faked act of memory and mourning, to end in an afterlove depression that would make the touch of her, the nearness of her, hugely irritating.

Puss was too recent.

After I was in bed, I went back and forth across the same old paradox: Then if Puss gave of herself so totally, opening up all the girl-cupboards in the back of heart and mind, how could she leave? Why did she leave?

There was a little chill that drifted across the back of my mind and was gone, as before, still unidentified.

There had been one cupboard unopened, all those months.

But at least I could not stop making wistful fantasies about the little garden of delights in its yellow garment from Tokyo.

Hogamus, Higamus. Mary's polygamous.
Higamus, Hogamus. Trav is monogamous.

For a while. It won't be any good until big Red wears off more. It will be a drag. And when it seems time to begin to expect something of it, and the opportunity comes along, don't risk it with a Mary Smith, whose involvement would be about on the same order as all other kinds of occupational therapy.

11

On Saturday before noon I looked through the stowage areas for fifteen minutes before I found my gadget. It is called the McGee Electric Alibi. The two D cells had expired, so I replaced them with fresh ones and tested it. Once upon a time it was a doorbell, but I removed the bell and replaced it with a piece of hardwood that has exactly the right timbre and resonance.

I direct-dialed my love and hunched over the desk top so I could listen to the earpiece and hold the mouthpiece at the pretested and precalculated distance from the mouthpiece. It only rang twice before she picked up the phone, but twice was enough to give me the duration and interval of the rings.

"Darling?" she said. It was exactly noon, as promised.

I pressed the button, transmitting the raucous clatter of a phone that keeps trying to ring after you've picked it up.

Between the first two imitation rings I heard her say, ". . . dammit to . . ." and in the next gap, ". . . stinking thing. . . ." I heard the clicking as she rattled the bar ". . . n of a bitch . . ." I gave it eight fake rings and that made ten in all, as they instruct you in the yellow pages, and hung up.

Poor guy calls up all steamed up, right on time, and she isn't even home. Fine thing. So he thinks maybe her clock is wrong and she ran out for a paper or a loaf of bread or something. Five minutes later I tried again, and she answered, and I rattled her eager, frustrated, infuriated, helpless little eardrum and this time heard her cry over and above the racket, "Goddamn it to hell!"

So on the off chance, the guy would call the office, so I phoned at once before she would decide I might, and a subdued voice said, "Three one two one."

"Is Mary Smith there, please? Extension sixty-six."

"Miss Smith is not in today, sir."

"Well . . . if she should come in or phone in, would you tell her that Mr. McGee has been trying to reach her, and he'll phone her at home again at three o'clock."

"Is there a number where she can reach you, sir?"

"No. I don't expect to be here much longer, thanks."

She would know I had the right number, as I had reached her before. I had the bell on my phone switched off. I could make outgoing calls, however. So I tried her at twelve thirty. She hung up on the second rasp. At one her line was busy when I tried it. I had been hoping for that. It would be a help. A few minutes later it wasn't busy. She caught it on the first ring. "Hello?" Raaaasp. Cry of pure despair. Clunk as she hung up.

Snoopy the dog wears a guilty and evil grin from time to time. I couldn't work one up.

Meyer and I were in the lounge going over final details when I suddenly realized it was exactly three. I had no time to prepare him for the Electric Alibi. I heard a distinct sob before she hung up.

He stared at me as I came back to the chair. "Sometimes you worry me, Travis. It's something about the way your mind works."

"I often find it depressing." I stood up again. "Hell, we're all set. I'm going to drive up and see Janine and Connie. I'll stay over, and drive down to Sunnydale early Monday. You get there about noon and get a motel room somewhere, and go to the hotel I told you about for lunch. I'll show up with our pigeon. I think that sometime about maybe five or six o'clock Miss Mary Smith will show up and beat on the doors. I think I've described her well enough. Keep an eye out for her and intercept her and tell her you think I'm on the Alabama Tiger's cruiser and point the way."

"Consolation prize?"

"Who for?"

He gave up and sighed and left. I phoned To-Co Groves and Connie's cry of pleasure at my coming was convincing enough. I buttoned up, switched the Sentry on, and put my gear in the car. Then I walked to the Tiger's permanent floating houseparty. Even with the boat closed up, the Afro-Cuban beat was loud. When I opened the door to the big main cabin area the sound nearly drove me backward. The big Ampex system was blasting, and the regulars were all around the perimeter because Junebug had herself a new challenger.

She is a rubbery brown solid chunk of twenty-something-year-old girl, a sturdy mix of Irish, Gypsy and Cherokee. She wore a pink fuzzy bikini, and she was a go-going dervish, black short hair snapping, face and eyes a blur, body flexing and pumping to the beat, which Styles was sharpening with a blur of hands on the battered old bongos. The challenger was one of the king-sized beach bunnies, one of the big young straight-haired blondes about nineteen who look so much alike lately they should wear numbers on the side like stock cars. The money was in three piles on the deck by the Tiger's big bare feet. The big bunny was beginning to lag and flounder, miss the beat and catch up. Her mouth hung open. Her hip action in her zebra bikini was getting ratchety. The Tiger sat in a high glaze, swaying on the stool, smiling to himself, glass in hand. Muggsie Odell gave me her big smile, and I pointed at my watch and raised an eyebrow. She checked her watch, then flashed me seven sets of ten fingers plus four. Except for being so sweaty her body looked oiled, the Junebug looked absolutely fresh after seventy-four minutes of it. Maybe the challengers can go all day long to the beat they're used to, but they don't realize the additional demand on stamina of the Afro-Cuban tempo. One of them is reputed to have lasted over two hours before hitting the deck, but the Junebug wasn't even close to her own limit.

I crooked a finger at Muggsie. She nodded and followed me out and closed the hatch against the noise.

We sat on the wide transom and Muggsie said, "She's good for five more minutes, if that. I'd just as soon not be in there. They're waiting for her to fall down, and she's a stubborn kid and she'll keep going until she does drop. I just don't like to see them fall down like dead."

"A favor?"

"Depends. Probably yes, McGee."

"I'm going away for a couple of days. A very very nice little package is going to come right here looking for me. I'm having her steered here. The name is Mary Smith."

"No kidding!"

"Tell her I was here with the group, but I went away and you think I said I was going to come back, so it would be best for her to wait. Meanwhile, has Hero been around?"

I was interrupted by a yell from the group. The door burst open and somebody stopped the tape. The Junebug came out, yelling Ya

HAA, Ya HAAA, and jumping into the air with every third stride. Through the open door I could see the bunny facedown on the deck trying to push herself up, with people reaching to help her. Junebug gave a great leap to the dock, spun the valve on the dock hose and held the nozzle aimed right at the crown of her head. After it had streamed down her face and across her smile and pasted her dark hair flat, she stuck the nozzle under her bikini top for a few moments and then under the elastic of the bikini bottoms and, with an ecstatic smile, worked it slowly all the way around to the back and around the other side of that muscular body to the front again.

"Anybody else?" she yelled. "Any new pigeon, step up and put your bread on the deck! The old Junebug is ready."

"I'd watch *her* fall," Muggsie said grimly. "I'd watch her fall and hope for a couple of good bounces. What's this with Hero? What are you asking about Hero?"

"Has he been around?"

"Who can stop him? You know Hero. Every hour, cruising in and seeing if there's any new stuff he hasn't seen before. With him it's a dedication. Are you saying aim Hero at this Mary Smith? What's the matter? You hate the girl?"

"Let's say they deserve each other. As soon as he starts trying to snow her, Muggsie, you go back to her and say you just heard that I came here in a bad mood and there was a girl who wanted to cheer me up and we went off together, so maybe there's no point in waiting."

"Why don't I just chunk her on the head and help Hero carry her back to his pad?"

"Because it is entirely possible she'll chunk him on the head and take him back to hers."

"Oh. One of those. Anyway, Hero certainly is a handsome guy, and he certainly has enough charm for a whole charm school, and he certainly has given an awful lot of lady tourists a vacation they'll never forget. I was saying just the other day, I could really go for that guy, if only he just wasn't a real rotten person through and through."

"You mean if you didn't know him."

"That's what I must mean. Wherever you're going, have fun, Trav. I'll unite the happy couple and get her off your hands for good."

As I left I walked by Junebug on the dock, toweling herself dry. "Hey you, McGee," she said, with the big white mocking grin. "Hey, you never tole me when we're gonna start to go steady. How about it?"

I looked at all that brown rubbery, arrogant vitality. "I told you, Junebug, the very next time I get a death wish, I'll look you up."

"Some coward!"

"You can believe it."

"Aww. Poor fella. I wouldn't kill you. Just cripple you up pretty good, hah?"

"I think your trouble is that you're too shy. You lack self-confidence. Get out and meet people."

When I was a long way away I could still hear Junebug cawing with laughter.

I made good time and got to the Groves an hour after nightfall. We had drinks by the fire of fat pine, and a good dinner, and good talk. Janine got up and came over to me, hesitated, then leaned and touched her lips to the side of my face, and went off to bed.

Connie asked me what I thought of how Jan looked and acted.

"Listless. Thinner. More bones in her face."

"She's not eating well or sleeping well. She'll start to read or sew and end up staring into space. I hear her wandering around the house in the middle of the night. She's not coming out of it the way she should. I don't know what to do to snap her out of it. She's a damned fine girl, Trav. She's turning into a ghost."

"It's good of you to have her and the kids here."

"Don't be a jackass! I told her she can stay forever and I mean it. Those are three good kids. Five kids make a good kind of noise to have in the house. It's been quiet around here too damned long."

She asked about my redhead, and why I hadn't brought her along. When I said we'd called it off, she was suddenly furious, saying she thought I had more sense than that. I had to explain that it wasn't my idea and I'd been given no chance to make her change her mind. Then she was merely puzzled, saying it didn't make any sense at all.

On Sunday the three of us went fifty miles in Connie's Pontiac at her customary Indianapolis pace up to Rufus Wellington's law office. He had had his elderly secretary come in, and she was just finishing the typing of the deed and other documents pertinent to my sale of the Bannon property to Preston LaFrance. I had the power of attorney with me that Meyer had given me, which, when signed by Janine and witnessed, would authorize him to buy and sell securities in her name in the margin account he was establishing for her at the brokerage firm he used in Lauderdale.

Rufus eyed me and said, "You sure LaFrance will pay forty for an equity that isn't even there? Young man, do me the favor of not telling me what kind of persuasion you're fixing to use on him. I don't think I would like to know. I don't even want to know who this Meyer is, thank you. Any member of the bar is an officer of the court."

"If I have any trouble with the bank approving of the transfer of the mortgage to LaFrance, can you help?"

"I can phone Whitt Sanders and remind him of something that would make him approve transferring it to a little red hen. But I don't want to use it less I have to, just like I didn't have to when Connie went on the note with you. I have the feeling LaFrance is going to have trouble making those payments on the mortgage."

"If you don't want me to tell you anything, Judge, why do you make leading statements and then wait for me to explain?"

"Because I guess I figure you're not likely to tell me, son. But I do have a couple of clients here. You, Connie, and you, Miz Janine, and it would rest my mind to feel sure that nothing would come back on these ladies from anything too cute you are figuring on working on some of those folks down there in Sunnydale."

"Rest your mind, Judge," I said.

He leaned back, looked beyond us into the misty places of memory and said, "When I was a rough, wild young man, which seems like it was all in a different world than this one, I ended up down in Mexico one time, near Victoria, on a horse ranch. You had to prove you were all man. There was a thing they did, called the *paseo de muerte*. Maybe I don't have the lingo just right, but it's close. It was just riding full out, a full hard run over rocky land on half-broke horses, and the one who wants to test you, he comes up on you on one side, and he grins and you grin back and kick your feet free of the stirrups and you change horses right there, risking the way the footing is, and spooking one of the horses, or losing ahold. Once you'd show them you were ready to do it anytime, then they'd leave you be, because they weren't any more anxious deep inside to keep doing it than you were. Any fool could see that every time a man did it, his odds got shorter." He shook his head and smiled. "Long hours and short money, and one day out of noplace I could imagine came the idea I could start reading for the law. Why did I start all this? There was some point I was going to make. Oh. You keep in mind, Travis McGee, that the money game is one wild horse, and the vengeance for murder is another wild horse, and you try riding them both, you can fall between and get your skull stamped with an iron shoe. Bannon was your friend, and Connie's friend, and he was your husband, Miz Janine, daddy of your boys. Murder can come in when the money game goes bad. But don't think of it as being black dirty evil, but more of it being sick and sad, of some stumbling jackass that didn't mean it to come out that way, and he wakes up in the night and thinks on it and he gets sweaty and he hears his heart going like mad. Well, you folks have refused my kind offer to come on home with me for kitchen whisky and side meat and fancy conversation, so you will forgive me if I tell you all to be careful, and speed you on your way."

I phoned Press LaFrance in the late afternoon and arranged to meet him in Sunnydale the next morning. He sounded cautious and nervous and he gave me the impression of a certain evasiveness. He assured me the forty was still waiting, and he was anxious to listen, but I had the uneasy feeling that something had changed.

I went out to the sheds and sat on the truck dock, feeling dispirited. I finally admitted to myself that I felt guilty about Mary Smith. I could rationalize it as an adroit defensive maneuver. Gary Santo had aimed her at me. Maybe the little code word had been "steak." He had evaluated me and decided there was enough chance of additional useful information to turn her loose. So I had sidestepped her and aimed her at Hero.

But, after all, she knew her way around. She was about as gullible, innocent and vulnerable as those limey lassies who had starred in the Profumo affair. It was a good chance that she would case Hero in about forty seconds and turn him off, because he could certainly never be a business assignment.

I wished, however, that one little comment about Hero had not lodged itself so firmly in my memory. He looked like the big, gentle, slow-moving, kindly star of a hundred Westerns, and he had the charm to make a woman feel admired, protected and cherished, until he could ease her back to his pad, or back to her place, or any nearby nest he could beg, borrow or rent.

And there he would tirelessly demonstrate that degree of satyriasis that stopped short of landing him in various kinds of corrective institutions. He cruised the festive areas and cut his quarry out of merry packs with easy skill and monomaniacal determination. The comment that lingered in my mind came from a weary man who came aboard Meyer's boat one hot Sunday afternoon and said, "Knowing Hero this long, I sure God should have had the good sense never to let him bring a woman aboard my ketch last evening, but with Myra and the kids off visiting her folks, and the forward cabin empty, and me a little smashed, I said okay and what he had was some young schoolteacher he'd found right over at the *Yankee Clipper* in a big batch of schoolteachers having a party before going on a five-day cruise to the Islands out of Everglades. The ship left this morning and she sure God isn't going to make that cruise. Giggly woman, kind of mousy and trying to get along without her glasses, and built real good, especially up front. His angle was showing her a Bahama-built ketch on account of she was going to the Bahamas. I left them aboard and that was nine or ten o'clock and I came back at midnight or later thinking they'd be gone. Honest to God, I'm dead for sleep, men. It would get quieted down and I'd be drifting off and it would start up again. With all that whinnying and squeaking and thrashing around, the nearest thing it sounds like, and it's still going on from time to time, is like somebody beating carpets with a shoat. One day Hero is going to nail him one with heart trouble and she just isn't going to last it out. I should have had more sense last night. Meyer, what would you say to me going below and getting a little nap?"

So maybe, I thought, Hero never came back to the Tiger's, or maybe Mary Smith never drove up from Miami to try to find me, and if she did, maybe Meyer missed her. Or little Muggsie could have decided she deserved better.

Janine came walking slowly from the house, hands deep in the pockets of a borrowed gray cardigan worn over white ranch jeans. She hadn't seen me, and when I called to her, she turned and came over.

"Have a good nap?"

"I slept a little." She sat on an upended cement block and reached and picked up a piece of lath and started drawing lines in the dirt with the sharp end. She tilted her head and stared up at me, squinting against the brightness of the sky.

"Trav," she said, "I keep wondering about one thing. It keeps bothering me. I keep trying to figure out what happened, but I can't seem to think of anything logical. It's sort of strange."

"Like?"

"How did Tush get out there? I had the car. He was going to come into Sunnydale by bus and phone me to come get him. Did somebody give him a ride, or what?"

"I never thought about that."

"Then, whoever gave him the ride could tell when he got there. They . . . found him at what time was it?"

"A sheriff's deputy found him at nine o'clock, approximately. The medical examiner estimated he had been dead from one to four hours at the time he was found."

"From five thirty to eight thirty, then. In there somewhere, somebody . . . killed him. But he was so strong, Trav. You know how powerful he was. He wouldn't just stretch out and let somebody . . . He was dead when they put him there. Maybe whoever drove him out there saw somebody hanging around."

"We're going to get to all that, Jan. Believe me, we're going to do our best to find out. But first we've got to do some salvage work for you."

She made a bitter mouth and looked down and drew a dollar sign. She reached a foot out and slowly scuffed it out. "Money. It got to mean so damned much, you know. Getting pinched worse and worse, and snapping at each other about it, and being so scared we were going to lose the whole thing we started with. And now it doesn't mean anything. Nothing at all."

"With those three kids to bring up? Shoes and dentists and school and presents?"

"Oh, I suppose it will be something I'll have to think about. But right now I'm just . . . nowhere. You're sure you can fix it so I'll end up with thirty thousand clear, and you seem so sure you can make me a lot more out of that stock stuff I don't understand at all. I ought to sound grateful and pleased and delighted and so on."

"Not for my sake. Or Meyer's."

"Everybody is doing things for me. But I ran. Everybody knows that. I'm a lousy person. I don't like myself. Trav, I used to like myself well enough."

I slid off the dock and took her hand and pulled her up. "Let's walk for a while." We walked and I gave her some dreary little sermons about how never quite matching up to what you want of yourself is the basic of the human condition. She heard, but I don't know if she believed. I was trying hard to believe my own hard sell, because I kept thinking of carpets and shoats and wide wide emerald eyes and a delicately provocative little pressure of teeth against the knuckles of my stupid right hand.

12

I ARRIVED in downtown Sunnydale at nine o'clock on Monday morning and parked in the bank lot, and walked toward the Shawana River Hotel, where I had arranged to meet LaFrance in the coffee shop.

When I went into the lobby, two men in green twill uniforms moved in from either side to position themselves with an unhurried competence between me and the glass double doors. A cricket-sized man of about sixty planted himself spread-legged in front of me and said, "Nice and easy, now. You just lay both hands atop your head. You're a big one, all right. Freddy?"

One of the others came in from behind and reached around me and patted all the appropriate pockets and places. I had recognized the sheriff's voice from having heard it over the phone. He wore a businessman's hat wadded onto the back of his head. Straight gray hair stuck out in Will Rogers style. He wore an unpressed dark suit with a small gold star in the lapel. The suit coat hung open, exposing a holstered belly gun small enough to be an Airweight. Small enough to look toylike, but in no sense a toy.

The legal papers, billfold and keys were handed to Sheriff Bunny Burgoon. From his voice I had thought he would be all belly, with porcine features. He opened the wallet, flipped through the pliofilm envelopes. He stopped at the driver's license and studied it.

"Your name Travis McGee? You can put your hands down, boy."

"That's my name."

"Now we're going on over to my office and talk some."

"Can I ask why?"

"It's my duty to tell you that you got no obligation to answer any questions I or any of my officers may ask you without the presence of any attorney of your choice, and you are in your rights to request the Court appoint an attorney to represent your interests in this matter, and anything you say in response to interrogation, with or without the presence of your legal representative, may be held in evidence against you."

He had run all the words together, like a court clerk swearing a witness.

"Is there a charge?"

"Not up to this minute, boy. You're being taken in for interrogation in connection with a felony committed in the county jurisdiction."

"If I'm being taken in, Sheriff, then it is an arrest, isn't it?"

"Boy, aren't you coming along willingly and voluntarily like is the duty of any citizen to assist law officers in the pursuit of their duty?"

"Why certainly, Sheriff! Willingly and voluntarily, and not in the cage in the back of a county sedan, and with my keys and papers and wallet in my pockets. Otherwise it's an arrest, and if so, my personal attorney is Judge Rufus Wellington and you better get him on the horn and get him down here."

"Read his name in the paper, boy?"

"Instead of bothering the judge, why don't you just ask Whitt Sanders if the judge represents me?"

I was watching for a shift of uncertainty in his eyes and saw it. Apparently he had not anticipated any connection with the local power structure. He motioned one of the two deputies close, stood tall, and without taking his eyes off me, murmured into the younger man's ear. The deputy walked out. Burgoon asked me to come over and sit on a couch in the lobby. The deputy was back in five minutes and the sheriff went over and talked quietly with him, then came over and gave me back my possessions. With one of the deputies ten paces behind us, we walked through the morning sunshine to the Shawana County Courthouse and around to the side and into the entrance labeled COUNTY SHERIFF.

I was aware of a particularly avid curiosity on the part of the desk personnel and the communication clerk as he led me back into his office. The slats of the blinds were almost closed. He turned on the ceiling fluorescence and his desk lamp. He had me sit in a straight chair facing his desk and six feet from it. The sheriff looked at the papers on his blotter, put them aside and sat in his big black chair. A portly man in deputy uniform came in and sighed and sat in a chair back against the wall. "Willie will be bringing it along, Sherf."

Burgoon nodded. There was silence. I looked at the framed testimonials on the walls, and the framed pictures of Burgoon taken with various political notables, past and present. Some file drawers were partially open. The contents looked untidy, with documents sticking up out of the file folders.

"Make that deal with Harry?" Burgoon asked.

The portly one said, "He give me an estimate of over seventeen hundred. And it was supposed to be a twenty-year roof. I told Cathy we could buy a lot of buckets to set under the leaks for seventeen hundred."

"Harry does nice work."

"Wisht I'd used him when I was building."

Burgoon looked at me. "You made up your mind about a lawyer yet, mister?" I had been promoted from boy.

"Sheriff, I think it would be easier for me to make that decision if I had more information about what you think I did. It could be something we might be able to straighten out without bothering anybody."

"Maybe. Maybe not."

"When and where did the alleged crime take place? That might give me something to go on."

"It took place, mister, on the morning of December seventeenth last, and it took place at a marina on the Shawana River just about eleven miles east of here."

"That was a Sunday morning?"

"Yes it was."

"Would you be trying to make a capital case, Sheriff?"

"Murder first."

I remembered that Sunday with no trouble. Puss, Barni Baker, Mick Coseen, Meyer, Marilee, in fact a lot more people than we had needed or wanted aboard, and a dozen ways to refresh their memories that it was that exact day.

"Just one more question and I can give you an answer. Am I supposed to be connected with it in some way, or are you trying to say I was there at that time?"

"There at that time and did commit an act of violence which resulted in the death of one Brantley B. Bannon."

"Then, I don't think I need a lawyer to straighten things out."

It seemed to startle Burgoon. He said irritably, "Tom, what the hell is holding up that damn Willie?"

"Right here, Sheriff. Right here," said a thin young man who came in carrying a tape recorder. He put it on the corner of the sheriff's desk, knelt on the rug and plugged it in. "Sheriff, you just push——"

"I know, I know! Get on back to work and close the door." When the door was closed, Burgoon said, "We took this with the court reporter and on tape at the same time, and there hasn't been time to transcribe it yet. You get to hear it on account of now we've got that damn new law on full disclosure, and the defense would get a certified copy of the transcript anyways, and the State's Attorney said it was all right I should do it this way. You listen, and then you answer questions and make a statement, and then we hold you and this goes to a special meeting of the Grand Jury for the indictment so you can be arraigned proper."

He punched it on and leaned back and closed his eyes and rested his fingertips together. The tape had a lot of hiss. Apparently nobody ever bothered to clean or demagnetize the heads. But the questions and answers were clear enough.

I recognized the flat, insipid, dreary little-girl voice before she even gave her name, saying that she was Mrs. Roger Denn, Arlene Denn, and that she had been living with her husband at the Banyan Cottages, Cottage number 12 ever since the tenth of December, that she was twenty-two years old and that she was self-employed, as was her husband, making and selling art objects to gift shops. Prior to that time they had lived aboard a houseboat the Bannons had rented them, tied up at the Bannon Boatel on the river, and had lived there eight months.

"What were the circumstances of your leaving?"

"Well, they had to come and take the houseboats back. They owed on them and some men came and towed them off, I don't know where. That was . . . early in December, I don't know exactly what day."

"What happened then?"

"We put all our things in the two end units of the motel just for a while, until we could find something, because Mr. Bannon said it looked like he might lose the place. We went looking and we found a place at the Banyan Cottages and moved in on the tenth, and we were making trips in the station wagon to bring our supplies and so on back to the cottages."

As she spoke on the tape, through the hiss, I could picture her clearly, pallid and sloppy and doughy, with dirty blonde hair and a mouth that hung open, and meaningless blue eyes.

"What was the occasion of your last visit to Bannon's motel?"

"It was because of missing some silver wire. We use it in the jewelry. On Saturday, that was the sixteenth, we looked all over for it and it was just gone. We knew then that the place was foreclosed out there, but we still had a key to the end units on account of Roger forgot to leave it off when we made the last trip. I kept thinking that maybe what could have happened to it, we had a lot of supplies piled on the beds and maybe the wire slipped down and caught somehow like at the headboard or the footboard, because I had crawled around looking to see if we'd left anything on the floor the last trip we took. Roger kept saying to forget it because it was real trouble going into a place sealed off by the court, and maybe they'd changed the locks. But it was twenty dollars' worth of wire and maybe seventeen left on the roll, and we don't do so good we can just throw away seventeen dollars. So we sort of had a fight about it, and I said I was going to go out there whether he was or not, so I went out when it was just getting to be daylight the next day, which was Sunday. I drove right on by, slow, to see if anybody was there and I didn't see anybody, so I went a ways up the road and put the station wagon in a little kind of overgrown place that used to be a cleared road once. I backed it in. You know, kind of hiding it, and I went back with the key and when I was pretty sure nobody was around, I tried the key and it worked and I let myself in and started hunting for that wire."

"What happened next?"

"I guess I was hunting for maybe ten minutes or fifteen minutes. I don't know just what time it was. Maybe sometime between seven and seven thirty and I heard a car coming, so I squatted down so nobody could look in and see me when they went by. One of the windows, those awning kind of window things, was open three or four inches. So I heard the car drive in and it stopped and then I heard a car door slam and then I heard another car door slam and I heard men's voices."

"Could you hear what was said?"

"No sir. They were loudest near the car and then kind of faded when they were walking toward the marina. I couldn't hear words, but I had the feeling they were mad at each other, almost shouting. I think one word that was shouted was Jan. That was Mrs. Bannon's name. Janine. But I couldn't be sure."

"What happened next?"

"I didn't know what to do. I was afraid to leave. I tried to peek out the windows and see where they went to, to see if it was safe for me to sneak out."

"Could you see the car?"

"No sir. But I knew I would hear it if it started up."

"Then what happened?"

"Somebody shouted a lot louder, and further away, and I knew they were real mad. It sounded to me like Mr. Bannon. Then it was quiet. Then maybe five minutes later I looked out the back window that looks toward the river, and I saw a man dragging Mr. Bannon across the ground. He had his arms wrapped around Mr. Bannon's ankles and he was leaning forward and pulling hard and pulling Mr. Bannon along. I was kneeling and looking out a corner of the window, like with one eye. He dragged him right to that old hoist thing and then kind of rolled and shoved and pushed him under the motor. Mr. Bannon was real limp, like unconscious or dead. The man stood up and looked at him and then he looked all around. I ducked down and when I got up enough nerve to look again, he was walking toward the hoist thing again from the marina and he was carrying something small, some wire and something. I watched him and he kneeled down and did something to Mr. Bannon I couldn't see, and then he worked some more at the hoist thing. Then he turned the crank and the motor went up real slow. I could hear the clickety sound it made. Then he stood near the gear part and bent over and did something and . . . the motor fell down onto Mr. Bannon. There was a rackety sound when it came down and the wire ropes slapped around and hit those poles and made a ringing sound."

"And then?"

"He cranked it up halfway and looked at Mr. Bannon close, and cranked it up the rest of the way and let it fall on him again. When he cranked it up again, Mr. Bannon looked . . . kind of flattened out. He didn't put it all the way up again. He just let it fall from there and he left it there and picked up something off the ground and then kind of stopped and dropped it and then picked it up and wiped it on some kind of a rag and dropped it again. He was nearly running when he left. And 'then I heard one car door slam and after a little while the car started up. I stayed way down until it was gone."

"Which way did it go?"

"Back this way, toward Sunnydale."

"Did you get a good look at the man?"

"Yes sir, I did."

"Had you ever seen him before?"

"Yes sir."

"Would you recognize him if you saw him again?"

"Yes sir."

"Do you know him by name?"

"Yes sir."

"What is his name?"

"His name is Mr. McGee."

"Under what circumstances did you first see Mr. McGee?"

"I only saw him two times before that, both on the same day. It was back in October. I don't know the exact day. He was a friend of theirs and he came in a nice boat to visit them. He took them over to Broward Beach in the boat that night for dinner and I sat with the little boys. So I met him when I came over to sit, and then I saw him again when they came back."

"Did they seem friendly, McGee and the Bannons?"

"I . . . guess so."

"You seem hesitant. Why?"

"I had the feeling it was Mrs. Bannon he came to see."

"What gave you that feeling?"

"Well, actually I saw him three times that day. It was an awful hot day. Mr. Bannon and Mr. McGee had fixed Mr. Bannon's car. Then Mr. Bannon went off to get the boys from school. I saw Mrs. Bannon taking a pitcher of iced tea to one of the units. I wanted to ask her about something she was going to bring me from town, to save a trip. I needed it in my work and I went down there to where she took the iced tea, thinking she would come right out. When she didn't, I sort of looked in the window. I didn't know his name then, not until later. But I saw Mr. McGee and Mrs. Bannon laying on the bed, kissing."

"Did you notice anything else that day in October that seemed odd or unusual to you?"

"No sir. Nothing else at all, sir."

"What did you do after McGee drove away?"

"Well, I thought I better wait a little while in case he forgot something and came back. So I looked for the wire some more and I found it. I left and made sure the door was locked and then I ran all the way to our car. I threw the key in the bushes when I was getting into the car, the room key."

"Why did you do that?"

"I was very frightened, I guess. I didn't want anybody to know I'd been in the motel."

"I show you a motel room key. Is this that same key you threw away?"

"I think so. Yes sir. That's the key."

"Did you relate all this to your husband?"

"No sir. I didn't tell him anything."

"Why not?"

"Because he said I shouldn't go out there, and even though I did find the silver wire, he was still right about that. I wish I hadn't gone out there that Sunday morning."

"Will you tell us why you finally came forward, Mrs. Denn?"

"I thought they would catch Mr. McGee. But they didn't. I worried and worried about it and the other night I told my husband the whole thing and he said I had to come and see you. I begged him not to make me do it, but he said I had to. That's why I'm here."

Sheriff Burgoon turned it off. "There's more. But it covers the same ground. It doesn't bring up anything new. It's an eyeball witness, boy, with nothing to gain or lose. We took her out there and she showed us the window and you get a real good view from there."

He had demoted me back to boy, heartened by his evidence.

"I think she saw almost exactly what she says she saw, Sheriff."

"Want to change your mind about a lawyer?"

"Motive, opportunity, weapon, and an eyewitness. Sheriff, don't you think it's all wrapped up just a little too neatly?"

"A man can be damn unlucky."

"How true. I wonder just who he is."

"Suppose you make a little sense."

"Okay. Here is something that the unlucky man, whoever he is, had to take a chance on. He had to take a chance on there being some probability or possibility of my being in this area at that time, and my having no way to prove I wasn't."

"It's going to take a pretty good piece of proof."

"I can place myself aboard my houseboat where I live, *The Busted*

Flush, Slip F-18, Bahia Mar, Fort Lauderdale, at nine o'clock that Sunday morning. Does the rest of the tape establish her best guess as to the time I'm supposed to have left after the murder?"

"Maybe eight thirty, give or take fifteen minutes," he said. "But let's get to just how you place yourself there and how come you'd remember it so good."

"Because I arrived at Bannon's place the following afternoon and found out he was dead. I found out he had died the previous morning. Somehow you remember what you were doing at the time a good friend died."

"And just what were you doing?"

"Socializing, Sheriff Burgoon. Being a jolly host, right out in front of everybody. I think that I could probably come up with the names of at least twenty people who saw me and talked to me between nine and ten o'clock that morning. Some of them are totally unreliable. I don't pick them for social standing and credit rating, and I wouldn't ask you or anyone to believe them if they swore on every Bible in Shawana County. But there are a half dozen well worth believing. Suppose you write down the names and addresses and pick a couple of names off the list and question them by phone right now any way you feel like. Try any trick or trap you can think up."

"What did you mean saying she saw almost exactly what she says she saw, mister?"

"She saw everything except me doing it. She saw somebody else do it, and that changes your theory about nothing to gain or lose."

"How do you mean?"

"Somebody prepped her pretty good, Sheriff. I might even have thought that she saw somebody she sincerely mistook for me. But the iced tea sequence was a little too much."

"Didn't happen?"

"I got hot and sweaty helping Tush fix the spring shackle on his car. I showered in the motel unit they loaned me. I had just finished dressing when Jan brought the pitcher of tea and two glasses. We talked about the problems they were having. Maybe fat-girl even looked in the window. But no bed and no kisses. Nothing like that between us. Not even any thought of it on either side. At the moment I happen to own the Bannon place, Sheriff. I bought it from Jan Bannon. Why in hell would I do that?"

"*You* are the one bought it!"

"I'm here today to try to resell it to Press LaFrance."

Burgoon looked very thoughtful. "He's surely been wanting it so bad he could taste it. Trying to put some kind of parcel together for resale. Don't he own a patch out there, Tom?"

"Fifty acres right behind."

Burgoon nodded. "Probably could move it if he had river frontage to go with it."

Tom scrubbed his snow-white brush cut and coughed and said, "Bunny, that Bannon woman didn't seem to me to be that kind of woman when I had to go out there and roust her and the kids out and seal it up. That's one part of this job I surely hate. We tried to make it easy as we could, but there isn't any good way to make it easy. She was one upset woman and you can believe it."

The sheriff asked me for the names of my witnesses and wrote them down.

I thought of something else. How come they had been waiting for me at the hotel? And did that have anything to do with LaFrance's evasiveness when I had phoned him?

"Who told you I was coming to the hotel, Sheriff?"

"Wasn't it Freddy dug that up, Tom?" Burgoon asked. When Tom nodded, Burgoon said, "Didn't you say you were coming here to see Press LaFrance? Then, that answers it, sure enough. Freddy Hazzard is Press's nephew, his sister's eldest boy. He's my youngest deputy, mister. You saw him at the hotel, the lanky one."

"Is he the son of one of your County Commissioners?"

"Sure is. Monk's boy. But that's got no bearing on me taking him on. Freddy came out of service with a good record in the M.P. and he earns his pay right down the line."

"Didn't somebody say that it was somebody named Freddy who found the body?"

"That's right. On a routine patrol at nine thirty. You see, I had a note for Bannon from his missus, and she'd left a suitcase here for him, and I didn't know but what Bannon might hitch a ride to his place or come by boat or something. She'd said he was planning to be back Friday or Saturday, so I had the boys keeping an eye on it out there off and on." He peered at me. "You getting at something?"

"I don't know, Sheriff. I'm going to check out all right. You have a hunch I will, and you hate to admit it to yourself because it's such a nice neat painless little case."

He slapped his hand on the desk top. "But why would some other damned fool, if somebody else besides you did it, why would they want to pick *you* for it? They should know there was a chance you'd be in the clear. Why not some description to fit somebody we'd look for and never find?"

"Suppose this person heard, second hand, that I had a theory somebody had done too good a job of working Tush Bannon over and killed him, then dropped the engine on him to hide the traces, and fixed the wire to make it look like suicide?"

"If you can prove you said that to anybody at any time, mister, it might be more help than this list of folks I wrote down."

"I told that same person that maybe it was somebody who was trying to do him a favor and do Monk Hazzard a favor, by trying to take some of the spunk out of Bannon so he would leave quietly. Because the person I was talking to has been trying to get that land."

"LaFrance?" Burgoon said, almost whispering it. "Tom, you think Press ought to come in for a little talk?"

"Can I make a suggestion, Sheriff?" I asked.

"You mean you've got another way to make things worse than they are right now?"

"Isn't the weakest place the fat girl? She lied and she'll know who made her lie. Don't you think she could be brought in to make a positive identification?"

"You ever been in this line of work?"

"Not directly."

"You got a record, mister?"

"Four arrests. No convictions, Sheriff. Nothing ever even came to trial."

"Now, just what would those arrests have been for, mister?"

"Assault, which turned out to be self-defense. Breaking and entering, and it turned out I had the owner's permission. Conspiracy, and somebody decided to withdraw the charges. Piracy on the high seas, dismissed for lack of evidence."

"You're not exactly in any rut, are you? Tom, send somebody after that Arlene Denn."

After he left, I said to the sheriff, "When did she make that statement?"

"Saturday, starting about . . . maybe eleven in the morning."

"Did you try to have me picked up in Lauderdale?"

"Sure did."

"And Deputy Hazzard found out yesterday in the late afternoon that I would be at the hotel this morning?"

"He got the tip last night and phoned me at home."

"Did he have any objections to the way you set it up to take me?"

"Well . . . he did say maybe if I stationed him across there, like on the roof of the service station with a carbine, it would be good insurance if you smelled something and decided not to go into the hotel at all." He shook his head. "Freddy is a good boy. It doesn't fit the way you want me to think it fits."

"I'm not trying to sell you anything."

In twenty minutes Tom brought her in. She stopped abruptly just inside the door and gave me a single glassy blue look and looked away. She wore a paint-spattered man's T-shirt hanging outside her bulging jeans, and apparently nothing under the T-shirt.

"Move over near Tom and let her set in that chair," he said to me. She sat and stared at Burgoon, her face so vapid she looked dim-witted.

"Now then, Arlie," said Burgoon, "we had a nice talk day before yesterday and you helped us a lot and we appreciate it. Now, don't you be nervous. There's another part of it you've got to do. Do you know that man setting over there by Tom."

". . . Yes sir."

"What's his name, Arlie?"

"The one I told you about, Mr. McGee."

"Now, you turn and look at him and be sure and if you are sure it's the man you saw dropping that engine onto Mr. Bannon, you point your finger at him and you say, 'That's the same man.'"

She turned and she looked at the wall about a foot over my head and stabbed a finger at me and said, "That's the same man."

"You had a clear view of him on the morning of December seventeenth? No chance of a mistake?"

"No sir."

"Now, don't be nervous. You're doing just fine. We've got another little problem you can help us with. It turns out Mr. McGee was way down in Fort Lauderdale that same identical morning at the same time you think you saw him, and he was on a boat with some very important people. A federal judge and a state senator and a famous surgeon, and they say he was right there at that same time. Now, Arlie, just how in the wide world are we going to get around that?"

She stared fixedly at him, her mouth sagging open.

"Arlie, are those big people lying and are you the one telling the truth, so help you God?"

"I saw what I saw."

"Who told you to make up these lies, Arlie?"

"I told you what I saw."

"Now, Arlie, you recall what I said before, about you having the right to be represented by a lawyer and so on?"

"So?"

"I'm telling you again, girl. You don't have to answer any questions. Because I think I'm going to hold you and book you."

She shrugged plump shoulders. "Do what you feel like."

Crickety little Burgoon glanced over at Tom and then looked at the fat girl again. "Girl, I don't think you rightly know just how much trouble you're asking for. You see, I *know* you're lying."

Tom, responding to his signal, came in on cue. "Bunny, why in God's name you being so kindly to this fat dumb slut? Let me run her on out to the stockade and turn her over to Miss Mary. Leave her out there three or four days and Miss Mary would purely enjoy sweatin' off fifteen pounds of slop and teaching her some manners. She'd have a nice attitude when you have her brought back in."

Arlene Denn turned and stared at Tom. She bit her lip and swallowed and looked back at Burgoon, who said, "Now, if we have to come to that, Tom, we'll come to that. But this isn't any ninety-day county case. And this isn't any one to five up to the state women's prison. What the law of the State of Florida says is that giving false testimony in a capital case, or withholding evidence in a capital case is punishable by a maximum sentence of imprisonment for the rest of her natural life."

She stiffened as much as her figure permitted, sat up straight and said, "You've got to be kidding, Sheriff!"

"You know how to read, girl?"

"Of course I know how to read!"

He dug a battered manual out of a desk drawer, licked his thumb and found the right page. He handed it across to her. "Second paragraph down. That there is sort of a short form of everything against the law. It's what new deputies have to study up on and pass a test."

She read it and handed the manual back. She looked over at me. The look of vacuous stupidity was gone, and I realized it was the mask she wore for the world she was in.

"Now, without me saying I *would* change my story, Sheriff, let's suppose I did. What would happen to me?"

"Would the new story be the exact truth, Arlie?"

"It would be."

"Would it have you out there seeing anything at all?"

"Let's say it would have me seeing somebody else instead of Mr. McGee. Let's say that when I looked in the window, Mr. McGee and Mrs. Bannon were just talking."

Burgoon said, "What do you think, Tom?"

"I think she ought to do some laundry work for Miss Mary for thirty days."

"Maybe. Maybe not. I'd say it's going to depend on *why* she showed up with those lies."

"Regardless," said Arlie, "would you bust me for any more than thirty days?"

"Only if it turns out you're telling more lies. We are going to check this new one out every way there is, girl."

"Okay, then, here is the way it really was . . ."

The sheriff told her to wait a moment. He spoke into his intercom and got hold of Willie and told him to bring in some fresh tape, and told him the Denn girl was changing her story, and stop the transcript on the old story. Willie groaned audibly. He came in with the fresh tape, took the old one off the machine and set it for record.

"It's mostly all still good what I said before," Arlene said. "I just have to change some parts. I mean it would save doing the whole question bit right from the start, wouldn't it?"

"Then, save that tape, Willie," said Bunny Burgoon, "and close the door on the way out."

He started the tape rolling, and established time and place and the identity of the witness.

"Now, Mrs. Denn, you have told us that you wish to change portions of your previous statement."

"Just two . . . no, three parts."

"What would be the first change?"

"I didn't hear anybody say anything that sounded like Jan. The two men were mad at each other, but I didn't hear any word like that."

"And what is the second change you wish to make?"

"What if you decide to protect your own and throw me to the dogs, Sheriff?"

"What is the second change you wish to make?"

"Well . . . it wasn't Mr. McGee I saw. The man I saw did everything in the other statement the way I told it. But it was Deputy Sheriff Freddy Hazzard."

"Oh, God *damn* it!" said Tom.

"Hush up," said Bunny. "And the third change?"

"I looked in the window back in October but they were just talking. Drinking tea. That was all."

"Now, hold it a minute, girl. Tom, you go tell Walker and Englert to pick Freddy up and bring him back here and . . . Damn it, tell them to take his weapon and put him in the interrogation room and hold him until I can get around to him. When does he come on duty, Tom?"

"I think tonight he's on the eight to eight again. But you know Freddy."

"Sheriff?" the girl said as Tom left the office. "You weren't having me on, were you? About how big I could get busted for telling something that didn't happen?"

"I never said a truer thing in my life, Mrs. Denn."

"Why box me?" I asked her.

The vacant blue look she gave me was a total indifference. "Every straight one looks exactly alike to me."

Tom came back in looking distressed. "Damn it all, Bunny, he was out there checking the skip list when you came over the box telling Willie this girl was changing her story. And he walked right out and took off. He's in uniform, driving number three. Terry is trying to raise him on the horn but no answer. All points?"

Burgoon closed his eyes and rattled his fingers on the desk top. "No. If he's running, there's eighty-five back ways out of this county and he knows every one of them. Let's see what more we've got here." He leaned wearily and put the recorder back on.

"Who induced you to lie about what you saw that Sunday morning, Arlie?"

"Deputy Hazzard."

"What inducement did he offer you?"

"Not to get busted for possession, and some other things he said he could bust us for."

"Possession? Do you mean narcotics, girl?"

"That's your word. That's the fuzz word. But all we had was acid and grass. Booze is a lot worse for you."

"Arlie, are you and your husband addicts?"

"What does that mean? We're affiliates with the group up in Jax. And we get up there now and then. We take trips sometimes here, but it's a group thing. You couldn't comprehend, Sheriff. We all have our own thing. We don't bug the straights, and why shouldn't they leave us alone?"

"How did Deputy Hazzard learn you'd been a witness?"

"Like an accident. Last Thursday night out at the Banyan Cottages there was a complaint from somebody, and I guess it would be on your records here someplace. I didn't even know Hazzard's name. But he was the one who came there. Five of the kids had come down from Jax, three of them gals, in an old camper truck in the afternoon, from the Blossom Group in Jacksonville, and they had some new short acid from the Coast that never gives you a down trip and blows your mind for an hour only. We had almost two lids of Acapulco Gold, and we just started a lot of turn-ons there in the cottage, relating to each other, that's all. At night, sometime, I don't know what time, maybe the music got too loud. An Indian record. East Indian, and the player repeats and repeats. Maybe it was the strobes. We've got one and they brought two, and each one had a different recycle time, so there was a kind of pattern changing all the time. I guess you have to know the way it was when Hazzard came busting in. We had the mattresses and the blankets on the floor, and one of the gals was a cute little teeny-bopper and I'd painted her all over eyes."

"Ice?" said the sheriff.

"Eyes," she said impatiently. "Like eyeballs and eyelashes. All colors. And one boy and girl were wearing just little bells and rattles. You do whatever. Who are you hurting? It was blossomtime. A love-in, sort of, and our own business. Just with the strobe lights and the sitar music and he came breaking in because maybe we didn't hear him. Him and his gun and his black leather evil thing for hitting and hurting. You can't turn off a high like in a second. So he found the lights and ordered things in a big voice and nobody did what he said or cared. So he starts yelling and chunking people. The teeny-bopper wanted to tune him in and turn him on I guess and she started throwing flowers at him and he chunked her too. Of the seven of us he chunked the four that were turned on to the biggest high, chunked them cold, and he chunked the record player, busted it all to hell and got the other three of us finally sitting in a row on the cold bare bed springs holding onto the backs of our necks. Not scared or angry or anything. Just sorry there's no way of ever getting through to that kind of a straight. All he thinks of is busting people and busting things. And he chunked all the three strobes and broke them up. They're expensive and hard to find ones that don't over-heat and burn out when you keep them cycling a long time. In my high I understood all about him. He was breaking things and hitting heads because he hated himself, and I had seen him mushing Mr. Bannon with that heavy motor, and I knew that was why he hated himself. He collected up all the grass and the three little vials of powdered acid, and he picked up all the color polaroids laying around that a boy had taken earlier to take back to Jax to the group on account of the girl painted all over eyes was a big turn-on for him."

"Lord Jesus God Almighty," said the sheriff in a hushed voice.

"He was going to radio for help and take everybody in and bust them, and I just felt sorry for him being so empty of love and so I said to him that he hated himself for what he did to Mr. Bannon. He looked at me and he picked up a blanket and wrapped it around me and took me out in the night. He shoved me up against his car and I told him the whole thing, just the way I saw it. I told him he could trade in his hate for love, and we could show him the way. I could feel myself beginning to come off the high, because I began to think about it being a lot of bad trouble, and it was a poor time to get busted because of orders Roger and I had to fill. He kept wanting to know who I'd told about it, and while I was coming off the trip I got smart enough to say maybe I had and maybe I hadn't. So he said he was going to keep the evidence and think about what he was going to do, and we should cool it and he would come talk to me the next day.

"So in the morning the kids headed on away in the camper truck and the first thing I did was tell Roger the whole thing. That was Friday, and Hazzard came out in the afternoon and sent Roger out of the place and talked to me. He said he'd put the evidence away in a safe place, and in the pictures he had proof on both Roger and me on the teeny-bopper on corrupting a minor, and lewd and lascivious conduct. Then he questioned me over and over on what I saw that Sunday. Then he brought up if I knew a friend of Bannon's named McGee. I told him about just that one day, and he made me re-member every little part of it. So he walked back and forth and then he told me I was going to come in and make a statement and what I was going to say. I asked him why I should do anything he said, because if he left us alone, I wouldn't say anything about him. He said if I didn't do it, he would bust us both good, and he had enough proof and enough charges to get us both five to ten anyway. And I said if he tried to bust us that way, when he took us in, I'd tell what I saw him do. And he said then it would be pretty clear to everybody that I was making it up just to try to get him in trouble for doing his job and nobody would believe it because nobody ever believes an acid head about anything, and those pictures would make a hog sick. He said if I did my part, then after McGee was convicted, he'd give back everything he took. Then he gave me a chance to talk it over alone with Roger and for a while we thought maybe we ought to just take off and go merge into a colony someplace, but we went that road for a while and we relate better like plastics."

"What? What?" asked the sheriff.

"Take the group thing now and then, and have a square thing we do for bread. We take off and we lose the trade we've built up that comes to maybe a hundred and fifty a week on average, and then maybe that Hazzard could get us brought back anyhow." She combed the fingers of both hands back through the dark blonde stiffness of her long hair, shook it back and said, "So we decided okay, only what we didn't know is how I could get busted a lot bigger for the statement than for what he's got on us, and I didn't know McGee would be in the clear, because he said maybe McGee might not even get to answer any questions at all. So where are we?"

"Where are you?" the sheriff asked. "Honest to God, I don't even know *what* you are, girl."

I looked at my watch. It was just eleven o'clock. The sheriff told Arlie he'd like to hold her and her husband in protective custody on a voluntary basis, and she agreed. I knew that part of the case against Freddy Hazzard would be Press LaFrance's testimony about whatever conversation he'd had with his nephew, triggered by my comment to LaFrance about the possible reason why Tush had been killed. But had I reminded Burgoon of that point, he was going to mess up my timing, which was already two hours off. So I wondered out loud if Tush could have come in by bus early Sunday morning and if Hazzard, cruising around, had picked him up near the bus station and driven him out there.

Arlie had been taken off to the female detention tank. Tom, the chief deputy, said that if anybody could place Hazzard and Bannon together in town at dawn on Sunday, it would lock it up tighter.

"Tighter than the way he run?" Burgoon asked. "He was a *good* boy. He worked harder than any two others I got. Just a little bit too handy with that mail-order pacifier sometimes. But you take a county where you got some hard cases back in the piney woods, a little head-knocking keeps things leveled off. He lived clean and straight. It must have shook that boy when he checked out that complaint, walking in on that. Like looking into a bucket of mealy grubs. What's going wrong with folks lately, McGee?"

I had neared the ultimate promotion, to Mr. McGee.

"It's a mass movement against head-knocking, Sheriff."

"What kind of a joke is that?"

"All kinds of head-knocking. Commercial, artistic and religious. They're trying to say people should love people. It's never been a very popular product. Get too persistent, and they nail you up on the timbers on a hill."

He stared at me with indignation. "Are *you* one of *them?*"

"I recognize the problem. That's all. But the hippies solve it by stopping the world and getting off. No solution, Sheriff. I don't seek solutions. That takes group effort. And every group effort in the world requiring more than two people is a foul-up, inevitably. So I just stand back of the foul line and when something happens that doesn't get called by the referees, I sometimes get into the game for a couple of minutes."

"Around here today," he said sadly, "it's beginning to seem to me like in my sleep last night I must have forgot half the English language."

"Can I go take care of my business matter?"

He looked at Tom, got some signal in reply, and said, "Stay in the area, Mr. McGee."

13

I SAW Preston LaFrance sitting at his desk inside his little real estate office in a converted store on Central Street. He had his head in his hands, and he was alone.

When he heard the door open, he looked up with the beginnings of the affable show-you-a-fine-parcel smile, and it froze there partially developed. He jumped and boggled and said, "McGee! You . . . you're alone? But I saw you with . . . you were . . ."

"Sorry I couldn't keep the coffee date, Press. I had to go answer some fool questions the sheriff wanted to ask me."

"Bunny . . . let you go?"

"What's the matter with you? Are you disappointed?"

"No! Hell, no! Sit down! Sit down, Trav! Cigar? Take that chair. It's more comfortable."

I sat down. "Did you have the same weird idea Burgoon had? Did you think I killed Bannon?"

"But Freddy said an eyewitness had turned up, and they were going to grab you down there in Lauderdale and he was going to go down and bring you back."

"It would have been an exciting trip."

"What happened? What about the eyewitness?"

"Burgoon satisfied himself that she was lying and I wasn't."

"Freddy said everything fitted together."

"It did."

"What? What do you mean?"

"It worried you a little, Press, when I told you that maybe somebody was trying to give you and Monk Hazzard a lot of cooperation in rousting Bannon out of his property, and maybe they busted him up too much. And you said that there wasn't anybody involved who'd do a thing like that, but you hesitated a little. So you were thinking of Nephew Freddy, the head-knocker. So you came back and laid some very indirect questions on him and he convinced you he was absolutely innocent, and then you told him who had been feeding you such crazy ideas. So, lo and behold, the eyewitness was brought in and she changed her story and the sheriff let me go."

"I guess then we can . . . talk business?"

"Sure, Press. That's what I'm here for. By the way, the eyewitness identified Freddy as the killer. He heard about it by accident and took off. They're running a manhunt right now. So it was a pretty good guess."

"I got the money together, but first I have to . . . What did you say? Freddy? Come *on!*"

"He ran, Press. He took off. Check it out. Call Burgoon."

He reached for the phone, hesitated, then picked it up and ran a thumbnail down the typed list of numbers under the desktop glass. He dialed and asked for Burgoon. "Okay, then give me Tom Windhorn. Thanks. . . . Tom? This is Press. Say, Tom, is Freddy in some kind of a . . . Huh? No kidding! But look, it couldn't really be that he would . . . Oh. . . . I see. . . . Yeh. . . . Boy, some mess. Anybody get hold of Monk yet? . . . Oh, that's right, I forgot. . . . No, Tom, I don't even know what route they were taking. Monk said he was going to take his time and see the sights. Sis will be out of her mind. Tom, is everybody absolutely *positive* he . . . All right. Sure. I'll be over later." He hung up and shook his head in bewildered fashion. "I just can't believe it. He's a nice clean-cut boy."

"I'm afraid you've got too much on your mind. This is no time to talk business. We've got another deal we can work out. So let's forget the whole thing. Okay?"

"But I . . . but I need——"

"Just hang onto your fifty acres and use the forty thousand to pick up that Carbee land. The way the area is going to go, you ought to make a nice profit in a couple of years. Just sit tight."

His smile was slightly ghastly in its attempt to be reassuring. "Listen, Trav. Believe me, I can keep my mind on your proposition. I mean this is a terrible tragedy in the family and all, but it isn't going to do anybody any good for me to lose out on something."

"Maybe you won't like it anyway," I said. "Give me a piece of paper and a pencil. I'll show you how it works."

I wrote down a little tabulation on the sheet:

Carbee	200 acres @ $2000 =	$400,000
LaFrance	50 acres @ 2000 =	100,000
McGee	10 acres @ 2000 =	20,000
Total purchase price		520,000
Cost to LaFrance:		
McGee 10 acres	$ 90,000	
Carbee 200 acres	40,000	
	$130,000	130,000
Total available for split		$390,000
To LaFrance	$265,000	135,000
McGee (+ 40,000 from LaFrance)		95,000
×		60,000
		390,000

"Who is this X? What does your ninety-five thousand come out of? I don't understand this."

"Mr. X is the man we're going to meet at the hotel for lunch. The point is, I don't trust him completely. But he has the authority to buy—from one single owner—those two hundred and sixty acres at two thousand an acre. And because he's going to the top limit authorized, he wants a cash kickback, under the table. The trouble is, he wants it now. And I don't think we ought to turn it over until we get the full amount on the land. If something went wrong, we couldn't prove a thing. Right?"

"Yes, but——"

"Listen, can you get my forty thousand in cash instead of by certified check?"

"I . . . I guess so. Sure. But—"

"Then, maybe there's a way we can work it so we won't end up with the dirty end of the stick, Press."

"But what's this ninety-five thousand for you?"

"For putting this thing together. You are going to sell me a twenty-five percent share of that option for five thousand."

"The *hell* I am! I can sell that Carbee land for——"

"Forget it. Forget Calitron. You'll see why when you see the correspondence X has. If X can't deal with us, he'll deal with Gary Santo and we'll be out in the cold. Why are you crying anyway, LaFrance? You get all your bait back, all hundred and thirty grand, plus a hundred and thirty-five on top. That's fifteen thousand over a quarter of a million."

We had lunch with Meyer at the hotel. He was superb. He told us where he was staying. I went to the bank with LaFrance and got the papers on our land sale signed and notarized, and he got the forty thousand cash. I drove him to the motel where Meyer was waiting, and before we went in, I unlocked the trunk compartment and dug out the little package of currency I had taped to a far dark corner. It was my total war fund, and it made me feel uneasy carrying it around. Meyer showed us the rest of the correspondence and the overlays. He took them out of the bulky dispatch case. He was properly arrogant, properly shifty. LaFrance bought the con. I could read it on his face and in the sweatiness of his hands, leaving damp prints on the papers.

"So, if we can settle the last little detail, gentlemen?"

"Doctor Meyer," I said, "we get . . . I mean Mr. LaFrance gets the point five two million check or definite confirmation from topside that it has gone through, then you get the money we agreed on."

He stared at me with a heavy, convincing contempt.

"And sue you if I don't get it, Mr. McGee? Where? In Small Claims Court? You see the correspondence. You see the authorizations. It will go through. Believe me."

"And at the last minute they change their minds. What have we got to make you give it back, Doctor?"

"There will be nothing in writing. You understand that. You have my word."

"But you won't take ours, Doctor?"

"So forget it, gentlemen. Impasse. I'll resume the negotiations for the other tract."

"There's one possible solution, Doctor, that might satisfy both sides. It would be safe for both of us."

"Which is?"

I took out the two packets of money and dropped them on the coffee table. "Seventy-five thousand dollars, Doctor Meyer."

"So?"

"Let's seal it in an envelope and we can put it in the hands of a local attorney, and give him instructions about it."

"To do what?"

"I'll tear a dollar bill into three pieces. We each keep a third. The attorney is authorized to surrender the envelope to whoever shows up with the three pieces, or to any two who, between them, have all three pieces."

"Kid games!" said Meyer. "Nonsense games!"

"The extra fifteen, Doctor, is a bonus for doing it this way. Does the game sound better?"

He nodded. "A little. But you can save fifteen by giving me the sixty now."

"We'll pay the extra fifteen for insurance, Doctor."

"Sometimes being too careful is stupid," he said. "I'll play your game."

The good doctor had a fresh Manila envelope in his dispatch case. He handed it to me. I put the money in it and sealed it and handed it to LaFrance, saying, "Which lawyer do . . ."

"I think," said Meyer, "as long as we are not trusting one another, I will choose not to trust any lawyer of your selection, gentlemen. The old hotel where we lunched has a safe, no doubt. And some sort of claim check arrangement. The claim check could be torn into three portions, and the manager instructed not to surrender the envelope except for an entire claim check taped back together. Satisfactory?"

"Suits me," I said. "Press?"

"Sure." So we went back downtown in my car, Press beside me, Meyer in the rear. I parked and we went in. Meyer hung back while Press and I went to the desk. The girl greeted him by name and Press asked for the manager by name. He came out of his office.

"Can I help you, Mr. LaFrance?"

"Harry, this is sort of a wager. Can you put this in the safe for me and give us a claim check. We're going to tear it into three hunks, and don't surrender it unless you get the whole claim check."

Harry was affable about the whole thing. He took the envelope into his office and came back with the other half of the perforated tag he had affixed to the envelope. I had a five-dollar bill ready and reached and laid it on the counter and said, "For your trouble," and he gave me the tag, telling me it wasn't necessary to . . . uh . . .

"Go ahead, Harry," I told him. I turned away, and walked over to Meyer, with LaFrance hurrying to keep up with me. I tore the tag into three parts, making them irregular, and ceremoniously put a third on each of their outstretched palms.

Meyer sighed. "Games for children. An expensive game for you, my friends." We walked out and stood by my car. I offered the doctor a ride back to his motel. He got into the front seat. I closed the door and turned and held my hand out to Preston LaFrance.

"Press, I think we're really in business. I'll be seeing you in a few days. You draw up the agreement on the Carbee option."

"Sure, Trav. I'll sure do that." His expression was doleful and earnest and anxious, like a dog hoping to be let in out of the rain.

"I hope you get your trouble worked out all right."

"What? Oh, that terrible business about my nephew."

"The boy just got too eager, I guess. He knew you and his father were using every legal means to run Bannon out of business. He probably tried a different way of discouraging him."

"That's probably it. And he tried to cover up. It was sort of an accident, I'd say. Freddy wouldn't want to kill anybody. When they find him, I think if he tells exactly what happened, they might agree on letting him plead guilty of manslaughter. Monk has got a lot of leverage in this part of the state. Trav, how . . . how soon do you think our deal will go through?"

"A matter of days. Don't worry about it."

"I think I'll go over to the sheriff's office and see what's happening."

He walked away. I walked around the car and got in and drove away. "Pigeon drop, smigeon drop," said Meyer. "How was I?"

"Like a pro. Great natural talent, Doctor."

I reached into my breast pocket and took out the intact green claim check and handed it to him. He took the little tin tape dispenser out of his pocket and tore the check in thirds and stuck it back together with the tape.

I made two right turns and parked on the side street behind the hotel. He gave me the claim check and said, "So soon?"

"Why not? While we know Harry is still in the office and we know where ol' Press is. Wait right here. Don't go away, pro."

I walked around the corner and went in the side door of the hotel and across the old-fashioned lobby to the desk. Harry was alone, sticking mail into the room boxes.

I handed him the check and said, "The winnah!"

"That was a quick one, sir."

"Wasn't it, though!"

He brought me the envelope and I said, "Harry, if you want to keep on being friends with Mr. LaFrance, you'd better not mention this little fiasco to him. He was so sure he was right he's going to be *very* grumpy about the whole thing."

"I know what you mean, sir."

I walked back to the car and drove Meyer to the motel. I gave him the forty thousand, and taped my emergency fund back into its inconspicuous place in the car trunk.

It was just three thirty. When I walked back into the motel unit, Meyer was on the phone talking with his Lauderdale broker. He hung up and looked at the figures he had scribbled down.

"I think the answer is right here, Travis. I don't think it has to come from Mary Smith. Fletcher Industries moved up one and an eighth today, to sixteen and three eighths on a volume of ninety-four hundred shares. So Janine Bannon has made eleven hundred and twenty-five bucks today."

"Today?"

"Well, so far. I mean the final returns for the day aren't in, but it will be pretty close to that. The Dow is off a little over five points. You look astonished. Oh, I see why. This morning before I left I opened her margin account with cash money, pending the power of attorney that you forgot to give me. I put in enough to buy her a thousand shares, and I got them at fifteen and a quarter."

I gave him the power of attorney. He put it in his dispatch case, and took out all the fake correspondence to My dear Ludweg and the fake reports on plant location data.

"So," he said, "it was worth the chance and now I reimburse myself out of this money and put the rest into her account to cover the order I placed for the opening tomorrow. Another twenty-five hundred shares. That will commit her account up to maximum. Then I have to go sit and stare at the tape, day after day, ten in the morning to three thirty in the afternoon. Bring me sandwiches." He waved the sheaf of counterfeit letters and documents. "When these are confetti and flushed away, my heart might slow down some you think?"

He went into the bathroom with them and I placed a credit-card call, station to station, to the Santo offices, and after a short wait I got Mary Smith.

The approach, to be convincing, had to be that of the male who'd been brushed off.

"McGee here," I said. "What was Santo's decision?"

"Oh. Trav. I've been *so* impatient for you to call, darling."

"I bet. What did he decide?"

"I want to tell you something else first, because I have the hunch that if I tell you first, you'll hang up."

"Can you think of any good reason why I shouldn't?"

"Darling, I can think of a *very* good reason. My darned telephone was acting up. I *knew* it was you, but it just kept making a horrid ringing sound in my ear when I picked it up." Her voice was intimate, cheery, persuasive.

"Nice try, kid."

"But I'm telling the *truth! Really* I am. What could make you possibly think I wouldn't *be* there? If you want to be such a grouchy old bear, you can call the phone company and ask them if a certain Mary Smith raised absolute *hell* with them Saturday afternoon. I got the message you left at the office, and I left one for you, hoping you'd call back."

"At least you make it sound good, Miss Smith."

"Travis, I *know* how disappointed and angry you must have been."

"How come the phone company couldn't fix the phone?"

"Actually they swore there was nothing wrong with it. They tested and tested, and when I made them come back the second time, they took out the instrument and put in a new one."

"Which didn't work either. Which didn't work on Saturday night."

"I . . . wasn't there."

"You said you had the weekend open. So why didn't you hang around? How about four o'clock Sunday morning, kid?"

"I . . . I was told you'd made other plans, dear."

"By who?"

"To tell you the truth, I drove up to Lauderdale just to find you. I saw that fantastic boat of yours, dear. It must be a marvelous way of life. A man told me you might be at a party on another boat and I went there, but a very odd-looking girl told me I'd missed you and you might come back. So I waited there. You can ask those people. A lot of them are your friends, I guess. It is quite a . . . lively group. Then that strange girl came and told me that she found out you had left with another girl, so you probably wouldn't be back. So . . . you see, I really tried."

The persuasive lilt of her tone was dying away, fading back into the monotone of a deadly exhaustion.

"So even at four in the morning, you weren't home yet? I guess you had a good time."

"Not terribly. But it was pleasant. I . . . called up an old friend and she invited me over, and it got to be too late to drive back, so they put me up for the night, dear."

"So when did you get home?"

"I think it was about . . . ten o'clock last night. I spent the day with them. Why, dear? You had a date, didn't you? There was hardly any point in roaring home and sitting panting by the phone, was there? Listen, dear, I don't *blame* you for having a date. After all, it was perfectly reasonable for you to assume I stood you up, and so you said the hell with Mary Smith and her lousy steak. Don't I get any points for driving all the way up there to find you?"

I said in a marveling tone, "And all it was was a phone out of order. You know, there must be a hex on us."

"I guess there must be," she said. She sighed audibly and heavily.

"So expect a man at about nine tonight, honey. Okay?"

"Oh no, darling! I'm sorry."

"What now?"

"Well . . . I guess the hex is still working. I . . . uh . . . my friends have this little boat at their dock. They live on a canal. And they were going to take me out in the boat, and like a clumsy idiot I tripped somehow and fell headlong, right off the dock into the boat. Honestly, I'm an absolute ruin. I was waiting for you to call so that I could get out of here and go home and take a hot bath and go to bed. I've been tottering around here today like a little old lady."

"Gee, honey, that must have been a nasty fall. Where did you hurt yourself?"

She gave a tired laugh. "Where didn't I? There were a lot of . . . you know . . . fishing tackle things in the boat. I must have hit my mouth somehow because it's all puffed out, and when I looked at myself head to toe in my mirror this morning, I swear I didn't know whether to laugh or cry. I'm battered and bruised from head to toe. I *couldn't* let you see me like this. I'm a fright."

"That could be dangerous, Mary, a fall like that."

"I know. I strained my back somehow, I think. It's such a shock I guess it takes a lot out of you. My bones ache even." She sighed again. "Darling, give me time to get all well again, just for you. Please?"

"Sure. Take care of yourself, kid. Sorry our luck was running bad."

"Friend McGee, you are not one-tenth as sorry as I am," and there was total conviction gleaming through the drag of her words. "The decision was yes, by the way."

"Good. How much?"

"He said it depends on how it goes. At least one and a half. Maybe up to three, or anywhere in between. He said to tell you he'll be doing it through different accounts, scattered across the country. He wondered if you mind the amount being a little vague."

"I expected that. If it gets too much play from the traders, he won't be able to slow it down enough."

"Dear, may I wish us better luck next time?"

"You may indeed. Hurry home to bed, honey."

I hung up and looked into the bathroom in time to see Meyer sprinkle the last of his confetti and flush the toilet.

"The evidence is destroyed," said Meyer, with big smile and big sigh.

"And Santo has climbed on."

"May he enjoy the trip in good health. May he have asked a few friends to join him even."

I gave him my third of the other claim check and he put it carefully into a pocket of his wallet. "So tomorrow," he said, "I drive up to Broward Beach and go out A-One-A and find a place called the Annex, and at seven I am sitting at the bar, waiting for the pigeon. Correct?"

"Looking important and shifty. Correct."

"Shouldn't you ask me what it is I checked when I arrived for lunch? Don't you care?"

"I do now. Now that I know it must be interesting."

"Here is the scene. Mr. LaFrance rushes to the desk at the hotel. He has the three parts of the claim check taped together. He is panting, right?"

"His hands are trembling. He can't wait for Harry to give him the money," I said.

"So Harry takes the check and he doesn't come back with a big brown envelope. He comes back with a small white envelope. Number ten. Greeting card size. The envelope I checked when I arrived for lunch, so I could get a claim check, so you could make the substitution and tear it up into three pieces and give him one."

"Meyer, remember me? I *know* all this."

"Shut up. Let me enjoy. So he asks Harry, where is the brown envelope? Where is the money? So Harry says the other fellow claimed it ten minutes after it was checked. Yes, Mr. LaFrance, he had the right three pieces stuck together. He said I shouldn't mention to you that you lost the bet. I *know*, Mr. LaFrance, this check is torn in three pieces too, but it isn't the check for the money. It's the check for this card."

"And so," I said, "stunned, bewildered, shocked, our Mr. LaFrance wobbles over to a lobby chair, falls into it and thumbs the white envelope open. Come *on*, Meyer! What does the card say?"

"Don't rush. It says on the front: 'Congratulations from the Gang at the Office.' You open it. Inside it says: 'It couldn't have happened to a nicer guy.'"

"That is very wicked, Meyer."

"But the signature. That's the good part."

"What did you do? Forge my name?"

"Not exactly. He saw your houseboat. He saw the name. Inside the greeting card he finds five playing cards I took out of a deck. I threw the rest of the deck away. The five, six, seven and eight of hearts. And the king of clubs. Right? A busted flush?"

I looked at him admiringly. "Meyer, you have great class. You have an instinct for this kind of work."

"It was nothing, really. Just innate good taste, a creative mind, and high intelligence. It will make a nice signature anytime you want somebody to know who gave it to them good."

14

AT NINE that evening Sheriff Bunny Burgoon sent word out from his office that he could see me.

His chief deputy, Tom Windhorn, was planted in the same chair against the wall as before. They both looked as if they'd had a very hard day.

"From the talk out front I know you haven't gotten him yet. But have you gotten any kind of line on him, Sheriff?"

"What I got doesn't exactly boost up my spirits, mister. And it's no joy having every newspaper and TV and radio station yappin' on and on about Shawana County having a deputy that turned bad. And it didn't help any to have Monk Hazzard chewing me up long distance and telling me I was crazy as hell. But when I told him about car number three, it slowed him some."

"Where was it? I heard you found it."

"Just before sunset. The Highway Patrol chopper spotted it way over in the southwest corner of the county, run off into a marsh and bogged up to the top of the fenders. I got a call from the boys that went to check it out. There's little places along the lake shore there, spread out. They were checking all the driveways and heard somebody yelling in one of the places. Retired couple, trussed up, scared, and mad as puckered owls. Seems that Freddy drove in, knocked, real polite, a little after two in the afternoon. Asked to come in. Said it was on a complaint on the fish and game laws. Head-knocked them both, tied them up, stuck dishtowels in their mouths. The boys say it's a big tall old man, so his clothes fit Freddy good enough. Left the uniform. Put on the old man's best suit, packed a bag with other clothes and toilet articles. Picked up what money they had around. Thirty or forty dollars. Drove off in the county car. Came back on foot and drove off in their two-year-old Plymouth station wagon. Said he seemed nervous. Told them he was sorry he had to do them that way. Seemed right sorry about it. The old man tongued the towel out of his mouth after a while. When he heard the boys drive down his drive, he started bellering. So we put the car and the clothes on the wire. From there he's twenty miles from the Interstate. If he pushed it hard enough, he could have crossed into Georgia before we got the word out."

"Once they calm down," Tom said, "if we get all their stuff back to them and fix up anything busted or lost, and talk nice, they might not press charges."

"We sort of reconstructed the thing with Bannon," the sheriff said. "I say he must have come across Bannon on the road, hiking out to his place and told him he'd been foreclosed and his wife had took off on him, and he must have wanted to drive Bannon back here, but Bannon just wouldn't believe him and wanted a look, so when he insisted, Freddy drove him the rest of the way out. That would account for the fat girl thinking they were talking ugly to each other. Now I'd say Bannon lost his head and tried to bust into the place that used to be his. Now that's against the law and Freddy tried to gentle him some, but that was a lot of man and if he didn't drop with the first knock, and if he rushed Freddy, that boy in his excitement just swang too hard is all. Caved his head bone in, maybe. And he knew Tom and me had chewed him for being too goddang quick with that mail-order pacifier, and I guess Freddy just lost his head is all. Having that girl see how he covered it up was just plain bad luck."

"And was he in line to be the one to come to Lauderdale and bring me back if I was picked up there?"

The sheriff looked uneasy. "That was what was planned, mister."

"I guess I would have tried to open the car door and jump out when we were going seventy-five or eighty. After I got 'through bounding along the pavement, nobody'd find a little extra lump on my skull."

"Now you can't be sure that would have happened that way."

"I wonder why he told anybody about hearing from his Uncle Press that I was going to be here this morning?"

"Because," said Tom Windhorn, "he knows I play golf Sunday mornings in a foursome with Press LaFrance every week of my life, and Press knew we were hunting you, and Freddy knew there was no way in the world of stopping Press from telling me. So he brought it in first. And the fool thing about it is that Press never did play yesterday. He phoned in he was feeling poorly, too late for us to get somebody to fill out, and so they stuck some old coot in with us that couldn't hit the ground with his hat."

"That poor boy just had plain bad luck all the way around," I said. "He never did get a chance to kill me."

"He's no killer," the sheriff said. "He just lost his head some."

"Nice I get to keep mine. Find the stuff he picked up out at the cottages?"

The sheriff nodded. "It was at his place, under his clean shirts. The narcotics we got packed up to mail in for analysis. No case on that because without Freddy we can't prove the chain of possession." He opened the shallow middle drawer of his desk and then held an envelope toward me. I reached and took it.

The color prints were sharp and clear. I leafed through them. They did not leave the feral and cynical impression that the posed product of the hard-core studios induce. This was a tumble of aging children, most of them rather badly nourished. In spite of their placid, dazed, beatific smiles and grimaces, they were a kind of curious sadness, in their weird, bright patterns of love-paint on the scrawn of flesh, in their protest bangles and their disaffiliated bells, crushing the flower blossoms in a dreamy imitation of adult acts that for them had all been bleached of any significance or purpose. The rites of the strobe, frozen in such a sharpness it caught forever a wistful dirtiness of knuckles, the calico of bad bleach jobs, the moles and the blemishes and the sharp, helpless angle of shoulder blade. This was not a rebellion against mechanization, or emotional fraud. This was denying life itself in all eras and all cultures, and instead of being evil or outrageous was merely empty, bland and slightly saurian somehow, as though in a vain attempt to warm the blood that had begun to turn cooler in some gigantic and total regression that would take us all back through geological time, back into the sea where life began.

Said Tom, "Ain't that Arlie the damnedest sight a man would ever want to behold?"

"Unforgettable," I said, and put the envelope on the edge of the desk. "I've been waiting around to ask permission to leave your area, Sheriff. Here's the address where you can get me. I'll come back if you need me. But now I'd like to drive up to Frostproof and see Jan Bannon."

"Get your business done with Press?"

"Yes, thanks."

"Well . . . I guess there's no call to keep you waiting around. Thank you for your cooperation, Mr. McGee."

"Thank you for your courtesy and consideration, Sheriff."

When I phoned ahead, Connie said that Janine had heard the news and that she was very upset and puzzled. I said it would be well after midnight before I could make it, and she said that it had been too much of a long, hard day to wait up. I told her my day had been on the same order, and told her that everything had gone very smoothly so far.

It was ten after one when I got there and turned under the arch and through the glare of the gate light and drove to the big house. The night was cool and the stars looked high and small and indifferent.

Jan stood in the open doorway waiting for me. And she leaned up to rest her cheek for a moment against mine, with a quick, soft touch of her lips. "You must be exhausted, Trav."

"And you shouldn't have waited up."

"I couldn't have slept."

I went in and sat down into the depth and softness of a big leather couch. There were two red embers among the silvery ashes of the hearth. She wore a floor-length navy robe with a white collar. She said, "Connie left orders to give you a great wallop of bourbon to unwind on." I said it sounded great. She drifted out of sight and I heard the clink of cubes and the guggle of a generous dose.

"Water?"

"Just the ice, thanks."

She brought it over and fixed the cushions at the end of the couch and told me to lie back and put my feet up. She moved a footstool close. The light behind her from the corner lamp, the only one on in the room, shone through the fine ends of her cropped black hair. Her face was in shadow.

I sipped the strong drink and told her about Deputy Hazzard. "That's what I couldn't believe," she said. "He and the older one, with the funny name. Not the sheriff."

"Windhorn?"

"Yes. They were the ones who . . . came out with the padlocks and the notices. And he, the young one, seemed so very shy and nice and troubled about everything. There was no point in taking it out on them. They had their orders."

"Had he been out there before?"

"Several times, yes. To serve papers, and the time they checked to see about the licenses we have to have for the houseboats. A lanky boy with a long face, kind of a red, lumpy face, but sweet. But very official about what he had to do. All leather and jingling and creaking."

"That reconstruction of it doesn't fit," I said. "It doesn't fit Tush."

"I know. He never got mad that way. Not like me. I fly off the handle and want to hit everything I can reach. He'd just get very very quiet and sad-looking, and he'd walk slowly away. It's better for me to . . . to be absolutely positive once and for all that he didn't kill himself, Trav. But it just seems to be such . . . a stinking trivial way to die, to be killed by that harmless-looking young man."

"Most of the ways people die are kind of dingy and trivial, Jan."

"It just shouldn't have been that way for Tush. But how in the world did that Freddy person get Arlie Denn to tell such an ugly lie about you? She always seemed to me to be sort of dull and placid. She never seemed mean or vicious or anything. It must have been horrible for her—watching like that. I would think she would just . . . have never told anybody at all, ever."

And that took some explaining and finally I managed to make her comprehend it, up to a point. But comprehension was comingled with revulsion. "But we let that wretched girl sit with our boys a lot of times! She could have taken something . . . and hurt them."

"I doubt it."

"What kind of people were those others? How old were they?"

"I'd say Roger and Arlie were the oldest. The others looked nineteen and twenty. And the one girl about fifteen or sixteen."

"What are they trying to do to themselves?"

"Drop out of the world. Hallucinate. Turn on. Dig the sounds and colors and feels. Be at one with the infinite something or other. I can't lay too big a knock on them, you know. In another sense I'm a dropout. I don't pay for my tickets. I jump over the turnstile."

"I think I've *been* dropped out somehow. For good."

"Now I am supposed to tell you about how you're a young woman still in your twenties with most of your life still ahead of you."

"Please don't."

"A guy will need you in the right way sometime."

"Tell him not to *really* need me. That's when I run like a rabbit." She took my empty glass and said, "another?"

"No. That one is going to do it."

"I made you talk too long. There's more I want to ask. But I'll wait until tomorrow."

She got up and took the glass away. I decided I'd better get up and head for bed while I could. I closed my eyes for a moment and opened them again and a high sun was shining and her middle boy was standing holding a saucer with both hands, and he had his tongue sticking out of the corner of his mouth to help with the chore of keeping the coffee from spilling out of the cup.

"Everybody's been up a *long* time," he said disdainfully. "Mom said bring you this and if I stood here, the smell would wake you up. I think it's a lousy crummy old smell and I'm never going to drink that stuff. Oh. Good morning."

My shoes had been removed, belt loosened, necktie removed, collar unbuttoned. There was a blanket over me. The lady had given me bourbon and loving care. I hoped that it would be at least another full year before I had to put a necktie back on.

I sat up and took the coffee.

"*You* spilled a little bit," he said. "*I* didn't."

"Like it here?"

"It's neat. Today there's a teacher's meeting, so we don't have to go on the bus. Charlie's going to let me ride on the tractor again with him. It's real neat. I gotta go." And he went—at a full run.

I dialed Press LaFrance direct at twenty after ten. I wanted him to have a lot of time to make some collections. Just as I was ready to hang up, he answered, out of breath.

"Who? Trav? Where are you? What's up?"

"Miami, boy. And I'm getting a little sweaty. Maybe we're in trouble."

"How? My God, Trav, I thought everything was——"

"I've been making some long distance calls, Press. And it looks as if everything might go through okay. I was with Doctor Meyer a few minutes ago and he as much as admitted that he might wait until Gary Santo gets back from abroad and see if he wants to make a better deal on the side, a fatter deal for Meyer. I told you he's slippery."

"But what are we going to do?"

"If we play it his way, the way he suggested in the beginning, he'll move right ahead with it. But it has to be today. He's on his way up to Broward Beach. Do you know a place called The Annex?"

"Yes, but——"

"I had to take the chance, Press. I had to move fast. I gave him my third of the claim check. Now he's going to be at the bar at The Annex at seven o'clock tonight. I told him that you would meet him there and give him his damned sixty thousand in cash for the two thirds he's holding."

"Where am I going to get that kind of money before seven?"

"The minute after you get back to Sunnydale and walk into the hotel, you'll have it back, won't you?"

"Yes, but——"

"Scrounge it somehow. You could pay somebody a very fat amount of one-day interest out of that fifteen extra, couldn't you?"

"But, Trav, suppose he takes the sixty and then screws us and makes his deal with Santo? What can we do?"

"Absolutely nothing. But stop running around in crazy circles, man, and *listen* to me. I'm assuming the risk. Got that? It's my money sitting up there. Give me a week and I could scrape up three or four times sixty in cash, but I damned well can't do it today. If it falls through, what are you out?"

"There's . . . maybe one possibility."

"Now you're beginning to think. I'll phone you back. How long will it take you to find out?"

"I . . . I should know by . . . you phone me back right here at two o'clock?"

The shape of larceny is, in time, written clearly enough on a man's face so that it can be read. Constant greed and sharp little deals and steals had left the sign on Preston LaFrance. There is the old saying that God and your folks give you the face you're born with, but you earn the one you die with.

I went back into the house at two o'clock and phoned him. I knew just how he had probably worked it out in his mind. Get hold of sixty thousand cash to buy the claim check to seventy-five thousand in cash. Nobody ever gets hurt taking a profit. The small towns of Florida are peppered with old boys who don't like to have too much information on record about the deals they make. And they like to keep a little leverage around in the form of cash money. LaFrance would know a couple of those shrewd old hawks. He'd hunt one up, probably put up his fifty acres and the Carbee option as security, if the bank wasn't holding them, and pay the old boy a thousand dollars or five hundred for the loan of sixty thousand in cash for a few hours. Then he'd hike the interest rate as high as he dared when he reported to me.

"Trav?" he said. "I've been dreading this call, cause there's something I hate to have to tell you."

"You couldn't get the money!"

"No, no. I got the money. I got it locked up right here in my office. I got it from a fellow that keeps cash on hand. Trouble is, he knows I'm spread thin. Maybe I got too anxious. Anyway, he gave it to me good. The only deal I could make was to pay him the whole fifteen thousand. Honest to God, Trav, when a man gets the tights, all the money dries up on you. There just wasn't anybody else who'd give me the lend of it."

"Pretty damned steep, Press."

"Like you said, this is an emergency."

It was the perfect example of the philosophy behind all kinds of con, big and small: You can't cheat an honest man. I gave him a B in the course. B for Brass.

"When I get back," he said, "that old boy is going to be right there in the hotel lobby with his hand out, and there won't even be any point in unwrapping it, except he'll want to count it slow and careful, and then go on rattling home in his old pickup truck, smiling like a toad in the moonlight. Trav, it was the pure best I could do on short notice, and that's God's truth."

"Okay, then. Tote it over to The Annex and give it to Doctor Meyer, and don't lose it on the way. Then we'll just have to keep calm and wait for the corporation check to come through."

"How long will it take?"

"Ask the Doctor."

I hung up, knowing it was going to work. The secret of the big con is to move the victim, bit by bit, into increasingly implausible situations. At last, in the act of plucking him clean, you have him performing such a damned-fool act he will never understand how he came to do it, why he didn't see through it. He was blinded by the conviction he couldn't possibly lose a dime. And when he learned he'd been conned, he couldn't take it to the law. He'd have to tell them he had been taking a sixty-thousand-dollar bribe to a man pretending to be a field representative of a huge corporation. He would have to tell them he'd paid forty thousand dollars for a worthless equity in a defunct marina. If a story like that got out, every member of the Sunnydale business community would laugh himself sick. So he didn't have a chance. Poor LaFrance. Exactly the same situation he put Tush in. Smashed flat, plucked clean. No mercy for Tush. No mercy for LaFrance.

I walked out and found Connie by the equipment barn. We strolled over and sat on the mossy old stone bench under the huge banyan tree in the side yard.

I told her that our fish had gobbled the hunk of ripe bait, and the hook was perfectly set. A very greedy fish, that one.

Her weather-beaten face twisted in mocking amusement. "Maybe he's just greedy enough so your friend should be a little careful leaving that place, Trav."

"He's got a self-addressed envelope with him, and he walks right from The Annex through into the motel lobby and drops it in the slot. It's got more than enough stamps on it. It'll be solidly sealed with tape, and the money will have cardboard and a rubber band around it. Connie, again thanks. I'm going to head back."

"You come anytime, hear? Are you going to make our gal rich?"

"Let's say reasonably comfortable, if all goes well."

"And you'll have sixty more to fool with?"

"Meyer wouldn't like that verb."

"Ahh, McGee, all those poor bastards who'll wish that Tush Bannon never had a friend like you. Anyway, when things get just a little quieter—if they ever do—please let me know because then I think would be a good time for you to phone Jan and tell her that there are papers to be signed or something, any excuse for her to come down there. I'll talk her into it and keep the kids here, and when she gets down, you make her stay awhile. She needs a change. She needs to get away from the kids and away from here. She ought to get a lot of sun, and walk on a beach and swim and catch a fish and hear music and be near happy people. Okay?"

"Okay, Connie. Soon."

At eight thirty that evening the bing-bong announced that somebody had stepped over the gangplank chain and come aboard. I looked out and saw Meyer. I let him in.

He had a grin like a piano keyboard. He fell onto the yellow couch and said, "Build me one of those death-dealing in-and-out jobs named after somebody who's name escapes me."

"You'll get maudlin."

"So?"

"Any trouble at all?"

"None. You know, I have seldom seen or touched a greasier, grimier wad of money. I didn't know hundred-dollar bills ever got so cruddy. They must have come from a fondler."

"LaFrance was calm?"

"He stammered and sweat and his eyes bulged and he spilled his drink and mine. Otherwise, a cucumber. By now he's got the greeting card. By now he knows how it was done, by you switching claim checks as you turned away from him to walk over to me. By now he knows you picked it up ten minutes after it was checked. By now maybe he has leaned across the desk and hit Harry in the mouth. What a pity not to see him read the nice card I bought him."

"You'll get to see a certain amount of agitation."

"You can arrange that?"

"The phone is turned off. He'll be here in the morning. Count on it. Come over early. We'll play a little chess."

"I should be down watching the board. Today it moved almost too good. Volume is picking up. Very close to two points. Seven grand, practically, for the widow. I've got a friend on the floor of the exchange keeping in close touch with the fellow who maintains the position in Fletcher, and he calls me at my brokers the minute anything starts to look sour. And I should put in some orders for her out of the sixty. We'll have five days to meet the margin call. I don't think the mail takes that long from Broward Beach to here. At least not usually."

"We could be having a little game on the sun deck. The forecast is warm and bright. We invite him aboard. We have a little chat. He goes away."

"So I could phone in the first order. So it isn't as risky now in the beginning as it is going to get. Also, there is a variation of the queen's pawn opening I think I can break your back with. You know, you don't look so great."

"I brood a lot."

He finished the last of the drink in one huge gulp. He shuddered and got up and said, "Now if I can be standing by the bunk when that hits me . . ."

15

We had placed the chess table and chairs near the rear of the sun deck so we could look down onto the dock. We surveyed the morning traffic between moves. At one point Hero went by, swaying his big shoulders. The usual lock of hair was combed to fall just right over his forehead. He was taking a morning saunter through the game preserves, just in case he might flush something even at an unlikely morning hour. His gray slacks were tightly tailored to his narrow hips, and the broad belt was cinched tightly around his improbable waist.

He crinkled up at us and said in his mellow bass-baritone, "Morning, gents. Nice day out today."

"Getting any?" Meyer said contemptuously.

"Can't complain, gents. It's the best season for it."

He came to a momentary point and then lengthened his relaxed stride. I turned and saw two girls in beach togs with pale northern faces and legs, heading from the dock area toward the shops. Just as they disappeared from sight beyond the palm fronds Hero was ten feet behind them and, I suspected, clearing his throat and checking the third finger, left hand. That was his quaint little conceit, his only concession to any rule of human behavior. He proclaimed it often, with great conviction and emphasis. "I hold marriage sacred, and never in my life have I knowingly courted nor touched a lady united in the holy bonds of matrimony, no sir. It's something no gentleman would do."

A little later Meyer went below and phoned his broker and came back acting less restless. "It opened up a whole point, and then a couple of pretty good blocks came on the market and knocked it down to an eighth below yesterday's close. Insiders unloading, maybe. If so, in another week or two, they'll be slitting their throats at what they could have gotten."

At a few minutes before eleven, Preston LaFrance came along the dock at a half lope. He looked rumpled. He hadn't shaved. He came to a lurching halt and stared up at us.

"Doctor Mey . . ." It came out falsetto, so he coughed and tried again. "Doctor Meyer!"

"Hidey, Press," I said. "How you, old buddy? Come on aboard. Ladderway up here is on the port side."

He came clambering up and came over and stood beside us. We studied the chess pieces. "Doctor Meyer!"

"Just Meyer," he said. "Plain old Meyer."

"But don't you work for——"

"Work? Who should work? I'm an economist. I live on a little cruiser that has a case of dry rot lately. If I decide to get out the tools and go to work on it, then I'll be working."

"Then there isn't any . . . offer for the land?"

We both looked up at him. "Offer?" I said. "Land?" said Meyer.

"Oh Jesus, you two were in this lousy racket together. You are a stinking pair of con men. Oh Jesus God!"

"Please!" said Meyer. "I'm trying to figure out why he moved his bishop."

"I'm going to have you two bastards thrown in jail!"

"McGee," said Meyer, "let's finish the game after the noise stops." He stood up and leaned against the rail. Meyer in his white swim trunks reminds me a little bit of a man who is all dressed to go to a masquerade as a dancing bear. All that is left to do is put on the bear head and the collar. He stared at LaFrance. "Jail? For what?"

"You two took a hunnert thousand dollars away from me! More than that! That Bannon place isn't worth half the mortgage on it!"

"Mr. LaFrance," I said, "the records will show that I paid a legitimate fifteen thousand for Mrs. Bannon's equity in the Bannon Boatel, and then I turned around and sold that same equity to you for forty thousand. And I think that your banker will remember how anxious you've been to get your hands on Bannon's ten acres on the river."

"But . . . but . . . damn it, that was because you said . . ." He stopped himself and took a deep breath. "Listen. Forget the forty thousand. Okay. You suckered me. But the sixty thousand I gave this man last night, that's something else again. I've *got* to have it back."

"You gave me sixty thousand dollars!" Meyer said in vast astonishment. "Look. Stop standing in the sun. Get some rest."

He stood there, blinking, clenching and unclenching his bony fists. His color was bad. He smiled what I would imagine he thought was an ingratiating and friendly smile. "You took me good, boys. Slick and perfect. You made a nice score off ol' Press LaFrance. And I guess you're not going to give it back just because I say pretty please with sugar. But you don't understand. I had to put up the Carbee option to get the sixty thousand. Now, if I had it back, I could go ahead and make my deal with Santo. That's what I got to trade with, boys. We'll draw it up legal. You'll get the sixty thousand back that you stole off me, and twenty more to sweeten the pot."

"If I had sixty thousand," said Meyer, "would I be hanging around with such riffraff? I would be riding around in a white convertible with a beautiful woman in furs and diamonds."

"How can you lose?" LaFrance said. "There's no way you can lose."

"No thanks," I said. "What shape does that leave you in, buddy?"

He wiped his mouth with the back of his hand. "I just plain can't afford to get left in the kind of shape I'd be in. Why, I would be worse off than dead broke. I would be a mile underground, boys. I would be attached and garnisheed the rest of my natural life. I would never have one dime to call my own the rest of my days."

"Now you know how it feels, Press."

"How what feels?"

"How some of the people felt who got in your way. Like Bannon."

He peered at me. "You bleeding for Bannon? That was straight-out business. He was squattin' right in the way of progress, and he was so dumb it took him a long time to catch on, is all."

"It would have helped him a lot if he'd had a brother-in-law on the County Commission."

"What in the wide world is eating on you, McGee? My God, there's a whole world full of Tush Bannons stumbling around, and they get et up left and right, and that's what makes the world go 'round. I put Monk onto some good things and he owed me a favor."

"And you and Monk let Freddy Hazzard know you'd appreciate him leaning a little hard on Bannon any chance he had?"

"Now, we never meant anything like *that!*" He smiled. "You're just trying to sweat me up a little. Isn't that right? Look, boys, it won't improve the deal any. Twenty more on top of the sixty is the best I can do."

He was such a weak, miserable, unsatisfying target. He still thought he was one of the good guys. I tried to reach him, just a little.

"If you could bring in a thousand-percent profit a day, LaFrance, I wouldn't throw pocket change on the deck there in front of you. If I was on fire, I wouldn't buy water from you. I came prowling for you, LaFrance. If the thing you cared most about in the world was that face you wear, I would have changed it permanently, little by little. If your most precious possession was a beautiful wife, she'd be right down there below in the master stateroom waiting for you to leave so I could get back to her. If you juggled for a living, friend, you'd now have broken wrists and broken elbows."

"What the *hell* is the matter with you?"

"Get off the boat. Go ashore. Tush Bannon was one of the best friends I ever had. All you give a damn about is money, so that's where I hit you."

"Best . . . friend?" he whispered.

And I watched the gray appear. That gray like a wet stone. Gray for fright. Gray for guilt. Gray for despair. His mouth worked. "You . . . rooned me, all right. Ever'thing I worked all my life for is gone. You finished me off, McGee."

"Wait a minute," Meyer said. "Maybe I've got an idea."

LaFrance came to point like a good bird dog. "Yes? Yes? What?"

Meyer smiled at him benignly. "The answer was staring us right in the face all the time. It's so simple! What you do is kill yourself!"

LaFrance stared at him, tried to comprehend the joke, tried even to smile, but the smile fell away. Meyer's smile stayed put. But not one gleam of humor touched Meyer's little bright blue eyes. And I do not know many people who could have stared into that smile for very long. Certainly LaFrance couldn't. In the same soft persuasion a lover might use, Meyer said, "Do yourself a favor. Go kill yourself. Then you won't even know or care if you're broke. Maybe it hurts a little, but just for a split second. Use a gun or a rope, or go jump off something high. Go ahead. Die a little."

It is a kind of rat-frenzy I suppose, that dreadful and murderous fury of the weak ones when the door of the trap slams shut. With a mindless squalling he plunged at Meyer, long yellowed ridged thumbnails going for the meat of the eyes, knees jacking at belly and groin. The squalling and flailing and gouging lasted perhaps two and a half seconds before I clamped my forearm across his throat. I pulled him back away from Meyer, spun him and let go. He ended up against the far rail.

Obscenities are tiresome. He kept repeating himself. I cuffed him quiet and he went down the ladderway and I helped him along the way and onto the dock.

He stayed there perhaps three minutes. He was going to come back with a gun. He was going to bring friends. He was going to have my boat blown up. He was going to have it burned to the waterline. He was going to hire some boys from back in the swamps to come with their knives some dark night and turn us into sopranos. We were going to be awful sorry we'd ever messed with Preston LaFrance and you can by God believe it.

His eyes bulged and his voice had hoarsened and the saliva shone on his chin. And finally he hitched up his pants and walked away. His walk was that of a man wearing new bifocals and not being very sure of how far away the ground might be. Meyer was able to stand up straight without much discomfort, and I dabbed iodine on the thumbnail gouge under his left eye. He seemed troubled, thoughtful, far away. I told him LaFrance wouldn't make any trouble. I asked him what was bothering him.

Meyer, scowling, pinched the bridge of his nose. "Me! Did you hear me? On the sidewalk if there is a bug, I change my step and miss him. For me the business of the hooks almost spoils fishing. Me! I don't understand it. Such a rotten anger I had, Travis! Thick in the throat like a sickness. Oh, he won't kill himself. Not that one. He'll live on and on so he can whine. But it was like changing your step to squash the bug, not flat, just a little squash so he can crawl a little bit, slow, leaking his juices. McGee, my friend, I am ashamed of that kind of anger. I am ashamed of being able to do something like that. I said to myself when I first got into your line of . . . endeavor, I said—forgive me for saying this to you—I said I will go only so far into it. There are things McGee does that somehow hurt McGee, hurt him in the way he thinks of himself. I talked to Muggsie. This business of the pretty little woman who just somehow happened to go off with Hero, that wasn't pretty, and you were punishing something in yourself. Now I find myself a little bit less in my own eyes. Maybe this is a bad business you're in, Travis. Is there this kind of ugly anger in a man that waits for some kind of virtuous excuse? Was it there in me, waiting for a reason only? Travis, my friend, is this the little demonstration of how half the evil in the world is done in the name of honor?"

He wanted help I couldn't give him. One does not pat a Meyer on the head and give him a lollypop. He had overturned one of the personal stones in my garden too, and I could watch leggedy things scuttling away into comforting darkness.

I said, "You still didn't figure out why I moved my bishop."

He sat down and fixed a total concentration on the board. He gave a little nod at last and pushed a pawn one space forward, spoiling the sequence I was planning. He pinched at the bridge of his nose again, then smiled across at me, a hairy Meyer-smile, and said, "You know, I think I must have taken some sort of a dislike to that fellow."

Two days later, Friday afternoon, Meyer came aboard the *Flush* at four thirty, just after I got back from the beach. A mass of that arctic air that Canada sends down free of charge had begun to change the day a little before noon. It had come down so swiftly I knew the grove people would be worried. There were frost bulletins on all the broadcasts. An edge in the crisp northeast breeze had cleaned the long beaches of everybody except diehard Yankees and one masochistic beach bum named Travis McGee. I had been taking out all the kinks, in the muscles in both body and brain, of too many sedentary days, swimming parallel to shore, in and out of the surf line, for all the distance, endurance and occasional speed sprints I could manage. It had been hard work to even stay warm, and I had ground away at it, breaststroke, backstroke, crawl, until on my chattering lope back to the *Flush* I felt as if I had pulled most of the long muscles loose from the joints and sockets and hinges they were supposed to control.

Any persistent idiot, like Hero, can strain away at the doorframe isometrics and build impressive wads of chunky fibrous muscle with which you can lift the front end of any sedan to make the girls say Oooo. But if you want the kind of muscle structure that will move you from here to there very very quickly, that will enable you to slip a punch, snatch a moving wrist, turn a fall into a shoulder roll that will put you back on the balls of your feet, balanced and ready, then you'd better be willing to endure total expenditure over long, active and dogged periods. I was going to be slowed down by time and attrition, and maybe it had begun, but not to a degree as yet for me to notice, nor to a degree to make me doubt myself—and doubt, of course, is more fatal than slowed reflexes.

I had the heat going aboard. Meyer drank coffee and worked on his investment figures while I hot-showered the salt away, dressed in ancient, soft, treasured, threadbare checked shirt, gray Daks, and a pair of Herter's Two-Point woodsman's shoes, of oiled, hand-treated bull hide, worn to a condition as flexible and pliable as an Eskimo wife. In the shower I had begun to raise tentative voice in song, but had remembered another day, another shower, when that same song had been interrupted by a lady named Puss handing me in a well-made sample of the drink known as a McGee. So that song clogged and died, and I dressed and made the drink myself and took it into the lounge.

Meyer looked up from his work and said, "You look grotesquely healthy, Travis."

"And your eyes look grainy, and you look tired, and how long do you have to go five days a week and sit and watch the board like a great hairy eagle?"

"Not as long as I thought."

"Indeed?"

"Sit and listen. Without a glaze in the eyes, please. Try to understand."

"Proceed."

"These Fletcher Industries earnings statements. Look, accounting is flexible. There are choices. Each one is legal. However, say there are fifteen ways to handle different things to make earnings look a little bit better. So this outfit uses all fifteen, right up to the hilt. The last published quarter, it looks like they made forty percent more money than the quarter before that. I rework the statement and I come out with earnings not even flat. But down a little, even."

"So?"

"At fifteen dollars a share it *looked* as if Fletcher was a bargain for a growth stock, selling at maybe twelve times anticipated earnings for this year. So on top of that—which you call the fundamental picture, then there is the technical picture of the stock in the market. This buying pressure improves the technical picture. It becomes very desirable. Big volume attracts attention. Today I saw how it was going, how it was reacting, and so I took the risk, and I committed her all the way. Here is where her account stands. She's got seventy-four hundred shares. Average cost per share is eighteen dollars.

Today it closed at twenty-four and a quarter. So, right now, a short-term gain of forty-six thousand dollars."

"Of what!"

"She holds shares worth right now a hundred and eighty thousand, less the margin account debit. The supply is shrinking and the demand is increasing. It is moving too fast. The *Wall Street Journal* yesterday had a statement from management saying they don't know why all the big interest in their stock all of a sudden. It got out of hand too fast. I made this projection about where it is going to go next week. I have a used crystal ball an old gypsy gave me. I say a minimum eight points next week, so it will close between thirty-two and a half and thirty-seven. Traders will grab profits and get out. Usually I would wait, buy on the correction, and ride up with it again. But we get a trading suspension, maybe an investigation of corporate books. I think they used all the accounting gimmicks they could, and then they lied a little. It went up too fast and next week will be faster. So I start moving her over into that nice one I found for her to keep."

"You're telling me or asking me?"

"Telling you. What else? You are the expert on pigeon drops. I am the expert on the biggest crap game in the world."

"But you have to talk to her and explain all this."

"I do? Why?"

"Because she ought to come down here."

He cocked his head. "Connie suggested?" I nodded. "I should discuss all this with her. It is only fair to her."

"And she should sign some papers, maybe?"

"Very important-looking documents." He scratched his chin, tugged at his potato nose. "One part of your thinking I don't understand. That lousy fellow, that LaFrance, it makes some sense he should go to Santo to see if he can get bailed out by maybe peddling him the option he's got on the Carbee land. So doesn't he mention you?"

"If he mentions me, it's the same as telling Santo that he was a damned fool. If he admits he's smashed and trying to salvage something, the price from Santo will go way down."

"How can you be sure of how that idiot will react?"

"I can't be sure. I just make my guess and live with it."

The freeze hit low spots well to the west and north of the To-Co

Groves, hit them hard enough so that all the smudge pots and airplane propeller fans and bonfires of old truck tires failed to save the dreams of a lot of the smaller growers. They expected the same on Saturday night, but the upper winds changed and a warm, moist breath began coming up from the lower Gulf and the Straits of Yucatán, moving across the peninsula from out of the southwest, and after some unseasonable thunderstorms, the afternoon was clear and warm and bright on Sunday when Janine Bannon arrived in the car Tush and I had fixed a quarter of a year ago.

I was watching for her, knowing when she had left the groves, and went and took her small suitcase from her and brought her aboard. She had been aboard before, when I had taken the *Flush* up the Shawana River, back when the Boatel was doing well, and they had told me their plans with an air of pleasure and excitement, so she knew the layout.

She looked trim and attractive in her green suit and yellow blouse, but thinner than she should have been. The difference in her was the way the vitality had gone out of her, deadening her narrow and delicate face, making her move like a convalescent, taking the range and lilt and expression out of her voice. Even her dark hair had lost luster, and there were deep strainings under her eyes, fine lines around her mouth.

I took her back to the guest stateroom and she said, "I don't want to be a bother. I should have found a place."

"Which would be a very good trick right now. No bother. You know that. Get yourself settled in. Meyer will be over in a while for drinks and talk, and then we'll go out and find some beef, or Chinese, or whatever you feel like."

"Oh, anything is all right. Trav, it'll just be for overnight. I have to get back."

"That will depend on what Meyer has set up for you to take care of."

A little while later I heard some small clatterings in the galley and the chunk of the refrigerator door. I went forward and found her bending over and frowning into the little freezer. She turned and said, "I'd feel a lot better about all this if you'd let me earn my keep, Trav. Connie has all that help, and they have their own ways of doing things, and I feel like a parasite. You have lots of stuff here. Honestly, I *like* to cook."

"Never volunteer, lady. Somebody will take you up on it. So you're hooked."

She smiled. "Thank you. You know things, don't you? Like you know what people really want to do. Now go away and let me just potter around and find out where everything is and how everything works, all by myself."

I went in and looked at the tape labels and picked out one of a lot of classical guitar with Julian Bream and started it rolling, adjusting it to that level that is not quite background and not quite for listening only. It wasn't until Meyer was aboard and I called Janine in from the galley that it occurred to me that they had never met.

She put her slim hand into his paw, and she had that speculative reserve that women seem to have for the first twelve seconds when confronted with the rather outrageous presence of Meyer.

He peered at her, shaking his head slowly in a disconcerting way and then said, "Tricked again! Janine, my dear, if I had been told you were beautiful, I wouldn't have been working so hard to make you rich."

"Beautiful! Now *really*."

He turned to me. "See? A fishing expedition even. She protests so she can hear it again. Okay, Janine. You are a beautiful lady. I am very sensitive to beauty. A man who makes children run and hide behind mommy is very receptive to beauty."

"You should see the wolf pack of little kids," I said, "following this character up and down the beach, listening to his lies."

Suddenly her dark eyes looked lively. "Meyer, you too are beautiful. I do not know how you are doing it or why you are doing it even, but if you are making me rich, I will be very pleased and grateful."

"I am doing it because McGee nags me. That is a good guitar to drink by. And how long do we stand around with no drinks?"

She cooked up a great kettle of a delicious thing that she called "Sort of Stroganoff." I found some red wine that, for a change, Meyer approved of. After she had cleaned up, she and Meyer went into a huddle at the desk over the papers he had brought over. I sat on the yellow couch, reading and digesting, hearing them with half an ear.

At last she came over and plumped down beside me, sighing. I put the book aside. "That fantastic man keeps telling me fantastic things, Trav."

"Meyer is like that."

"He says you are supposed to tell me where so much money came from to start with. I *know* you somehow tricked Mr. LaFrance into paying such a price for our place. But there's a lot more."

"He made a donation, Jan. Press LaFrance made a nice gesture."

"But . . . if you stole it from him, I don't——"

"Meyer, did he give you that money willingly?"

"Willingly!" said Meyer. "He could hardly wait to get rid of it. That is the truth, dear lady."

"Okay. I give up. But apparently I might end up . . . Tell him, Meyer."

"It's an estimate only. At the end of this year, after all taxes are paid, you should have, I think, about two thousand shares, free and clear, of G.S.A., General Service Associates, worth seventy dollars a share now, and more then. The dividend income will be six to seven thousand a year. All your eggs in one basket, but a very nice basket. Great ratios, great management, fantastic promise. Meyer will have his eye on the basket. With little kids, and you a young woman, you need growth and income. Tomorrow we see some people, start setting up some basic living trust structures."

"I have to stay over another night," she told me.

"Or more," said Meyer. "Depending. A three-year program and you will be on a five-figure income with a nice reserve, with insurance trusts maturing for the college expenses. The boys grow up, get married. You can go abroad, go to Spain, rich and foolish, marry a bullfighter, buy fake paintings. I'll be right here. A little trembly old man, feeling terrible because I ruined your life."

And I wondered if it was the first time she had laughed loudly and long since Tush had died.

16

ON THE following Tuesday night at ten thirty, after Janine had once again fed us well, I strolled with Meyer back to his boat to check on the strategy.

"A piece of genius," he said, "that call from Connie."

I had arranged it earlier with Connie, while Meyer was taking Jan to mysterious appointments with lawyers and trust officers, and Connie had called back at six and asked Jan if it was all right if she took the boys with her for a few days. She would take Marguerita with her to look after the kids. There was an Association meeting in Tampa, and then she wanted to go up to Tallahassee for a few days, and stop and visit some other growers on her way back. She'd be gone a week, and why didn't Jan stay right where she was?

"Once she gave in," said Meyer, "you noticed the relaxation. You noticed she ate better too? You noticed she laughed a little?"

"Conspiracy."

"The best kind," he said. "Today I unloaded a thousand shares of Fletcher at thirty-one and moved the funds into G.S.A. It's the critical time right now. I don't know how high the rocket goes. Ninety-two thousand shares traded today. Suppose in the morning I call her and tell her the men we have to see will be available Friday morning. No. Saturday morning. So you should move that hunk of ugly luxury before it congeals to the slip. A nice little cruise someplace."

"I'll try it. Don't count on it."

I went ambling back and went aboard and into the lounge. Janine was standing in the doorway at the forward end of the lounge, the companionway dark behind her.

"Trav?" she said, and her voice was all wrong. It was a sick sad scared voice, and the belt she was wearing was a sinewy, sun-reddened forearm. "Trav? I'm . . . sorry."

A knuckly hand appeared at her left side, at waist-level, aiming a short barrel of respectable caliber at my middle. "I'm sorry about this, Mr. McGee," he said. I could make out a tallness behind her, a relative pallor of the face against the gloom behind her.

"Freddy?" I asked.

"Yes sir."

"I'm sorry about this too, Freddy."

"Just you stand quiet," he said. The arm left her waist. A set of regulation handcuffs arched toward me, gleaming in the light, and fell on the lounge carpeting with jingling thud.

The arm quickly clasped her waist again. "Now you move all the time like slow-motion movies, Mr. McGee. You get down on your knees and take those cuffs there slow, and you edge over slow and reach both arms around that pipe thing and put them on and press them nice and tight."

"Or?"

"I think you know the corner I'm in, Mr. McGee. It has piled up on me, and no way to stop it or change it. I couldn't stand being locked up anyplace even for one month without being turned into some kind of animal. So I've got no choice. I'm sorry about everything, but sorry doesn't help. So do it right now, start moving, or I'll lay one slug right through your forehead, Mr. McGee."

Freddy had been worn thin. He was on the edge, and the truth was in his voice. It made me very obedient. Very humble. I moved the way the specialists move when they are lifting the fuse out of a bomb. I snapped the cuffs snugly, taking a faint remote comfort in the knowledge that given ten seconds alone in the lounge I could brace myself, wrench the stanchion loose and get my hands on the revolver in the desk.

He walked Janine out of the doorway and into the lounge. As he put the handgun away, I heard him sigh with the release of tension. He released her and gave her a little push. She stumbled forward, her body slack, head bowed in her despair. "I'm sorry," she said in a low voice.

His hand went to his hip pocket, then reached out toward her quite casually. There was a barely audible sound of impact, a hairsoftened, leathery little thopp. She took half a broken step, face emptying. She started to lift her arms to break the fall, then pitched onto her face, jelly-slack, with a tumble of cushioned bone against the lounge carpeting.

I had seen something odd in his face just as he had flicked the lead against her skull. It had been a moment of change and revelation, showing a pleasure of erotic dimensions, of sensual pleasure. It is not an unusual way for the mind of a man to turn rancid. Cops fall in love with the hickory nightstick. Prizefighters forget to pace themselves, going for the sweet knockout. It is a pull that takes some twisted ones into anesthesiology, or into preparing the dead for burial, or into scut-work in asylums. They are the dark brothers of the slackened flesh, turned on in some soiled way by a total vulnerability.

He looked down at her, stepped over her and sat in a chair just out of my reach. He yawned hugely. There was a faint family resemblance to LaFrance. He was a big, stringy, slope-shouldered boy, and he looked stone tired. He held the spring-handled tranquilizer in his right hand and gently bounced the leaden end off the open palm of his other hand. It was of black leather, intricately woven, greasy with much handling.

The only time I had seen him was when he and another deputy had backed up Sheriff Burgoon when he had picked me up in the lobby of the old hotel.

I sat and hitched around to where I could lean my back against the bulkhead, the stanchion between my flexed knees, forearms resting on my knees.

"Why did you come here, Freddy?"

He was so exhausted his mind was moving slowly. "I remembered two days ago my Uncle Press telling me about this houseboat of yours. I was trying to sneak aboard one of the freighters heading out of Tampa. They watch them too close. I figure I can get out of the country somehow, I can get myself all sorted out and get some time to think what to do next."

"What you ought to do next is pick up that phone over there and call Sheriff Burgoon and tell him where to come get you."

"Too late for that."

"You've got a lot of friends in Shawana County. They'll work things out for you. They think you were defending yourself from Bannon and hit him too hard and got scared. They'll make sure that old couple where you got the clothes and car won't press charges."

"I tell you, Mr. McGee, it's too *late*. I had some more bad luck. That's the only kind I've had lately. There's a woman I killed not meaning to, over west of Dade City. I tunked her perfect, light and easy and just enough, and she took two steps more than she should have been able to and when she fell, it was right on a garden rake acrost her throat, and no way in the world to stop all that blood. God, there was a lot of blood! He ran into the brush and I don't know if I winged him at all. Anyway, I couldn't find him and I had to get out of there. No sir, it's too late for anything but running and hiding. Things start to go wrong, they just seem to keep right on."

"How did they go wrong with Tush Bannon?"

"I was patrolling and seen him at just about first light walking the shoulder of the road, carrying a suitcase. I stopped and he said he'd come in on the bus and phoned out to his place and no answer at all. He was worried about Miz Bannon. It's easy to know later on what you should have done. My daddy had said Mr. Bannon was sure a hard man to discourage. I should have taken him in where we were holding the stuff his wife left and the letter from his wife, and told him his place was all foreclosed and sealed up with the notices and all. Uncle Press had to have that ten acres, and he was sure going to get it. It had been a real quiet night, so I decided what I'd do was run him on out there so he could see with his own eyes, without me telling him, how he'd lost the whole works for good. I think I wanted to do that because he didn't act whipped at all. He acted like he had some way out of the mess he was in. So I said maybe the phone wasn't working and took him out. We got out there and he got ugly when he figured out I had to know that he'd been all foreclosed. Then I told him his wife had left him and left his stuff and a letter with the sheriff and he called me a liar. He walked at me, half yelling at me and I tunked him on the skull. It should have taken him down, but it just bent his knees some and he shook his head and kept coming. So I knew he had a hard skull, and he was big, and he felt ugly, so I made sure the next one would take him down. I put a lot of wrist in it and I figured to lay it right onto his forehead, but he was quick for a big man like that, and he tried to snap his head back." He sighed. "I hit him right square on the bridge of the nose, Mr. McGee. That's a real bad place because it drives two little thin bones right back into the brain. I squatted there beside him in the morning light, sweaty and cold, and held my fingers on his wrist, and felt his heart go slower and slower and softer and softer and then it stopped all the way and he shivered sort of, and after a while I figured out it would seem likely he had enough troubles to want to kill himself, and figured out how to make it look like he did and at the same time cover up the places I'd tunked him. You see, I knew if I had to tell what happened, I'd get run out of police work for good, maybe, and it's the only way I feel good, with the uniform and people listening when you tell them something."

"But Arlene Denn saw you."

He shook his head slowly. "All those weird kids. I thought I was in the clear on Bannon. Then she said she watched. I stood out there in the night trying to think of some way I could kill all of them. Like tunk them all on the head and an overdose or something. Or a fire. But I was on the dispatch book because they gave me the complaint. I had those pictures, and I had that stuff I took off them. She didn't want trouble. I could give her a lot. So when she was off her high and made sense, I asked about maybe if Mrs. Bannon was playing around, or if there was some friend she could say she saw instead of me. So . . ."

There was a stir beyond the yellow couch, a grunting sigh. Freddy got up quickly and went to Janine. When he bent down over her, he was out of sight. I heard the tone of his gentle voice but not the words. It sounded as if a lover were murmuring to his beloved, comforting her fears. I heard the tiny thud once more.

When he came back and sat as before, I said, "That isn't going to do her any good, Deputy."

"Or no harm, Mr. McGee. I know just where and how hard. It just kind of puts a jolt onto the brain, with hardly even a headache afterward. I'll be thinking on what I should do so I can get some sleep without worrying about either one of you. You know, if you'd only been right here on this boat when Shawana County made the request to have you picked up and held, everything would have been all smoothed over."

"Don't count on it. No matter how good you make it look, Freddy, the people I was with at the time you killed Tush would have come forward and cleared me and left you with a lot of explaining."

"By then there would have been no Arlie to change her story. It maybe would be a big mystery, but there'd be no way to get me mixed up in it."

"So Tush was an accident, and the woman with the rake in her neck was an accident, but Arlie Denn was going to be on purpose."

"You get pushed so far there's only maybe one little narrow way out of the corner. I better get you two . . ."

I awakened lame and sore, with no knowledge of time or place. Daylight came from overhead, around the edges of a hatch cover that did not fit as well as it should. I had what I thought was a hang-over headache, and when I realized that I was in the forward bilge area of the *Flush*, curled close to the anchor line well, the old frame members of the hull biting into my side, I thought that only a sorry drunk would pick that as a place to sleep. But when I tried to bring my right hand up and rub my face, it stopped with a jolting clink of chain. I turned my head and saw that my right wrist was handcuffed to one of the forward braces made of two-inch galvanized pipe, braces I had installed long ago to give her more forward rigidity in rough water. And I wasn't going to yank one of those loose, not without a chain hoist and a power winch.

I fingered my skull with my left hand and found a tender area above the right ear and a little behind it. I could not remember being "tunked," or where the conversation had stopped. My thinking gear was sluggish. It took me a long time to realize that my houseboat could not be moored at Bahia Mar. The motion was wrong. She was at rest, bow into a gentle swell, lifting and falling. Sometimes she would get out of phase with the swell and I could feel the soft tug of the anchor line snubbing the left of the bow.

I sat up and shifted and found a better place to stretch out, where no white oak ribs dug into me. I kept telling myself that Janine was perfectly all right. There wasn't a thing in my pockets of any earthly use to me. And there was nothing I could reach. I managed to doze off a few times. The motion was restful. At eleven fifteen by my watch I awoke and heard the latch on the small hatchway entrance to the forward bilge click.

Freddy Hazzard came crawling through, wearing a pair of my fresh khaki pants and a clean T-shirt. He nodded and reached back through the hatch and lifted a half bucket of water through and put it within reach. He reached again and brought in a brown paper bag and put it beside the bucket.

"Mr. McGee, there's milk and bread and cheese in the sack, and a roll of toilet paper. You'll have to make out best you can with a bucket, because I'm not about to let you loose until there's a good reason."

"Where Mrs. Bannon?"

"She's just fine. I found some chain and a padlock, and I got her chained in the head by one ankle, and I took her some food first."

"Where are we?"

"Anchored in the flats just off Sands Key, way east of the channel, maybe twelve miles south of Miami. I had me a time working this thing out of that big marina. The wind takes it. I fished commercial about every summer I was a kid in school. Mr. McGee, I found your fuel tables in the drawer next to the chart rack. With the fuel aboard it figures out to maybe four hundred miles range. Does that sound about right to you?"

"Why should I tell you anything, Freddy?"

He squatted on his heels, balancing easily to the motion of the hull. He looked at me in a troubled way. "I got that little runabout boat in tow. That's what gave me fits getting clear of the boat basin. I've been checking her over, and I think she's got maybe three hundred miles in her because the tanks are topped off full. Cuba would be easy, but I've got the feeling it would be another kind of jail. I've been checking weather and there's a good five-day forecast. I think I could just about get to the Caicos Islands. There isn't much of any red tape or government there because, like a friend explained to me, they used to belong to Jamaica and when Jamaica went independent, the Turks and Caicos Islands weren't in that deal. I've got your papers and I can scorch them up some like this boat burned, and leave enough to read so I can pass for you where nobody knows you. I'm sorry about the way it has to be, but if I'm going to be you, I'm going to have to leave you and her fastened tight to this thing when she runs out of fuel and I open her up and let her go down. I thought of all other ways and there just isn't a one. Now, I'm telling you this, how it's going to be, but I'm not telling her because she'd come all apart. And you won't be telling her because you and she aren't ever going to see each other again. It's the only chance and I'm sorry about it, but I have to give it a try. Now you want to know why you should tell me anything. It's because when the time comes, I can lay one on your skull bone and hers too and you'll drown without knowing a thing about it. And I'll make you comfortable as I can meanwhile. Her too. But every boat has cranky ways, and when this thing isn't acting right, I want to ask you what to do and you tell me right. If you don't, you aren't either one of you going to be comfortable hardly at all. And you should know that when I was carrying her into the head and getting that chain fixed on her leg, I thought about how full-grown women like that always made me feel dumb and clumsy and afraid to even think of touching them. But since she's going down to the bottom anyways, it wouldn't matter what happened to her beforehand. I might mess with her and I might not. I couldn't say right now, but there's not so much chance of it if you act right. So right now I want to know just where to put those tacs to get the top range out of this thing."

"It isn't going to work."

"It's the only chance I've got. What rpm, mister?"

"Eleven hundred."

"Where's the switch on the automatic pilot?"

"Up on the topside controls, under the panel, over on the port corner."

"Where's your compass correction card?"

"Pasted to the inside lid of the box where the rule and dividers are."

He nodded. "I got a nap, but I need a lot of catching up. I'm going to sleep out the rest of the day and move on out of here about dusk. I'll bring you down some blankets so you can rest better, Mr. McGee."

"Don't knock yourself out with favors."

He left. It was just a wild enough idea to work, if I'd been alone aboard. But Meyer would know Janine had been aboard, and so would Connie Alvarez. They would never quit, not until they found out what happened. Small comfort.

So this had to be the time. During this long afternoon. Don't count on his getting careless later on. Because even when pooped, he wasn't careless. He's been on the run. His two shipmates are latched up tightly. The bed is deep and soft. The sea rocks him. He may never sleep as deeply again.

So get to it, McGee. Get something working, mostly your dull head. Nothing in the pockets. Escape needs tools. Like a belt buckle? Ah yes. A careful young man. The old jail training. Belt and shoelaces were gone. What have you got that's made of metal, fella? Well, you have a corroded old bucket and you have a wristwatch, and you have some fillings in the fangs, and that is it.

And if you had metal, what could you do? You might try to pick the lock on the cuff. Think nothing of the fact that they are designed to be pickproof. Or if you happened to have a very thin and fairly narrow piece of spring steel, you could maybe work it into this little aperture where the cuff clasps together and maybe free the ratchets somehow. Except the good sets, like this one, have little knurled places designed to keep you from doing just that.

The hatch latch clicked and it opened and he shoved two blankets in far enough for me to reach them and slammed it again. Nice gesture, fella. Thanks a lot.

More appraisal. The cuff would slide along the heavy pipe bracing. They were in the shape of the letter X laying on its side, and I was cuffed to the one with its low end on the starboard side, the high end on the port. They did not quite touch at the center of the X. There was room to get the cuff between them. I could stand up, if I kept pretty well hunched over. I gave myself very good grades in the handyman department, at least in that bracing chore. I had hacksawed them to fit snugly, then slipped the collars over them, each with a base about four inches across with four big bolt-holes. Even with the biggest wrench aboard, I would have had trouble. The rust looked as solid as the steel.

Suddenly I remembered that they were just friction collars. They were not threaded on. And the lip was about one inch deep. So, if a man could put his back into it, and put enough of a bend in one of them to make it an inch shorter, it would slip out of the bolted collar and that intelligent fellow would be free.

I made a blanket pad to protect my back. I hunched under the cross pipe, got myself nicely braced and tried to bend it. I tried until the world turned jet black with little streaks of red flickering through it. I tried until my ears were full of blood roar and my jaws ached and the pipe was grooving my bones, but it did not bend a quarter of an inch, if that.

I sat down and panted for a time. My ears stung with sweat. Impasse. The only possible way I could get myself loose, other than chewing my hand off at the wrist, was to bend the pipe brace. And I couldn't bend it.

Give me a lever and a place to stand, somebody said. Or was it a fulcrum? Anyway, he was going to move the earth. If a reason had been given, I had forgotten it.

Sure. With a lever or a winch or a truck jack, no problem at all. I drank some milk and ate some cheese. Okay, McGee. Sit here and make yourself a truck jack out of some bread, cheese, a watch, a pail and two blankets. The old know-how.

And something went skittering across the back of my mind so

swiftly I didn't catch it. A frail ghost of some kind of a frail idea. I lay back and tried to think of nothing at all, and when it appeared again I grabbed it. I shook it, but it didn't have anything to tell me. It muttered something about a turnbuckle and I let it go.

There are two ways to move something. Push it or pull it. I sat up and looked at my equipment. I took one blanket and, starting at one corner, I rolled it as neatly and tightly as I could. There was a squat thick short timber brace on the port side near the bulkhead, but it was a foot beyond my best reach. I soaked the ends of my blanket rope in the water bucket. I took off my shoes and socks and stretched out and fumbled the end of the blanket rope around the brace and clapped it between the soles of my feet and pulled it through and toward me. I looped the other end around the pipe brace to which I was fastened, and pulled it as tightly as I could manage and knotted the wet ends together. I poured the water out of the bucket, put my boat shoes back on and trod upon the bucket until the side seam parted and the seam that held the bottom on tore loose. Then I stomped and folded and grunted and sweated until I had a clumsy metal club about two and a half feet long. I wrapped that up in the other blanket as tightly as I could and tied it with strips torn off my shirt. Then I stuck six inches of the padded lever between the two strands of the blanket rope and began winding.

It was easy—at first. The blanket began to twist and knot like the rubber band in a toy airplane. The timber brace made alarming creaking sounds. Each full wind took more effort. I had wrapped my lever in the blanket to try to keep it from bending. But as I began to have to hold it right out at the end to get enough leverage, it began to take on a curve. When I noticed that the pipe brace was taking on a curve too, I began to worry about what might happen when all that accumulated force was released. The sweat ran. I turned my lever. The blanket was so taut I could imagine I could hear it humming. What is the breaking strength of the average blanket?

Suddenly it was like being dropped into the middle of a threshing machine. The pipe sprang out of the collars and banged me on the shoulder. The lever spun free and hit me on the elbow and numbed my forearm and hand. The pipe spun and rang against my skull and knocked me down and tried to twist my arm off by the cuffed wrist. It was an ungodly din, and Freddy was going to come charging down. I slipped the cuff off the end of the pipe. I clawed the shirt strips off my lever and knelt by the hatchway with the raw, flattened chunk of bucket held high, silently begging him to stick his head in, and wondering if he was on the other side waiting for me to stick my head out.

So I went creeping cautiously out, holding the loose cuff in my right hand with enough tension to keep the chain from clinking. I went up through the other hatch forward and moved silently aft. I stopped every few steps to hold my breath and cock my head and listen. At the mouth of the corridor I heard a buzzing snore, deep and slow and regular. The door of the master stateroom was ajar. The door to the head was closed, and I could hear a faint clinking of chain.

Procedure:—Go to the lounge. Get the weapon from the desk. Go charging in and blow one of his kneecaps off just to be on the safe side. Liberate the lady. Head for Dinner Key and radio the police to meet us.

But again he was careful. He had shaken the place down. No 38. I checked the pilothouse and the shark rifle was not in the spring clamps where it belonged.

Revised procedure:—Silently liberate the lady and get her the hell out of there and into the *Muñequita* and when we had drifted far enough, start her up and leave in a big hurry.

Chain. So the quickest, easiest way would be with the great big nippers, a brute set with handles a yard long. And they were right where I hoped they would be, in behind the tool locker, wedged in place.

I enjoyed his snoring as I moved like a ghost past the door to the master stateroom. I opened the door to the head slowly. She was sitting on the floor. She snapped her head around and looked at me with a madwoman's face, eyes and mouth wide and round, breath sucking to scream. But comprehension came just in time and I eased in and closed the door just as silently as I had opened it. She had found some greasy medication in the medicine locker and she had greased her bare ankle and foot and had been trying to work the chain off of it. She had gouged through the skin and her greasy ankle and the floor was speckled with blood.

I slid one jaw of the nippers under the ankle chain and applied pressure. The jaws bit through and the chain fell away, rattling on the deck. I put the nippers down and helped her up. She clung to me. I whispered to her and told her he was asleep and we were going to go aboard the *Muñequita* and release her tow line and drift away. She bobbed her head in violent agreement.

When we had crept to within two feet of the partly open door we had to pass, I suddenly knew what was wrong. I couldn't hear him snoring. So I took her by the arm to try to make it a fast run, but the door swung open and there he was. I shoved her along the corridor and in the same violent effort I tried to jump him. But a big soft hot red hammer hit the meat of my left shoulder and that much impact at that close range spun me and drove me back through the open door of the guest stateroom. The spinning tangled my legs and I fell heavily, remembering as I went down an old lesson painfully learned long ago. When you are shot, you are dead. Bang, you're dead! So be dead, because it might be the only chance you have left in the world.

I heard him come in to stand over me. "You damn fool!" he said. "You sorry pitiful damn fool." And he put his toe against my hip and nudged me to see how slack I was. I swung both legs and swept his feet out from under him and clawed my way onto him, yelling at the same time to Jan to get off the boat, swim ashore, run like hell.

It was very busy work. My left arm wasn't part of me, and he kept trying to work that revolver around to get it against me, and I kept trying to stay behind him and get the cuff chain around his throat. He managed to struggle up with me, which was a demonstration of an impressive amount of wiry strength, but I yanked him off balance and toppled back on the bed with him. It had taken only a very few seconds. I gave up the chain bit and got my right forearm across his throat, but he kept his chin tucked down well. I got the gun wrist with my left hand, but the left arm was getting worse by the moment, and slowly, slowly he was turning the muzzle to where he could be sure of putting the next slug in my head without even having to look back at me.

It was then that Janine came through the door screeching, and bearing on high, in both hands, the small red fire extinguisher she had apparently yanked out of the clips on the corridor wall. Screeching, face contorted, she ran directly at us, starting the great descending blow when she was at least three steps from the bed. He wrenched the gun wrist free and there was the great slamming sound of a shot in an enclosed place, and I saw her head wrench sideways as she struck her fearful blow, then a jostle of great weight made such a sickening pain in my shoulder and arm, the world shrank down to a little white thing and winked out.

I don't know how long I was out. Thirty seconds, fifteen minutes. I came struggling up aware of great urgency, aware of being pinned under great weight. Freddy Hazzard seemed very heavy. I fingered his slack throat with my right hand and couldn't find a thing. I wormed partway out from under him and saw one good reason for the weight. Janine lay spilled across us, supine, the small of her back across his loins, her dark head hanging back over the edge of the bed.

I squirmed out from under both of them and stood up. I did not want to feel any more dead throats. The left side of her head was toward me. Her hair was clotted heavily with blood. I stared at her and when I saw the rise and fall of her chest, I risked the finger on the throat, found a place going bump, bump, bump.

Then I looked at him. Nobody was going to be able to feel any pulse. He had a grooved head. Diagonal. From one temple across to the opposite eyebrow. A groove as wide as the fire extinguisher and maybe an inch deep. The eye bulged with a blank astonishment greater than any astonishment in the living world.

The faintness came over me and faded away slowly. I stood three stories tall and I would sway in the slightest breeze. Toy fellow made of broomstraws and flour paste. My left arm hung there, and I looked down and saw the blood dropping busily from my fingertips.

Things to do, McGee. Got to take care. Got to tidy ship. Grab the buckets and brooms, men. Clean sweep fore and aft. So start moving, because you don't know how much time you have, and it might not be enough. I fingered Hazzard's pockets and found the cuff key and managed to turn it with numb fingers and get my right wrist free. The metal had rubbed it raw.

I could not make myself hurry. I felt thoughtful. It was a kind of faraway game. Amusing and not very important. I might be able to do what might keep me from falling off the edge for good, and I might not. Interesting.

On my slow way to the head I ripped my shirt off. I turned my left side toward the mirror. The entrance hole was three inches below the top of the shoulder and on the outside of the upper arm, but deep enough so that I couldn't tell if it had done bone damage. The slug had tumbled apparently, and torn one hell of a hole on the way out. I lifted my left arm with my right hand, braced the left palm against the wall and locked the elbow. I took my time putting the gauze pads on the wounds, winding it very neatly, tearing the surgical tape with my teeth.

"Nice," I heard myself say in a voice that seemed to come from the next room. "Very neat."

So I went floating blissfully to the galley. Shock. Loss of blood. Replace fluids. Use stimulants. There was a quart jar of orange juice in the icebox. I found an unopened fifth of Wild Turkey in the liquor locker. I put them on the booth table and eased into the seat and wondered what a good name would be. An Orange Turkey? A Wild Screwdriver? The white mist began moving in from the edges and I realized nobody was going to come along and serve me. I picked my left arm up by the wrist and put the arm on the table. It wiggled its fingers when I sent the message down the nerves. I drank a third of the quart of juice. I took four long swallows of the bourbon. Second third of the juice. Another deep drag on the liquor. Polish off the juice. Then enough bourbon to just begin to tickle the gag reflex.

Come on, white mist. Take another shot. Here is McGee.

But it had edged so far back I couldn't see it anymore out of the corners of my eyes. I got up without thinking of my arm. It slid off the table and flapped me on the leg. And I thought about Janine, and she had a slug in her skull, and the bump, bump, bump would be over. I picked up my left arm and turned it and looked at my watch. How had it gotten to be three in the afternoon?

The throat was still knocking away like a good little engine. I tugged at her and got her off Freddy and straightened her out on the bed. I did not want to move her too much. But I did not want to take the chance of her waking up all of a sudden and finding herself right there side by side with what had been Freddy.

I got an old tarp and put it on the floor beside the bed, on his side, reached beyond him and got hold of the bloody sheet and yanked it out from under her, and tugged on it until it rolled him off and he fell onto the tarp with a lanky thudding, face-down. I left the sheet on him and flipped the ends and side of the tarp over him. I turned on the bright reading light and fingered her crusted hair apart and found where the bullet had grooved her skull in an area an inch and a half long and the same distance above her left ear. There didn't seem to be anything you could pull together or sew together. It had punched out a strip of scalp meat, hair and all, and had clotted over and stopped bleeding. I soaked gauze in antiseptic and patted the wound very delicately, then tied the pad in place with more gauze.

Then, in a moment of pure genius, I got a piece of sheeting and made a sling for myself, so my arm would stop swinging around and flapping at me. It was much better. I didn't want her to wake up and look in that tarp. I found the fire extinguisher in the corner where it had rolled. I wiped it off and put it back in the clips. I sat on the floor and put both feet against the tarp and shoved Freddy half under the bunk, where he was less noticeable.

I went above decks. We were riding well at anchor. Sea calm. Skies clear. I went below and stripped and cleaned myself up. I wasn't bleeding through the gauze. Good sign. I put a robe on. The empty sleeve flapping was less troublesome than the empty arm.

I made two giant peanut butter sandwiches and yonked them down and washed them the rest of the way with a quart of cold milk. What every healthy American kid needs after being shot.

At four thirty, after some mental practice, I warmed up the set and got through to Miami Marine and put through a credit-card call to Meyer aboard his boat. She told him she had a call for him from the motor vessel, *The Bustled Lush*.

"Travis? Say, I see you must have talked her into it without too much trouble, huh? Over."

"It was spur of the moment, Meyer. Crazy wild kids taking off on a magic adventure. Over."

"Are you maybe a little smashed, old friend? Listen, I can't talk about the other thing, not with half this transmission open for anybody who wants to listen. Tell her things are going well. How about the next time you call me, make it from shore and I can tell you the news. Over."

"Will do. I don't know how long we'll cruise around. Maybe I can keep her out a couple of weeks. Over."

"It will be great for her, Travis. And it won't hurt you. Have some fun. Catch fish. Sing a little."

As soon as I signed off, the reactions began. Somehow you do what you have to do, and somehow the machinery accepts the abuse. But when you've forced your way through it, all the gears and wheels start to chitter and grind and wobble around on the pinions. I felt icy cold. I knew it was all sour. She would never come out of it. Something would be bleeding in her head and that would be the end of it. Or somebody had seen him coming aboard, or seen him taking the houseboat out. My arm would start to rot. The hook would pull out of loose sand and we'd drift aground.

I went back below and looked at her and went into the master stateroom and slipped out of the robe and into the giant bed and wished I wasn't too old to cry myself to sleep . . .

I heard her saying my name for a long time before I let it wake me up. She sat on the edge of the bed, facing me. She wore a short beach robe and she had fashioned a turban affair out of a pale blue towel. It was night. The light was behind her.

"Trav? Trav?"

"Mmm. How's your head, Janine?"

"I'm all right. I'm perfectly all right. Trav, how badly are you hurt?" She had bared my shoulder and she was looking at the bandage.

"It's just a scratch."

"Please. How bad is it?"

"I don't think it's too bad."

"I want to look at it."

"Let me wake up. I didn't mean to sleep so long."

"Get waked up, then. I'll be right back."

She came back with a towel, a first-aid kit and a basin of hot water. I rolled onto my right side. She went to the other side of the bed, spread the towel and equipment out, and snipped the bandage off.

I heard her insuck of breath, and said, "That bad?"

"I . . . I think it looks worse than it is. I'll try not to hurt you."

She busied herself. She was very gentle.

"Travis?"

"Yes, Jan."

"He was going to kill us both, wasn't he?"

"Maybe."

"I know he was. From the way he looked at me. After he . . . I thought when you came in and snipped me loose, it was him coming back."

"Did he give you a bad time?"

"Sort of. After he chained me up, he hit me on the head again. Very very lightly, and it was just enough so everything seemed to go far away and I couldn't move or speak or see. I wasn't awake or asleep. I could feel what he was doing. Just with his hands. Sort of . . . to see what a woman was like there. And when I could move, I grabbed his hands and pushed them away. And he looked at me and blushed and then sort of half smiled and shrugged and I knew he knew I wouldn't ever be able to tell anybody about whatever he decided to do to me. I knew he'd come back . . . but it was you. And then I was sure he'd killed you like he killed Tush and . . . I knew I could kill him. I knew he couldn't stop me. And so . . . I did."

"You didn't quite make it, honey. I took care of it."

"Don't try to be sweet and protective and all. I looked at him in there. I had to touch him and turn him over to make sure. I even felt it in my hands when it hit him, a kind of looseness, the way his head went. I'm not proud of it or full of joy or anything. But I can live with it. . . . There. I think that's better than the way it was, Travis."

"Thanks," I said and rolled onto my back. She took the basin and towel and gear away.

When she came back, she stood at the foot of the bed and said, "What do we do now?"

"I called Meyer while you were still out."

"And told him about this?"

"No. I said we might cruise around for quite a while."

"You did?"

"Until we're both healed up enough so people won't ask questions. If we go back, we make statements. Everybody will want to see how much front-page space they can get, how many times they can get their pictures taken with us. What good will that do you or your kids?"

"No good at all."

"Or do Freddy's people?"

"They might as well think he's alive in the world, somewhere."

"And I couldn't take that kind of hot publicity, Jan. I can't start wearing a public face. It would put me out of business. I don't need a lot of official interest. There's a little bit now. All I can handle. So we deep-six him and say nothing. Not a word, Jan. Not ever, to anyone. Can you handle that?"

Her face was quiet, her eyes thoughtful. In the sea-night there was the tangible presence of death aboard. A head-knocker whose luck turned very bad, who'd never make it to the Caicos, who'd had something rancid going on in the back of his mind, some warped thing all mixed up with darkness and helplessness and sexual assault. The sickness had begun to stir and move under stress, had begun to emerge, but his life had stopped before it had gone out of control.

She said, "What if you don't heal right? What if we have to find a doctor?"

"We have a story. We were potting at beer cans with a thirty-eight. The kick startled you. It slipped out of your hand, went off when it hit the deck."

"Does . . . anyone but us know he was aboard?"

"Not likely."

She nodded. "I'll be all right, Travis. I'll be fine."

I got up and went on deck and discovered I had completely forgotten the anchor lights. We were well away from any course a small boat might take, but a darkened boat at night invites investigation. I put us back onto legal status. We were riding well. The night was soft, the stars slightly misted. Miami was a giant glow to the north.

I stayed topside a long time. When I went below, she was curled up on the yellow couch in the lounge, sound asleep. I looked down at her and hoped that she would have enough iron in her to help a one-armed man with some curiously ugly chores. She had dark patches under her eyes. I turned off the small dim lamp nearby and felt my way through dark and familiar spaces back to the master stateroom.

I didn't really know if she could last, if she could handle it, until the next morning when I sat on the edge of the freshly made bed in the guest stateroom and watched her using the curved sailmaker's needle and the heavy thread, sewing Freddy into his sea shroud. She had cleaned and dressed my wound afresh. I had wired a spare anchor snugly to the deputy's ankles, and tucked his gun and cuffs and the black leather strap in beside him.

When she ran out of the hank of thread, and clipped it off and took a fresh end from the spool and moistened it in her lips before threading the needle again, she looked up at me for a moment. It was a flat, dark look, and it made me think of old stories of how warriors dreaded being taken alive and turned over to the women.

At the end of the day she wrested the anchor free when I ran the *Flush* up to it, and brought it aboard. We ran outside, creaking and rocking in the swell. I put it on automatic pilot at just enough speed to hold it quartering into the sea, and together we clumsied him up and out onto the side deck. She held the book and tilted it to catch the light from where the sun had gone down, and she read the words we thought would be appropriate to the situation.

She laid the book down and with my one arm and her two, we lifted the stiffened body upright, and as she held it propped against the rail, I bent and grasped the tarp at the feet and lifted and toppled it into the sea. It sank at once. And then I took the wheel and came about and headed for the buoy that marks the pass back into Biscayne Bay.

17

ONCE SHE accepted the need to stay by ourselves, to heal in order to avoid questions, a strange new placidity came over her. She had long times of silence, and I could guess that now that she knew what had happened, and how it had happened, part of it was over and the part about finding an acceptance of Tush's death had begun.

She began to eat well and spend some of the sun hours basting and broiling herself to the deep tan her skin took readily, and she began sleeping long and deeply, gaining the weight that softened her bone-sharp face, that filled out the long concave line of the insides of her thighs, that made her fanny look a great deal less as if it had been slapped flat with a one by six.

I called Meyer from shoreside phones. I wore the arm out of the sling for longer periods each day, reslinging it when the knitting muscle structures began to ache.

She phoned Connie when the trip with the kids was over, and Connie accepted the notion that a little more time cruising would do her good. She talked to each of the boys. They were fine. They missed her. She missed them.

Meyer eased out of the last of her holdings in Fletcher on the Wednesday, the last day of January, at a good price, and when we talked again the following Monday evening—I had phoned him from Islamorada—he said with undisguised glee that Fletcher had gotten up to forty-six dollars a share at noon, and the Exchange had suspended trading in it fifteen minutes later, pending a full investigation of a tip that the earnings reports had been misstated, that a syndicate of speculators had been boosting the price, and that the company officers had been quietly unloading all their own holdings at these false and inflated values. The word on the Street was that it might be another Westec case, and it was rumored that a Florida-based speculator named Gary Santo was deeply involved in the artificial runup of the price.

"If they ever approve it for listing again," Meyer said, "it will open at about six dollars, and even that is more than a realistic book value per share."

The next morning the *Flush* was tied up at the marina dock at Islamorada, and after breakfast I had Jan peel the final dressing off the wound. The entrance wound was a pink dime-sized dimple, vivid in the middle of the surrounding tan. She made careful inspection of the exit area, held the back of her hand against it to check for any inner heat of infection and said, "This last little piece of scab is going to come off any day now. If we could have had it sewn up, there wouldn't be so much scarring, Trav. It looks as if . . . somebody stabbed you with one of those wood rasp things."

"I got through the whole day without the sling yesterday. And I can hold that smallest sledge out at arm's length for fifteen seconds. And so I keep a shirt on till the scars bleach white and match the old ones."

"You would make a very low-grade hide," she said. "They might find three or four sections that would make nice little lampshades, but they'd have to throw the rest away."

"Just accident-prone, I guess. And you pass inspection now, lady. Keep it combed that way and you're fine."

"You see, I was aboard this funny houseboat and it got rough and I lurched and took this great gouge out of my scalp on some kind of sharp thing sticking out."

"We can head back so Meyer can help you count your money."

Late that afternoon she went below and came up with two cold uncapped bottles of Tuborg and sat close beside me and said, "A sort of an announcement, Travis McGee. There won't be another chance to talk, probably. I wish to announce that you are a dear, strange, ceremonious kind of guy, and I didn't like you very much at all before Tush died and didn't know why he liked you, and now I do, maybe."

"Tell me. Maybe I can use it."

"It made me jumpy to be alone with you, because the way I had you all figured out, you were going to comfort the little widow woman. Life goes on and all that. Let me bring you back to life, darling. A woman always knows when a man finds her physically attractive, and I am flattered that you so do."

"I so do."

"I expected some of the gooey rationalizations of the chronic stud, including how Tush would approve, and besides it's so healthy. But you have been very stuffy and proper and dear. Thank you."

"You're welcome."

"Maybe I would have gone along with it, out of some kind of self-destructive impulse. I don't know. I don't know if I was a one-man gal. I sort of think so. Maybe that part of me—the privacy part—will come alive again. Anyway, I'm glad you didn't give me a chance to make any choice. Physically I'm a lot better than I was. Better nerves. But I'm still half a person. And so damned lonely, and the world is so . . . flattened out." She reached up and kissed me under the ear. "So thanks for not trying to be God's gift to the bereaved, dear."

"You're welcome aboard anytime. You wear well."

She smiled a bitter little twisty smile and, eyes wet, took my hand and clenched it tightly. So we were a couple of kids in an abandoned barn and the big storm was hammering down, and we held hands for comfort. Tush was her storm, and perhaps Puss was mine.

On another Wednesday, the day of the Valentine, Meyer came over at high noon and interrupted my project of cutting and laying some Nautilex that was a clever imitation of bleached teak on a portion of the afterdeck.

"So I am here and I have brought you a Valentine," said he.

"Sometimes, Meyer, when you act like Porky, you make me feel like Pogo."

"Read the card."

I put down the knife I was cutting the vinyl with and thumbed his card open. Homemade. He had drawn a heart pierced by an arrow, with a dollar sign dangling from the end of the arrow. His verse said, "Roses are red; violets are blue. Unadulterated, unselfish, unrewarded efforts in behalf of even the grieving widow of an old and true friend are not like you."

"It rhymes," he said.

Inside the folded card was his personal check made out to me for twenty-five thousand dollars.

"What the hell is this?"

"Such gratitude! It hurt me to see you lose your professional standing, McGee. Like you were going soft and sentimental. So, through my own account, I put us into Fletcher and rode it up nicely and took us out, and split the bonus right down the middle. It's short-term. It's a check. Pay your taxes. Live a little. It's a longer retirement this time. We can gather up a throng and go blundering around on this licentious craft and get the remorses for saying foolish things while in our cups. We had a salvage contract, idiot, and the fee is comparatively small but fair."

"And you are comparatively large but fair."

"I think of myself that way. Where did the check go? Into the pocket so fast? Good." He looked at his watch. "I am taking a lady to lunch. Make a nice neat deck there, Captain." And away he went, humming.

And not over four minutes later a half-familiar voice said, "McGee?" I looked up from the tricky bit of fitting the vinyl at the hatch corner and saw the three of them lined up on the dock, staring at me without much affability or enthusiasm. Gary Santo on the left. Mary Smith in a bright orange minitent and a little-girl hat standing in the middle. A stranger on the right, medium tall, of that hunched, thin pallor that looks like sickness, even to the little watermelon pot, with a face like a bleached mole, glasses with massive black frames, a briefcase in hand.

"Howdy do there, Gary boy," I said. "Miss Mary."

"And this is Mr. D. C. Spartan, one of my attorneys. May we come aboard?"

"Why, surely. Please do."

I took them into the lounge. There was no handshaking going on. I excused myself and went and washed the grime off my hands, pulled the sweaty T-shirt off, swabbed chest, neck and shoulders with a damp towel, put on a fresh white sports shirt and rejoined them, saying, "Coffee, folks? Booze?"

"No thanks," said Santo.

Spartan said, in a voice like a talking computer with a slight honk in the speaker system, "It might be advisable for you to have your attorney present, if you could reach him quickly."

"Now what would I need lawyers for? Somebody suing me?"

"Don't get so damned cute!" Santo said. His face looked slightly mottled and puffy, as if the facials weren't working well lately.

"Please, Mr. Santo," Spartan said. "Mr. McGee, we are facing what might shape up into a very exhaustive investigation of Mr. Santo's role in the speculation in Fletcher Industries. And it may well become necessary to have you testify as to your part in bringing this . . . uh . . . investment opportunity to Mr. Santo's attention."

"Why?"

"There seems to be an unfounded opinion that Mr. Santo knew of the precarious condition of Fletcher Industries and conspired to run the stock up, and then short it, and that this scheme was interrupted by the suspension of trading in Fletcher common. To show Mr. Santo's good faith, we will have to subpoena your trading records and show that you had taken a position in Fletcher and then went to Mr. Santo to elicit his interest, and that Mr. Santo then made a cursory investigation of the company's condition before beginning a very active trading in the common stock."

I shook my head. "Mr. Spartan, you lost me there somewhere. I never bought a share of Fletcher. I don't own any stock at all. Never have."

"Come off it, friend," Santo said in an ugly way. "You better be able to show me you took a real good bath in Fletcher. You better be able to show me you got stung."

"I've never owned a share of stock in my life!"

Spartan looked sad. He dug into the briefcase. He took out the stapled Xerox copies of the fake margin account with Shutts, Gaylor, Stith and Company. "Come now, Mr. McGee! Surely you know that your account records can be subpoenaed from the brokerage house."

I looked at them and handed them back. "I'd say that's going to be a very confused bunch of brokers, folks. If I had to guess, I'd say these were Xerox copies of some kind of forgery, or there's somebody else with my name. I just don't know what the hell you're talking about."

"But Miss Smith can testify to what you told her and to you giving her the originals to Xerox. Do you actually want to deny that you went to Mr. Santo's offices and talked about this whole matter to Miss Smith?"

"Oh, I went there all right. I didn't have any appointment, and I had a hard time getting to talk to anybody, even this pretty little quail. Now, I suppose whatever we said was taped, just as a matter of convenience, you know, for reference. But I don't think you can introduce that kind of a tape, and even if you can, it would have to be the whole tape, not just some edited parts of it."

"There is a tape, of course," Spartan said. "And we can prove it predates Mr. Santo's interest in Fletcher common."

"Spartan," said Gary Santo, "I think this son of a bitch is too cute. I think he was working for somebody. I think he was setting me up."

"Sometimes I work for people," I said. "But not for long. Mary, you remember the long talk we had about that Gary's parcel he holds up there in Shawana County under the name of Southway Lands, Inc.?"

"What?" she said. "There wasn't anything like that."

"But, honey, you confirmed the rumor that Southway was going to sell out to Calitron for a nice price, if a fellow up there by the name of LaFrance could assemble the rest of the acreage."

"But what are you trying to *do* to me?" she asked.

"Say! If I've spilled the beans and gotten you into some kind of trouble or anything . . . I guess we didn't talk about it up in the offices. That was later, honey."

"We *never* talked about that!"

I shook my head. "But you told me how Bannon got through to you, and you had a drink with him at the airport, and he told you how he was being squeezed and wanted Santo's help, and you decided you couldn't take a little thing like that to Mr. Santo and waste his time with a little guy who got caught in the middle."

She caught her little lip in her teeth the same way she had when talking to Tush.

I continued. "Remember, honey? You said that you thought Mr. Santo had mentioned how, up in the hotel penthouse in Atlanta, LaFrance had tried to get Santo to buy Bannon out and Santo told LaFrance that it was his problem and he should handle it? That was the same night you told me you'd give me a clean bill with Santo."

I moved just fast enough. Santo got up and got over to her and got his hand back for a slap that would have loosened her teeth. I caught his wrist. The position gave me very nice leverage. I swung the wrist back and over and down and ended up in about the same position as a pitcher after letting go of his best fast ball. Santo boomed into the yellow couch hard enough to snap his head back, and then bounced forward onto his hands and knees on the rug.

"Now just a minute. Gentlemen! Just a minute!" Spartan said.

Santo shook his dazed head. I picked him up by the nape of the neck and sat him on the couch.

I stood in front of him and said, "Fun time is over, Gary baby. I didn't get a damned word of this from pretty-bit over there. She's devoted. She's energetic. She just never got a chance to get close to me. I made sure of that. Tush Bannon was a damned good friend. Your pressure, second-hand, drove him into the ground. And it went a little wrong up there and they went further than they had to and killed him."

He stared up at me, very attentive.

"I squashed LaFrance. I would have squashed you too if I could have figured a way. But you're too big and too spread out. All I could do was sting you a little."

"A little?" he said wonderingly. "A little? You cut my venture capital right down to the nub, friend. You fixed me so I'm associated with any new stock issue and it never gets off the ground. Sting me a little! God damn you, I might never take up the slack you put in me. And all of this was over some . . . dreary little small-time buddy of yours?"

I leaned over and slapped his face sideways and backhanded it back to center position.

"Manners," I said.

I moved back to give him a chance to come off the couch. He thought it over. Then he took out a frosty-white handkerchief and patted the corner of his mouth and examined the dappling of blood.

I turned to Spartan. "Tell him how he stands if it checks out that I've never owned a share of Fletcher."

"Well . . . it would eliminate one possible way to ease the present situation."

I turned back to Santo and looked for that tinge of gray under the barbered, lotioned, international complexion. Saw a little. Not like LaFrance. Saw enough of it, and enough slump of resignation. He dabbed at his mouth again and got up.

"Come on, Spartan," he said. He stopped so close in front of Mary Smith's chair there was not room for her to get out of it.

"You're fired, you stupid bitch!"

"But you heard him say I didn't——"

"You didn't do what you're overpaid to do, which is to stick close and check every little thing out. You could have saved me going into the tank for enough to buy five thousand of you for a lifetime. And that makes you too damned expensive. I'll have your office stuff packed and dropped off at your place. I'll have your check mailed. I couldn't look at you again without feeling sick."

"Gary, you just don't know how mutual that feeling is."

His arm came halfway up. "Uh uh!" I said. He lowered it and left swiftly. Spartan hurried behind him, and gave me a single despairing glance as he left.

She slumped in the chair. "Hooo, boy," she said wearily. "They told me there'd be days like this." She gave me a look through the emerald lenses. "Thanks heaps, McGee."

"I didn't exactly intend it that way, Mary Smith."

"But that seems to be the way it is. In many respects that was a very very very nice job, lad. It did have its cruddy intervals. You know, I didn't realize how much enjoyment I'd get out of seeing the great Gary Santo get clouted around. Funny. In three years he's popped me in the face three times. And I told myself that one more time, brother, and that's it. Would I have quit, though? I wonder? I am going to believe I would."

"Will he send any muscle around to teach me I can't do that?"

She looked at me, head cocked, wearing a little frown. "I'd say not. I mean if he thought you were absolutely alone in this, I think he would. But when he thinks it over, he's not going to believe that a person of your type could con him so completely. He'll think you're a front man, and I think he'll leave well enough alone. Besides, he's got a lot to think about."

"Do you think I'm a front man?"

"I am inclined to doubt it somehow. How about buying an unemployed girl a drink and then some lunch? You know. Like no hard feelings. You know, this is quite a setup you've got here, McGee. I couldn't tell much from the outside that time."

"Bourbon straight, water with no ice on the side?"

"Exactly."

As I was fixing the drinks Johnny Dow hallooed and stuck my mail under the corner of the deck mat. I gave her her drink and went out and brought the mail in, flipped through the customary junk and came upon an airmail one from Chicago in Puss's broad, round scrawl.

"Excuse a little mail-reading?"

"Sure. I'll just sit here and plan my future."

Old dear darling, I said one time that I would write it down to get

*it straight for you, and so I have and even have the eerie idea you
might be able to read all the words between the words. The name
was right. I lied about that. But the town wasn't, and Chicago
isn't the town either. And there was no divorce. And I love Paul
very dearly and have all along, and love you too, but not quite as
much. That lousy Meyer and his lousy Law. Get a pretty girl to
kiss Old Ugly and tell him he was absolutely right. You see, my
dear, about six months before you met me on the beach with that
living pincushion stuck into the sole of my foot, they took a little
monster out of my head, maybe as big as an English walnut almost, and with three stumpy little legs like a spider. Half a spider.
And the men in white dug around in my head to try to find every
little morsel of the beast, because he turned out to be the bad
kind. So . . . I got over confusions and got my memory all
straightened out again, and my hair grew back, and I pinned an
old buddy of mine to the wall of his office and he leveled because
he has known me long enough to know I have enough sawdust to
keep me solid. His guess was one chance out of fifty. No treatments possible. Just go off and get checked every so often, bright
lights in the eyes, stand and touch the tip of your nose with your
fingertip while keeping the eyes closed. That stuff. And pens drawing lines on little electric charts. I could accept it, my dear, because life is very iffy and I have busied up my years in good ways.
But I could not accept the kind of life that went with the waiting.
Dear as Paul is, he is a sentimental kraut type, and we had the
awareness of the damned time bomb every waking moment. So
life became like a practice funeral, with too many of our friends
knowing it, and everybody trying to be so bloody sweet and com-
passionate during a long farewell party. I began to think that if I
lucked out, I'd be letting them down. So I finally told Paul that if
it was the end of my life, it was getting terribly damned dreary and
full of violin music, and I am a random jolly type who does not
care to be stared at by people with their eyes filling with tears. So I
cashed in the bonds for the education of the children I'll never
have, and I came a-hunting and I found you. Was I too eager to
clamber into the sack? Too greedy to fill every day with as much
life as would fit into it? Darling, I am the grasshopper sort, and so
are you, and, bless you, there were dozens of times every day I
would completely forget to sort of listen to what might be happening inside my redheaded skull. Be glad you jollied and romped the*

redheaded lady as she was coming around the clubhouse turn,
heading for the tape. She loved it. And you. And how good we
were together, in a way that was not a disloyalty to Paul! He is one
of the dogged and steadfast ones. Can you imagine being married,
dear, to Janine, great as she is, and having her know you could be
fatally ill? She would mother you out of your mind until you ran.
As I ran. But there was the little nagging feeling I was having it all
too good. I kept telling myself, Hell girl, you deserve it. And then
hairy old Meyer and his damned Law about the hard thing to do
is the right thing to do. I suppose you have been wondering about
me and maybe hating me a little. I had to run from you exactly
when I did and how I did, or I couldn't have left at all. You see,
the dying have a special obligation too, my dear. To keep it from
being too selfish. I was depriving Paul of his chance of being with
me, because it is all he is going to have of me . . . all he did have
of me, and I was forgetting that I had to leave him enough to last
him long enough to get him past the worst of it at least. The darling has not done the interrogation bit, and if he thinks or doesn't
think there was a man in the scene, I couldn't really say. You
would like each other. Anyway, the female of the species is the
eternal matchmaker, and I have written the longest letter of my
life to Janine, all full of girl talk, and about living and dying, and I
have, I hope, conned her into spinning a big fancy pack of lies
about the Strange Vacation of Puss Killian, because I am leaving
her name and address with Paul, saying that she could tell him
how I was and what happened among people who didn't know. It
is a devious plot, mostly because they would work well. He is a
research chemist, and perhaps the kindest man alive. Anyway, last
week all of a sudden the pupil of my big gorgeous left eye got
twice as big as it should, and they have been checking and testing
and giving me glassy smiles, and I am mailing this en route to the
place where they are going to open a trap door and take another
look. So they may clap the lid back on and say the hell with it. Or
they may go in there and without meaning to, speed me on my
journey, or they may turn me into a vegetable, or they may manage to turn me back into me for another time, shorter or longer.
But from the talk around the store, the odds on that last deal
make the old odds seem like a sure thing bet. Do you understand
now? I'm scared. Of course I'm scared. It's real black out there
and it lasts a long time. But I have no remorses, no regrets, be-

cause I left when I had to, and Meyer got me back in good season. Don't do any brooding, because if I can try to be a grownup, you ought to be able to take a stab at it. Here's what you do, Trav my darling. Find yourself a gaudy random gorgeous grasshopper wench, and lay aboard the Plymouth and the provisions, and go fun-timing and sun-timing up and down the lovely bays. Find one of good appetite and no thought of it being for keeps, and romp the lassie sweetly and completely, and now and again, when she is asleep and you are awake, and your arms are around her and you are sleeping like spoons, with her head tucked under your ugly chin, pretend it is . . .

> *Puss, who loved you.*

"Is something wrong?" a voice said.

I looked at Mary Smith, realizing that it was not the first time she had asked me. "Wrong? No. Just a letter from an old friend."

"You looked funny."

"I guess it was . . . because the old friend decided to cancel an old debt." I got up and got the bottle and refilled her shot glass.

She lifted it in toast. "Here's to vacations without pay. Oh, Christ, that was such a great job! Such a sweet lush life, dear. But you know, sometimes you get an instinct. I think other things are going to go bad for Santo. I think he's going to strain too hard to catch up, and he'll choke, and he'll lose his style, and in a couple of years he'll be one of those whatever-happened-to people."

Puss's letter said, *"It's real black out there and it lasts a long time."*

I could feel my heart fall. It dropped a certain distance and there it would stay.

I could look at Miss Smith as if I'd never seen her before. She sat with a little inward smile of satisfaction, thinking of what she wished for Gary Santo. She dipped at the shot glass for her little butterfly sips. The edge of the minitent came to mid thigh. Exquisite legs, honey-tan and matte finish, were crossed. The light of early afternoon came through the window ports, highlighting the lustrous brown-auburn fall of hair, a healthy pelt. The secretive lashes half veiled the vivid plastic green, the secret half smile curved the corners of the plump mouth.

She got up and wandered over to look at the titles on the sleeves of the records on the shelf by the player. "Do we get music with the booze?" she asked.

I went over dutifully and when I stood beside her, I realized she had suddenly fixed her attention elsewhere, so totally that she was unaware of me and unaware of the music. She was standing looking diagonally through the starboard aft port toward the dock, and following the direction of her intent gaze, I saw Hero ambling along, looking for fresh game, the meat of his shoulders slowly rolling, one thumb hooked into the tightness of the broad leather belt.

I looked down at her face, saw that the lips, now parted, looked almost swollen. Breathing deeply and slowly through parted lips, eyelids heavy, head nodding slightly, she watched Hero.

Then she turned to me and it seemed to take her a moment to remember who I was. In a voice pitched lower than usual, and with a huskiness, she said, "Darling, forgive me if I uninvite myself for lunch? Thank you for drinks and entertainment. Thank you for saving me from a shot in the mouth. I think I'll . . . look up those friends I have here. Some other time, dear. You have a lovely boat."

She put on her huge black sunglasses and put the empty shot glass down, and smiled and left. I went out on the afterdeck and watched her go hastily in the direction Hero had taken. Swing of the purse. Quick clip-clap of the sharp little heels on the cement. Rapid bouncing of the weight of the rich brown mane. Unseen, tented hips swinging. And, I could guess, a crawly butterfly awareness of the silky brushing of the softening thighs together, awareness of the prickling tickle of erectile tissues, of labial weights and thickenings, and a feeling of being unable to take a breath quite deep enough—as she went tocking and bobbing in her scurry to fall under the brutalizing, tireless, impersonal hammer of the Hero, to be once more the bedbeaten shoat, to be spent and lamed and emptied as before.

So I walked slowly to Meyer's boat and sat on the bunk with my head in my hands while he read Puss's letter. He finished it and coughed and honked and wiped his eyes. So I told him that we were going to take his little cruiser because it could take more sea than a houseboat, and we were going to take the *Muñequita* in tow, and we were going to go as far down the Exuma Cays as the range of his boat would allow, and then we were going a lot further down in the Little Doll. I told him I was sick unto death of miniwomen, miniclothes, miniloves, minideaths and my own damned minilife. I wanted empty cays, gaudy reefs, hot sun, swift fish, and maybe some talk when it was time for talking.

And Meyer said, "So give me a hand with the lines and we'll take this crock over to the gas dock and top off the tanks."

Dress Her In Indigo

1

On that early afternoon in late August, Meyer and I walked through the canvas tunnel at Miami International and boarded a big bird belonging to Aeronaves de Mexico for the straight shot to Mexico City. We were going first class because it was all a private and personal and saddening mission at the behest of a very sick and fairly rich man.

We had the bulkhead seats on the port side because I am enough inches beyond six feet to cherish the extra knee room.

Tourist cards in order, cash in the moneybelts, underseat luggage only. And the unfamiliarly sedate wardrobes of the airborne businessman because there is a constant flow of them back and forth, the systems analysts and the plant location experts, the engineers and the salesmen, importers and exporters, con men and investment specialists.

The Mexican peso is rock solid, the economy roaring, and the population zooming past fifty million. So it is protective coloration to join the flock, as most trips combine business and pleasure, and the pure tourist is fair game for every hustle in the book.

But in one respect we were not entirely plausible. We'd spent the last few weeks aboard my houseboat, *The Busted Flush*, puttering around Florida Bay and the Keys with a small, convivial, and very active group of old and new friends aboard. When you get your clock adjusted to the routines of anchoring off shore, you keep the same hours as the sea birds, and the long hot bright days of summer had been full of fishing and swimming, walking the empty beaches of the off-shore keys, exploring in the dinghy rigged for sail, diving the reefs. So we were both baked to the deep red-bronze that comes from the new deep burn atop the years of deep-water tan, hair baked pale on my skull, salt-dried and wind-parched, the skin sea-toughened. Even Meyer's heavy black pelt had been bleached a little and now looked slightly red when the light hit it the right way.

So if we were of the business breed, it was something to do with engineering and the out-of-doors, like pipelines and irrigation projects.

He had the window seat. We sat in the sweltering heat of the tin bird until finally they unsnapped the umbilical tunnel, swung the door shut, and taxied us out toward takeoff. Then the warm air that had been rushing out of the overhead vents turned to cool, and white shirts began to come unstuck.

Meyer shrugged and smiled in a weary way and said, "That poor sad son of a bitch."

No need to draw a picture. The memory of my short visit with Mr. T. Harlan Bowie was recent and vivid. Maybe any complex and demanding life in our highly structured culture is like that old juggling routine in which a line of flexible wands as long as pool cues is fastened to a long narrow table and the juggler-clown goes down the line, starting a big white dinner plate spinning atop each one, accelerating the spin by waggling the wand. By the time he gets the last one spinning, the first one has slowed to a dangerous, sloppy wobble, and so he races back and waggles the wand frantically and gets it up to speed. Then the third one needs attention, then the second, the fifth, the eighth, and the little man runs back and forth staring up in horrid anxiety, keeping them all going, and always on the verge of progressive disaster.

So Mr. Bowie's white spinning plates had been labeled Vice President and Trust Officer of a large Miami bank, Homeowner, Pillar of the Community, Husband of Liz, Director of This and That, Board Member of The Other, Father of Beatrice known as Bix, the lovely daughter and only child.

He kept the plates spinning nicely, and I imagine he expected to eventually take them off the wands and put them down, with each deletion simplifying the task that remained, until maybe there would be just one plate called Sunset Years, placidly spinning.

But somehow life is arranged so that if one plate wobbles too much and slips off the wand tip and smashes, the rest of them start to go also, as if the sudden clumsiness were a contagion.

One morning Liz had asked him if he had time for another cup of candy. She became furious when he couldn't seem to understand what she meant, and she got the steaming pot and poured another cup and said, "Candy!" She hesitated, frowning, and said, "Coffee? Of course it's coffee! What did I call it?"

By the time she was scheduled for all the neurological tests at the Baltimore clinic, she had lost the differentiation between genders, using he and she so interchangeably she had a fifty percent chance of being right at any given time, and she had admitted to having had sudden and severe headaches for several months, but had paid as little attention to them as possible, because she had never believed in babying herself. They took the top of her skull off like a lid and got some of it but knew they could not get all, and stuck a cobalt bead in there for luck, even knowing she had no luck left. She kept talking for half the time it took to die, but the words didn't go together in any pattern anyone could translate. It took five months to kill her, if you start counting the morning she poured her beloved husband a cup of candy. It was hideously expensive and, to Harl Bowie, hideously incomprehensible. She died on Columbus Day. Daughter Bix had spent the summer at home and had stayed on, of course, rather than going back in September for her senior year at Wellesley. After Liz died, Bix told her daddy she would probably go back at mid-term.

He was not paying much attention, not only because he was stunned by the loss of his wife, but also because there had been a merger of certain banks, and there was a new imperative computer system for the handling of trust account investments, and Harl Bowie had to keep running up to Atlanta for a week at a time to try to find out what the hell the quiet young men who had been posted in the trust department were talking about.

But he paid a lot of attention when she told him right after Christmas that she had decided not to go back. She had decided to go to Mexico for a while "with some kids I know." He had tried every bit of leverage he could think of, and he couldn't move her an inch. He couldn't even get any display of emotion out of her. She reminded him gently that she would become twenty-two in another month, and there was the twenty thousand left her by her mother, and said it would be nice if he could stop being so manic about it because she was going, with or without approval.

So she went, and he got some infrequent postcards, and in April he was driving through thunder to the airport for another bout with the systems analysis people in Atlanta, and a big semi coming the other way got a big blast of wind and lost it, and came piling and jackknifing across the medial strip into heavy oncoming traffic. They said it was a miracle half a dozen or more people weren't killed, instead of just one man seriously injured, a local bank executive.

T. Harlan Bowie had to be prybarred and torch-cut out of his squashed Buick, and there was so much blood the rescue people were in a big hurry. As it turned out, they would have done a lot better taking it slow and easy rather than turning him and twisting him and working him in muscular style out of the metal carapace. Nobody could prove anything afterward. The lacerations were superficial. But there was a fracture of the spine, and between the second and third lumbar vertebrae the unprotected cord had been pinched, ground, bruised, torn, and all but severed. Nobody could ever say whether the accident had done it, or the rescue efforts.

And it killed him—from the fracture point on down to his toes. Meanwhile the fates were laughing dirtily in the wings at another aspect of the treatment they were giving the poor, sad, sorry son of a bitch. T. Harlan Bowie had always been both shrewd and lucky with what Liz used to call "Harlie's funny little stocks." He liked to put his eggs in a couple of baskets and watch the baskets like an eagle. The day they told him they wanted to take the top of Liz's skull off, he stopped watching the baskets. They were a couple of little technology companies. He had about an eighty thousand investment in them, evenly split. It was not savings, because bank officers don't make enough to save money like that after taxes. It was the pyramided gains of a dozen years of those funny little stocks.

His personal broker would call once in a while and try to report what was going on, but Harl didn't want to talk about it or hear about it or even know about it. After Liz died, he was too upset about being so damned alone, and about Bix, to have even the slightest stir of curiosity about his two little dog stocks. Then, of course, there were the weeks in the hospital, and by early July they moved him from the hospital to an elegant place that was a combination rest home and therapy center. When he found out that the tab was running seventy-five a day plus extras, it stimulated the money-nerve and he began to check things out. An old and good friend had emptied out the house on Cricket Bayou, the redwood and coquina stone house Liz had loved so, had stored Harl's personal stuff, and had gotten a very good price for the house the day after it was listed. The personal accident and disability and major disaster insurance was paying off handsomely. His attorney had negotiated a surprisingly fat settlement from the company which handled the trucker's liability insurance. The premature retirement benefit and the bank insurance disability income clause were spewing more money diligently.

So he called his broker finally and heard the awed, hushed and respectful tone, and finally comprehended that the two funny little technology stocks had both come out with a couple of earnings quarters of a fantastic richness, that they had valuable patents in areas Harl had never even heard of, that one was listed on the big board and the other one had applied, and the stock of both of them had been generously split a couple of times. So in one of them, what had cost him six dollars was worth two hundred and fifty, and the laggard had gone only from eight dollars to a hundred and twenty. So there was upwards of two million two, or an aftertax one million six.

He laughed after he found that out; he laughed himself sick. He had his broker arrange a negotiated sale through the floor specialists, and he put the tax money aside in treasury bills, and he stuffed the rest of it into tax-free municipals, and there he was all of a sudden with a tax-free income coming in on the basis of like two hundred and forty dollars a day forever, and it was money he didn't have to touch because what was coming in from all other sources was more than sufficient to his needs, even in Garden Suite Number Five in Tropicana Grove Retreat.

His lawyers had been trying to locate Bix in Mexico to tell her that daddy had been badly injured. But the last plate had to smash and did so when a man with a polite and careful voice tracked T. Harlan Bowie down by long distance from the State Department to tell him that Miss Beatrice Tracy Bowie had been killed near Oaxaca when the vehicle in which she had been riding had gone off a mountain road, and the Mexican authorities wanted to know where the body was to be shipped and who would arrange and pay for the shipment.

Poor sick sorry rich and sad son of a bitch.

All you can say is: Well, that's the way it goes sometimes. It goes very bad sometimes because they give you the bad in great big indigestible wads. As if they want to write you off in a hurry. As if the idea is to tear down your whole scene and sow the area with salt and acid, and be off looking for the next fellow who happens to be standing and smiling and thinking that life is pretty good lately.

So only-daughter was airfreighted back to eternal rest beside mother Liz in one of those happy-vale places where the markers are flush with the ground level, the walks and gates have names, and stereotaped organ music comes wafting out of the pole-mounted guaranteed weatherproof high-compliance speaker systems.

Nobody knew whether she had enjoyed Mexico.

So three days ago T. Harlan Bowie got Meyer on the phone and they had a long talk, and then Meyer said I should accompany him to Miami and talk to a friend of his. I said I did not want to talk to anybody about anything, because it had been a very nice cruise and I wanted to slob around and savor it in full measure.

Meyer then reminded me that I had met Bix Bowie, and that last year, a week or so after her mother's funeral, he had brought her around and we had gone with her and some other people on the *Flush* up the waterway, and the girl had seemed to have a good time, but it was hard to tell. He explained that he had been a sort of unofficial godfather to the girl when she was smaller, before she had gone away to school.

It stirred my memory, but I could not get a clear image of the girl herself. The world seems overful of quiet pretty blondes lately, and the trouble is that when they are silent and withdrawn one no longer knows whether it is shyness, total disinterest, or a concealed and contemptuous churlishness.

But I could see that it had racked my friend Meyer, and that if I continued to drag my feet, he was going to say please, and then I would be unable to help myself, so I agreed before he had a chance to say the magic word friends should not have to use on one another.

On the way down he talked a little about how Liz used to ask him to show up at school when there had been some kind of bring-a-parent situation and Harlan Bowie was too tied up to make it. He thought Bix was glad he would show, but he could never be certain. He had never been able to reach through to her. She had extraordinary composure and control. He and Liz had attended her high school graduation together, because Harl had an appointment in Tallahassee that day.

I said I thought a father should be able to manage at least a graduation for an only child and only daughter. And Meyer said it had often seemed so to him, too.

So we drove on down to Tropicana Grove Retreat, and Meyer was so troubled, I found myself getting emotionally hung on this blonde

I couldn't remember. By God, anybody who cruises with McGee deserves better treatment than the fates, or her father, had apparently given her.

The establishment was in a quiet area in Coral Gables, with low buildings, a lot of very handsome old banyans, lots of plantings, summer birdsongs, and old parties being wheel-chaired along curved walks. They made a phone call from the office. A stocky woman in a gray and white uniform appeared and introduced herself as Mrs. Kreiger and smiled in pleasant recognition at Meyer, and led us back through garden walks to Garden Suite Five. T. Harlan Bowie sat in a wheelchair in the air-conditioned, carpeted living room, watching a cable television picture of the changing prices on a brokerage house board, while a man was talking about the rails confirming the Dow. He turned it off with the remote control.

Tall thin frail man. His handshake was fragile and tentative. His eyes had that look. It is not so much a haunted look or a hollow-eyed look. It is a look of constant and thoughtful appraisal that keeps going on and on in spite of all conversations, all diversions. Any man who outgrows the myths of childhood is ninety-nine percent aware and convinced of his own mortality. But then comes the chilly breath on the nape of the neck, a stirring of the air by the wings of the bleak angel. When a man becomes one hundred percent certain of his inevitable death, he gets The Look.

He had a long face, high forehead, the fine-bodied white hair of the erstwhile blond. Mrs. Kreiger told him she would be back in an hour to take him to therapy. She had broad pale lips, lovely eyes, a tidy muscularity in the way she moved. She told us happily, in a little more than a trace of German accent, that Mr. Bowie had moved the toes on his right foot.

He flushed. Part irritation. Part Aw shucks, it was nothin', guys.

He looked at the door she closed behind her and said, "Und soon, Herr Bowie, ve vill haff you running races, nein?" He asked us to sit. He said to Meyer, "Did you tell Mr. McGee what we discussed?"

"Some of the background, Harl. Not what you want done."

He turned the chair slightly to face me more directly. "Mr. McGee, I know damned little about what my daughter, Bix, felt and thought and believed. I've had a lot of time to think. And a lot of the thinking has been painful. Appraisal of myself as a father—very, very poor. I know that when she was a toddler we were close. She adored me. That was the good part of it. Our only chick. Liz had had a bad time. Couldn't have more. You know, Bix never went through any ugly period at all. Beautiful baby, lovely little girl, hand-some teenager. No acne, no braces, no gawky period. Liz and I were too aware of her being an only child, I guess. And awed by how damned pretty she was, and upset at all the admiration she got. So we were too harsh with her. Two against one. United front. She had to strain like hell to get our approval, and we were too chinchy about giv-ing it out. We made her obedient and docile and sweet, and we probably made her unsure of herself. But how can you tell? How many chances do you get to raise a child? I was very, very busy. So I wasn't paying attention, not to Bix as a person. She was an object. Beautiful child.

"Then when Liz . . . got sick, Bix came down. She stayed with her mother right through it. And it wasn't pretty. Bix was a rock. I took her for granted. I took her strength for granted. God only knows how badly it tore her up. She never let me know. Without Liz I was a zombie. I went through the motions. It should have been the two of us then. Father and daughter. But each of us was alone in a private way. I had my own hell. I don't know where she was spend-ing her time. She was just . . . around."

He gave me a despairing look, and made an empty gesture with his hands. "I'm dithering. I'm not saying it. Look. I don't even know how she lived when she was here with me in Miami. I'd find her in the house with friends. Pretty oddball-looking kids. I'd go through and they'd stare at me as if I came from Mars, as if my house were a bus station and I were some strange type in transit. Empty eyes, loud music. She went to Mexico in early January this year. Seven months later she was dead. I want to know . . . what it was like. I want to know—Oh God help me—I just want to know if she was having a good time." His voice broke and he put his hand across his eyes.

Meyer said, "Harl had an agency do a little investigating. But the reports are facts without any flavor. He'd follow the back trail him-self, if he could. He tried to think of somebody who could get away, somebody without a regular job or a family and he thought of me. When we talked about it, I said you were the man for the job. He wants us both to go. All expenses. Take our time and do it right and come back and tell him how it was for her."

"And find out," Bowie said, "what kind of people she was running around with—find out if they could have played . . . some kind of cruel game."

I questioned him, and he explained. After he had had word of his daughter's fatal accident, he had received a letter that had been written and mailed at least a week before she had died, but had been sent to the house that had been sold and had taken a long time in transit. He took it out of the drawer and handed it to me.

Ordinary mail. Sent from Oaxaca in July, with a date stamp so blurred it could have been the 23rd or the 28th. Cheap envelope, cheap paper. Blue ballpoint. It was small untidy writing, half script, half printed, with no clue to the sex of whoever wrote it. No salutation or date or signature.

You want Bix to come back ever, or ever want to come back even, you better come after her or send somebody pretty quick because she doesn't have any idea what's happening to her lately.

"My daughter always knew exactly what was happening," Bowie said. "Somebody was trying to create a problem for her. I don't know why. A cruel little game of some kind. The part about her not wanting to come back certainly means that this note has no relationship to the accident."

So we had talked a little longer, but by then I knew it was for no other reason than to have us report on the end of the short and happy life of Miss Bowie. But he did not look as if he really wanted to hear anything too ugly.

Maybe it wasn't very pretty for Bix Bowie.

Maybe it was a dingy way to die.

So we had the brief reports from the investigation agency, and we had the translation of the Mexican police report of the death, and we had some duplicate prints made from a negative Harlan Bowie had given us. The picture did not restore my memory of her. Full face, half a smile. A flash picture taken the last Christmas the family was intact. Home from school. Without a schoolgirl look. Mature woman. Long creamy spill and fall of thick, ivory-blond hair. Watchful eyes. Meyer told me they were dark, dark blue. Mouth curved with secrets untold. The expression was contradictory. She looked bland and reserved, almost content. But the slant of the flashbulb light picked up a little bulge at the corner of the jaw, a little knot of muscle, a look of tension held under the clench of teeth, under iron control.

The tin bird whoofed down the runway and lifted sharply, while everybody played the habitual game of total indifference which hides the shallow breathing and contracted sphincters of the Air Age.

I looked across the blue bay at the fantasy known as Miami Beach. Cubes of maple sugar. Candy minarets. Special low summer rates. We were off to start at the end of her life and work back.

2

THE TWO Mexican stewardesses in first class were tidy, handsome, efficient, and very polite. It was restful to find they had apparently not been programmed to smile constantly. The drink cart was well stocked, and it stopped as often as you wanted it to. Lunch was late, fairly heavy, and though no gourmet feast, was served in a manner which had more of the illusion of permanence than is created by the disposable plastics of the domestic airlines in the states.

The plates were heavy cream-colored china with a gold band. Tablecloth and napkins were thick linen. The cutlery was massive silver plate, and the cream, sugar, salt, and pepper came in chunky, permanent, cut-glass containers.

Meyer found the whole thing pleasantly inconsistent. "The jet aircraft is a limited life-support system. It hangs up here, above the thunderheads, heated, pressurized, ventilated, with food and water and waste disposal. The duration of the system depends on the fuel supply. So, if one comes down at the wrong place at the wrong speed for the wrong reasons, the logical debris should be of disposable items. Travis, the mind boggles at visions of a wooded hill littered with broken pieces of dinner plates, cups, saucers and silver tableware. As if a dining room fell out of the sky. Those horrid little plastic compartmented plates and cardboard shotglasses for the cream and salad dressing are more apt for scenes of disaster. So the whole bit is an affirmation that it can't possibly fall out of the sky. Subtle and interesting. Now if they could cover these jukebox plastic bulkheads with a very thin layer of teak or library oak . . ."

"Mighty guru, take your bulging brain off the psychology of air travel and put it on your old buddy, T. Harlan Bowie. He did not ring loud and clear. There is a crack in the bell somewhere."

Meyer shrugged. "Sure."

"What is that supposed to mean?"

"He rings true enough, as what he is. What you sense is that his concern seems a little faked. It isn't. It's limited by his own limitations. He's using us to buy a kind of emotional respectability. He's using us to pat his image back into shape. Oh, he adored her when she was a toddler. Tiny girls are cute and huggable, like puppies and kittens. Lots of people adore kittens, and when they get to be cats they take them for a nice ride and dump them out in the country somewhere and imagine them living in a nice barn, catching mice. McGee, the world is full of reasonably nice guys like Harl. They go through all the motions of home and family, but there is no genuine love or emotion involved. There is an imitation kind. They are unconscious practicing hypocrites. They're stunted in a way they don't and can't recognize. If I had to nail it down, I'd say that people like Harl go around with the unspoken, unrealized conviction that nobody else in the world exists, really, except as . . . bits of stage dressing in the life role that they are playing. So wife and child and job and home are part of the image, and he kept it burnished and tidy, but without any deep involvement with anybody but T. Harlan Bowie. Now he's studying his way into his new role. Tragic, crippled figure. So the dramatics are off key just a little. And now the tears are not quite real. Our mission is part of the new image. But don't fault him. He believes he is really in the midst of life and always has been. He doesn't know any better, because he's never known anything else. What a limited man believes is emotional reality is indeed *his* emotional reality."

"Doesn't everybody fake a little in their own way?"

"Sure. And you're aware of it when you do, aren't you?"

"Uncomfortably."

"But he isn't. And that's the difference."

I thought it over. "Question answered, Meyer. What was his wife like?"

"A nice woman. Comfortable. Adjusted."

"Would Bix have been able to understand what you've told me about him?"

"She would have known it existed. Whether or not she understood it is something else. Maybe she thought it is what people mean when they talk these days about the generation gap. I imagine it would have given her the feeling that no matter how hard she tried, she could never really please him. She would believe, maybe, that there was some well of warmth and understanding and love that she couldn't ever reach, without realizing that she couldn't reach it because it wasn't there, not for her, not for anybody."

I retrieved the investigation reports from the inside pocket of my jacket and studied them carefully, looking for any lead I might have missed the other times I had gone over them.

The group had left Miami on January third, five of them traveling in a blue heavy-duty Chevrolet pick-up truck, two years old, Florida license, registered in the name of Walter Rockland, who, up until Christmas, had been a swimming pool attendant at the Sultana Hotel on Miami Beach. A few days before Christmas Miss Beatrice Bowie had withdrawn eight thousand dollars from her savings account, leaving a balance of thirteen thousand two hundred and eleven dollars and sixty cents, twelve thousand of which had been part of the twenty thousand from her mother's estate. She had purchased a new camper body for the truck, and the group had purchased a great deal of camping equipment and supplies—sleeping bags, a shelter tent, hatchets, camp stove, netting, gasoline lanterns, flashlights, first-aid kits.

They had shown up on January 10th in the public records at Brownsville, Texas, where they had applied for and received tourist cards good for six months. The other three members of the group were Minda McLeen, age twenty, occupation student, address Box 80, Coral Gables, Florida; Carl Sessions, age twenty-two, occupation musician, listed at the same address as Miss McLeen; and Jerome Nesta, age twenty-six, occupation sculptor, home address Box 2130, Key West, Florida.

The agency had come up with only a few additional facts about the quintet. Miss McLeen had stopped going to classes at the University of Miami in May of the previous year. Walter Rockland had been fired by the Sultana Hotel, and though the personnel manager would not state why, there was reason to believe that the hotel management thought he was implicated in some way in a series of robberies of the winter guests at the hotel. Jerome Nesta had been arrested three and a half years previously at Marathon, Florida, in a narcotics raid, had been charged with and had pleaded not guilty to possession of marijuana. When the case came to trial, there was insufficient proof that the marked and tagged container presented in court was in fact the same container taken from him when he was taken into custody, and a defense motion to dismiss was granted by the judge.

And that, of course, is the tragic law in the narcotics laws—that possession of marijuana is a felony. Regardless of whether it is as harmless as some believe, or as evil and vicious as others believe, savage and uncompromising law is bad law, and the good and humane judge will jump at any technicality that will keep him from imposing a penalty so barbaric and so cruel. The self-righteous pillars of church and society demand that "the drug traffic be stamped out" and think that making possession a felony will do the trick. Their ignorance of the roots of the drug traffic is as extensive as their ignorance of the law.

Let's say a kid in Florida, a college kid eighteen years old, is picked up with a couple of joints on him. He is convicted of possession, which is an automatic felony, and given a suspended sentence. What has he lost? The judge who imposes sentence knows the kid has lost the right to vote, the right to own a gun, the right to run for public office. He can never become a doctor, dentist, C.P.A., engineer, lawyer, architect, realtor, osteopath, physical therapist, private detective, pharmacist, school teacher, barber, funeral director, masseur, or stock broker. He can never get any job where he has to be bonded or licensed. He can't work for the city, county, or federal governments. He can't get into West Point, Annapolis, or the Air Force Academy. He can enlist in the military, but will be denied his choice of service, and probably be assigned to a labor battalion.

It is too rough. It slams too many doors. It effectively destroys the kid's life. It is too harsh a penalty for a little faddist experimentation. The judge knows it. So he looks for any out, and then nothing at all happens to the kid. Too many times harsh law ends up being, in effect, no law at all. All automatic felony laws are, without exception, bad law, from the Sullivan Act in New York State, to the hit and run in California. They destroy the wisdom and discretion of the Court, and defeat the purposes they are meant to serve.

I wondered if Jerry Nesta, sculptor, knew how close he had come to the edge. I wondered if it had marked him in any way. And I wondered if I'd ever get a chance to ask him.

So they had crossed over into Matamoros, Mexico, on January 10th, and some seven months later, on August third, a Sunday, according to the translations of the police report, Miss Beatrice Bowie, twenty-two years old, American tourist, had been driving at dusk down State Highway 175, heading southwest toward Oaxaca. At a steep and dangerous part of the highway, the vehicle left the road at a spot fifteen miles from the city. A bus driver on a switchback on the opposite side of a valley saw the bloom of flame and reported it when he reached the bus station in Oaxaca. As night had fallen, the police were unable to locate the automobile until the following morning. She had been alone. The car was a British Ford with State of Oaxaca plates, owned by a resident American named Bruce Bundy, age 44, of 81 Calle las Artes, Oaxaca.

He stated that on Saturday afternoon he had loaned his car to a young man, an American tourist, known to him only as George. He did not know why there was a girl alone in the car, or why she had been on that road. Police could find no identification. On Monday afternoon a woman came to the funeral parlor and made a positive identification of the body as that of Beatrice Bowie. She made a statement to the effect that Miss Bowie and Miss McLeen had been staying in the guest apartment at her winter home on Avenida de las Mariposas in the section known as La Colonia. The woman, a French national, Madame Eva Vitrier, told the police that several days earlier her guests had evidently quarreled, and Miss McLeen had left for Mexico City. She said that Miss Bowie had seemed upset and depressed. When she did not return to the guest apartment on Sunday night, and when on Monday she heard of the recovery of the body of the unidentified woman, she had thought it might be Miss Bowie, and discovered that indeed it was. She knew Mr. Bundy, but did not believe that Miss Bowie knew him. The name George did not mean anything to her. But it was probable that Miss Bowie knew him. All the young American tourists seemed to become known to one another.

The police had returned to Mrs. Vitrier's home with her and had there picked up Miss Bowie's personal effects, including her purse and her tourist card which, on the day of her death, was almost a month overdue for renewal. Their search for the young man known only as George had been unsuccessful.

As I put the papers away again, Meyer said, "Anything new?"

"Just more questions. When did she send for that bank draft to clean out her account?"

"Harl said it was in late March."

I had the address where they had sent it. She had been at Los Tres Rios Trailer Park at Culiacán, over in the State of Sinaloa, on the

Gulf of California, and it had been made out to her, payable at the Culiacán branch of the Banco Nacional.

"My question right now, Meyer, has something to do with it being one hell of a trip from Brownsville to Culiacán, and another hell of a trip from Culiacán down to Oaxaca. And did they all go, and did they go in that camper, and where and when and how did they split up? And the Mexicans are very touchy about people getting their vehicles back to the border in six months. You can renew and go back in again, but don't get cute about overstaying your tourist card deadline. Why did she want the money, all of it, and why did she overstay her permit?"

"Shut up," said Meyer, "and look out at the nice volcano, McGee. I mean at the three nice volcanos. No, by God, there are four of them."

"Citlaltepetl, Malinche, Ixtaccihuatl and Popocatépetl."

"Travis, do you have something caught in your throat?"

"If you want to cheat a little, you can call that one over there Orizaba instead of Citlaltepetl."

"I did not know you had any expertise on Mexico's snow-capped peaks."

"Once upon a time there was a roof garden in Puebla, and a little tile stairway going up to it, and the biggest mesh hammock you ever saw in your life, old friend. And when the moonlight was right and the night balmy, a fellow could go padding up the tile stairs and stretch out in that hammock, and one Maria Amparo Celestina Rodriguez de la Vega would take up her warm one third of said hammock and make a fellow name each volcano and name it right."

"Is that where you got your pidgin Mexican, señor?"

"It helped."

So fasten seat belts, and, in the late afternoon, head down and into that misty, poisonous, saffron smutch that fills the mountain bowl of that great city half full. Better than six million of the fifty million Mexicans live on that swampy plateau seven thousand five hundred feet high. An inaccurate comparison would be twenty-four million Americans living in Denver. Mountains rim the Mexico plateau, enclosing and holding the exhaust fumes of unaccounted thousands of trucks and buses ranging from brand new to items so ancient they have a sidelong, clattering shamble, steaming and groaning. And the exhaust of a bedazzling number of Volkswagens. A big new plant on the Puebla highway stamps them out like production-line tacos, and every boulevard is a combination scrambling road rally, dodgit game, and demonstration of machismo. Add the smoke of a few hundred thousand little charcoal cooking fires, and the city is in an unending haze, saffron-gold on the sunny days, purple-brown when it is cloudy.

Our cab driver was a large, loud, jolly type with a dashboard covered with religious statuary and medallions. With graceful little flourishes of hand and wrist on the wheel, he slid through openings that opened just as he got there, closed just as he got through. He said we were very lucky it was not yet five o'clock, because we would make the trip to the Hotel Camino Real in perhaps twenty minutes, and a half hour later it might take an hour and twenty minutes. I translated for Meyer. Meyer sat with his eyes shut and said he would have preferred the hour and twenty minute version.

Once he got to the Paseo de la Reforma heading out toward Chapultepec, he was able to play the chicken game at each traffic circle—at Colón, Cuauhtémoc, Independencia, Diana. To play the game properly you get into five-abreast traffic and accelerate to fifty as you enter the traffic circle, then all go screaming and swaying around the monument in the middle and find room to peel off and out of the group and exit from the circle at the street you want.

Meyer had opened his eyes. They were too far open. I tried to take his mind off the chicken game by telling him bits of lore—such as the fact that Chapultepec means Grasshopper Hill. But all he could say, watching the traffic inches away, was a barely audible "Dear kindly Jesus." He said it several times.

We popped out of the flow at Diana, sped across the bow of several buses, and gradually slowed down as we went along Mariano Escobedo. The driver turned into the hotel entrance, stopped abruptly, hitched around to face us, looked at his watch, and with a big grin said in semi-English, "Twenny-toos minootis!"

"I'll just sit right here for a while," Meyer said.

But a large young man garbed like an Ecuadorian admiral handed us out and got us and our luggage into the incoming flow. My first look at the Camino Real. Twenty-five million dollars worth of it. Seven connected buildings, the tallest only five stories. Entrance lobby the size of a football field, paved with little oblongs of gleaming hardwood, each piece smaller than the end of a pack of cigarettes. Bold colors, daring architecture, startling vistas, all of it a maze of shops and bars and lounges, fountains and pools and restaurants, stairways and corridors and carpeted luxury. Seven hundred and something rooms and suites.

The reservation was in order, the bellhops brisk, and after a very short elevator ride and a very long walk, we were deposited in a pair of interconnecting singles on the third floor of a bedroom wing. Drinks came swiftly. I unpacked. I heard Meyer's voice raised in sonorous melody, and wandered into his place and found him in his giant tub, his drink on the broad marble encircling slab, the black pelt on chest and shoulders foamed with soap.

"About those last lions," he said. "Too damned fat and sleepy and indifferent. Send the boys out to get some lean and hungry lions. How can we put the fear of God into those Christians unless we use faster lions?"

"Anything else?"

"Who catered that last orgy? There were only three dancing girls apiece. An austere orgy is no orgy at all."

"I'll make a note of it."

"And get me my fiddle."

"So soon? We haven't put out the last fire yet."

He hoisted his glass. "Here's to primitive, backward Mexico. Here's to hardship."

I left him there, paddling happily, soaping and singing, and went back into my room and looked up Ron Townsend's number in the oversized phone book. The hotel operator told me I could dial direct. There was a little gadget on the phone. Push the gadget and dial.

A girl answered and I asked for Ron.

She had a good voice, husky and very personal. She got my name and came back and said, "Hang in there while waterboy gets the soap out of his eyes, friend."

He came on the line, properly enthusiastic. He is a young partner in a Miami advertising firm. He was born and partially raised in Cuba. He is the agency expert in Mexico and doing well. I had made a good recovery for them some time ago when a secretary, unbonded, took off with enough cash out of the safe to sting them pretty good. He was delighted to learn Meyer was with me, and apologetic about having a date he couldn't break. But he said he could stop off on the way, so in thirty minutes or so he joined us at the bar in the Camino Real which he favored, named Azulejos, bringing with him the voice on his phone, a young girl at least five ten, suitably spectacular, and clad in mini-leather fastened with big brass chains and galoshes snaps. Her name was Miranda Dale and she had just finished a bit part in a West German motion picture they had shot at Mazatlán, on Mexico's west coast.

I told Ron our problem, and the girl listened to it with a pretty and sympathetic show of interest. I asked him if he could recommend a useful and influential contact in Oaxaca, and he came up with one named Enelio Fuentes and wrote it on the back of his business card and slid it across to me. He said Enelio was an old friend, had a big VW agency and other business interests scattered around the State of Oaxaca. But he couldn't help with a name in Culiacán. He said he would phone Fuentes and tell him to take care of me if I had to look him up.

Then I asked him how he would go about checking on the Chevrolet truck and camper with Florida plates, registered to a Walter Rockland, and he said he wouldn't even try. In theory you get car papers at the border, and they keep a copy at the place where you enter, and if you leave at some other border town, the stamped papers are supposed to go back to the place where you entered, and then the set is supposed to be sent to Mexico City and filed somewhere, possibly by some branch of the Mexcian Tourist Bureau. But that was only theory.

I said we'd be back in Mexico City sooner or later, but right now the most useful thing to do was get down to Oaxaca while there was still a good chance that friends of Miss Bix might be around.

They had to leave. Went across the dim and crowded room. Those long, sweet, taffy-sleek legs, from boot leather to mini-leather, seemed to gather available light and reflect it. Three mariachi types were on the stand, one singing a ballad, and he inserted an improvisation I could not catch. Ron turned, grinning, and called something to the musicians, and there was laughter and applause.

Meyer and I stayed on. He had discovered that *tequila añejo commemorativo*, with *sangrita* on the side, is one of the world's most pleasant drinks. The añejo—the "j" pronounced like a gutteral cough —means old. The commemorativo means a very special distillation. It is drunk straight, pale amber in color, strong, smooth, and clean. The chaser's full name is *sangrita de la viuda*, which means for some reason I have yet to learn, "little blood of the widow." It is tomato juice, citrus juices, with several varieties of pepper and spices. It changes the taste buds, readies them for the next sip of the tequila. Meyer crooned and beamed and ordered more.

But later his mood changed. "Vulgarity can be many things," he said. "It can be having a good time while en route to where the daughter of an old friend died. Dead young women are a pitiful waste."

We had finished a late dinner. "Tequila shouldn't make you morose," I told him.

"Without it, I would probably be crying," he said.

3

WE WERE reserved on an early Mexicana flight. It was an elderly Douglas with four genuine propellers and a full load of passengers. Noisy engines, with oil stains on the housings, littered floor, some popped rivets, lots of vibration. My turn at the window seat. Went roaring and clattering down the runway and lifted off. You get conditioned to that steep upward slant of the jets. This thing lifted off and seemed to hang there, fighting for every slow foot of altitude. Lots of time to look down into the streets. At seventy-five hundred feet as a starting place, and with a full load, we did a lot of clawing before we finally came up out of the last of the bright morning smutch and made a long slow turn.

A very plump stewardess in a soiled uniform served us paper cups of coffee and sweet rolls, and she did a lot of bantering with the customers. Then we went between Popo and his sleeping lady, Ixtaccihuatl. The blazing white summits of the dead volcanoes were easily a thousand feet above us, and vivid against the indigo sky. We were close enough to see snow plumes trailing off the cliffs of Ixta in the morning winds.

Then down along the torn and crumpled country, old stone spilled from the spine of the Sierra Madre. A day so clear you could see tiny villages, see the pale narrow marks of burro paths along the ridges. Too harsh a land to sustain life, but it does. Spaniards could never have taken it from the Indios without all those cute political tricks, turning them against each other. Travel-worn old DC grinding slowly down the side of the rocky world, a tin impertinence making its rackety noise across the stone indifference of the volcanic land. So eat the sweet roll and look down at the world of a thousand years ago. Mexicana Airlines sells tickets on a time machine.

So we came down into the valley of Oaxaca—pronounced wuh-HOCK-ah—beginning the descent at the upper end of the valley, some twenty miles from the airfield. Green valley encircled by old burned brown rounded hills. It is a plateau valley, five thousand feet high, in the Sierra Madre del Sur, and the Pacific is not far away. Skimmed lower. Saw a broken, abandoned, stone church amid corn-fields. Saw a man scratching a groove in brown soil with a wooden plow pulled by slow oxen. Saw village children, bright as spilled flowers. And our pilot set the old crock down with such precise and loving delicacy that there was but one small yelp of rubber, and not the slightest jar.

A neat little terminal, wine warm air, a confusion of greetings and luggage and taxis and hotel vehicles. The man from our hotel made himself known by pacing through confusion, calling "Veeeek Tory Aaaah! Veeeek Tory Aaaah!"

So soon we were off in a VW bus, the other passengers two stone-faced ladies with blue hair, large satchels, and guidebooks in German, and one young Mexican couple. The girl was in a smart travel suit of painful newness. The boy looked everywhere except at her. New gold rings gleamed.

We passed a sign as we approached the city, asserting that there were eighty thousand people therein. We skirted an edge of it, and climbed steep grades, then, in lowest low, ground up the long, steep, divided driveway to the parking area at the top, and the portico over the entrance to the Hotel Victoria.

The modern hotel, five stories tall, stretched along the top of a ridge, looking out across all of the city. Down the slope, in random array, beyond a huge swimming pool, were individual bungalows, each with carport, each landscaped with brilliant flowers and flowering vines. Rough stone steps and walks and stone driveways wound down through the bungalow community, all of it behind a guarded security fence.

The bungalows had girl-names instead of numbers, and they put us in Alicia. There was one large, tiled, plain room, simply furnished, two double beds, a bath, a dressing room, and a small porch in front overlooking the panorama—a porch with a tin table and poolside chairs. Alicia was two hundred and fifty pesos a day for two. Twenty dollars. I had explained to Meyer the quick easy McGee system for keeping track of the pesos. A fifty-peso bill is a four-dollar bill. A ten-peso bill is an eighty-cent bill.

Meyer stood on the porch and looked at the city and the mountains and the blue, blue sky. He looked at the flowers. He sniffed the flavors of the summery air. Then he turned to me and said, "I would have this handy little magic wand and I would take one little pass at you. Kazam! Suddenly you are Miranda Dale, looking at me like she looked at Ron Townsend."

"Didn't all those legs make you feel insecure?"

"And so did the age of the child. But this is the sort of place where I could try to overcome minor obstacles."

"You are a hairy, over-educated, lecherous old man."

"Flattery will get you nowhere, McGee. It's eleven-fifteen. What now?"

"Our wheels." We took a cab down into the city. The Hertz office was on a side street near the *zocalo*—the public square. The man was pleasant enough, but had absolutely no record of any reservation. He would have a lot of nice cars soon. Maybe in a week. He said he felt desolated by being unable to serve me. I said I would like to give him a four-dollar bill to ease his desolation. It was not to spur him to greater effort on my behalf, I said, because I was certain he would give me every possible help. It was a token of my understanding. He said there was, in truth, a car, but it would be a pity to rent it to me, because I obviously was used to better, and deserved better. It had been many, many *kilometros* and needed small repairs and was unclean. A boy with a Le Mans psychosis brought it around.

It was a Ford Falcon, from the Guadalajara assembly plant. Made in Mexico by Mexicans. Pale green. Four doors. Standard shift. It had been thirty-five thousand kilometers, and had been grooved on both sides by near disaster. And it had been traveling some very dusty roads. I signed for it. I took it on a test run, with Meyer copiloting, using the street map they had given us at the airport. Either the Ford engineers have decided Mexicans are a smaller race, or the cars shrink in the dry climate. With the seat as far back as it would go, my knees were on either side of the edge of the steering wheel, and unless I remembered to swing the right knee out of the way, each time I shifted into high I gave myself a sharp and painful rap on the inside edge of the kneecap. When we hit the first potholes I found the front shocks were gone. The front end hit the frame with a metallic thunk, and then a rumbling chatter.

So I asked directions, and found the Ford garage about seven blocks west of the zocalo. It was then a little past noon. The boss man took it for a turn around the block and came back shaking his head, and said I could have it at four.

We walked to the central square, along narrow sidewalks on narrow streets. The plaster-over-stone fronts of the two-story residences and shops formed a solid wall along the walkway, and they had been painted and repainted with pure strong pigments. One blue wall brought Meyer to a stop. Maybe it had been painted and patched fifty times. Layers had cracked, peeled, faded. It was all the shades of blue there are.

"Fix that with transparent epoxy," he said, "peel off a rectangle eight feet long and five feet high, frame it in rough-cut cypress with a white stain, and take it to any decent gallery—"

"And somebody will tell you their little daughter could do it better."

"The creative act is in selecting *which* rectangle to frame. It is very damned beautiful, Travis. And that talented daughter is a rotten kid."

Buses, trucks, cars, bicycles, and the ubiquitous popping and snorting of the Mexican plague—the motor scooter. So we went out of the sun heat into the cool shade of the gigantic trees of a splendid zocalo. It had its ornate circular bandstand in the middle, a crisscross of wide walkways and a perimeter walk past gaudy riots of flowerbeds. Traffic circled it counterclockwise. There were men, women, children selling serapes, shoeshines, chewing gum, straw baskets and straw animals, black pottery, fresh flowers and wilted flowers, serapes, cigarettes, fake Indian relics, silver jewelry, junk jewelry, firecrackers, aprons, serapes, ice cream, soft drinks, and hot tacos stuffed with God only knows what kind of meat. And serapes.

There was evident poverty, beggars with twisted limbs, sick children, stray mongrels, but there was a sense of great life and vitality, of enduring laughter. We found an empty bench. Meyer sat and saw everything, soaked it up, and smiled and smiled. And it was Meyer who spotted a little group on one of the diagonal paths, carrying purchases from the public market, walking toward the largest hotel that fronted on the zocalo, an old ornate stone and plaster structure with a sign proclaiming it as the Hotel Marqués del Valle. There was a long, narrow roofed porch across the front of it, a couple of steps up from sidewalk level. Fat cement columns supported arches that held up the overhanging bulk of the hotel. The porch was two tables wide and about thirty tables long, about half of them occupied, with white-coated waiters hustling drinks and food.

It was a group of four young men and three girls. The college-age men were wearing faded Mexican work shirt, bleached khakis. Two of the men and one of the girls were barefoot, and the others wore Mexican sandals. The girls wore shorts with bright cotton Indian blouses, and the boys were extravagantly bearded, long-haired. This, as Meyer pointed out, was clear indication they had been in Mexico for a long time. The government had long since closed the border to what were called "heepees," so the shorn locks and whiskers had to be regrown south of the border.

We got up and followed along. The waiters pushed two tables together for them. Meyer and I took a table about twenty feet from them, which was as close as we could get. The tempo of the public square was diminishing visibly. Shops were closing. It was siesta time, and not until two-thirty or three would the town begin to stir again. Only the serape salesmen along the sidewalk stayed in business, holding up the rough-woven gaudy wools, trying to catch the tourist eye, the tourist interest. And a dirty, big-eyed child roamed from table to table, trying dispiritedly to vend her "cheeeklets."

The young seven were a closed circle, totally indifferent to everything and everyone around them, relating and responding to one another. Too many for any initial contact. So I looked at the menu. Meyer had to trust me. The waiter was very patient with my verbless Spanish, and I was equally patient with his rudimentary English. So I managed to find a good solution—chicken enchiladas covered with Chihuahua cheese and baked. He said they had no Dos Equis, but if we wanted a dark beer, Negro Modelo might please us. And it did, and we were into the second bottle before the enchiladas came, bubbling hot in oval steel dishes.

After some thoughtful mastication, tempered with the dark beer, Meyer said, "Offhand, what are the immigration laws?"

"I'll just leave you here, and you can take your chances."

"I'll send you a card every Christmas."

Another student couple had appeared, a huge boy with a small head and a sensitive delicate face, and the blond silky hair and beard style of the Christus. He was with a small wiry black girl with a skin tone like dusty slate, sporting an African blouse and a tall tightly kinked African hairstyle through which she had bleached several startling amber-gold streaks.

"Wish me luck," I told Meyer, and with beer in hand went ambling over to their table. There was one extra chair.

"Join you for a couple of minutes?"

They looked up at me with a quick, identical wariness, and looked away again, and kept talking as if I was not there. Bad tactics. Should have asked the stranger to go away.

So I sat down, smiling blandly, and cut into their conversation, saying, "I am not on vacation, kids. I am not looking for fun and games. I am not drunk. I am not fuzz."

She stared at me with a hot, dark-eyed hostility and said, "Did you catch the strange word, darling? This fellow seems to have some sort of in-group syndrome."

"Fuzz," the boy said thoughtfully. "Wasn't there some sort of quip about that we never understood, Della?" Boston accent.

"I don't recall at the moment, dear."

He put on a minstrel show, end-man accent, doing the Sambo thing very badly. "Hey, you all hear 'bout what happen to Jemima?"

"No!" she said. "Whut happened to ol' Jemima?"

"Got herself picked up by the fuzz."

"Lordy me! That sure musta stung."

"Hyuck, hyuck, hyuck," I said, unsmiling.

"Just go away," Della said. "Be cooperative. Go back to your friend."

"If you had to make a guess, why would you say I came over here?"

They glanced at each other. The boy shrugged. "I guess the most likely thing would be one of those little speeches about tolerance and miscegenation and all that, so that you can pretend to be so terribly understanding and get some queasy little kick out of it, and get some barroom conversational gambits back wherever you come from, and also, let's see, delude yourself into believing that there is something so awfully swinging about you that you can bridge the communications gap."

I laughed. I couldn't help it. He was bright. He was so damned right and so damned wrong, all at once. I rocked the chair back and laughed. They looked startled, then angry, then they fought the temptation to smile, and then they were laughing. She had a piercing giggle, and he had a deep, rhythmic bray. We were being stared at. Finally, when I could get my breath, I said, "My name is Travis McGee. Fort Lauderdale, Florida."

"Della Davis," he said. "I'm Mike Barrington." His was a large, hard, muscular hand.

"Equal time?" I asked. He nodded. She had the hiccups. "I'm loaded with a lot of kinds of tolerance and intolerance, and the only time I get defensive is when I identify some kind of tolerance or intolerance I didn't know I had, or thought was something else. The only people who need queasy kicks are the ones with the sex hangups, and I think I was a little hung up when I was twelve years old, but not lately. I don't need a new supply of small talk. And if I did, I wouldn't look for the raw material on a hotel veranda. Anybody who gives it any thought knows that there has always been a communication gap between everybody. If any two people could ever really get inside each other's head, it would scare the pee out of both of them. I don't want to share your hopes and dreams, Mike. I just want to communicate in a very limited way, politely, with no stress on anybody."

"I guess they aren't with the mining company after all," Della said to him. She turned to me. "We noticed you two and decided you weren't tourists. There's a mine up in the hills northeast of the city. Okay, Mister McGee, let's communicate in our limited fashion."

"If you two haven't been here a month, communication ends."

"We got here . . . the second of something. May or June, dear?" she asked.

"May," said Mike, "and I change my guess. You're looking for somebody's baby darling, so in your nice, personable, reasonable way you can talk baby darling into coming back home to daddy. Or maybe that's daddy you were sitting with over there. And you locate her—or him—and lay on the tickets, the kind you can't cash in."

"Closer. But that isn't daddy over there. Daddy is back in Florida because he got nearly, but not quite, torn in half. And baby darling went home already. From here. In a box, early this month."

"Oh sure. The one with the country-day-school nickname. What was it they called her, Del?"

"Hmmm. Dox? Nax? Bax? . . . Bix!"

I put one of the prints on the table, facing Della Davis. She pulled it closer. "That one?" I asked.

"'Tis she," said Della. "We saw her around. You know. Stay here a while and you see everybody. Nod and smile. Didn't socialize. The group she was in, or better the groups she ran with, we don't make those scenes. I've got nothing for or against, you understand. Freedom is being left alone to do your own thing. Mike is a painter."

"Wants to be a painter," he corrected.

"And he doesn't want to talk about it. He gets up early and he works all day and he goes to bed. And I prowl around driving hard bargains for tortillas and beans and rice and thinking up new ways to cook them. So today I got a little check from my sister in Detroit. So we're living it up. I mean we aren't here much, so we don't keep good track. Anyway, she's dead. What are you after?"

Mike Barrington said, "If old dads wondered if somebody pushed his baby darling off the mountain, he might send somebody like Mr. McGee to come and snuff around."

"Oh, he doesn't doubt that it was an accident. It was a pretty good police report. They were out of touch since last January, when she came to Mexico. He wants to know what the last six months of her life were like. How she lived and what she thought and how she died."

"And," said Della with an acid sweetness, "I suppose she was always a very good girl."

"Kept her room neat," I said, "got good grades, remembered names, thanked the hostess, brushed her teeth, and said her prayers. I guess he'd like to know who the hell she was."

"None of them know who we are," Mike said. "Or care much, really. Hang in there with an image they can live with, and they love it. You don't know who they are, and they don't know who you are."

"So who was Bix Bowie?"

"A girl who died young," Della Davis said.

"If I had to guess why," Mike said, "and understand I'm not knocking her, I'd say she was probably turned way on. She was high and she was flying, and she was coming down the mountain without knowing if she was there or she was dreaming it, and it turned out she wasn't dreaming it. In a dream, when you hit bottom, you wake up. The thing about Mexico, the stuff that's on prescription in the states, here you can buy it in any drugstore. All you have to know is the name of what you want. Little lists circulate. The right names for Thorazine, Compazine, oral Demerol, Doriden, reserpine, Mardil, Benzedrine, other amphetamines. And in the public market, at the herb stalls, you can buy a kilo brick of very good, strong pot. It's all a big lunch counter. You mix them up in brand new ways and wait and see where and how it hits you. If you like it, you try to find the same combination again."

She put her wiry black hand on his and said, "That *used* to be the name of your game, sweetheart."

"There's a better high," he said, smiling into her eyes. "I don't ever have to come down off this one."

She gave me a bawdy wink, which somehow was not bawdy at all, and said, "Like the old saying, man, I changed his luck."

"It needed changing," Mike said.

"Was she any kind of hooked?" I asked them.

"I wouldn't know," Mike said. "I didn't know her. It's unfair to make guesses. Maybe one of those damned cows came clumping onto the road and she swerved and lost the car. But it's fair to say she was some kind of user, because it was users she was with, mostly, but I don't know how much or how often, or even what."

"Those seven over there at that table. Would any of them know more about her?"

Della leaned back and made a careful inspection. "I just don't know. If any of them, it would be the girl facing this way, with the round face and the reddish hair and the big sunglasses, and the skinny fellow sitting on her left. I think they've been here the longest."

"Got a name for either of them?"

"Mike, isn't that the girl they call Backspin?"

"Yes. God knows why."

I used my little notebook to refresh my memory. "Here are the names of the ones she came into the country with back in January. Stop me if I come to anyone you know. Carl Sessions? Jerry Nesta? Minda McLeen?"

"Whoa," Della Davis said. "Little bit of a dark-haired girl. She and that Bix were usually together. Strange-acting girl. Haven't seen her around lately. But that doesn't mean anything. Mike, darling, that horrible bore of a man with the funny hat. Wasn't his name . . . ?"

"McLeen. I went to the public market last week with Del and he introduced himself. Said he was looking for his daughter."

"He still around?"

"I have no idea."

"Walter Rockland?"

They both looked blank, both shrugged.

"They came down in a Chevy pickup, blue, with a new camper body on it."

She looked at Mike. "Rocko?" she asked.

"He says the name is Rockland, and the truck fits. Mr. McGee, is he a little older than the rest of the bunch? Husky?"

"That fits."

"Then Miss Bix came down here in bad company if she came with that one," Della said. "That one is one mean honkey son of a bitch. That one is a smart ass and a hustler. When did we have that fuss with him, honey?"

"About the fourth of July, I think. The day after the fourth." They took turns telling me about it. They'd gone to visit a couple they knew, who were living in a travel trailer at the trailer park over near the Plaza de la Danza. Rocko's camper was in a nearby site. Evidently someone had pried open a little door in the side of the camper and stolen his little tank of bottle gas. He came over to the travel trailer in an ugly mood, acting as if it was the fault of the friends of Mike and Della for not seeing it happen. Mike told him to take it easy. Rocko looked the situation over and told Mike he didn't need any advice from him *or* his spade chick. They were standing outside the travel trailer. Mike swung on Rocko and missed, and Rocko tagged him as he lunged forward off balance.

"And," said Della, "Mike was out of it right then. And that mean bastard knew it, but he hit him three more times before he could fall down, and then kicked him in the side. I jumped on his back and reached around to claw his face, and he bucked me off right into the side of the trailer. It sprained my neck and I went around for a week with my head way over on the side like this."

"Is he still there?"

"Our friends left not long after that. We had no reason to go back. Maybe he's still there." They told me how to find it. It was on the west side of town. It was near a street carnival. It was near a school. It had an iron fence around it. It was near the Ford garage. Oh. And called Los Pájaros Trailer Court.

With considerable animation, Della said, "We've got a crazy pad, built like into a corner of a walled garden where there used to be some kind of tourist home that burned. We met such a sweet guy in Mexico City at the art school, and we were running out of money, and he said we could stay there. Outdoor plumbing, and a well with a pump that Mike fixed, and all the tame flowers have gone wild. It's about a mile along the Coyotepec road. You ought to come and see us and . . ."

She froze, and her eyes changed and narrowed. "You are some kind of sneak, man. What the hell am I saying? Who knows you?"

"We know him, honey," Mike said gently. "You have to go along with your own reaction. We can't keep all the walls up all the time. We can't demand credentials."

"Easier for you," she said obliquely. "The man can be so dear, and then his partner takes over and raps you on your kinky haid until your ears bleed, and then the dear man takes his turn with sweet talk."

"Come and see us if you get a chance. On the left on the way to the airport," Mike said. "Look for an old red jeep parked under the trees by the wall."

"I'm sorry," Della Davis said.

"I'll stop by and say hello. Thanks for the invitation. One thing I forgot to ask. The man who owned the car she drove off the road. Bruce Bundy. Know him? Or the woman who identified the body, the French woman, Mrs. Vitrier?"

They did not know them. Mike said, "There are some eerie people living in these little resort spots in Mexico. Here and in Cuernavaca and Taxco and San Miguel. Some are loaded and some are just making it. And the summer is hunting time, both ways. All the kids come flooding down, and there are weirdo types who stalk the kids, and hard kids that stalk the resident crazies. I used to make that scene. Now I don't need it. I can't use it. Depending on what hangups you run into it can go all the way from laughs and kicks to nightmares you couldn't believe."

Their waiter came with the tab. I made a foolish move to pay it, and nearly lost both of them. I relinquished it to Mike, saying, "It was going to be a deductible contribution to the fine arts."

They softened, their pride undamaged.

We said good-by, see you around, see you soon, and I went back to Meyer.

4

Just as I was finishing my factual summary to Meyer, four departed from the group of seven. One of the girls and three of the boys took off and headed slowly along one of the shady walks that angled across the zocalo, in the somnolence of the warm siesta afternoon. Only a half dozen tables on the porch were occupied. The sun was slanting in. The three who were left—the round-faced redhead with the curious nickname, the very skinny boy, and a muscular girl with a tight cap of brown curls and sunglasses with blue lenses—moved back to an empty inside table out of the sun. A yawning waiter went over to them.

A red jeep went by, with Mike driving. Della was talking to him, gesturing with little chopping strokes of a slender black hand. The windshield was down, and the breeze of passage streamed back his silky hair and beard.

Our waiter brought us more Negro Modelo, and when I glanced again at the three of them, I saw that after the departure of their four friends, they were no longer turned inward upon themselves, making their own closed world of talk, but were now aware of what was around them. They had become interested in us. The redhead, staring at us, said something inaudible to the others. The boy laughed and laughed. The big-shouldered girl in the blue glasses did not react. It was idle interest, and we were fair game. Business types. Establishment. She was pretty good at her little jokes. She kept the boy laughing, never taking her eyes off me. The quite obvious intent was to make me uncomfortable, and if they could get a reaction it would improve the game. So I provided the reaction.

I gave Meyer a warning wink, and got up and walked over to

them, properly stuffy and irritated, and said, "Something seems to be very, very funny. How about letting me in on it?"

They were delighted. The victim had walked right up to the gun. The skinny boy took it. He said, "Think maybe big tourist fella like to make bang-bang with nice clean American college girl? This one here name Jeanie. Nice big strong girl. Three hundred pesos maybe? Take her up to your room right now, big fella. She give you a good time. She likes you. Right, Jeanie? You like the big fella, sweetie?"

The girl's head turned very slowly and I could not see her eyes behind the blue lenses as she looked up at me. I pulled the extra chair out and sat down. The skinny boy and the redhead waited in mildly pleasurable anticipation for the shocked reaction. This was called blowing the mind of the random member of the establishment. I let my mouth sag in stupefaction as I appraised them, looking for clues to the best approach. At such close range they were far less attractive than at a distance. The bigger girl looked less muscular, more suety, and smelled slightly rancid. There was grime in the creases of the redhead's neck, and stains on the front of her Indian shirt. The dark boy's hands were filthy. The two pair of eyes I could see were not quite right. They were subtly out of focus, with that slightly glassy and benign look of the mind behind the eyes being skewed a degree or two off center.

There were several ways to go with it. I picked the one I thought might sting the most. I shoved my chair around so that I could call to Meyer and at the same time keep the edge of my eye on the trio.

"Hey, Charley!" I called to Meyer.

"What do you want?" he yelled.

I said to the trio, "My buddy is a little hard of hearing." I raised my voice to a pitch that startled the serape sellers. "Charley, there's nothing here worth fooling around with. The big one with the blue shades he wants twenty-four bucks for. The redhead would maybe go for thirty. But, honest to God, Charley, they're both of them so damn dirty it would turn your stomick. The redhead has spilled food down her shirt, and you should see her neck."

"Knock it off!" the boy said in a pinched little voice.

"Charley, the big one here is named Jeanie, and she doesn't take baths. And all three of them are stoned out of their skulls on something. The kid has got the dirtiest hands I ever seen. Scrawny little bastard. If you ever could get him cleaned up, I don't think even old Crazy Eddie would grope him."

"Get away from us! Get away from us! Get away from us!" It was the redhead, in a dismayed little whine. All the waiters were wide awake. Pedestrians had stopped to admire the volume of sound. Some tourist tables were staring, eyes bulging slightly. Out of the corner of my eye I saw the boy make the move, snatch at the bottle. So I gave him full attention, snapped my hand up and let the bottle slap into the palm. I twisted it away and put it carefully back on the table and gave him a wolf-smile and said, "That's lousy manners, sonny."

I stood up and said, "Charley, maybe a couple of years ago these fatso broads would have been worth a free jump, but now they're so far over the hill . . . Charley! Can you hear me, Charley?"

"Just barely," he roared.

"Even if they were cleaned up and dressed nice, they couldn't even make expenses at a hardware convention in Duluth."

I dropped all the way back to merely a hearty conversational tone and smiled down at them and said, "Thanks anyway, kids. You got any slim clean pretty little friends who need more vacation money, send them on up to the Victoria and tell them to ask for McGee. But don't send any turned-on slobs like you two sorry girls. Fun is fun, but a man likes to keep his self respect. Right? See you around."

I went back to Meyer. He rolled his eyes when I sat down with him. I slid down in the chair, ankles crossed, thumbs hooked in my belt, and smiled amiably at the three.

They tried to brass it out for a little while. But the redhead started snuffling and choking. They gathered up their market bundles and took the route that got them around the nearest corner and out of sight.

Meyer sighed. "In a queasy kind of way, I think I enjoyed it. Did you?"

"The target was the redhead."

"And?"

"She won't be able to leave it alone, Meyer. She'll have to pick at it. She's not as far gone as the other two. She can't endure anybody having that reaction to her. They have to be wrong. So she'll have to tell me how wrong I am. Ruptured pride. And then I can ask about Nesta, Rockland, and company. What if I'd asked them today?"

He nodded. "I keep forgetting how devious you are at times. McGee, it was one of your better performances. You were in good voice. But . . . it was brutal."

"Because it was too close to the truth. Let's go."

The car was ready when we got back to the Ford garage. The shift still whammed me on the knee bone, but everything else was fine. I found a place to park it not far from the Ford place, and we walked over to the street carnival area and then located the Los Pájaros trailer park. There was a spiked iron fence around it, crumbling stone pillars. There were big old trees with dusty leaves shading unkempt flower beds. Paths had worn the grass away, and nobody had picked up the scraps of litter in a long, long time.

The bossman was a jolly fat little type in a ragged blue work shirt and paint-spotted khakis. He had a big gold-toothed grin, and more English than I had Spanish. We went into his little office-store and he looked the information up in his registration notebook. When he pronounced Rockland, it came out "Roaklawn."

"Ah, yes. The Señor Roak-lawn, on place *número* seexteen, from . . . ah . . . twenny-four of Abreel to . . . ah . . . twenny-three in Zhuly? Yes. Tree month. He was having a camper here, was Chevrolet trock of Florida, color . . . how you say? . . . *azul.*"

"Blue."

"Ah, yes. Blue!" Suddenly his smile dwindled. "Ah! Yes, it was *that* one. You his fren?"

"No. I am not his friend, señor."

"Then I say. Many, many people here. Nice American *turista* people. That one, that Roak-o, the only one I must ask to leaving when the month is up. Too much the fights and noise. Too many times he called me bad words. This is not right, that is not right. Nothing is right for him. I have to get *policía* to make sure he is going."

"Where did he go from here?"

"Who knows? Away from Oaxaca, for surely."

"Who was with him when he left?"

"Who knows. Different people live with him here the two month. One two three four. Different girls sometimes. Boys and girls. I have no names, nothing. It is nothing to me. So, he is going now for . . . wan month and six day." The grin was broad as he said, "I am not missing him moch, you bet. One other señor was asking the same things, maybe it is two weeks ago, I think. And he is asking about his daughter."

"Was his name McLeen?"

"Ah, yes. Señor McLeen. But I do not know of the girl nothing. To me, señor, a father is never letting his daughter go off far away in these times. All is changing, no? Some of these young American, they are very nice and good. But there are the ones such like Roak-o, doing bad things."

"Are there any young people here who were friendly with Rockland?"

"Some would know him, I think maybe. Some are here many month. Perhaps the young ones, the señor and señora . . . I cannot say. Here, look, is the name."

Mr. and Mrs. Benjamin Knighton, of Kerrville, Texas.

They were in space number twenty. It was a travel trailer with canvas rigged to make an extra area of living space. But whatever towed the trailer was not there, and the trailer was locked. Happy Fats explained that the young man was an amateur archeologist who was writing a novel about the Zapotecan civilization in pre-Columbian Mexico, and said that the couple went on a lot of field trips in their "Lawn Roover."

"Very young. Very nice. Very hoppy."

So it was then a little past five on that twenty-ninth day of August, and I asked Meyer if it might not be a good time to chat with that expatriate American, Bruce Bundy, who had loaned his car to some unknown named George, who had loaned it to Bix, who had died in it, or near it.

"I used to be young and nice and hoppy," Meyer said wistfully.

"So now you are old, and nice, and hoppy. And you don't listen. Bundy. Bruce Bundy. Now?"

"Why sure."

I studied the map and found Las Artes, a short street about ten blocks north of the zocalo, toward our hotel. I parked at the end of the street and locked up, and we went looking for number eighty-one.

It was a very narrow two-story house squeezed between its bulkier neighbors. Its plaster front was painted in a faded hue of raspberry. Grilled iron doors were locked across the arched entrance, but the inner doors were open. We could see down a long shadowy corridor to the sun-bright flowers of the rear courtyard. I tugged a woven leather thong and a bell hanging in the archway clanged. A man, slender in silhouette, appeared and came swiftly along the corridor, and then slowed as he saw us, and stopped, frowning, in the edge of daylight, one long step inside the doorway.

"Are you looking for someone?" he asked.

"For a Mr. Bruce Bundy."

"I am he," he said, and it surprised me because he looked no more than thirty-four, and the police report had said he was forty-four. "What do you wish to see me about?"

"It's about the fatal accident involving your vehicle on the third of this month."

He shook his head and sighed. "Oh dear Lord, I will *never* come to the end of the bloody red tape. I have answered *endless* questions, and have filled out *endless* reports. What is your part in it?"

"This is my associate, Mr. Meyer. My name is McGee. I'm sorry to bother you, but this is a necessary part of the insurance investigation. Could we come in."

"Now *really!* Are you men trying to be terribly tricky or something? The whole matter has been settled. And I must say that it was terribly unfair. I should have gotten full value for my marvelous little car, but they kept talking about my not putting that fellow, George, on the list of people authorized to drive it. Actually, I shall never loan *anyone* a car, ever again, no matter how nicely they ask."

"Insurance," I said, "on the life of the deceased, Miss Beatrice Bowie of Miami, Florida. There is an accidental death clause in the policy."

"And you came here from *Florida!*"

"A large sum of money is involved, Mr. Bundy."

"And I'm sure it's all terribly important to you and your company and the beneficiary and all that, and I suppose you are here to practically lunge at any hint that the pretty child killed herself so that you can save great wads of money, which I suppose is what you are paid to do, but I am expecting guests, and I was just about to make my famous salad dressing. So why don't you plan to come back tomorrow, Mr. McGoo? But I won't be able to tell you a thing, actually. I did meet those girls, but I knew them so slightly I had the names mixed up. I thought it was the little dark one they called Bix, and I was surprised to find it was the tall, quiet blond one."

"It will only take a couple of minutes."

"Sorry. Tomorrow would be far more convenient. Come at about . . . eleven-thirty in the morning, please."

He turned away and had gone two steps before I tried my hunch. "From talking to Rocko, I thought you'd be more cooperative, Bruce."

He stopped in his tracks and turned very slowly. "To whom?"

"Walter Rockland."

He moved closer to the gate and looked up at me, his head tilted, lips sucked flat. He wore a coarse cotton hand-woven shirt, offwhite, with full sleeves and silver buttons on the tight cuffs. He wore a yellow silk ascot, and snug lime-green slacks, and strap sandals the color of oiled walnut. He had brown-gray bangs, a slender tanned face, eyes of pale amber brown.

"Now where would you have encountered *that* creature?"

"If we could come in for a few moments."

"What did he say about me?"

"I promise we won't take too much of your time."

He unlocked the gate. I followed Meyer in. Bundy locked the gate and told us to go straight ahead to the garden and he would be along in a few moments. He said he wanted to make the dressing and get the woman started on the main course. He told us to help ourselves to a drink.

There was a high wall around the small courtyard, a fountain in one corner. The courtyard was paved in a green stone, and the flowers and shrubs were in huge earthen pots. The furniture was of dark heavy wood upholstered in bright canvas. There were bright birds in bamboo cages.

I poured some of his Bengal gin onto ice. As Meyer fixed himself a whiskey soda he said, "From whence came that inspiration, Mr. McGoo?"

"I'd rather not try to find out. I might not get any more inspirations if I knew."

I dug through the back of my wallet and found one of my Central General Insurance cards and showed it to Meyer so he would at least know who we were working for.

Bundy came into the courtyard carrying a glass of wine. He sat on a low stone bench and looked at me. It was a look familiar to any veteran poker player, when someone is debating whether or not you have the gall to check and raise.

"I think you'd better tell me, Mr. McGoo—"

"McGee."

"Oh. Terribly sorry. McGee, then. Tell me just when and where you saw Charles Rockland."

"*Walter* Rockland."

"Terribly sorry. Charles didn't sound quite right, did it? Rocko suits him better than either, of course."

"We saw him in Mexico City the day before yesterday, Mr. Bundy."

"Really."

"Just routine. After all, he *did* own the Chevy truck and camper that entered Mexico last January tenth, and Miss Bowie was one of the group. Miss Bowie, Miss Minda McLeen, Carl Sessions, and Jerome Nesta. He wrote to a friend in Miami and gave his Mexico City address. So we looked him up, of course."

"Naturally. Part of your investigation. Go on."

It was turning sour. You can take only so many chances. But when it does turn sour, at least you know at what point it started to go bad, and that can be useful. "Go on with what?"

"With what he said to you about me, of course."

"Just that if you seemed uncooperative, to mention his name."

He finished the wine, licked his finger, ran it around and around the edge of the wine glass until he created a thin, high musical note.

He smiled at me. It was a mocking and flirtatious smile. "Bullshit," he said softly.

I smiled back. "At least I gave it a try, Bruce."

"Dear fellow, little games of intrigue, little fabrics of deception, they're too much a part of my scene. I had years of stage design in New York, and years of set design on the Coast. I'll give you one little gold star for your forehead, though. You are a *little* more subtle than you look. Your type, all huge and hearty and outdoorsy, I expect just a kind of clumsy blundering about. Rocko, for example. Dear God, if at this stage of my life I hadn't learned how to protect myself from anything any piece of rough trade could dream up, I'd be terribly vulnerable and innocent, wouldn't I? Don't you think you'd best leave now?"

"Never argue with the umpire. Come on, Meyer."

He walked us out to the gate. As he unlocked it he said, "I suppose that if you are really what you claim to be, and you really want to know whether it was an accident or suicide, I'd think that that little brunette friend of the Bowie girl's would give you the most clues. Actually, her father is clomping all over town trying to locate her. A perfectly dreadful, dreary man from one of those ghastly midwest states that begin with a vowel. Product of Kiwanis and Dale Carnegie, and once he affixes himself to you, you have to pry him off as if he were a fat little pilot fish."

As I thanked him his two guests arrived, spectacularly, in a little

custom Lotus Elan convertible in bubblegum pink with black upholstery. The woman came out from under the wheel, leggy, slender,
tall, nimble, in light-blue linen sheath dress to mid-thigh, sleeveless.
She had a wild and riotous ruff of wind-spilled lion-mane hair, high-
heeled sandals and was twenty something, but then in the light
across her face she was thirty-something, with a twenty-odd body.
The boy was in his early twenties, in white shirt open at the throat,
crisp khakis, and a powder blue jacket that was a precise match with
the lady's dress. He was brick-red from the sun. His hair was cropped
to a copper bristle. He had a sullen face, heavy features, and he
moved with the indolent indifferent grace and ease of one of the
big hunting cats, or one of the many imitations of Brando.

"Brucey!" she cried in joyous greeting.

"Becky darling!" he cried.

Giving us a sidelong questing glance, she ran to embrace the host,
saying in a British accent, "David had the most fascinating day at
the dig. They came upon a whole pocket of tiny beads of bone and
jade, and the poor darling had to spend practically the entire day on
his knees in the bottom of a monstrous hole, brushing the dust away
and picking them up with tweezers. He desperately needs a huge
whiskey, don't you, darling?"

The sunbaked boy grunted, and Bruce tried to move them inside.
We had gone a half dozen steps when Becky gave that upperclass
commanding caw. "You! I say, you two! Wait up a moment! Bruce?
Dearheart, why must one set of guests leave when the next arrives?
Your house is rather small, I grant that. But not *that* small."

I saw the way it might go, and came back as he murmured protes-
tations to her. I said, "It really wasn't a social call, ma'am. In fact we
wouldn't have even got inside the gate if I hadn't tried a little
doubletalk. But it only worked for a little while. Mr. Bundy called
my bluff. So I don't believe he'd be very happy about having us come
back in as guests."

She measured me with vivid emerald wicked-gleam-of-mischief
eyes through the rough spill of the red-blond-gold-russet hair and
made up her impulsive mind and cried, "Nonsense! We are just too
terribly inbred around here. One says the same old things to the
same old faces in the same old places year without end. Bruce, dear,
these gentlemen would make it a more lively evening."

"But Becky, they are *insurance* types, from Florida. And it's all a
very dull bit about the dead girl, the Bowie girl, and they know she

traveled here with that Rockland boy. Apparently there was some sort of policy on the girl's life."

"But Brucey, what if they *are* assurance types? Does that mean we have to sit about talking about premiums? Let us widen our horizons a bit, dear."

He hesitated and then, from the little lift and fall of his shoulders, I could see that he had given up. He said to us, "Lady Rebecca Divin-Harrison is one of our most attractive local institutions, and she has, as you may have detected, a whim of iron. Becky, may I present Mr. McGee and Mr. Meyer. Gentlemen, please come back into my home as my invited guests."

"Bravo!" said Becky. "That was really gracious, Bruce. Like a child taking medicine. Mr. McGee, I am Becky and you are . . ."

"Travis. And Meyer is Meyer."

"And this is David Saunders, who is down here on a grant, grubbing about in the ruins. Bruce, dear, are you going to keep me out here on the street? I'm beginning to feel like Apple Mary."

So we went back in, with Meyer giving me an amused little wink, a little nod of approval. We went out onto the twilight patio, sweet with the evening song of the birds, heavy with the scent of flowers that were just opening for the hours of the night, with fleshy pink petals, and a smell something like jasmine.

Each little group of strangers establishes its own set of balances and unspoken agreements. Tentative relationships are made and broken until the ones are found which are durable enough to last the evening, at least. From long habit, Meyer and I could talk on one level while maintaining an elliptical kind of communication on a level inaccessible to the other three. Bruce and Becky were doing the same thing, wherein innocent expression had subterranean values.

Bruce bustled about, happily hostessing, making drinks, lighting the patio lanterns, summoning a solemn little Mexican woman to present the trays of hors d'oeuvres, with Bruce anxiously awaiting our verdicts on each delicacy.

Becky was all animation, in constant movement, making wry and bawdy judgments, with hoots of harsh laughter. In her evident maturity, she was still totally girl, that special kind of girl who does not have any self-conscious awareness of herself, but can fling herself about, leggy and lithe, laugh with an open throat, comb her casual hair back with splayed fingers, scratch herself, kick off her sandals, stand ugly, lick crumbs from her fingertips. She was teeming and

burning with endless and remarkable energies, with taut slender vi-
brating health. One could not imagine her ever being bored. Her
drink was a pale Spanish sherry, in an old-fashioned glass with a single cube of ice, and she seemed able to make one last indefinitely.

David Saunders was a familiar type, muscular, burly yet feline. He
moved with languid grace. He sat immobile, thighs bulging the khaki
slacks, apparently in total disinterest and indifference to anyone and
anything about him. It was that special arrogance which relieves the
possessor of any responsibility to communicate with anyone or please
anyone. He could have been in a bus station, waiting for an overdue
bus. But he did not become inconspicuous or invisible. There was a
surly presence, an assurance, that made people try to please him, to
bring him into the conversation. His drink, to Bundy's apparent dismay, was bourbon and Coke, and he knocked them back with stolid,
metronomic efficiency.

I decided that I could risk, for the sake of possible returns, casting
a large doubt on our insurance story, and Bruce's statement of having done stage design in New York and set design in California gave
me the opening. So at a handy opening, using that-reminds-me, I
brought up a Famous Female Name in the Industry.

"*That* wretched bitch!" Bruce said. "The most self-important little
slut in the world, believe me. I did one totally commercial job for
her. One of those period piece things, where they wrapped her little
ass in crinoline, and had her bang her way through half the Confederate Army. I went a little camp with the decor, not to cut the picture, but to make a little gentle fun that only the cognoscenti would
catch. So she raised stinking hell about my color patterns being
wrong for her. She wants to act, direct, produce, write the script, and
design the sets, and she doesn't know thing one about her own
trade. The only acting she does that seems authentic is when they
have her horizontal. She is one of the reasons, dears, why I tucked
away all their abundant bread into very good little securities, and
when I had enough to live nicely on for the rest of my years, I told
them all what they could kiss." He paused and looked at me with a
suspicious glint. "But don't tell me *she* was buying her insurance in
Florida."

"It was something else, Bruce. She partied on a sun deck with a
mixed bare-ass group, and somebody with a good telephoto lens tried
to get rich quick."

He nodded. "I remember a rumor that she was in that kind of trouble, but nothing happened."

"I got lucky."

"But why would you get involved in something like that, Travis?"

"Because she came around and asked me."

"Why would she come to you?"

"Because I solved another kind of problem for someone she knew."

"Then you aren't really in the insurance business?"

I smiled upon him. "Hell, I don't know. I guess that lady would be willing to say it was a kind of insurance."

"But what are you trying to do here? Who are you . . . trying to insure, Mr. McGee?"

"I think that if I had gone around telling people what I was trying to do for the actress, it wouldn't have worked out as well as it did."

Meyer broke in and said, "We just go around helping people, Bruce. I think it's some kind of guilt syndrome. Trouble with those windmills, you stick a lance into one in a good wind, and it will purely toss the hell out of you."

Bundy, after a few moments of narrow-eyed consideration, dropped it. And soon he began moving in on David Saunders' blind side. But first there was a little exchange between Bruce and Becky that went over David's sullen head.

Bruce said, "Becky, darling, Larry told me last week that you practically *gave* him that marvelous ceremonial mask from Juchatengo."

I saw her eyes go blank and her mouth purse, and though she recovered in a sparkling instant, I felt reasonably convinced that there was no mask, perhaps not even anyone named Larry.

"He seemed to want it."

"It upset him a little. I mean he knew how terribly acquisitive you had felt about it when you first got it, and he didn't want to take advantage of your friendship."

"How silly!" she said. "I was cleaning out my little gallery and I remembered that he seemed to admire it, so I took it over and asked him if he'd like it. My word, had I wanted to keep it, would I have taken it to him?"

"I guess he wanted to be certain it was not just an impulse you'd regret later."

"When you see him, tell him not to worry his little head. Actually, you know, I was very fair with him. I told him when I took it over there that it was really not as first class as I had thought at first. It's very primitive, of course, and quite authentic, but it's just one of those things you tire of seeing every day, I suppose because it hasn't much subtlety."

"It's probably more Larry's sort of thing than yours."

"Very probably. I sensed that, I suppose."

Transfer accomplished, in good faith. And so Bundy engaged Meyer in amateur archeological talk, saying, finally, "I just cannot *imagine* how those priest types could bring the Indian peasants into this terribly inhospitable and certainly waterless countryside and establish a whole culture without losing untold thousands of them."

And that hooked Saunders into his first conversation of the evening. "From what we know now, the system was to send out a large party of specialists, carrying water supplies, just before the rainy season. If they couldn't find reliable wells or springs, they would dig giant cisterns deep in the earth, wide at the bottom and narrow at the top, like gigantic bottles made of stone and waterproofed with clay. Then around the top of the bottle, they'd make a hard surface, round, fifty or sixty feet across, and sloping toward the mouth of the bottle. The rains would fill the bottle and they'd put a big clay stopper in place to prevent evaporation. Next they would bring in the Indian families with grain and fowl and tools and tell them where to build the village and where to plant the grain."

Bruce cried that the information fascinated him. How clever those ancient peoples were! And how clever the ones who were now so carefully reconstructing all that lost marvelous history!

And he kept him going a little while until it was time for dinner. I said we had to leave just to see how much he would protest. And he did, with an earnest vehemence, because it was obvious that if there were just the three of them, he couldn't focus on David.

So we, with show of reluctance, accepted the warm invitation.

5

THE FOOD was excellent. Candles flared and flickered in the night breeze. He served a good and heady Greek wine.

A round table. Superb silverware, table linen, glassware, pottery. Muted music from a good tape system somewhere in the house. Bundy had Lady Rebecca at his right, David at his left, with me at Becky's right, and Meyer between me and David.

Rebecca had begun to make an elegant presentation of herself to me, managing in her casual careless way of handling herself, to artfully establish all the sensory awarenesses—of vision, of scent, of apparently inadvertent touch. But more importantly, she knew well that most important ingredient of all charm, all seduction, the art of so listening and responding that she made me feel as if I were the most exciting and rewarding and important man she had met in untold years, that if I had not come along, her life would have continued in its drab and dreary pattern. It requires not only the ability to listen so carefully no word, no nuance, is missed, but also the ability to sense when a contrary opinion will further the growing sense of closeness. I knew what she was doing and knew some of the devices she was using, but that awareness did not prevent my growing feeling that this was, indeed, one hell of a lot of extraordinary woman and nice to be with and worth arranging any further closeness possible.

Bruce Bundy, in another way and on another level, was targeting in on David Saunders. And it was interesting to see how much more masculine Bruce had become, in voice, gesture and opinion. And both Bruce and Becky were using Meyer as that necessary little dilution factor to mask their acquisitive intensity, directing questions and comment to him in much the same way the stage magician makes a great show of letting you look up his sleeves and into his top hat.

Their eyes gleamed in the candlelight, and their faces were smooth and youthful and animated, and their voices were clever, articulate, and amusing. The pretty predators, using their tested skills for the newest stalk.

David Saunders seemed to make, at table, a slightly porcine prey. He would dip his head almost to the plate, shovel in a heaping forkful, chew heavily with rolling bulge of muscle at the jaw corners, and then slosh it down with a gulp of wine, the throat bulging and shifting with the bulky swallow.

So, half in self-defense, half in the interest of moving ahead with the mission, I found a hole in the conversation and ran it off at a new angle. "I'd like to meet and talk to Eva Vitrier. Can you arrange it, Bruce? Becky?"

An instant of wary stillness, such as might happen to the smaller scavengers when they hear the carnivore coming back through the jungle toward the kill.

"Oh, it would have to be Bruce. He seems to get along quite smashingly with the creature. And by the way, dear, her first name rhymes with favor rather than with fever. Shockingly rich, that one. And she doesn't, as we say, mingle."

Bundy said, "I really don't see very much of her. She comes and goes without much warning—I should say with *no* warning. She's not a very social animal. Even were she here, Travis, it would be quite a feat to arrange an introduction. But I understand she left right after identifying that ghastly body. I could hardly blame her for wanting a change of scene."

"Where would she have gone?"

"She's never given me any other address," he said.

"But," said Becky, "it's rumored she has several of her little fortresses scattered about the world. The woman has this secrecy thing. Absolutely barmy."

"But she had those two girls at her place as house guests," I said. "Seems like a sort of friendly sociable act."

"On the same order, one might say," said Becky, "as that touching friendliness and sociability in a dinner invitation from the Borgias."

"Wear the big ring," said Meyer, in nostalgic tribute to Lenny Bruce. It drew blank looks.

I took a sneak shot at Bundy. "Didn't you say you had to protect yourself from something Rocko dreamed up?"

He pressed his gray-brown bangs with the palm of his hand. A ring fashioned of gold mesh gleamed in the candlelight.

"Why do you strain so hard to be clever, McGee?" he asked.

"Answer a question with a question," I said, "and you buy time to sort things out."

"I used the name Rocko in a generic rather than a particular sense. The Rockos of the world are always scheming, aren't they? Just as you were when you first arrived. I merely said that I feel competent to protect myself against the schemes of . . . the Rockos and the McGees."

"But you met the girl, didn't you? Bix Bowie?"

"Should I have?"

"Through Rocko or through Eva Vitrier, one or the other. Why not?"

He smiled. "I went through deep analysis *ages* ago, my dear man, with a very fashionable New York shrink. He had this quaint trick of trying to stir up guilt by asking questions in *exactly* that manner. One *does* lie to one's psychiatrist, you know. The truth is so utterly rancid sometimes. One wants to look better. But with all that endless talking, it is terribly difficult to remember what one might have said a dozen afternoons ago. No, I did not meet the lass. Nor do I see any reason why I should be expected to have met her, or have any memory of her if I did. What are you *really* looking for?"

"All the reasons why the girl drove off the mountain in your car, Bruce."

"I shall never never forgive the little bitch. That was a marvelous little car. Very loyal and dependable."

David Saunders yawned, belched, reached for the wine bottle.

"See?" Becky cried. "We're *boring* poor David. A lovely meal, Bruce. Do you have any of that marvelous brandy? The kind I like? I can't remember the name. Good! Just a tiny bit, no more than a tablespoon. And can we leave table? Thank you, darling."

As we got up, Meyer said, "Mr. Bundy, I appreciate your hospitality and your kindness, but I think that I am beginning to feel unwell. The altitude and the wine, I think. The best thing for me would be a walk in the fresh air. I can walk down to the plaza and take a cab back up the hill to the hotel. No, Travis. Don't bother. I'll be fine."

Gracefully and shrewdly done, old friend. After he left the brandy was served, and I noticed that Bruce gave David Saunders the opportunity to pour his own, and a snifter that gave him enough scope to be foolhardy. They went off into the house. Bruce wanted to show David some of the artifacts he had collected.

Becky and I went into a far corner of the patio, sat together on a stone bench near a small, persistent fountain.

"You were very naughty, Travis, really."

"What did I do?"

"Ah! Such innocence. It was a lovely little party and then you made poor Bruce so awfully uncomfortable and nervous. He was terribly upset by the whole Rockland affair. Actually, it's the last thing he wants to have mentioned."

"And you know all about it?"

"He talks over his problems with me. He asks my advice. He's not a bad sort, you know. Sometimes he is quite foolish and impulsive and he encounters . . . problems that are typical of the world he lives in. I think that because I never condemn him, we've been able to become friends."

"Such good friends you brought him a little gift."

"A gift?"

"One husky, sunburned young archeologist."

"Of course, ducks! We are frightfully nasty degenerates who go about handing our discards to our chums. And I imagine that quite puts you off, doesn't it?"

"I don't know enough about it. Or about you."

"Me? I am just a wicked old woman with a ravenous appetite for strong young men. They are generally sweet and touching and grateful. But this chap was . . . out of focus somehow. He fancies himself as some sort of overwhelming stud. But he has that talent for little bits of brutality that betrays him for what he really is. I had begun to suspect him, and then he told me a horrid little story about beating up homosexuals and taking their money when he was at school. Such chaps are usually hiding their own tendencies from themselves. I had decided to cut him loose because he is really dull. He has no sense of fun. But I had described him to Bruce, and Bruce said that were I to bring him around, he could quickly tell me if my suspicion was correct. After ten minutes Bruce knew and let me know. So . . . it might be rather nice for Bruce after such a fiasco with that Rockland person. Bruce is quite lonely this year. The chap who used to stay with him drowned last year in the surf at Acapulco when they were down visiting friends. It was a terrible shock to Bruce. Do I sound as if I were pleading for forgiveness and understanding? Hardly! After all, I did not exactly bash him upon the head and gift wrap him and put him on the doorstep, did I?"

"What did happen with Rockland?"

"My dear, you are very, very nice. But, my word, you are tiresome at times! Here we are, quite alone, both of us with that marvelous knowledge that we would be awfully, awfully good in bed together, and all you seem to want from me is a long tiresome story—far too long to tell here. I *know* you respond to me. We're becoming quite deliciously aware of each other. Shouldn't you be trying to bundle me off into my lonely bed instead of leaving the advances to me? I am quite sick of the young, young men. They are in endless supply, and unlike poor David, they are terribly sweet and earnest and dear. But too sweet. Like endless desserts. They cloy. But one accepts, because the mature ones with any style and presence are usually married. And I have a rule about that. It is too much like theft."

"But what about my wife and five kids?"

"You lie, sir! A woman leaves her mark, her scent, her shape upon what is hers, whether it is her furs, her underthings, or her man. You are not married, and I doubt you ever have been. Though I was once, several centuries ago."

"Here I come again, tiresome as ever. How do I find out about Rockland?"

"Why, I should imagine that you would have to sit down with Bruce and have him tell you, dearie."

"Correction. How do I find out about Rockland from you?"

"Let me see now. You are asking me to betray a confidence. That means that I would have to have some good reason for breaking faith. I should have to know exactly why you wish to know all this, and understand your motives. And, of course, I would have to believe you. That is the tricky part, because you lie so much. And you lie so *well!* No woman ever knows a man, or ever really trusts him until they have made love. Then, of course, she often discovers she has trusted some absolute scoundrel. But then it would be too late, would it not?"

"Let me see. You picked me off the sidewalk in front of this place. You have not had enough booze to cloud the mind of a mouse. You are damned attractive, Becky. And I am sitting here on a fag's patio in lovely Oaxaca letting you put a ring in my nose so you can lead me off to the sack. Such things don't happen."

"Such a horrid, suspicious, nasty little mind. You are a towering chap, showing signs of rough use, and I find you monstrously attractive. Your pale eyes and your big hands and the way your lips are made and the way your voice sounds, all these things have just made me terribly randy. So I choose not to blush and simper and flirt, because men are horribly anxious to protect their pride and quite often never make the attempt for fear of failure. And life is awfully short, and each day it is shorter by one day. And there is something else about me which I might or might not tell you later. It depends."

"All right. Such things happen."

"But in case you feel overwhelmed or anything, we don't have to make it definite, not at this moment. I can provide a nightcap and we can cast ballots or something. But let's find those two dear boys and say goodnight."

When we were halfway across the patio, David and Bruce appeared in the corridor, walking toward us. Bruce had hold of David's arm. David Saunders was staggering, mumbling, making sweeping gestures, tripping on the irregularities of the tiles.

"Whas'm never'n standa menshunenny."

He peered at us, feet planted wide, and wrenched his arm out of Bruce's grasp. He started to say something incomprehensible and made another big gesture which swung him off balance. He melted down onto the tile and sagged over onto his back and began to snore.

"I think he drank a little too much," Bruce said.

"Would it be too much of an imposition for you to put him up for the night, dear?"

"Gracious, no!"

"Want me to help you with him?" I asked.

"Thanks, I can manage. Becky, the gate is on the latch. When you shut it, give it a try to be sure it's locked, will you?"

"Of course," she said. We thanked him for the dinner. He acknowledged it in absentminded fashion. He sat on his heels, worked one arm under David's shoulders, another under his thighs, poised for a moment, and then came up smartly with the slack meaty burden. The head lolled and an arm swung limply. In sleep the sullenness was gone. David was a large dreaming child. His burned features looked more delicate. Bruce's feat had been impressive and I suspected it had been done for my benefit. He could indeed feel quite able to take care of himself.

We went in her Lotus. She said my rented car would be quite safe where it was parked. She drove through the dark streets alertly and competently, sitting tall, chin up, hands solid on the wheel, through the rush of wind, past dark buildings.

She said her place was in La Colonia. Wider streets. High walls. Gates. She swung in and stopped, the headlights shining on an iron gate. She gave me the keys, indicating the one for the gate. I unlocked it and swung it open. She drove in and waited while I closed and locked the gate. Then along a curving drive paved with white gravel. Night lights on in the house. Left the car in front. Went through large formal rooms and out into a walled area in back. She turned on lights, little spots and floods and the lights below the water level of a large curved pool.

"I know," she said. "It left rather a bad taste. But Brucey will not be sordid about it. He'll undress poor David and tuck him into a big bed and leave him quite alone. In the morning he'll be tearful and terribly upset and accuse poor David of all manner of amorous aggression, and claim he is going to register a bitter complaint with me. Poor David will be beside himself with shock and fright and shame. And sometime tomorrow they will kiss and forgive, and I expect that after the weekend David will be moving in, and in a few months he will have rather a pretty little lisp. He might become a much nicer person, actually. Just stop looking so broody and accusing about it, darling. Open that cupboard door and you'll find ice and all kinds of liquor. Cheer up, dammit!"

So I made my drink. She refused one. She sat beside me for some silent moments, then got up from the chaise and walked to the far end of the pool. Without posing, posturing, or artifice, she kicked her shoes off, pulled the mini-dress off, floated a wisp of brassiere onto the pile, stepped out of sheer pants, hooked her bare toes over the curbing. Her figure was riper than I would have guessed, but solid, smooth and firm as that of a circus girl, tumbler, or ballerina.

"Goes with the nightcap or not," she called to me. "Whatever you choose, my good man."

And in she went, in a flat sleek slapping racing dive.

Well, you came down here, fella, to find out about Bix Bowie. And, by God, no sacrifice is too great once a fella gives his solemn word, right? And the way you get to know a country is by getting to know the people, right? And even though there's a pretty good size to that pool, what with the pool lights and all, you ought to be able to catch her sooner or later. So I think the answer ought to be that if it really goes with the nightcap, then . . .

But I discovered I was already trying to pull the trousers off with the shoes still on, so I sat down again and untied the shoes, thus solving that problem with hardly any trouble at all.

She clung, sweat-misted, still breathing deeply, and ground the scratchy ruff of her tawn-crisp hair into the side of my laboring throat; she gave her small crow-caw of delighted laughter.

"You *do* have to say something, you know," said Lady Becky. "Some observation. Some passing comment. I rather like to remember the better ones."

"Okay. Passing comment: Quote. Holy Mackerel. Close quote."

She rolled up onto an elbow. "I think you are very nice, McGee. I think I will tell you what you just enjoyed."

"I wouldn't want to try to describe it myself."

"I have to confess how ancient I am, darling. I am terribly old. I was married before the Battle of Britain. I was in London for the whole bit. Dreadfully earnest and devoted and valiant. Family tradition. All heroes. Volunteer nursing service. Stiff upper lip. So my beloved husband was in Spits, and they pranged him early on. And the others went, bit by bit. The chums and brothers, the family and the sister. Stiff upper lip, lass. Strive on. So it ended, you know. And peace came, and two days later some damned delayed action thing went off, and it was my last duty call. Collapsed a row of flats and they burned. And I held two screaming tots, one after the other, on my lap, charred little things, trying to pop morphine into them before they died. Managed with one and didn't with the other. Dreadful stench. Total pointlessness. Walked all night, said odd things. They put me off to rest. I was expected to pick up the loose ends of my life and start over, somehow. Do good works. But there were no loose ends, lamb. And I had a bellyful of good works.

"So one makes an accounting of sorts. I had, God knows, money enough, and time, and a strong body. And I was in a world that charred tots, and I wanted no more of it. What I had most adored with Robin was all the lovely free marital fornication. Never could get enough. He used to say I had great natural talent. So I vowed solemnly, ducks, to become the jolly best piece of Anglo-Saxon ass in all Christendom. It is sad and remarkable that people really know so little about it. They sort of fumble about and trust to luck. I knew that all I had to work with was my body. I had to keep it as enticing as possible, because one must arouse intense desire, or the game is lost before it is begun, what? I haven't changed an inch or a pound in twenty years, my dear. I stay on the most strict routine of diet and exercise. And I go twice a year to a Swiss clinic for hormone balance, and there is a clever little Japanese doctor in your California who does clever little operations when they're needed. To know how to use the body, one must go to Yoga. God, how I labored, and then suddenly it fell into place. I have absolute and independent control now of every muscle in my body, even all those reactions that are supposed to be involuntary responses to erotic stimulus. And all this time, my dear, I was studying all the books on the arts of love that I could find. Hindu, Arabic, Ancient Egyptian. I am now a repository of all that learning and skill. And I know some astonishing things, luv. It is a responsibility, actually. I had to learn a great deal about anatomy, neurology, glandular functions, all that. So you see what's in store, my good man? You've had a taste. And now I shall destroy you, bit by delicious bit. Because you shall respond again and again after you are quite certain you are finished. I need merely do some odd thing like . . . this?"

And as I was tumbled back into my role of awed participant in the second strenuous, virtuoso performance, I realized I had come upon a prime example of that uniquely English phenomenon, the true eccentric. Some of them build cathedrals out of bits of matchstick. Some of them count the number of stalks of hay in the average haystack. Some write a hundred letters a week to the London *Times*. Some catalogue all the birds in fifty meadows. They are all quite mad, but do not know that they are mad, since they find a socially acceptable outlet for their monomania. This woman had been driven mad in a mad war, and had retained one little ledge of sanity and built the rest of the structure of her life upon it. But I could not carry my realizations any further, because something hitherto unknown had begun to happen, and it felt as if my head were starting to fry at the hair roots. I thought I heard her laughing, but then all I could hear in some far corner of the most primitive part of my mind, was myself roaring, atavistic and lonely.

There was another time of respite when, halfheartedly, I asked about Bruce Bundy and Rockland. She told me that they had met on the veranda of the Marqués del Valle many weeks ago, and that Bruce knew Rockland had let himself be picked up. Bruce had told her that Rockland was not exactly inexperienced. He had then begun to ask Bruce to lend him money. Some large amount. Ten or fifteen thousand. It was to be some sort of investment scheme. Rockland had hinted that it was illegal but quite safe. He would double Bruce's money. He then got very surly when Bruce said he would not cash in perfectly good securities in order to lend money to an animal off the streets. Then apparently Rocko had to leave the trailer park. Bruce let him bring the truck and camper and put it in the shed beyond his wall where Bruce garaged his little English Ford. There was room for both. He had moved into Bruce's house on an apparently permanent basis. But he had spent Thursday, the last day of July, away from the house all day and a good part of the evening. When he came back he had asked Bruce to lend him a smaller amount. Three thousand or even two. When Bruce refused, Rockland had accepted it too calmly. In the small hours of Friday morning, Bruce had heard the distant sound of Rocko trying to start his truck. Bruce put his robe on and hurried out. She said Bruce had taken something out of the motor and hidden it. Rocko got out of the truck and tried to hit Bruce. But Bruce had won some sort of belt for some sort of way of fighting, and he kept in splendid shape, and so he had hit Rocko and knocked him unconscious, but when he fell he had hit his nose on the stone floor and bled, and it had made Bruce ill. When Rocko could walk, feeling very weak and shaky, Bruce had helped him into the house and into bed, and then he had gone back and searched the truck and found his little Picasso bronzes, and the solid gold amulets from Yucatan, and the prints and drawings by famous Mexican artists, and some of his better silverware.

Out of an increasingly hazy state, I interrupted her at this point in her narrative to ask her what she was doing.

"Dearest, don't tighten up like that. Trust your Becky. There. Turn just a little bit more this way. That's a dear. This will rest and relax you. It's something Japanese women used to know, thousands of years ago. Just don't think about me. Don't think about anything. Just let your mind drift."

So, though curious, it was restful, relaxing, soothing. It was indeed. For quite a while. And then it began to have quite another effect. And when that effect was sufficiently and unmistakably evident, Lady Rebecca Divin-Harrison swung triumphantly and exuberantly aboard, with spurs, whip, check-rein, and posted tirelessly and happily across the endless moors.

I lay dead, yet managed to say, "Then what happened?"

"Weren't you paying attention?"

"I mean to Bruce and Rockland."

"No, dear, I've told you much too much. No more for now. I shouldn't have told you a bloody thing, you know."

"Then I think I am going to sleep."

"Really? Really? . . . Really?"

"Cut it out, Becky. Whatever ancient rite that happens to be, cut it out. Because it is not going to do any good. Look. I am not ashamed to admit I'm finished. All done. I haven't got any desire at all to set any records. And I don't feel any childish urge to prove anything to anybody. Okay? I *have* to go to sleep, Becky."

"Yes, darling. I agree. Utterly. I've quite finished you off, poor darling."

"Then stop."

"Don't writhe away from me like that. It is awfully impolite. Travis, darling, let me just prove to both of us that we are both absolutely correct, that there is nothing more you can possibly contribute to the evening."

"It's been proven."

So she hummed to herself. She kept busy. Adjust spark and coil. Hop out and run around to the radiator and try the hand crank. Thumb out of the way in case of backfire. Back to spark, coil, mixture. Prime carburetor. Crank again. What the hell is she humming? For God's sake, *Roll Out the Barrel*. Should be humming *Bless 'em All*. Ancient engine catches, sputters, stops, catches again. And then, by God, settles into a deep-gutted roar. Hop behind the wheel, kick it into gear. And I once again enwrapped all that hot limber skill, endured her delighted chuckling, romped her onto her spring-steel spine, and tried in my endless, mindless, idiot frenzy to hammer her down through the damn silk sheets, down through the foam and springs, down through the carpeting and the tile and the beams and down into the deep black Mexican soil under the lovely and formal old house, where I could be buried without fanfare and sleep forever and ever and ever.

6

MEYER WAS gone when I woke up at ten o'clock Saturday morning. When I came out of the shower he was sitting on his bed with a bright red flower tucked behind his ear, beaming at me.

"I heard you come in," he said. "Just after daylight. I think I should say I heard you come *tottering* in. I never heard so much heavy sighing. You sounded like a leaky truck tire."

I pulled my shorts up and turned and said, "I never noticed what really nasty little blue eyes you have, pal."

"What happened after I left?"

"Poor David passed out and was promoted to the status of house-guest."

"Make a note that I am not astonished."

"And I went to Lady Rebecca's house with her for a nightcap."

"Again, no surprise. And then?"

I sat on my bed to rest up a little. "I gathered a few bits of information about Rockland which I shall shortly impart to you, Meyer. I do not make a practice of discussing a lady. I just wish to tell you that the few bits of information were *earned*."

Bland astonishment. "Really, old chap? Why, to look at the lady, I should have thought her a jolly amusing romp, what? All slap and tickle. Good earthy sport, what?"

"If I had the strength, I swear, I would reach over and hit you right in the mouth, dear friend."

He faked sudden comprehension. "Aha! Oh! Like that, eh? It wasn't because it was distasteful, eh? You mean that she was tasteful and somewhat on the demanding side, old man?"

"Meyer, believe me, I will never try to explain it to you or describe it to you. I do not want to think about it. Here is what you do for me. Some day, two or three years from now, hire the most luscious, unprincipled, hot-blooded wench you can find. Have her strip down and sneak aboard the *Flush* and climb into the master's bunk with the sleeping master. Then you wait outside. If you hear an ungodly thump, it will be her girlish rump bouncing off the deck after I kick her out of bed. When you hear that thump, take the girl away, wait a year, and try again."

"Is this the McGee talking?"

"McGee, the misogynist. From now on, buddy, every broad in the world is going to look as enticing as a rubber duck. I would rather have one handful of cold mashed potato than two handsful of warm young mammalian overdevelopment."

"Did you get too much sun yesterday?"

"Just help me through the day, Meyer. Help me and shut up. Catch me when I start to wobble. Keep me out of drafts. Order me good nourishing food and get me to bed early. Now get me up that hill to the dining room."

At breakfast I told him about the Rocko-Brucey affair, as much as I knew of it. We agreed it fit with Bruce Bundy's asking us in when I used Rockland's name on him. He had to know if Rockland had devised some way to make him unhappy and had sent us around to set him up.

Meyer worried at it, hairy dog with an old meatless bone. "Then we go another step. Bundy had to believe Rocko *could* make trouble."

"It begins to look," I said, "as if Rockland knew just how to make trouble for people. I think the hotel covered up the ugly truth with those hints about theft. I think he was scavenging the older lonely ones. Hustling them. Setting them up with pot, hustling them with sex, male and female, and then putting the squeeze on."

"So a type like that comes to Mexico in a truck and camper? Roughing it?"

"Bix drew out part of the money before they left. She drew out the balance from Mexico. Twenty isn't a bad score."

"If he knew she had it," Meyer said.

"And he could lever it out of her easier out of the country. But we have to find one of the others to find out what went on, dammit. Either Rockland himself or the musician or the sculptor or the other girl."

At this stage of the game it seemed to be a good idea to split up. Meyer acquires people as easily as a hairy dog picks up burrs. He smiles and listens carefully, and the little blue eyes gleam with good humor and personal interest. He says the right things at the right time, and surprisingly often the random stranger tells him things he wouldn't tell a blood relative or a psychiatrist. No bore, no matter how classic, ever manages to bore Meyer. It is a great talent, to be forever interested in everyone.

We agreed that the best thing to do would be for me to drop Meyer downtown and then go off and see what I could learn at Eva Vitrier's place. I got lost twice in the Colonia district before I located Avenida de las Mariposas. A man driving a delivery truck helped me locate the home of Eva Vitrier.

It was an estate, enclosed by a high stone wall. The morning sun shone through the shards of glass of the ten thousand broken bottles cemented into the top of the wall. I found a vehicle gate, double-chained and locked. I rattled the gate and hollered, to no effect. I could look through the bars at a curve of driveway paved with brick, disappearing into the trees and plantings, but I could see no part of any building inside the compound. I located the main pedestrian entrance, a solid and massive door of ancient wood, iron-studded. There was a bell button set into the recessed stone beside the door. No one answered.

Around the corner, on a narrower street, I found a smaller wooden door and, beyond it, a double door which could open wide enough for a good-sized truck. I pushed another bell button by the smaller door and heard a distant ringing. As I was trying it for the third and last time, a hinged square set into the door swung open and a broad, bronze, impassive Indio face looked out at me.

I asked for the señora. He said she was not there. I asked when she would be back. He said he could not know. Tomorrow? Oh, no. Maybe many weeks, many months, maybe a year. Where is she, then? One does not know. Who *does* know? One must ask el Señor Gaona. Who is he? He is the lawyer of the señora. Where is he? In his office, doubtless. Where is his office? It is in the city. In this city? Where else? On what street is his office? It is on Avenida Independencia. What number? One cannot say. It is near the corner of Avenida Cinco de Mayo.

As I started to thank him, he slammed the little opening. It startled me. A rude Mexican is a great rarity.

I had to wait fifteen minutes before Señor Alfredo Gaona y Navares could see me. I waited on a rump-polished wooden bench in a musty ten-by-ten office dominated by a large old lady at a large old typing desk, operating a machine that looked as if Mark Twain had invented it. At last two women in black came out of the inner office, arms around each other, sobbing softly. I was directed to go in.

Señor Gaona was elderly. He had a small pale face and an expression of weary distaste. He did not get up or extend a hand. Complex aluminum crutches leaned against the wall behind him.

"What is your reason for wishing to see Señora Vitrier?" The English was precise, unaccented, with a delivery that sounded like a programmed computer.

"I wanted to talk to her about the two American girls who were staying with her as her guests."

"With what purpose?"

"Señor Gaona, I am doing a personal favor for the Bowie girl's father. He was injured in an automobile accident, or he would be here himself. He was out of touch with his daughter for seven months. He is curious about how she lived here, where she lived, what kind of life it was for her."

"Señora Vitrier would not care to discuss it."

"What makes you so sure?"

He hesitated. "I do not have to explain, but I will. Out of her generous heart she offered the two young women lodging when they had no place they could go. This was not a wise thing to do. One cannot judge by appearances. The young women might have been of a kind one does not want in the home. After they quarreled and one departed, the other one was killed, as you must know, in an accident in the mountains. Señora Vitrier appeared and performed the duty of identifying the dead young woman, and turned over her possessions to the police. It was a very ugly experience for her. I am quite certain she would not care to be reminded of it, or to discuss it."

"Couldn't you let her decide that? Where can I get in touch with her?"

"She is a very, very wealthy woman. The house she maintains here is one of several in various parts of the world. I am retained by her to keep her from being approached by strangers, and also to keep her house here in good order so that she can return, unannounced, and begin living here at any time."

"What would happen if I were to write her a letter?"

"It would come here to this office and I would open it and read it and decide if it is a matter which she would wish to know about. If I so decided, I would mail it to her bank in Zurich and they would forward it to whatever address she is using at the time."

"What would you do if her house here burned down?"

"So advise Zurich."

"And my letter would not get past you?"

"Assuredly not, sir. She gave explicit instructions to me that she did not want to hear any more of this affair, not even if the surviving young lady attempted to reach her by letter."

"And has she tried?"

"No."

"Has anyone else tried, I mean in relation to the death of the girl?"

"I have explained the situation to you, sir, in more detail than is my habit. There is no way you can approach Señora Vitrier, no way whatsoever. So we must consider the matter closed. Good day."

And indeed it was good day. The old lady had entered behind me, unheard, and she startled me when she said, "Theees way ow." I was on the sidewalk nine seconds later. And ten minutes after that I was in a briskly modern office where mini-skirted darlings came beaming in and out, emptying the "out" baskets and putting documents in the "in" baskets, and I was shaking hands with Ron Townsend's friend in the local power structure, Enelio Fuentes. A glass panel in a wall overlooked, from about a thirty-foot height, about two acres of concrete shop space where bug-swarms of Volkswagens were being tuned, inspected, and repaired.

Enelio was thirty, or a little over, ruggedly handsome, with a yard of shoulders, a contrived casual lock of black hair across the forehead, a narrow waist, a big friendly grin, a massive and powerful handshake.

"Ol' Ron phoned me about you. Hey, sit down. How you like our town? How about that bird Ron has got himself? You meet her? That big Miranda. Fonny goddam thing. Ron spend half his life running like hell every time any bird looks at him with that marriage look. This big Miranda, she doesn't want not any part of it, and he wants it so bad he can't breathe deep. That one is some batch of girl, I tell you. Hey, you want a bloody mary? Good. Hey you, Esperanza, go make bloody marys for Mister Travis McGee, here, and me, and stop making the hot eye at him and waving that little butt around. Mr. McGee isn't interested in short, ugly little girls." She was a lovely little thing, and she went running out, giggling. "Soch a one that is," he said fondly. "Can't type, can't file, can't run the switchboard. But she can make any drink you ever heard of, man. My old man says, 'Nelio, why the hell did I waste my money sending you to the Graduate School of Business at Stanford University, all you do is hire pretty girls all the hell over the place?' Me, I don't say a word, just give him the quarterly breakdown, show the profit we're turning, ask him if he'd rather give it back to his brother, my oncle, hired women looked like dogmeat, worked their ass off on overtime, and sometimes didn't even break even. Now my oncle is crapping around with the little feeder airline we bought las' year, Aeronaves Fuentes, and from the way the books look, I got to pretty soon go shake things up over there. Hey, here she is. Try that, Travis McGee. Delicious? Don' stand around bugging the boss fellas, girl. Go file something in the wrong place so nobody ever finds it again." He looked out through the glass wall and suddenly stiffened, the smile gone. He pressed the bar on a call box and bent toward it, and the Spanish was much too fast for me to follow. I looked out at the shop area and suddenly saw a man in a white jacket heading at a half run toward a couple standing helplessly beside an old black Volkswagen.

Enelio grinned and stretched. "Chrissake, tell them five million times anybody comes in, you find out what the hell they want right away. Quick. Then you tell them how long it takes and how much it costs. And you do it in the time you say, and you charge what you say, and get them out on the street fast." I saw something I had overlooked. The big grin did not change the eyes. They remained cool and shrewd and appraising.

A tall solemn girl came in with letters for signature. He nodded and motioned her closer. He read the letters swiftly, scrawled his big signature on each and handed them to the girl, then slapped her smartly across the seat of her skirt as she turned. She yelped and jumped, and he said something in swift, slurred Spanish. She spoke in tones of protest. He spoke again. She smiled and flushed and walked swiftly out.

"That one," he explained, "that Rosita, she had the unhoppy love affair and now she has the long face. I told her I wanted to see if there was any feeling left in the back side. She told me I should have more respect. Then I said something, it doesn't translate. But it made her face hot and it made the smile, no? Hey, anything you want, just say what it is. Okay?"

I briefed him on the situation, and on what we were trying to do, and showed him Bix's photo. He caught on quickly. He understood the father's need to have all the blanks filled in.

He looked in the phone book and gave his switchboard a number to call. In a few moments his desk phone rang. He picked it up and, after a few minutes wait, got through to somebody he called Roberto. I could make out a word here, a phrase there. He asked some questions and then thanked the man and hung up.

"The sergeant who did the investigation has no English at all. *Nada.* Here is how it will go. At two o'clock today he will come over to the Marqués del Valle. We close this place at noon today. I will come over in my car. You and your friend and the sergeant, we will go up into the mountains and he will show us the place and I will tell you what he says."

"I don't want to put you to—"

"*Silencio, gringo!* How do you know it doesn't give me the chance to get out of something I didn't want to do, eh?"

"Okay. Next problem. How do I get to talk to Mrs. Eva Vitrier?"

"That one is one rich lady. I remember it was maybe eight, nine years ago, that place was sold. Nearly two million pesos. And then a lot more to fix it up. All the other ricos out in the Colonia, they can't wait to find out who the owner is. They think there will be entertaining. They want to see how the house has been fixed. All of a sudden they find out the owner is there, this Frenchwoman. They go calling. She will not see them. They leave cards. Nothing. Oh, she has guests come in sometimes, very few, from far away. Sometimes she is seen in the city. She shops, and has servants with her to carry packages to the car, and a man to drive the car. People say crazy things. Maybe she is the mistress of a king. Maybe she is a political refugee. Maybe it is stolen money. I think it is easy, man. I think the lady wants to be left the hell alone."

"What does she look like? Have you seen her?"

He leaned back, eyes half closed, a gentle smile on his lips. "She has no age. She could be thirty. She could be fifty. No difference. She looks like that queen of Egypt, you know. The one with the nose."

"Nefertiti?"

"That one. Very proud. Head high. Very hot eye. One day, three or four years past, I walked behind her from one jewelry store to her car. Black hair. Cool day. Had on a dark red wool dress. She walked slow, like music, man. Long narrow back, narrow little shoulders. Not much in front, but one truly fantastic ass. Firm, round, heavy but not too heavy. Wide but not too wide. It moved just right when she walked. Nothing under that dress, man. She had some great kind of perfume. It came floating back. You know, she got in that car and it drove away, and what I wanted to do, I wanted to lean against a building and pant like a dog. Hell, I tried to meet her. She was worth a good try. Twenty good tries. I never got to first base. First base! I never found the road to the ball park. I tell you, one long look at her, and that Miranda bird of Ron's looks like somebody's brother."

"So there's no friend of hers here who could put me in direct touch?"

"She has some friends, I think. I don't know exactly. Those friends would not be my friends. People I think who tuck their lives behind walls here, like she does. Because here they are left alone, and it is a freedom for them. I know that Gaona won't help you. That is one tough old man. Long ago there was an election when there were strong feelings. He wanted to be a politico. Somebody shot him in the spine. He dragged himself home in the night. Four miles. Took him all night. Wore his hands to ribbons. Would not say who shot him. If I had to trust a secret to any lawyer in the world, it would be Alfredo Gaona."

"About Mrs. Vitrier's friends. One of them would be Bruce Bundy?"

He looked startled, then impressed. "Yes, it was his car. He loaned it to someone who loaned it to the Bowie girl. I know Bundy by sight. Three or four years he's been here. There's a little group of them here. Nobody pays much attention, if they stay out of trouble. But if one of them starts taking little boys from the public market home, then the police will make their life very ugly. To find out so soon that Bundy and the French lady are friends, something I did not know, means you are very quick with these things, eh?"

"I tend to go in like a bull, Enelio. Or like a kid busting into a room full of slot machines. I pull levers and kick things and usually end up with pure lemons. So I found that Bundy is a friend of Eva Vitrier, and Bundy is a friend of Lady Rebecca Divin-Harrison, and Lady Becky doesn't like Eva worth a damn."

He looked at me with a speculative appraisal, head cocked slightly, and then a slow grin came and widened and then he threw his head back and laughed and slammed the desk top with a big hand.

When he caught his breath, he said, "So! You do not always have those black circles under the eyes, amigo! And that mark on your neck is not a strawberry birthmark. And maybe your hands do not always tremble a little, eh? My God, you are a rare one, McGee! You and me, we are members of one club now. Goddam, there are plenty members, and I joined—let me see—fifteen years ago, and she looked exactly, I swear, the way she looks today. She had a beautiful car and she asked me if I would like to drive it. I was young. I could conquer anything. Car or woman. Perhaps it is good to learn humility when young. Four days I was not a part of the world. Four days and nights, and then ejected, blinking, weak as a new kitten, dazed, damn near destroyed. Ah, that one is legend, my friend. *Muy guapa.* As much woman as there can be. Too much woman. The club is big, but she selects with great care, believe me. One cannot ask to be a member. One must be invited. Some day, McGee, we will be wheeled into the sunshine with the blanket over our knees, and we will have that memory, and we will smile a nice and dirty-old-man smile. There is an old saying among the Oaxacaños: The most bitter remorse is for the sins one did not commit. She is quite mad, of course. But it is an agreeable madness, no?"

"If I recover, I'll let you know."

"One always recovers. I even wished to see if it had all happened as I remembered, or if I had dreamed portions of it. But she patted my face and she said, 'Nelio, you are a dear boy and I am very fond of you, but I have turned the page you were written on. It is a very long book, and I do not have time in my life to reread any part of it if I am to finish it.' For a time I was hurt and angry. Then later I understood. She was written in my book too, and by then I was writing a new chapter.

"About Bundy being friends with such total female creatures as Becky and Madame Vitrier, I think it is a common thing among women who do not have tea-party friendships with other women, to have a Bruce Bundy to make girl talk with. And I think he helps them with decorating things in their homes. Look, maybe it is like this. Can Becky have a close friend who is a normal man or normal woman? Bundy is, for her, neutral ground. A relaxment? Bad English. A . . . relaxation. I do not pry. How is it now with Becky? Not ended, I would think."

"*She* thinks it isn't. She thinks she told me just enough to keep me on the hook." I told him about Walter Rockland moving in with Bundy, trying to hit him up for a large loan, and then trying to clean out Bundy's little store of art treasures and getting a quick education in karate.

I said, "She told me I'd made Brucey very nervous, but there isn't enough there, in her story, to make him nervous, so the best part is yet to come. So I am supposed to drop in, alone, for drinks and dinner tonight. And be spoon-fed another little fragment. By the time I know it all, she'll be able to bury me at the foot of her garden, so it will be less wearing to find out what color belt Brucey earned from Brucey himself. Anyway, I'm imposing. I'm taking up too much of your time."

"No. There are some small things I must do here, then it is enough for this day. Let me say one thing. In the picture you showed me, that is one lovely little chicken. I have respect for what you do, Travis. A father should know more of how such a one came to die. He will never understand why. But to know a little—not too much—will help."

7

Most of the tables on the hotel porch were full when I got there. I spotted Meyer at the far end, sitting at a table with a portly man wearing a pale tan suit and yellow sports shirt.

While the waiter was hustling me a chair, Meyer introduced him as Wally McLeen from Youngstown, Ohio. Mr. McLeen's handshake was moist and unemphatic. His hazel eyes were magnified by the thick lenses of glasses with thick black frames. There were steel-wool tufts of hair on his sunburned skull.

Meyer said that Wally had sold out his business and had been in Oaxaca since August first, looking for his daughter, Minda.

"It's more than just looking for her, Mr. McGee. It's trying to understand more about what the young people are looking for. Way back in January she wrote me that she was going to Mexico with some friends. Just like that. Well, I wrote airmail special to the University of Miami asking them if she left any forwarding address or anything like that, and they wrote back that she'd stopped going to classes way back last year, before summer started. She came on home last summer for about ten days and then went back. She told me she was doing extra work over the summer. I sent my little girl money every month. Then I just didn't know where to send it, or where she was or anything.

"You know, I got to thinking, Mr. McGee. I had four establishments, located real good in nice shopping centers, turning a nice profit. I worked hard all my life. Connie died three years ago. We had one other daughter, older than Minda, but she died in infancy. I got to wondering just what the hell I was working for. My little girl came home and didn't have much to say. She acted sour, sort of. It was like lying to me, her not telling me she'd already dropped out of college. Once I decided, it took me a long time to make the right deal on the stores. I figured this way. The only thing I've got in this world is my daughter, Minda. And if I can't communicate with her, then there's no point in anything. If I kept working we'd be in two different worlds. She couldn't or wouldn't move into mine, so what I have to do is move into hers. It's the only way I'll be able to talk to her when I find her."

"You expect to find her soon, Mr. McLeen?"

"Wally, please. Yes, I've got it pretty well pinned down that sooner or later she's coming back down here. I'm right in this hotel, right in the center of things. Room number twelve, on the second floor, looking out over the zocalo. When she gets back, I'll be here."

"Where is she?"

"Someplace in Mexico City, but there's six million people in that city. . . . What do people call you?"

"Travis. Trav."

"Trav, you're one hell of a lot younger than I am, but you're older than these kids. I don't know what you think about them. But I've been talking to them now for a long time, and I've changed a lot of my ideas, like I was telling Meyer. It used to make me so damn irritated just to look at those young boys with all the long hair and beards and beads. I figured them for fanatics and dope addicts and degenerates. I can't stand that rock music and those songs about freedom. All right. Some of them are nuts, so far gone on pills and drugs, they're dirty, dumb, sick, and dangerous as wild animals. But most of them are damned good kids. They care about things. They've taken a good long look at our world and they don't like it. They don't like the corruption, and the way the power structure takes care of its own, and the way we're all being hammered down into being a bunch of numbers in a whole country full of computers. They believe that each individual person is getting so insignificant you can't really change anything by voting for a change. You get the same old crap. So what they want to do is get away from all the machinery that makes Vietnams and makes slums and discrimination and legalized theft and murder. How do you get away? Well, you have to go against the establishment in visible ways, so nobody will have any chance of ever thinking you are a part of it. And so you can identify the other people who don't want any part of it either. You pick ways to dress and act and look that turn the establishment people off. You're against the idea of accumulating money and things, so you cut life down to the simplest kind of food and shelter you can scrounge. Because establishment morality is a lot of hypocrisy, like Lenny Bruce pointed out, you say and you write the words that shock the establishment, and you turn sex into something simple and natural and easy. The art and the music—everything has to be something the establishment can't stand. Because, little by little, or maybe in one big fire, you're going to tear all the false fronts down and start everything over again, in a lot simpler and more decent way, without a lot of hangups about money and race and sex and war. I didn't see where pot and pills and LSD fitted in for a while, but I think I do now. They want to turn on because they believe every person has the right to do anything to himself that doesn't harm others. Society makes laws about that because society doesn't want people to make themselves unuseable to the power structure. If everybody turned on every day, what would happen to industry? They're saying this, Trav. They're saying, 'I don't want any part of things the way they are, man. So don't tell me I'm ruining my life because I'm ruining just that part of me that you'd want to use up if you had a chance. The rest of me belongs to me to do what I want with. And what I want is everything you despise. So don't make a lot of value judgements about a scene you can't dig. You are all caught in the machinery, and you want everybody else to get caught in it, too. I make you uncomfortable, old man, because I get more out of every week of my life than you ever got out of a whole year of yours.'

"You know, they *will* talk to me about these things once they find out I'm not just trying to tell them the same old crap they've always heard. When they find out I want to *learn* what this is all about, then they'll talk about it. And I'll tell them how I feel about my life. What was so great about my life up till now? Mortgage payments, inventories, worries, sickness . . . and so damned many *things!* Color television and the new car every two years, and a lawn mower to ride on. Your friends die and you die, and what's the point of any of it? Who ever misses you? Yes sir, like I've been telling Meyer, when I see my Minda again, I'll be able to talk to her like I never could before. I talk too much about all this, and I guess I bore people, but I have the idea I want to spread the word about these kids. I want to be a sort of . . . a messenger." He looked at me with a goggle-eyed earnestness. "Do you understand what I'm saying?"

"Sure, Wally," I said, comfortingly. "We dig you."

He smiled. "Jesus! When I think of how the guys back in Youngstown would take it, I get the idea nobody over twenty-five can understand what I'm trying to say."

"Wally, I understand you've been trying to locate Walter Rockland too."

"To see if he knew anything about Minda. She was with that group for a while. The groups that travel together keep changing. People split and new ones join. I told Meyer that my Minda and that girl that was killed, Bix something, they left at the same time and took a cheap room at the Hotel Ruiz. That's over there, diagonally across the zocalo on Guerrero. They moved in sometime late in May. I saw the room. It's on the second floor in the back. There's a bath down the hall. There's four kids living in that room right now. But only one was there when Minda and Bix moved in. One from the present group, I mean. He thinks there were six or seven kids there in the room while Minda and Bix were there, and as he remembers it, they left at the end of June or early July when Mrs. Vitrier invited them to stay in her guest house. Such a small room, and pretty beat up. You try to give your girl the best of everything. It hurts to think of her living like that. But what you can do? They just don't want the things you can give them. Not this new bunch of kids. They've turned their backs on the whole thing." He shook his head slowly. "Maybe it wouldn't be nice for you men to go back and tell Bix's father about things like that little room in the Hotel Ruiz. It could give him the same feeling I had, thinking of my daughter there at night, in some dirty sleeping bag in a dark corner, and some boy with a dirty beard laying her, and the others sleeping so close, or hearing it happening. Maybe he should think it is all like the posters and the travel ads. . . . A daughter is not like a son."

Meyer tried him on the other names. Carl Sessions, musician. Jerry Nesta, sculptor.

Wally McLeen said he might have met them and talked to them, but he didn't remember those names. He had asked everyone about Minda. He had shown them her picture. And he had added up the little crumbs of information. She had gone alone to Mexico City. She would be back one day. He would wait. If, instead, she showed up in Youngstown, a friend would cable him. He looked at his watch. Some of his new young friends were expecting him. He said he would look us up and let us know if he learned anything interesting, anything that might make that poor girl's father feel better.

Enelio Fuentes appeared promptly at two, and he had Sergeant Carlos Martinez with him. Martinez, a squat, broad man with very dark skin and several gold teeth, was in civilian uniform. We all got into Enelio's car, a new Volkswagen squareback sedan, custom-painted a strange metallic purple. Enelio took the wheel. Meyer and the sergeant sat in the back. Siesta traffic was light, and Enelio wasted no time scooting north to Route 190, the Pan American Highway, where he turned right on the road toward Mitla. About a mile beyond the city limits he turned left on State of Oaxaca Route 175, and began streaking across the flats at astonishing speed toward the lift of the high brown mountains.

"I didn't know these things had so much snap," I said, speaking loudly over the sound of wind and engine.

"They don't. We put a Porsche engine in this one, race tuned, man. Heavy duty springs and shocks. Disc brakes. I can make Mexico City in five and a half hours. Hey, how do you like it? See? One eighty kilometros which is . . . a hundred and ten."

When we hit the first curves and began climbing, I was able to relax. Roaring along the straights proves nothing. On the curves he proved the nice mating of man and machine. He found the right track around every curve. He was showing off and enjoying himself, and it was a pleasure to watch. But it certainly was one hell of a road. It was very narrow asphalt and the climb grew steeper and steeper, with switchbacks, cuts, and no banking on the turns, and not a sign of a guardpost. Ahead I would get glimpses of our road halfway up the next mountain, a little man-made ledge with a rock wall on one side and mountain air on the other. Sometimes I could see where we had been, and it was like an aerial view of a road.

We met two buses hurtling down the mountains, and passed one old truck grinding its way up in low-low-low, radiator steaming. The sergeant told Enelio we were getting very near the place. Enelio slowed down and soon found a place to pull off the road, on the outside of a curve where the car was visible from both directions. We got out and chunked the doors shut. The silence was enormous, the air thin, chilly and very pure.

We followed the sergeant about a hundred and fifty yards further up the road to the next curve. He sat on his heels and pointed at a black rubber skidmark on the asphalt. The mark ran off the asphalt and he pointed to some small bushes with broken branches. The branches dangled and the leaves had turned brown. It was easy to see where the car had come back onto the asphalt. We walked back down the slope and saw where she had gone across into the wrong lane and off the road. He pointed to the yellow paint marks on the rock wall and, a hundred feet further, to some oddly shaped skid-marks on the road, like gigantic commas. He made a fast circular gesture with his hand, fingers down, like somebody stirring something in a bowl. Then he made a thrusting gesture with his hand toward the precipice indicating how it had shot out over the edge. Giving me a broad golden grin, he said, "Too fasssss!"

Yes indeed. It was vivid. She lost it on a downhill curve to the left, maybe because the curve was sharper than she had anticipated. She fought for control but went across at a long angle and hit the stone cliff, bounced off it into a spin, and shot backwards or forwards—it didn't matter which—over the edge at maybe a forty-five degree angle, and maybe a hundred feet short of the next curve, also left-hand, where the purple tiger was parked.

The sergeant led me to the brink and pointed down. I could not see what he was pointing at. He spoke to Enelio. Enelio shaded his eyes and looked. "Hey, I see it. Travis, you see those three little bushes that grow out of the edge of shale down there, near that round rock? Okay, now about ten feet to the right of the three bushes, and a little way back up the slope . . ."

I saw it. A few smears of yellow paint on sharp edges of rock, and a twinkling of broken glass among the rocks, and a gleaming piece of twisted chrome trim. So that's where it hit first, but the next bounce had to take it out of sight of where we were.

The sergeant walked us down past the purple car, and pointed down at an angle toward the valley floor. From there it was easy to spot the car, or what had been a car. If you took one of those match-box toy cars and put it on top of the charcoal and cooked steaks for a whole party, then retrieved the little car and stepped on it with your heel, you'd have a pretty good imitation of what was lying in the valley.

"How did they ever get the body?"

"They came down from the other side. There's our road over there. That's where the bus was when they saw the flame when she hit. You can see from here it's not as steep to go down, or as far."

"How was identification made?"

"By Madame Vitrier."

"That's in the report, Enelio. I mean what condition was the body in?"

He questioned the sergeant. Finally he turned back to me and swallowed in a sickly way and said, "She was half in and half out of the car, charred from the waist up, and chopped up pretty bad, man. There was a silver chain on her ankle Madame Vitrier identified, and a red shoe that was hers, fifty feet maybe from where they found the car and the body. Didn't find the other shoe."

"Why was she way up in these mountains? Enelio, this damned road must climb four thousand feet in fifteen miles."

He turned and pointed. Through a notch in the hills we could see the far valley and the smoke-misted shimmer of the city. "Five thousand feet above the sea. Up here we are . . . maybe eight thousand and a half? Yes. Ten, twelve kilometers more and we are at the top. The puerto, like the gate or the pass. At Relon. Ten thousand, two hundred and seven. I remember from the sign. Little houses here and there. Mountain people. Very sweet. Very cruel. Ah, this is one evil road, Travis. Every year two, three, four vehicles go over. Most of the time everyone dead. Six years ago a bus with eighteen persons. Why would she come up here? Maybe for the same reasons when I was . . . seventeen? Yes. On an English motorcycle. Early, early in the morning, I went down this crazy road, man. I was yelling. It was a great excitement. It was speed and death and terror. It was a rhythm, Travis McGee. Lean into one curve, lean into the other. *Fantástico!* Like when it is the very best of sex, like the mountains are all parts of the body of a great brooding woman. Way down, near the bottom, somehow the wind got under the goggles, blew them crooked, one eye covered, one eye in the wind, so the tears were running. I think there was a little stone I did not see. Zam! I am turning in the air. Smash into trees. Fall. Broke this wrist. See? It is never quite straight again. Blood running out of my hair. Hey, I walked down the road, holding this broken wrist like so. I walked with a big grin and I was singing, and they came out of the huts and stared at the crazy fellow. I had been to visit death, my friend, and had a taste of it and I was alive and I would live forever, and finally see death again and say, 'Remember me! You had me once, old woman, and you let me go!' " He grinned, picked up a stone, threw it over the edge. A truck came grinding and popping and grunting by us, and he waited until it went up around the corner Bix had missed and he could be heard again. "I think it was something like that for the girl. When you are young you drive up in the mountains and you drive back down again."

He turned and questioned the sergeant, listened and then interpreted. I had caught about half of it. "He went on up the road and asked the people about the yellow car. He found a boy who would talk about it. The boy was herding two burros back to the little farm. He'd been in the woods that Sunday, cutting wood and making two big loads for the burros. The yellow car was parked off the road in the late afternoon, about a kilometer this side of Guelatao. The pavement stops there. Beyond that it is gravel and stone all the way to Papaloapan, and from there paved again until it ends on Route 140 on the Gulf of Mexico, south of Veracruz. It can be driven in a Rover or a Jeep or a good truck. No matter. The boy said a big foreigner was leaning against the yellow car, and a young foreign woman was sitting on a stone. He said they spoke greetings and he replied. Because of what the boy said, the sergeant came back with a dozen men and they searched every inch of the slope to be certain the man had not been with her and been thrown clear. They looked in the tops of trees to see if he was wedged there. There was no sign of him."

"Ask him if he got any description of the man from the boy."

After the sergeant replied, Enelio shrugged and said, "The boy told him that all foreign people looked exactly the same to him, as identical as kernels of dried corn."

"Did anybody else see them?"

"Perhaps. Who knows? These mountain people. They say very little to anyone from the valley, and they say nothing to the police. Look over there. See that place where the top of the smaller mountain seems to be flattened?"

"What is it?"

"In this light you can see faint lines running across, below the flat part, like terraces. If we went up there, Travis, and dug where those lines are we would find old, old walls. We would find shards of Zapotecan pottery, maybe splinters of obsidian. Under the soil of the flat top will be stone paving. There could be tombs there, but if there are they will be broken open, because that site is easy to spot. It overlooks the valley. Maybe it was an outpost for soldiers, maybe a place of the priests. There are maybe twenty thousand archeological sites in Mexico. Some say fifty thousand. Maybe five hundred have been investigated by the professionals. Here is how it was. Five, six, seven hundred years ago, these mountain people, who had been led into this place by the priests and the soldiers, they climbed to that place you see, and they made offerings of food, and they worshipped. They built the temples, dug the wells, carried the stones, made the pottery, cut the thatch. But the priests got too far away from the people. They thought they owned the people forever. They lost common understanding. So one day the people went up to the high places and killed the priests and killed the guards and pulled down the temples and never went back. They did not talk about it. They did not have elections. They just got tired of slave life, of catering to the demands of the priests for food and women and children to train, and tired of work that became more meaningless to them. They went up and killed them and put an end to it, and did not talk about it, or make legends, or write about the revolution. These are hard, enduring people. I am proud to have this Indian blood in me. Do you know the kind of men who come out of these valleys? Benito Juárez! Porfirio Díaz! This small place of Oaxaca breeds great men who dream big dreams and then act on them. Hey! Sorry, I am not teaching school here. But listen to the silences here! They never shout, these mountain people. The greeting is adios, said so softly city ears can hardly hear it. Shall we go?"

And so we went back down that insane road, with Enelio driving conservatively, automatically, far away somewhere in thought and memory. Down to the flats and across to the intersection of the main road. There was a small industry on the right, where men baked adobe brick in rough ovens, then stacked them in the sun, in shades ranging from brown-orange to yellow-gold.

"Ask him if the American students cause him many problems," Meyer said. The sergeant talked at considerable length.

Enelio translated. "Martinez says that as a group they are like all people. Most of them create no problems. But there are always the very few who get drunk and break things, and there the ones who live foolishly and become sick and require help. Some go into the wrong places with valuable things and become the victims of thieves. Some take drugs and act irrationally. Some act in a very improper way, which upsets the simple people."

"Improper how?" Meyer asked.

"A boy standing in the zocalo, fondling and kissing a half-dressed girl in front of a hundred Mexicans who have come in from the villages for a market day upsets them. But suppose you take some bearded, ragged, dirty kid, loaded with pot, digging the village scene, just floating and smiling, the village people will treat him with great gentleness and courtesy and consideration. Know why? It is tradition to be very nice to all madmen. The ancient gods have put a spell on them, and to be mad is to have been touched by the gods."

"Does he get requests to find specific students?" Meyer asked.

"He says that the American Embassy makes the request of the Federal Police, and then the information is sent down here. Then the registration list at every hotel and motel and trailer court is checked. If the student is found, he is told to get in touch with the Embassy in Mexico City. If he is not found, then that is reported."

"Do they keep a list?"

I congratulated Meyer for clear thinking. In the city, Sergeant Martinez brought a stack of papers out to the car. It was not a list, but rather a sheaf of faintly imprinted carbon copies of the Embassy requests, about forty of them.

"He says it is for all of this year up until now," Enelio explained.

Meyer went through them swiftly, with minor pauses, and then stopped at one and showed it to me. *Request to locate Carl Sessions, age 22, five foot eleven, one hundred and forty pounds, fair complexion, blond hair. Request contact Mr. Lord at the American Embassy, Extension 818.* It was dated the ninth of June. There were some notations and numbers written on it in red ink. Enelio asked the sergeant to explain the notations, then interpreted for us.

"They couldn't find this boy and they made a routine report. Okay, on July seventh, on a Monday morning, the boy is found dead in a doorway on Arteaga Street, in a bad section over beyond the public market. There wasn't anything left in his pockets, probably taken by kids who thought he was drunk. If his clothes hadn't been so ragged and dirty, they would have taken those too. A doctor took a blood sample. There were needle marks on his arms and thighs. Some were infected. He was badly undernourished. The cause of death was an overdose of an opiate. They found out he had been sleeping in a little place he had made out of cardboard boxes in the back of one of the market stalls. The owner of the stall had locked some of the boy's stuff up for safekeeping. There was a guitar case with a guitar and some personal papers in it. They found his name from the papers."

He asked Martinez another question, listened, and then said, "A lieutenant called the Embassy in Mexico City and reported it. An embassy employee flew down and took care of the details. The body was sent by air freight to the boy's sister in Atlanta, Georgia."

I was suddenly aware of the way I was being studied by Sergeant Carlos Martinez. It was the cop look, flat, narrow, hard, and thoughtful. I didn't need any translator for that one. We showed an interest in two young travelers, and both of them were dead. Cops do not believe in coincidence. It offends their sense of orderliness. They find it hard to believe, for example, that every DWI they arrest has had exactly two beers.

We all thanked him for his time. Enelio shook his hand in that special way which inconspicuously transfers a folded bill from pocket to hand to hand to pocket.

As we drove away I said I wanted to replace the gift.

"Hey, you are pretty fonny, McGee. What time is it? Five o'clock already! Hey, Meyer and me will leave you off at the car, and by the time you get up to the Hotel Victoria, hombre, you will find us sitting at a shady table by the swimming pool looking at the lovely little birds in their wet little bikinis, and you will be one drink behind."

8

THERE WERE indeed some delicious little morsels making energetic use of the giant pool, getting the last of sun and water and squealing games of tag before the shadows of the mountains moved in and the evening chill began.

The drinks were good, and Enelio was sufficiently well known to get very earnest service. For a time Meyer scribbled on the back of an envelope, pausing to squint into the distance and think. When I asked him what he was doing he said he would show me in a couple of minutes.

Finally he handed it to me and said, "Timetable. If I screwed up anything, let me know." I held it so Enelio could read it also.

Jan. 10   Five cross into Mexico at Matamoros in camper.

Mar. 25   (*approx*) $13,000 + sent to Bix in Culiacán, Sinaloa.

Apr. 24   Rocko w/camper checks into Los Pájaros.

May 25   (*approx*) Bix & Minda move from Los Pájaros to room in Hotel Ruiz.

June 9   Official request to locate Sessions.

June 30   (*approx*) Bix and Minda move to Mrs. Vitrier's guest house.

July 5   Rocko beats up Mike Barrington.

July 7   Sessions found dead.

July 10   Camper permit & tourist cards run out.

July 23   Rocko leaves Los Pájaros, by request, moves in with Bruce Bundy.

July 30   (*approx*) Bix & Minda quarrel & Minda goes to Mexico City.

Aug.	1	Before dawn, Bundy stops Rocko from leaving with loot.
Aug.	1	Minda's father arrives, looking for her.
Aug.	2	Bundy lends his yellow British Ford to unknown person called George.
Aug.	3	Bix killed.
Aug.	4	Mrs. Vitrier identifies body.

I said, "Meyer, it makes it look a lot neater and more orderly than it is."

Enelio took the envelope and frowned at the timetable, and then said, "No sense to one thing here, men."

"Such as?"

"He couldn't have stayed in the trailer park after the permit and cards ran out. You have to show your car papers when you check into any trailer park. They put the date and so forth on their records. The police are very fussy about car permits. They check the books. So then their papers were still good on July twenty-three . . . which means this first date is wrong, when they came in."

"No, Enelio. It was pretty well checked."

"Okay. Then sometime before April twenty-four, they went up to the border and got everything new again. New car papers, new tourist cards. I think . . . maybe seven days from the border down here to Oaxaca. So the date on everything could be April seventeen, eh? Good until October sixteen. You can look in the office at Los Pájaros. They will have the permit number and the place of entry. It is not so necessary to go to the border to get the tourist card new. It is not supposed to be done, but it can be newed . . . *re*newed in Mexico City, if there is a little gift to the right clerk. But not for a vehicle. One *must* go to the border. Where were they? Culiacán? Shortest way is up to Nogales." He grinned at us. "And I know why they went there. Pretty stupid thing to do."

"How could you know?" Meyer asked.

He tapped the side of his head. "Very smart fellow, this Enelio Fuentes. Sessions died from drugs. Okay. Sonora has a lot of poppies growing. The crude opium—it's called *goma*—is sold in one ton lots to the little factories where they reduce it to heroin. I think the biggest operations are in Sinaloa. And some very rich men there in fine houses, you believe me. What was stupid was having money sent to Culiacán. But maybe not. How was it sent?"

"Bank draft."

"Dumb stupid, man! A few years ago, okay. Now the Mexican Narcotics Bureau is pretty smart. They find out who is making a deal. Then they tip their people on our side of the line. So they get searched and, okay, suppose there's four kilos of heroin. Tell them they are going to be tossed into a Mexican jail for ninety-nine years. Scare them all to hell. Then take three kilos, and a big bribe to let them keep one, then tip the customs men on your side of the line. They get . . . what's the damned word . . . saw-hammered?"

"Whipsawed."

"So a bank draft is like hanging out a sign. I wonder what the hell happened."

Meyer said, "I can't see Bix Bowie as a smuggler of narcotics."

"So? That sister probably couldn't see little brother Carl stone cold dead in the market, full of old needle holes."

I asked him, "Could anybody go to Culiacán and buy heroin?"

He shrugged. "For double the going price, and never seeing the face you buy it from. Why not? Double the going price is maybe one tenth the wholesale price in the states. One hondred and thirty thousand dollars, U. S., is . . . one million, six hondred twenty-five thousand pesos."

"In a very dirty business," Meyer said.

Enelio laughed. "Sure. But don't you know how the whole world thinks about dirty business? Everybody says, 'Oh, I know it is a bad, bad thing. But it is going to happen anyway. I can't stop it all by myself. So long as *somebody* is going to do it, it might as well be me.' Meyer, I like you. You could not do bad things. Me, I do terrible things, believe me."

"Oh, so do I, Enelio. Unspeakable things."

Enelio made a sad face. "But for me, instead of involving money, always it involves women. That is my burden."

He looked at his watch. He said he had to go and change and go out. We thanked him for everything. He said he would phone us tomorrow, and maybe we could find something amusing to do.

The pool was shadowed, and most of the birds had flown. A batch of American youngsters in their late teens came whooping down from the hotel, smack-diving into the pool. Brown little girls, rangy boys, firm young flesh.

"You have to understand that all these kids are in revolt against the establishment," Meyer said in earnest imitation of Wally McLeen.

"Oh for chrissake, Meyer!"

"I found Wally quite touchingly simplistic. And that *is* a very funny tourist hat he wears."

I yawned. "And they translate ancient tables inscribed three thousand years before Christ and find out that way back then the young were disobedient, had no respect for the old ways, and everything was going to hell in a handbasket."

"Spoken like a true member of the establishment."

"Old friend, there are people—young and old—that I like, and people that I do not like. The former are always in short supply. I am turned off by humorless fanaticism, whether it's revolutionary mumbo-jumbo by a young one, or loud lessons from the scripture by an old one. We are all comical, touching, slapstick animals, walking on our hind legs, trying to make it a noble journey from womb to tomb, and the people who can't see it all that way bore hell out of me."

"You're snarling, McGee. So it is either the effects of the altitude, or post coital depression. Or nervousness at round two coming up."

"Or frustration. I want to know where Rocko is. I want to know who was up on that mountain with Bix. I want to find Jerry Nesta. I want to talk to Minda McLeen. I want to talk to Mrs. Vitrier. I can scratch Carl Sessions. Thin blond guitarists shouldn't live in cardboard boxes and use dirty needles. And I want to bounce the rest of Brucey's story out of him."

"And you should be busy prettying yourself up for Lady Rebecca."

"I keep thinking of all the other people who would have been so happy to come to Mexico with me. You're getting so nervous about my date, I better make a phone call. Don't move."

I walked down and put the call through from our cottage.

"Darling McGee person!" she said, breathy and husky. "God, I feel so overall delicious! I'm humming and tingling and I hardly touch the floor when I walk. I ache for you so terribly, I feel hollow. Hurry, hurry, hurry! Please!"

"Becky, I'm afraid there has to be a change of plans."

"You monster! I can't *endure* it!"

"A chance has come up to move ahead a little, to get some more questions asked and answered. And I realize it was unfair of me to try to get you to tell me things told you in confidence by a friend.

That was the wrong way to go about it. I won't pester you that way any more."

After a pause she said, "You are precisely what I need, you know. The young, young men would come to me at a dead run. Maybe that's what cloys. Having such total control over them. One gets so accustomed to getting exactly what one wants, right on schedule. Darling, I bow to your sense of responsibility. I shall wait here very, very patiently, if I must. And when you are finished with your chores, come to me no matter what hour it is."

"If it's possible at all."

"What are you trying to *do* to me? Could it be that I was just a bit too mischievous last night? Darling, you *were* a challenge, you know. What is that silly thing they shout when great trees fall? Timber! Then they stand aside, smiling. Suppose I make a solemn vow not to be aggressive, and even teach you some special ways to absolutely destroy *me*? Fair is fair. Now will you promise to come here?"

"If I knew exactly what was going to happen, I'd promise. But I don't know how long it will take me to do the things I have to do."

"Could another woman be involved in all this work, dear?"

"It might turn out that way."

"If it does, kindly do not bother to come here. Is that quite clear?"

"From the tone of voice, Becky, abundantly."

"You're trying to spoil things. I'm not accustomed to that."

"All change is beneficial, honey. Take care."

I heard her start to say something as I hung up. I felt slightly weak in the knee. Say you are driving through on a green light and out of the corner of your eye you see a crazy running the red, about to hit you broadside. So you step on it hard and your car jumps ahead far enough so there is just a little clink as he ticks the rear bumper on his way past. So you drive three blocks and park carefully and get out. And the knees feel strange.

So we drove down into the center of the city. The military band was playing marches on the ornate stand in the center of the plaza, and people were walking slowly around and around the perimeter walkways. The traffic sounds, roar of conversations on the veranda, motor scooters, and vendors hawking everything salable overpowered the band, reducing it to an occasional cymbal-clash, and oompah now and then.

It was so crowded we had to take a table at the far end, near the jewelry-store corner. By the time we'd put a drink order in, and I was about to bounce my Bundy-plan off Meyer's more temperate outlook, the Backspin redhead came out of nowhere and plumped down at Meyer's left and glowered across the square table at me.

"You put on a great rap, you sneaky bastard!"

"*Well* now! All fresh and clean and pretty as a picture. See, Meyer? Her eyes focus and her neck is clean. Carrying a little too much weight, but trim her down and she could cut it at anybody's convention."

"Mark was making a joke. That's all. I want to tell you I didn't appreciate the floor show you put on."

I smiled at her. "What were we supposed to do, honey? Sit there and let three heads think that the laughing was a great put-on? Should I have plucked that scarecrow stud out of the chair and booted his scrawny tail out into the traffic? Should we have ignored you and spoiled your fun? Should we have gotten up and walked away? Name it."

"We had some Mardil caps with a Coke was all."

"All for Jeanie?"

"That's something else again."

"Yes indeed. She is long gone. It looks like barbs to me. What's she using to come back? Speed? Is she popping it or eating it?"

"She is *not* long gone. She'll be okay."

"Get her when she's leveled off, kid, halfway between, give her a little kiss, and say good-by."

"You know so *damned* much, don't you?"

"I tried to sweat the whole thing out once upon a time with a very dandy little girl named Mary Catherine. She went onto reds and blues. Tuinal. They used to hate to see her coming, because the ward nurses hate the barbiturate addicts worse than the drunks or the ones on horse. Took her up to North Carolina to a cabin to get her once and for all clean. I'd go in for groceries and come back and find her gone way on some kind of high. Sneaked back and watched through a window. Draining gas out of the lantern, heating it and sniffing it. Lovely sweet faraway smile. Busted in. Tears, promises. Never again. Then she took off. Couldn't find her. Pretended to look. Pretended I had the broken heart. But you know, Red, that look on her face had killed it. I was the most relieved lover in contemporary history. I have no idea what Jeanie is to you."

"My best friend. My roommate at school."

"Take my word. She'll never make it back. Not from where she is."

"So what if she doesn't? It's her life, isn't it?"

"If you want to call it living."

"Hah! That big act of yours, mister. It so happens I found out you're nothing but some kind of rotten private fuzz, both of you. Private pigs for the establishment, down here to make trouble for people. That's some kind of living, isn't it?"

Meyer hitched around and leaned toward her. "Listen to me, my dear. And believe me. We came here as an act of friendship to find out how a lovely girl died. Just that. Nothing more. It seems like such a waste. Your friend Jeanie seems like a tragic waste to me. And to you too, I think. You are being very defensive and impertinent because you are very troubled. I think more has happened than you can handle. If I can help you, privately, personally, no strings attached, if I can help you in any way, just tell me what you need."

She shook her head. "Oh, for chrissake. You kill me. Honest to God, *me* need help from *you!*" And she began to laugh. Very merry. Very young and jolly. Ha ha ho. Meyer sat looking at her. Very patient. No change in the concerned, benign expression. And the laughter took on a thinner edge, a shrillness that suddenly broke into a sob. She slumped, face in her hands, crying quietly. I opened my mouth to speak. Meyer gave me a warning look, a quick lift of the hand. She was straining for control, trying to smother the crying, trying not to be conspicuous.

"What do you need?" he asked.

She reached blindly, head bowed, chin against her chest. She grasped his bulky forearm with both hands. "Can you . . . can you get us out of here? Jeanie and me. Please. . . . Tickets. I can . . . pay you back."

"Where to, dear?"

"Oklahoma City."

"Where are your people?"

"In Europe with my youngest brother, traveling."

"How soon do you want to get out of here?"

"Now! Tomorrow!"

He borrowed a blank sheet from my pocket notebook, and put it and his pen in front of her. "Write your names and addresses."

She hunched over the paper, snuffling. She gave it to Meyer. He said he'd be back in a few minutes.

She wiped her eyes with a paper napkin and sat up and sighed deeply and made a wry mouth. "He isn't kidding?" she asked in a small voice.

"No. Not Meyer."

"I have run into so many lousy rotten people."

"Who briefed you on me?"

"Oh, there was a man around like an hour ago, maybe even two hours. Sort of handsome and elegant and faggotty. He was speaking real good Mexican to one of the waiters and he came over to the table with the waiter and the waiter pointed me out. So he asked me to come back to his table for a minute. So what the hell, why not?"

"Brown-gray hair, good tan, bangs, gold mesh ring."

"Yes, that's him. He lives here. He described you and, boy, did I ever remember *you!* He said he found out there was some kind of scene and wanted to know what went on. I asked why, and he said that a girl had died accidentally, the Bowie girl, and I knew about that, of course. Everybody who was here knew about that. And he said you were an investigator trying to turn it into a murder or something so you could make more money off her parents, and you were trying to make trouble for innocent people who live here. So I told him that what happened had nothing to do with anything like that. He wanted to know who else you talked to, and I said you had talked to the big fellow named Mike, with the Jesus beard, the one who paints, and the black girl named Della who's living with him, but I didn't know what you talked about to them. And that was all."

Meyer returned and gave her a pat on the back of her hand and said, "You can pick up two air tickets at the travel desk in the lobby after eleven tomorrow morning, dear. For your protection more than mine, I'm arranging it so that they can't be turned in for cash."

She nodded. "I think that's the best way. I . . . I won't believe it until I've got the tickets in my hand."

"You leave here at two tomorrow afternoon. You'll have three hours in Mexico City, so you better stay in the airport."

She tried, almost successfully, to smile. "Is there anybody you want killed? . . . Sorry. I guess that isn't very funny."

"You might be able to help us with one little problem. We're looking for three people Bix Bowie traveled with. There were five all together, but the Sessions boy died. We'd like to find Minda McLeen and Walter Rockland, known as Rocko, and Jerry Nesta."

"Those last two, Rocko and Jerry, if anybody wants to kill those two, I'll help. They are rotten human beings, especially Rocko. Look, I'm not going into any details about it. A bunch of us went back to that camper with those two, for like a fun party for one evening. So that Rocko gave me something that ran me up the walls. It ended up a girlfriend of mine named Gillian and me, we were there for I think it was three days. It taught me why the blond and the little dark one split and lived in that crummy hotel room. Mostly that lousy Rocko had me. He is strong as a bull. I mean I knew that if I went there I might end up getting balled, and that it would be taking that risk, right? Look, there are things you say you won't do. You know. Stopping points. But when people keep hurting you and hurting you, then it's easier to do any sick thing than keep getting hurt. It was all rotten. The kids who should have gotten us away from those two didn't do a damn thing. They just left us there. Jerry wasn't so bad. Gillian had the idea he'd be all right if he'd get away from Rocko. Jerry has this fantastic black beard. It's the biggest, blackest beard I ever saw. All that shows are his eyes and a little bit of cheekbone and the end of his nose. I saw her in the market two or three days ago and she said they'd been out to Mitla and she saw Jerry walking along with a kind of ugly little Mexican woman walking behind him, so she made Ricky stop the car and she went back, but he was very strange. He didn't want to talk to her at all. He's living out there someplace, but he wouldn't say where. I haven't any idea where Rocko went, and I couldn't care less. I heard that the dark one— Minda?—yes, Minda. She's supposed to be up in Mexico City and her father is here waiting for her to come back. So that's all I know."

She got up and smiled good-by and said she couldn't say thank you or she'd start crying again. But she bent over and kissed Meyer in a very quick, shy, small-girl way. And fled.

"How did you know she'd grab at it?"

He shrugged. "I didn't. But sometimes you can smell despair. Besides, all generosity is selfish. It made me feel good all over."

Quickly I told him about Bruce Bundy's quest. It was logical, Meyer agreed, that Bundy would have a good contact among the waiter staff, because it would be useful to know what was going on at all times.

"But," asked Meyer, "what is he so damned jumpy about?"

"That is what we now go to find out."

He looked doleful. "A minute ago I felt good all over."

9

So I left the car at the end of the block and once again, this time by night, we walked along Calle las Artes, to the narrow front of number eighty-one.

Hundreds of years of dedicated and diligent theft have made Mexican homes very hard to crack. They grill everything you can reach. They put that busted glass into the tops of their patio walls. And they listen for thieves all the time without knowing they are listening. Thievery is a recognized, though not highly respected, profession. Artists use a limber length of bamboo with a hook at the end to snag the tourist trousers and pull them through the bars of the bedroom window.

There was a light upstairs, and the patio area, seen through the entrance corridor, was lighted. We stood in the shadowed darkness across the narrow street, and I said in a low tone, "I do not think we can talk our way through the gate. He won't buy a drunk act. He won't be bluffed, and he won't be hustled. And it would take a trampoline or a Tarzan act to pop in there uninvited."

"I'm still afraid you'll think of something, Travis."

I was afraid I wouldn't. And then luck took a hand. If you sit still, you don't give that lady much of a chance to operate—for or against you. But if you move around, she can get into the act oftener. She sent the tired old clattering cab down the street to pull up in front of Bruce's house. When the back door opened the dome light went on. Bruce got out. David Saunders was in the back seat. Bruce went a few steps and looked back and then came back to the cab. He leaned in. The rough idle of the motor made it impossible to hear what he was saying. But his expression, seen through smeared glass, was animated, amused, coaxing. He made little shrugs and hand ges-

tures. And at last David hitched himself along the seat. Bruce
reached in and lifted a large suitcase out, put it down, paid the
driver. The cab drove away. They moved toward the gate, Bruce carrying the suitcase. They talked outside the gate in low tones. Bruce
unlocked the gate and swung it open. He began to lead David
through the gate, with a quieting, comforting arm across David's
back in such a way that it reminded me of that classic, *The Specialty
of the House*, when the plump customer is being taken into the restaurant kitchens.

So I was on my toes with good knee action, angling across, hoping
Meyer was reasonably close behind me. When Bundy spun, hearing
the sudden unexpected sound, I was coming through the gate full
out, shoulder already dipped, and a tenth of a second from impact.

Karate, judo, boxing, jiujitsu, wrestling—not one of the formal
schools of unarmed combat prepares a man for the special problem
of suddenly catching a sack of bricks that has fallen out of a third
story window. It was a driving, rolling block coming in from the
blind side, and the impact was impressive. It took us both ten yards
down that tiled corridor, right to the end of it where it opened up
onto the patio. We picked up a small table en route, along with
some decorative crockery that had been on it. I rolled up onto my
feet, my back toward him, and spun and was bemused and discon-
certed to see him bounce up in a springy way and land in the dangerous balance of the expert, hands low and slightly forward. I did not
want him to start that business of *Hah!* and *Huh!* The table was on
the corridor floor between us, the three remaining legs aimed toward
me. So I punted it at him, getting a lot of leg into it, and getting a
nice lift on it. He got his hands up in time, and as the table fell
away, I was right there to pop him with a short overhand right,
slightly off target, and correct the error when he came back off the
wall. He had been obliging enough to wear a leather thong as a belt
for his vermilion stretch slacks, and I yanked it loose, rolled him
onto his face and took two fast turns around the wrists and two fast
hitches that would hold long enough for me to go solve Meyer's
problem, even if Bruce woke up right now, which didn't seem plausible.

I came upon the Mexican woman standing crouched in terror,
wringing her hands. I smiled broadly and told her that it was a game
Americans play. Don't worry, señora. We are all very happy.

Meyer was between the gate and the entrance to the central corridor. He was clumping around in a small circle, taking quick steps to the side now and again to catch his balance. He was shaking his big head and muttering to himself. David Saunders sat spraddled like a chunky little kid. He was swaying from side to side, cradling something against the lower part of his big chest and making a small thin keening sound. He looked like he was rocking a little dolly, and he couldn't carry a tune in a basket.

I got the gate shut and latched. I caught Meyer as he came around his circle. He stopped and shook his head violently and knuckled his eyes.

"Violence is vulgar," he said. "It offends me."

"You won, didn't you?"

"By giving him a frightful blow on the fist with my forehead. The expression is, 'I ducked into it.'"

I helped Saunders up and walked him past Bundy into the bright area of the walled court and eased him into a white iron armchair. I pulled the hand away from his chest. It was beginning to puff. Broken hands are unpredictable. There are ten thousand nerve bundles, and if the break doesn't involve them, you don't feel a thing until later on. But if the broken bone or bones grind into the right nerves, it is an agony that prevents you from thinking about anything else in the world, and keeps you right on the twilight edge of a faint.

I plucked Brucey off the floor and put him on a purple chaise, rolled him onto his side and neatened the thong. The maid stood staring at us. I smiled at her. Meyer smiled at her. After a few moments she smiled back and scuttled away.

Bruce lifted his head, coming awake all at once. He swung his feet to the floor and sat up. He worked his jaw from side to side and licked his lips and looked at me and said in a totally masculine manner, "You are pretty goddam impressive, McGee. Men your size are supposed to be slower." He looked at David and frowned. "What's the matter with him?"

"He broke his hand hitting me on the head," Meyer said. "Terribly sorry about that."

"But he's in *agony!*" Bruce said. "He's *terribly* hurt. He needs medical attention immediately. *Look* at his poor hand!"

"He'll get it, after we have a little chat."

"What in the world do we have in common worth talking about, McGee?"

"The subject of discussion is what makes you so nervous about my asking questions about Walter Rockland and the Bowie girl."

"Am I nervous?"

"Nervous enough to talk to that redhead earlier tonight and tell her I was trying to make something out of nothing."

"Aren't you?"

I kicked a chair closer and sat facing him, about four feet away. "Brucey, the trouble with playing games is that you never know how much the other party knows. Rocko moved in here with you at your invitation, and put the camper in the shed out in back, and tried to hit you for a large loan, and then he tried to make off with a lot of valuable little goodies, but you'd read him right and disabled the truck. Took the rotor, probably. He jumped you and you black-belted him pretty good."

He tossed his head to throw the bangs back. He turned pale under his golden tan, and the odd brown eyes turned to dingy little slits. At that moment he looked his age.

"I shall *never, never, never* forgive that treacherous, rotten British bitch." He continued at some length. He had a truly poisonous mouth.

"All through? So why are you so edgy about it?"

"I can't afford to get involved in anything."

"What is there to get involved in, Bundy?"

He hesitated. "What if I happen to know that someone saw Walter Rockland and the Bowie girl together just a week ago? Ah . . . at the airport, getting on a flight to Acapulco."

Misdirection. Nice footwork. Toss in a thought that warps the mind. Maybe it was true. So how to test it?

It took me quite a segment of silence to come up with the leverage. "You are a clever man, Bruce. Look at it this way. Nobody knows where Rocko is. It wouldn't be hard to prove he lived here with you. You are very nervous about the whole thing. I can get the information to Sergeant Martinez that you fought with Rockland. I can tell him that he can find traces of human blood on the stone floor of the shed out behind this place. I can tell him your story about Rockland going to Acapulco, and I guess they could check that out and see if he did. Then I would suggest that they take this place apart looking for a body and take you apart to see what you know about it."

"You are *such* a cruel son of a bitch."

"So?"

"All right! All right! All right! I nearly moved away from here after the first four months. I had a stupid mishap with the car I had then. A drunken old fool on a bicycle ran into the side of the car. And so I . . . enjoyed the hospitality of the local prison. My dear friend Freddy, now deceased, tried frantically to get me out, but they managed to hold me there five days. Police the world over seem to have this compulsion to mistreat men of my particular sexual pattern. They treated me with contempt. I did not mind that. I considered the source. The brutality from the jailors could be endured. But each night I was locked into a very large cell with the very dregs of Mexico, who had been informed, of course, of what I was. And so I was used and abused. They degraded me. It put me into a depression that lasted for months. Freddy talked me out of leaving Mexico. He said it would be the same anywhere in the world. That is a valid observation. We have no recourse in the law, really. And Walter Rockland knew that when he tried to make off with some very valuable things. He knew that I would not report the theft, that I would not dare report it for fear they'd think of some pretext for locking me up again. I don't think I could endure that a second time. If you understand that, Mr. McGee, and understand my absolute terror, then I can tell you what happened."

He told us that Walter, as he called him, had stayed in bed all day Friday, and had said on Saturday morning that he still felt unwell, but begged to be allowed to leave. Bruce told him to rest. At noon on Saturday while Bruce was in the kitchen fixing something for a light lunch, he had been struck from behind and knocked unconscious. When he regained conscousness, Walter was gone. So were his car keys, a couple of hundred pesos from his wallet, and his yellow English Ford. At first he had been afraid Walter had broken in and taken the valuables which he had locked up after the first attempt, but they were still there. He had no intention of reporting it as a theft. He still had the truck and camper, and they were worth more than the car Walter had taken.

On Monday, in the middle of the morning, the police had come to see him. They had asked him about his car, asked him where it was. He had thought they had picked Walter up, and he remembered Walter's hints about needing the money for some illegal act. He could not be tied in with any illegality, so he had invented the fictitious young American named George, and had described him in a way that would fit half the young Americans in Mexico on summer vacation. Only after they had made him go over the story several times did they tell him that an unidentified girl had gone off the mountain road, that his car was a total loss and the girl was dead.

Later that day before learning that Eva Vitrier had identified the body, Bruce had gone to Becky and told her the whole story and had asked her what she thought he should do. He was frightened that Walter was involved somehow in the girl's death, and that if they picked up Walter he would manage to involve Bruce somehow.

Becky thought it was logical that Walter Rockland would come back after his truck, and that Bruce should leave the shed unlocked and leave the keys in it, and replace the rotor. Maybe somebody would steal it, or Rocko would retrieve it. And if neither happened, she would help him get rid of it some dark night, follow in her car while he parked it somewhere else in the city, and bring him back. In the small hours of the night, at a little after two o'clock on Tuesday morning, he heard the truck start, heard the backing and filling in the narrow alleyway, heard it speed away, the drone fading into the normal night sounds. And he did not care whether Rocko had taken it or a thief had taken it. He thought he was out of it.

"So weeks later," he said bitterly, "you show up at my door, telling your lies about insurance. I had to let you in, because I had to be certain Rocko hadn't sent you on some kind of blackmail project. But you didn't say the right things because you had no way of knowing."

"Like I have no way of knowing that all this is true."

"It *is* true. And the Bowie girl is dead. Eva telephoned me to say good-by. She said she did not know when she would be back."

"Where did she go?"

"She never says. I have no idea. I know she was very upset. It was unlike her to . . . identify the body. I think she had to be certain in her own mind that it was the blond girl, and she was too impatient to wait for them to identify her in some other way. I think it was quite a strong and unusual infatuation for poor Eva."

"Infatuation?"

"You aren't as aware as I thought, McGee. It seemed to me that Becky made it obvious last night that Eva and I are opposite sides of a very old coin. But the approach is not the same. She is very rich and quite impersonal about her . . . requirements. When she arrives here she will usually have a personal maid with her, never the same one. Girls of a certain type. Bovine, Nordic, bursting with health, quite young, tailored drab uniforms, terribly submissive and polite and humble. Northern Europeans. I suppose it is a great deal more efficient and less wearing than forming emotional attachments, and of course she can afford it without pain. I must say I did get a certain dirty satisfaction out of hearing how distressed she was, and realizing she is just as human and vulnerable as the rest of us. My hands are getting awfully numb. And poor David is in misery. And I have told you the whole thing."

I looked over at Meyer. He had several small purple knuckle-lumps on his forehead. "Do you buy it?" I asked him.

"I buy it."

"How terribly kind!" Bruce said acidly.

"Meyer, I would not like to untie him and have him start making out like we are pine boards and cinder blocks and going into that yelling and grunting bit. So why don't you just take that same walk again, and take a cab from the square to the hotel, and if I'm not there by the time you think I should be . . ."

So I gave him five minutes and then untied Bruce. He flexed his hands and went at once to David, turned and asked me where my car was and would I please bring it to the front.

They sat in the back. I heard Bruce coaching him in what to say at the hospital. Bruce told me the turns to take. They talked in low tones. I heard Bruce say at one point, "But *really!* Somebody is going to have to wait on you hand and foot, and shouldn't I have that right? Besides, Davey, it was all settled, wasn't it? And your things are at my place, aren't they? Be *practical,* darling!"

They got out. Bruce said he could manage from there on, thank you. He gave me an absent nod, and walked David slowly toward the ambulance entrance.

I managed to get lost and end up back in town rather than out on the Mitla Road. I got lost because my mind was too busy trying to make order out of too many fragments. I went up the hotel hill and around past the lobby entrance and down the cobblestone drive to the cottage carport.

Meyer hadn't left any lights on. I stumbled on the steps to the front porch of the cottage, and I heard the legs of the metal porch chair scrape on the cement as he moved. I groped for the other chair and sat down, feeling a few twinges from the tumble along the tile, and wondering if they would turn into morning aches.

"Hoo, boy," I said. "Dandy little village they've got here. These sweet kindly folk tear me up, they really do. I'm even beginning to wonder about Enelio Fuentes. He'll probably turn out to be a retired female wrestler going around in drag."

"Near fear," said Lady Becky from the neighboring chair. "Enelio is *muy hombre*. I can so certify."

"How the hell did *you* get here?"

"That's what I like, dearest. A warm welcome."

"Where is Meyer?"

"He's really a dear man. Did you know that? Oh, I packed him off. I expect he's settling down for the night in one of the cottages. Things are thinning out, you know. We had a nice little visit, and he went puddling off carrying his little kit. He's marvelously tactful and understanding."

"And treacherous."

"I was driving around and about looking for you, darling, and saw him walking toward the zocalo, so I gave him a lift back here. Thought you might spot my car and turn into a ninny and drive away again. So I parked it discreetly. Travis dear, such a lot of nuisance and nonsense for you to hammer poor Bruce about. All you had to do was come to me. I should have told you all the rest of it."

"If I lived long enough to hear it all."

"But darling, you'll want to hear it from me too, to see if it all matches up, won't you? So doesn't it come out to the same thing? You *do* struggle so. One would think I was quite sickeningly ugly or a horrid bore."

"If you would kindly be ugly or boring, I would be very grateful."

"But I shall be both soon enough! Any day now one ghastly wrinkle will appear, and all of a sudden I shall be . . . Doriana Gray? Or like that carriage one of your sentimental poets wrote about. Quite suddenly I shall dwindle into a scruffy little old lady in tennis shoes, peering through bifocals, fussing with her hearing aid, who, in a quavery little old voice, will bore everyone with her memories of lovemaking. I am here because I forgave you."

"Thank you very much, Lady Rebecca. But you see, I wrote you down in one of the pages of my life, and now the pages have been turned, and we cannot go back and reread them because . . . because . . ."

"Because the book is very long and life is very short. Nice try, ducks. But *I* did the writing, and all I wrote was a preface. I told you. I was being a horrible show-offy person. I shan't be like that at all. Promise. Besides, you would be cheating me dreadfully. I granted myself a few little moments of climax, dear, but then I nipped the poor struggling things in the bud because, should I let one get truly started, it goes on and on and on, quite unendurably. It is so terribly lasting and intense and exhausting that I have to ration myself carefully. Even so, I go dragging about for days, looking quite puffy and done in. It would be wicked at this stage to deprive me."

I stood up slowly and made a wide circuit of her chair to reach the door. "It may be wicked, Becky. It may be unforgivable. It might even be a shocking lack of courtesy. But I am going to deprive the hell out of both of us, and I am going to get a long night's sleep, alone. Sorry about your pride and all that. Someday I may think back and kick myself. Sorry. Go drive that bubblegum car home. Good night, Lady Rebecca. Bug off, please."

I opened the screen door and reached in and found the switches for the room lights and porch lights and clicked everything on. She stood up and turned to face me, eyes sparkling green through the sheepdog ruff, mouth broadened in a delighted bawdy grin.

"You know, I *thought* you might be stuffy and standoffish and difficult. So one does what one can to make it a *fait accompli*, what?"

She wore a wine red hotel blanket gathered closely around her. She laughed and said, "It would take you *hours* to find where I hid my clothing, dearest."

She dropped the blanket to the porch floor. "What is that quaint Americanism you people use? Peekaboob?"

I flapped a weak and frantic hand at the switches until I hit them back the way they were and we were in darkness. Well, shucks. And puh-shaw, fellas.

"That's right," I said, as she found me, locked on, and strained close. "Exactly right. Peekaboob. Very quaint old saying."

10

I SAT out on the cottage porch in the Sunday-morning clang-bang on the church bells and rooster announcements. Blue-gray smoke of breakfast fires hazed the morning bowl of the city.

Meyer came tentatively around the corner and looked up at me on the porch. Dopp-kit dangled from one hairy finger.

"Yoo-hoo," he said.

"Yoo-hoo to you, too, my good man."

"I didn't see her car, so I thought . . ."

"Come on up. You live here, Meyer. Remember?" So he came up onto the porch, started to say something, and changed his mind and went silently into the cottage. He came out in a few minutes and sat in the other chair.

"McGee, I thought that you had gotten back and somehow managed to send her on her way, implausible as that may seem. But I can see from the . . . the wear and tear . . . that she stayed for a while."

"She went tottering out of here about forty minutes ago, Meyer. She claimed she could walk to her car unaided."

"But . . . how do *you* feel?"

"Vibrant, alive, regenerated, recharged."

"I . . . I'm sorry I let her talk me into moving out for the night, Travis. But I guess you know you can't argue with that woman. She doesn't listen. And after all, it was your personal problem and—"

"Stop apologizing, my good man. No trouble at all. Quite a pleasant night. Active, but pleasant. Now if you would pick me up and take me up to breakfast, we can begin the long day."

We went back to Los Pájaros Trailer Park. The office and store were closed and locked. We left the rented car outside the gates and walked in. In the space numbered twenty, a Land Rover was parked under a tree with dusty leaves, near the travel trailer of Mr. and Mrs. Benjamin Knighton. The Rover was battleship gray, dusty and road-worn, with tools and gas cans strapped aboard.

He was sitting at an old table, typing with two fingers at respect-able speed, apparently copying from yellow handwritten sheets. She was hanging some khaki shirts on a line to dry. They could have been brother and sister, slat-thin young people, deeply sun-weathered, small statured, with colorless eyes, mouse hair, that elu-sive pinched and underprivileged look around the mouth that seems typical of slum people, swamp people, coal mine people, and moun-tain people. He wore steel-rimmed glasses, and she had a plastic clothespin in her mouth.

"Good morning!" I said.

He took off the glasses and she took out the clothespin. "Howdy," he said, in a voice more appropriate to a seven foot cowboy. "'Morn-ing," she murmured.

"Sorry to bother you. My name is Travis McGee. This is my friend Meyer. The manager said you were acquainted with a man who stayed here for a while, right over there in number seventeen. His name is Rockland."

"Why do you want to talk to me about him?"

"I thought you might have some information that would help us locate him, Mr. Knighton."

"Why do you want to find him?"

"To ask him about a girl who came into Mexico with him."

"Afraid you're wasting time, Mister McGee, covering ground al-ready covered. I think he should have told you he was already here over two weeks ago."

"Who was here?"

"That girl's father. What was his name, hon?"

"McLeen," she answered softly.

"This isn't about the McLeen girl. This is the girl we're asking about." I moved over to the table and handed him the picture.

He looked at it, tilting his head, squinting one eye. "I don't want to tell you something that isn't true. Maybe could you tell me this one's name?"

"Bowie. Beatrice Bowie. She was called Bix."

He was quick. "*Was* called. Then I wouldn't be breaking news, would I? You know she's dead."

"Yes."

"But you want to ask about her? You related to her?"

"No. Friends of her father. He's unable to travel. He wants to know what things were like for her down here, before she died. They were out of touch."

His wife had hung up the shirts. She came over to the table to look at the photograph. "Never knew she'd been such a pretty one," said Mrs. Knighton.

"We don't want to interrupt your work," Meyer said.

Knighton studied us in turn. He shrugged and stood up, hand out. "I'm Ben. This here is Laura. Hon, you want to bring us out some of that coffee?"

"Surely," she said. "We take it black with a little sugar." We both nodded acceptance, and she responded with a thin smile and went into the travel trailer. The three of us moved over to the cement picnic table and benches that were, with the fireplace, part of the permanent installation at each site.

"Set," Ben Knighton said. His wife brought coffee, poured it and sat with us. They were comfortable people. He explained that he was on a sabbatical year from Texas Central University, and it was nearly over, and they had to leave in a few days.

He was obviously fond of young people, and he was also well acquainted with the drug scene on campus. It was natural that they would be curious about the five young people who had arrived in the camper back in April.

"Some of them dabble a little, without knowing the least damn thing about what the direct effects and the side effects might be. And some of them turn into heavy users. So you give them what help you can, what help they'll take from you. After a while you learn the categories. There's the predators who get their kicks out of turning the weaker kids on and taking monetary advantage or sexual advantage of them, or both. And some of the kids are such victims natural born, they seem to be looking for their personal predator. You can tell when a kid is so susceptible he is too far gone before you can manage to get to him. There's a faculty expression. D.T.O.D. Down The Old Drain. Black humor, but so true. They slip through your fingers. I watched them, those five. Rocko is a predator, and one merciless son of a bitch."

"Ben!" she said.

He smiled at her. "Honey, I've been writing this novel for a year. I have to talk like a novelist, don't I?"

"But you don't have to sound like the dean of men."

"Rocko seemed clean as far as I could tell. He hit the bottle sometimes, which is a good indication he was clean. And he is one mean drunk. Jerry, the one with the black beard, I'd label a semi-predator. He was on something, and getting closer to getting hooked on it every week. That's the way the predators turn into victims. The guitar player, Carl, was already way down the old drain. The blond girl, Bix, didn't look much like her picture any more. She wasn't too many steps behind Carl. The McLeen girl seemed to be on stimulants of some kind. She was burning herself up."

Mrs. Knighton shuddered. "That Carl used to sit over there under that tree and think he was playing a guitar. But there weren't any strings on it. And when the wind was from that direction, you could hear his long dirty fingernails rattling on the wood where the strings should have been."

"Cats tire of crippled mice that can't scamper any more," Ben said. "Sessions left, and then one day the girls were gone. But there was a fresh supply available in town and they used to bring them back. They'd stay three or four days sometimes and then they'd leave. Rocko and Jerry weren't a pair anybody'd want a permanent home with. Rocko was mostly bluff though. See those two tanks fastened there to the yoke of our house trailer? Gas tanks. Cooking gas. Twenty gallons each. That camper had been jacked off the truck and was on blocks. One day after Jerry had left, too, and Rocko was there alone, he drove back from town and found out somebody had pried open a little locked hatch in the back of the camper and stolen his bottled gas. He went storming around to all the sites, fussing about whether anybody saw the theft. He came over here, ugly, loud and mean. I was adjusting the fan belt on the Rover. I kept working and told him I didn't know a thing about it. I guess he thought I should stand at attention when spoken to. So he grabbed my shoulder and pulled me up and spun me around, and I came right around with the lug wrench I was using, and rang it off the top of his skull."

"Ben doesn't like people grabbing hold of him," Mrs. Knighton explained with a little air of pride.

"He walked back on his heels with his hands clapped on top of his head. Then he shook himself like a wet dog, and I knew from his eyes he was going to make a try for me, so I walked into him while he was getting organized and popped him again the same way but harder. He went down onto one knee and I told him to stay off my site from then on. I could tell from his color it had made him sick to his stomach. He looked at me and knew I meant it. He went away and I went back to tightening the nuts under the hood. Then he pulled out about two weeks later because Tomas wouldn't rent to him for another month."

"How bad off was the Bowie girl?" Meyer asked him.

"Bad. Passive, dirty, confused. Disoriented."

Laura Knighton said, "She seemed withdrawn and full and listless. Stringy hair and a puffy face and bad color. I'd say she looked fifteen years older than that picture you've got. One of the retired couples hitched up and moved out because of her. She had . . . a habit they didn't take to."

"Don't get so fastidious, darling, nobody knows what you're trying to say. If that girl was walking slowly across that site over there and had an urge to pee, she'd pull up her skirt and squat wherever she was, unconscious as a dog in a cemetery."

"Then," said Laura, "there was that one day she had a blouse on and forgot her skirt or pants or whatever she was going to wear. And the little dark girl came running out and got her by the hand and tugged her back and got her inside and got her dressed the rest of the way. The poor lost thing is dead now, and I can't help saying it. I think it's for the best, just as I think the guitar player is better off dead, no matter what sorrow his folks may be feeling for him. They'd have no way of knowing how bad off he got toward the end."

I said, "It would be a help if you knew how we could locate any of the others, Rocko or Jerry or Miss McLeen."

"I wish we could help you," Ben said.

"I *did* see that truck and camper that day, dear," she said.

"You *maybe* saw a blue truck with an aluminum camper body."

"That is *exactly* what I saw!"

He went into the trailer and brought out a large map of the State of Oaxaca, and also brought along his work journal to pin down the date. In one part of the historical novel he was finishing, a young Mixtec priest from Mitla flees all the way down the long slope of the Sierra Madre del Sur to the Pacific coast a hundred and fifty miles away. He had decided the imaginary priests would follow the dry bed of the Rio Miahuatlán, and so on Tuesday, August 5th, over three weeks ago, they had driven the Rover south along the road to Puerto Angel as far as Ocotlán, and then headed east on a road that was barely more than a dusty trace. Where it was blocked by a rock fall, they had gone ahead on foot. They had climbed a ledge and surveyed the country to the east with a pair of seven power binoculars. When he had gone wandering off, she had picked up a dust swirl far to the east, appearing and disappearing across rolling country. She had steadied the glasses and identified it as a blue truck with an aluminum truck body or camper on it.

"I was terribly curious about it because it was going so *fast*," she explained earnestly. "Mexicans will drive like maniacs on paved roads, but when they get onto dirt roads they positively creep, because if they break springs or anything in the holes or on the rocks it is so terribly expensive to replace them. And tourists in this country drive very carefully when they get off the paved roads. And anyway, what would there be over there to attract a tourist. I mean it was just so unusual I was interested and I wondered about it. I decided the driver was drunk or it was some terrible emergency."

He showed us on the map about where the road had to be, but there was not even a dotted line on the map. It had been headed south, Mrs. Knighton said. It had to be some road that turned south off 190 somewhere beyond Mitla, maybe as far as the village of Totolapán. Distances, he said, were very deceptive in the dry, high air. "But the chance of it being Rockland?" He shrugged.

We thanked them for the good coffee and the talk. He talked a little bit about his book. We wished him luck.

As we walked out, Tomas, the manager, was unlocking the store and the office. He was delighted to serve us by looking up the date he had copied from the vehicle papers on Rockland's truck. Yes indeed, the permit had been issued at Nogales on April 10th, and was thus good for yet another month and a half.

As we drove away Meyer made listless agreement with my observation that the Knightons seemed like nice people. He seemed dejected. I knew what was wrong with him. The picture they had given us of Bix Bowie had been vivid, ugly, and depressing. I could not get him to talk. He did not feel like going to Mitla to look for Jerry Nesta. He seemed to want to go back to the cottage at the Victoria, so I skirted the center of town, drove up there. He plumped himself into a porch chair, sighing. I put on swim pants and walked up through the noon sun and swam slow lengths of the big handsome pool, staying out of the way of the young'uns who came squealing down off the diving tower. I dried off in the sun on a towel spread on the fitted stones of the poolside paving. The high altitude sun had a deep stinging bite to it that went all the way down through all the old layers of Gulfstream tan.

I opened small gates and let the immediate sensory memories of Becky flow into my mind. By rights I should have felt even more surfeited and exhausted than before. But though this weariness was deep, it seemed more gentle, with a spice of male arrogance, of satisfaction, of knowledge of satisfaction given in full measure.

She had been simpler, softer, more feminine somehow. She had been involved more with herself and her own reactions and timings. Before, we had used me, and at last in a final full measure which had been, she said, more than she had wanted to spend.

Later we had talked in a sleepy way of half sentences, and the sound of her shower had awakened me. I slept again, and was awakened by the kiss that was good morning and good-by, sat up to see her standing tall and smiling nicely, dressed in orange linen, white leather hatbox in her hand.

"You were very wicked, darling. I am utter ruin. It will take a week to mend my puffy old face. But I feel buttery delicious. And you are very dear. Afterward, remember, we chuckled together at nothing. Just at feeling nice. That is rare and *very* nice."

"And now you turn the page, Becky?"

"Yes. But I shall turn the corner down. One of the special pages that I go back and look at sometimes. Take good care, lamb."

When she got to the door I said, "You are . . ."

She turned, waiting for the rest of it. "Yes?"

But how to tell her she had achieved her aim in life? And wouldn't she be aware of it anyway? "You are completely Becky."

"Hmm. Rather nice that. Some are totally barmy. And I am completely Becky. Really no other way to say it, is there? Keep well, luv." She waggled her fingers at me, slammed the door smartly, and soon thereafter rammed the Lotus up the slope with thunderous verve.

I walked back to the cottage. Meyer said, "Would it be possible for you to stop smirking?"

"You have a foul manner today, Meyer."

"Let's give up on the whole thing, Trav. What the hell good are we doing? We can't tell Harl any of this. She was on a gay adventure, full of plans and excitement and fun. Until the tragic accident. Let's rehearse it. I don't want to know any more about it. I *knew* that girl. She was a quiet, calm, decent kid. So she tripped and fell into this damned septic tank, and we don't have to follow her any further into it, do we?"

"Can I tell you one thing I want to know?"

"You get compulsive about these things."

"The sergeant found a boy who saw a man that afternoon back up in those mountains with Bix. Everything we've learned thus far tells us she was in no shape to drive down a six-lane highway across Kansas at high noon. But somebody let her bring a car down that mountain, or try to, at dusk. Is it any different than pushing her off a bridge? And with Harl, which would fester the longest—pure accident, self-destruction, or contrived murder. I think it's something we ought to know before we leave this place."

I watched him work it out. Finally he grunted and rubbed his eyes.

"So, I won't get off just yet. I'll ride to the next stop. But I don't think I'll like it any better than the whole ride up till now."

11

AFTER a hotel lunch, a few miles out of the city on the Mitla road we came upon El Tule, and Meyer said that he wanted to be a tourist for a few minutes, and look at the biggest tree in the world.

It was not far from the highway, a hundred yards perhaps. It dwarfed the old church nearby. I was astonished to see how rich and vital and green it was. Seemed to be of the banyan family. Elephant-gray bark. Glossy dark leaves. There was a low iron fence all the way around it. The trunk was maybe a hundred and fifty feet in circumference. It made better than an acre of shade.

Meyer stood absolutely still, staring up into the cool green shadowy places beyond the giant lower limbs. When he turned smiling toward me, I knew that the tree had restored his nerves and composure.

"At the time of Christ," he said, "nobody was giving this tree a second look. It was just an ordinary little tree."

"It looks as if it has decided to stay around awhile."

"And I am going to come back here," he said, "and I am going to paint myself blue, and I am going to live up there in the top of that tree forever."

"Come on, Meyer. Ya vamonos."

The knowledge of the huge black beard on Jerome Nesta simplified the search.

"*El americano con una barba negra y grande. Un escultor.*"

Ah, yes. I have seen him. Yes, he goes often to the ruins. Also to the Museo de Arte Zapoteca, near the plaza and central market. No, I do not know where he lives.

We found an American student at the small museum. He was an exchange student working on the continuing excavation and restoration program at the Mitla ruins. His name was Burt Koontz, and he was out in the rear courtyard, carefully washing and brushing the fragile shards of an old broken vase. He was burned to the rough red shade of roof tiles. He wore a white T-shirt, khaki shorts, and G.I. boots.

"I know Jerry. I mean as much as I guess you can get to know him. They let him come in and make sketches. He's been sketching some of the old stone heads. I haven't seen him around the last few days though. Maybe even a week. I couldn't say for sure."

He told us, as he worked, that he had been curious about Nesta. He was big and he moved carefully, as if he were convalescing from a serious illness. A Mexican girl always came with him. Young, but not pretty. One of those broad stocky ones with the same kind of Indio face you see in the old carvings. She would sit with infinite patience under one of the trees and wait for him, then get up when he came out, and follow him, a few steps behind, usually carrying one of those baskets they take to the market.

He had the impression that Nesta was living over toward the south side of town, up one of those steep dirt streets to the left of the main road as you come in.

So Meyer and I trudged up and down a lot of steep little streets, and met with varying degrees of suspicion, indifference, and secret amusement. But with the help of pesos and persistence, we finally found the place, on Calle Alivera, halfway up the hill. There was a pink house that seemed to be crumbling away. There was a walled courtyard with a broken gate. In the courtyard were mounds of litter, a couple of dozen small noisy children, and some women squatting around a pump, several of them nursing the future members of the gang.

We had a twelve-year-old businessman who led us across to a room in a far corner with a door that opened onto the roofed gallery that extended along the side of the courtyard. It was a dark little room. There was a cement and plaster fireplace-stove built into one corner. There was a raised platform along the opposite wall, where pallets could be placed for sleeping. The little room was entirely empty. I could not get it through the boy's head that I wanted him to speak slowly and clearly. So I had to make him repeat everything over and over until I thought I had the general idea.

The wife of the Americano was Luz. They had lived here many weeks. Then they had gone away. Three days ago. Four. Maybe they were married, maybe not. It was the same. They were poor. For marriage the priests and the government charge too much money, so one waits. The Americano had little Spanish. Luz had been married to a baker and had three sons. The baker and the three sons had died of enormous pain in the belly. Luz had the pain but had not died. The Americano seemed often sick. The room was five pesos a week. Maybe the Americano had sold his . . . I could not understand what it was that Nesta was supposed to have sold. He said it so many times he was getting discouraged and angry before I caught on. It was a gigantic head made of wood, taller than a man. The señor worked on it each day. It was a very curious thing. It was very ugly.

As near as I could tell, the giant head had been carried away by the señor and another big Americano, with great difficulty. And the tools and the cooking pots and the clothing and the beds. They all went away in a heap-di-row. In a what? Heap-di-row. What? Heap-di-row! Again, please? Heap-di-row! Heap-di-row!

He was close to tears with frustration. So I brightened his face with pesos. Once again as we crossed the courtyard the children fell silent, stopped all movement, and stared at us. The women pulled the edges of serapes together to hide the sleepy suck of small mouths.

And then, twenty-four miles back to Oaxaca, feeling glazed and unreal. When you stack into one day the biggest old tree in the world, a gigantic ugly wooden head, a magical disappearance in a heap-di-row, and a page with the corner turned down in the Book of Becky, it is time to start searching the hedgerows for Alice and that well-known rabbit.

I had been counting on a therapeutic Sunday siesta, one which might have lasted right through to Monday breakfast. But when we got back to the hotel, there was a message to call Enelio Fuentes and a number where he could be reached. He was at a party at something that sounded less than interesting, called the Commercial Club. I tried to beg off but he insisted. It was atop a great big new farm equipment agency building set back off the Oaxaca-Puebla highway a mile or so beyond the city limits. He had said to drive around in back and go up the stairs in back. The cars were varied and impressive, parked back there.

When we walked out onto the gigantic roof, I saw why he had insisted. That part of it was called the Beach Club. There was a gigantic swimming pool with some kind of infernal device that created pretty good waves which broke on a realistic slope of sand beach. The high wall beyond the pool was painted to resemble a seascape. There were areas of lawn, small trees, fountains, cement sculpture, big bright beach umbrellas. There were several bars, and there were waiters in red coats, and there was a good trio working hard in the waning day. There were tennis courts and badminton courts, and the whole happy busy place was aswarm with jolly tanned Mexican businessmen with the same stamp of success as Enelio, but generally smaller and heavier, and the entire scene was bubbling and dancing with platoons of the vivid young girls that Enelio variously described as either cheeklets or crumpets. There seemed to be a difference, but I could not identify it.

"Just a simple, warm, primitive people," Meyer muttered.

Enelio found us and took us to his table. He had been playing tennis. Pretty soon he would change. He recommended the tall sour rum drink he was having. He said, "An old friend, Ramón, he put up this dull building here, and one day we realize here is the hell of a big roof, and we can have the storage floor underneath too. So we made the initiation big, and big dues, because where else can they go, and we brought down a crazy man from Mexico City, told him to go ahead, make a place to have fun. Three million pesos! By God, you find out everybody uses the club to get back the fun for the money. Hey now, over here, you *pollitas*. These soaking wet crumpets, they are here on vacation from Guadalajara. This one, she is Lita, short for Carmelita, and has very little English so she is with me, okay? And these two here in pink, they are the sisters del Vega, the tall one Elena, the not so tall one Margarita. Darlings, this big ogly one is Señor Travis McGee, and this round hairy one is Meyer. They are my friends, so they are evil dangerous fellows, eh? Now we sit. Elena, you are to be with this McGee, and Margarita, here, dear, between me and Meyer. Now smile and greet my friends."

Elena was spectacular. "Yam ver' please to knowing you, Meester McGee," she said with a five hundred watt smile.

"You will have one little drink with us now, and then you will run away and play in the pool, while we make man talk, and we will summon you when we want you back. Waiter! And you will not make friends with any sly fellows or never, never, never again will Enelio Fuentes fly his little airplane to Guadalajara and bring you here for such a nice vacation from that insurance company office."

They had their drink, and they giggled, and then they went trotting off in their little sopping bikinis back to the artificial waves breaking on the artificial beach.

So we gave Enelio the full report of our activities. Meyer and I took turns filling him in on the details. He was particularly interested in the information about the truck being seen by Mrs. Knighton, heading south on a distant road at high speed.

"Yes, it fits the time," he said. "It is taken from Bundy's place before dawn on the fifth, that same day. Tuesday. I know those little roads. I used to hunt there. I used to kill small things in that burned country. One day I said, Who are you, Fuentes, killing things that breathe the same air, walk the same earth? What gives you the right? Who said you are more important, and other life is just for your sport? So I stopped. No matter. Those roads do not go to anyplace. Interesting. I think it would be nice, we go down there in my jeep. Not tomorrow. Some damn engineers are coming in to spoil my day. Tuesday, eh? Maybe in the morning. I will phone to you. Now I am wondering what things can be true and maybe not so true in the story Bundy tells you. I think you were great fools to do what you did, but it worked, eh? A man like that, it is easy for him to twist things a little, change things a little, the way a woman can do."

I said, "It's exactly the same story he told Lady Becky."

He looked puzzled. "But, my friend, I do not understand. You talked with Becky *before* you got all the story from Bruce."

"Well . . . I talked to her last night again."

"You are some kind of man to go visiting Becky again."

"Well . . . she visited me. By the time I got back from the hospital, she was at the cottage and Meyer was gone. Nice fellow when you get to know him, this Meyer."

He shook his head slowly and then he began to grin. "Oh boy. And how did you feel when you meet Elena, eh? Strong, young, handsome girl, eh? Look, I am not the kind of man who hands you out a sure-thing cheeklet, man. Just only a nice girl who if she decides she likes you, and if you make the struggle to be nice to her, then there she is, without teasing. Oh boy. One time in California on television I saw a contest, many men at tables eating apple pies as fast as they could. An ugly scene, truly. The winner, I don't know, eight or nine whole pies maybe. He walks careful. When he is getting the prize, the poor fellow looks sick. So here you are, McGee. You win the contest. So here I come with your prize, eh? Know what it is? Piece of apple pie. This is very, very fonny."

"Look at McGee chortling," Meyer said.

"Pretty girls are nice to be with," I said. "You are a very considerate man, Enelio. We will have drinks and we will have dinner, and they will brighten the table and the hours. And I will make excuses and slip away and you two can work things out."

"Just a minute!" Meyer said. "That girl is just a child!"

Enelio and I agreed she looked grown up. We reconfirmed the Tuesday date. Enelio went to shower and change, and when he came back the Guadalajara girls were with us, and Margarita was studying Meyer's palm and telling his fortune, and Meyer, so help me, was blushing.

So off went the girls from Guadalajara and they came back in their vivid little shifts and high-heeled sandals and with their big handbags and fun-sparkle eyes, all golden sun-glowing in the blue dusk under the festive lights strung across the roofed dining areas and umbrellaed bar areas. The trio had become a quartet with the addition of a muted trumpet of great clarity and passion, and they played a lot of Augustin Larra's romantic ballads. Meyer was the light-footed tireless dancing bear, and Enelio Fuentes was the good and amusing host. The world of Bundy, of Rockland, of Carl's stringless guitar, of plane tickets to Oklahoma City that Meyer had arranged in the early morning—all were far from the elegant roof where they had stopped the wavemaking machine and the colors of the lights stripped the still water of the giant pool.

I, too, had my fortune told. Elena studied for a long time, biting at her lip, and then looked at me, head cocked to the side, unexpectedly solemn.

"I do not know how to say. Bad things happening. You are smile but you are sad. It is a . . . a evil time for you in your lifetime, Trrrravis."

12

Monday was hiatus. A quiet day, useful as a compress on an ugly bruise. Meyer was up early by prearrangement and braved the traffic in our rental to go down to the Hotel Marqués del Valle and pick up Lita, Elena, and Margarita, who were staying there, and take them all the way out to visit the ruins at Mitla, stopping on the way to admire, once again, the great tree in which he had vowed he would one day live.

I slept so deeply that when I awoke I had that rare and strange feeling of not only being unable to figure out where I was, or what month and year it was, but even who I was. The dregs of dreams were all of childhood, and in the morning mirror I looked at the raw, gaunt, knobbly stranger, at the weals and the pits and the white tracks of scar tissue across the deepwater brown of the leathery useful body, and marveled that childhood should turn into this—into the pale-eyed, scruff-headed, bony stranger who looked so lazily competent, yet, on the inside, felt such frequent waves of *Weltschmerz,* of lingering nostalgia for the lives he had never lived.

After long showering, I went up the hill and sat out on the high deck of the hotel and ate enough breakfast for any three people, then sat in delightful digestive stupor, making the pots of coffee last. When I began to wonder how the waiters would react if I went over and did a handstand on the wide cement railing, I realized that I felt very, very good indeed, felt better than I deserved to feel, felt as if I had a sudden dividend of youth, available for the misspending. Then I decided, for like the ten thousandth time, that I was one rotten contradictory fellow, that my talent for dissipation should have long since turned me into a slack, wheezing, puffy ruin, had it not been combined with that iron Calvinistic conscience which, upon noting too much progressive decay, would drive me into the kind of training the decathlon boys seem to enjoy, punishing myself back into the kind of fitness that makes you feel as if no maniac could dent you with a sledge hammer.

Meyer arrived at one-thirty with the three crumpets, complete with swim togs. While they changed in our cottage, he explained to me that a crumpet was a cheeklet with a warm muffiny heart, whereas a cheeklet was a crumpet with a talent for creating special problems. I told him that was worth knowing, certainly. He told me his tree was fine, and he had driven with raceway verve, and he could understand why the Mixtecs took Mitla away from the Zapotecs. He said that he had checked with the girl at the hotel, and that the redhead had picked up the two tickets and had made the flight.

We lolled the long afternoon, with sunshine, hamburgers, beers, and pleasant, sidelong, inconspicuous admiration of the tender textures of the maidens of Guadalajara. Enelio arrived at rum-time, full of such fury at the arrogance and ignorance of visiting engineers that he had to swim a dozen thrashing laps before he could get the scowl off his forehead. Before he left, taking Lita with him, he brought a map from his car to the lighted cottage and spread it out and showed me, by drawing a pencil line, the road which the Chevy truck had probably been on when Laura Knighton had seen it.

On Tuesday morning at a little before eleven, Meyer and I were standing out in front of the lobby entrance to the Victoria when Enelio, in a yellow jeep, came roaring in low gear up the steep hotel driveway. It was the earliest he could get away from the agency. Enelio looked very elegant and dashing in his white-hunter hat. He came to a flashing grinning stop within a few feet of us. The jeep had those special fat low-pressure tires useful for traversing open country full of stone and sand.

As we clambered in, two little Mexican boys who had been vigorously rubbing a tourist sedan with greasy rags came trotting over to examine the vehicle with their quick, bright obsidian eyes. They looked at the gas can racks and the power takeoff winch and the big spotlight.

One asked the other one a question, and got the authoritative answer, in the slightly contemptuous tone of all authority, "*Es un heep especial, seguro.*"

Enelio spun it in a tight turn and went charging down the hill. He stopped at the bottom to wait for truck traffic on the highway. The word had been echoing in my head.

"Wait a minute," I said. "Please wait right here a minute."

Enelio turned and looked back at me. "Forget something?"

"Remember something. Any 'j' is pronounced like any 'h'. Jalisco. Jugar. And so, by God, we are riding in a heep."

"Very fonny joke. But very old," Enelio said.

"I know what he's getting at," Meyer said. "That kid at Mitla. You couldn't understand that thing he was saying."

"Heap-di-row. Jeep de rojo. Jeep de color rojo."

"Yes indeed," said Enelio. "A red jeep. And this is a yellow one. Is the game over?"

Meyer had hitched almost all the way around so as to look directly at me. "A painter and a sculptor. Why not? What's Mike's last name? Barrington?"

"And Della Davis."

"Too much sun at this altitude," Enelio said, "and the brain gets cooked and people don't make sense."

"Enelio, what's the name of the road toward the airport?"

"The Coyotepec Road."

"And about a mile out, is there some kind of a tourist place that burned?"

"I know the place. It burned a long time ago."

"Can we go out there?" I asked. "I want to check something out."

I leaned forward and hollered the explanations over the wind roar and tire whine as Enelio pushed the jeep hard.

The place had been surrounded by a thick high adobe wall, enclosing about an acre of land. There were shade trees inside and outside the wall, but the land around it was bare and flat, and planted with parched and scraggly corn. Over the wall, which began back about a hundred yards from the highway, I could see the broken and sooty stone walls of the structure, open to the sky, with an angle of charred, leaning beam that had rank green vines clinging to it. The old red jeep was parked close to the wall over at the left, under the shade trees. Several little groups of people sat and squatted in the shade, at respectful distances, looking toward the wall. Two police cars were parked with their noses toward the red jeep, and at an angle to each other, as though snuffing it.

"Something bad is going on here," Enelio said. "Those are people who have stopped working the fields to come and wait and watch.

They don't do that for a small thing. Something very bad, I think."

Both doors of the entrance gate in the side wall stood open. A very shiny black Mercedes sedan was parked inside the compound. An adobe cottage was built into the corner of the compound, so that the encircling wall formed two walls of the cottage. Two wooden sheds had been attached to it, one on either side, braced against the wall.

A big young man sat in the sunlight on a scarred wooden bench. He was hunched forward, elbows on his knees, face in his hands, shoulders thrust high. He wore dirty gray denim work pants and a clean white shirt. He was barefoot. The fringe of a huge glossy black beard curled inward around the edges of the hands he held against his face. A bald man in a black suit was standing in front of him. Three uniformed policemen stood off to one side. Our acquaintance, Sergeant Martinez, in civilian clothes, stood a couple of paces behind the bald man.

All except the man on the bench looked toward us as we came through the open gate. I saw a startled look cross the sergeant's face, immediately replaced by that cop look I had seen before, but this time considerably reinforced by this new coincidence.

The bald man said, "Enelio! Using you for speaking here, maybe?"

He came several steps to meet us. Enelio introduced us to Doctor Francisco Martel and then the doctor launched into such rapid Spanish I gave up trying to catch the meaning of any part of it. He did much gesturing and pointing, and spoke with dramatic emphasis. The sergeant joined them and there was discussion for a time, then Enelio came and told us what had happened.

An hour ago a man had run out and waved a city-bound bus down and told the driver people were dying behind the wall. The driver stopped at the first telephone and reported it. The police sedan had arrived just before the ambulance. The young black girl was just inside the gate, sprawled in the dust, killed with a single blow that had apparently come from behind, and had so ruined her skull that brain tissue had made a spatter pattern in the dust. The big blond bearded American youth had been over beyond the shed, the whole upper left side of his forehead smashed inward. There was a heartbeat but it had stopped before they could load him into the ambulance. Near him lay the Mexican woman, dead of a similar single stupendous blow over the left ear, eyes bulged and staring by the force of the hydraulic pressure created within the brain case. And the black-bearded one was sitting on the ground with her head in his lap, weeping. He claimed he had arrived minutes before the police, and found them like that.

"Have they identified him?"

The sergeant brought the tourist card over. It was sweat-stained and dog-eared. The ink on the signature had run. He was Jerome Nesta. Enelio said, "Martinez knows he's guilty of being in Mexico illegally. The card has run out. Guilty of one thing, guilty of everything. That's how the official mind works, eh? So I have the permission to ask some questions. Come listen. Maybe you two think of some, help me out a little."

Enelio sat on his heels in front of Nesta. "Jerry?" he said softly. "Hey, you. Jerry!"

The head lifted from the hands. The eyes did not match the virility and vitality of the great black beard. They were gray-blue, hesitant, uncertain. And reddened by tears.

"How you making, boy?" Enelio asked.

"All . . . all three of them. Jesus! All three of them. I just can't start to believe it's true."

"Who did it, Jerry?"

"I don't *know!* There wasn't anybody here. I didn't see anybody. I came in, calling Della on account of I wanted to know where to put the stuff."

"What stuff?"

"The stuff I brought back from town. It was my turn to go in. Nobody felt like coming along. Luz was doing washing, and Mike was going on a painting, and Della had a headache."

"You drove the jeep to town?"

"Yes, sir."

"What time did you leave here?"

"I don't know. Maybe a little before ten. I bought fruit and radishes and beans, and a kilo of masa for Luz to make tortillas. I guess I was gone most of an hour probably."

"How soon after you got back did the police come?"

"I don't know. Like two minutes."

"Jerry, can you think of any way we could pin it down, what time you got back here, man?"

"I don't know how I can."

Enelio got up and went over and spoke to the doctor for a little while. They walked over near one of the sheds and the doctor indicated a dark stain on the dust and stones. Enelio came back and sat on the bench beside Nesta. "Did you see anything unusual or hear anything unusual on your way out of town or on the highway?"

"I can't remember anything."

"Nothing interesting at all?"

"Oh, wait a minute. There was something. Right near the edge of town, where the railroad tracks are, there was an old truck pulled over and the engine was on fire, and people were running around yelling, and they were throwing dirt on it and a man beating at it with a blanket."

Enelio said, "You are one lucky fellow. The cops saw it too and stopped for a minute. They were just putting the fire out. So they were, like you said, a minute or two behind you."

"What difference does it make?"

"This wasn't robbers, Jerry. Nobody touched a pocket or a purse. From the blood over there, it had to have happened at least twenty minutes before the police got here, according to the doctor here."

Jerry stared at Enelio. "Would these damn fools think I'd kill my friends?"

"That's what most people kill. Their family or their friends. Very few people kill strangers. I got to tell what you said to the sergeant."

I sat where Enelio had been. "How come you and Luz moved in here with Mike and Della?"

He looked at me, puzzled. "Who are you?"

"My name is McGee. I've been trying to locate you. I found where you had been living, out at Mitla."

"Why have you been looking for me?"

"Just to see what you might know about Bix Bowie."

"Bix got killed in an accident."

"I know. And Carl Sessions died of an overdose. So the only ones left to talk to are you and Minda and Rocko."

"Why should anybody know anything about Bix? Minda, maybe. It happened after everybody had split."

"A girl named Gillian saw you in Mitla and told a friend. Gillian talked to you and she said you weren't very friendly. She asked you where Rocko was and you said you didn't know."

"I didn't and I don't. I was the last one to split. I had to get the hell away from Rocko. I got pretty sick there. I had to try to get clean. I'm not in real good shape yet. I get this ringing in my ears, and I get shaky, and my eyes blur sometimes. I have real bad night-mares, but I don't hallucinate any more. Luz took care of me when I was real, real bad. I don't even know how I got to Mitla. It was all part of a bad trip. She pulled me out of a ditch and got some friends to help her get me under a roof. I had the idea Rocko was trying to kill me, you know, like paranoia, and I had to cut out. Jesus! Why would anybody kill Luz? You know she had a beautiful smile? When she smiled . . . I tell you it was something else."

"Was it better here than it was in Mitla?"

"Oh sure. I ran into Mike out at the ruins and we started talking, and I took him back to the place and showed him the big timber head I've been working on. So he came out to see it and he liked it. I mean there are too many people around just *talking* about doing something. I told him I was trying like hell to work, because it had been too long. I leveled with him. I said I had been on things that didn't do me much good, but now I was clean and I was going to stay clean. I said it was lonely, me not being able to talk much of Luz's language, and he told me about his free place, and how there was room, and Della might like having another woman around to share the scut work. So why not? We got a guy to help and we loaded the big head on his jeep and packed and came here. Luz was pretty weird about Della for a little while, until she got used to her. Then they started to get along. But . . . they haven't . . . didn't have much time to get acquainted. Oh goddammit all anyway! It's such a lousy waste. Della was pregnant. That's why she was having headaches."

Enelio sauntered back and said, "Jerry, they want to investigate further, but because the time you got back checks out and because they can't find any kind of a weapon, you ought to be okay."

"One of them was looking at one of my sculptor's mallets."

"And he would like to cry because it was such a nice thing for somebody to use, but there would have to be blood. Blood and skin and hair. And fantastic strength. But they have to take you in anyway."

"Why?"

"Your tourist card is no good. Got money to get home?"

"Hell no."

"So they hold you and ask the American Embassy to make arrangements."

"Look, I forgot the card ran out! I didn't even think about it. I don't want to sit in any Mexican jail."

"Nobody sitting in one wants to be there."

I took Enelio aside. "I want to talk to this kid, alone and in the right relaxing surroundings. Any way to keep him out?"

"Want to pay for his trip to the States?"

"If it'll help."

"Want to give a little gift to the police welfare fund?"

"Like?"

"Five hundred pesos?"

"Sure."

"Then let them keep him overnight and we'll see what we can do tomorrow. Tomorrow they are maybe going to be happy to get rid of any little problems. Newspaper people will be here today from Mexico City. This will be one big stink. The Tourist Bureau will be very ogly about it. This is supposed to be such a nice safe country, eh? But always there are damn fools going off into primitive places where los Indios are still damn savage. No Spanish at all. Cruel land and cruel people. Canoe trips. Hiking. Go see the interesting Indios and get your interested throat cut, and get thrown naked into an interesting river, man. So that is one thing, and that is something else. One and a half million cars cross the border and stay for a time. God knows how many more go over into border towns for the day. It is big industry. Come to beautiful Oaxaca and get a big hit on the head. Travis, my friend, to get this bearded boy with the sad eyes loose, I must make some little kind of guarantee all will be well. You think everything will go well?"

"I'll know better after I talk to him. If I don't like the vibrations, he better go back in."

Meyer came over to us and said, "Come take a look at something." He took us over to a space against the adobe wall beyond a wooden shed. The wooden sculpture stood there. A head five feet high, carved and gouged and scraped out of old gray beams that had been bolted together. It was the same sort of Zapotecan face of the ancient carvings in stone. It had the same cruel, brooding look of lost centuries and forgotten myths. It was the size and weight and texture of the old timbers that gave it impact. There was no neck. It sat solidly on the great hard width of jaw. It could have been just a kind of self-conscious trick, but somehow he had given it a presence that made you want to speak softly.

"Son of a bitch," Enelio said slowly.

Jerry Nesta came up behind us, a man in uniform with him. He said, "I had to find hunks of metal and make the tools. I kept them sharp by rubbing them on stone. I kept thinking of the whole figure, and the way he would stand, so the head would carry the look of the whole figure. I thought of it as being something that would stand at the corner of an old temple, looking out. Not a priest or a soldier, but one of the laborers that built all these ruins and died building them. Like maybe the priests decided those unknown people should have a statue, but not out of stone. Mike thought it was . . . said it was . . ."

He turned away. Pretty soon they put him in a car and took him in. They left a car and two men to keep watch over the place. As we drove away, the silent people were still under the trees, looking toward the place of murder.

13

THE HOURS spent on the Coyotepec Road had taken too big a piece out of Enelio Fuentes' available time, and he said we would have to delay the exploration of the unmarked road until later.

He drove us into the center of town. The girls from Guadalajara had planned to spend the morning shopping and have a late lunch on the veranda at the Marqués, where we were to join them if we got back in time. Otherwise we would see them after the siesta time. But it was too early for lunch. Enelio said he might as well clean off another square foot of his desk and see us later. We let Meyer off near the big camera store on Hidalgo and Enelio took me around the zocalo to drop me in front of the hotel. There was, by some freak of chance, a parking space available, so he braked and swung in.

"*Momentito*, my friend." He sat with his big hands on the wheel, looking straight ahead, frowning. "One thing I did not know. I did not know I would be so busy, so many things would happen to keep me busy. So what I have done, I have made you two hombres into tourist guides and taxi drivers for the three little crumpets. I had been telling my conscience, why not? What man could not have pleasure to be with the tiny little flock of bright birds? But I forget. You are here on a sad and serious kind of business, eh? My God, that blood on that dusty ground is enough to wake me up. What I am saying, if they are a burden, arrangements can be made."

"No burden, amigo. They are a good contrast."

"You are certain? Good!" He grinned and winked. "I tell you, those sisters they are ver' pozzled by you two. I am old and good friends with Lita a long time. They tell her the pozzlement and she whispers it to me. These girls on vacations, McGee, they are having a beautiful time. But what soch pretty ones want on a vacation is the chance to say yes or say no. They do not know what it will be. Much depends on the asking, eh? But they look back on a vacation, they can say, well, I am sorry or I am glad I said yes, or I am sorry or I am glad I said no. Margarita thinks Meyer is one of the great men of our time, and Elena is beginning to think maybe she is ugly, or she is using the wrong toothpowder. I tell you one thing, with these girl, if you do not know the new Mexican working girl, maybe you are afraid they are wanting a permanent thing, hunting for keeps. Forget it. This is a vacation. They take care of themselves pretty good, and they were upset with me I should find dates with Americans before they met you, because the Americans they meet, they are too much interested in one thing only. Do as you please. I just say they are pozzled. But if you ask, if they say yes, I tell you it will be one hell of a distraction from this serious matter you are doing here. No, I do not want answers or conversation, please. See you later on, my friend."

And he went swinging out, putting the fear of the hereafter into a bevy of bicycles and motor scooters. I claimed a table for four on the hotel porch. Though it was nearing the busiest time of day, it was not as crowded as usual. There were far fewer of the college young. It was time to head home, sort the gear, and head back to school. I could overhear the tourist conversations, and quite a few of them were exchanging very lurid and distorted versions of sudden death on the Coyotepec Road. One beflowered matron was explaining loudly to her friends as she walked by that some hippie had shoved a knife into five fellow drug addicts and had been killed resisting arrest.

Suddenly Wally McLeen scurried up and plopped into one of the empty chairs. "Remember me, Travis? Wally McLeen? God, wasn't that a terrible thing that happened! Did you hear about it? Two wonderful kids were killed this morning . . ."

"Mike Barrington and Della Davis. And a Mexican girl."

"Their skulls were crushed. Absolutely crushed. I knew those two kids. Not well, of course, because they didn't come into town often. They knew my Minda, just casually. They were very nice to me, actually, because they knew I was trying sincerely and honestly to keep from making any emotional judgements about a white boy and a black girl living together. I mean it is rough enough for any young couple to make it, even when they have the same heritage, isn't it? But you have to respect genuine emotion wherever you find it, I say. No one could be with them without seeing that they were in love and were so terribly anxious to make it work. Now the difference in race doesn't seem important at all, does it? Dying is the same for everyone. I understand that they think a boy named Jerry Nesta did it while deranged by narcotics. Do you remember when either you or Meyer asked me about Jerry Nesta and Carl Sessions? I since found out that they were in the same little group that came down together, that my Minda was in! Did you know the Sessions boy died?"

"We heard about it."

"From drugs, I understand. Well, if they were using drugs, I'm certain that's the reason Minda left the group the first good chance she had. Even if we couldn't communicate, I know she respected her body too much to abuse it with narcotics, but I will have to accept the very real possibility that she uses marijuana and probably LSD. I've been trying them from time to time, without really very much effect. But I have had some periods of a new kind of self-awareness, a sort of spiritual feeling of kinship with all living things and all of history. Knowing the effects gives me a better chance to relate to Minda when she comes back here, I think. I thought that Jerry Nesta might have known when she was coming back or where to get in touch with her, so I'd been looking everywhere for him. Do you know, I rode my Honda right past that place twice this morning, where it happened, once on my way to the airport and once on the way back!" His eyes looked goggly behind the thick lenses.

"Wally, Wally. A Honda yet."

"I got one, a rental, as soon as I got here. It was pretty hairy for a while, those trucks and buses, but now I'm getting quite confident with it."

"And those beads, Wally?"

"Well . . . they're from the market. They're made of the vertebrae from the backbones of little fish, stained with vegetable coloring."

"And that is, or will be, a goatee?"

He laughed unhappily and felt his chin. "Guilty. I don't know what the boys would say back home. But it's like . . . a protective coloration, Trav. These kids, if they peg you as a square, they are absolutely cruel and merciless. That's the part I don't understand yet—the cruelty. The very first evening I was here a boy made an absolute ass of me, just for sport, I guess. I'd been up and down this veranda all day and all over the zocalo and the market, asking every kid I saw if they knew Minda McLeen. I had just flown down from Mexico

City that morning, a Thursday morning. And this young man asked me if I was the one looking for Minda, and he took me back into that bar lounge there, to one of those circular booths. The place was absolutely empty. He was very mysterious about it and very cautious. He said he might know Minda and he might know where she was, and she might be in some kind of a jam, and so what was it worth to me to have him see what he could do to get her out of the mess she was in and turn her over to me. I must say I was suspicious. We finally made a deal that if he'd bring me some proof, like a note from her, I would give him five thousand dollars, and then give him five thousand more when he brought Minda to me. But he just never showed up again. It was a game, a story to tell about how he blew my mind. It's hard to forgive him, but I think I can."

"So the beads and the Honda and the goatee are just a disguise, so they won't try so hard to put you on?"

"Oh no! It's more sincere than that. I mean they'd see through that in a minute. Why, last night there must have been thirty or forty kids milling around this porch at midnight having a good-by party. Most of them went out this morning. And I was genuinely part of it, Trav. They talked to me freely. They knew I was trying to find Jerry Nesta, and one girl told me that he was in bad shape and living in some Mexican hovel in Mitla, hitting up the tourists for money to live on. But I thought he might have *some* crumb of information about where my Minda is and what day she planned to come back here. Do you think they would let me talk to him at the jail?"

"Why not?"

"But isn't he in isolation or anything?"

"No. He was able to prove he was here in town when it happened. He came back in the jeep and found the three of them dead."

"Then why would he be in jail? Answer that, will you."

"Because his tourist card ran out and he's an indigent, Wally."

"Oh. Then what everybody is saying about him—"

"Is inaccurate."

"How do you know so much about it, McGee?"

"I dropped in. A social visit, but I got there too late."

"Oh. Well, I suppose I better try to see Nesta then. Well . . . thanks again." He got up. "And if you happen to hear anything about my Minda, anything at all, I'm right here in the hotel. Room twelve. You can leave a note in my box. I would appreciate it so much."

He'd been gone maybe two minutes when Meyer, with a straw bag full of little gift-wrapped items, sat down at the table and said, "Guess who nearly ran me down?"

"Wally McLeen on his Honda."

"If I didn't like you, McGee, I'd find it very easy to hate you. So you saw him. Okay, what struck me about him? What item?"

I tried the beads, then the goatee, but he smugly said no. "The best thing, the unforgettable thing was what I saw as he thundered by, jaw clamped. They glittered in the sun. Old-fashioned bicycle clips, by God, with his trousers neatly furled and held in place thereby."

"I envy you that vision," I said. I reported our conversation. I found that Meyer wanted to know more than I thought worth telling. He made me go back twice to the fellow who had conned Wally with the wild tale about Minda, and try to tell it in Wally's words.

"Whoa! Let me up, or at least tell me what you're after."

He gave me his most infuriatingly smug Buddha smile. "I would hate to think that a certain lady of noble blood romped you into permanent semi-consciousness, old friend. Nor would I like to believe that yesterday's lazy sun cooked the protein in your head. So why don't you take it from the top all by yourself, with one little clue. Just imagine that the fellow who wanted to peddle Minda to her father was named Rockland." And when he spoke again, several minutes later, he said, "Your face is all aglow with a look of rudimentary intelligence. Now try it out loud."

"McLeen said he'd been here since the first. So he could have arrived on the last day of July. That was a Thursday. It was the day that Rockland stayed away from the little nest on Calle las Artes all day long and part of the evening, and came back and asked for a loan of three thousand and made Bruce Bundy suspicious by not being sour about being turned down. So all of Rockland's troops had deserted him, and he had been tossed out of the trailer park, and he was trying to hustle a sizable piece of money anywhere he could find it. So maybe he spent a lot of time that same Thursday trying to establish contact with Minda McLeen. He would know where she was, but that house is a fortress, the Vitrier house. And neither girl would be very anxious to see Rockland for any reason, I'd assume. But let's say he did get in touch, or find out how he could get in touch later."

"You're recovering nicely," Meyer said.

"So Rockland had written off Bruce Bundy, at least as far as any willing donation is concerned. So he decides to leave with the things that look most valuable, going on the basis that the Bundys of this world seldom blow the whistle. They would rather write off the loss than make it police business. But Bundy was too cute. And when Rockland tried to jump him, Bundy was too rough. Rockland got black-belted all to hell. It probably made him pretty sick. But he had to get out of there on Saturday to meet Minda."

"What would he be most worried about?" Meyer asked.

"I guess he would realize that if Wally McLeen located his daughter, that would end any chance of selling the information and delivering the girl to him for a price."

"So we have a gap in the sequence. Better than twenty-four hours, and we have Bix and an American up on that mountain Sunday afternoon, parked and both out of the car and talking. Because it was Bundy's yellow car, we can assume it was Walter Rockland with Bix. He had to have a way to get down off the mountain. He could walk it after dark. But it would be full daylight before he could get down to the valley floor."

"Or somebody picked him up, by arrangement."

"He'd run out of people," Meyer said. "And if it was by arrangement, then there would have to be the assumption that he knew she would take off with the car and wouldn't make it all the way down. How could he be sure she wouldn't? What would the motive be?"

"Then there's the next gap until Tuesday morning, when he took the camper out of Bundy's shed."

Meyer shook his head. "It doesn't fit together. None of it. We just don't have enough of the missing pieces to even be able to guess how many other pieces are missing. Unless Jerome Nesta is willing to talk freely, we might as well go home. And maybe even if he does talk it won't be helpful."

Just then the Guadalajara sisters came clattering and squealing down upon us, laden with purchases, and there was much arrangement of girls and packages. They were still avid with the lust and fury of shopping, and they made expensive burlesques of total exhaustion, then dived into the bags and bundles to open the small ones for the reassurance of our admiration, and pluck open the corners of the big ones to show the pattern and texture of bright fabric.

And where is Lita? Ah, there was someone here in this city she had to call, an old couple who were friends of her mother, and she had been putting it off, so at last she called and they had asked her to come to have lunch with them, and it seemed as good a time as any, so she had phoned Enelio and informed him and had gone to meet the old couple. So Enelio would not join us either.

The sisters were both thirsty and famished, so as soon as a drink came they ordered lunch, and then went chattering on up to their little hotel suite to drop their purchases and freshen up.

They had made crackling inquisition of the waiter, and so we had ordered what they had ordered. It was very, very good indeed, and not at all heavy.

After lunch Margarita, the one with the best command of English, said, "Meyer, I wish to ask of you one great favor, a selfish thing, a very dull thing for you. I am silly. You can say no, please."

"I say yes. Okay."

"Without knowing, even! You remember at the place coming into Mitla at the right side, how I saw the mos' lovely color shawl and cried out to all to look? There is *no* such color in the market here. I must have, Meyer. I must go and buy it in Mitla or it will be gone forever and never, never will I see another one."

"So we will all go to Mitla. Right, Travis? No problem, ladies."

"Please, wissout Elena," said Elena. She put the back of her fist in front of a gigantic yawn. "You three are going. I am sitting and then up above sleeping, I think."

"Okay," I said. "Wissout McGee too, if you don't mind."

They didn't mind. They took a cab up the hill to the hotel after I told Meyer to look for the Falcon keys on my bureau. We watched the people, few and slow-moving in the time of siesta.

"Asking one favor too? Okay?"

"Sure, Elena."

"Maybe one little swimming in the so beautiful pool as before we were?"

I agreed. She went up and came down quickly with a little blue airline bag. We strolled over to the cab row on the post-office street and took a cab up to the hotel. She changed first in our cottage named Alicia, and came out in a narrow bikini that was a froth of rows of crisp horizontal white ruffles, and by the time I got up to the pool she was swimming, wearing a swim cap covered with vivid plastic daisies. People were baking in the sun, except for some children in the shallow end, we had the pool to ourselves. She was an unskilled and earnest swimmer, rolling and thrashing too much, expending too much effort and trying to hold her head too high. I told her a few things that would help, and swam beside her. She learned quickly and was very pleased with herself and kept at it until she was winded and gasping. We climbed out and she pulled the cap off and said, "Now enough I think. Okay?"

We walked back down to Alicia, among the cottages below and beyond the pool, and I unlocked the door for her and sat on the porch while she went in to change. I heard the clatter as she closed the blinds.

"Tuh . . . rrrravis? *Por favor, ayudarme?* Thees dombo theeng is es-stock."

So if something is es-stock, one must go in and un-es-stock it for the lady. She was between beds and bath, back toward me, still in bikini, and she looked over her shoulder and indicated the snap or fastening or whatever at the back of the bikini top was es-stock.

So I went to her. She pulled her long dark hair forward and stood with head bowed. She held the bikini top against her breasts with her hands. There were two snaps hidden by ruffles. I put a thumbnail under one and it popped. I put a thumbnail under the other and it popped and the two straps fell, dangling down the side of her rib cage. She stood without moving. It was a lithe and lovely back. Droplets of water stood on her back and shoulders. Crease down the soft brown back. Pale down, paler than her skin, heaviest near the vertical furrow. The bikini bottom came around her just a little above the widest part of her hips, leaving bare that lovely duplicated tender concavity of the girl-waist, leaving bare two dimples in the sun-honeyed brown, half a handspan apart, below the base of her spine.

So the response is an acceptance, a dedication, a tenderness expressed by very slowly, very precisely, very carefully placing the male hands upon the slenderest part of the waist, thumbs resting against the back, aimed upward, parallel to the center division of the back, edges of the hands resting against that soft shelf where the hips begin to bloom. She shivered at the touch, then lifted her head and leaned back against me. I bent and kissed the top of her shoulder, close to her throat, felt the dampness of some tendrils of hair which the swim cap had not completely protected. She was breathing very steadily, audibly, deeply, and her eyes were heavy and almost closed when I turned her around and kissed her on the mouth.

"But . . . they might come back here," I said.

She gave a little shake of her head and spoke through soft blurred lips. "No, no. She will taking Meyer to the Marqués to see dresses she bought. She trying them on for him, no hurry. Ah, she bought one hell of a lot of dresses, that sister mine."

So you go over and bolt the door, and the room is golden with the sun through the tiny cracks of the closed slats. She wants to be looked at, yet is at the same time shy. She is avid and timorous. She is experienced to a small degree, yet unsure. There is a musky-sweet, pungent scent of herself in her heat, distinctively her own. She has a secret inward smile when the pleasure is good for her. She has a long strong belly and rubbery-powerful hips and thighs, yet there are no feats of astonishing muscle control, no researched ancient trickeries, and that is a sweet and simple relief. Approaching climax her body heats and her breasts swell and her mouth sags. She deepens her strong and heavy beat and her eyes roll wild in the dim room, as if in panic, and she rolls her head from side to side and has the look of listening, and of being afraid of what is rolling up out of the depths of her, and then she is into all of it, making a very small and very sweet whimpering, and holding tight, like a child on a high scary place.

Siesta is sweet when the light is gold, and when the vivid young face on the pillow looks into yours, beside her, inches away, and smiles the woman-smile older than time, her exhalations warm against your mouth, as with slow fingers she traces your brows, lips, and the shape of cheek and jaw. There is nothing more es-stock. It has all been unfastened, all turned loose, with a guile that was so sweetly planned it could not be denied, even had there been any thought of denying it. Elena, you are the Mexican afternoons forever.

14

AT ELEVEN on Wednesday morning Enelio Fuentes brought Jerome Nesta to our cottage at the Hotel Victoria. Nesta acted sullen, uncommunicative. He wore the same clothes, but otherwise I would not have recognized him.

Enelio said, "They gave him a choice with the big bushy beard. Take it off himself, or they'd strap him down and take it off with a dull knife. The haircut was done by a jailor with no talent, eh?"

"Have your laughs," Nesta mumbled. The area where the beard had been was blue-white and nicked in a half dozen places. His scalp shone pale through a half inch of black bristle. Without the beard he looked older. I remembered he was twenty-six. He looked thirty. There were deep lines bracketing his mouth. Also, without the beard he looked almost frail. His hands were big and heavily calloused from the work with the mallet.

"One thing they forgot," Enelio said. "Out in the open if you stay upwind from him, it's not bad. In the car you keep the window open and stay close to it, very important. In this room, this size, he is impossible. It cannot be endured."

"Screw yourself," Nesta muttered, eyes downcast.

I went into the dressing-room closet and picked some tan slacks I'd never liked much, and the white sports shirt that had been, despite all instructions, starched, and some laundered jockey shorts and socks which had seen dutiful valiant service. I handed him the bundle and said, "Go in and scrub."

"Screw yourself," he said again.

"Enelio," I said, "can you give this thing back to the law, or don't they want him either?"

"As a favor to me, they'll give him his same cell back."

"Then take him along. Thanks for your trouble. I don't need to talk to him. Not right now. Not this way. When they fly him into Miami, I'll have him picked up there."

"For what?" Nesta asked.

"We'll think of something," I said.

"How about air pollution?" Meyer asked.

"Dade County loans able-bodied prisoners to Collier County for road work," I said. "Sheriff Doug Hendry's people give a short course in manners and personal hygiene."

Nesta looked at me, then at Enelio. It was a quick, flickering glance of appraisal. Without the beard he had the con look, the loser look. He had been there before, and knew he would be back there again, and it didn't make too much difference whether it was going to be a valid rap. He had the cronkey look, that flavor of upcoming trouble that alerts any cop anywhere. I don't know what it is. It is a combination of facial expression, posture, gesture—and the experience of the cop who sees the stranger and sees that indefinable thing he has seen so many times before. The animal behavior experts report that something similar exists in those wild animals who have some form of community culture. Certain individuals will be run off by the others, will be killed, or will be left to roam alone.

He picked the clean clothing off the floor and went into the bathroom and slammed the door.

Enelio said, "The shock yesterday opened him up. He talked pretty good, remember. So now he closed the doors and locked them. I don't know if he'll talk to you. I know damn well he won't talk if I'm here. The chemistry is not good. I better go. You know, one funny thing. You types from the Estados Unidos, too many talk about dirty Mexicans, right? Okay. Those little huts over there on that hill. Poor people. Carry water a hell of a distance. And take a bath every day, and the women wash that long hair every day. Clean, clean, clean. So we talk about dirty heepies. There is an old dirty heepie in there, showering. But I have had the pleasure of knowing some of your little heepie crumpets, and they have been, my friend, deliciously fresh and sweet and clean. Clean and shining as the beards on some of their boyfriends. So, big conclusion. There are dirty Mexicans and dirty heepies. But it is not a characteristic, hey?"

"Thanks for getting him out."

"Use your judgment. If there's a chance he'll make trouble, we better stick him back inside fast. He looks to me as if he wants to take off."

"The bathroom window has bars on it too."

"I noticed. If you decide he's trouble, take him in yourself and give him to Sergeant Martinez, okay?"

We thanked him and he left. Room service, as a concession to the standard issue American tourist, has hamburgers with everything all day long. I phoned up for two for Nesta, and a pot of coffee. He showered for a long time. At last he came out. My stuff was big for him, except around the waist. He had to turn the bottoms of the slacks up. He had wadded his old clothes up. Meyer told him to stuff them into the wastebasket and put the wastebasket out on the porch. Nesta looked guarded and self-conscious. Before he had come out, anticipating problems, I had told Meyer we had better go into the good-guy bad-guy routine if he seemed too uncooperative.

"Sit down, Jerry," I said. "I want you to start at the beginning. How did the five of you get together originally and decide to come to Mexico?"

"Maybe we answered an ad."

I glanced at Meyer. We'd have to try the routine. The hotel waiter arrived with the tray, and that gave me my opening.

"Did you order this stuff, Meyer? For him?"

"When you walked out with Enelio. Yes."

"Out of the goodness of your heart? Your motherly instinct? You want gratitude from this dreary bastard?"

"I don't imagine he got much to eat in jail, Travis."

"That's one part of the hotel bill we don't split down the middle. That little gesture is all yours."

Nesta took a small, tentative bite, and then wolfed the two hamburgers down. He was taking a gulp of the coffee when I asked him the same question again.

"Maybe we had this real great travel agent," Nesta said.

I waited until he set the cup down, then took a long reach and backhanded him across the chops. It was quick and substantial. It rocked his head and emptied his eyes.

Meyer jumped up and yelled at me. "What are you trying to do? You've got no right to do that! Give him a little time. He'll explain it all."

"I know he'll explain it all. Because somewhere along the line the message is going to get through to him. He's going to talk it all out or I am going to keep bending him until something breaks. And he is going to tell it straight because he doesn't know how many ways I have to check it all out. I know this slob beat a possession indictment three years ago. I know he was inside the Bowie house at Cricket Bayou on several occasions. I know they all crossed in on the tenth, from Brownsville into Matamoros, and I know exactly when the Bowie girl got the money in Culiacán, and exactly how much. And I know a lot of other things that better match with what he says, and if they don't match, you'd better take a long walk, Meyer, because there are some things you don't like to watch. They upset your stomach."

"That's no way to talk to him!" Meyer said.

"Look at him! Look at the expression. It's the only way to talk to this pot head."

"I think *you* better take the walk, McGee," Meyer said.

"I'll be right on the porch, because you're going to need me, my friend."

I slammed the door. I sat in one of the porch chairs and put my heels up on the brick railing. Meyer would take it as far as he could, and then it would be my turn, and between the two of us we had a chance of whipsawing him.

From the porch I could hear the tone of their voices without being able to hear the words. I heard Meyer mostly, and then I began to hear more and more of Nesta's voice. It was the Meyer magic at work. I looked through the window. Nesta sat on the end of Meyer's bed, leaning over on one elbow. Meyer had turned the desk chair around and he sat facing Nesta.

They say that only a small portion of personal communication is verbal, and that the rest of it is posture, expression, gesture, those physical aspects of man which antedate his ability to speak. Meyer constructs somehow a small safe world, a place where anything can be said, anything can be understood, and all can be forgiven. We are all, every one, condemned to believe that if we could ever make another human understand everything that went into any act, we could be forgiven. The act of understanding bestows importance and meaning, encouraging confession.

After a half hour I knew he was going to get all of it, and so I went for the walk. I went up to the hotel and picked up a cold beer at the bar, which had just opened, and carried it out onto the porch overlooking all the cottages and the summer city beyond. The scent of flowers was heavy. Gardeners were working on the green lawns. Sprinkler heads were clicking their big slow circles, and birds hopped and preened in the falling mist. A lithe lass, deeply sunbrowned and wearing a vivid orange bikini, stood alone on the diving tower, using the railing to practice the standard exercises of ballet. She was moist with her efforts, smooth skin gleaming in the sun. Her hair was tucked into a plastic swim cap clustered with plastic daisies.

The cold dark beer stopped halfway to my lips, and even before I could make the mental association—yes, that is the kind of swim cap Elena wore yesterday—there was such a violent surge of desire for the girl from Guadalajara that it startled me. Becky diminished need. Elena compounded it. Elena had, with a splendid earthiness spiced with innocent wonder, so emphatically superimposed herself on the memories of Becky, I would have to carry those memories into a bright light to see who the hell they were about. After those dedicated decades striving to become the very best, thinking she had attained it, it would have crushed her to find out a sweet Latin amateur was, in the light of memory, by far the better of the two, more stirring, more fulfilling, and far more sensuous.

So make a note, McGee. There are some things which practice does not enhance. Thunderstorms never practice. Surf does not take graduate lessons in hydraulics. Deer and rabbits do not measure how high they have jumped and go back and try again. Violinists must work at it and study. And ballerinas. And goalies and shortstops and wingbacks and acrobats. But that business of acquiring expertise in screwing turns it into something it wasn't meant to be.

Beer finished, I went back to the cottage to see how Meyer was doing. I was amused at Meyer and at myself. We were very formal with each other today. Remote, thoughtful, and formal. I had bought Elena a late dinner the night before at the hotel and sent her home in a cab—at her insistence on not being a nuisance. Meyer had arrived as I was getting ready for bed. Yes, he had eaten in town. Not bad, actually. Car had run fine. Margarita had found the shawl. Sleep well. Good night.

I looked through the window. Nesta had a hand over his eyes. Meyer waved me away.

Back up the hill. Drifted around. Watched the happy vacationers at play. Kept out of the line of people taking happy pictures of each other. Admired shrubbery clipped into the shapes of animals. Elephant. Ostrich. Donkey. Tried to remember the name for that particular art form. Couldn't.

Sat on a stone bench and tried to bring back some specific memory of Bix Bowie the day Meyer brought her aboard the *Flush*. Couldn't. Brain apparently failing along with everything else. Premature instant senility. But Meyer had the vivid memories of the girl. Vivid and now painful. And some more painful images to put on top of the heap.

Finally went back. Meyer was on the porch, sitting in a kind of slack, dumpy solemnity. I looked through the window. Nesta was sprawled on Meyer's bed, with a blanket over him.

I sat down beside Meyer. "So?"

"I feel sick."

"That bad?"

"Bad. Yes. And . . . pointless. Wasteful."

"Did you get all of it?"

"I don't see how there could be anything more. He's exhausted, physically and emotionally. And he's not alone."

"How did the group get together?"

"Bix had some friends at the University of Miami, kids she went to public school with in Miami. After her mother died, she looked them up. She met Carl Sessions at a party. They started going around together. Carl knew Jerry Nesta. Jerry was Carl's connection for marijuana. Jerry was living with Minda McLeen. And he also made deliveries out to the Beach, to Walter Rockland, as a go-between. He and Rockland talked about some way to make a big score someday. The four of them, Carl, Bix, Jerry and Minda began running around together. Rockland found out Bix had some money from her mother's will. Rockland talked Nesta into helping him promote the Mexico trip. Sessions had already turned Bix on to pot, and she obviously took to it all too well, as some will. Rockland claimed to have a good contact in Mexico where they could buy pure heroin at Mexican wholesale prices. The idea was to get Bix down there, talk her into financing it, smuggle it across the line and peddle it to a wholesaler in Los Angeles. So Nesta helped Rocko develop some enthusiasm among the other three to take a Mexican vacation. Bix was willing to buy the camper and the supplies and pay expenses. She did not seem to care about the money one way or another, or really care much whether she went or stayed. So when Rocko was fired, they moved the timetable up and got ready and left, and there was absolutely nothing Harl Bowie could do about stopping her."

"But she didn't know the real reason."

"Not until later. And by then I guess you could say it was too late for her to do anything about it. You see, Rockland was the only one of the five who was not a user or anything at all. In fact, not even liquor except very rarely and then too much. No cigarettes. A physical culture type. But he had a couple of mimeographed sheets he'd paid five dollars for in Miami. They give the trade and generic name of a list of pharmaceuticals available over the counter in Mexico. Opposite each was the Spanish name and the phonetic pronunciation. They bought good strong pot the minute they were over the border, and at Monterrey they loaded up with items off the list. Rockland was in charge, ostensibly to keep people from taking too much when they were too stoned to know what they were taking. He kept the drugs locked in the tool compartment of the truck, but the pot was available at any time. Rocko set a slow pace across Mexico. It was the cold season. He and Nesta shared the driving. When they found a good place to camp, they would stay two or three days. They went from Monterrey to Torreón to Durango to Mazatlán. Nesta doesn't know how long it took. He said it could have been a year or a week. He said it was all pretty blurred. Rockland would dole them out a mixed bag of opiates and stimulants, barbiturates and mescaline, and he said you didn't know what kind of a high you were going into until you were there, and some of them were bad."

"It's a wonder he didn't kill somebody."

"I know. In the beginning Bix was paired off with Carl Sessions, and Minda McLeen with Jerry Nesta. Those relationships fragmented. It didn't turn into some kind of orgy, even though repeating what he told me makes it sound that way. Apparently the first deviation was when Rocko made love to Bix. Carl was angry and upset about it at first, but he got over it when Minda slept with him because she felt sorry for him. Then Jerry Nesta fought with Minda, and then got even with her by sleeping with Bix. Except for the tension in the beginning, it seemed to all iron out into a kind of casual and, except for Rocko, infrequent thing. Nesta told me that Bix was totally placid and submissive. It didn't matter to her which of the three had her. She seemed to accept and endure. Once when Carl was still reasonably lucid Nesta asked him if Bix had ever been passionate with him, and Carl said no. By then Minda was taking care of Bix. Unless prodded and helped she wouldn't wash, brush her teeth, blow her nose, change her clothing. It was a process of disintegration for all of them. Except Rocko. Each was hooked in his or her own way. Rocko was the ground control. Sessions apparently became even more hopelessly addicted to methadone, moving in a fumbling, stumbling, hazy dream, losing all sexual drive. Nesta was on pot and mescaline. Minda McLeen was on stimulants, amphetamine and dexedrine compounds, getting ever more shaky and thin and nervous, and becoming even more physically dependent on Rockland. Do you see the pattern, Travis?"

"In the kingdom of the blind, the one-eyed man is king. And a five way split is a lot of ways to split it."

"But Nesta apparently didn't suspect. As they neared Culiacán, Rocko took Bix's indispensable pot away from her, and so she behaved exactly as directed, sent for the money, cashed the draft, turned the money over to Rocko, and was rewarded with a half-dozen joints and swiftly sucked her way back into her waking dream. Rockland's contact had been reliable. They got pure heroin in full quantity. Rocko, working alone, transferred it into small sacks made of thick transparent plastic tied with nylon cord, and took an inside panel off the camper and stowed it in the shallow space between the inside and outside skin. He was nervous on the way up to Nogales. Sessions got on his nerves, playing the same chords over and over and over on the guitar, until one evening Rocko took the tin snips out of the tool box and cut the strings off. But Sessions kept playing as if nothing had happened. All they could hear were his fingernails on the frets and the box. Ten miles out of Nogales, Rocko decided that it had all been too easy. He decided to make a dry run. So he tied all the little bags up in a raincoat and buried it in the dirt near a flowering bush. He took Bix with him to the border, taking her off pot for a full day first. He left the three others with the supply of pills and pot in a cheap motel with orders to wait until they crossed back in. They came back four days later. He had new papers on the truck and camper, and new tourist cards for himself and Bix. But Rocko was savagely angry. The sellers had apparently tipped the customs people. The total search took fifteen hours, and they had to reassemble the truck and camper when it was over. The border people knew the names of the five of them, said they knew they had made a large buy, and said that no matter how they tried to bring it back across, they would be nailed, all together, or one at a time."

"Very thorough."

"They went back down Route Fifteen and recovered the heroin. Rocko concealed it in the camper. They made camp well off the road by a dry stream bed another ten or twenty miles down the road. Rocko was in a foul mood. Minda, humming and burning with energy, was doing the cooking, washing, laundry, mending, housekeeping, and taking care of Bix, her hair and her person. During the second day at that place, she began complaining to Rocko that they were nearly out of cooking gas, that the gauge was way down. When would he get it filled? She was sick of having to make fires with sticks when they were out of gas. He paid no attention. And then she said that at least the border people hadn't let the gas out of the tank, and she should be grateful for that much. He jumped up and ran and examined the tank. The fill valve and the outlet valve were part of the brass assembly that was fastened onto the top of the tank. They drove south and at Hermosillo he bought two small pipe wrenches and got the whole assembly off. The orifice was just large enough so that by rolling the plastic bags between his palms he could make them small enough to drop into the tank. He put one in the tank and had it refilled at Hermosillo. Three days later he let the gas escape and, with some difficulty apparently, got the bag out. It looked and tasted fresh and unharmed, so he loaded the bags into the tank and got it filled again. Nesta thought he would start for the border right away. But Rocko was unexpectedly relaxed and unhurried. There was a pretty good piece of Bix's money left. They might as well see the country. He became very charming."

"Life of the party."

"Sure. He even had a special little treat for Carl Sessions. On the way south in Ciudad Obregon he picked up a hypo and some distilled water, some cotton swabs and some alcohol, and he fixed his good friend Sessions a nice little pop and injected it under the skin on the underside of his forearm. Sessions got very sick from it. But Rocko kept helping him out until finally Carl could inject himself and feel very good. Then when he had worked up to injecting it directly into the blood stream and felt very, very good, Rocko talked him into sharing his new talent with Bix."

"I know why you said you feel sick."

"That Walter Rockland is a real charmer. All heart. So our little caravan came wandering through the mountains on down here to Oaxaca. And the flavor changed, or, I might say, the alignment.

Minda got sick. Nesta was appointed by Rocko to look after Bix. When he refused, Rocko beat the hell out of him. He said he got to sort of like it after a while, scrubbing her and washing her hair. But he'd lost any physical desire for her. She and Carl Sessions had gone off into some country of their own, nodding and popping. Minda, scared by being sick, was stubbornly taking herself off the stimulants. I suppose as they are habituating rather than addicting, a person with enough will could do it. And she apparently, as if compensating, became ever more infatuated with Rocko in a purely physical way. After they were here a while, Rocko started to cut off the supply to Carl and Bix. He would let them get sick before he would dole out a very small amount. One day Nesta took Bix off somewhere on some errand. He had wanted to get out of Rocko's way because Rocko was on one of his rare drunks, when he was inclined to get violent and nasty. When he came back, Carl wasn't there. Rocko was asleep, snoring loudly. Minda was in some kind of shock. For a long time Nesta couldn't find out what happened. Then he learned that Carl had come pleading and begging to Rocko. Rocko, in Minda's presence, had asked Carl if he would do anything in the world for a fix. Carl said he would. And after he had stripped down, as Rocko asked, Rocko boosted him up into the double bed over the cab and climbed up in there with him, and Minda went running out. She heard Carl crying. That apparently finished it for Minda. A few days later she left and took Bix with her. Nesta said Rocko seemed perfectly content to have them gone for good, all three of them. Nesta stayed on. But he began to have the feeling that Rocko was watching him and planning how to kill him. It could have been an induced paranoid hallucination. But he took off, by then in very bad shape, and gradually came out of it in Mitla, with the woman Luz taking care of him just the way he had taken care of Bix."

"So now we know," I said, "why Rocko reacted the way he did to having somebody pry that little door open and take that tank of gas. He knew it had to be taken by somebody who knew what was hidden in it. The first guess would be Sessions. So he would go looking for him."

Meyer nodded. "Let's say he didn't find him. Sessions was found dead on the morning of the seventh. He could have stolen it, emptied it, hidden the stuff away, and died of an overdose."

"Or once he found him, maybe he was satisfied Carl knew nothing about it. And it would be fair to assume Rocko had enough left on hand to stick much too much into Sessions."

Meyer thought that over. Then he shook his head. "I can't buy that, Travis. I can't buy the idea that Rocko would kill anybody. Not then. Not at that time. Maybe now. Maybe he has been coming closer and closer. I think he gave it a lot of thought after he discovered a hiding place the border search had overlooked on the dry run. He knew that if he tried to cross with the whole group, five minutes of interrogation would crack any one of the other four, and the five of them would be busted. So they camped out, in wild areas. He knew that alone he could make it. Maybe he had plans of marketing it at ten times his cost, hiding the cash in the same place, crossing back with it, and running another batch over again, for the big final score. I think he must have thought of the obvious way out. Chunk them on the head and bury them out in the wastelands. It's so completely efficient, he *had* to think about it. And if he didn't do it, it is because he couldn't bring himself to do it."

"Because he is such a nice guy."

"Because he decided they would destroy themselves if he nudged them in the right direction. And check his track record so far. Carl and Bix are gone. We don't know about Minda McLeen. We know he's batting five hundred. It could be seven fifty."

"So who stole the little gas tank, Meyer?"

"You force me to guess? I would say that Carl Sessions talked about the Americano with a fortune in junk in the bottled gas tank, and I would guess that his addiction would put him into contact with some very rough local types, and it would be natural for them to check it out. And easy enough. So then Rocko would be compelled to pick up another stake, so he could go make another buy, hide it in another tank, and take it across alone. So he went cruising, and he let Bruce Bundy pick him up, but it didn't work out the way he planned it. When he saw he wasn't going to con any cash out of Bundy, he went cruising again, and came up with Minda's father, Wally McLeen. So he would have heard by then that Bix and Minda were guests of Eva Vitrier."

We were both silent, trying to appraise the possibilities. I said, "Remember? The girls quarreled. Minda left for Mexico City. So Rocko couldn't contact her. Assume that when he took the Bundy car, he went right to the Vitrier place in La Colonia. And the next thing we know, it's Sunday afternoon and he and Bix and the yellow car are way the hell up in those mountains."

"It would be nice to talk to Eva Vitrier," Meyer said.

"It would indeed. A total recluse, using a hell of a lot of money to buy total privacy, to build big walls. And she's gone. Try and find out where."

"Somebody could get into her place and look around."

"Like me?"

"Well, any large, curious, agile fellow, let's say."

"And I get slapped into a cell out in that Zimatlán jail."

Meyer shrugged. "I'll be there every visitors' day. Speaking of jail, what about our friend in there?"

"You're in the best position to decide."

"I just don't know. He seems docile. I might take the risk if I had to take the blame, too. But if I make a bad guess, then Enelio is in trouble. It's just a hunch, my friend. I sense a kind of animal wildness, a potential for unpredictability. Talking to him, even when he wept, was like sitting in a zoo. I didn't want to make any sudden motions. I would have felt better with bars between us."

"So, I go with your instinct, Meyer. Your average is too good. We can get in touch with Enelio and find out if he wants us to take the package back to the store."

We got up. Meyer went through the door first. The blanket was thrown back. The bathroom door was closed. I could hear water running. No reason at all why I shouldn't accept that obvious conclusion, that Nesta had gotten up and gone into the bathroom. I did accept it, and in a sudden surge of adrenalin, rejected it a microsecond later, rejected it as I was in motion, going through the doorway. To reverse motion meant vulnerable stasis for too long an instant, so I dived forward, and just as my palms hit Meyer in the middle of the back, knocking him onto and over the nearest double bed, something chunked very solidly and painfully into the meat of my back, just under the right shoulder blade. I used the leverage of Meyer's solidity to thrust myself to the right, and the momentum took me across the tile floor, scrabbling on all fours for balance, and simultaneously trying to turn so I would be facing the doorway when I came back up. I made and saw Nesta going by the windows. He was out on the porch and moving fast.

I caught him on the road, about seventy yards up the hill. He was in no shape for uphill running. He turned, gasping and gagging, and

swung some kind of dark club at my head so off balance I had time
to step back and let it go by. It carried him halfway around. So, in
that tiny interval of time when he was almost motionless, trying to reverse direction, I hit him a very nice right hand shot right on the point
of the shoulder. It is that ancient and effective torture of schoolyards
and playgrounds. The nerves run over the bone of the arm socket
right at that point. He dropped the weapon. Something inside a
sock. It made a metallic thud. His arm hung slack, dead and useless
and he cupped his shoulder in his big left hand and looked at me
with the twisted face of a child fighting tears, chest heaving from the
effort of running.

"Naughty, naughty!" I said and reached out quickly, caught the
end of his nose between thumb and the bent knuckle of the
forefinger, and gave a long hard pull downhill, stepping aside and
releasing him. He ran a half dozen jolting steps and stopped, his
back toward me. I picked up the improvised weapon and gave him a
gentle push. It got him in motion and he walked the rest of the way
to the cottage, up onto the porch, and into the room, not looking at
Meyer as he passed him. Meyer stood outside the door, fingers laced
across the nape of his neck, grimacing as he turned his big head
from side to side.

"Whiplash, maybe," he said.

"Officer, he stopped dead right in front of me." I spread the opening of the dark sock which belonged to Meyer and peered down into
it and said, "Tsk tsk tsk! Little present for you."

He took it, reached down into it, and pulled out his sturdy little
travel alarm. Sturdy no longer. The case had burst open and there
were a lot of little loose parts down in the toe of the sock.

He dumped them out on the metal top of the porch table, quite
sadly. "McGee, I have to assume you reacted first. It will never cease
to make me feel insecure, the way you do that. What alerted you,
dammit?"

"I haven't any idea. Something subliminal. Something smelled or
heard or seen, on an unconscious level."

"And if I were a more primitive organism, I could perform such
feats also?"

"Flattery won't help."

We went in. Nesta sat on the foot of Meyer's bed. His right arm
was cradled in his lap and he was looking down at it, slowly flexing
the fingers.

"They'll be interested in knowing you like to pop people on the skull," I said to him.

He did not raise his eyes. "The law likes to get cases off the books. It takes the heat off them. I thought I better get going before I got elected," he said.

"You're going back inside."

"So?" he said in a toneless voice.

"I can tell them about your little try here, or I can keep it between us."

It brought a quick and wary glance before the eyes dropped again. "What'll it take?" he asked.

"Something important that you maybe left out of your confession hour with Meyer. We think there's a good chance Rockland could have set Bix up to kill herself trying to drive down the mountain alone at dusk."

"I didn't even know about that until just the other day, when Mike and Della told me about it. I didn't even know she was dead."

"How did you feel when you heard it?"

"I didn't feel much of anything. A long time ago she was something else. That was one pretty girl and that was one hell of a body. I was willing to trade off Minda for the chance to start balling her. But it was like nothing. Like one of those plastic things in a store window. All you had to do was lead her into the bushes or take her into the camper and she'd lay down on her back. Then a long time later when she'd lost a lot of her looks, and nobody was hacking her any more, I sort of got to like taking care of her. I don't know why. Making her look a little better, making her eat, making her walk around. But she was gone anyway. She was dead before she was dead. Even pot took her too far out of her tree. When Carl turned her on with horse it was too late to make any difference one way or another. What did I feel? Nothing, I guess. Nothing at all."

"Would Rockland want her dead?"

"Why would he? She didn't know who the hell she was or where she was or who we were. Her memory was shot. The way she was just . . . around, like a lump, used to get on Rocko's nerves. He used to try to get some kind of rise out of her. One time . . . I don't know where it was, I think maybe someplace south of Puebla, outside one of those little towns, some Mexicans came around in the evening, mean-looking bastards in those white pajama suits and straw hats, one with a shiny new rifle, and the others with machetes, a dozen I guess. They had eyes for Bix. So Rocko started laughing and grabbed her by the wrist and grabbed a blanket and took her over into the cornfield and peddled her ass for two pesos a trick, and came back with her and told me the banker's daughter had earned herself thirty-two pesos. He gave me the money and told me to buy her some penicillin in the next town. Why would he kill her? She was less than nothing. Good Christ, by then she looked forty years old."

"When you left you were giving up your share of the Los Angeles loot?"

"I didn't even think about it, man. I was hallucinating bad. I could shut my eyes and feel my hands melting and dripping off my wrists. Rats were running around under my clothes, eating me. Hairy red spiders as big as airdales kept jumping out and jumping back in any direction I tried to walk. And Rocko had sicked them on me and he was making my hands melt, and I just had to get the hell out of there. And I did. I wish I could help you with something. But I don't know anything I didn't already tell."

"What would you have done if you'd nailed me with that clock when I came in the door?"

"Hit him next. Take your money and your car keys and get out onto one ninety and head southwest, because they'd expect me to head for Mexico City. My best bet would be to try to get to Vera Cruz and stow away aboard some crock heading across the Gulf."

"And if you hit us hard enough to kill?"

"I start running. It looks like I killed the others, so what difference would it make?"

"It might make a little difference to you," Meyer said softly.

"To me? Well . . . yes. A little difference, I guess. But not a hell of a lot."

I sat on the bed and phoned Enelio. I said, "We don't want to take any chances with this one. He got cute, and he'll get cute again."

Enelio said that Chief Alberto Tielma of the Zimatlán jail would give me a nice official receipt for him. He asked me if we got anything out of Nesta, and I said we got a history of the little Mexican hayride those five took that would gag a weasel, but nothing that helped with the primary problem of how come the girl drove off the mountain.

"So," he said, "when something pozzles me, I find out anything I can find out, and I still see no reason under God for anybody to drive a camper going like hell down into that lousy country down there, except somebody wants to get rid of a camper, which is a large object. If, God forbid, I wanted to get rid of a large object on wheels, I mean without selling it, which is always possible, no matter what kind of papers you have on it, maybe I would take it down that way."

"So you'd consider going on another expedition with Meyer and McGee?"

"My trouble is I am impulsive. Also I never make the same mistake once. I think . . . Yes, if it's okay with you, I pick you up maybe at the Marqués tomorrow afternoon?"

It was agreed. We toted Nesta back to jail. He had the contrived indifference of the born loser. He had not a word to say all the way.

15

MEYER and I had just finished a late Wednesday lunch on the veranda of the Marqués del Valle when Enelio Fuentes arrived, by prearrangement, in the jeep. As we went out the Mitla road, Meyer and I, taking turns yelling against the wind, filled Enelio in on the little talk with Nesta, and the subsequent problem of talking him out of leaving.

I said that after due deliberation, and weighing of all factors, I had told the police chief, with gestures, about Nesta's antisocial behavior. I had finked on him.

"Hey, how can an animal like that one," Enelio roared, "carve that strong glorious wooden head? How is it possible?"

"All great artists lead placid, humble, gentle lives," Meyer hollered. "They are all celibates and never drunk or violent. You know. Like your own Diego Rivera was."

Grinning, Enelio took his right hand off the wheel and made that unique and expressive Mexican gesture of consternation, like trying to shake water from the fingertips.

The road he was looking for began about twenty miles beyond Mitla. It was a dirt road that, about four miles from the main road went through a village, and then continued on, dropping perhaps a thousand feet before reaching dry stony flats. Sometimes he could get up to twenty miles an hour before braking, putting it in low, and lurching through rain gulleys and across a moonscape of potholes. Then the road became straighter and smoother, and he was able to make good time. A long high dust plume was kicked up behind us in the windless hot afternoon.

He slowed and stopped and we got out. He took binoculars out of a case and looked west. He said, "Yes, the smaller road out of Ocotlán runs down through those ridges. When I was small we hunted rabbits over there. But not over here. This is the burned land. Sand, rock, cactus. Only by the dry rivers are trees. See. Deep roots. They drink deep only after the rains. You know, it is maybe a little bit too much, those Texas schoolteachers just being there at the right time and looking way over here and just happening to see what she thinks was the camper, and he thinks was not."

"But the dust would draw your attention," Meyer said.

"And this," I explained, "is the kind of coincidence—if she *did* see it—that is not a coincidence at all. Because the world is jammed with people, and if you talk to enough of them, you usually find that the unseen things were seen by someone. And if they are a little out of the ordinary, like the vehicle she saw going too fast, they stick to the edge of memory. Had it been going slower, she would never have examined it so carefully through the glasses, and she would have forgotten it by the next day. She claimed she saw blue, and saw glintings that could have been the aluminum camper body. But it is a hell of a way over there."

"One hell of a way indeed. And the road goes nowhere," said Enelio. "So what went down it had to come back, or still be somewhat ahead. And the wind blows the sand and dust so there are no tracks."

The road dwindled away to nothing in about six more miles. Enelio told us to hang on. He turned sharply right and soon I realized what he was going to do. He made a big circle around the rocky landscape. It had to be an irregular circle due to the contour. A couple of times he had to back and shorten the diameter of the circle.

When we were two thirds of the way around I tapped Enelio on the shoulder and pointed ahead and to our left, inside the arc of the circle. He drove over and stopped and we got out again. It was a clear and distinct tire track in the lee of an outcropping of red-brown rock. It had run through some kind of crumbled clay, and though some sand had blown into it, it was unmistakable.

Enelio sat on his heels and crumbled the claylike substance between his fingers. "*Animalitos.* Damn, we call them *hormigas.* Some are red. They bite. They make little hills."

"Ants?"

"Yes! The tire went through the middle of this little one and along the edge of this big one. They brought up the dirt from underneath the sand, and it is moist almost."

He stood up and shaded his eyes. "Back there is the last of the road. So draw a line from there to these tracks . . ." We turned and looked, and Meyer suggested we fan out a little and walk it, looking for any clue, not taking any route a vehicle could not take.

After a hundred yards my route ended in impossibility. I backtracked and cut over to the other side, beyond Meyer. Then I came to a place where the earth dropped away. It was a deep meandering crack, perhaps twenty feet across and fifty feet deep, with round boulders and brush at the bottom of it. Enelio shouted. We hurried along the brink to where he stood. He was at the edge of a semicircular bite looking down at where the landslide had choked the bottom of the dry wash. There was an uncommon amount of loose brush on top of the barrier.

Enelio widened his nostrils and sniffed the breeze. He crossed himself and said, "Death." I caught it then, too—the sweet, rotten, sticky smell of decaying meat.

We stumbled and slid down the slant of sandy soil. We pulled the brush away, exposing the upper half of the rear of the camper. It was nose down into the stones, the landslide drifted high around it. The smell was sickeningly strong.

"The McLeen girl?" Meyer asked in church tones.

"Somebody our boy Rocko took a dislike to," I said.

"You get the dirt off the door while I go get something I know about," Enelio said. He went plunging up the loose slope and disappeared. I started digging the door out with my cupped palms, and with Meyer helping me. We heard the sound of the jeep overhead. It stopped. After a few minutes Enelio came sliding back down. He had a thin piece of rag tied around his head so that it came across his upper lip. He had another piece for each of us. The center portion that came across the lip was damp with raw gasoline.

"One time when we had to go into the mountains after bodies from a plane crash, one of the medical people taught me this thing. Gasoline numbs the smelling. It overpowers everything. There was one trouble. For nearly a year afterward, each time I would smell gasoline, I would start gagging. Also it makes a burn on the lip. But it is better than the only other choice, eh?"

The camper body was out of line and the door was jammed. But it was on such a steep angle I could stand on the aluminum beside the door and bend over and take hold of the handle. I yanked it open and let it fall back. There was enough reflected sunlight so that we could see quite clearly into the dark interior. Enelio grunted, spun, jumped down and trotted twenty feet along the bottom of the wash, then bent over and vomited explosively.

"You can move too," I told Meyer. "I want to make sure."

"I should help you."

"Get going."

"Thanks, Travis."

I took a deep breath and clambered down into the camper. He had been wired up with considerable loving care. Extension cord wire. Spread eagled, on his back on the narrow floor, head down, feet up toward the doorway. Wire snugly knotted to each wrist and ankle and angling off to whatever was sturdy enough and handy enough. Dead mouth crammed with something and taped in place. Bulky roll of the sleeping bag under his back, to keep him arched. I tried not to look too closely at him. I found his trousers against the bulkhead up front. The wallet was in the hip pocket. I turned the identification toward the bright light that streamed down, and got my verification. I put the wallet in my pocket and climbed carefully up to where I could hoist myself up and out with one final effort. Then I took that long close look at him, and left in a hurry. I went up that slope like a giant jackrabbit and hit a pretty good stride as I passed the jeep. I stripped the gasoline rag off and dropped it as I ran. I stopped and faced into what little breeze there was and started hyperventilating.

The jeep stopped behind me. Over the motor noise I said, "Make no jokes."

"There is no intention, señor," Enelio said.

I knew they would not want to touch the wallet. I turned and held it so they could read the drivers' license through the yellowed plastic.

"Rockland!" Meyer said loudly. "Rockland?"

"The description matches what . . . what's left."

"Was he shot, or what?" Meyer asked.

"I don't think the question is material. I do not know everything that was done to him. But I think he was tapped on the head and then stripped, spread and wired in place and gagged. Then various things were done to him. The most impressive, perhaps, being a knife line drawn across the belly, then down the tops of the thighs, then across the thighs about six inches above the knees. Then the entire area thus outlined was carefully flayed, skinned like a grouper. I would guess that he was not blinded until a bit later on."

"I would be very grateful if you would not continue this," Enelio said.

"I am glad to stop right here."

I climbed in by going over the back of the jeep, as I sensed they did not want me too close.

Meyer said, "Not even Rockland should be . . ."

"Are you sure of that?" I asked.

Meyer gave it thought. "Not entirely sure. But if we could understand all the formative influences on Walter Rockland—"

"We would learn," I said, "how come he turned out to be a wicked, contemptible, evil son of a bitch."

And by then it was too late for more talk. Enelio wanted to be home. He wanted to be there very badly. He was willing to sacrifice our kidneys, our discs, and our silver fillings to that desirable end.

But near Oaxaca, Enelio suddenly braked, swung over to the curb and cut the motor off. He turned in the seat to address me and Meyer simultaneously. "I am a respected citizen of the State of Oaxaca," he said. "I have a certain amount of influence. I am a happy man. I enjoy my work. I enjoy my friends. I enjoy doing a favor for a friend. McGee, I was glad to welcome you to Oaxaca as a favor to my good American friend Ron Townsend."

"And I appreciate it."

"But I am *not* going to go to the officers of the law and try to explain to them just how we happened to find that body. They look at me strangely already. They look at you even more strangely. I am not a man who has this big thing about killing and bodies and investigation. I am going to be a bad citizen. If you report it, I never heard of this trip today. A dear little crumpet will swear I spent a long, long siesta with her. In fact, it was my plan. In fact I should have been with her. I do not like to throw up. It gives me a severe headache. But you, of course, are at liberty to report it."

"It would be nice if they knew about it," Meyer said.

"I think that tomorrow one of our pilots for our little airline will see a gleam in that arroyo and so advise the police."

"In that case, Don Enelio," I said, "I too have lost my taste for civic duty. I think that sergeant of yours would like to knock my head a little."

"He implied as much. He is known for enjoying such small pleasures."

"What about this wallet?"

"If I had it, I would wipe it off very carefully and put it in the mailbox by the Hotel Marqués del Valle."

"Consider it done, but after I see what's in it."

He waited. They did not turn around to watch me. Three hundred and sixty-two pesos, which is twenty-eight dollars and ninety-six cents. A Mexican peso, after it goes from hand to hand in the public market a few times can turn into something that looks like a piece of Kleenex rescued from the bottom of a pot of very stale and very greasy bean soup and then used to patch a manifold in a sloppy garage. Florida driver's license. Truck registration slip, a couple of months overdue for re-registration. Tourist card. A small squashed notebook with a soiled red plastic cover containing addresses, phone numbers, notes to himself. It seemed to be in the order in which he had written the items down. It was better than half filled. I scanned the last few pages and found Bruce Bundy, with address and phone. What they did not know had been there, they would never miss, and it needed longer and more careful study, so I put it in my pocket. I found a Miami Beach health card certification, with thumb print and picture. The picture confirmed a positive identification of the thing suspended in the tipped camper. I found two keys, obviously vehicle keys, probably spares. I found three folded color Polaroid prints quite ancient and faded and featuring obscene acts so unique, so improbable, that after an instant of surprise, the performers no longer looked obscene or shocking, but looked instead strangely comic and forlorn. Nobody I knew. All strangers, even the sheep dog. I put them back in the wallet with everything except the red book, thinking that the prints might well end up taped on the inside of the door of some local cop's locker. Some daring sociologist should someday publish a collection of the art work found on the insides of locker doors of cops, firemen, ballplayers, and resident golf pros.

So we went roaring ahead again, back to the downtown hotel where he had picked us up. The car was parked over beyond the post office. On the way I felt a stupid smile appearing on my stupid face from time to time. Perhaps more rictus than smile. It is one of the many curious phenomena of reaction. There is a dreadful jolly animal hidden inside us all who keeps reminding us we are alive and somebody else is dead. It kept telling me to remember how deeply the wire had eaten into the wrists of Walter Rockland, impacted there by the spasm of powerful muscles reacting to unspeakable pain.

No more hustling towels for the guests around the pool. No more two hundred percent markup on funny cigarettes. No more decisions, boy. All problems are solved forever.

Fuentes double-parked in front of the hotel and signaled the strolling cop that he would be but a moment by holding up thumb and forefinger a half inch apart, and the cop touched his cap in proper deference to the local power structure.

Enelio said firmly, "You are very nice fellows. You are splendid fellows. Lita tells me that the delicious sisters from Guadalajara have dreamy eyes about you two, and say now that it is the best vacation of all. For that the sisters and I am grateful, and my faith and trust is justified. But no more of death, eh? Maybe I am not a true Mexican. I am not enchanted by death. Do not tell me any more you learn. Do not ask my advice on any such matters, eh? In fact, let us not see each other as planned tonight. In exactly . . . forty minutes I shall be in one big deep hot tub, and pretty soon I will give a big yell and Lita will come scampering in with very, very cold wine because I like it very cold when I am in a hot tub, and she will pour a glass, and when I have drunk it all she will take the big brush and the special soap and scrub my back, and then she will pour me another glass, and soon then maybe I will begin to sing a little. I shall tell her that we are going to stay in, because with a woman in my arms I can stop thinking about death. I know I will live forever. So there is the place at this hotel, and there is the other place at the other hotel, and Lita will stay with me. So I advise you, kind gentlemen, to stay apart, to stay with your loving girls, to lose the stink of death in the sweetness of girls, and have food and drink sent in, which is possible in both places, and make the girls of Guadalajara laugh and also, in time, make them cry, because laughing and crying are very living things. Tomorrow, perhaps, you will hear from me. Adios, amigos."

So he sped off. It was after five. Meyer grabbed a table. I went inside to the men's room and scrubbed my hands and face and neck and arms, and looked at myself in the mirror and saw I was still wearing that stupid smile. It is the smile of the survivor. A man walks away from the pile of tinsel junk that was once an airplane, and which for some unknown reason failed to explode and failed to burn, and he wears that smile. I wiped the wallet off and dropped it into the mail box. Meyer had a cold Negro Modelo waiting on the table for me.

"I'm trying not to think," he said. "I don't want to do any thinking, please."

"So don't."

"But the stinking wheels go around in my head. I keep remembering that day aboard the *Flush*, and trying to say something to Bix that would make it easier for her, somehow, to accept Liz's ugly death, and those beautiful deep blue eyes of hers were absolutely bland and indifferent, no matter what polite thing her mouth was saying. There was a . . . a challenge there. Something like that. I wanted to try to reach her and get some reaction, some genuine reaction, no matter how. To say or do some . . . ugly thing, to shock her awake maybe. Travis, I wonder if there are people in this world who are appointed by the gods to be victims, so that they bring out the worst in everybody they touch. And the perfect victim would have to be surpassingly lovely, of course, to be most effective. I keep wondering if she was the catalyst, not Rockland. And maybe, that day, if I hadn't become irritated at being unable to get any reaction, if I had tried harder."

"Meyer, Meyer, Meyer."

"I know. I have this thing, like the disease of kings. A bleeder. The internal wounds do not clot well. All my life is remorse. If I had done this, if I had done this . . ."

"And if your aunt had wheels she'd have been a tea cart."

"Where *are* we, Travis? Just *where* the *hell* are we?"

"In Oaxaca. The Chamber of Commerce motto is 'Stay One More Day in Oaxaca.' "

"Perhaps I do not care to."

"A pity to spoil a nice girl's vacation just when it is shaping up, Meyer."

"Now Travis."

"My God, when you get the shys you look just like Howland Owl."

"Well . . . she is quite young, and . . . and, dammit, McGee, anything that pleasurable has to be shameful, sinful, and wicked. I am a lecherous old man, shaken by remorse. We should go home."

"So we can go back to Lauderdale, land of the firm and sandy young rump, home of the franchised high-starch diet, and appraise the cost and the seaworthiness of all the playtoys that churn up and down the waterway, and criticize the way they are being handled.

And we can wonder who did what to whom and why, and wonder why we didn't stay just a little bit longer and find out."

"Or *not* find out."

"Somebody wasn't in it for the money. Somebody wasn't worried about little incriminating items in the wallet. So Rockland has been dead in that aluminum hot box since August seventh, and I think maybe whoever did it parked the truck on the rim, worked on him for a long, long time, then rolled it over, pried dirt down on it, piled brush on it, and went away. It was a punishment which somebody devised to fit the crime. It was a very sick mind at work. Very sick and very savage."

"As with Mike Barrington, with Della Davis, with Luz?" Meyer asked. "As with my travel clock which is now junk?"

"Mr. Nesta? You had what we'll call an exploratory session with him. Do you buy him?"

"No. Not for that. Maybe, without the alibi, for what happened on the Coyotepec Road. Hallucination, violence, amnesia. But not what . . . was done to Rockland. It's fallacious to try to assess what any human being is capable of, naturally."

"You know, Meyer, my friend, what has put us into cerebral shock is knowing that Rockland was probably capable of doing to others just what was done to him. He was the sweet guy who led Bix Bowie out into the cornfield. He was the charmer who did the one thing that would finally destroy Carl Sessions. And he—possibly—set Bix up to fly off the mountains."

Meyer shrugged, massively, slowly, expressively. He wore that inexpressibly mournful look of the giant anthropoid, of the ape who knows there is not one more plantain left in the rain forest.

"There's Bundy," he said without conviction. "We don't know if Bundy told us the whole story, and . . . Forget it. It was a stranger. It was somebody who took a dislike to him, for some strange reason."

Lady Rebecca Divin-Harrison came up behind me and pressed my shoulder affectionately. "Travis darling! How lovely to see you again, dear." I came to my feet, feeling as clumsy and oppressed as the big-footed kid who has to come into the living room to meet mother's bridge friends. I mumbled the presentation of Meyer. She had a friend with her, a sunburned youth of sufficient inches over six feet to be able to look me right in the eye. He was rawboned, shy, with cropped blond hair and a face and manner from the midwest farm belt.

"I want you to meet Mark Woodenhaus," she said. "Isn't that a precious name?" The boy suddenly looked even more sunburned. "He's been working out in a primitive village doing some kind of sanitation thing with the . . . what is the name of it, dear?"

"The Friends' Service Committee, ma'am."

"And I found him trudging down the highway all hot and dusty and carrying a monstrous dufflebag because he couldn't spare bus fare. It's volunteer work, isn't it, dear?"

"Yes, ma'am."

"And I truly believe that parasites like myself should take every chance to express their deep gratitude to marvelous young men like Mark, don't you, Travis?"

"The best is none too good," I said. I could not see through the dark lenses of her glasses very well, but thought I saw a significant wink. "Would you like to sit with us?" I asked her.

"Oh, thank you so much, but I think not. We have some errands to do, don't we, Mark darling? Some bits of luxury for those poor young people slaving away out there in the bush. So nice to see you, really. Do hope you'll be about for a time, Travis. Come along, Mark."

She looked, as one might well say, smashing. Vibrant and saucy and a-hum with improbable energies. Happily predatory, she scurried along in her lime-yellow slacks beside the gangly, unsuspecting prey, with his plowjockey stride. The solid and shapely behind swung in graceful clench and cadence, and as I watched it disappear down the long aisle between the evening tables, I remembered the tag line because of its aptness.

I'd been out in the placid Gulf of Mexico off Manasota Key in a small boat with a good and longtime friend named Bill Ward. We were trolling slowly for anything interesting and edible. But there was no action. A gull came winging by, and in the silence, out of boredom, Bill aimed a forefinger at it and said, quietly, "Bang!" At that precise instant the gull, spotting a small meal on the surface, dropped like a stone. Bill, eyes and mouth wide in amazement, turned toward me, inadvertently aiming the lethal finger at me. "Don't aim that thing at me," I told him.

"And there you sit," Meyer said, "steeped in jealous envy."

"Smiling, the boy fell dead."

"Well, he has found a Friend. And the magic word is Service. But it will play hell trying to get back to that primitive village, carrying that dufflebag."

"And on his hands and knees. Where were we? Hell, let's write a finish for it, Meyer, for a bad movie. Harl Bowie is really not confined to a wheelchair. And that German nurse of his got her basic training in concentration camps. So, as a cover story, he suckered us into coming down here openly. He knew the whole story, snuck into town with the German nurse, and took care of Rockland before ever sending us down here."

Meyer smiled and then sobered. "Remember my saying that one shouldn't guess about what people are capable of? I think if Harlan Bowie knew the whole story, he could possibly do that to Rocko."

"So let's write the part for Wally McLeen. Minda didn't make as many bad scenes as Bix, but it wasn't exactly a fond daddy's idea of a nice vacation for dear daughter."

Meyer chuckled. "Poor Wally. What's the word for what he's trying to do? He's trying to get with it. Or maybe that expression is already passé."

"And for a man devoting his whole time to tracking down his daughter, he isn't very well organized. He hadn't even nailed down the names of the original group."

We sat in our silences, watching the people.

Meyer said, "Somebody had a hell of a long and lonely and conspicuous walk back from the place where we found the camper. Unless, of course, they had a rented Honda to offload before running the truck into the dry gulley."

"Come off it, friend. Wally is trying to establish communication. He is a very earnest little guy. Boring, obvious, comical . . . but earnest."

More silence. Then it was my turn. "So he reports a conversation with Rockland. He *says* he didn't know it was Rockland. He *says* the mysterious stranger tried to con him out of money in return for producing darling daughter. It accounts for the two of them being seen together in a public place . . . how long before Rockland had his little misfortune?"

Meyer half-closed his eyes and turned his computer on. "Wally McLeen claimed they talked on the . . . we figured out that it had to be the last day of July. Rockland lived five more days. But could that puffy little man immobilize Rockland long enough to wire him and gag him? Unlikely. And could he have done the mischief on the Coyotepec Road? Three of them?"

So I thought that over and finally said, "Item. Let's say, just for the hell of it, that Wally went into that compound believing that Jerry Nesta was there with the others. He could have taken Mark by surprise, then got the two women before they could run. Then he could have scurried around and found that Jerry wasn't there. Item. He made a point of telling me he had been out on the Coyotepec Road that morning on his rented bike."

Meyer shook his head. "No, Travis. We're playing bad games."

"Agreed. But he *is* a common denominator, and so what we do is get him off the books because if we don't he'll muddy up the logic of the situation. And we get to throw two stones at one bird, because maybe he knows something useful, without knowing how useful it is."

"But we will have to listen to the communication lecture again."

"And admire the progress of the chin whiskers."

Meyer remembered the room number and went and checked and came back and said the key was in the box, so Wally McLeen was out. I took a stroll down the porch and couldn't spot him. I put a note in his box to call me at the Victoria. By then it was five minutes past the time we had all agreed to meet on the veranda. And the sisters appeared, newly and too elegantly coiffed, high heels, gloves, evening bags, dresses more suited to the night life of Guadalajara or Mexico City than to a September night in Oaxaca.

Their festive smiles and dancing eyes dimmed when they saw that Meyer and I were still in the rough dusty clothes of the expedition to the burned land, and they exchanged a meaningful sisterly glance. They came to the table and were seated. I said that I was sorry that we had not yet had time to change. I said that it had been an evil day, and they would have to forgive us if we seemed solemn and tired. I said that Enelio Fuentes was also tired, and that he and Lita had decided not to join us.

Any affront Elena may have felt was erased immediately by the concern in her eyes as she searched my face. She moved her chair closer, laid her hand on my wrist. In a little while I noticed that Meyer and Margarita were gone. I had not seen them leave. I told Elena, in our special clumsy mixture of English and Spanish, that I was sorry she had taken such care to dress for a dinner party. She said she had dressed to please me. I said there could be no question of that. She said that whatever I wished—*cualquier tu quieres*—that would be the evening that would please her. I said that I wished to go up the hill with her, to have a quiet drink with her, to have food together, and to have love. She said she had planned on love in any case.

The last angle of the sun before it slipped over the mountains found her face with a single shaft of orange light. She looked at me, her eyes moving back and forth, focusing on each of my eyes in turn, and she wore a small, questioning sensuous frown. Black pupils set in deepest brown, whites of her eyes blue-white with superb health, long fringe of wiry black lashes, long oval face, matte golden skin, microscopic beads of moisture in the down of her upper lip above the broad solid mouth. Then suddenly her eyes looked heavy and her mouth loosened, and her head bowed slightly. She took a deep and shuddering breath and exhaled slowly. Her nostrils flared and the enameled nails bit into my wrist. She smiled and said, "Why we are sitting here so long time, *querido*?"

I could have reported to Enelio—but I knew I would not—that a back can be effectively scrubbed in a tiled shower stall, and that there is no real need for a special brush and special soap. Also gin over ice is cold and pleasant and goes with a hot shower in a very Sybaritic way. I could have reported that soon I came to believe that I would live forever, and even sang a little.

Good steaks came down the hill from the hotel, and when we were done we put the cart outside at the end of the porch, turned off the lights and sat comfortably and quietly and had coffee and looked at the stars. Wally had the grace to phone at that time, and I went in and took it in the dark, sitting on the turned-down bed.

"Trav? This is Wally. I just found your note in the box a little while ago. What's it about? Have you . . . have you heard something about Minda?"

"I wish I had, Wally. No. This is something else."

"Well, what is it?"

"Meyer and I would like to have a chat with you when it's convenient, Wally."

"What about?"

"We think it's a good idea to pool everything we've all learned up to this point. What do you think?"

"Well . . . I guess it couldn't do any harm."

"When would be a good time? Now?"

"Oh, not now. I'm going with a bunch of the kids up to Monte Albán to see the ruins by moonlight again. Say, how about tomorrow morning? Have you ever seen the ruins at Yagul? It's only about ten miles down the Mitla Road, and there's a sign where you turn off to it."

"I saw the sign the last time we were out that way."

"I'm getting turned on pretty good by these ruins. I mean they are sort of timeless, and your own troubles don't seem to mean so much. They don't really know much about Yagul. It's so quiet there, you can sit and . . . contemplate things. I was planning to go out early. I'll be there all morning. Why don't you and Meyer come out any time tomorrow morning? It will be a good place to talk. I think a place that is very, very old and peaceful and dead is a good place for really talking, don't you?"

"Sure, Wally. We'll see you there."

As I talked I had heard her close the door and click the night lock. I had heard a tock of heels on the tile, then felt a dip of the bed as she sat on the other side. Whisk-whisper of nylons, then slap-pad of bare feet. Zipper-purr, rustle of fabric, click of snaps. Dip of bed again. I hung up. Hand on my shoulder to urge me around and pull me down to a mouth that fastened firmly and well, while a hand plucked at the tied belt of the robe I had put on after showering. Voice making a tuneless little contented *ummming* sound, way back in the strong round throat.

"This you want?" she whispered. "Turn some bad day to good things?"

"This I want."

"This you have, Tuh-rrrravis."

"You are fine."

"Sank you ver' motch. You are doing some thing in Mexico . . . how you say? . . . *peligroso?*"

"Dangerous? I don't know. Maybe, maybe not."

She held me tightly and made a small growling sound in her throat. "Some person hurting you, Elena will fix. Tear out some eyes. Cut out some tongue. Breaking all bones, *verdad?*"

Something came flickering in through the back door of my mind, but by then everybody had become too busy to notice, and so the thought sat patiently out there in the back entryway until somebody had time to notice it.

I got around to noticing it when she lay purring into my throat, tickling weight of long heavy dark hair fanned across my chest. I eased the blanket up over her without awakening her. The thought that had come into the back of my mind was a memory of how the primitive warriors of history dreaded being handed over, alive, to the women of the enemy tribe. There had been a very convincing savagery in Elena's threats about what she would do to whoever harmed me.

Rockland had gone to Eva Vitrier's estate in La Colonia, and he had managed to take Bix Bowie away in Bundy's car. Bundy had been wickedly pleased to learn that Eva could become emotionally involved, infatuated, with a girl she saw on the street and contrive to invite the girl and her friend into her home. The two girls had been her guests for a long time. It would seem plausible that they might tell Eva Vitrier some of the rancid highlights of their vacation in Mexico, the same things Nesta had told Meyer.

So sooner or later Mrs. Vitrier would reveal, calculatingly or accidentally, her desire for the Bowie girl. In view of Bix's passivity about being used in physical ways, perhaps an actual affair had begun. Safe to assume that Minda McLeen would be opposed, and also fair to state there was very little she could do about it. So the note to Harlan Bowie about coming to get Bix may have come from Minda. Perhaps the girls quarreled over Eva's attentions to Bix, Minda demanding that Bix leave, Bix refusing. So Minda left.

Knowing Rockland's past abuse of Bix, knowing Rockland was responsible for her addiction, knowing Rockland was responsible for her death that Sunday evening, what would happen to Rockland if he went back to the Vitrier house? She could very well have mutilated him in exactly the ways I had seen. The flaying and blinding could even be said to be a symbolic expression of her attitude toward male sexuality. And perhaps her wealth enabled her to employ muscle she could trust—muscle that could overpower him, truss him up, leave him alone for her savage attentions, and then dispose of truck, camper, and body in one package.

So then Wally McLeen would be a waster of time. But it was set, so we'd lose nothing by going through with it. I thought of a twelve-second system for opening him up, and knew it would draw a wide dazed blank. He was one of the nice little people you meet on a Honda.

Elena suddenly began to jerk and twitch and make muffled little yelping sounds. I woke her up, and tenderly and gently quieted her down. She said it had been a terrible, terrible dream. I had been broken into tiny bits, and if she could put them together in time I would live. But the little wet pieces kept crawling away in every direction as she tried to reconstruct me.

16

THURSDAY WAS another bright, hot, beautiful morning. I had spent the time after driving Elena to town, sitting at the desk in the room and going through Rockland's little red notebook. There were Miami and Miami Beach addresses, and addresses all over the country, presumably people who had stayed at the Sultana and who had subscribed to one of Rockland's services—in one way or another. It would be logical for him to keep such a record.

The notes and reminders were too cryptic to be of any use. Things like "L. 2 Sat aft"; "2 doz, suite 20B"; "100 Reb in 7th." As they were chronological, I could get enough hints to figure out when notes were made. He didn't make many. There was a notation of the cost of new tires in pesos and dollars, made before they got to Oaxaca. And just a few addresses after that, Bundy, the Vitrier estate, the hotel where Bix and Minda had stayed, and one that read, "I. V. Rivereta, Fiesta D, Mex City." All the rest of the pages were completely blank. On the inside back cover was his social security number.

At breakfast I checked out my twelve-second system with Meyer. "If I start edging up on him, he has time to adjust, assuming he's our nut, which I doubt. So I will drop it on him suddenly and from considerable altitude, and we will watch his throat and his mouth and his eyes like a pair of eagles, and no man living can make a fast enough recovery to hide every part of it, especially when I come on very amiable and kindly and understanding."

I told him the approach. He approved. He had watched me do it before. He had seen it work and seen it fail.

So we drove out to the turnoff to Yagul. We could see it a couple of miles north of the main road as we turned off, old stone patterns atop a rounded hill which bore faint traces of the old horizontal terracing. I drove across flats and then up the steep winding road to a wide paved parking area. There was an old sedan there with Mexican plates, and the small Honda. That was all.

As we got out, a large Mexican family came down the worn path from the ruins and started getting into the sedan, arguing about who would sit where. We went up the path. A gnarled little man came trudging out of a shady spot to collect the small government fee and give us our handsomely printed tickets. He went back to his place in the shade, his back against raw rock. From there he could look out across the valley, with all the ruins behind him.

The morning sky was a deep rich Kodachrome blue. A buzzard wheeled in the updraft from the hill slope, making sounds very like a pig. Tall clumps of cactus with big red blossoms grew out of the stony soil. It was indeed quiet. Two buses moved along the valley floor toward Oaxaca, stolid, silent beetles.

We came upon the traditional ball court, a long sunken rectangle with sloping sides of carefully fitted stone, with the high place where the priests sat and watched, and the lower places for the other spectators. Tricky bounces off those side walls. Iron rings set into the stone at either end, now long rusted away. Archeologists believe that the captain of the winning team was beheaded. It was some sort of honor to strive for. It meant a permanent place in the record books. It would keep a team from running away with the league. Perhaps the same theory as the cellar team getting first draft choice.

We looked at the front of the long temple, at the altars, at the peak of a distant knoll beyond the edge of the temple front wall, and saw, silhouetted against the sky, along with some twisted little trees, a dumpy figure semaphoring its arms at us, and a faint hail came upwind.

We found the stone steps that would lead us up to the temple level. A lot of it was restored. When they restore, they stick pebbles in the mortar between the new courses of stone. The academic mind saying, "See? This is all fake. We stuck it on the way we *think* it used to be."

Behind the temple façade there were small courtyards and unroofed stone walls forming a maze of small rooms and corridors. After we came to two dead ends, I found a toe hold and climbed up and picked out the right route toward Wally's little hill. We came out the back of the temple complex and went up a narrow and winding footpath, puffing a little in the unaccustomed altitude.

Wally McLeen beamed upon us. "Isn't it great? See, from up here you look over into the next valley too. Pretty strategic place. These holes here, these were tombs. The big shots got buried at the highest place. They bust into every one they can find because there's gold jewelry in some of them. Now look back at the whole thing. Gold, sacrifices, underground passages, astronomy, brain surgery, it blows my mind thinking about it."

He wore a market shirt of coarse unbleached cotton, a pale blue beret acquired from God knows where, burgundy-colored walking shorts cinched around his comfortable tummy by a belt with a lot of silver knobs affixed to the leather, and market sandals. His goatee was coming along nicely. He carried a bag woven of yellow fiber, shaped like a two-handled market bag. He had flip-up sunglasses fastened to his thick eyeglasses, and the cycle was turning his previous angry red to a red-brown, with some pink patches on forehead and nose where the early burns had peeled.

"When Minda comes back, I want to show her all these places, Trav, on account of I know she'll flip. I remember when she was a little kid, one summer at the lake she found an arrowhead and I read to her all about the Indians, and you'd be surprised how much she remembered, a little kid like that. Just turned five years old. They can bolt another seat on that Honda and we can travel all over this part of Mexico."

Meyer had moved around into position, so that we were both facing him.

"But that won't work out so good, Wally," I told him.

"*Sure* it will!"

"For a while. But then sooner or later the cops are going to find that village kid that saw you dump the camper into the ravine, and find out what you did to Rocko, and start adding things up and nail you for Mike and Della and the Mexican woman, too. So you better aim that bike for the nearest border crossing, Wally."

It is like that lousy frog routine I had to do in high school biology lab. You hook up the battery and touch the wires to the right place and that slimy dead leg makes jumping motions.

He stared at me and he stared at Meyer. And his mouth hitched up into a weak little smile and then opened into an O. Not a big O.

About twice the size of the one you use to whistle. It went through the same pattern again.

"What the hell are you *talking* about?"

"Too long, Wally," Meyer said sadly. "You took too long finding the right way to play it. Too much was happening in your head. You froze. You had too much to add up."

"I . . . I've *got* to wait for Minda! You can understand that. I've got to wait for her to come back here!"

It was hard to believe it, looking at him, even though it had come through as clear as a ten page confession.

"Wally," I said, "I can understand the thing with Rockland, sort of. You're over the edge. You found out too much. Those three—Sessions, Nesta, Rockland—they turned your little girl on, and they banged her, and they degraded her, and something went wrong then in your head, Wally. This is a hell of a long way from the weekly Kiwanis meeting and the shopping center stores. What you did to Rockland means you've been taken sick. It means you've got to go into town and tell people about it and get help, because there was Mike Barrington and there was Della Davis and there was Luz."

"I know. That went wrong. I mean I wouldn't feel bad about it if I got Nesta too, because I thought it might have to be that way. I went in from the back, over the wall. The jeep was there when I went by, but when I came back to look for him I found it was gone. I should have waited for him to come back. But I got scared. I have to get him, you know. And I will. I made a vow. I've been working it all out. Mike and Luz were so close together, I got her before she could take a step, after he went down. But the nigger bitch could run like the wind. If she hadn't stumbled and fallen, she would have been out the gate and gone." His voice was small and thoughtful, the words half lost in a small warm wind that gusted and died.

"What did they do to you . . . or Minda?" Meyer asked.

The shadow of the buzzard angled across the stony earth between us. Silent, awkward tableau. Wally McLeen bent over and picked up a small triangular shard of Zapotecan pottery. He looked at it with care and flipped it aside.

"I like the ones with designs," he said. "I like to think of them out here, hundreds and hundreds of years ago, scratching little designs in the clay to make the pots prettier. Funny thing about that. This morning, maybe an hour ago, over there down the slope of the hill, I found a piece that reminded me of an ashtray Minda made for me in the first or second grade. She made the same kind of wavy lines in the clay. I've got it here in the bag." He opened it and peered down in, reached in.

My alarm system went off too late. He yanked out some kind of a weapon, swinging it so swiftly I could not see what it was. From where he stood, his first choice was a backhand slap at Meyer. He should not have been able to reach him, but he did. There was the sickening solid thonk of a hard object striking the skull. Meyer went down in a bad way—a boneless sloppy tumble. There was no interval, no half-step, no attempt to break the fall. In a fluid continuation of the same motion, McLeen took a forehand shot at me and I sprang back, leaning back at the same time, and even so felt the wind of it across my upper lip, heard its whistling sound. He stood nicely balanced, slightly crouched as I moved back cautiously. Meyer had rolled over twice, down the slope, slowly, but it took him to a steeper slant and he rolled more rapidly for perhaps fifteen feet before the upper half of his body dropped into one of the small open tombs. He was wedged there then, the legs spraddled, toeing in, the substantial bottom turned toward the blue sky.

The weapon was at rest. I could see what it was. He held a hardwood stick about two feet long, gray with age, greased with much handling. A leather thong, heavy, tightly braided, was fastened to the end of the stick. The end of the thong was fastened to a crude metal ring that had somehow been affixed to a stone, round, polished, irregular, a little smaller than a peach.

He came at me with a little rush of quick light steps, bouncy and balanced. I feinted to run down the slope, then dodged and ran uphill, angling away from him. The feint had been a mistake. He missed my head by an inch. I realized I had seen smallish portly men like Wally McLeen moving very lightly and quickly and well on many dance floors in years past. Long-waisted men like Wally, and with the same short, hefty legs.

"I bought this in a stall in the public market," he said. "One of the kids told me it was a fake. But it's just like the soldiers used to use. It's tricky. You have to practice with it. The handle is limber. See? So all you need is good wrist action. I practiced on trees. You have to get the range right."

"Let me go help Meyer. Please, Wally."

"You can't help him. He's dead. Or dying."

When again he came bouncing toward me, I spun and ran up the slope all out, thinking to get far enough away from him so that I could circle around and go down toward the temple. But as I started down the other side I took a quick look back and saw that he was only thirty feet behind me, moving too well. There was a crumbling, unrestored wall to my left and I angled toward it, snatched up a chunk of rock and turned and hurled it at him. He scrambled to the side and it gave me enough leeway to pick up another jagged piece and, in too much haste, overthrow him. He backed away quickly.

With more time, I was able to pick up one of better size and heft. I turned it to fit the hand, and took my best shot. He was fifty to sixty feet away. I put it on a good line, right toward the middle of his face. He moved just his head. He moved it quickly to the side and just as far as was necessary.

A rock fight. Too many years since the last one. I might be able to get away from him, but that wasn't enough. I had to get to Meyer, and I had to get to him soon. I didn't like the choices. If I picked some good rocks and charged him, trying to get close enough to chunk him, he was going to have just as good, or better, a chance to bust my skull as he had with the three in the old compound on the Coyotepec Road. He was too good with that thing, and he could make it whistle.

A madman is curiously deadly. When the strictures and restraints of civilization and conscience are wiped away, the animal can move with ancient shrewdness. Man is a predator.

He stood downhill from me, slowly swinging the stone ball from side to side at the end of the stick, planning what to do next. Stocky little storekeeper in blue beret and new goatee, and just as calmly intent on killing me as a Bengal tiger would have been.

I squatted by my wall and picked up a rock the size of my head and held it in both hands and arched it at him, like taking a shot from the foul line. He squinted up at it and stepped to his right. It hit, bounced and rolled down through the coarse grass and brush toward the temple level below. All the ruins were silent. For perhaps the first time in my life I desperately wanted to see a chattering flock of tourists, festooned with Instamatics, leaving a spoor of yellow boxes.

I knew that if I didn't come up with something workable, fat Wally would, and I wouldn't like it.

Misdirection is the name of the game. I couldn't point behind him and yell, "Hey! Tourist!" and hope to bounce a rock off his skull as he turned and stared.

But he had looked up at the big rock, hadn't he? Indeed he had. So I palmed a couple of good small ones, holding them in place against my palm with ring fingers and little fingers, and picked up another big melon of a rock and gave it as much height and distance as I could, and as he looked up at it, I let fly with the first small stone. He glimpsed my movement and looked at me, moving swiftly to his left along the slope. He ducked away from the first small one, had to check the one in the air again to be sure he was out from under it, and moved forward, taking the second small rock high on the forehead and going ass over teacup into a backward somersault as I came bounding down the slope. He peered up at me, on hands and knees, a bright rush of blood on his face. He had lost the ancient fake weapon and the blue beret and his glasses. But he reached and grabbed the weapon and took a blind full-arm swing and got me on the outside of the left thigh, just below the hip bone. It felt to me as if he had smashed the hip. I fell and rolled and got up, surprised to be able to get up. He wiped blood out of his eye and started toward me and I made ready for him, telling myself I would catch that damned rock, catch it in my teeth if I had to, and take it away from him and feed it to him. He hesitated and ran down the slope. I saw him fall and roll and get up and disappear into the maze of walls behind the temple façade. I was trembling with reaction. I picked up the sweaty beret and the eyeglasses with the tilt-shades attached, and saw that one lens was shattered.

I went hobbling on my broken, ground-glass hip to the opened tombs and heard myself saying, "Sorry. Sorry, Meyer. Sorry."

I got him by the belt and pulled him out of the tomb. He seemed very heavy. I rolled him onto his back. He was very loose and sloppy. He had a lump over his ear the size of an apple. His cheeks and forehead were scratched and torn from rolling down the slope. I put my ear against his chest, and the mighty old heart of Meyer said, reassuringly, "Whup tump, whup tump, whup tump."

So I thumbed an eyelid up, and a blank, sightless, and bright blue eye stared out, stared through and beyond me.

The other one opened, unaided, and slowly the focus came back from ten thousand miles in space, down through all the layers with fancy names, and stared at me. Tongue came out and licked dusty lips. Rusty voice said, "So? So hello."

"Are you dying?"

"The point is debatable. What happened? I saw McLeen way up on the hill. We started up. Here I am. I fell?"

"You got hit on the head with a rock."

A slow hand came up and the fingers touched the lump. "This is part of my head? Way out there?"

"Do you want to sit up?"

"I would like to think about it. We economists have very thick skulls. It is a characteristic. Everybody knows that. But we are happy people with a great sense of rhythm."

"You are talking a lot."

"It keeps my mind off my head. So let's try this sitting up part."

He sat up and spent a little time moaning. And then he stood up, and we started down the slope, very slowly.

"Why are you limping?" he asked.

"I, too, got hit with a rock."

"What do you have there in your hand?"

"A blue beret and a pair of broken glasses. Shut up, Meyer."

"Ask a stupid question and you get . . ."

"Shut up, Meyer."

"Sit up, Meyer. Stand up, Meyer. Walk, Meyer. Shut up, Meyer."

I had been listening for the snoring sound of the Honda heading down the hill, and I hadn't heard it yet. It made me thoughtful. So I made Meyer sit on a short, wide, restored wall, and hold the beret and glasses. I went over to the side and climbed up onto a high wall. I could see a portion of the parking lot. I could see the Falcon and the cycle. I looked around. I could see the pattern of the maze, but not down into the rooms and corridors.

I dropped down from the wall, and managed not to scream out loud. Just silently, in the brain. I listened for a long time. I moved a few feet and listened again.

With an explosive grunt of effort he came scuttling out of a doorway, blinking and swinging, forgetting that part about the wrist action, and forgetting how tall I am. I stepped inside the arc, so well inside it that the lethal rock which I had expected might wrap around me and splinter a rib, smacked the wall behind me instead. I got one paw on the stick and the flat of my other hand against his chest, pushed and yanked and took away the toy. He ran backward, kept his balance, turned, and kept running. I went after him with no hope of catching him—not on a leg that felt as if I were wearing it backwards—but to see where he was headed, and if there was anyone interested in stopping him.

He came out onto the wide stone plaza that ran along the front of the temple façade. By the time I got to the end of the unroofed corridor and made the turn, he was scooting along toward the nearest set of big steep stone stairs leading down to the lower courtyard level, to the same level as the ball court a hundred yards away.

As I came hitching and galumphing along, I saw him make his turn and slow to go down the stone steps. He tried to take the steps in stride, but he had not slowed quite enough, probably because perceptions of depth and distance were flawed without the thick lenses. So momentum carried him to the outside edge of the stairs. There was no railing. And he flailed his arms to recover balance but momentum took him over, leaning further and further, his feet trying to stay on the edge of the steep stone.

He dropped out of my sight. I heard a single cry which could have been "Oh!" and which could have been "No!" The sound ended with a whacking, dusty thud. I went down the steps and around and back to where he lay, half in white sunlight, half in black shadow. He lay on his right side in white dust, using a rock for a pillow, left arm curled around the pillow.

I went down onto one knee with some difficulty, and as I placed the pads of three fingers against the big artery in the side of his throat, I could see into his half-open mouth, see the neat gleam of a reasonably new filling. The dentist probably belonged to the same luncheon clubs and called him Wally, told him jokes and told him when to spit. The artery throbbed once, and in about three seconds throbbed again with half the vigor, and then did not ever move again. Escaping air rattled in his throat. All my life I had heard about the death rattle. Thought it was a myth. Now it was confirmed. A classic sample. A collector's item.

I stood up and walked beyond the steps. No tourists. A thousand years worth of silence. Baked rocks. Shards. Dust. A lot of Indio blood had soaked into the soil of Yagul, enough to chill the back of my neck. And I had to go up and get Meyer and did not relish the climb.

But Meyer was sitting up on the stone plaza, his feet on the top stair. His color was pasty.

"I told you to stay put."

"I came to tell you I feel very dizzy. And . . . in all truth, a little bit frightened."

I got up those stairs and got him down them, taking a lot of his weight. I then put the blue beret next to the stone pillow, and tucked one bow of the broken glasses under Wally's cheek. I had shoved the wooden handle of the weapon down inside my belt, above the right hand pants pocket, and put the stone ball in the pocket, so that only the braided leather showed.

Walked by the ball court, out along the path. No new visitors. Tourists go to Monte Albán, to Mitla, not often to Yagul. I shouted the gnarled little ticket-taker out of his shady nest, and pointed back in agitation, and then at the Honda, saying in my pidgin Mexican that the man had fallen, the man was hurt. He looked absolutely blank, and then there was sudden comprehension and concern. I said I would have the *ambulancia* come, the *Cruz Rojo, los doctores*. He went trotting to find the dead daddy of the dear daughter, and I wedged Meyer into the Falcon and took off. Before we got to the main highway, he toppled over against the door on his side.

The large modern hospital was on the fringe of La Colonia, toward the city. I was glad I had taken Brucey and Davey there. I left rented rubber on every turn, using one hand to hold Meyer in place when I made turns to the right.

A birdlike little nurse came hurrying out of the emergency entrance. She ignored my linguistics. She looked at Meyer, sucked air audibly as she saw the lump on his head. She directed the attendants who lifted him onto the stretcher and rolled him in. I refused to understand their instructions to get my car out of the way, knowing it was perhaps the quickest way to contact somebody who could speak English.

A big brown man in a white smock appeared and said, "Would you please move your car out of the ambulance gate, sir. You can park it in back."

"My friend and I saw a man fall from in front of the temple at Yagul. While we were hurrying to tell the man who sells the tickets, my friend fell and struck his head. The man who fell was an American tourist, and I think the fall may have killed him, Doctor. What about my friend?"

"He is being examined right now. If you will move your car and then go to the office and help with the admission papers . . ."

"Is he in bad shape?"

"*Please* move your car."

And so I did. Then a large, billowy, benevolent lady in the office helped me interpret their form and put Meyer's name, rank, and serial number in the right spaces. I caught Enelio Fuentes just as he was leaving the agency. I was using the phone on her desk. Enelio came through with that clout and speed that only a certified member of the local establishment can provide. A Doctor Elvara arrived twenty minutes later to be a consultant on the case. He was young, brisk, authoritative, and emotionless. After fifteen minutes he came back to the waiting room and made his report.

"There is no fracture. The patient regained consciousness and seemed rational, and then lapsed again into a comatose condition. It is obvious there is a severe concussion. The question of tissue damage cannot be resolved as yet. Pulse, respiration and pressure are good. It is safe to say there is no major area of hemorrhage in the brain, according to present symptoms. There could be a slow seepage from small blood vessels and torn capillaries. If so, the indication will be a deterioration in pressure, respiration, and pulse. We have no mechanized intensive care installation, and so the procedure here is to use student nurses on one hour shifts, constantly taking the pulse rate and the blood pressure and the rate of respiration and marking them on a special chart form which carries a column for cumulative change. If percentage change exceeds specified limits, she will immediately alert surgery. I will be on call and be here by the time the patient is prepared. The chief resident in surgery will assist me. In almost every instance the seepage is subdural, evident, and readily accessible, with a favorable prognosis. When a deeper area is traumatized, the problem becomes more grave."

"Do you think you'll have to operate?"

"I do not make guesses."

I knew he would make his guess if I could word the question correctly. "Doctor Elvara, if you had ten patients with exactly the same test results as my friend, the same lump on the head, how many do you think would require surgery?"

"Hmmm. Ten is too small a sample. Make it a hundred. At least twenty would require surgery, perhaps as many as forty."

"Out of a hundred operations, given the same conditions thus far, how many wouldn't respond?"

"Perhaps five, perhaps four."

"How long does it usually take before you know whether you have to operate?"

"There will be a deterioration in the first twelve hours. But we would keep close watch for eighteen to be safe, then two more days of observation before the patient would be discharged."

"Thank you, Doctor."

"You are most welcome." He stopped outside the door and turned and looked in at me. "You . . . ask very nice questions," he said. It was probably his compliment for the whole calendar year.

So then, three chances out of ten they'll have to open your skull, Meyer, and if they do, it's twenty to one in your favor. Your friendly neighborhood oddsmaker can thus put up fifty bucks against the dollar you don't make it, and still have a twenty percent edge in his favor. But with your pants showing above the edge of the tomb, you didn't look all that good.

But nothing in the world could keep it from being a very very long twelve hours.

17

At eleven on Thursday night the twelve hours were up. Enelio, Margarita, and I got in to see him. Small room. Hospital gown. Side bars on the bed up. Blue beard on Meyer's jaws. White compress on the head lump. A squatty little girl in gray and white, skin color like old pennies, was pumping the bulb on the blood pressure gadget and reading the levels.

"Well, well, well," said Meyer.

Fuentes said, "Meyer, if you were a gentleman, you would tell the young lady there is a beetle crawling right across that little nurse cap." When she did not move, Enelio smiled and said, "No English."

"Some day," said Meyer, "kindly tell me what happened. Memory stopped. Travis, you are not limping as much."

"They stuck something in there that works like novocaine."

The girl posted her chart and started taking his pulse, moving her lips as she watched the sweep second on the gold watch pinned to her uniform.

"Meyer," I said, "it now appears that they do not have to open your skull and examine the contents."

His eyes went wide. "They were thinking of it?"

"All day long."

"Too bad," he said, "to deprive them of the chance. Better luck next time."

"Now we're going to the Victoria and celebrate. We'll order drinks for you too and take turns drinking yours."

"Salud, and happy days."

Margarita, however, was not going. She had pulled a chair close to the far side of the bed. The squatty student nurse made querulous objection. Margarita blazed up and exploded several packages of Spanish firecrackers around the girl's head. It backed her up and shut her up, and she soon resumed her testing.

Margarita looked content as a cat on a warm hearth. She held Meyer's hand, and with her free hand, she gave that odd little Mexican good-by wave, which looks more like a summoning than a dismissal.

Meyer gave us an inordinately fatuous smile. I told him I'd be back in the morning. He told me not to put myself out. Elena was waiting in the Falcon. She did not seem at all surprised that her sister had stayed with Meyer. I got the feeling it would have astonished her if Margarita had not stayed. Enelio followed us back to the Victoria. I left Elena off at the main building and told her to wait for me in the lounge. I parked the car there, and concealed the weapon once more, and walked down to the cottage with Enelio. Inside the cottage, with the blinds and draperies closed, Enelio stood and held the handle and let the stone ball swing from side to side, then swung it a few times, cautiously.

"Hey, one hell of a thing. I have seen the *autenticos*, in collections. Very much the same thing. Any weapon, they keep changing it, changing it, until it is as dangerous as they can make it. I think you better throw this thing away, my friend."

"I have that feeling about it too."

"By God, they were a bloody people. A thing like this, there's no halfway. What it does is kill."

I took it and put it in the closet on a shelf. I got out a bottle of genuine bottled-in-Guadalajara House of Lords gin, and phoned up for ice for both of us, and some mix for Señor Fuentes.

"What about the camper?"

"Fonny thing. One of our pilots saw something shiny in that arroyo and reported it to the Federals. Maybe they went out today. Maybe in the morning. No talk about it yet. I tell you, Martinez and Tielma are getting damn sick and tired of dead American tourists. Telephone calls come from Mexico City. 'What are you trying to do down there, you *estupidos!* Ruin business?' But I think the little fat man is no problem. Mexico is full of pyramids and temples and they are all of stone, and Mexico is full of tourists, and some of them are feeble and some are careless and some are dronk, and some have bad hearts and faint and fall, so it is not something special, one more little man with a sack full of pieces of pots, eh?"

"If anybody else had shown up, it would have been a different ball game."

"Not so many go to Yagul. Some days probably nobody. Maybe two or three days, nobody."

The ice and mix came. We fixed our own. He give a little lift of his glass and gave that Spanish toast that covers everything there is. "Health, money, love, and time to enjoy them." I've never been able to think of anything it doesn't cover.

"So," said Enelio, "your friend will be all right, and now it is finished, and now you go home and you tell nice pretty little lies to the father, eh?"

"Is it finished? All day I've been worrying about Meyer with half my mind and using the other half to list the questions I would have asked Wally McLeen but didn't get a chance to."

"What do you need to know from some fat little madman?"

"I wanted to know who crazed him. Somebody had to give him enough sordid and factual information to actually arm him like a bomb, to turn him into a deadly weapon."

"You told me he talked to that Rocko?"

"Yes. Apparently on the first night he was here. So he came here knowing who to look for. So I think it's fair to say that somewhere along the line Minda dropped him a letter or a postcard, telling who she was with and their destination. Otherwise, he and Rockland got together too fast. Too big a coincidence. I can see how Rocko would see it as a way to come up with some quick money. That would be his style, to sell a man his own daughter. But there wouldn't be any point in Rocko talking about what shape the girl was in, or talking about what kind of a trip they'd had, or telling him his daughter was hooked on speed."

"Speed?"

"Stimulants. Amphetamines. Dexedrine. People develop a physical tolerance but not a mental tolerance, so they hit it heavier and heavier and they can get pretty nervous and erratic. If they get so dead for sleep they try to balance it off with barbiturates, then the real trouble starts. Look, Enelio, Wally McLeen came here to find his daughter. He went looking for Rockland and found him. So Rockland said that, for a fee, he might be able to produce her. He knew the girls were guests of Eva Vitrier, and we can assume he knew her place is like a fortress. What he would have to do is get to Minda, con her into writing a note to her father, peddle the note for

half the money with the balance on delivery of the girl. But according to what Mrs. Vitrier told the police when she identified the body
of the Bowie girl, Minda and Bix had quarreled, and Minda had
gone to Mexico City a few days earlier. So Rockland went back to
Bruce Bundy's house and tried to leave in the middle of the night,
but Bundy had different ideas. So he didn't get to leave until Saturday, a little past noon. That leaves the rest of Thursday evening, and
all day Friday, and half of Saturday, for Wally McLeen to find out
where his daughter might be. I think he could have managed it. I
think he could have gotten to the Vitrier estate without any help
from Rockland. That's as far as I can take it. It's a point of focus, for
Wally McLeen, Minda, Rockland and Bix. So the Frenchwoman
must know something that will make sense out of it. What's the
name of that little lawyer again, on the crutches?"

"Alfredo Gaona y Navares."

"And I can't get past him to locate Eva Vitrier. Can you?"

"I would think no."

"But he does communicate important things to her."

"Maybe not direct. Anyway, I have told you—I don't want to play
very much of these games of yours, McGee."

"What if he can communicate with her directly? Is there anything
that anybody could tell him that he'd think important enough to
bother her with?"

Enelio got up and fixed a new drink. He shrugged. "I suppose he
is responsible for the house here, and the staff. It must always be
ready for her at any moment, I understand. I cannot think of any
problem of the house he could not take care of without bothering
her. Unless it is totally destroyed. You want me to burn it down, no
thanks!"

"There must be some way."

"He is a tough old man and he is being paid *not* to bother her,
Travis."

"And he is a very sharp-minded old man."

"Very."

He roamed the room, scowling, pausing to sip his drink. He
stopped in front of me. "One small idea. No good, maybe. From everywhere in the world it is possible to telephone to Oaxaca. I say possible. Our great *larga distancia* service makes grown men cry. But if
he can be in touch with her, he would follow instructions if there
was an order from her to him to phone her at once. Then, if some-

how you could learn to where the call is placed. . . . But how can we do that? Hide under his desk? Damn!"

"Suppose the message came to him by phone, Enelio."

He looked blank. "So?"

"Long distance connections are frequently bad, aren't they?"

"Bad? They are unspeakable sometimes."

"And local lines are out of order sometimes?"

"If it is only once a week, it is a very good week."

"So what if that old lawyer *thought* he was talking to the long distance operator."

"I think I begin to see . . ."

"And she said she had an urgent call for him from Señora Vitrier, person to person, but when she tried to get through his line was not working, and then the long distance call faded before she could get the place of origin of the call and the number. Perhaps, if he had the number, she could try to put the call through to the lady."

A slow smile spread across his face. "Señor McGee, you have a great talent. Of course, you have one loathsome disease, which is the need to know everything. But it is a beautiful talent. I have the correct little girl for this improvisation. Very bright, very lovely, very, very naughty. And to be trusted. . . . Why am *I*, Enelio Fuentes, helping you with this nonsense?"

"Because the disease is contagious."

"And it is also a very Mexican disease, you may have noticed."

So we agreed that I would come to the agency at ten-thirty Friday morning and he would have the girl briefed, and we would see what happened.

In the morning I went to the hospital first. Meyer was sitting up, eating a large bowl of hot oatmeal. The compress had dwindled to a small bandage, and the swelling was down. But his bright blue eyes peered out through two slits in puffed flesh of deep purple and cobalt blue. It made him look less simian—and more like a hairy, dissipated owl. The girls had stopped checking his condition on a continuous basis. He had a dull headache. He said he felt as if he had been rolled downhill in a barrel. He said everyone was being very nice to him. He said that everybody seemed to have the idea that if they were not nice enough to him, the señorita from Guadalajara would say a few little things that would make their hair smoke. She had gone off to the center of town to buy some things for him which she said would make him more comfortable. He had little idea what they might be.

He asked about Elena, and Enelio, and Lita, and I said that last night we had celebrated his thick skull by stopping at Enelio's bachelor penthouse apartment and picking up Lita and a hamper of cheese and fruit and wine, and the four of us had picnicked in the moonlight at the ruins at Monte Albán, and had toasted his health frequently, invented new lyrics to old songs, and identified the constellations. Now, Elena and Lita were resting, having vowed to slay anyone who woke them before noon. He said wistfully he was glad everybody was having such a nice time. Then he wanted to hear about Wally. He still was blacked out by a traumatic amnesia covering that period. I told him he wasn't ready yet. He should rest.

When I got to Enelio's office he was ready and impatient to get started. He closed and locked the office door. The chosen girl was named Amparo. She wore a pink mini-dress, had cropped hair and huge dark eyes and an amused, mocking mouth. She was not the least bit nervous about the chore. She used Enelio's private line, which did not go through the switchboard.

Though her Spanish was faster than I could follow, she had adopted, for the occasion, that flat, impartial, decorous tone of long distance operators the world over, and the overly careful enunciation of all numerals.

She spoke, listened, spoke again, wrote on the pad beside the phone, said something else, then sat for several moments with her palm over the mouthpiece. She then said something which ended in *momentito*, thanked him, and hung up.

Enelio went over and ripped the top sheet off the pad. He bent over the girl and kissed her heartily. She beamed and bridled and went switching out, giving Enelio a solemn wink after she had unlocked the door.

"She is close," Enelio said. "Mexico City. Hotel Camino Real. Extension F.D."

We shook hands. Successful conspiracy warms the blood. He told me that the girl had pretended to place the call, and had told him the circuits were busy and she would try again in a little while. So, when Alfredo Gaona did not hear, he would try again, and it would go through normal channels, and there would be a certain amount of confusion and apology.

He checked the schedules and discovered that if I could get to the airport in fifteen minutes, I could be in Mexico City at twenty after twelve. He said he would explain to Elena. I was not dressed for the trip. He ran me back into the suite of bedroom, dressing room, and bath off his office, grabbed some clothes, and jammed them into a small suitcase.

I gave him my car keys and told him where I was parked. He said he would inform Meyer and have the car taken up to the hotel and the keys left at the desk. I changed to his shirt in the car on the wild ride out, and finished putting the necktie on as we got there. I knew the jacket was going to be uncomfortably snug. They were so close to departure they would not have waited for me. But they were all pleasantly glad to do a favor for Señor Fuentes. He slipped a tip into the hand of the stewardess, patted her on her behind, said he would sign inside for my ticket. We got on, and the stairs came up, and she spun the lock, and I got the belt buckled as the aircraft reached the end of the runway and turned for final check and takeoff.

I checked into the Camino Real at five after one on Friday afternoon. No reservation. A single. Any single. Yes sir, of course sir, thank you, sir. Twelve twenty-eight for the gentleman. Enjoy your stay with us, Señor McGee.

I unpacked the assorted garments. I sat on the bed and read the instructions on how to dial other rooms in the hotel. But there was no clue as to how to dial F.D. I tried the operator. With hardly a pause she said, "I am ver' sorreeee, but I am ask to put no calls to that number, Señor."

Hmmm.

Sat at the desk and used the elegant stationery and elegant envelope. *Am very anxious to speak to you on a matter of the greatest importance.* Name and room number. Sealed it. Señora Eva Vitrier. Took it down to the desk. The man checked the indexed list of guests. Handed it back.

"I am sorry, sir. We have no one of that name in the hotel. Perhaps if you check the reservation desk, they might know if she is coming in."

Thank you very much.

Hmmm.

So I went down to the shop near the coffee shop and bought razor, toothbrush, and the other essentials. Went into the coffee shop. Hamburger and coffee. Very tourist-like.

Obviously the lady had built walls here also. She liked walls around her, with broken glass on top.

Big money plus a passion for privacy makes an effective combination. How long since anyone has seen Howard Hughes?

Went back to the lobby area and roamed about until I found a bellhop with a very amiable expression. Laid ten pesos on him to tote my little sack of toiletries up to twelve twenty-eight. It was enough to make him look even more amiable. It established me as a guest. When he came back down I intercepted him again, my hand in my pocket. He looked delighted.

"Say, all these rooms have numbers, but there seems to be phone numbers with letters instead of numbers."

"What, señor? What, please?"

"Suppose a phone number is F.D. Where is that?"

"What, señor? No understands."

"*Si el número de teléfono es effay day, donde está el cuarto?*"

"Oh! Oh, yes, señor. Isss not a room. Isss a suite. Other part of hotel, that way. Effay means is Fiesta Suite. Effay ah. Effay bay. Effay—"

I thrust another ten onto him and told him that was very interesting. And something was nibbling at the frayed edge of my memory. Yes indeed. Fiesta D, in Rockland's little red book. With a name I could not remember. I found a writing desk and made some tries at it. I. V. Rivatera. I. V. Traviata.

Close. But not close enough.

Eva Vitrier. And there is the old game of anagrams. So take out an "i" and a "v," and you have the letters E A V T R I E R. And in three tries they assemble into Rivereta. I. V. Rivereta was exactly right.

New envelope. Same note. Tear open and reseal. Mrs. I. V. Rivereta. Walk to desk.

"Would you please see that this is delivered?"

Checks the index. "Yes sir. Thank you, sir."

"Thank *you*."

Walk back up to room and turn on the television and watch an episode of *Gunsmoke* and wonder how come they all speak Spanish; and wait. And wait. And wait. Start to give up and wonder what the hell to try next.

Quarter to five. Got the phone on the second ring.

"Mister McGee?" A throaty and charming voice, with that strange

French bit with the vowels, and the little clickety R's of the Parisian.

"This is he." Grammar reassures.

"I 'ave your note. What is this thing of so much great importance?"

This was a crucial moment. I had the feeling that if I said the wrong thing she would hang up, and that would be the end of it for good and all.

"It concerns Beatrice Bowie, Walter Rockland, Minda McLeen, Walter McLeen and, of course, you."

"Perhaps it is important to you, yes? But not to me."

At least I had not lost her yet. "I want to remind you that it is a matter of record in Oaxaca that Miss McLeen and Miss Bowie were staying with you. It is a matter of record that you identified the body. It is a matter of record that Miss Bowie was under suspicion of complicity in an attempt to smuggle narcotics into the United States."

"This has nothing to do with me. Nothing. I should not have . . . done the kindness of helping them find out who that poor child was, and giving them her possessions to send home to her family. I do not become involved in such matters."

"But the point is you *did* become involved. I agree with you, Mrs. Vitrier. Things should always be handled privately and with discretion. I find myself in an awkward position. I must return to Florida and report to the Bowie girl's father. He wanted to know the circumstances of her death. If I go back to him with a lot of unanswered questions, he has the resources to pursue this matter through diplomatic channels. I have talked to your attorney in Oaxaca, Alfredo Gaona. He refused to give me any help in getting in touch with you. But from talking to him, I think I know how much you value your privacy."

"Do you now have a desire to threaten me in some way, Mister McGee?"

"No. But should Mr. Harlan Bowie pursue this further because I could not give him any answers, I would think that the Mexican government would make a complete and official investigation, as a matter of diplomatic courtesy. And I do not think that you could . . . stay behind your walls under such circumstances."

There was such a long pause I began to be afraid she had hung up very quietly. Then she said, "I have always enjoyed this country. But you see, it is not entirely necessary to me, is it? There is nothing to prevent my leaving tomorrow and never coming back here. What I have would be sold without difficulty."

"I think that would be a very odd thing for you to do."

"I cannot be impressed with what you might think of what I do or do not do."

"I merely meant that it seems like such an extreme reaction to a very simple thing. I just want to fill in the blanks. It would not take much of your time. And then I would leave you alone, and I could make my report to Mr. Bowie. It's that simple."

"I think . . . you are a clever person, Mr. McGee."

"Not particularly."

"To learn the name I use here was a clever thing. Poor Alfredo was dreadfully upset to learn there had been no call from me. So it is to understand you found where I am by tricking that old man. But certainly he did not tell you this name I invented."

"Sometimes there is luck."

"Luck is something one makes for oneself, I think. Mr. McGee, I think I will give you that little time to ask your questions. You will present yourself at this suite at seven promptly?"

"Thank you very much."

"This is done only because I must believe you are a person of some discretion and privacy."

"I will be there at seven."

The wing of the hotel that was given over to the suites had wider and more luxurious corridors, was more deeply carpeted, more boldly decorated. The Fiesta Suites were on the fourth floor. I had gone in and talked to the reservation people about accommodations and had learned that suites were available from forty dollars a day to three hundred dollars a day. The wing was five stories high, and the several Fiesta Suites were duplex, with the living areas on the fourth floor, opening out onto spacious, walled roof gardens, and with two bedrooms and two baths on the fifth floor, and an internal staircase. The reservation girl was friendly, not busy, willing to chat.

She said that the largest suite, the presidential suite, had four bedrooms, a servant's room, a baronial dining room, and, on its larger roof garden, quite large shade trees and a large heated swimming pool. She said that several of the suites were permanently rented, some by businesses, some by individuals who had taken them when the hotel had opened and either lived there most of the year, or used them whenever they visited the city.

I pressed the bronze button by the door. I noticed one of those little peepholes set into the door, a wide angle lens, and I repressed my usual impulse to put my thumb over it.

The door opened six inches, as far as the heavy brass safety chain would let it. Eva Vitrier looked out through the gap at me. Enelio's description had been apt. Her face had all the striking thrusts and angles and slightly vulpine harshness of Nefertiti. Black hair piled high. A long muscular throat, graceful but not delicate. It was as broad as the slender face. The mouth was small and plump and fleshy. Her eyes were set oddly, one more sharply tilted than the other. She was wearing some sort of hostess gown, deep aqua, floor-length, with a wide scooped neck, a metallic golden rope belting it at the natural waistline. She had a look of extraordinary sensuous vitality kept under such exacting control, such practiced control, that she was an immediate challenge.

I could see beyond her into a hushed and handsome room, with a high ceiling and glass doors beyond, through which I could see a patio garden so verdant and substantial it was difficult to adjust to being on the fourth floor. Sizable trees, and muscular flagstones winding through heavy plantings.

"You *are* Mr. McGee? I do not care to ask you in, or feel the need to apologize. I am quite alone here. There is no reason why I should even give you this much time. But I was curious to . . . put a face and body with your voice, perhaps."

"I'm what you imagined?"

"Does it matter? I thought you would be a large man, but with more of the American look of softness and baldness and the quick clever eyes behind glasses, the look of the ones who find their way to the money so easily. I would rather you looked like that, because as you look now you disconcert me. To be so muscular and fit and brown, and to have about you a look of laughing at me somewhere inside you, and to look so . . . indolent—perhaps it is a part of cleverness to create an illusion of being a faithful dog one can scratch behind the ears, and send bounding off to fetch some object or to kill some animal. Now if you will tell me the blanks I will give you the little words to fill them, and everything will be tidy and proper for your report."

So the day was fading quickly, the room darkening behind her, and I was sorry I could not be reassuringly balding and soft with the little shrewd economic eyes so she would be reassured.

"Okay. What day did Minda McLeen leave and go to Mexico City?"

"The twenty-eighth day of July. A Monday."

"What did they quarrel about?"

"I have no idea. She was a tiresome girl, nervous and restless and irritable. She asked me to lend her money so she could leave. I was glad to."

"How much?"

"I do not know exactly. Perhaps two thousand pesos."

"How did she travel?"

"I have no idea. Something was said about someone driving to Mexico City. I did not listen. I was not interested. I do not know if she even came here, nor do I care."

"Why did you invite them to stay with you, when it must have been obvious to you that Miss Bowie was on drugs?"

"I felt sorry for them. One makes certain impulsive gestures from time to time, and usually regrets them. I had room for them, or for a dozen of them, at my Oaxaca home. And servants and money. It was a human impulse. I thought I might help them."

"Did you try to do anything about the Bowie girl's addiction?"

"Of course! I had a discreet doctor fly in and give her a complete physical examination. She was in very bad shape from the addiction, malnutrition, intestinal parasites, several small chronic infections. The McLeen girl needed medical attention too, but mostly rest and nourishing food. Soon she was able to help with the Bowie girl. I gave her much personal care. I have had some practical experience. My first husband was seriously ill for a year and a half before he died, and he would not permit anyone else to care for him. I gave her the prescribed injections to quell the withdrawal symptoms of heroin addiction."

"And you knew what you were taking on?"

"One becomes bored and feels a bit . . . unnecessary from time to time. Then it is an affirmative act to make oneself needed. I would not have gone on and on with it, certainly. I had planned to have someone take her back to Florida to her home when she was well enough."

"When did Miss Bowie leave your home?"

"She was becoming more alert and responsive. On Saturday in the early afternoon, a young man came asking to see her. I told my gate man that he could see Bix. Then Bix came to me and asked me if she could go for a ride with the young man. She said he was a friend. I thought it would be constructive to give her a test of her will and her desire to be cured. So she left with him. When she did not return Saturday night I was annoyed and disappointed, and quite alarmed. She had become a likable personality. But I had no reason to report it. One cannot keep a houseguest locked up. Then she did not return Sunday night either. My cook went to market Monday morning and came back and told me of an unidentified girl killed on the mountain road. I had her identification and her belongings at the house. I do not care to be involved in such things. I summoned my attorney, Alfredo Gaona, and explained the situation, and sent him to make arrangements with the police so that it could be done as quickly and quietly as possible. The body was sickeningly damaged, of course, but I knew at once from the chain she wore on her ankle and the red shoe that it was Beatrice Bowie. The police came to my home and claimed her belongings. And I did not care to stay there in the house longer. It was very depressing. So I came here the same evening. I have maintained this suite since the hotel opened."

"She was over her addiction?"

"She had been addicted intentionally to several compounds, each less powerful. It is a common method of treatment. Perhaps she could have been cured entirely. I do not know. There seemed to be in her a great need to escape herself, to blot out her known world."

Neat blanks, neatly filled.

"What day did Mr. McLeen come to you, asking about his daughter?"

"Let me think. Was Bix there? No, because he wished to question her about where Minda might have gone. I believe that it was quite late on Saturday afternoon."

"Then you must have told him to come back, because at that time you thought Bix would be back from her ride."

"Then I am mistaken, and it was late on Sunday afternoon, because I did not ask him to come back. He is a very tiresome and talkative man."

I was running out of blanks. So there was left only what I expected would be the doorslammer.

"Mrs. Vitrier, did Minda McLeen try to prevent your having an affair with Miss Bowie?"

She stared at me, so motionless I could believe she had stopped breathing. Then she gave a husky, earthy, single bark of derisive laughter.

"Do you wonder that I close the world out, Mr. McGee? There is always some kind of obscene poison, isn't there? Can you look at me and believe that?"

"Well, it isn't easy."

"I have buried four husbands, Mr. McGee. They were all elderly and extremely well off. I respond to older men. Perhaps that is a weakness. I do not know. I loved them. There was poison then, too. Each time. Snickerings about how I had seen to it that they would die in bed. The world is nasty and cruel. Fortunately they left me with all the money I shall ever need, and nasty gossip cannot touch me."

"Maybe the gossip started because you've brought so many big, healthy, pretty maids down there with you, one at a time of course."

"Oh? Yes, I *see*. That could do it, couldn't it? But how grotesque! It is a kind of work I do for an institution in Brussels, Mr. McGee. The rehabilitation and training of disadvantaged young girls. I give them a year of training, and when each one leaves my service, she is competent and disciplined and polite. I must confess that I select ones who are attractive to look at. I select paintings and lamps which are attractive to look at. And I try to see that they are sturdy enough to do a hard day's work. Do you understand? One cannot protect oneself against idle malice. I am a mystery. They seek answers. They will not accept the idea that there is no mystery at all. But I believe you will. You are, I think, an understanding and complex man. You look like the sort of man who is paid to strike a ball with a stick, or to fly to another star. But you have an easiness, an awareness of pleasure, no? And a life style which contents you, I think. You disconcert me. And you intrigue me."

"Which makes us even, Mrs. Vitrier."

"More blanks?"

"If I think of any, I'd like to come back and stand out here in the hall and have a nice little chat."

"Sorry. This is the only chance you will have."

"And. . . . I've run out of blanks."

She smiled, and without another word she closed the door. I stared at it and wondered if she was looking out the little peep hole at me. I walked back down the corridor. Nice going, McGee. Handled it real swell. And besides, you've got a life style which contents you. But not very much right now. You are pure hellfire with an insurance secretary from Guadalajara, but to the pretty French lady you are as impressive as a bag boy at the A & P.

Something about her was so vivid and so directed and so strong, it was difficult to think clearly in her presence.

So I adjourned the meeting to a metal table on the wide deck outside Azulejos. One was a quorum.

All right. Meeting come to order. What was wrong? Standing out in the hall. She's alone, she likes privacy, too many people could be on the make for some of that money from those four old dead boys. So she is alone, eh? Where are all the servants? All right, this is one of the great hotels of the world, and they can give you service until you drown in it, particularly if you maintain a suite like that permanently, and if you demand service, which I imagine she would. And it could be the maid's night out.

When I came to the doorslammer, why didn't she slam it instead of explain herself? What would she have to lose? Maybe she has so much pride in being 110 percent woman, she doesn't want anybody to believe she likes girls.

So why hadn't I tried to break up *that* act by bringing in Bruce Bundy? Because I knew she was lying anyway. And how did you know that, McGee, you subtle, clever, complex fellow? Nothing but pure instinct. Don't knock it. Meyer says it is made up of things you saw without knowing you saw them.

So what did I see that I didn't know I saw? Close the eyes. Focus on the room behind her. Whoa! Scan back. Change focus. Something there. Corner of coffee table. Fancy box. Candy box. How do you know it's candy? Because, dammit, there were those things on the floor there. What things? Well, candy litter. Wadded up pieces of that kind of red tinfoil and yellow and blue they wrap up good candy in. And some of those little pieces of brown paper.

So she has a sweet tooth.

And throws the debris on the floor under the coffee table?

Maybe she isn't neat.

But wasn't the rest of the room, what you could see of it, so neat as to be practically sterile?

She was sitting on the couch eating chocolates. Why not?

But I'd been aware of two scents coming from that woman. One was perfume, faint and astringent, and the other was gin. Gin and candy? Ech!

So the servant eats candy.

And throws the wrappers on the floor?

Well, it was a big hotel and they would take very good care of the monied guests, and they would make a practice of not handing out information for the hell of it. But a big hotel has to have a big staff, and there are always new people who haven't learned how to keep the mouth entirely closed. And guests have room service, maid service, laundry service, dry cleaning, television repair, dog-walking service. All in Spanish, no doubt.

If you skulk, you attract attention and suspicion. If you have to sneak, be loud and brash and confident about it.

My approach drew a blank with the guest service director's staff, and it drew a blank with the travel agency office, and I struck out with the switchboard girls, and then I started hitting the shops, all open at that time of the evening, on the lower level, showing my white teeth and finding out which clerk had the most English. I varied my pitch to fit the shop situation.

"You do speak English? Good. Golly, I sure hope you can help me out of an awful spot. I just had a drink up in Fiesta Suite D as a guest of Mrs. Rivereta, and she did me a real important favor. Now what I want to do, honey, is send up a couple of little gifts. But I must be losing my mind, because I've drawn a blank on any name except Mrs. Rivereta, and I thought maybe you might have sold stuff and sent it up there and know the names."

So you walk and talk, and it goes clunk, clunk, clunk, and in a little silver shop it goes DING!

She was a brisk, cute little thing and she had pale streaks dyed into her black, black hair, and she frowned and went thumbing through records, and asked questions of the other girl, and then finally pulled a card out.

"Yessss! I *thought* I remember something. But I don't know if this is a guest living there or it is something she is taking outside the hotel to a fiesta, a birthday. These things Mrs. Rivereta signed for and they are put on her hotel bill. Very nice. Let me show you one thing." She scampered off and came back with a thing that at first glance looked like a silver cigarette case, but turned out to be a purse gadget, with space for coins, notebook, pencil, identification.

"Across here, inside, people like the name engraved. We can give two-day service. And here, see, on this copy is the name. Meenda McLeen. Also, many, many sets of our initials for lugguage and personal things. M. M. In silver and gold, different es-styles. And also one bracelet with the initials. I can show you the kind of bracelet. Señor? Anything is wrong?"

"No. You've been a big help to me. Yes, you've been a big help, and I certainly appreciate it more than you can know."

She was glad she had helped. Her smile was eager and pretty. I found the door without walking through the glass, and went down a corridor and came upon the coffee shop and sat at the counter and had coffee.

So it sorted out with a dismal and feral logic. Lose the first choice off a mountain road, so pick up the trail of the little brunette and cut the loss by settling for second choice. The door had stayed chained. Maybe second choice wasn't exactly a willing guest? Want to indulge in a dramatic rescue attempt, McGee? Adolescent emotions. The thing to do is talk to Minda, because she was the one who was closest to Bix, and she would know the story and be able to guess how it must have ended.

I did some exterior surveying. I found a place where I could walk from the end of one of the buildings, parallel to it, far enough out to look up and see the night-lighted green of the fourth floor garden patios, and, above them, the narrow balconies outside the fifth floor windows of the bedrooms of the Fiesta Suites. So I got back up to the fourth floor and paced the long straight corridor, counting the strides to her door, took my count back outside and paced from the same basing-point and found that the bedrooms of Fiesta D had to open out onto the seventh and eighth balconies from the end.

18

THE ROOF areas by the tennis courts and the heliport were too popular as a place to get kissed and a place to gawk at the great humming city. The chill of nighttime at seven and a half thousand feet didn't seem to discourage either pastime.

And there was one of the hotel guard staff wandering around from time to time, on no schedule. I spent almost an hour and a half, noodling around, knowing exactly the route I had to take, but unable to make my start because people get very edgy about watching other people go over the edge of a roof.

When the crowd was down to one couple and they moved toward the stairs, I moved to my drop zone, and as I did not know how long the privacy would last, I swung over, hung by my fingertips, kicked myself away from the wall, and dropped, landed on balance, and scuttled over and stood behind a bank of floodlights waiting for somebody to start yelling.

Of course somebody could have been looking out of the window of one of the rooms and might now be phoning the desk to complain about people sneaking around at midnight. So move along, aware of the residual stiffness in the leg where Wally had popped me that good one. Down the cornice, behind the spots and floods, over to the higher one. Jump and grab. Hear the shoulder gristle pop as I pull myself up. No lights on the roof at this level. Angle across. Look down, count the shallow balconies. Seven and eight. Pick any number from seven to eight. Because seven is lucky, I chose eight. High ceilings in their hotel. Looked like a thirty-foot drop into the fourth-floor roof garden.

Make it fifteen down to the floor of the little balcony. Cement railing maybe four and a half feet high, so call it ten and a half down to the railing. And it was about four inches wide and had a flat top. Drop to the balcony floor and it is not going to sound exactly like a stray birdfeather floating in. And hang by the fingertips and it is going to be a blind two foot drop to the railing.

Shoes off. Tie the laces. Hang around the neck. Check the pockets for any jingle-jangle of keys or change. Take a long long look around to see who might be watching the fun. Wave and see if they wave back. Momma, momma, look at the funny man on the roof!

Get it over with. And, for God's sake, McGee, in the future why don't you try to believe what people tell you? Just pray for a nice landing, drawn draperies, and an unlocked door.

I let myself down, hung, rehearsed it in my head and let go. I turned toward my left to land with feet at right angles to the balcony edge. Less chance of straddling it, which would sting like crazy. Landed, by design, leaning in, off balance. Landed on the railing, then dropped like that birdfeather to the balcony floor. Looked through a screened gap eight inches wide into a room with a brighter focus of light than I could have guessed from above. It did not illuminate the balcony because it was a recessed prism light in the bedroom ceiling. It shone straight down onto a tufted blue carpeted area. Beyond it I could see, in the dim glow, an open door and bathroom fixtures beyond. To my left I could see a low couch, a chair, a coffee table. To my right I could see the bottom corner, apparently, of a bed that was against the wall to the right, said corner perhaps six feet from the narrow opening created by opening the sliding door that far and pulling the draperies open to the same distance.

It seemed a little bright for a night light. But maybe it would serve. More probably the room was empty. I stayed down below the railing height. Less chance of being noticed from a nearby building or from one of the other balconies.

Knelt and found the edge of the sliding screen and gave it a very gentle and cautious tug. It opened silently, a full inch. Another. Another. And somebody made a groaning sigh. Just as I was getting back into my skin, somebody said something, half mutter, half whisper, and I had to steady myself down again. Whoever you are there, talking in your sleep, why the hell did you leave the light on? One small advantage, however. Enough light, maybe, to be able to distinguish one dark head and be able to see whether it was Eva Vitrier. If so, I could then make my well-known death-defying leap across empty space to the other balcony.

I got the screen open as far as the door, and knew I would need a few more inches before I could go through it sideways. Had just put my palm against the edge of the door and the screen when I heard breathing. Not the deep breathing of sleep. This was more like the long distance runner. Bellows, getting deeper and faster, a huffing and a panting, then a cough and then the unmistakably, wide-open-throated, strained, soft, have-mercy cawing of woman in climax. It ended. There were some whisperous murmurings, too faint to catch. Then silence. A new set of rules had just been posted.

The bed creaked and suddenly a pale shape moved past the corner of the bed and stopped in the light, facing the balcony. I had pulled back quickly, but one instant had stamped it into memory for as long as memory would last. Naked, skin so white it seemed to blaze in the downthrust of the ceiling spot. An incomparable figure, simultaneously rich and delicate, without blemish. Nipples of that rare youthful pink, soft pubic bush, a color paler than old pennies. And it did what the picture could not do. It brought her into the focus of memory, of almost a year ago, when Meyer took the wheel and I went forward to bend a line on the new anchor. She was the one who stood at the bow in white shorts and a red top, and had looked out across Lake Worth with almost the same soft, brooding, dreamy, inward expression. The wind had tangled her hair that day as much as bed had tangled it a year later. Welcome back from your damp Florida grave, Miss Bix.

The throaty, French-lady voice from the bed corner said, "Darling? You're too sweaty to stand in that cold night air. You'll get chilled."

"Can we go out on the balcony and look at the stars, Eva?"

It was a little-girl voice, humble and obedient.

"Of course, darling child. But we'll have to put something on."

I wondered if there was a gap at the other end of the draperies, where I could look in through the glass, from a darker area. I moved over and stood up and found a slit just wide enough. I saw Eva come to the edge of the light and hang some kind of floor-length cape or cloak over the girl's shoulders. It was a dark, rich-blue, a violet-blue. She kept her hands on the girl's shoulders and I could hear her distinctly as she said, "Did I make you happy?"

The taller, younger girl turned quickly into Eva's arms, eagerly, gladly. Murmurous love-words. A soft, triumphant little laugh. Long kisses. And then Bix went off into shadows while Eva stood in the edge of the light, half-smiling. Hers was a slightly more spare and forthright body, as feminine, but with more of a look of function, so that naked she seemed more naked. Swarthy skin tones, sharp breasts with broad umber-dark nipple areas, long downsweep of muscular belly to the wide, vital spread of curly blackness, a look of compacted sinew along the tops of the thighs.

Bix brought a tailored gray robe and held it for Eva to slip on. My mind had been caroming around amid probables and improbables, bouncing off obstacles, like the shiny ball finding its way down the pinball machine, looking for the bumper that would ring the bells, flash the lights, award me some free games.

As Eva Vitrier looked down to fasten the belt of the robe, taking her first step toward the balcony, I pulled the doors wider and stepped into the room.

"Hate to bust in like this," I said.

Bix Bowie moved back into the shadows and stood staring at me without expression, yet with a kind of market-dog wariness which says that to find out if stones will be thrown, or food, one must wait, ready to run and ready to eat.

Eva Vitrier leaned forward in fishwife fury, backs of her hands against her waist, elbows cocked forward. I think that had I been able to understand French, the words would have chopped out little chunks of my flesh and left smoking craters. As I waited for her to run down, she whirled and dived to grab the nightstand phone. I clapped the cradle back down an instant after she lifted it. She hit me in the middle of the forehead with the earpiece. I clopped her on the side of the head with a cupped palm. It knocked her onto her hands and knees. She rose slowly, touching her hair, and said, "Bixie sweetie, go into the bathroom and close the door."

"I want to watch, Eva."

"Mind me! Or there'll be no surprise tomorrow, and no candy."

The girl turned and went into the bathroom and closed the door. And Eva came after my eyes with ten long nails. A wiry, furious, unrestrained woman can be dangerous to all men who, out of some notion of chivalry, try to quell her furies, hold her wrists and avoid her kicks and bites until she gives up.

Chivalry is pretty flexible. And sometimes it is dead.

So I hooked her a pretty good one in the stomach as she was coming in, and it was on a slightly upward angle, so her heels lifted off the floor, her legs swung up, and the first thing that hit the floor was that rear end which Enelio had found so delectable long ago. Momentum rolled her over onto her back, and her legs went up and over and she ended on her knees, the gray robe forward, and all entangled about her head and arms, which were resting on the floor. Enelio might find that angle even more entrancing. She rolled onto her side, sat up, smoothed the robe down. She reached and caught a chair and pulled herself up and sat on it, making inhalation groans to try to suck enough air back into herself. Hit a woman, would you, McGee? I surely would, now and then.

All the spark and snap were gone. I saw switches by the door and went over and turned on the rest of the room lights. I closed the glass doors and pulled the lined draperies shut. I sat on the foot of the tousled bed.

She straightened herself. "You know, I could have you killed for that."

"If you know where to go and how much to offer."

"I can find out."

"And I can walk you into the bathroom there and try to teach you to breathe underwater, and I might have to do just that if I don't like the answers."

"There won't be any answers."

"Suit yourself, French lady."

"What are you looking for?"

"Something to knot you up with. Nylons are great. Stronger than steel. Then we'll see how much of this Kleenex we can cram into your mouth, and I'll tie that in place, roll you under the bed there, get Miss Bowie into some clothes and take her to the Embassy and phone her father from there. So forget the answers. I don't need them."

"Wait a minute. Sit down. Stop opening drawers, please. Listen to me a minute. I brought her back from living death, Mr. McGee. You don't know what she was like. Even I didn't know how lovely she would look."

"What is she blasting lately? She's way off center right now."

"She can't get along at all without something. I don't think she ever will. She's on charas. An agent brings it in for me from Calcutta. It's like marijuana, but very, very powerful. They use just the resins. I let her smoke three tiny cigars of it a day. We make a ceremony out of it. Don't you understand? She's been too badly damaged. She can't exist in the real world."

"But your world is just dandy. Best thing for her."

"She gets love and protection, and I keep her in good health. We have silly little games we play. I make her keep herself clean and pick up her clothes."

"And you get her her distemper shots and keep her coat glossy, and some day you can bury her in the foot of the garden and put a mossy little headstone up. Bix. Beloved pet. But that would be a little sentimental, huh?"

"You are certainly a cruel bastard. All right! So maybe I don't want any more challenging human relationships."

"After four old husbands?"

"You meet the simple young ones who can introduce you to the important young ones who can introduce you to the important and rich old ones. And you work at it, you know. You give fair value. All of them use you like a waste bin, a conveniently shaped receptacle, just as males used Bixie. But there is tennis and sailing and all the vigorous games in bed, and the old ones do not last long. The money was earned. The privacy was earned. The freedom was earned."

"I might pop you another one, just for luck."

"I don't think it would astonish me, actually."

"So she gets love. From you."

"I saw her and Minda in the zocalo. I followed them. They had to keep stopping at benches so Bix could rest. There was something about her. I had to know her. They needed help. The word probably doesn't mean anything to you, but do you know that she had never been sexually awakened? Can you imagine how much restraint and patience it took? But now she is more easily stimulated each day. She's very sensual. But she lives on Lesbos forever, because it is the only island she has ever known."

"That's pretty poetic there, French lady. What are you getting at? You want to keep her around the house?"

"She can never endure any contact with any part of her old life without reverting. I arranged to have her tourist permit renewed, in Minda McLeen's name. It was expensive. I am taking her . . . to another country where identities can be purchased, I intend to see that if anything should happen to me, she shan't want for anything."

"So Minda went off the hill in the yellow car. That's why she doesn't need her own papers. And Bix's papers went to Florida with the body and the personal effects. Was it expensive getting Minda bumped off the road, French lady?"

"It wasn't that way."

"What way was it?"

"Minda began to get suspicious after Bixie began to improve. And she began spying on me, and finally caught me . . . caressing Bixie in a way that couldn't possibly have been anything except what it was. She made a very ugly scene, and said some very ugly things. She said she would not permit it. Permit it! Can you imagine the impertinence? She tried to stay with Bix every moment, day and night. I asked Minda to my room to discuss the problem. I tried to seduce her, because I knew that would shut her mouth, but she acted as if I were some sort of sickening animal. She said she was going to get in touch with Bix's father. So as I was afraid I might lose Bix, the next time Minda left the house, I had a trusted friend of mine come at once in her car and pick up Bix and bring her up here to the city; I asked her to stay here in the suite with Bix until I could arrive. I informed the hotel they would be using the suite. I knew I could trust my friend to be careful and discreet, but I knew she would never be able to keep from making love to such a lovely child. But I had to accept that, even though it made me feel wretched. So when Minda came back I asked her if she had seen Bix. I pointed out that all her things were still in her room. I said she had wandered out and that I was worried. Minda knew it was a trick of some kind. She said she would stay with me and I would lead her to wherever Bix was."

The bathroom door opened and Bix came wandering out. "I'm tired of staying in there, Eva."

"Just a little bit longer, dear. Please."

"Well . . . all right." She went back in.

"On Saturday, in the early afternoon, that Rockland person came to my home demanding to see Minda. She did not know of it. She was in her room. I had Rockland brought to me, at the garden house beyond the pool, and I had Ramón and his nephew stay close by. I told you before, it was easy to see he was a low type, crafty and arrogant. One must exploit their greed to find out what plan they have. He so was obviously relieved to find no one else had been there before him, asking about her. It took a little time and a few simple threats, but I found out that Minda's father was in Oaxaca and had looked for Rockland and found him. Rockland had made an arrangement to deliver the girl to her father for money. He thought he could get ten thousand American dollars if he managed the affair skillfully. Nothing could have been more obvious to me than that if he did manage it, Minda would seek aid from her father in taking Bix away from me. One cannot tell how much resource an American businessman has in such matters. It would be obvious that at the very least he would feel an obligation to acquaint the other father with the state of affairs. I would want neither the notoriety nor the legal problems, nor want to take the chance of losing the girl. So I offered him twice what he expected from Mr. McLeen, if he would take Minda away with him on some pretext and leave her far enough away so that by the time she made her way back I could be gone and there would be no way to reach or find me. Then, if he chose, he might be able to continue his arrangement with her father.

"We set the schedule. I gave him five thousand dollars and suggested he take her to Coatzacoalcos on the Gulf of Campeche, on the pretext of taking her to where Bix was. Transportation is awkward from there to Oaxaca. He had a car. He could drive far into the night. It is something over three hundred miles from Oaxaca. He was to abandon her there, without funds, and return quickly. I would wait until a nine o'clock flight out of Oaxaca Monday evening, I would give him the rest of the money then, and he would, if ever questioned, swear he had loaned Bix money to fly back to the states."

But, she related, she had been awakened at midnight on Sunday night to be told that the young American was back, that he was on foot, that he was at the gate demanding to be let in. She dressed and went down to the gate and they talked in the courtyard. He said he had been too tired to drive so far. He thought it would be just as good to take her up into the mountains. She had gone willingly when he said that Bix needed her and he was taking her to where Bix was. But she became suspicious. He had found a place to pull off the road when night fell. He had kept her there with him. He had wanted to wait long enough so that she, Mrs. Vitrier, would think he had taken Minda a long way away. He had not wanted to lose track of her because of her resale value. It was his plan to tie her to a tree or something, out of sight of the highway on Monday, and go down and get the money and come back and pick her up again and make his deal with Wally.

Late Sunday afternoon while she was napping in the back seat of the little car, he had fallen asleep in the front seat. He had slept so heavily that apparently she had been able to work the car keys out of his pocket, put the key into the ignition, silently open a front door, brace her back against the other door, put her feet against him and suddenly shove him out onto the ground, yank the door shut and lock it. As he tried to break in, she got it started and pulled out and headed down the mountain, accelerating. He had picked a spot, after a long walk, where trucks would have to shift way down to negotiate a steep uphill curve. He had to wait hours before one came along with a tailgate he could climb onto. He had dropped off in the city and made his way to Eva's house. When he found that Minda had never arrived, he was certain she had gone off the mountain. And if she had, she was dead.

"I took him to the sitting room which adjoins my bedroom. We discussed the possible repercussions of this event. It had been a car he had taken without permission, but he was quite certain the owner would give very little if any information to the police, and he explained why. By then, you see, I knew that a car had gone off the mountain, and they would look for it by daylight. It sickened me to think of it. She was being very difficult, but I had not wished *that* for her. But it had happened. And in many ways it simplified things. One must be mature and accept facts, yes? So he said he must have the rest of the money because it had been promised. He was looking at me strangely, I thought. He said that in addition, I would give him the ten thousand he would have gotten from the father. I told him that was not my affair. He said it had become my affair. I had given him money to get rid of the girl and he had gotten rid of her. He said it would all be difficult to explain.

"By then I began to see that he could be of some danger to me. He was greedy and crafty and brutal, but not intelligent. It had been a mistake to make an arrangement with him. I knew that to disarm him I had to appear to be . . . manageable. I said I did not have so much in American dollars in the house, but I could make up the difference in Swiss francs. I got it all for him and explained the rate of exchange. I even told him the name I use in this hotel. He counted the money too many times and, also, too many times he told me that it was the last time I would have to give him money. It meant that he was thinking that he would ask again.

"He began looking at me in another strange way and said that we were now associated in this affair. He said he knew from Minda what I was, but that it would please him to come into my bed and use me as a woman, just to verify our trust and friendship. I told him there would be no pleasure in it for me, and he said that it did not particularly matter whether there was or not. At such times one must be very careful. And so I pretended fear and begged him not to, then seemed to accept the inevitable, and asked him if he minded if I had some brandy before all this would take place. He said, as I expected, that he would enjoy some also, and that we could drink a toast and seal the bargain. I got a special bottle kept in a special place, and silver glasses so that he could not tell that I would let it run out my mouth back into the glass. In a little while he smiled foolishly and his words blurred and soon his head toppled forward and he began to snore. I took the money from him and replaced it in the wall safe in the back of my bedroom closet. I felt as if I were moving through a dream. I had quite a lot of the meperedine left, which we had sometimes given Bix when she became unmanageable. Ten little ampules. I had been taught how to administer hypodermics when my first husband was dying, and of course I had given Bix injections. I prepared him properly, with an alcohol swab, and knelt by his chair. But I could not. One wonders if it is possible to kill a human being. I had a dozen reasons to do this thing. But I could not. I could touch the point to the vein on the inside of his arm, but I could not shove it through the skin, no matter what I told myself."

So in the end she had tied him securely, binding his wrists and ankles to the heavy chair. She had paced the floor until dawn, wondering what to do. When he began stirring, she had sedated him heavily. On Monday morning, early, Wally McLeen had arrived, having at last tracked his missing daughter to her house. She had taken him to the garden house and had given him some of the vivid highlights of Minda's Mexican vacation, throwing in incidents that had happened to Bix as though they had happened to Minda, including how Rockland had taken her into the cornfield to service the men who had showed up out of the night at the campsite. From his reactions she was afraid he was having a massive coronary. When he was at last more normal, she had said that it was possible that Minda was dead and that Rockland was responsible. She did not say more than that. She said that if he would get hold of some vehicle and if he would come to the vehicle gate at ten that night, there was a possibility she might be able to deliver Rockland over to him, so that he could take Rockland to the police. She showed him where the vehicle gate was. She would not answer his questions.

She had then decided, later on in the day, hearing that the body could not be identified, that if she made an appearance and made the identification and then said that the last she had seen of the girl was when she had driven off with Rockland on Saturday, it would help insulate her against any future accusation.

"But when I saw how . . . the terrible condition of the body, I knew that one could identify it as almost anyone. There was the chain, of course, that Minda wore about her ankle. But who could say that Bix did not wear one and it was not that one? Or could say those were not Bix's red shoes. I had the personal papers and personal things of both of them. My mind raced. I stood holding the perfumed handkerchief against my nose. I saw how it could be. If it was Bix who died, she would be mine without question. So I identified her and the police came to my house and I gave them Bix's things. I brought Minda's papers here, and I arranged to have the permit renewed under Minda's name without Bix having to appear. I sent all the servants out that night. I opened the gate for Mr. McLeen. I helped him get Rockland down and into the trunk of an American sedan Mr. McLeen had rented. Mr. McLeen was very strange. He whistled and he walked on his toes, and he said that everything was splendid, that Minda was going to come back to Oaxaca and he would wait around for her until she returned. Rockland was very groggy. When he was curled up in the trunk compartment on his side, Mr. McLeen gave him little pats on the back and called him son and said everything would be arranged properly. I thought I was all right. I thought I was not feeling much of anything. But when I had shut the gate again, all of a sudden without warning, I vomited. Afterward, I felt so faint it took me a long time to finish packing the last few things. I flew from Oaxaca Tuesday on the early schedule. Bix was happy to see me, happy as a Christmas child."

She was watching my face carefully.

Bix came out of the bathroom again. "Please?"

"All right, dear girl. Sit over there on the couch and be quiet. Mr. McGee, does she look abused? Surely you must have the right to make choices in your work. I am fond of her. I cherish her. I will take her to lovely secluded places. Look how splendid that color is for her. It makes those deep blue eyes look almost deep violet. I will dress her in indigo, and in the good blues and greens and grays. Cool tones suit her kind of beauty. I can control her . . . need for escape into drugs. She will not be sick, or lonely, or institutionalized. Can anybody else in the world promise that? Can her own people promise that? What do you return to them if you do your nasty little job, Mr. McGee? A young girl with a drug-retarded mind. A committed and incurable addictive personality. A committed and incurable Lesbian. A person the police of your country will be watching closely, as they promised. You will be taking back heartbreak. Isn't it kinder, by far, to let her stay dead?"

"Dead?" asked Bix.

"The kid asks a good question, French lady. So do you."

"Think about it carefully, please."

So I sat and thought about it. It was nice and easy, her way. Let the dead stay dead. Tell a happy story to good old Harlan Bowie. Feed Meyer the story Eva had fed me through the chained door. Go back and romp away the final few days of Elena's vacation. Mission accomplished. But should the father have the chance to undo the damage that he had started and others had finished? He had a lot of money, enough to buy penance, good clinics, sleep therapy.

"I have a wall safe here," she said. "In that closet. I think there is the equivalent of about forty thousand American dollars. I can give you that now, and I can have an additional hundred and sixty thousand here by the day after tomorrow."

"You buy the girl for two hundred thou?"

"That is a clumsy way to put it. I buy her happiness, and mine. I can afford it."

"I know. You earned it. The hard way."

I walked over toward her. She stood up and looked up at me, and I saw the hard mocking confidence in the back of her eyes. She was wearing the small smile of the winner. So I smiled too, and I sighed, and I wondered if it was getting to be too attractive a habit as I steadied her with one hand, chopped the side of that long muscular throat with the other, caught her as she dropped, and slung her onto the bed.

Bix had stood up. "Now what are you doing?"

"I am going to take you for a nice little ride in a nice murderous taxi, sweetie."

"To the movies?"

"Maybe. Why don't you go put some clothes on? Where are they?"

"In there. In that other room in the closet and all over."

"Go get dressed."

"Sure."

She went into the next room. I wanted to fix French lady so she would stay put for a nice long time, but not too long, in case nobody dared unlock the suite unless asked. I yanked the sheets out from under her and took them in and dropped them in the tub and got them sopping wet. I took them out and spread them out on the rug, took her out of her gray robe, put her down at one end of the soaked sheets, and rolled her up in them like a window shade. I put her back on the bed with the last wet end tucked neatly under her. As long as they stayed wet, she stayed still. When they dried out, she would wiggle loose.

I pried her jaw down and found that in spite of the plump little meaty mouth, there was room in there for a hell of a lot of Kleenex, if you packed it carefully. I knotted a nylon stocking in place, webbing it between her teeth and against the Kleenex so she couldn't tongue it out of the way and start yelling.

Then I went in to see how Bixie was progressing. She had lost ground, because she had shed the robe and added one lacy pale-green bra. So I told her I expected her to shape up better than that, which at the moment was the wrong expression, and I started digging around trying to find what you put on a naked young lady to take her to the Embassy in the middle of the night.

I heard some kind of disturbance, but by then I had found where the skirts and blouses and sweaters were. So I took time to match them up reasonably well. Bix had gone back into the first bedroom. I heard a lovely gasping delighted giggling, and I heard some kind of muffled grunting and thrashing.

When I hurried in I saw that Bix was bending over the bed, and she had grasped Eva Vitrier firmly with thumb and first two fingers, right by the Nefertiti nose, thus cutting off all air except what the woman might try to suck through all that Kleenex. French lady's face had turned very, very dark. Her eyes were bulging and blind, and she was spasming and grunting and flapping, looking very much like an oversized, dying whitefish in the bottom of a skiff. And, believe me, she did not have very far to go. Like twenty seconds more, possibly. I snatched Bix's playful fingers off lovergirl's nose, and Eva subsided, breath whistling as she hyperventilated through that noble beak. She opened her eyes and looked up at me, in combination loathing and appeal. Her effort had burst a blood vessel in one eye, and half the white had turned bright crimson.

I tucked her wet sheet firmly under her, patted her on the cheek, took Bixie in, and crowded her into her clothes. She passed inspection. In the elevator on the way down she said, "Wasn't Eva funny? Wasn't she funny, though?"

"She was a scream, kid."

"I wish you hadn't made me stop."

"So do I, sort of."

So we taxied to the Embassy, not far down Reforma, and stood on the wide sidewalk as the cab went away. She yawned.

"Is this the movies?"

"Bixie baby, things can get very, very rough for you. I don't even know if you can understand how rough they have been, or will get. I would feel a lot better if I thought maybe you could cut it."

"Oh hell yes," she said. "Let's go in."

19

MEYER WAS at the Oaxaca airport to meet me when I came back from Florida via Mexico City five days later.

He looked fit and smug and amused, and he wore a straw hat from the market and a blue shirt covered with zippers with metal rings in them.

I peeled out of the inbound line and said, "Relapse? What the hell kind of relapse are you having?"

"It's no worse than a bad cold."

"Then you could have all by yourself gotten on a plane and all by yourself flown home, right?"

"But I don't like to travel alone. Anyway, are you paying for the extra trip?"

"No. But this isn't the happiest place in the world to come back to, for me. I guess you know that."

"Oh, I guess I do. But I don't have to get depressed just because you do. That wasn't such a great phone connection. How did Harl take it?"

"How the hell did you expect him to take it? He's bursting with joy and hope and all that, in a good effort to hide the fact that what we took back there to him might be, in his code of values, better off dead. She started coming apart. She was very, very raggedy by the time the reunion happened."

"Nothing out of the Vitrier woman?"

"What could she do? Why should she try to do anything? And they had to buy my story. I saw the girl wandering around near Sanborne's. I was sure I recognized her as Beatrice Bowie, who was supposed to have died. In fact, I was in Mexico at her father's request, finding out how she died. Here you are, Embassy. Straighten things out. They would rather have had me hand them some armed infernal device. They hated it. They kept looking very Princeton and sighing and hunting for new forms to fill out. Meyer, goddamit, pack! I want to be home. I want to be on the *Flush*. I want to go to some island no developer has ever found yet, where no beer can has yet washed ashore."

"Enjoy beautiful Oaxaca."

And she hit me at a dead run, grabbing and laughing and saying if we were going to stand out here all day, she, Elena, could not wait for the surprise.

I told her she was supposed to be back at work.

She told me she wanted a little more vacation, and so did Margarita, and so they took a little more.

"But can they just do that?" I asked Meyer.

"When Enelio Fuentes owns that much of the insurance company they can, buddy."

So we had drinks and dinner at the Victoria, abundant and long and I tried to be festive, but it kept slipping on me. I kept worrying the whole thing. Picking at it. Meyer said impatiently, "Will you kindly get off that tiresome point of no return, McGee? Please? For me? And for these Guadalajara girls, and for your own sake? A grown-up man must make a lousy decision from time to time, knowing it is lousy, because the only other choice is lousy in another dimension, and no matter which way he jumps, he will not like it. So he accepts the fact that the fates dealt him two low cards, and he goes on from there. Or better, why don't you two go on from here. I seem to have been moved into another cottage, and only this insurance friend of mine seems able to find it after dark."

But it still kept nibbling and chewing at me. It kept me just a little apart from all the joy of Elena. And it woke me near dawn, thinking again of that look in Harlan Bowie's eyes, and wondering if the son of a bitch would clap her away somewhere forever, for her own good, of course.

Dawn-thoughts are the bleak ones. And these took me back to T. Harlan Bowie's arena—Garden Suite Number Five in that quietest part of Coral Gables. As a medical precaution they had put him on a tranquilizer and then told him I was on the way, bringing back his only chick, alive. I left Bix with his nurse-therapist, Mrs. Kreiger, while I tried to prepare him for her.

I tried, but I don't think he was listening closely. "Look, Mr.

Bowie, she went down there with rotten people. It was a setup. She could put her hands on twenty thousand, and they knew it, and they conned her out of it, every dime of it. Some people, Mr. Bowie, have too much of a taste for marijuana. It takes over. They just float and they don't give a damn."

"My daughter isn't that kind of person, McGee."

"She was fogged over, believe me. In the early part of the trip the three men were all banging her, and the other girl too—the one you buried."

"Then they were taking her by force, and I am going to see that they are prosecuted."

"This wasn't kid games. Two of them are dead. She's under suspicion of conspiring to smuggle heroin across the border. She got hooked on heroin, Mr. Bowie. She was an addict, or is an addict. A woman gave her a home cure. She cycled her down through some other opiates and got her over onto something that's not physically addicting. It was a lot of trouble. The woman wanted her."

"Wanted her?"

"And got her, as a girlfriend, as a female homosexual partner."

"Are you out of your mind?"

"I'm just trying to tell you that this is a different girl. She's an addictive personality, and she isn't going to be able to handle any part of this without getting back onto some kind of a high. And you can't reach her because she bombed herself so long and so big, her mind is not on our wavelength anymore. I'm trying to tell you that—"

"McGee, I think I'm a little tired of you telling me things. I want to see my daughter, please."

Bixie was down off the charas high, and was being threatened with all the hard edges of reality, and she wanted no part of it. She was mean, edgy, suspicious, and unpredictable. She was vulgar and sullen and semipsychotic. And she was not about to rush in and kiss dear old daddy and cry tears of joyous welcome, and express any sympathy for his being in a wheelchair.

She came scuffing in, glanced at him, and went over and slouched into a chair. Mrs. Kreiger saw him having problems with the wheelchair and hurried around and wheeled him over to the girl. He reached and grabbed her hand. He was weeping. "Bix. Oh, Bix, honey."

But Bix honey looked narrow-eyed at me. "Is this the big treat, you rotten, dirty bastard? You bring me back to this silly old fart?

Where's Eva. What have you done to Eva? Look, I've got to have a surprise. Honest to God, I've got to have a surprise or I'm going to go up the walls screaming."

"You're home now!" he said.

"Somebody get him off me," she said.

"I thought you were dead, honey."

She looked at him with the coldest dark blue eyes in town. "And I wish you were, old man. I wish to hell you were."

Mrs. Kreiger said, "Doctor Kohn wants to have a look at her. Should I . . . take her along now?"

"Yes. And . . . let me know what they suggest, please."

When they were gone he wiped his eyes and shook his head. "It isn't possible she could change so much. What can . . . be done?"

"I think maybe you've got to make her able to live with somebody she despises. She despises Bix Bowie, and always has, but didn't know there was a way to escape. It will take a lot of love, a lot of patience, a lot of motivation to make her ever believe that the Bix Bowie of the real world isn't a total failure. Excuse me, but what else have you got worth doing?"

"It . . . it's a second chance?"

"And very damned slim."

"It's the only thing I can do."

So maybe he would and maybe he wouldn't give it the big try. Or it might last only so long. I wondered about that look in his eye. Maybe I'd only imagined it was there. Second try, second rejection. But maybe, just maybe, he might have the guts for the job.

I heard a rooster crow a long way across the silence of the predawn morning in Oaxaca.

Near dawn, and Elena was curled into me, fists against my chest, round knees pressing against my belly. So I kissed the sleeping eye that was nearest and handiest.

She grunted and came but partway up out of sleep, far enough to begin a slow and determined worming and squirming, trying to work the undermost leg under me, under my waist. When I saw what she was trying to do, I made it easier for her. She slid the leg under, and then hooked her calf back against me. She lifted the other leg over me, the drowsy weight of it coming down across my waist. She uncurled her fists and slid her hands around my ribs, one under me, one on top, and flattened her palms against my back.

So then there was the unseen questing, and a guiding touch, and then a snubbed pressure increasing until—celebrated with a little snuff of sudden insuck of air through her nose—we were suddenly, sleekly, deeply coupled. She hitched herself a little higher, changed her position, moved her hands further around me, and made her small warm sound of contentment.

I slid my hands down her back until they reached and cupped the warm, smooth, solid buttocks. And like some familiar, faithful, trusty, loyal little machine, that touch and pressure was enough to start the slow, rhythmic pumping of her hips, rich and sleepy and demanding.

So with gray at the windows, and her mouth turning upward for the kiss, with the slow deep steady beat that would begin to change only when we neared climax, *this* became the reality, *this* became the life-moment, *this* became the avowal, the communion, the immortality. The private rhythm of our need, a small and personal and totally shared thing, was that special thing in the world and in time which changed the Rockos and Evas, the Jerrys and Wallys and Bruceys and Carls, the Bixies and Beckys to scare-masks fashioned of cardboard and spit, empty things which hang on strings from an empty tree, turning in the parching wind that blows across the empty heart.

"Ah," said the tireless, tawny, loving engine.

Bless all the sisters, wherever they are.